TRUE COLORS

TRUE COLORS

a novel by

Doris Mortman

~

CROWN PUBLISHERS, INC.
NEW YORK

Published by Crown Publishers, Inc., 201 East 50th Street, New York,
New York 10022. Member of the Crown Publishing Group.

Random House, Inc. New York, Toronto, London, Sydney, Auckland

CROWN is a trademark of Crown Publishers, Inc.

Manufactured in the United States of America

Library of Congress Cataloging-in-Publication Data
Mortman, Doris.
True colors:a novel/by Doris Mortman.—1st ed.
p. cm.
I. Title.
PS3563.08818T78 1994
813'.54—dc20   94-13068
                                CIP

ISBN 0-517-59262-2

10 9 8 7 6 5 4 3 2 1

First Edition

For my mother—
a never-ending source of strength and inspiration—
with love.

PROLOGUE

Santa Fe, New Mexico, 1990

Behind La Casa, fireworks electrified the dusky sky with paroxysms of color and ribbons of smoke. As clusters of green, orange, red, and blue rained down on a frenzied crowd, a mariachi band played, its blaring trumpets and rhythmic guitars amplifying the excitement. In the center of the large terrace, pink and turquoise lights transformed a towering stone fountain into a liquid bouquet of color. A quick volley of rockets whistled into the darkness. The sky thundered. Sparkling strands of incandescent glitter streaked across night's black canvas, fizzing and flaming like shooting stars. People screamed their approval, applauding and chanting a name, demanding an appearance of their own special star.

A young woman was urged onto a platform. Tall and trim, she smiled as she took her place behind a long table festooned with crepe-paper flowers. Silver arrows tipped in turquoise dangled from her ears, hammered silver bangles encircled her wrists. Her body was lightly tanned, the white of her ankle-skimming dress toasting her skin even more. The neckline was low, the rest of the garment loose, revealing a gentle swell of cleavage, hiding a small waist and long, shapely legs.

She wore little makeup—a touch of mascara, a bit of blush, a hint of gloss; her chocolate-brown hair hung straight and loose, dropping just below her shoulders. Her eyes—a rich blend of coffee and emeralds—appeared almond shaped at first glance; close up, the lower lid was straighter than the upper, convincing the two to convene with a slanted edge that seemed visually to affirm the aura of mystery that had always surrounded the woman named Isabelle de Luna.

She flushed at the sustained applause and laughed at the gibes being thrown at her.

"Let's see if you've finally learned to say *gracias*," someone shouted, reminding anyone who might have forgotten that Isabelle's Spanish was softly accented Castilian rather than the harder sound heard throughout the American Southwest.

Isabelle indulged the heckler. *"Gra-see-as,"* she said, elongating the word, exaggerating the strain it placed on her not to pronounce the "c" as "th."

"Maybe when she's fifty, she'll get it."

"Don't count on it!"

Isabelle laughed again, basking in the warmth coming from the audience. While there were some faces she didn't recognize—friends of friends, she assumed—she had literally grown up with everyone else. Standing before her, in the guise of grown-up women and men, were the girls with whom she had shared everything from the shock of the first menstrual period to the insecurity of their first kiss; the boys who had teased her about being skinny and shapeless and then had embarrassed her when she wasn't. These people had made her feel welcome when she'd first arrived in Santa Fe many years before, and they had never stopped. Yet despite the hundreds who had come to share this night with her, the most conspicuous guests were the ones who had stayed away: Tía Flora, who was fighting a fearsome battle she was destined to lose; Nina, who was waging a savage war she was determined to win; and the man who had conquered Isabelle's heart but hadn't been able to subdue her fears.

Before she could dwell on any of them, someone handed her a stick. Enthusiastic voices shouted above the music, urging her to feed the child in every adult there by whacking the piñata that hung from a tree branch above her. Her eyes searched the crowd for the faces that gave her strength. Off to the side she found the Durans, the couple who had raised her, the people she thought of as mother and father, even though she called them Miranda and Luis. Miranda smiled at her. Luis waved his hand and nodded. "Go ahead. Do it!" his gesture seemed to say.

Encouraged by their approval, Isabelle raised the stick and brought it down on the papier-mâché donkey that dangled before her. Once. Twice. Three times she hit the hand-crafted animal before it burst open, spraying those nearest her with candy and trinkets.

"Make a wish!" a young woman in the first row called out, waving a bouquet of multicolored streamers in Isabelle's face while others clamored for the piñata's bounty.

"What could she possibly wish for?" said another woman in a tone laced more with wonderment than bitterness. "She has everything."

Isabelle overheard the comment and winced. She supposed she did appear to have everything. She was an artist with an international reputation, an enviable bank account, an uptown apartment and a downtown studio in New

York City, an ancestral home in Barcelona, Spain, and a private casita at La Casa. Her paintings hung in prestigious museums around the world. Her picture had graced the covers of every major magazine in the United States and Europe—from *Vogue* to *Newsweek* to *Paris Match* to *Tatler*. She had been interviewed by such broadcasting luminaries as Barbara Walters, Ted Koppel, Sam Donaldson, and David Frost. She had even done a solo hour on *The Oprah Winfrey Show*. She was the reigning *enfant incroyable* of the art world, the most accessible, understandable, sensual, deeply emotional painter America had produced since Georgia O'Keeffe.

To the casual observer, she supposed she did have it all. But just then, all that Isabelle treasured was in jeopardy.

Sighing, she reached back, pulled her hair off her face, inhaled deeply, and, in a single breath, blew out the candles on her birthday cake: thirty-four for each year of her life, plus the one she needed most, the one for good luck. As fingers of yellow flames dissolved into puffs of gray smoke, shadows began to take shape within the sulfurous fog. Isabelle closed her eyes and grabbed hold of the table in front of her for support, fighting to stave off the nightmarish attack she knew was coming.

They had begun several months before. At first it was an occasional lapse of consciousness, a sudden, inexplicable moment when things went black and the world disappeared behind an opaque curtain. Lately, however, the spells were lasting longer; the aftereffects were more disturbing. Stranded for an immeasurable time in the disquieting purgatory of unwelcome visions, she'd awaken with no memory, only shaking hands, a body dampened with sweat, and the insidious feeling of having been kidnapped from the present by the ghosts that inhabited her past.

A strong arm encircled her waist. Her eyes snapped open. Her breath, coming in short, anxious puffs, calmed when she saw that the arm belonged to one of the few she felt she could trust. Luis Duran smiled and squeezed her waist, confirming that he was by her side if she needed him, just as he had been since she was seven years old.

Allowing Isabelle time to regain her composure, Luis raised his glass and turned toward the crowd.

"It's always a special event when Isabelle comes home to Santa Fe, but today is even more special because the occasion is a celebration of her birth. Certainly, all who respond to the genius of her art are thankful she was put on this earth. For Miranda and me, it's the beauty of her being that inspires our gratitude."

His voice wobbled with emotion. Needing a moment to compose himself, Luis turned to Isabelle and tilted his glass toward her in a gesture of tribute.

"She is the most wonderful daughter a man could ever hope to have. The fact that God thought I was worthy enough to be her father is a miracle I thank Him for every day of my life."

Isabelle smiled, but just as she leaned over to kiss Luis, she heard it: the snap of footsteps crunching fallen twigs. Her smile froze on her lips. It had come from behind her. She turned but saw nothing. Quickly her eyes scanned the perimeter of La Casa and searched the faces in the crowd. If only she knew whom she was looking for and why he was stalking her, she might have been able to alleviate some of the terror, but this pursuit was unnervingly anonymous. She had no known enemies. There had been no overt threats. Yet with the same certainty as one sensed a hurricane about to land, she knew someone was after her.

Worse, Isabelle suspected that somewhere, deep in the recesses of her mind, she knew who he was, but hard as she tried, she couldn't bring his face forward. He was a blur that visited her in the night, teasing her with a second of near focus, then quickly retreating into a dense fog of memory obfuscated by fear. She couldn't point to a physical form and identify him; she couldn't confront or accuse him; but she took him and his menacing presence very seriously. She had to. The one thing of which she was certain was that he had killed before.

Nina stared at a photograph the publisher had selected to use on the cover of her forthcoming book: *True Colors, an Intimate Biography of Isabelle de Luna.* It was a color portrait of Isabelle that was far more flattering than any Nina would have selected. Annoyed, she flipped the book over and studied the black-and-white photograph of herself that would occupy the back cover.

Scavullo had done it, and she looked fabulous! Her blond hair—blunt cut to her shoulders—shone as if she had just rinsed it in sunshine. Her gray eyes had snared enough light to glimmer like polished silver. Though Scavullo thought she had a devastatingly sexy smile, she had chosen a more serious mien. She didn't think it was appropriate to look gleeful about revealing the darkest secrets of Isabelle's past. Too ghoulish, she had decided. Besides, she looked more sophisticated with her lips in a subtle moue, more in keeping with the persona she had created for herself.

Knowing that Isabelle had been photographed wearing white, Nina had worn black: a cashmere sweater, round neck, long sleeves, very Smith. She had toyed with the idea of a strand of pearls but had decided not to press the image. After laying the two pictures side by side, she studied them with a critical eye, examining contrasts, weighing impact. Her mouth spread in a broad smile. It was so Shakespearean, so blond versus brunette, so good versus evil, so Rosalind and Celia. And, if the truth be known, so Isabelle and Nina.

Isabelle was color. Nina was black and white. Isabelle produced paintings. Nina collected photographs. Isabelle was an artist who created images in brilliant hues and emotional shadings. Nina was a journalist—of sorts—who said what she thought, reported what she saw, and repeated what she heard, all hard edges and bold lines. Isabelle looked to clarify herself through her work. Nina hid behind hers. Isabelle was shy, wary of public attention, and had a tendency to retreat into the solitude of her art. Nina defined the word *assertive* and had found a profession where aggressive behavior was a plus.

Though Isabelle's inner circle was small, it was tight and close-knit. Nina was always surrounded by people, always attending benefits or openings or luncheons or dinners, yet there was no one she could call in the middle of the night when she was frightened, no one in whom she could confide, no one she could honestly claim as a friend.

Nina's eye caught sight of the calendar on her desk. Today was Isabelle's birthday. Checking her watch, adjusting for time differences, she estimated that Isabelle was blowing out the candles on some enormous cake just about now. She could see the fireworks, the mariachi band, the crowd, the buffet table groaning with chile con queso, *chicharones, carne adovada,* frijoles, enchiladas, and dozens of other southwestern dishes.

Typical Duran fiesta, she thought, pushing aside the unbidden remembrance of times when she had found them fun, preferring to turn up her nose and dismiss the party as boorish and ethnic and completely beneath her.

An unexpected twinge surprised her. Maybe she should have gone, shown them who she was now, what she had become. It would have felt good to see respect in their eyes, to hear jealousy creep into their voices as they offered phony greetings and reluctant compliments on her success. But going there would be going back. And, as they had been for most of her life, Nina's sights were fixed upward. To many, the attainment of great wealth was the driving force behind that oftentimes tedious climb to the top, but it wasn't money Nina wanted; it was an acknowledgment of personal worth.

While it was true that penning an unauthorized biography about a national icon was a risky route to acceptance, Nina suddenly had found herself wedged into a very uncomfortable corner. The only way out, as she saw it, was to chance having the media come down on her or to serve Isabelle up as the *scandale du jour*.

As always, Nina chose to save herself.

"Eccentricity" was a word attributed to either the very rich or the very old. The young and those of the working class who acted in an unconventional or unorthodox manner were derided as weird, bizarre, curious, odd, and even sometimes freakish. Only the dignity of age or the accumulation of great wealth allowed a more elegant label to be applied.

Flora Pujol personified the word *eccentric*. She was out of the ordinary, she behaved in an unusual manner, and it was readily apparent to all who knew her that she did not have the same center as those who moved in her circles. What made Flora even more unique was that she had been eccentric for all of her eighty-nine years.

Born into the uppermost strata of Barcelona society, she had defied just about every convention associated with the aristocracy. A quixotic artist who had remained deliberately single, but definitely not celibate, she had been a puzzle to her father, an inspiration to her grandniece, a source of strength for her siblings, a pariah to those who resolutely cleaved to custom, and an icon of envy for the doyennes of her social set who whispered behind her back, raised outraged eyebrows to her face, and secretly wished they had the courage to say and do everything for which they criticized Flora Pujol.

Although this appeared to be the last of her days, Flora saw no reason to take a sudden turn toward tradition. It hadn't appealed to her in the past. It held no lure for her now. Besides, she thought, a girlish giggle bubbling inside her ancient chest, the two people she cherished most in this world— Alejandro Fargas and Isabelle—had always told her that she was the measure against which normal was judged. Without her idiosyncrasies, they argued, how would they know what was typical and what was unique?

Her lower lip quivered. It was only the thought of leaving them that saddened her. Nothing else. She didn't mind the notion of leaving this world and going on to the next. If her current existence was dry and unappealing, it was because she had wrung out of this lifetime every drop of living it had to offer.

As she lay in her bed, physically weakened by a failing heart, she surveyed her domain, a grand suite filled with the touches of color and whimsy that had become part of her legend. Her large four-poster loomed as an elaborate confection, its spiraled posts enameled with red blobs, fuchsia splashes, turquoise streaks, and tangerine squiggles, abstract forms that glistened from numerous coats of shellac and twinkled from an occasional dash of glitter.

Overhead hung a canopy that, like the tie-back drapes in the doorway separating her sleep area from her sitting room, was made of cellophane. Flora loved cellophane. To her it was the essence of illusion. It was sheer, but not soft; rigid, but not inflexible; translucent, but not without substance. She liked the way it crinkled when she touched it, the way the sun refracted into spears of color when passing through it, the way its folds seemed to hold light within it, and especially the way it shocked those who never would have thought to use it as a decorative medium.

To the unenlightened, cellophane was something ordinary, a pedestrian material used for gift wrap and food storage. To Flora, cellophane was a metaphor for art. Those who had no desire to explore beyond that which they could see and touch, could never appreciate the heart of a painting or the soul of a sculpture. Only those able to cast aside preconceived notions and look past the obvious would be able to access the magic art offered.

"Beyond the surface lies the spirit," Flora was fond of saying to those who sought her advice. "Don't accept what you see. Reach out and embrace what you feel."

As the sun inched its way toward the west and the shadows of afternoon lengthened, Flora summoned her nurse.

"My beads," she whispered, wondering why the voice in her ear sounded so delicate and frail when the voice in her head was so loud and strong and clear.

Quietly, unobtrusively, the young woman hired to tend to Flora's needs fulfilled the request, placing a primitive chain in Flora's hands. As she backed away toward her place in the corner, she crossed herself instinctively.

Flora's eyes lodged a protest, but her mouth was too weak to verbalize a correction. The dear girl thought these were rosaries and that Flora was about to seek God's blessing. She was a sweet thing, well meaning and well intentioned, but extremely misguided. These beads did not aid prayer; they did not represent Aves and paternosters and Glorias. These were counters for the breaths one needed to transcend the corporeal and attain the clarity of vision possible only through the third eye. Meditation was the succor Flora sought, not penance.

Almost desperately her fingers clutched at the necklace, her arthritic digits trembling as they tried to hold on to the strand of small, dried *Rudraksha* berries. Her thumb and index finger gripped the first bead, the one nearest the gold silk tassel. In, she breathed, drawing the breath through her nose, listening as it echoed throughout the cavern inside her skull. Out, she exhaled, cleansing her body of its tensions. A single breath became a gentle rush of wind, blowing through her, carrying with it a sense of peace and calm.

With each breath her fingers moved from one bead to the next in a rhythm composed four thousand years before. A round of one hundred eight breaths equaled a *mala*. When she was young she easily completed the ten *malas* of a full meditation. These days, if she completed one, she considered it an accomplishment. One hundred eight beads. One hundred eight breaths. Twelve cycles of nine. To the yogis of ancient days, nine was the number of truth, because no matter how you multiplied it, it always came back to itself: $9 \times 2 = 18$, $8 + 1 = 9$; $9 \times 5 = 45$, $4 + 5 = 9$, etc. It always came back to the truth.

Flora tried to still her brain so she could experience the ecstasy of total tranquillity. Yet each bead reminded her of what she had to do before her brain was stilled forever. Calling out to the spirits of those who had gone before, she sought their advice and their support. Suddenly switching ecclesiastic gears, she sought God's help as well. Instead of chanting a mantra, she recited an Ave. Instead of seeking a higher consciousness, she invoked the Eternal Being. Though she had forsaken the formal rituals of the church many, many years before, Flora often vacillated between offering traditional prayers and seeking a different realization. To her, the avenue wasn't nearly as important as the destination.

Eyes closed, breathing slow and deep, her hands glancing the tops of her beads, Flora lifted herself beyond that which was earthly and beckoned to the keepers of secrets.

"It's not safe," she said to them. "I can't leave until she's safe!"

Inhale. Exhale. One hundred one. One hundred two.

"There are things Isabelle knows . . . bad things . . . awful things . . . things that could hurt her."

Inhale. Exhale. One hundred five. One hundred six.

"*He* knows what's locked inside her mind. *You* know, too. Please! Let it go! Let her go."

Inhale. Exhale. One hundred seven. One hundred eight.

Flora held the last bead between her fingers. A tear squeezed through a tightly clamped eyelid and lingered above her cheek.

Life. Lies. Secrets. Beads. What was existence except a series of cycles that went from beginning to end, then back to the beginning again? It didn't matter who you were, what you were running from, whom you were trying to protect, or what you were trying to hide: there was only one possible route to inner peace.

Like the number nine, it always came back to the truth.

The room was dark. Rain slapped against the windows, pelting the glass with unrelenting insistence. The sky rumbled. Seated on a chair facing the window, he watched in terrified silence. He hated thunderstorms. They frightened him, made him edgy. Tonight, the sound of the squall was particularly jarring, clanging inside his brain like a lighthouse bell warning ships away from the rocks. It was an apt analogy, because just then he felt like a small craft caught in the swell and pitch of a raucous tide.

Control, he reminded himself. It was all about control: having it, using it, mastering it. For so many years it had been the prime motivation behind every move he made. It had determined his friends, his enemies, his business partners, even his lovers. Control. Of himself and others. Most of all, of his emotions.

Once, many years before, anger and rage and frustration had formed an alliance so forceful, it overrode his governance, inciting foolish acts that had sired disastrous consequences.

It had taken years to recover from that catastrophic lapse, years to bury that failure in the recesses of his mind, years to convince himself that it had been an aberration, a mad, deviant incident that had nothing to do with the rest of his life. Yet every now and then, when he was alone and it was very dark, particularly when it was very stormy, that heinous memory surfaced, bringing with it an inescapable reality: he had not been the only one to witness his digression.

So much time had passed without a confrontation, it seemed obvious that she had been muted by fear, that the terror and anguish created by what she had seen had constructed a wall of repression around the truth. Clearly it was a high wall, thick and sturdy enough to have hidden his monstrous secret for twenty-seven years. Yet he had never found her silence reassuring.

Even seemingly impenetrable walls had a way of cracking and crumbling.

The party had ended hours ago. Isabelle should have been sleeping, but slumber eluded her. One reason was the thunderstorm rumbling outside, its percussive sounds muffled only slightly by the thick glass of her window. Isabelle had never reacted well to nature's dramatics, and tonight was no exception. Each time a bolt of electricity jagged across the sky, she clutched at her blanket, wishing she didn't feel so foolish about wanting to hide within its folds. *One Mississippi . . . two Mississippi.* When she was a little girl, Miranda had taught her to count the seconds between the moment she sighted the lightning and when she heard the thunder. Each second equaled a mile, Miranda had told her, teaching the child a way to measure how far away lightning had struck. Miranda had meant it as a tool for providing comfort, but nothing would ever anesthetize Isabelle to her fear of storms. Thunder. Lightning. Powerful winds. Blinding rain. These were not elements of weather. To Isabelle they were the ingredients of violence.

Contributing to her wakefulness was the knowledge that in the morning she was due to board a plane bound for Barcelona. Her suitcases sat in a corner, packed and waiting. They were ready for the journey. She was not. Returning to the city of her birth had never been easy. She had not left willingly, and each time she revisited the site of the cataclysm, the pain in her heart grew more profound.

This trip loomed as particularly difficult. The thought of having to witness her great-aunt's slide from life was almost unbearable. Flora was the last of Isabelle's blood kin, but more than family ties would be severed by her passing. Flora had always been Isabelle's aesthetic mentor, her guide through the tangled jungle of imaginative thought. Though others had helped steer her along the road to greatness, Flora was the one who had shown Isabelle how to reach the visions that lived within her. The prospect of losing the woman whom Isabelle viewed as her creative wellspring evoked a sense of void almost impossible to comprehend.

Trembling slightly, she switched on a light and reached for her sketch pad, hoping that by busying her hands she would distract her mind. As her pencil skittered across the blank page, it struck her—not for the first time—how ironic it was that Tía Flora's home was called El Castell de Les Bruixots, the Castle of Ghosts. For months Isabelle had felt like a ghost: restless, wandering, unable to settle in any one place. Much of her uneasiness sprang from the suspicion that someone was plotting against her. Yet whenever she tried to put those premonitory feelings into some kind of rational order, scenes of Barcelona projected onto her mental screen: The Castell. The Ramblas. The town house on Passeig de Gracia. Was she supposed to go? Or stay away? Was the danger there? Or here? Was there someone lurking on the borders of her life, waiting to end it? Or was she simply transposing her dread of Flora's death into an unsubstantiated apprehension?

Isabelle closed her eyes and leaned back against the headboard. That morning she had confided her fears to Miranda.

"Tomorrow's journey is a sad one," she had said, taking Isabelle's hands in her own and drawing her close. "Tía Flora is dying, but in truth, my darling, you are not mourning her death alone. You're still feeling pain from other losses, ones you have never been able to put to rest. No one is following you. What you're feeling is the past catching up to you."

Isabelle sighed as she recalled Miranda's words, acknowledging their veracity. In fact, she had spent most of her life running away from things that happened during her earliest years. She supposed she had always believed that if she ran fast enough and far enough, she would leave the past behind. That hadn't happened. Instead she was mired in her long-agos, stuck in a time warp that was slowly eroding any chance she might have for future happiness.

During her party, she had thought a great deal about happiness and how many definitions it had. To some it was one other person loving them. To others it was a family, a house, a small garden. To many it was money and all it could buy. To a few it was serving God or lending a helping hand to those in need.

Painting made Isabelle happy. The act of it. The feel of the brushes, the canvas, the paint itself. The energy. The effort. The orgasmic joy of completion. And yes, the acceptance of what she produced made her happy. Outside of her career, what else provoked a smile or a contented sigh? A weekend with her family. A quiet dinner with friends. Travel to a place she'd never been. Music. She grimaced. Everything she had mentioned was an external, something she experienced through others, something she could touch and feel with her hands but not her heart.

She was thirty-four years old. According to some, she should have been married by now, perhaps even a mother.

Isabelle's eyes opened and strayed downward to her sketch pad. Without conscious demand, her pencil had drawn his face. Using her finger, she traced the jut of his chin, so square and strong, the broad expanse of his brow, the carefully sculpted line of his nose, the deep set of his probing, intelligent eyes. She hesitated before following the curve of his mouth. So much pleasure, so much wisdom, so much passion, had flowed from those lips. No one had ever generated such intense heat within her. Probably because while others had caressed her body, he had connected with her soul.

Just then, she missed him terribly. She could have used a dose of his common sense, his strength, his ability to analyze a problem down to its most common denominator; she could have used a hug. But she had turned him away. What he had never understood—what the others had never understood—and what she could never fully explain, was that for her, love wasn't enough. She had to feel safe. And she didn't. Not with him. Not with anyone.

Isabelle hadn't been aware of her tears until they splashed onto her drawing pad, blurring the lines of his face. She stared at the distorted image and shivered. Her tears had redrawn his eyes and revamped his mouth. Why did *this* face bother her? she wondered. Hastily she ripped the sketch off the pad, crumpled it into a ball, and tossed it across the room, as far away from her as she could get it.

It landed near her luggage, making her wonder whether it was an omen. Outside, the storm raged. The sky exploded with electricity and thunder. Suddenly Isabelle was more frightened than ever to return to Barcelona. All around her were harbingers of violence, the promise of impending evil growing stronger every day. She couldn't see it or touch it or put a name to it, but it was there, spreading, gaining strength, ravaging her soul like a metastasized cell.

Something terrible was going to happen. She shivered at the thought, petrified because it wasn't the first time she had felt this way.

Then, someone she loved had died a brutal death. Now Isabelle feared she would be the victim of the same savage hand.

CHAPTER 1

Barcelona, Spain
August 26, 1956

Althea de Luna felt a peculiar twinge at about five in the afternoon, but since it was eight days before her due date and her doctor had cautioned that "first babies don't fall out," she paid little attention. Later that evening, during a dinner party in Campíns, the twinge intensified. Trying not to draw attention to herself, she took a few deep breaths until the feeling passed. When it returned ten minutes later, she excused herself, motioning to her husband to follow her into the hall.

"Martín, I think my labor is beginning," she whispered, not wanting to disturb the others.

Her husband's green eyes narrowed. His hands went immediately to her shoulders, as if to steady her. In truth he was the one in need of support.

"You're not due until next week. If I had thought . . . we . . . I never would have suggested we come out here. It's over an hour to the hospital."

Althea smiled, reached up, and brought Martín's face close to hers so she could kiss his cheek. Even though she was five feet five, at six feet four Martín towered over her. Big and strapping, he always made her feel petite and protected, something that these days, being so cumbersome and large with child, was not easily achieved.

"It could be a false alarm."

"We should have stayed in town. This was stupid! Whatever possessed me to bring you here?"

"I asked you to," she reminded him. "This dinner was important to me."

Althea was both painter and patron. Unlike many Spanish artists—including the giants, Picasso and Miró—who years before had opted for expatriation rather than risk having their creativity stifled, Althea had not fled the country. Instead she had made it her personal cause to circumvent Franco's censorship squads.

One way was to transpose her artistry—and her politics—onto fabrics. As head designer for Dragon Textiles, a company owned by Martín's family that produced cloth for clothing as well as home furnishings, she was acutely aware that textiles could be used as a subtle but effective ideological tool. Popular themes translated into abstract patterns created powerful subliminal messages: books in flames reminded Catalans that Franco had burned their national literature; renditions of the dragon—Catalonia's symbol—or George, their patron saint, reinforced a sense of national pride.

Outraged by the treatment afforded their fellow artists, Althea, along with Martín's aunt, Flora Pujol, became underground champions of Catalonian art. Flora's home in Campíns, a small village nestled in the hills outside of Barcelona, was a large structure with many rooms and many secret passageways, the perfect place to harbor those whose creative visions clashed with the arid landscape of Franco's Spain. Several artists—whose studios had been destroyed by the police—painted up in the tower of the Castell. Others used the Castell to store their work. Many had their incomes supplemented by generous gifts. And whenever possible, Althea and Flora conspired with several of Barcelona's more courageous gallery owners to mount exhibitions that ran counter to the politically correct aesthetic decreed acceptable by the state. This particular evening Flora had invited several young painters to the Castell to discuss just such an exhibition.

Althea felt another contraction begin. Her full, ripe lips tightened into a grimace of pain.

"That's it!" Martín declared, completely unnerved by Althea's obvious discomfort. "We're leaving."

Taking great care not to jostle her, he guided his wife to a nearby chair, settled her, headed for the dining room, and returned in seconds with Flora in tow. Though Althea protested, Martín lifted her in his arms and carried her outside. When he put her down and she noticed the car idling in the driveway, she squealed like a delighted child. Martín's passion was classic automobiles, and while his collection included some of the most exquisite machines ever engineered, none could compare with the beauty before her.

"Whatever possessed you?" Althea asked, completely stunned.

"Love," Martín said, grinning and bending in a chivalrous bow. "This is a very special occasion. You're about to bear our child. You deserve to be treated like a queen."

Living with Martín, Althea had learned enough about cars to identify a Rolls-Royce Phantom I. Long, sleek, its body gleaming black, this was truly a chariot fit for a pharaoh. While the chauffeur's coach remained open to the sky, as was customary with many luxury touring cars of the era, the passenger compartment was enclosed and exquisitely appointed: a brass-framed sofa upholstered in petit point made in Aubusson, as was the carpet that covered the floor; small crystal vases; windows draped with gold damask curtains; gilded metal fittings; a cabinet of richly grained walnut.

Had Althea not been interrupted by another contraction, she would have examined every last detail of this automotive gem, but her body was demanding that she postpone her inspection for another time. While Martín eased her onto the sofa, pulling out one of the auxiliary seats for her legs, Flora arranged a stack of pillows and towels; her maid, Consuela, replaced the frippery in the bar with bottled water and bandages. Flora positioned herself next to Althea and held her hand as Martín started toward Barcelona.

As the car accelerated, so did Althea's labor. They had traveled less than five miles when Althea announced her water had broken. As the Phantom rolled down the hills of Campíns and through some of the smaller villages that made up the environs of Barcelona, her contractions increased in intensity.

"Breathe," Flora said, mopping Althea's brow, acutely aware of the fact that they might not reach the hospital on time and that she might have to midwife this child. "Keep breathing."

Though Flora knew little about the birthing process, yoga had taught her that breathing in a certain way could soothe pain and relieve stress. Fortunately she had instructed Althea in these breathing techniques before. All she had to do now was reinforce what Althea already knew and pray that Martín got them to Barcelona sooner rather than later.

Up front, Martín pushed the Phantom as hard as he could, but there was no way he could convert a Rolls-Royce into a Lamborghini. This engine was meant for touring, not racing; this car had been built for those who craved elegance, not speed. Gripped by frustration and self-recrimination, he pressed the accelerator to the floor, stomping down as if to frighten it into going faster. Unfortunately for Martín, in this particular battle between man and machine, the machine won.

"It's coming," Althea said, wincing in pain as her body tried to accommodate the mounting pressure.

Quickly Flora helped shift Althea's position, lifting her slightly yet keeping her body slanted downward. She had read somewhere that in primitive cultures, where women squatted to give birth instead of lying flat on their backs, the pain was less intense. Carefully she lowered Althea's legs so that gravity would assist and not fight the baby's birth.

"I can see the baby's head," Flora said, her voice filled with a mix of astonishment and worry.

"I've got to push," Althea said, her hands gripping the sofa with such ferocity that her knuckles were bone white.

"Not yet. Just keep breathing. Soon, you'll push."

As she waited for the next contraction, Flora searched her memory for diagrams and pictures, trying to recall steps and procedures. During the past several months, she had informed herself on the process of childbirth—not because she ever expected to be in the position of bringing this child into the world, but because she had wanted to be part of the most significant event of Martín's and Althea's lives.

Althea's face was streaked with sweat. Her hair was soaked and clung to her skin. Flora mopped her brow and begged her to remain strong.

"Soon," she said, lifting the curtains, praying that she would see the lights of the hospital.

"Now!" Althea screamed, straining against the pain, tearing at the needle-point of the sofa.

Suddenly the car stopped, the back door opened, and Martín climbed inside.

"I heard Althea scream. I had to help." His voice was small, scared.

"You can help by getting us to a hospital."

He shook his head. "We're too far away. We'll never get there in time."

"Martín!" Althea moaned and reached for her husband.

The contractions were more painful and more frequent, coming every other minute. Responding to Flora's crisp commands, Martín climbed onto the seat and slid behind Althea, straddling her, allowing her to lean against his chest. He gripped her under the arms and held her as she pushed. Althea shrieked as her skin ripped to allow the head to push through. The contraction subsided. Exhausted, she whimpered in pain. Martín whispered in her ear, encouraging her, soothing her, loving her. Another contraction began. Althea's keening filled the car.

"Breathe," Flora urged, unable to disguise her nervousness. "Push!"

Althea sucked in her breath and strained to rise above the heat and the pressure assaulting her loins. Pushing down, she felt another tear, another pop, as the baby's shoulders slid into Flora's hands. An eager silence descended as they waited for the miracle to complete itself. On the next push, Martín and Flora watched in awe as a tiny human being slithered out of its mother and became part of the world of man.

Flora remembered to turn the baby upside down and clear its air passages. As a lustful cry filled the cabin, she wrapped the child in a blanket, placed the newborn on Althea's abdomen, and watched as father and mother greeted their daughter with tearful gurgles of reverence.

"She's so beautiful," Martín whispered, his voice muffled by amazement.

"I love you," he said to Althea, brushing a strand of hair off her face and stroking her cheek, unable to express his gratitude any other way.

"I love you, too." Althea raised her chin, inviting a kiss, which was willingly given. "Just think," she said, looking from Martín to the child napping contentedly against her chest, "we're parents now."

"You're also in the backseat of a car," Flora reminded them. "You belong in a hospital."

Martín shook his head and laughed. "Is that a hint?"

"Consider it a command," she said, hugging him and then firmly shooing him out.

Later, after mother and child had been admitted to the hospital, Martín and Flora went to the de Luna town house on the Passeig de Gracia. After Flora retired, Martín closed the door of the library behind him. After lighting only a small lamp, he went to a portrait of his grandfather and lifted the frame. Hidden behind the painting was a wall safe. He twisted the dial, opened the steel door, and withdrew an old family Bible. Covered with an elaborate jacket of hammered silver and decorated with a large cross made of inlaid rubies and pearls, it dated from the eighteenth century.

With appropriate respect, Martín carried it to his desk, set it down, and splayed open the front cover. He ran his fingers over the delicate parchment pages on which were written the names of his ancestors. Slowly he traced the line of descent. His finger paused when he came to his mother's name.

If only you were here, he thought, wondering how the ecstasy over the birth of his child could suddenly turn into such intense longing for his mother.

Having lifted the cover of the brass inkwell on his desk, he dipped a quill pen into the black liquid and, beneath his own name—Martín Josep Ildefons de Luna—inscribed the name he and Althea had decided upon—Isabelle Beátriz Rosa de Luna.

Martín stared at his daughter's name. His daughter. He couldn't keep from smiling, thinking of her sweet face, her pink skin, her tiny bow-shaped mouth puckering as she slept. Recalling his last sight of her swaddled in that hospital cradle, he thought she seemed too small to carry the burden of such a long name. But, he thought with the resignation of one who understood that certain customs were inviolate, as the newest link on three dynastic chains—the de Lunas, the Pujols, and the Murillos—it was expected that she perpetuate the line. In keeping with tradition, she bore the names of Martín's mother and grandmother, as well as Althea's grandmother, Isabella, the only relation Althea thought of with any affection.

For a long while after Martín returned the Bible to the safe, he sat in the shadows and thought about family—what his had been like, Althea's, what they both wanted their own family to be. He ruminated about the relative merits of each limb on their respective trees, wishing he knew exactly what Isabelle had inherited from whom. He worried that she might have too much from one side, not enough from the other.

In the end, Martín acknowledged that no matter how perfect he wanted Isabelle's world to be, he couldn't alter the arrangement of her genes. She was the sum of many parts, blessed and cursed by those who had gone before.

She had a lot to live up to. And a lot to live down.

It would follow that one born in a Rolls-Royce Phantom would lead a charmed life, and Isabelle did. Enthroned in a nursery that used every shade of pink conceivable, Isabelle was pampered by all who attended her, particularly her parents. To them she wasn't a baby, she was an amulet imbued with magical powers. Touching her, caring for her, even simply being in her presence, was enough to chase away a headache or lighten a dark mood or make silence as lyrical as a song. She was more than God's most magnificent creation, she was an affirmation of their love for each other.

As Martín told Althea repeatedly, "Only a love as pure as ours could have produced a child as perfect as Isabelle."

While Althea tried to instill a modicum of structure and discipline into Isabelle's life, Martín was a hopeless spoiler. For the longest time Althea complained—albeit lovingly—that Isabelle would never learn to walk because Martín carried her everywhere, that she would never learn to speak because Martín gave her everything she needed and then some. Rarely did he come through the door without a surprise for Isabelle—a toy, a sweet, a new storybook, an invitation to take a ride in "one of Daddy's special cars." He liked to feed her and bathe her. He even liked to change her. If she was cranky, he soothed her. If she was restless, he played with her. If she was sleeping, he was content to sit and watch her. In whatever way he could be part of her life, he was.

Althea was just as attentive; her devotion simply took a different form. She took Isabelle on long walks in the country, waxing poetic about the glory of nature's artistry. She pushed Isabelle's stroller up and down the streets of Barcelona, talking to her about Antoni Gaudí, the flamboyant architect who had left his flourishing signature all over the city, about artists like Picasso, Miró, and Dali, and musicians like Pablo Casals. She took Isabelle to pick grapes in the family's vineyards and, when she was older, to the mill where Dragon Textiles were produced.

"Make a pretty picture for Mama," she said to Isabelle one day, seating her daughter on a high stool in front of a drafting table, supplying her with crayons and a sketch pad, and encouraging her to scribble away. Althea was hoping to occupy the four-year-old while she attended to a few pressing business matters.

A while later Althea gushed at the squiggly red lines and splotches of vibrant color that danced on the paper in front of Isabelle. "Can Mommy have this?" she asked, suddenly inspired.

"Do you want to hang it up?"

Althea chuckled. The walls of her office were tattooed with Isabelle's pictures. "Better than that," she said, studying the colorful abstract. "I'd like to turn it into fabric."

"You would?" Since Isabelle didn't fully understand what that meant, she remained cautious.

"I would."

Isabelle thought for a minute or two, shrugged her shoulders, and agreed. "Only if I can have a piece," she said rather seriously.

Althea laughed as she hugged her little negotiator. "It's a deal!"

Over the next several days mother and daughter spent their afternoons observing the process of creating cloth. Diego Cadiz, Dragon's foreman, supervised the tour, patiently answering all of Isabelle's questions about how cotton became yarn, why it was wound onto large spools, how the loom could turn hundreds of separate strands into solid sheets of cloth, who wrapped it on the tubes that soaked in the dye vats, and who got to pick the colors.

Althea took Isabelle into a smaller workroom, where she watched as a pattern based on her design was etched onto cylindrical screens that were then slipped inside porous metal rollers that would dispense the various dyes. When Diego activated the rotary machines, Isabelle's eyes widened as a river of plain cloth flowed in a steady stream toward the rollers. Gripped by invisible teeth, the cloth hugged the rollers, went up and around, and came out imprinted with a design Isabelle recognized instantly as her own. She giggled with delight.

It was with great ceremony that Althea presented Isabelle with the first cut. Kissing her daughter on both cheeks, she draped the swatch around Isabelle's neck like a scarf and declared the pattern a permanent part of Dragon's design inventory. Blushing, yet beaming with undisguised pride, Isabelle curtsied in response to the affectionate applause of the assembled staff, clutching the cloth square as if it had been spun of pure gold. To Isabelle it was that precious.

As a family, the de Lunas spent every Sunday they weren't in Campíns visiting Flora, strolling Las Ramblas. Running from the Fountain of Canaletas in the Plaça de Catalunya at the top, down to the Columbus Monument by the harbor, the Ramblas was Barcelona's spinal cord. With traffic moving up one side and down the other, the middle serving as a wide, tree-lined pedestrian esplanade, the Ramblas were a string of five connecting avenues that had its genesis as a river whose channel was used as a roadway during the dry season. In the fourteenth century this barely consequential waterway was paved as a means of linking the harbor and the old town. As Barcelona grew, so did the Ramblas, which eventually evolved into the nerve center of a very vital city.

During the day it was a place to shop, meet friends, enjoy lunch, discuss business, start or end a romance, have your palm read, or get your pocket picked. Rumors started on the Ramblas. Demonstrations began on the Ramblas. Protesters waved their flags of discontent on the Ramblas. Soccer fans celebrated victories on the Ramblas. Everything happened there, because there one could be a spectator and part of the spectacle, all at the same time.

From their town house on the Passeig de Gracia it was a short walk to the upper part of the Ramblas, but the distance was lengthened considerably by the number of passersby who used Isabelle as an excuse to stop and chat. While it was true that *en famille* they presented a stunning portrait, and Isabelle was an especially outgoing, friendly child, it was the endless curiosity about Martín and Althea that attracted attention.

For one thing, their lineage was impressive. He carried the bloodlines of two of Catalonia's most distinguished families; she was the daughter of Andalusian aristocrats who counted not only royalty among their ancestors, but also Bartolomé Esteban Murillo, one of Spain's most famous painters. For another, their life-style was one of wealth and indulgence, unusual at any time, an act of utter daring during the reign of Francisco Franco. Yet it wasn't lineage, life-style, or political defiance that had captured the imagination of Barcelona's citizenry; it was the gossip that had surrounded their courtship and continued to envelop their marriage.

Althea had shattered her parents' dreams by running off with a man they considered beneath their daughter's station; their response had been to disown Althea. Martín, considered by many to have been the most eligible bachelor in Catalonia, had broken dozens of hearts by eloping with a woman unknown to the doyennes of Barcelona society. Their response was to treat Martín's bride with guarded indifference and deny her welcome.

Ultimately Althea proved irresistible. First, there was the matter of her beauty. Althea was an incredibly sexy woman, long-legged and sinuously shaped. Her hair was a mélange of ash blond and coffee brown, a thick mane that fell past her shoulders and seemed always to have a tousled, just-got-out-of-bed look. Her eyes—dark and hooded and heavily lashed—described a woman who preferred the amorous glow of candlelight to the self-aggrandizing nature of the social spotlight. Her lips were full and lush, her nose straight and thin. Her cheekbones were high and sharply planed, her skin extremely pale and delicate. Whether in jodhpurs and boots astride a horse, a sedate suit kneeling in church, a silken dress at the opera, or lying naked in bed, she was, as Martín defined her, what a dream would look like if crafted in flesh.

While her physical appearance cast her as a man's woman, women found themselves drawn to Althea's generosity of spirit, her grace, the genuine warmth of her smile, and the magnetic aura of energy that seemed to surround her. Her critics found it hard to mount a case once they had spent time with her. Those who did found that Althea didn't intimidate easily. She was happy with Martín, he with her; everything after that was a bonus. If one chose to be her friend, she was welcoming. If one chose to be her adversary, she accepted the challenge. Eventually the list of her enemies dwindled until only two continued to disapprove of who she was and whom she had married—her parents.

Even after their initial novelty had worn off, people continued to find the de Lunas exciting. To those for whom passion was more memory than reality, Martín and Althea personified romance. If they were dining at a restaurant or having coffee at a café, they leaned toward each other, their eyes locked, their body language showing them to be engaged in the art of seduction more than the art of conversation. If they were at a party and there was music, they danced as if they were making love, their bodies joined in rhythmic union. Even touring the kiosks along the Ramblas, their appetite for each other remained on display: they never allowed themselves to be more than inches apart, Martín with his arm either around Althea or linked with hers, his hand holding hers or touching her shoulder.

Many had thought that Isabelle's birth would change the dynamics of their relationship, that parenthood would diminish their endless attraction for each other. When it became apparent that their delight in Isabelle had only increased their mutual fascination, some became infected with the virus of envy. Others simply acknowledged their uniqueness, granting that the inextinguishable flame of desire that fired the de Lunas' marriage burned for very few.

Despite appearances, sex was not their only adhesive. The notion of family made a stronger paste. Outside of themselves, Isabelle, Tía Flora, and her longtime companion, Alejandro Fargas, Martín and Althea had no relatives. Fortunately neither of them craved a clan, nor did they care about what others viewed as normal or standard or conventional. Since each was the product of a less-than-perfect childhood, both had entered the marriage determined to redefine the word *family* for themselves. While neighbors repeated patterns they had learned from their parents, Martín and Althea made theirs up as they went along.

Another commonality was art. Though Martín could claim no talent of his own, he allied himself with his wife and aunt, doing all he could to combat the cultural cleansing of the Franco regime. In addition to supplying Althea with whatever funds she needed to fight the smothering of Barcelona's artistic voice, Martín's personal charity became the Avda Gallery on the Consell de Cent. Rafael Avda was a boyhood friend. Martín's grandfather had granted the loan that had helped Rafael's grandfather open the gallery; Martín intended to help prevent its closing.

Friendship aside, Rafael was a sound investment. He was a man with an unerring eye for art and a head for business. In 1953 Avda saw an opportunity and seized it. Franco had accepted American aid in exchange for allowing the United States to use Spanish land for air bases. Taking advantage of an ease in restrictions, he traveled to the United States in search of new artists. The American Southwest, in particular, overwhelmed him.

His first exhibition was small, a test to help gauge the reactions of both his clients and the censors. When the former responded favorably and the latter didn't respond negatively, he set about mounting a larger show. As insurance, he billed it as a cultural exchange, inviting several American dealers to come to Barcelona to exhibit their artists' work and then to select works of Avda's Spanish artists that they would exhibit in America. It was an exhibition that was meant to open eyes as well as doors.

And it did.

Miranda Duran arrived in Barcelona feeling rather insecure. All the other dealers in the delegation had long-standing reputations. While it was true that for the past five years Miranda had managed her Enchantments gallery quite successfully, until she paid off the purchase price—which, the way things were going, would probably take ten years—she was the owner in name only.

The night of Avda's opening, she was a nervous wreck. It wasn't simply that this was her first foray into the international art market; it was the stark contrast between Santa Fe and Barcelona. Though art was taken seriously in Santa Fe, the life-style was far more casual, the dress more informal, the chat breezier. Miranda found Barcelona's more formal atmosphere intimidating. She fretted about her dress (black, but maybe a bit too basic), her hair (thick, black, and plaited into a long braid), her height (five feet one), and her conversation. She worried that she would spend the entire evening being overshadowed by her compatriots, until she realized she could do something the other American dealers could not—she could speak Spanish. Though the accents were different, the language was the same.

Infused with a sudden burst of confidence, Miranda separated herself from the pack and began to snake her way through the crowd, standing next to the works she had contributed to the exhibition, speaking to whoever stopped and expressed admiration for her artists. Some prattled and moved on. Miranda identified them immediately as lookers, not buyers. Several lingered long enough to prompt Miranda to believe that she and Rafael might actually be able to record a sale. The one who lingered the longest was Althea de Luna.

Miranda had noticed her hours before. It was hard not to. Swathed in a tight white dress that looked as if it had been engineered rather than designed, her deep blond hair twisted into a deliberately precarious knot, her legs positively endless, she was a stunning creature who dared inattention. As she approached her, Miranda anticipated a great deal of eyelash fluttering and very little substance. Instead she was confronted with a woman on a mission.

"The colors are extraordinary," Althea said, leaning closer to an abstract painted by a young Native American new to Enchantments. "I like the way he creates the illusion of transparency by superimposing one tone on another."

She took a few steps backward, squinted, walked forward again, and spoke without actually looking at Miranda.

"Do you think . . . what's the artist's name again?" she asked, scanning her program.

"Ben Fireside."

"Right." She nodded and smiled. Miranda had never seen lips that red or teeth that white. "Do you think Ben Fireside would consider designing fabric for me?"

"Fabric?"

"I'm Althea de Luna," the woman said, extending her hand. "We own Dragon Textiles here in Barcelona." When Miranda didn't respond, Althea explained further. "We produce some of the finest textiles on the continent. I serve as Dragon's design director. Though we maintain a small staff of textile artists, I try to enlist outside talent whenever I can. Uniqueness, you know."

Miranda nodded and tried to look sophisticated, but in truth she didn't know a thing about textile production.

"I'm eternally fascinated by different cultures and their motifs," Althea continued, oblivious of Miranda's confusion. She walked several paces to another painting. Miranda followed. Althea tilted her head, squinted her eyes, and studied the canvas. "What are these called?" she asked, pointing to several sticklike figures.

"They're petroglyphs," Miranda explained, "the religious symbols of the Pueblo people. Mostly they represent the Indians' dependence on the land and its bounty, and their reverence for Mother Earth."

"Are you an Indian?" Althea asked with sudden boldness.

Miranda smiled. Foreigners often mistook her lightly tinted skin and licorice hair to mean that she was of a tribe. "No," she said.

"Oh." Althea sounded disappointed. "Rafael said there were a lot of Indians where you come from. I guess I just assumed that's what you were."

"I'm Spanish-American. There are lots of us in New Mexico, too."

"Forgive me for sounding so stupid." Althea was truly embarrassed. Changing the subject quickly, she said, "Rafael told me Santa Fe was a wonderful city."

"Why don't you come and see for yourself? You could stay at our hotel." Miranda surprised herself with the invitation. "I could show you around and introduce you to Ben Fireside and several other artists whose styles might interest you."

"What a wonderful idea! Martín and I have never been to America. My daughter, Isabelle, will love it! Do you have any children?"

"Yes," she said. "I have a daughter also."

"How old is she?"

"Nina's six."

"Isabelle's not quite four, but very bright and very sophisticated for her age. Do you think they'll get along?"

Miranda smiled. "I don't see why not."

"If they connect as quickly as we did," Althea said, taking Miranda's hand and squeezing it, "they're going to be very good friends. We're all going to be very good friends."

"I hope so," Miranda said honestly.

Suddenly the sunny expression on Althea's face clouded. She stared at the small, dark woman for a moment.

"My husband's aunt is a very spiritual woman. She believes there are no strangers in our lives; that everyone we meet for the first time is either someone we knew in another life and don't need anymore, or someone we need to know now." She paused. An odd chill hurried up her spine. "I know it sounds crazy, but for some reason, I think we were supposed to meet."

Isabelle perched on Martín's lap in the back of the car, her nose pressed against the window. While the adults talked, she watched the city of Albuquerque sink below the horizon. Gone were the neon signs and colorful billboards, the jagged skyline of the business center, the clusters of low-rise apartments, factories, and motels that flanked Interstate 25. In their place loomed an endless stretch void of people, houses, roads, and shops. Miles of flat land sprawled before her, a valley floor interrupted by occasional hilly swells that seemed to rise and fall with the gentleness of a breath. It was mid-December and the grass had yellowed, making the dark green of pine and piñon stand out in even greater contrast. In the distance she could see the outline of navy blue mountains sketched against the paler blue of a winter sky, a line of clouds floating in between the peaks like a puff of smoke.

Despite its location between New Mexico's largest city and its capital, this was a solitary landscape that spoke of isolation and remoteness, of something primeval and indifferent to the needs and desires of modern civilization. According to Miranda's husband, Luis, this was not a no-man's-land, but a succession of Indian reservations, each one a parcel of land owned by the people who had lived there for centuries and fought to live there still.

As they approached Santa Fe, Miranda told Isabelle that when the Indians first established a village there six or seven centuries before, they called it "the dancing ground of the sun."

Though Isabelle thought it a pretty name, she didn't know what to make of the small town the Durans kept calling a city. Barcelona was a city. There, thousands of tall buildings stood shoulder to shoulder, towering above sidewalks and streets jammed with people and cars and sidewalk kiosks. Parks and squares were grand affairs with fountains and decorative pavements and

elaborate plantings. Balconies boasted flamboyant ironwork, doors were ornate, courtyards were intricately planned and artfully designed.

Santa Fe's plaza was pretty but small, a few benches and a modest monument. Its buildings appeared plain and squat in comparison with those Isabelle was accustomed to. Made of mud and timber instead of brick or
concrete, shaped into squares with rounded edges and no ornamentation,
painted a color that reminded Isabelle of cinnamon and sugar, the houses
looked like large, child-designed cubes. The only fanciful touch she could
find was something Miranda called a corbel, a wooden piece the Spanish had
introduced to pueblo architecture to support the roof beams and lintels of
the *portales.* Some were rounded and looked like scrolls, some zigzagged like
steps; the ones Isabelle liked best were notched to look like the wings of a
powerful eagle, sitting atop each column of the *portale* as a symbolic sentry.

When Isabelle asked why so many of the window frames and doorways
were painted an almost electric blue, Miranda said it was to keep away the
evil spirits. Isabelle had wanted to ask how they knew which spirits were evil
and how many were around and what happened if someone didn't paint their
windows blue, but before she could ask even one of her questions, Luis
pulled up to La Casa.

Located at the far end of East Palace, La Casa stood sequestered behind
an undulating adobe wall on a small rise. Luis drove beneath a gently curved
arch into a small courtyard with a stone drive and several cottonwood trees
and two very distinguished giant elms. The main house was large and multi-
storied, yet again it looked nothing like anything Isabelle had ever seen
before.

There seemed to be no order to the building. One floor didn't rest directly
above the floor below but jutted to the right; another rose to the left; and
another pushed out toward the back. Yet each level was connected by a series
of elevated porches that Miranda called miradors.

As she followed her parents inside, Isabelle was relieved to notice that the
large wooden doors of the entrance were a blazing turquoise that even the
most nearsighted evil spirit couldn't miss.

The lobby was small and welcoming, the decor, though pleasant, would
never have garnered more than a single star in a guidebook catering to the
well-heeled traveler. Ocher-colored walls with rounded edges and a lumpy
texture common to Santa Fe interiors brought out the yellow tones in the
terra-cotta floor and the wooden ceiling. Covering much of the floor was a
slightly threadbare Navajo rug of clay red, coal black, and sand. A leather
couch that showed its age faced two cushy armchairs also in need of refur-

bishing. Tucked in the far corner opposite the reception desk was an adobe fireplace that bulged like a tumescent belly, filling the room with the cozy, country scent only a log fire could produce.

A little girl warmed her hands by the fire. She was standing so still and appeared so pale, Isabelle thought she might have been a statue. Her skin was the soft white of the finest pearls, her eyes the gray of kitten's fur, her hair the pale yellow of the silken threads that lined the husks of summer's corn. Everything about her appeared to be soft and delicate, yet her bearing spoke of a sterner spirit.

"Who's that?" Isabelle asked, remaining true to her reputation as the unquenchable questioner.

"This is Nina," Miranda said, walking over to the six-year-old, kissing the top of her head, and taking her hand. "Nina, this is Señor and Señora de Luna and their daughter, Isabelle."

"Welcome to La Casa. I'm very pleased to meet you," Nina said, delivering her prerehearsed greeting slowly and distinctly. She smiled politely, but her eyes had locked on the small, dark-haired girl sandwiched between the adults.

Isabelle smiled in return but shrank behind her father, out of the way of the penetrating gaze of Nina Duran.

"Want to see my room?" Nina said, having decided that Isabelle passed muster.

Isabelle wrinkled her forehead and looked up at her father. Nina was confused. Quietly Martín translated into Spanish what Nina had said.

"Isabelle speaks very little English," he explained.

"That's okay. I speak Spanish," Nina said rather assertively. "Don't I, Mama."

Miranda smiled and patted her daughter's head. "Yes, you do."

Martín and Althea exchanged a few words. They spoke quickly. Their accents were different. Nina caught only a few words.

"I'm not as good as Mama and Papa," she said, abruptly downgrading her fluency and, hopefully, the expectations of these strangers.

"Maybe Isabelle can help you with your Spanish and you can help her with her English," Althea said.

"Good idea!" Nina nodded in agreement, trying to hide her relief. Then she reached for Isabelle's hand. "Come!"

"Where are we going?" Isabelle said in Spanish.

"*Mi sala*," Nina said, pleased with herself for responding so quickly. "My room!"

Fully in charge, she led the younger girl away. All the way down the hall, they could hear her translating everything from Spanish into English: wall, floor, ceiling, door, chair, painting, flower, rug.

To Nina, the de Lunas were exciting, more exciting than anyone she had ever met. Aside from their looks, which were startling enough, the force of their personalities overwhelmed her. Althea was a veritable goddess. The way she looked, the way she dressed, the way she walked, the way she talked—everything about her was tantalizing and exotic. Though at first she inspired worship, she proved far too accessible for anything as standoffish as adulation. She was a hands-on woman who knew how to play with a six-year-old, how to roll on the floor with a four-year-old, and how to widen her embrace to include more than one child at a time. Best of all, she knew how much little girls liked to play dress-up.

One afternoon Nina, Althea, and Isabelle locked themselves in Althea's bedroom, trying on clothes and experimenting with makeup. Since Miranda wore only lipstick and a rare smudge of rouge, Althea's bag of tubes and pots and cakes of color looked like the inside of a pirate's treasure chest. While Isabelle watched and giggled, Althea used a variety of brushes, sponges, pencils, combs, and hairspray to create La Bonita Señorita Duran.

Next Althea put Nina in one of her printed silk dresses, wrapped a scarf around the tiny, childish waist, and bloused the dress so Nina wouldn't trip over the hem. Nina slid her feet into a pair of Althea's high heels and began to hobble around the room, feeling clumsy yet prettier than she had ever felt before.

While she was preening, Althea went to the closet and retrieved a beautifully packaged box.

"For you." Althea curtsied. Isabelle clapped her hands in anticipation.

Nina, surprised by the unexpected gift, opened the box slowly. Inside was an exquisite fan made of black lace and fine ivory.

"All elegant Spanish señoritas have fans like this," Althea said, showing Nina how to hold the fan so the back of her hand faced out, how to wave her wrist gently and seductively.

Striking an exaggerated sirenlike pose, she lowered her head, thrust her shoulder forward, and fluttered both fan and eyebrows, reducing the girls to fits of laughter.

Nina would treasure that fan—and that moment—forever.

Martín was more giant than god. Whatever he did, it was bigger or more or grander or greater than anything Nina had ever seen. He ate more than any three people she knew. He didn't sit on a chair as much as he overwhelmed it. If he laughed, it was louder and longer than anyone else. If he performed a kindness, it was more generous and unselfish an act than any she had experienced before. Years later, when she would be asked to give an example of what it was like to be around Martín de Luna, she would reminisce about the day he took them skiing at Taos.

An early snowstorm had covered the mountains north of Santa Fe, enticing skiers to taste the first powder of the season. Miranda and Luis had begged off, but Martín rallied Althea and the two girls, packed everyone into Luis's truck, and took off for the slopes. He rented equipment and arranged for half-day lessons for everyone, even Isabelle. After lunch, Althea took Isabelle to the bunny hill. Martín and Nina set out for more challenging terrain.

Nina wasn't a complete novice—she had skied at the Santa Fe basin many times—but there weren't many green beginner trails at Taos: this was a mountain of steep inclines and narrow passageways. Watching him studying the trail map, she feared that Martín, who probably could ski everything labeled intermediate blue and all but the most death-defying blacks, would take her somewhere she didn't belong. She was grateful—and relieved— when he sought easy terrain for their first run.

They cruised a wide expanse that snaked down the outer edge of the mountain. The snow was soft and fresh, making their skis fly a little faster than she might have liked, but Nina handled it. What she lacked in style, she made up for in speed and aggressiveness. They took three runs, but as they rode the lift for the fourth, it began to snow again. The light changed. Visibility decreased. When Martín raised the possibility of downloading on the lift and riding back to the base, Nina's expression was frought with such disappointment, he immediately suggested they play follow the leader down the mountain. He would be the leader, she would follow directly in his tracks. To make the game harder, he told her, they were both going to sing.

Nina didn't want to admit it, but she was scared. It was getting harder and harder to see.

"The winner is not the one who skis the fastest," he said, smiling reassuringly as he dusted snow off her goggles. "It's the one who sings the loudest."

Nina nodded, raised her voice in concert with his to the strains of "You Ain't Nothin' but a Hound Dog," and started down.

They had gone halfway when Nina caught an edge and fell into a huge snowdrift near a cluster of aspens. Her skis were twisted around each other.

Frightened, unable to untangle herself, she wondered when Martín would realize she wasn't behind him. It wasn't long before she heard him calling her.

"Here!" she yelled. All she could see was a sheet of white.

"Nina!"

The voice came from below, to her left. Again she shouted, "Here!"

Suddenly Martín appeared through the curtain of white, trudging up the mountain. Edging his skis into the hill for traction, he sidestepped in the direction of her voice. She bit her lip and tried to be brave and not cry.

"Okay," he said in a calm, even voice. "Let's get you out of here."

Quickly he snapped off his skis and began to dig her out, talking to her all the while to ease her fear.

"What happened? You decided you didn't like the song? Or maybe it was my voice you didn't like? I know I'm not as good as that fellow Elvis Presley, but I didn't think I was so awful you would run for the trees just to escape."

She tried to smile but couldn't. She was hurting and the strain was beginning to take its toll. Finally Martín freed her, snapped off her skis, and lifted her gently out of the snow. When she tried to stand, her left leg buckled and she cried out in pain.

"Okay, that's not going to work," he said, cloaking his distress behind a mask of nonchalance. "Let's try something else."

First he stuck her skis and poles into the ground, out of the way of other skiers but far enough from the trees to be visible to the ski patrol. Then he hoisted her up and told her to try to put one foot on each of his skis. Holding her tight against him, he said, "Let's see if two can ski as cheaply as one."

Nina nodded and attempted to screw her mouth into a courageous smile, but inside she was terrified. The snow was so thick and the light so flat, they could barely see three feet in front of them. Martín seemed unconcerned, despite the fact that he was gripping both his poles with one hand and Nina with the other.

As they wended their way slowly down the mountain, he told her what it was like to ski in the Pyrenees and the Swiss Alps. He sang Spanish ditties she couldn't understand but found funny anyway. They debated whether they should have hot chocolate or hot cider when they got to the lodge. And he put her in charge of trees and signs: if she saw either, she was to alert him. She was paying such close attention to her task, she never realized that her feet had left his skis. Martín was carrying her.

When they reached the base lodge, Althea and Isabelle were waiting out front. Isabelle saw them and started to cry.

"I was scared, Papa," she said, running toward him. "I thought something bad had happened to you and Nina."

Without letting go of one little girl, he lifted the other up into his arms. The instant they were eye to eye, Isabelle began to cross-examine Nina.

"What happened? Did you fall? Where does it hurt? Where are your skis? Did they break? Do you have a boo-boo? Is it bleeding? Can I see it?"

"Nina fell and hurt herself," Martín said, laughing at his daughter's verbal barrage, "but really, sweetheart, she's fine. Aren't you, my little pal?"

Nina's ankle was throbbing, but as she looked from Martín to Isabelle, saw how concerned her new friend was about her and how concerned Martín was about Isabelle's reaction, she smiled and said, "Yeah, we're great!"

Isabelle threw her arms around her. Althea kissed her. Martín hugged her. Her ankle was killing her, but it was one of the best days of Nina's life.

Miranda and Luis met the de Lunas at the emergency room of St. Vincent's. Despite their family doctor's assurances that Nina's injuries were minor, Miranda hovered over her daughter like a persistent cloud, watching, sheltering, guarding the child against some mysterious negative that only Miranda could see.

Althea watched the other woman with great interest, recalling a conversation they had had earlier the same day. They had finished their meeting with Ben Fireside and were having tea in the office at Enchantments when the conversation had segued into talk of children. Althea, who had been unsuccessful in conceiving a second child, had mused aloud about certain fertility treatments she had read about that were available in America and not in Barcelona, wondering whether she should ask Miranda's friend and physician, Jonas Hoffman, his opinion on the viability of such options, wondering too about adoption. Miranda had demurred, plainly uncomfortable with the conversation.

"Nina's adopted, isn't she?" Althea asked, believing it was too obvious to be an off-limits inquiry.

"Not officially, but we've filed the papers."

"Does she know?"

Miranda nodded. "We told her last year."

Althea sensed ambivalence. "Didn't you want to tell her?"

"I might have waited until she was older."

"Why?"

"I thought it would make her sad."

"Did it?"

Miranda smiled. "No. In fact, she seemed to like the notion that we had picked her out, that she was our daughter because we wanted her to be, not simply because she was born to us."

"What a lovely sentiment," Althea said, her eyes growing dark. "I grew up with parents who never made me feel loved or wanted. Believe me, I would have been better off with adoptive parents like you and Luis."

"You're exaggerating," Miranda said, certain that Althea had stretched the truth.

"I wish I were," she said. "My parents were meant to own animals and to have servants and to possess many beautiful objects. They were not meant to have children." She looked directly at Miranda. "Why is it that people who shouldn't have children do, and those who should can't?"

Miranda averted her eyes, her body language displaying an intense reluctance to continue the conversation.

"I'm sorry," Althea said, recognizing that she had trespassed into a private area. "I've intruded where I don't belong. Forgive me."

After a few moments Miranda said, "Luis and I had a child. He died when he was three years old."

"My God!" Althea was thunderstruck.

"His name was Gabriel. He was a beautiful baby, bright and bouncy, always running around and getting into trouble." She brought a hand to her eyes, wiping away tears that came from a bottomless well of grief. "When he was two and a half, the pediatrician felt a mass in his abdomen. After dozens of tests, they told us Gabriel had nephroblastoma, a cancer of the kidneys they call Wilm's tumor. They performed surgery, pumped his little body full of chemicals, and gave him radiation. Still, he died."

Althea wanted to comfort Miranda, but words could never soothe this kind of pain.

"It was years before Luis and I even tried to have another child. When we did, we couldn't conceive." Miranda gnawed at her lower lip. When she spoke, her voice resonated with the pathos of unwarranted guilt. "I always believed that after what happened to Gabriel, God had decided we didn't deserve another child. Then we found Nina."

"How wonderful, for all of you," Althea said, watching as Miranda struggled to climb out of her private darkness. "Did you get her through an agency?"

Miranda reacted as if Althea had aimed a flashlight at her. Her eyes widened, her body tensed. She had gone on alert, looking like someone alone in a house who heard someone breaking in.

"Sort of," she said, rising quickly and busying herself clearing away their teacups. When she turned her back on Althea and walked into the gallery's small kitchen, it was more than a gesture; it was a signal: the subject of Nina's adoption was closed.

Martín was very taken with the Durans. Hardworking, intelligent, generous people, they appeared on the surface to be simple folk with basic needs and ordinary dreams. Digging deeper, he found them to be incredibly substantial and complex. Miranda not only managed Enchantments and co-managed La Casa, she was also an accountant, an accomplished cook, and a voracious reader. Luis also was more than he seemed. Though extremely handy with a hammer and a wrench, he was also remarkably knowledgeable about things as diverse as the effects of modern dam construction on local irrigation and the importance of rethinking the national infrastructure.

It took a while for Martín to draw him out, but eventually he learned that Luis held a degree in engineering from a local university. He and Miranda had met in high school and married shortly after graduation. They had moved to Santa Fe so that Luis could attend school. To support themselves, they had taken jobs at La Casa: Luis as the night manager and all-around handyman, Miranda as a cleaning lady and part-time cook. As part of their compensation, they were allowed to live in a tiny casita on the grounds. Miranda and Luis had considered themselves blessed.

The hotel was small, only seventy-five rooms, but had been part of the Santa Fe landscape since the turn of the century. Unfortunately, the latest owner was more interested in pursuing a lounge singer in Roswell than in maintaining his property. When he defaulted on his mortgage, bank officials had no choice but to move for foreclosure. When word got out that La Casa was about to go on the block, a group of merchants got together and decided to back the Durans. Everyone knew that for years they had been running La Casa. With the bank's approval, the merchants put up the money to buy the hotel from the bank. The Durans would pay them back when they could. In eight years Luis and Miranda had never missed a payment. To them it wasn't simply a financial obligation, it was a matter of honor.

Though Martín had been born into money, his essence was that of a Catalan, an entrepreneur with the ability to appreciate and admire those who labored to turn dust into dollars. When he asked Luis about the strain of maintaining both the hotel and Miranda's gallery, Luis dismissed Martín's concern.

"We have too many loans to ever be rich in the conventional sense," he said, "but believe me, amigo, we're rich in other ways. We have a home, jobs, a wonderful daughter, and the respect of our neighbors. What's a little debt?"

Martín laughed with his new friend, but it was a hollow sentiment. He was becoming well acquainted with the concept of debt. The economy in Spain was a disaster. Properties that used to produce respectable profits had become red ink. The government had taken over the railroads and the steel mills and the banks, thereby eliminating private ownership by families like the Pujols and the de Lunas. Dragon Textiles and some of his machinery factories were still making a profit, but like most of his friends, Martín was forced to wonder how much longer he could stave off attacks against his fortune.

The de Lunas left Santa Fe several days before Christmas, leaving behind gifts and the promise to return, which they did—that summer, the following Christmas, and the summer after that. The bonds between the two families grew stronger, aided by a circle of friends that continued to grow with each visit.

Isabelle, the two Hoffman children, and Nina had become a foursome. Isabelle was the youngest, since Rebecca Hoffman was Nina's age and Sam Hoffman was two years older than that. Whatever she didn't know, they taught her; whatever she wanted to see, they showed her. By the time the de Lunas had spent their second year in Santa Fe, Isabelle knew how to ride western style, her English was almost as good as her playmates' Spanish, she had developed a passion for sopaipillas and tacos, and she was on a first-name basis with most of the Indians who camped beneath the *portale* of the Palace of the Governors.

While Althea ran off to the backcountry to paint when they visited New Mexico, Martín turned positively physical. Horseback riding and biking became daily activities, most often with Isabelle and her friends as his companions. Shopkeepers and townsfolk had grown so accustomed to seeing this giant of a man striding down the street with a flock of baby chicks scampering along behind him, they nicknamed Martín "Father Goose."

One particular morning the group had winnowed down to Martín and Isabelle. They decided to pedal to the top of Canyon Road, picnic in the hills, and then descend back into town. The climb wasn't terribly steep, but Isabelle was only six and her legs could pump just so hard. Recognizing her limitations, Martín attached a long rope that went from her bike to his. As long as she kept her balance and pedaled in tandem with him, they were fine.

The temperature was high in the eighties, not unusual for a Santa Fe summer. Though Isabelle and Martín had started out early, the sun rose quickly, drowning the city in a flood of dry, insistent heat. When they reached the top of Canyon Road, the path flattened out. Martín detached the rope so that both of them could ride at their own pace. Isabelle began to lag behind almost immediately, but because Martín was so huge, even from a distance she could see him clearly.

The sun blazed hotter. Isabelle was flushed from the heat of the day and the exertion of the exercise. Her legs hurt and begged her to stop, but she pressed on. Suddenly Martín's form disappeared from the horizon. It happened so quickly that Isabelle was certain her eyes were playing tricks. She studied the vacancy before her, blinking, waiting for his hulking shape to reappear. When it didn't, she pedaled as hard and as fast as she could until she reached the spot where he lay, long limbs tangled among tires and pedals and handlebars. His face was ashen. He wasn't moving. She wasn't even certain he was breathing. Panicked, she called his name and tried desperately to rouse him, but he didn't respond. She didn't know what to do or where to go. All she knew was that she was afraid to leave, just as afraid to stay.

Behind her, she heard a truck coming their way. Running into the middle of the road, she jumped up and down and waved her hands until the driver stopped. Luckily there were two men in that truck—one man alone never would have been able to lift Martín. After affirming to each other that indeed Martín was alive, they hoisted him onto the bed of the pickup and raced toward St. Vincent's. Isabelle held her father's hand, cried quietly, and prayed as hard as she could.

The horror continued even after they reached the hospital. They slid Martín off the truck and strapped him to a table with wheels. People were shouting. One man put tubes in his ears, ripped open Martín's shirt, and pressed a metal thing against his chest. Then they whisked him through a set of double doors that closed in Isabelle's face.

"Papa!" she screamed, banging on the doors.

She tugged at a few hems, desperate for attention. People stared at her, some scrunched their eyes into a look of concern, one or two promised to get someone to speak to her, but no one actually did anything. Finally a nurse asked Isabelle her name and where she lived.

Not long after that, Althea charged into the emergency room, her long legs moving with the speed of a track star, her blond hair flying behind her like a pennant on a yacht. The sight of Isabelle, crumpled in a corner of a vinyl couch, stopped her short. Her shirt and shorts were soiled, her hair was matted, and her eyes were puffed almost beyond recognition. Without saying a word, Althea lifted her daughter off the couch and hugged her tight.

"I'm so proud of you, my baby," she said, holding the frightened child close. "Papa's going to be fine. Don't you worry."

Despite a nurse's suggestion to the contrary, Althea carried Isabelle past the desk, down the hall, and into the examining room where Martín was. Both mother and child were relieved to see he was awake. Jonas Hoffman was at his side.

"Where's my little girl?" Martín said, forcing his lips to smile at Isabelle. "Come on over here."

Althea let Isabelle down, but before she went to her father, she looked up at Jonas, her eyes wide with fear and concern.

"It's okay," he said, nodding his approval.

Martín lifted Isabelle's hand to his mouth and kissed each of her little fingers. "I'm fine, sweetheart. It was the heat. Nothing to worry about."

Althea narrowed her eyes and stared at her husband. They would discuss this later, her look said, when they were alone. At Jonas's recommendation, Althea stayed only a few minutes longer and then took Isabelle back to La Casa.

It was several hours before Martín's test results were ready. They were seated in Jonas's office when his secretary handed him a stack of papers.

"Whatever it says on those reports, Jonas, is between you and me. Althea is not to know. Is that understood?"

"I will honor the doctor-patient confidentiality if that's what you want, but—"

"That's precisely what I want." Martín's tone was firm and absolute. "Now, tell me what's wrong."

"It's your heart."

"Serious?"

"Very." Jonas put down the papers and looked directly at Martín. Though he was gentle by nature, it was not his habit to sugarcoat diagnoses. "You have what's known as cardiomyopathy. It's a genetic disease that produces symptoms you've probably been experiencing for a while and have ignored."

"Like?"

"Shortness of breath, swelling of the ankles, fatigue . . ."

Martín shook his head. He had ascribed those symptoms to his smoking. He was young and active and, in his mind, physically fit.

"The muscle of your heart is deteriorating, Martín. Instead of being the healthy pump it once was, the muscle is softening, making it difficult for it to contract and do its job."

"Can't you fix it?"

This was the part of being a doctor that Jonas found most difficult—admitting that medicine had not yet found an answer to that question and, by conceding that fact, refusing a patient even that last resort, hope.

"No, my friend, I can't."

Martín's expression froze. His eyes fixed on Jonas's face. "How long do I have?"

"There's no way of knowing. It could be one year or ten."

Martín sighed and covered his face with his hands, as if to protect himself from the bomb that had just exploded in front of him. How would he tell Althea? Could he tell her? How would he adjust to what was happening to him?

And how could he ever accept that which most people denied—that life was limited?

CHAPTER 2

Barcelona, Spain, 1963

From the moment they returned to Spain, Martín's days became a desperate battle to retard the passage of time. He stretched one hour until it felt like three, cramming it with activities that exhausted whoever was his companion of the moment. Lunch with Flora, a biweekly ritual sacred to both aunt and nephew that once had served up equal portions of culinary and conversational spice, suddenly turned into a series of maudlin reminiscences: his childhood, her childhood, his mother's life and death, his life with Flora after that.

Meetings with Alejandro started off as they always had, with a discussion about Martín's various businesses and their wavering bottom lines, but began to segue with increasing regularity into inquiries about the advisability of consolidating several companies, liquidating others, shifting from maintaining a large manufacturing base in an unstable environment to making investments in foreign businesses functioning within more democratic, less economically volatile environments. While both Flora and Alejandro were confused by Martín's sudden solemnity, Spain's politics being what they were, his wasn't the only sober face in town, so neither pressed the issue.

Martín's nights became a private stage for tragedy, a darkened theater in which scene after scene of his personal horror was played out before him. Imagining his daughter needing a father and not having one was a daily torture. Equally painful were visions of Althea without a husband. The thought of her having to raise a child on her own, of her struggling to knit together the strings of their various interests within a society that found it difficult to respect women in entrepreneurial roles, of his absence making her prey to the interference of her parents—it was positively excruciating. Yet nothing hurt more than the knowledge that eventually she would fill the void his death would create with another man.

Before leaving his office on that fateful Sunday, Jonas had agreed to tell Althea that Martín's collapse had been exertion, nothing more. Martín had promised to put himself in the care of a cardiologist—which he did—and to tell Althea the truth, at home, when the time was right. Unfortunately the time never seemed right to say what he had to say. Althea had a right to know, but whenever he imagined her reaction, he recoiled, unable to bear the idea of witnessing her anger or pity or grief. So he said nothing, leaving her and others close to him to puzzle about the changes they saw in him. And there were changes.

The medicine the doctor had prescribed caused Martín's moods to become erratic. One minute he was charming, the next minute he was brooding and silent. Some days his level of activity was frenetic, other days he refused to leave his bed.

When Althea asked, "What is wrong with you?" Martín tried to explain, but the words "I'm going to die" simply stuck to his tongue like a toxic paste.

Althea wondered if Martín's strange behavior was a product of age: that she was beginning to show hers and Martín was not acting his. Flora disagreed with the first part but found merit in the second. For many men, forty was traumatic. Even Alejandro, that most stable of individuals, had found it difficult to adjust to the notion that at forty he was no longer a young buck. It never dawned on either of them that the problem was physical. Martín was young and virile and energetic and vital. Who ever would have diagnosed his bizarre conduct as a symptom of a man letting go?

July was so hot and humid and sticky, Isabelle couldn't wait to get to Majorca. She loved swimming in the calm, turquoise water of Palma's bay and playing in the soft white sand of the beaches that stretched along the coastline. Too, she couldn't wait to see her friends again. Over the years she had made met several other little girls whose families rushed to the Balearic Islands to escape the brutality of Barcelona's summers. They'd meet by the pool or on the beach and, under the watchful eye of whichever adults were closest, spend their days building sand castles, sunning themselves, and splashing about in the water. Sometimes, if they promised to be especially good, they were allowed to eat dinner at the same table—without their parents.

Aside from the fun she expected to have, Isabelle hoped that a change of scene might help her parents' marriage. Things were not right between them. Usually they were affectionate and caring. Lately they had been anything but.

The day after they arrived, Althea's best friend, Paloma Cervantes, appeared at the same hotel. Isabelle expected her mother to be surprised and delighted. She was neither. What was surprising was that Martín began spending a great deal of time with Paloma. Even Isabelle found his excessive attention to the lanky brunette annoying. Instead of playing with her on the beach, or having lunch on the terrace with her and Althea, or taking them on one of his famous shopping jaunts along the Avenida Rey Jaime III, he was off strolling with Paloma, his arm draped around her bare shoulders, his mouth close to her ear, whispering things that made them both giggle in a funny way. Isabelle didn't like it but said nothing. Althea didn't like it and told Martín so in no uncertain terms.

What struck Isabelle as odd was that when her mother began imitating her father, laughing and talking with several men drawn to her magnetic beauty, Martín responded with complete outrage. Though he railed at all of them, he seemed particularly vexed with one particular man, the one her mother called Paco.

His given name was Pasqua Barba. He was from Madrid and claimed to be a close childhood friend of Althea's. With his ebony eyes and coal black hair, he projected an aura of such intense sexuality that even Isabelle and her friends tittered nervously when he smiled at them. Though they didn't understand his effect, older women did. There was a provocative readiness about him that showed in the way he leaned in to a conversation, his body on the mark; the way his mouth pursed and his eyes fixed firmly on the speaker as he listened to whatever was being said, as if their words contained the keys to the kingdom.

By the end of the week, Martín had realized things had gotten out of hand. Paco wasn't merely catching up on old times, he was circling Althea, reconnoitering the territory like a general planning a midnight maneuver. Paloma was becoming more demanding, wanting more of him than he had ever intended to give. Suddenly he felt guilty and nervous and angry and jealous and repentant and scared, all at the same time.

After considering several alternatives, he decided to do what he should have done long before—tell Althea what was happening to him, as a way of explaining what was happening to them. The problem was finding a moment alone.

"Isn't it time for your nap?" Martín said, trying to shoo Barba from Althea's side.

Paco met Martín's fierce gaze with a taunting half smile. "Would you like to tuck me in, or should I ask Althea?"

"You don't want to know what I'd like to do to you."

"You're absolutely right," Barba said. "I don't want to know anything about you. I'm only interested in your wife."

Martín was stunned. He hadn't expected such bluntness.

"I'm glad to see you remembered she was my wife," he said, recovering quickly. "For a while it looked as if you'd forgotten that fact."

Barba laughed. "Watching you parade around Palma with Señora Cervantes, I'd say it looks more like you're the one who's forgotten."

"That's enough!" Martín was out of his seat and raging. "Get the hell away from us!" he stormed. "And don't let me catch you within ten feet of Althea or I'll break every bone in your smarmy little body!"

The smaller man stood, ignored Martín, and smiled at Althea. "I can see why you fell in love with him," he said as he bent over to kiss her hand. "He's charming."

Deliberately taking his time, Barba turned and sauntered toward the hotel.

Later that evening Martín and Althea quarreled again, this time in a crowded restaurant. The next morning, after yet another shouting match on the terrace, Althea went back to their room, packed suitcases for herself and Isabelle, and booked them on the first flight to Barcelona.

Instead of going to their town house on the Passeig de Gracia, or even to the castle in Campíns, Althea checked them into a suite at the Ritz Hotel. It wasn't that Isabelle didn't like the Ritz—going there for afternoon tea was one of her favorite activities—but that she couldn't understand why she and her mother were not at home with her father where they belonged.

It was several days before Martín tracked them down. Before heading over to the Ritz, he rehearsed his apology at least a dozen times. When he walked into the lounge and saw his wife and daughter having tea with Pasqua Barba, he exploded. Striding across the floor with targeted deliberateness, he stopped directly behind Barba and jerked his chair away from the table.

"It was very decent of you to save my place, but I'm here now. You can leave."

Without turning around, Barba returned his seat to its original spot and continued his conversation with Althea.

"I think Isabelle would love the ranch just as much as you always did." He laughed in an intimate, familiar way. "Do you remember when we tried to learn how to rope a calf and you lassoed my father instead?"

Althea started to smile, but it was an involuntary movement, halted by her sense of Martín's growing rage.

"Why don't you join us?" she said, reaching for Martín's hand and leading him toward the fourth chair in between herself and Isabelle.

As he sat, Isabelle climbed onto his lap. "Papa!" she squealed with obvious delight, snuggling next to him, her face bright and happy. "I'm so glad to see you. I've missed you terribly."

"I've missed you, too, little one." He hugged her tightly, rejoicing in the sheer pleasure of holding his child. Reluctantly he released her, but instead of shooing her back to her own chair, he let her remain on his lap, his arms still wrapped around her in a gesture that spoke with equal emphasis of love and possessiveness. Looking at her and then at Althea, he said, quietly but firmly, "I've come to take you and Mama home."

"What if Mama doesn't want to go?" Barba asked, needling.

"I can speak for myself, thank-you."

Both men reacted to the sharpness of Althea's tone.

"Then say what needs to be said. Tell him you're leaving him and coming with me."

Althea turned to Barba. "I'm not going anywhere with you, Paco."

"You're fighting your feelings, Althea."

"And you're fighting the truth." She leaned across the table and took his hand. "I never loved you. If I had, I would have married you when you asked me to. You're a friend, that's all."

"You heard the lady," Martín said, the triumph in his voice unmistakable.

Barba stood, shifting his gaze from Martín to Althea. His face was hard, his voice chilled. "You were promised to me, Althea. One of these days you're going to have to fulfill that promise."

"Or you'll do what?" Martín demanded, leaping up from his chair and grabbing Paco by the shirt.

Barba twisted free and backed away, mindful of the curious stares of those around them. Martín leered at him, but instead of cowering before the larger man, Paco laughed.

"Soon, de Luna, I'll take your wife away from you, too."

"Never!" Martín shouted, oblivious of the curious stares of those around them. "Didn't you hear the woman? She doesn't love you."

Barba turned toward Althea. His voice resonated with anger. "I don't care what she says. I know what I want. And I won't stop until I get it!"

Martín watched Barba leave with immense satisfaction. But if he thought the next scene was to be one of passionate reconciliation with his wife, he was mistaken. When he suggested that he come up to the room to help her pack, she rejected his offer. When he persisted, she lifted Isabelle off his lap and turned to leave.

"Just because I'm not going anywhere with him doesn't mean I'm going home with you."

Isabelle scrambled onto the bed and buried her head beneath a pillow. Her small hands clamped the downy puff against her ears, muting the angry sounds coming from the other room. Harder and harder she squeezed, but still she could hear her parents railing at each other, shouting terrible things about being unfaithful and deceitful and adulterous. Isabelle was too young to fully understand the acts that prompted such words, but even she knew accusations like those were aimed to hurt.

Isabelle peeked out from under the pillow to listen. The yelling had stopped. She thought she had heard a door slam, but she couldn't be certain. Outside, a loud thunderstorm had taken over the sky. Rain pelted the large windows that overlooked the Gran Via de les Corts Catalanes. Bolts of lightning pierced the black canopy of night that hung low over the city. Now and then a clap of thunder roared so ferociously, the room trembled. Isabelle was scared. She longed to seek shelter in her mother's arms.

Quietly, not wanting to disturb the momentary pocket of silence, she slid off the bed, padded toward the door, opened it, and looked into the sitting room. It was empty. On the other side of the suite, she heard water running. Her mother must have gone into her bedroom and was preparing to take a bath. She often chased her temper with a soothing soak. Again thunder shook the floor beneath Isabelle's feet. Again she thought about running to her mother, but she knew her mother didn't like to see her crying; lately she had been crying quite a bit. Isabelle assumed she was crying now.

She retreated to her own room, closed the door, climbed back onto the large bed, and reached under the pillow for her special security blanket: the fabric swatch she and Althea had created on her first visit to Dragon. Holding it next to her, Isabelle tried to lose herself in one of her storybooks, but disturbing memories of what had happened that afternoon in the tearoom dominated her consciousness. After a time, she thought she heard knocking and, then, the door to the suite being opened. She smiled. It was her father. He had returned, just as she thought he might, to apologize and make things right between him and her mother. It would take a while, she reasoned, but soon the anger would be gone; Martín and Althea would love each other again, and they could all go home.

Suddenly Isabelle heard Althea shout, "You have no business here. I want you to leave. Now!"

Isabelle leaned closer to the door. Again she heard her mother's voice demand that her visitor get out, but this time Althea's voice sounded strange. Nervous. Frightened, even. But that couldn't be, thought Isabelle. How could she be frightened of Martín? Even Isabelle knew that no matter what, her father would never hurt her mother.

The storm continued to rage, unleashing its fury in a continuous volley of sound and light. Isabelle tried to hear what was going on in the other room. A peal of thunder distracted her, but for a moment she could have sworn that the voice she heard arguing with her mother was not her father's.

Suddenly the lights went out—not just in her room, but throughout the city. Everything went black. In the next room her mother screamed. There was a thud, as if something had hit the floor: a crash and the sound of glass breaking. She heard clattering, as if people were scuffling. Her parents had always told her not to intrude where she didn't belong, but Isabelle was terrified.

Stealthily, her palms damp with fear, she turned the knob, opening the door a crack. She peeked in and directed her sight toward the noise, but her eyes hadn't adjusted to the darkness. Out of the murky shadows before her came muffled cries, an odd grunting sound, a slap, a hand pounding the floor. Her heart pounded in her chest. She remained frozen in the doorway, unsure about what was happening, even more unsure about what she should do.

With startling impetuosity, nature's power asserted itself. As lightning electrified the sky and shattered the blackness outside, the scene inside was illuminated by a quick burst of chilling blue light. In that instant Isabelle saw everything she wasn't supposed to see: her mother lying naked on the floor, a towel scrunched beneath her; a man in a dark jacket hunkered over her. She knew she was not meant to be a witness to this, but before she could escape behind the door, the man turned. He and Isabelle stared into each other's eyes.

Petrified, she ran back into the bedroom, seeking the darkest corner she could find. Trembling, her throat sore from swallowing her fear, she ran into the closet, squeezed her body against the back wall, and curled into a tight ball. If she could make herself small and unobtrusive and nearly invisible, she kept telling herself, he wouldn't be able to find her and punish her.

Please, God, don't let him find me, she prayed, holding her breath, believing that if she did, if she didn't make a sound, he wouldn't know she was there. She held her breath so long, she passed out.

When she opened her eyes, she was in Martín's arms. He was cradling her close to his chest, running down the hall, then down the back stairs of the hotel into the street, all the while kissing her and assuring her that everything would be all right. Isabelle was disoriented, her eyes glazed, her mind clogged by a throbbing headache. Before she passed out again, she asked about her mother.

She would never remember what her father answered. Nor would she remember anything else about that terrible night.

Despite Martín's best efforts to cushion her from the truth, the next day, in quick, brutal succession, Isabelle was assaulted by some very horrifying facts: her mother had been murdered, and her father was the prime suspect. Though Martín insisted he was innocent, the police continued to gather evidence and line up a string of witnesses they believed would guarantee a conviction.

Flora moved into the town house so she could tend her niece while Martín closeted himself with his lawyer, Alejandro Fargas, and tried to find a way out of the trouble he was in.

Alejandro was known for his keen mind and sharp tongue. Few who entered the court were as eloquent or persuasive as he. His only flaw, if it could be said he had one, was his complete honesty and total forthrightness. Often, according to his critics, he was so candid, so frank, and so pessimistic, he came off sounding like an alarmist. Alejandro's explanation was that he believed his clients needed to be prepared for the downside; the upside needed no preparation.

"They have witnesses who saw you and Althea fighting in the lounge of the hotel; witnesses who saw and heard you battling in Majorca; and witnesses who saw you leave the Ritz in a fury." Fargas flipped the pages of a pad, shaking his head as he read over his notes. "Your fingerprints are all over the suite."

"I was there," Martín said, frustration echoing in his voice. "I've admitted I was there. But I didn't kill her."

"There was blood on the carpet and beneath Althea's fingernails. It's B negative, same as yours."

"Thousands of people have B negative, Alejandro. That means nothing."

Martín pushed himself out of his chair and began to pace, shaking his head with annoyance. "Althea was my wife. We had a passionate sex life. Why would I rape her? It makes no sense."

Fargas narrowed his eyes and focused on his client. "Unfortunately, Martín, it makes a great deal of sense. You were cheating on her with Paloma Cervantes, blatantly so. You fought with her in public about a group of men who had gathered around her on the beach, yelling at her and Pasqua Barba like a jealous fool. Clearly you and Althea were having marital problems. It would be easy for a tribunal to assume that you hadn't slept together in some time, that because she was angry with you, she was denying you access to her body, that when she walked out on you in Majorca, you took it as an affront to your masculinity, and that when you went to her room that night, you asserted yourself."

"Why couldn't that same tribunal assume that Paco Barba asserted *his* masculinity?" Martín said, still stalking the perimeter of the room. "Everyone knows the man's been obsessed with her since childhood." Suddenly he stopped pacing and looked at Fargas.

"He was in the hotel, Alejandro, sitting there having tea with my wife and daughter. Paco Barba was there on the day of the murder. He rebuked Althea for breaking some kind of promise, insinuating that she had to make good on that vow. Why isn't that considered a threat? Why hasn't anyone tested his blood type? Why isn't he under suspicion?"

"Because you were the one putting on a grand display of temper," Fargas said matter-of-factly. "Not him."

Martín glowered at his lawyer. His green eyes blazed, but Fargas refused to be intimidated.

Instead he panned the length of Martín's massive form as he said, "The cause of death was a crushed larynx. The coroner has conjectured that during the rape, Althea struggled. Her attacker, presumably wanting her to lie still, pressed her to the floor with his forearm and, in doing so, crushed the delicate bones in her neck, killing her almost instantly."

Through gritted teeth, his hands curled into sweaty fists, Martín replied, "I didn't rape my wife, nor did I kill my wife. I fought with her. I offended her. And, God forgive me, I did cheat on her. But"—his voice cracked—"I loved her. I would never hurt her."

Martín collapsed onto a nearby chair, covering his face with his hands, allowing his grief to spill out. Alejandro rose and slowly crossed to the large man, placing his arm around his heaving shoulders.

"I believe you, my friend," he said in a voice choked with sadness. "The problem is no one else does."

The death of Althea de Luna was the talk of Barcelona. Up and down the wide, tree-lined Ramblas, all anyone spoke of was the Murder. On every street corner, in front of every kiosk, in every café, wine, and tapas bar, every restaurant and shop, Martín's guilt was debated endlessly. Some had converted rumors into fact and decided there was sufficient evidence to judge him guilty. To reinforce their opinion, they resurrected old stories about Martín's dissolute youth and the wild, uninhibited early years of the de Lunas' marriage.

Others dismissed the evidence as circumstantial and inconclusive, insisting that a man descended from the well-respected Pujol clan—Martín's mother's family—and the equally well-established de Luna line, couldn't possibly have committed such a heinous crime.

There was also the matter of Althea. Though she was a Madrileña by birth, the people of Barcelona had come to think of her as one of their own. Aside from breathing life into Dragon Textiles, one of the largest employers in Barcelona, as one of those who sheltered the keepers of the Catalan tradition, she had become something of a heroine.

It was no surprise, therefore, that the entire cultural community turned out for Althea's funeral. In accordance with her wishes, she was to be interred beneath a parasol pine in the small family cemetery at Campíns. In other places, at other times, it would have seemed unusual for one so young to have contemplated death and made specific requests for her burial, but in 1963 in Spain, premature death was not as unusual as it should have been.

Often Althea would stand on this particular hill, shading herself beneath this particular tree, and set her gaze toward the sea. Though the Mediterranean was barely visible from her perch, she liked knowing it was there, that at the end of the vibrant green line of woodland existed an equally vivid blue.

In addition to artists, architects, gallery owners, writers and publishers, friends and neighbors from both Campíns and Barcelona, city council members, and a few government officials, the entire work force from Dragon Textiles came to say good-bye to Althea de Luna. So did a team of detectives. As the mourners took their places, police rimmed the cemetery, noting every face in the doleful cortege so they could be interviewed at another time. As Martín, Isabelle, and Flora followed the casket toward the grave, the crowd parted out of respect for the bereaved. The detectives focused on the accused.

Martín was a study in tortured restraint. Though he felt as if his soul had been ripped from his body and were being lowered into the ground alongside his wife, no tears fell from his eyes, no sounds sneaked past his lips. When the casket hit bottom, his huge form slumped forward. He winced, his shoulders quaked, but still there was no audible admission of grief. As the priest invoked the blessings of the Holy Trinity on Althea's soul, detailing her goodness on earth so that she might gain admission to heaven, Martín silently detailed his sins. His mind begged Althea for forgiveness, pleading with whatever part of her still hovered over this world to understand that whatever his trangressions, whatever terrible things he had done, he had done them because he was mad with love for her, completely, insanely, possessively, and irrevocably in love with her. Despite what anyone thought, he still was.

On Martín's left stood Tía Flora, a sixty-two-year-old woman who had witnessed the burials of almost everyone in this small graveyard. She had grieved, in turn, for her parents and each of her three sisters. She had loved them all and missed them still, yet today her anguish was so great that it overwhelmed any sense of loss she had ever experienced. Certainly she mourned the absence of Althea, a woman who had been both daughter and friend, but also she mourned the absence of what had been. The past hadn't been perfect, but the future loomed disturbingly uncertain. Martín had lost his heart, his spirit, and quite possibly his freedom. Isabelle had lost her mother, which for any young girl should have been tragedy enough. But something deep inside told Flora that the gods who decided things like this hadn't finished with her darling Isabelle, that the full impact of this tragedy had not yet been felt.

At the moment, Isabelle felt numb. It had been five days since her mother's murder, and still she was having difficulty understanding what had happened. Each night she was assaulted by excruciating headaches and puzzling nightmares she couldn't decipher or repeat in any logical sequence. Each morning she awakened with the hope that after she had cleansed the sleep from her eyes, Althea would appear, the pain would go away, and all would be well. But Althea was gone and the pain remained.

Quickly she stole a glance at her father. His pain was carved on his face. He looked so sad and worried—but how could he not be, with policemen staring at him, watching his every move, calculating, judging, making it difficult for him to cry over his wife's death without the risk of incriminating himself in her murder?

It troubled Isabelle that she couldn't remember anything about that night. Everyone seemed to think she knew something very important, something vital to the case. The police had asked her. Tía Flora had asked her. Martín had asked her, over and over again. What did she see? What did she hear? Nothing, she told them. The storm had frightened her; she was reading storybooks in her bed; she must have fallen asleep. She didn't remember anything until she woke up in her bedroom at the town house.

The priest nodded toward Martín, motioning for him and Isabelle to approach the grave. Martín bent down and put out his hand. His fingers opened, ready to gather a clump of broken earth, but then they closed and his hand hovered in space, shaking, trying to postpone that wretched moment when he would have to throw dirt on the box that held his beloved Althea. Filling his lungs with a gulp of air, he filled his hand with soil and stood, preparing to finish the ritual of burial. As he did, the heavy silence that canopied the hillside was splintered by a piercing shout.

"Don't you dare!"

Everyone turned toward the man and woman who had emerged from the crowd and positioned themselves in front of Martín.

"You have no right," said the man, pushing Martín's hand so forcibly that the clotted earth fell from his fingers in a tight ball.

"What are you talking about? More to the point, what are you doing here?"

For the moment Martín forgot where he was and why; he forgot that he was surrounded by an audience. Anger had temporarily replaced grief.

Isabelle looked from Martín to Tía Flora, wondering who this couple was and why they had been able to provoke such a furious response from her father. Tía Flora moved behind her, placing her hands protectively on Isabelle's shoulders. Alejandro Fargas had joined them. Several policemen, also unsure about what was happening, left the periphery and moved closer to where the two groups had squared off.

"You are the one who should explain your presence, not I," said the man, baring his teeth so that they gleamed beneath his dark mustache. "I am Althea's father. This is her mother. You are her murderer!"

Whispers flickered through the crowd like fireflies as one explained to the other that the intruders were indeed Althea's parents, Count Javier and Countess Estrella Murillo. They were known to be close friends of Francisco Franco and sworn enemies of Martín de Luna.

"Althea has no parents," Martín said, fixing a steely gaze on the smaller man before him.

"Only because you took her from us," said Estrella Murillo, her contralto voice reverberating with hatred. "Now you've taken her life. You're not fit to stand on the ground hallowed by her presence."

As she lunged for Martín, Father Lorca and Alejandro Fargas stepped in, separating them, reminding them that a cemetery was hardly the place to air their grievances. The padre took the bereaved parents off to the side and spoke to them quietly. He soothed their tempers with assurances that there was a universal system of justice and that if they placed their faith in the Lord, good would be served and evil would be punished.

Alejandro's counsel was more pragmatic. "I don't care who they are and how you feel about them," he said. "The last thing you need is a display of violence in front of several hundred eyewitnesses, half the Barcelona police force among them. Now, get control of yourself!"

While Alejandro calmed Martín, Isabelle stood with Tía Flora, her eyes fixed on the couple identified as her mother's parents. Curious about them, a little frightened by their overt animosity toward her father, she studied their faces, searching for resemblances between them and her mother.

The woman was slender like Althea, with a fine complexion and a graceful neck, but her dark eyes were narrow and glinted; Althea's eyes had been open and glowed. Isabelle saw nothing of her mother in the man's face, but his hands reminded her of Althea's: slim, with long fingers and small, limber wrists.

It was when her gaze shifted back to the woman that she saw *him*. He was several rows back in the crowd, with a large hat shading his face; but the sun found its way beneath the wide brim, and for that moment, with his face spotlighted, Isabelle recognized the man from the beach, the man who had joined them for tea, the man her mother called Paco. He must have felt her staring at him because his eyes moved and locked on hers with an intense scrutiny that made her uncomfortable enough to look away. Several seconds later, when she worked up the courage to return his stare, she noticed he was gone.

Having positioned the Murillos on the left side of the grave and the de Lunas on the right, Father Lorca returned to his mission of laying Althea to rest. Holding Isabelle's hand gently, he whispered instructions into her ear, then let her go and smiled encouragingly. With great solemnity Isabelle did what he told her to do. She picked up some dirt and tossed it into the big hole that held the box in which her mother was going to sleep for eternity. As the dirt skittered across the wood of the casket, Isabelle heard Martín swallow a sob. Beside her, Tía Flora mumbled a few words and dabbed at her eyes with a handkerchief. Across from her, the woman swooned, the man caught her, and she buried her face into his chest; the two of them cried openly.

Isabelle remained silent and dry-eyed. She longed to talk to Althea, to tell her how much she loved her, how much she would miss her laughter and her wonderful bedtime stories, the afternoons they spent coloring, trying to create their own rainbows and landscapes, the mornings they spent exploring the hills around the Castell or the beaches by the sea, drinking in the exquisite genius of nature's brush strokes. She wanted to promise Althea that she would be well behaved and remember her manners and do all the things she knew would make Althea proud. She wanted to assure her that she would be good to Tía Flora and take care of her father, but she couldn't say any of it. Not now, not in front of all these people. She would come back some other time, when she could be alone with Mama.

Then she would find a way to say good-bye.

CHAPTER 3

That evening, when the Murillos returned to their estate outside Madrid, Estrella retreated immediately to her bedroom. Taking refuge in a deep-seated chaise longue, the large, heavily decorated space lit only by a small lamp, she stared at the roses that patterned the walls and windows. Drinking them in like a sedative, she waited for their delicate beauty to soften the harshness of the day, to soothe the rage she felt and filter out the cruel vision of the earth rent apart to receive the body of her only child. She dared not close her eyes, for if she did, she knew she would be confronted with the image of Althea wrapped in a burial shroud surrounded by the rocks and stones and dirt that would receive her when she became dust.

A maid brought her tea, but she couldn't bring herself to drink it. Too weak to lift the cup, she felt as if her strength, like Althea's life, had been siphoned from her. It didn't matter that she and her daughter had not seen each other in ten years or that they had been estranged emotionally for many years before that; Estrella mourned her loss intensely.

Javier joined her, taking a chair next to the window. Below him, illuminated by spotlights, was a formal garden worthy of a palace. Normally Javier felt a strong kinship with his flourishing preserve. Like the multifarious retreat below him, he was characterized by a certain predictability, a constancy, and a demand for harmony. As he often did, Javier searched for solace in the ordered rows of box hedges and standard roses, for comfort among the neat lines of iris, lavender, violas, and delphinium, but for once his garden failed to soothe him.

Estrella sought consolation in the symbols of her aristocracy, the antiques and paintings and lavish appointments that graced her surroundings. Neither spoke to the other, but that was hardly unusual. The Murillos weren't good with words unless they were commands or statements or declarations. If words were required to express an emotion or a sentiment, both had difficulty finding them, both were uncomfortable using them. Instead they harbored feelings, mooring them so they stayed in place, rather than allowing them to unfurl and catch the wind the way more adventurous souls did, the way their daughter had.

The butler knocked softly. Javier bade him enter.

"Señor Barba is here to pay his respects."

"I don't wish to receive any visitors," Estrella said.

"I'll be right down."

Javier nodded to his man, who receded as quietly as he had come.

"Paco must be grieving terribly," he said.

"He should be." Estrella's voice was cold. "This is his fault."

"How can you say such a thing!" Javier said, startled by his wife's accusation.

"He let Althea get away. He accepted her rejection instead of fighting for her. It was all planned. He was supposed to have married her. If he had, *this* wouldn't have happened!"

She spoke in a carefully measured cadence, her sentences paced like marchers in a cortege. Though her eyes remained fixed on her florals, her back had stiffened and her mouth had tightened into a taut white line.

"You're being too hard on Paco."

As he spoke, Javier wondered why he was bothering to mount a defense. He could tell by the emptiness in her eyes that she wasn't listening. It was difficult to move Estrella when she was in a mood. And this was not an ordinary mood: this was mourning. This was shock. This was undiluted fury. There was no argument strong enough to penetrate the barricade she had erected. Accepting the futility of further discussion, Javier left Estrella to her private sorrow and went to condole with the young man he had groomed to be his son.

With her husband gone, Estrella rose from her chaise and went to the skirted vanity table that occupied the far corner of the room. She opened a drawer below a tier of pink velvet and withdrew a fabric-covered box tied with ribbon. She returned to the chaise, carrying the box as carefully as one would carry a cinerary urn, which was fitting considering that the contents were all Estrella had left of the child she had borne thirty-five years before.

Slowly she removed her treasures, laying them out with near mechanical precision. There were pictures of Althea as an infant, large brown eyes overwhelming a cherubic face. There was Althea sleeping in her christening gown, Althea propped against the pillows on the Murillos' bed, perched on a pony, at a birthday party, in her white communion dress, standing between her parents in the living room, on the staircase, outside the cathedral, inside the Madrid apartment. Estrella didn't notice that Althea wasn't smiling in any of these keepsakes. She didn't see that each photograph was simply a recording of another pose, rather than a precious moment captured. Then again, Estrella had never been overly concerned with moments. She was a women dedicated to the larger picture. Her guiding principles had little to do with self-esteem and self-fulfillment and fun, and everything to do with training and grooming and the importance of station and order.

Order. That was what was distressing her so. Children were supposed to follow prescribed patterns. They were supposed to progress through a series of recognizable stages, stepping along the path laid out for them by previous generations, extending the path for future generations. They were supposed to marry and reproduce, mixing blood with an eye to improving as well as continuing a line. They were supposed to honor their parents and add dignity to their parents and bring joy to their parents through their achievements. But most of all, children were supposed to outlive their parents.

Althea had been doomed the day Martín de Luna entered her life, because she had allowed him to upset the order. He had destroyed the pattern. He had rerouted the path.

Estrella held up a picture of Althea and Paco when they had been about eighteen. They were in riding clothes, standing arm in arm in front of their mounts, she very slim and blond, he very dark and handsome. They were so elegant, so noble, so well suited. They would have made a divine couple, as Estrella had told her daughter innumerable times. Finding another picture of them—this one at a formal dance—that again displayed their obvious affinity, Estrella bristled as she recalled her daughter's reluctance to accept Paco as her destiny and her refusal to succumb to the wisdom of tradition.

When her parents had introduced her to Javier, Estrella had been delighted with their choice. He bore the name of one of Spain's most revered artists. He hailed from one of Seville's most prominent families. He had a title. His appearance was not unpleasant. And his manners were exquisite. It never would have entered Estrella's mind to wonder, as Althea had, about compatibility or common interests or passion.

For years both sets of parents nurtured the relationship, bringing the youngsters together with monitored frequency. No papers were ever signed or anything declared, but in accordance with customs well-known to and accepted by members of the upper class, Althea Murillo and Paco Barba were pledged to each other. When they reached the proper age, they would wed. Making the situation even more desirable was everyone's impression that the parties involved actually were attracted to each other. They flirted with each other. They blushed when the one's name was mentioned. They were secretive and excessively silent about their feelings. And they showed no interest in anyone else.

Until Martín de Luna ruined everything.

Estrella rummaged through the box, searching for the only picture she had kept of Martín and Althea. It had been taken at the reception for the newly-weds hosted by Martín's maiden aunts. Althea had sent it to her mother along with a letter pleading with Estrella to accept her marriage and her husband.

Hot tears singed Estrella's eyes as she looked at Althea and her groom. Even then she had thought they were ill matched. He was too tall for her, too big, too common. Yes, he had money. Yes, his family had a certain promi-nence. Yes, he might be considered handsome (if one did not consider large-ness a negative, which Estrella did). And yes, there appeared to be a certain magnetism between them. But so what! That was nothing but sex, and sex was unimportant in a marriage. Marriage was a contract. It was a negotiated merger between equals, not a simple joining of bodies.

Estrella tossed the photograph back into the box, unwilling to accept her daughter's happiness, even now. The photo landed on top of a picture that had been attached to a letter. Estrella picked up the package gingerly, hold-ing it slightly away from her, as if it possessed a curse. Perhaps it did. The picture was of an infant, the letter another appeal from Althea to acknowl-edge her life with Martín, plus a special plea for her parents to acknowledge her child, their grandchild.

Estrella stared at the photograph, seeking Althea in her daughter's daughter.

What she saw instead was an instrument of revenge against her daughter's killer.

Less than a week after Althea's murder, Alejandro Fargas joined Martín at breakfast and served him another helping of bad news.

"The Murillos have filed a custody suit demanding that Isabelle be turned over to them."

"Never!" Martín slammed his fist on the table, scattering silverware and rattling plates. "They didn't want their daughter and they're never going to get mine!"

"They've been very clever, Martín," Alejandro said. "Obviously they have sources at police headquarters, and they know that an indictment is imminent. It would be difficult for you to fight battles on two fronts, even more difficult if you're locked away in jail."

"I don't care if I'm swinging from a tree. They will not get Isabelle!" Hot tears flooded Martín's eyes. His huge body trembled with a storm of emotions that refused to be contained any longer. "She's all I have, Alejandro. You can't let them take her from me."

Fargas patted his friend's hand and nodded his understanding. "I may not have a choice, Martín. If you're convicted, the likelihood is you'll be sentenced to life in prison. Someone would have to take care of Isabelle, and whether or not you want to acknowledge the fact, they are her grandparents."

"I'll name Flora her guardian. Isabelle and Flora adore each other, and everyone knows it." Martín was thinking out loud, trying to convince himself of the soundness of his argument, so that if need be, he and Alejandro could convince a court. "Isabelle has practically grown up in this house. She's never even met the Murillos. I don't think she even knows who they are. Besides, Flora's been more of a grandmother to her than Estrella could ever hope to be."

"Their claim is not based on the assumption that you will be convicted," Fargas said quietly. "They want Isabelle even if you're acquitted."

"What!"

"They have asked for custody of their daughter's only issue. The basis of their suit is that you are an unsuitable parent and that they could provide far more in the way of parental guidance and devotion than you could."

"Bullshit! Those people don't have the faintest idea how to spell devotion, let alone lavish it on a child. They're cold, heartless bastards. Always have been. Always will be."

"That may be true, Martín, but with Althea dead, it's your word against theirs, and unless we can find evidence implicating someone else, you are about to go on trial for the murder of Isabelle's mother."

"In this case, the law is on my side," Martín insisted.

Alejandro nodded his head in agreement but said, "If we were only talking about this suit, that might be so, but we're not."

"What if the prosecution can't mount a case against me?"

"You're forgetting Javier's friendship with Franco. May I remind you that your beloved father-in-law is one of the Generalissimo's favorite aides?"

"So what!"

Fargas stroked his chin and emitted a frustrated sigh. He knew Martín was not as naive as he sounded, but still, a reality check was in order.

"This is not a democracy, Martín, it's a dictatorship. Right now, Franco *is* the law, and whoever can get to him wins."

"In other words, I don't stand a chance."

"Not much."

Martín left the Castell just minutes after Alejandro, having told Flora only that he would be gone for several hours and to keep a close watch on Isabelle. When he returned he invited Flora into the library. After closing the door behind them and settling beside her on the couch, he repeated what Fargas had revealed that morning about the Murillos filing a custody suit and the probable outcome of such an action.

As she gasped in shock, he took her thin, delicate hands and closed them inside his fleshy paws. "Will you help me?"

Flora looked deep into his eyes. "That depends," she said, squinting as if trying to get a better view of the soul that dwelt beneath the surface of those soft green orbs.

"On what?" He hadn't expected any hesitation. His entire life, he never remembered Flora thinking twice about giving him whatever he asked.

"On the answer to one simple question."

"Ask me whatever you want," Martín said, suddenly as nervous as he was curious.

"Did you kill Althea?"

Her words rebounded off the walls of the tall, bookcased room, bouncing from one side to another, back and forth like an echo in a canyon.

"No," Martín said.

Flora studied his face as he heard the question and spoke the answer, alert for a twitch, a bead of sweat, a telltale movement, anything that might indicate a lie. Having seen none of those things, she decided to believe him. Then again, she had always believed him.

"What do you want me to do," she said at last.

Martín smiled and hugged her. "I want you to take Isabelle away from them, before they take her away from us."

By the time most children were seven years old, they were too big to ride their father's shoulders. Thanks to Martín's size, he and Isabelle had been able to extend that particular pleasure. The hillside that surrounded the Castell was their favorite place to walk, especially in late afternoon when the sun dipped slightly over the forest of cork oak, creating a sensation of absolute peace and tranquillity.

While Martín strolled leisurely through the woods, Isabelle hunted for birds hiding among the branches or watched the clouds move across the sky, billowing now and then into shapes that reminded her of airplanes made of cotton balls or pudgy dogs or beds covered with overstuffed comforters. Sometimes she and Martín made up stories as they went, he giving the first line, she the second, he the third, and so on. Often they became so silly, the two of them collapsed with laughter. Today they walked in silence, neither of them able to find anything funny to say.

When they came to their favorite clearing, one that afforded a spectacular view of Barcelona sprawling toward the sea, he lifted Isabelle from his shoulders and seated her next to him on the grass. Taking a cluster of grapes from a pouch he had carried on his belt, he began immediately, wanting to quell the nervousness he read in Isabelle's eyes.

"You know that the police think I'm the one who hurt Mama."

Isabelle nodded and looked away. She knew he was embarrassed about his behavior preceding Althea's murder; she didn't want to embarrass him further.

"I did hurt her, but not the way they think." He gazed at a spot far away, but his vision was unfocused. He saw nothing in front of him, but much that was behind him. "I hurt her here," he said, tapping the spot on his chest where the heart was, "and I'm sorrier for that than I can tell you, but I didn't kill her, Isabelle. I swear to you I didn't."

For a moment roles reversed as the child patted the hand of the father, assuring him of her faith and her unwavering love.

"Someone else came into your room that night, someone who fought with Mama and hurt her very, very badly. I don't know who that someone is. What's worse, I don't know if the police care enough to find him."

Isabelle's eyes pooled. Quickly, so Martín wouldn't see, she lowered her head and sniffled. He placed a finger beneath her chin, lifted her face toward him, and wiped away the lingering tears. With an intensity that came from a sudden impulse to memorize her features, Martín stared down into Isabelle's wide-set eyes, delighting in their deep hazel color, a genetic blending of his green, Althea's brown. He marveled again at the pure ivory cast of her skin, the long, thick, silky mane of brunette hair that Althea had never wanted to cut. Though her nose appeared a bit too prominent right now, overshadowing a wide, softly arched mouth and a delicate, slightly cleft chin, Martín knew that in time, when age evened the dimensions of her visage, Isabelle's beauty would equal and probably exceed Althea's.

His hand trembled as the thought crossed his mind that he might never see her gain maturity. He shook his head, damning the thought, rejecting it, refusing to grant it residence in his brain.

"This is the worst time of our lives, Isabelle. We've lost the woman we both adored more than anyone else in the world, the woman who gave meaning to both our lives. We need to cry and to mourn and to be together while we do so, but the police won't let us alone with our grief."

Isabelle frowned, recalling her interviews with those men from the detective squad. "I told them everything I could, Papa, but they keep coming back, asking the same things over and over again. I don't know what they want, and it scares me."

Martín took Isabelle in his arms and held her close to his chest, protecting her, if only for the moment. He knew very well what the police wanted from her. They wanted her to place Martín at the scene of the crime at the time it was committed. Though he, like the police, suspected that Isabelle had seen more than she acknowledged, they believed she was protecting him; he believed she had repressed the truth and honestly could tell them nothing. For him that memory lapse was a double horror: her inability to recall the events of that night eliminated an eyewitness account of his innocence. Worse, her recollection of the battle that took place between him and Althea earlier in the evening was condemnatory testimony, especially coming from his own child.

"Come," he said. "Sit in the castle."

From the time she was a baby, her favorite place, the place she felt the safest, was inside Martín's make-believe castle. He bent his long legs so his knees pointed upward, rested his arms on his knees, and clasped his hands out in front. Isabelle crawled into the space between his legs and snuggled against him, looking out yet feeling hidden away, safe in the soft shadows formed by his massive body.

"Feel better?" he asked, relishing the warmth of her.

She looked back at him and smiled. "How about you?"

"I'm fine now, but I'm afraid that soon things are going to get nasty."

She knew nothing about the Murillos' custody suit, and he intended to keep it that way. The prospect of him being put on trial for Althea's murder was already too great an emotional burden for a child to carry. He took a deep breath, knowing that what he was about to say would upset her.

"That's why I've asked Tía Flora to take you to visit the Durans."

Isabelle kept her face forward, uncertain as to how she should react.

"Remember how much you liked it at La Casa? How kind and gentle Miranda and Luis had been? How much fun you always had with Nina?" Martín said.

Isabelle was trying very hard to be grown-up, to understand why her father would want to send her so far away, why he wouldn't want to keep her near so she could comfort him and love him and support him. But at her age most of her inner responses were those of a frightened child. Yes, the Durans had been wonderful; yes, she had liked Santa Fe; yes, she and Nina had become friends and it had been fun; but no, she didn't want to go there.

"It's too far away," she cried, unable to hold back her tears. "I want to stay here with you!"

"That's what I want, too," he said, his words caught in a sob. "I love you, Isabelle. You're the only person in this world who can bring a spot of sunshine into this terrible darkness I'm living in, but I don't know what else to do. I don't want the police bothering you. I don't want them to bully you in the hope of making you do or say something they can use against me. I want you to be safe and away from all this."

"But I don't want to go."

"It'll only be for a short time," Martín said, trying to comfort her, "just long enough for me to straighten out this terrible mess. Then you'll come back, we'll put our lives in order and be a family again. I promise."

Usually, when Martín hugged her, Isabelle was able to siphon off some of his extraordinary confidence, thereby shoring up her own. This time, despite the strength of his embrace, despite the sincerity of his promises, Isabelle's fears remained firmly in place.

The next morning, Consuela Serrat, one of Flora's most trusted servants, arose earlier than usual. Carefully she donned the clothes that had been left on her bed, clothes that had come from Señorita Flora's wardrobe: a black, long-sleeved dress befitting a woman in mourning, a lacy black silk shawl with long strands of hand-tied fringe to drape around her head and shoulders, dark stockings and shoes, black lace gloves, and a large black leather purse.

Consuela's daughter, Teresa, was ten years old but small for her age, which was fortunate, because Isabelle's clothes fit her perfectly. Though she knew she was about to take part in something very serious and very important to Señorita Flora, Teresa couldn't help but smile. Teresa had never worn anything made of cloth that felt this soft and this smooth against her skin, and for the moment, as long as she was alone and no one was watching, she allowed herself to enjoy the sensation of seeing herself in the puff-sleeved, narrow-waisted blue dress with the delicate white lace collar and cuffs. Though it was nice of Señorita Flora to let her keep this dress—it was brand new—it would never be missed because it was one of at least two dozen.

Since Señora Althea's murder, Isabelle had worn only dark blue dresses. From what Teresa had heard, Señor Martín had forbidden his daughter to wear black. Evidently Althea had once said that she hated seeing children in black, even at funerals, that it was too dark and too somber and that was not what childhood was supposed to be.

At around eight o'clock Consuela and Teresa took the big Mercedes, drove to the Barcelona airport, and boarded a plane for Venezuela.

Half an hour later, Consuela's husband, Pedro, loaded luggage into his pickup truck, covering the elegant leather bags with a dirty tarp. The way it had been explained to him, Señor Martín was concerned about the safety of Señorita Flora and his daughter, Isabelle. While no one appeared to be watching the house or tracking their movements, Señor de Luna was certain that surveillance of everyone connected with him would begin at any moment. Before that happened, he wanted Isabelle out of the country.

Using underground sources, Martín secured false papers for all four players in his little drama. Consuela and Teresa were supplied with passports identifying them as Flora Pujol and Isabelle de Luna. Flora and Isabelle were given completely phony passports with made-up names that would become untraceable once customs had checked the ladies through. After their safe arrival had been confirmed, Alejandro would forward their legitimate passports by special courier. A problem could arise only if passport control had been put on alert; one overly zealous customs officer could spell the difference between success and failure.

As Pedro escorted Señorita Flora from the house, Martín lifted Isabelle into his arms and hugged her close. She had been so upset the night before, he had slept in her bed, cradling her, smoothing her back, and talking to her each time the nightmares came. This morning her eyes were red and swollen, her lower lip seemed stuck in a frozen moue, her chin was unable to cease its quivering, and her hand refused to release the piece of cloth she and Althea had made a lifetime ago.

Her misery sliced into Martín like a steel-edged blade, releasing anger that flowed from him like blood. It was a red rage directed at God, the Murillos, the Barcelona police force, and, most of all, himself for having to send his daughter away from everything she knew and everyone she loved.

Slowly he carried her to the truck. After lifting her up and placing her on the seat, he leaned over, bringing his face inches from hers.

"Know that I love you, Isabelle," he said in a voice that commanded she remember those words for a lifetime. "Know that if I could think of any other way to help us, I would."

Isabelle nodded, struggling to restrain the torrent of tears she felt rising to the surface.

"I promise to call you every single day." He demanded that his mouth form a reassuring smile. "Before you know it, you and Tía Flora will be back with so many exciting stories we'll have to stay awake for a week to hear them all."

Her lips curled upward, but only for an instant. He kissed her cheeks and murmured softly, "Just remember how much I love you and how much I'll miss you."

"I will, P-Papa," she stammered as Flora and Pedro climbed into the truck alongside her.

Unwilling to cede even one second with her father, she turned around, scooted onto her knees, and pressed her face against the back window. As the truck started down the hill, Martín blew Isabelle a kiss, smiled, and waved as casually as if she and Flora were off to the market or church. If only they were, he thought as the truck ducked over the horizon.

Though she could see his arm long after she could no longer make out his smile, Isabelle never saw the tears that trickled down his cheeks. Nor could she see the hollow in his heart widen with every meter the truck traveled. Nor would she ever know just how alone and frightened and vulnerable Martín de Luna felt without her.

When Martín had called, explained the situation, and laid out his plan, Miranda Duran had agreed to help without any second thoughts. Once she had recovered from the shock of what had happened, she and Martín talked at great length about Althea, the tragedy of her murder and its aftermath, what this was doing to him, and most of all, what it was doing to Isabelle. Though he was loath to burden Miranda with the full and weighty measure of his woes, there was no way to avoid telling her about the Murillos and their determination to steal his daughter from him as well.

"If I sent her anywhere inside Spain," Martín said, "they'd know where she was before she ever arrived."

Miranda trusted Martín, yet she could not understand the intensity of his feeling against them even seeing Isabelle. Merely disapproving of him as a mate for their daughter didn't seem reason enough.

"They were abusive parents," he said with granite simplicity when she probed further. "Javier used to beat Althea savagely for the slightest infraction of his twisted rules. As for Estrella, Althea doesn't remember her mother ever touching her, or holding her, or kissing her good night. Are these the kind of people you would choose as guardians for Isabelle?"

Miranda's stomach lurched. She had lost a child. She remembered how her arms used to ache just for the feel of that baby's flesh. She remembered how welcome Nina was, how she had held on to her for days, unwilling to let her go even for a moment. It sickened her to think that Althea had managed to survive a brutal childhood only to die a brutal death. No, she didn't want Isabelle to have to repeat any part of Althea's tragic cycle. Certain legacies were not meant to be passed on from mother to daughter.

In the end, Miranda had concurred with Martín's opinion that with his situation so precarious, a temporary change of scene—and address—was, indeed, a good idea.

Two days later, however, when Miranda and Luis met Isabelle and Flora's plane, Miranda began to doubt the wisdom of separating Isabelle from her father. She had expected Isabelle to be upset. What she found was a child dangerously on the edge. In each of the de Lunas' previous visits, Isabelle had been affectionate with both Miranda and Luis; now, when they rushed toward her with their arms outstretched for an embrace, she shied away. Isabelle's incessant questioning had gained her a certain fame at La Casa, but there were no questions now. There was barely any verbal communication. Throughout the ride from the airport in Albuquerque to Santa Fe and for the rest of that first day, Isabelle refused to leave Flora's side. She spoke only when absolutely necessary, interacting with Luis and Miranda and Nina as little as possible.

When, finally, Isabelle fell into an exhausted sleep, Flora joined the Durans in their private quarters. She was too tired to absorb the smaller details, but as she seated herself on the well-worn sofa, her artist's eye swept through the sala. It was the unusual backgrounds that struck her first: the creamy plaster walls with their swirling texture and rounded corners; the sculpted doorway that extended several feet from the entry toward the windows with a half wall that held a collection of Pueblo pots; the thick tree trunks the Durans had called vigas, which stretched across the ceiling to define the space; the Navaho rugs, which spilled riots of color onto the hardwood floor; the old Apache baskets, both large and small, which lent texture and design to tabletops and windowsills; and the large corner hearth, which glowed with the flames of a crackling piñon fire, casting an orange glow on the unpretentious room.

"Is Isabelle asleep?" Miranda asked as she too settled on the couch.

"For the moment," Flora said, fatigue evident in the lines on her face and the slowness of her speech. Because her English was limited, the conversation was in Spanish, Flora's soft Castilian accent sounding curiously formal and exotic. "Since Althea's death, she's been plagued by nightmares."

Miranda shook her head. "She's awfully young to endure something like this. Losing her mother is horrible enough, but to have to worry about whether or not her father will be imprisoned seems excessive."

"I agree. I wish I could tell her her concerns are an overreaction, but in all good conscience, I cannot."

"How strong is the case against Martín?" Luis asked, drawing a pigskin-and-cedar *equipale* chair nearer Flora and Miranda.

Flora emitted a mirthless laugh. "In a dictatorship, the prosecution's case is always strong."

"Do you believe in Martín's innocence?" Though her question might have seemed rhetorical, Miranda felt compelled to ask it anyway.

"To be honest, immediately after it happened, I wasn't completely certain. They had been having a difficult time of it, and it had crossed my mind that perhaps things had gotten out of hand."

"What changed your mind?" Luis said as he walked toward a cabinet on the far wall and poured sherry for them all. Though Flora resisted, he encouraged her to take a sip, feeling rewarded when color returned to the older woman's cheeks.

"Martín's anguish," she said after some consideration. "So often grief is tinged with other emotions: guilt, remorse, anger, panic, even relief. Martín's grief was undiluted and so potent it immobilized him for days. It was only after Alejandro force-fed him the facts that he realized he had no time to mourn. A crime had been committed, and it appeared likely that he would be charged with that crime."

"Are there any other suspects?"

Flora sighed and offered Miranda a weak smile. "There is one man who was at the hotel the day of the murder who should be questioned and tested for blood type, but as far as Alejandro can tell, he hasn't been."

"Whom does he know?" Luis surprised Flora with his astuteness.

"The Murillos. According to Martín, Pasqua Barba was the man they had handpicked for Althea to marry. Not only is he rich and titled, but the two families are old friends. No doubt the Murillos are protecting him."

"Do you think he needs protection?" Luis asked. "Do you think he's guilty?"

Flora shrugged.

"Do the Murillos have reason to think he's guilty?"

"I don't know the answer to that," Flora said, finding it an interesting question. "What I do know is that they definitely want Martín to be guilty. They want him put away. And they want Isabelle."

Miranda patted her arm, offering what little comfort she could. "Isabelle is safe with us," she said quietly.

Flora nodded, but tension continued to line her face. "For now," she said, knowing it was impossible for the Durans to completely understand what life was really like in Franco's Spain or how far the Murillos were willing to go to achieve their ends. "But will she be safe tomorrow?"

Martín's lower back was pinched in pain. For three hours he had been forced to sit on a small metal chair that was much too low for someone his size. The pupils of his eyes had contracted to tiny dots, the effect of staring at a white light for a protracted period of time. His mouth was cottony from too many cigarettes, his bones creaked from the dampness of the basement interrogation room, and his bladder begged for relief, but he refused to succumb. Asking for a drink of water or a trip to the bathroom would give his examiners too much pleasure.

"It's a simple question, de Luna. Where were you between seven and nine-thirty on the night of August fifteenth?"

Manuel Garcia was the chief investigator of the Barcelona police. Placed in his job at the behest of Francisco Franco, he had a reputation for meanness, usually exhibiting a penchant for cruelty and barbarism. He seemed to be showing remarkable restraint with Martín. Martín wondered why.

"I've told you a dozen times, I was at home."

"You were seen leaving the Ritz at six-thirty," Garcia said, circling Martín, his hands behind his back, his eyes tracking his progress on the stone floor. "Did you go directly home?"

"Yes."

"Was anyone there with you?"

"No."

"Can anyone verify your whereabouts?"

"I made several phone calls."

"To whom?"

"Alejandro Fargas."

"Your lawyer. How convenient."

Martín ignored Garcia's sneer as well as the chuckles of his two cohorts. "Señorita Pujol."

"Your aunt." Another sneer. More chuckles. "Who else?"

"François LeVerre in Cannes." When Garcia paused, Martín explained, "He's a dealer in antique cars."

"You had a public row with your wife, stormed out of a hotel in a rage, and one of the first calls you made after you got home was to a car dealer?" Garcia issued a sarcastic laugh. "I find that curious."

"I was looking to sell several of the cars in my collection. Whenever I'd used Monsieur LeVerre in the past, I'd gotten good results."

"You sound desperate for cash. Are you?"

"As a matter of fact, yes."

Garcia laughed. "I believe that almost as much as I believe your alibi, which is not at all."

Martín de Luna's wealth was well-known and much envied. At one time the Pujols and the de Lunas were the richest families in Barcelona. Their fortunes had their genesis in textiles, but as their profits from cotton had increased, so had their reach. By the time Martín's parents, Beátriz Pujol and Jordi de Luna, married and merged the two dynasties, they controlled nearly every foundry, railroad, mill, and bank in Catalonia. But that was before Franco.

"Believe what you want," Martín said, knowing better than to recount his charges of government harassment. "It's the truth."

"I think you were setting up your escape. I think you planned to go to France, and this was your way of having money ready and available when you got there."

"That's ridiculous!" Martín said with a mirthless laugh. "First of all, transactions like that take weeks, not minutes, to conclude, so unless I intended to hang around Barcelona for a month or more after I committed this crime, your theory doesn't work.

"Second, those phone calls were made several hours before Althea was killed. If, as you said at some point in this tedious inquisition, this was not a premeditated murder, but a crime of passion, why would I be planning an escape for a crime I never had any intention of committing?"

"Who was your visitor?"

The abrupt change of subject represented a minor triumph for Martín. Garcia was conceding that Martín's argument contained enough logic to discourage debate.

"What visitor?"

"Someone entered your town house at approximately two o'clock that afternoon. Who was it?"

"Althea was murdered sometime between seven and eight o'clock at night. What difference does it make who I saw at two o'clock in the afternoon?" Even Martín heard the edge in his voice.

Garcia was surprised. His question was meant to be annoying, not revealing, yet Martín's tone suggested an unexpected uneasiness. "Who was it?"

Garcia had been standing in front of Martín. When he moved, Martín raised his hand to block the glaring light from his eyes, at the same time erasing the beads of sweat that had drawn a dotted line across his forehead.

"Pasqua Barba."

Garcia bent down so that his ear was close to Martín's mouth. "Did I hear you correctly? Did you just say that Pasqua Barba visited you at your house the day of your wife's murder?"

"Yes."

"The same Pasqua Barba who was pursuing her on Majorca? The same man you fought with later that day in the tea room of the Ritz?"

Martín's only response was a reluctant nod. Garcia pressed on. "And what exactly was the purpose of this visit?"

"He wanted to inform me about his role in a business transaction."

"What kind of transaction?"

"I had put Dragon Textiles up for sale."

Garcia rubbed his chin. Dragon was the cornerstone of the Pujol empire. "My, my! Things must be bad if you were about to sell the flagship."

Martín said nothing, but he was visibly fatigued. His eyes were half closed, and tears hid in the corners. His guard was down. He was weakening. Garcia was certain of it.

"What did Barba have to do with Dragon?"

"I had been negotiating with a Señor Ramirez for several months. That morning, we had signed off on a deal. Barba stopped by later that day to tell me Ramirez was merely a front for him."

Garcia's eyes widened. "Barba bought Dragon from you?"

"So he said."

"That must have made you angry."

"It didn't make me happy."

"Is that why you called Señor Fargas? To see if you could get out of the deal?"

"We did discuss the possibility."

"And was there a possibility?"

"None that we could see at the moment."

"So you called this LeVerre in France? Surely even a collection as prized as yours couldn't have netted enough money to buy Dragon back."

"It would have been a start."

Garcia resumed his pacing. Martín lit another cigarette. He had gone through two entire packs. His lungs were beginning to burn. He felt a tightness across his chest.

"Why would Barba want a textile company in Barcelona when his businesses are in Madrid and Seville?"

"Althea was Dragon's head designer. He wanted to own the company because he wanted to own her!"

"If Dragon meant so much to Althea, why would you sell it?"

"Some of our real estate properties are apartments with elderly tenants. The government wants them, so they hiked our taxes as a way of *encouraging* us to sell. The old people would have had nowhere to live. We decided to save these buildings by selling off something else. Dragon would have fetched the biggest price. Althea understood that."

"Did she?"

"Yes. She did."

"But you and she were at odds. Perhaps she thought you had put Dragon up for sale as a way of punishing her. Perhaps Barba told her he bought Dragon as a present for her. He looks good. You look bad."

Martín fought an instinct to scream. "You're wrong, Garcia!"

"Am I?" Garcia brought his face so close to Martín's, their breath intermingled. "You fought with her. People saw you. They heard you."

"Barba fought with her. People saw and heard that, too. Why aren't you interrogating him?"

Garcia stepped back and reined his temper. How dare Martín question his thoroughness, especially in front of subordinates!

"He never forgave her for marrying me. When I joined their table, he was pleading his case yet again. I admit I was not happy to see him there, but he was just as peeved to see me. We had words, but when Althea refused to leave with him, Barba was the one who was furious! He's the one who was rebuffed. And he's the one who killed her! Don't you see that?"

Garcia homed in on his prey. "What I see is an irate, jealous husband.

Barba outwitted you. He came to your house to laugh in your face. Then he went to the Ritz to tell your wife of his triumph. You were angry and humiliated. You hadn't been able to prevent him from taking your company, so you decided to prevent him from taking your wife."

"I didn't kill Althea." Martín's response was quiet and calm. Garcia was disappointed. "Paco was angry, Garcia. Althea made him look like a fool, and he didn't like it. Why don't you ask *him* where he was between seven and nine?"

"I did," Garcia said with a victorious smirk. "He was having tapas with your in-laws, of all people. We have a list of people who saw him with the Murillos at a café on the Rambla. Later, the three of them dined at Reno. I have affidavits for that as well. Sorry, de Luna. Barba's story checks out. Yours doesn't. So let's go over it again.

"Why did you wait so long to call the police?" Garcia asked, returning to his pattern of skipping around. "You called at nine-thirty. The coroner says Señora de Luna was killed between seven and eight-thirty. What were you doing? Admiring your handiwork?"

"I wasn't in her room between seven and eight-thirty. I was home," Martín said, swallowing his frustration, refusing to allow it to surface. "Sometime after nine o'clock, I decided to return to the hotel and apologize. When I got there, Althea was dead. I was afraid Isabelle was dead as well, but I found her asleep in a closet in the next room."

He paused. Despite his ability to control his emotions, he trembled at the memory of coming upon Althea's body—naked and twisted, ghastly white, and utterly motionless—and finding his daughter hidden away in a closet.

"I didn't want Isabelle to see her mother that way," he continued, his voice strained and scratchy. "I called the police and then took her out of there, back to the town house."

"Speaking of your daughter, my aides say that several days ago, she and Señorita Pujol boarded a plane for Venezuela. Do you have relatives in Venezuela?"

"Not that I know of."

"If they're not visiting relatives, it must be a vacation."

"Must be."

"Isn't this an odd time for a vacation?"

"I don't think so. Isabelle is a child. This situation has been horrible for her."

"We're conducting an investigation into her mother's murder. What if I need her for further questioning?"

"You've asked her a thousand questions already."

"If it takes a thousand more for Isabelle to tell me what she saw, then I guess I have a thousand more."

Two hours later, despite incessant grilling, Martín was released. No matter what Garcia had thrown at him, he had stuck to his story. The only way Garcia was able to rationalize his failure was to remind himself that he had been under orders to refrain from implementing his usual methods of persuasion.

As he watched Martín leave the police station, his mouth stretched into a feral smile. Even without a confession, the big man's days were numbered. By the end of the week Martín would be officially charged with the murder, arrested, and jailed. He would be brought to trial quickly, and whether it was a one-day affair or a long, drawn-out event, the outcome would be the same: Martín de Luna would be convicted.

One afternoon Nina found Isabelle scrunched up on the window seat of the living room. Her body was tight, curled like a fist. Clutching her security swatch, she stared out at the Sangre de Cristo Mountains, which rose in the distance and defined the horizon in and around Santa Fe, yet Nina could tell she wasn't admiring the awesome beauty of her surroundings. She was gazing far beyond the panorama, looking deep into the darkness of the mysterious infinity that cauled the earth. Nina, unable even to imagine what it was like to be in Isabelle's place, felt an overwhelming rush of sympathy for the sad little girl by the window.

To Nina, Althea had been a paragon, a woman blessed by the gods with everything wonderful. She had been physically beautiful, emotionally nurturing, witty, talented, adored by her husband, cherished by her child, admired by her peers, and, as if that weren't enough, had borne a noble pedigree. Too, Althea had fussed over Nina, extolling her pale, blond looks, delighting in her powers of observation and her ability to tell a story. Most important, she had marveled at Nina's height, turning something that Nina had always viewed as a minus into a plus.

"God doesn't make mistakes," she had told Nina when once the child had confessed to feeling gawky and much too conspicuous. "You were given this height because you were meant to stand out, so stand tall!"

For that alone, Althea would be sorely missed.

But, Nina thought, Isabelle still had Martín, and he was magnificent! Huge, like a giant, he had a carriage and bearing Nina couldn't help but envy. Martín never just walked into a room, he took it over, filling the space with the enormity of his presence, dwarfing everyone and everything in sight. He never stooped his shoulders, or bowed his head, or crumpled so much as an inch of his massive frame. Instead he affected an almost defiant stance, one Nina couldn't help but interpret as pride and confidence. Naturally he, too, had become one of her idols.

Nina had many idols, but Althea and Martín were the only two she had ever met in the flesh. The others were names and faces that appeared in movie magazines and on the covers of *Life* and *Look*. Paul Newman. Elizabeth Taylor. Natalie Wood. Warren Beatty. Rock Hudson. Marilyn Monroe. Jackie and JFK. She was enthralled by celebrity, intrigued with every aspect of their lives: how they lived, whom they loved, where they had come from, how they had gotten to where they were, what they had to do to stay there. She read every snippet in every fan magazine and newspaper she could find, devouring information on her favorites as if they were long-lost kin. Sometimes, late at night, she liked to think that maybe one of them was.

"How are you?" she said, approaching Isabelle and taking a place next to her on the window seat.

When Isabelle turned her face toward Nina, it was clear she had been crying. The clock behind Isabelle showed it was nearly four o'clock. Martín usually called around three. Isabelle must have just gotten off the phone with him.

"Is everything okay?" Nina asked again, afraid Martín had been arrested.

Isabelle nodded, but she was not convincing.

"I heard you crying last night." Isabelle and Flora were staying in the room next to Nina's. Sometimes, when the nightmares were particularly bad, Nina was awakened by Isabelle's sobs.

"I'm sorry," Isabelle said, blushing. "I don't mean to disturb anyone. I can't seem to help it."

Nina knew Isabelle had been in the suite the night of the murder. She also knew Isabelle claimed she was asleep when the actual deed was done. The drama of it all had Nina fascinated.

"What are they like?" she asked. "The nightmares, I mean."

"I'm in the blue," she said, her forehead furrowing as the hazy images reasserted themselves.

Nina, thinking Isabelle was having a language problem, moved to correct her. "Do you mean to say you're feeling blue? Like unhappy?"

The younger girl stared at her, but her eyes were focused on scenes Nina couldn't see.

"It's an easy mistake," Nina continued, unsure whether or not Isabelle was listening, a little nervous about the faraway look in the other girl's eyes. "I mean, it is true that in English if you're feeling good, you say you're 'in the pink,' but when you're feeling bad, you don't say you're 'in the blue.' You're just 'blue.'"

Though Nina's tone was light, Isabelle's answer was dark.

"You asked me what the nightmares are like," she said, the look on her face turning intense. "I'm trying to tell you. In them, I'm in the blue. Everything's colored a deep royal blue. Nothing looks right. Faces. Places. Things. Everything's blurry, everything's blue, like someone poured a can of paint over my dreams." She trembled. "That's what makes them so scary. The blueness."

Nina had never heard anyone speak like that, with a voice that echoed, as if it were coming from another place.

"Do you think your father did it?"

She hadn't meant to be so blunt, but to her amazement, Isabelle didn't even flinch. Obviously she had been asked that question often enough for its shock value to have been greatly diminished.

"No," she said with a certainty Nina found admirable.

"But you were asleep."

"I know, but Papa says he didn't do it, and I believe him."

As a devotee of the tabloid press, Nina had a hard time accepting a statement like that as anything but blind faith.

"Isabelle, your father's a great guy, and I don't think he could've done it, either, but if he did, he's not going to tell you. He's not going to tell anyone."

Isabelle's anger was instantaneous. "My father is not a liar! If he says he didn't do it, he didn't!"

Nina hadn't meant to upset Isabelle. When her friend jumped off the window seat and started for the door, she followed.

"I'm sorry," she said, catching Isabelle by the wrist, "truly I am. But you know me, Is, everything's a story. I got carried away. I'm sorry."

Isabelle nodded, but she was unable to stop shaking.

To Nina and the rest of the world, this might have been nothing but a story, but to Isabelle, this was her life, and just then she didn't foresee a happy ending.

Martín lit one cigarette from another. Alejandro winced as Martín's body quaked through another coughing fit. "You really should cut down," he said, concerned about the rising frequency of the attacks.

"Why? So I don't die of lung cancer?"

Martín's anxiety level was high. After his session with Garcia, he had been followed constantly. Guards were posted outside his house. Everyone who had ever had anything to do with him, either personally or in business, had been called in for questioning.

"Have they run a blood test on Barba yet?"

"They say they did, but the results mysteriously disappeared."

Martín gaped at Alejandro for a moment and then burst into hysterical laughter.

"That's great! A crucial piece of evidence that might have turned the spotlight of suspicion on someone else is missing." Despite another coughing spasm and a tightening across his chest, he lit another cigarette and dragged deeply on it. "I'll bet the signed affidavits validating that trumped-up alibi about him being with Javier and Estrella are safely locked away, though. Nothing's going to happen to them!"

Alejandro wished he could disagree, but he couldn't. They both knew that no matter what statements the police issued about conducting a thorough investigation, Martín was their target.

"The one thing I can't figure out," Martín said, pausing for a moment in his circumambulations, "is why Garcia was so hands off with me. It's not his style."

"That's easy," Fargas said. "This isn't a crime against the state, and you're too well known for them to justify beating a confession out of you. The last thing they want is for you to become a martyr."

"No. What they want is for me to spend the rest of my life rotting away in one of their stinking jails!"

Alejandro sighed. He loved Martín like a son and would have gone to any lengths to spare him the fate he'd just described, but even he knew Martín was beyond protection. The wheels of justice were about to roll right over him, and there was nothing Fargas could do to prevent it.

Their worst fears were realized later that night when Garcia and his team came to arrest Martín. Just before they took him away, he called Fargas.

"Get in touch with Flora," he said, his voice hoarse with apprehension. "I need her to come home and testify for me."

"What about Isabelle?" Alejandro asked. "Should she come home as well?"

"No," Martín said emphatically, ignoring the faint click that signaled someone had come onto the line and was listening in. "Not until everything is finished."

Fargas knew Martín meant not only the trial, but the custody suit as well.

As he prepared to leave his house so he could call New Mexico from a safe telephone, he worried that when everything was finished, Isabelle wouldn't want to come home.

When it came time for Flora to leave, Isabelle was inconsolable. Tía Flora was her anchor; without her, all sense of mooring fell away, making Isabelle feel very alone, very disconnected from the people and places who represented her security. Everyone who mattered to her was in Barcelona, yet she was being forced to remain thousands of miles away in Santa Fe. Events were taking place in Spain that were going to affect her drastically, yet she was not permitted to participate. It was like standing on the sidelines of one's life, while others took to the playing field and determined your fate.

After Flora returned to Barcelona, she called every day at a prearranged time to report on the progress of the trial, but their conversations did little to allay Isabelle's fears. Sensing that Tía Flora's narrative was heavily edited, Isabelle came away with more questions than answers, prompting her imagination to fill in the blanks. As the days passed and the information given her remained sparse, Isabelle's sense of uneasiness grew. Unaware of her grandparents' suit, she saw no reason for her banishment other than a universal anticipation of doom. With the simplistic logic of a child's mind, she had decided that those in charge of her father's case might view her absence as evidence of Martín's guilt; if she were there, standing beside the man accused of killing her mother, his assertion of innocence would prevail.

Miranda and Luis shared her concerns, but their attempts to calm her, based on vague explanations about Martín's case being more complicated than Isabelle supposed, only increased her sense of burden. If she were back in Barcelona, she said, perhaps she would remember something that could help free her father. Though Miranda didn't discount that as a possibility, she reminded Isabelle that the reason she had come to Santa Fe in the first place was so that the police couldn't force her to say something that would hurt him.

For weeks Isabelle remained listless and remote, coming to life only for a few moments around three-thirty in the afternoon when Flora called with news about Martín. One Tuesday morning the telephone in the Durans' private quarters rang. Nina was at school, Miranda was at the gallery, and Luis was somewhere in the the hotel. Isabelle wasn't sure what to do, but after several rings she picked up the phone. She recognized the voice immediately.

"Tía Flora? What's wrong?" The pause at the other end was so long, Isabelle thought they had been disconnected. "Tía Flora? Are you there?"

"Yes, but I have terrible news for you, my pet."

"Papa! What's happened to Papa?" Isabelle's heart thumped inside her chest. She held her breath and squeezed her eyes shut, as if that would soften the impact of what she feared was coming.

"He's dead." For a moment Flora's control abandoned her. Though her grief spilled out in a paroxysm of sobs, all she heard from Isabelle was silence. "Isabelle," she said, gathering her self-control, "did you hear me?"

"Did they kill him?"

Her voice was so small and so pathetic, Flora wanted to reach across the distance, wrap her in her arms, and hug her until the pain went away. But there were too many miles between them, and even if there weren't, Flora realized, there was too much pain for an embrace to soothe.

"No, darling. Papa had a heart attack."

When Isabelle collapsed, Miranda was there to catch her. She had returned to La Casa just moments before. Since the house phone also rang at the front desk, Miranda had picked it up. When she heard Flora's voice, she knew something terrible had occurred. Shouting into the phone for Flora to hang on, Miranda carried the limp child to the couch. She was able to revive Isabelle by taking water from a nearby vase and wiping it across her brow, but nothing was going to stem the tears that flowed without ebb.

As soon as she could, Miranda retrieved the phone and asked Flora for details. Martín had died in his jail cell of a sudden heart attack. After a quick autopsy, doctors concluded he had a genetic weakness that had been exacerbated by the combined stress of the investigation, his arrest, his incarceration, his trial, and the impending verdict. Naturally, his incessant smoking had not helped his condition.

"I don't question the doctors' findings," Flora said. "What they say is probably true, but none of that killed him. It was the pain of Althea's death and being separated from his daughter. Martín's heart didn't give out, Miranda. It broke."

"His is not the only one," Miranda said, carrying the phone to the couch and looking at Isabelle's quaking body. "What do you want me to do?"

"For now, just keep Isabelle with you. Alejandro and I need time to find out what the Murillos are planning." Miranda could hear Flora straining for control over her emotions. "I can't lose her, too, Miranda. Please. Watch over her. Take care of her. Be good to her."

"I will, Flora. You know I will," Miranda said, stroking Isabelle's back, feeling the young flesh shudder from the intensity of her sobs. "But you be good to yourself. Like you, she couldn't handle any more losses." As she watched Isabelle cry and curl her body into a bow, Miranda said softly, "I'm not sure she can handle this one."

For months Isabelle retreated into a world of tormented silence, burying herself in a dark depression surrounded by walls so thick and so tall, no one could reach her. She spent most of her time in her room, on her bed, staring out the window at the mountains, as if they held answers to the questions that haunted her dreams. Miranda would bring her to the table for meals; occasionally she ate, but most times she simply picked at her food. Each morning Luis tried to interest her in some activity that would take her out of her room and out of her mourning, even if only for a little while; but she rejected every suggestion. Each night Miranda sat with her and rocked her when she cried herself to sleep. Even Nina came in now and then and tried to get her to talk. Though she was aware of all the efforts made to draw her out, and in her own way appreciated them, Isabelle had nothing to say, so she said nothing.

The shock of Martín's death had thrown her into a spiritual tailspin. Coming so soon after Althea's, his death felt like a cosmic dare, a divine examination meant to assess her emotional stamina and psychological fortitude. It was an unfair test. She was far too young and ill equipped to take on such a mighty challenge. She tried, but especially where it concerned Martín, the task proved insurmountable. With Althea she had been able to participate in the ritual of burial, to be part of closing the book on her mother's life.

She had heard of her father's death over the phone. He was being buried without her, thousands of miles away. She was to be allowed no sense of finality, no images of ending, no visual aides to assist in the process of grieving. She was expected to accept the fact of his passing, stow it away in an emotional locker alongside the fact of her mother's passing, and move on.

Isabelle couldn't do that. In a period of less than two months she had lost both her parents and, it appeared, her home as well. Her base and her ballast were gone. And she was only seven years old.

CHAPTER 4

When Alejandro Fargas arrived at La Casa, he was shocked by Isabelle's appearance. Slight by nature, now she was gaunt. Her skin was dull and gray, her eyes void of all light. Though he could tell she wanted to run into his arms, her legs were too weak to carry her. With small, mincing steps, she started toward him, her lower lip unable to maintain a steady line, her eyes overflowing with big, sad tears. Alejandro, unable to bear the sight of her suffering, bridged the distance, lifted her in his arms, and held her close, unprepared for the swell of emotion that enveloped him. As her head snuggled into his shoulder and her spindly arms laced around his neck, he thought his heart would burst.

Though she called him *Tío,* he had always fancied himself her grandfather. Before, it had been an easy role to fill—sharing milestones and holidays, telling stories, introducing her to stamp collecting, teaching her to ride—easy because Isabelle was an affectionate child who had accepted his love without question and returned it without reserve. While his relationship with Martín—and Althea—had been solid right to the end, Alejandro thought of Isabelle as his special dividend for all that he had invested in her family.

His entanglement with the de Lunas and the Pujols began when he was twenty and fell in love with Flora. In the early years, when he was actively courting the young Señorita Pujol, Alejandro's advances had been stymied by Flora's three older sisters. As the youngest in a traditional family, Flora would not have been allowed to marry before them. Unmarried, unwell, and to his eye immensely unappealing, they became romantic albatrosses for him because they were marital obstacles for her.

The eldest of the sisters, Beátriz, did eventually marry, and when she died, her son, Martín, became the barrier. Flora became devoted to her nephew, and Alejandro was once again relegated to the second tier. It took a while, but finally he accepted reality: her sisters and her nephew were covers for the truth. Though she and Alejandro were best friends and loyal lovers, intellectual soul mates, and well-suited companions, Flora continuously rejected his proposals because in her mind, "husband" and "wife" were words that contained requirements and limits and expectations, none of which she felt would better her life. She loved him and wanted him, but she wanted Martín *and* her independence as well. Though she left him free to marry someone else if he chose, Alejandro never found anyone else. (If pressed, he would admit he never really looked.) He remained a bachelor with a difference—he enjoyed a strong, fulfilling relationship with the woman he loved, all the joys and dividends of a family, and none of the strings and obligations that usually accompanied that sort of package.

But, he realized as he held Isabelle in his arms, love created its own strings. He had loved Martín and Althea as if they were of his blood, and he mourned their deaths like a father, but this was worse. Seeing this child so emotionally ravaged was more devastating than watching her parents' coffins being lowered into the ground. Religion taught that the dead were at peace. Alejandro, though not a particularly religious man, liked to think that that was so. But what about those who remained behind? For Isabelle, there was no peace, only the vast, unquenchable loneliness of the orphan.

"*Tío,*" she said, uttering her first words since the call about Martín, "have you come to take me home?"

Alejandro had anticipated the question. Prepared as he was, he still had difficulty delivering the answer.

"No, *mi periquita,*" he said suddenly, almost unwillingly recalling the day he had bestowed this nickname on her. He had brought her a parakeet for her fourth birthday. She had been very excited and told him she was going to call the bird Alejandro, in his honor. Delighted, he had said he thought it was a fair exchange because he had always thought of her as his pet, his parakeet.

"Why not?" Panic shirred the edges of her voice. "Why can't I go home?"

Alejandro carried her to the couch and sat down, keeping her on his lap. Miranda and Luis retreated to a corner, remaining as unobtrusive as possible, staying in case they were needed.

Throughout the long plane ride, he had debated the wisdom of what he was about to do. He and Flora had discussed it thoroughly, approaching it from a thousand angles, but in the end both felt Isabelle deserved the truth. Unfortunately, like many truths, this one was unpleasant.

"Since Papa died, there's been a lot of confusion and a lot of arguing about things like property and money and bank accounts and who owns what. Tía Flora and I are trying to straighten it all out, but we're fighting the government, and you know how hard that is."

Isabelle nodded and wiped her eyes. Alejandro was speaking to her like a grown-up. She wanted to behave like one.

"We're fighting another battle as well," he said, gently pushing a damp lock of hair off her face. "Do you remember the people who disrupted Mama's funeral? The Murillos?"

Again Isabelle nodded, but her eyes narrowed with apprehension.

"You know who they are?"

"Mama's parents," she said. "My grandparents." Her lips curled over the words in an unconscious gesture of distaste.

"That's right." He paused long enough for a nervous smile to flit across his mouth. "They've decided they want you to come live with them."

"No!" She shook her head almost violently. "I don't like them. They were mean to Papa. Please, *Tío*, don't make me go to them."

"Shh." He kissed her cheek and stroked her head, wishing he could be more reassuring. "I wouldn't do that, *mi periquita*. But El Caudillo is their friend, and Tía Flora and I are worried that they might convince the government to make you live with them."

"No!" She was trembling. Her entire body was convulsed with fear.

"That's why we want you to stay here, with Miranda and Luis."

Isabelle's eyes widened. At first Alejandro thought she was beyond the ability to fully comprehend what he was saying, but when her face paled to a ghostly white, he knew she understood exactly what he was saying.

"If I bring you back to Barcelona, they could take you. Right now, they can't because they don't know where you are."

He had come to Santa Fe via Nice to Paris to Chicago, to avoid whatever tail they might have put on him. But, as he had explained to the Durans, Martín's will had named them as her guardians but had not listed any address. For all the Murillos knew, the Durans lived somewhere in Europe or South America. If, however, the Murillos located Isabelle, the likelihood was they would file for extradition.

For several minutes Isabelle didn't say anything. She appeared to be considering the situation and weighing her options. Because Alejandro and the other adults recognized that to a seven-year-old everything was exaggerated, both the positive as well as the negative, they remained silent. There was so little that was positive, it would have been cruel to dampen what was; there was so much that was negative, even the most excessive exaggeration was not far from the mark. Alejandro would have offered a more detailed explanation if he'd thought it would be helpful, but compassion cautioned against full revelation. Why tell her the Murillos were contesting Martín's naming of

Flora as guardian if the Durans were unable to fulfill their obligations, or that despite Martín's death, they continued to slander his name in the press and in the courts, proclaiming his guilt every chance they got? Isabelle had enough tragedy on her plate.

"When?" she said abruptly, her voice so low Alejandro had to lean down to hear her. "When can I come home to you and Tía Flora?"

"As soon as we're certain that you would be coming home to us." He knew she wanted a definite time frame, a specific number of days she could cross off a calendar, but the best he could do was, "I don't know how long it will take, but you have my word and Tía Flora's word, we'll make it as quick as possible."

"I know you'd rather be home in Barcelona with Tía Flora," Nina said, sitting at the foot of Isabelle's bed, "but I'm kind of glad you're staying with me. Now we can be like sisters."

Isabelle tried to smile, but just then it was a difficult maneuver.

"Are they really awful?" Nina asked, referring to the Murillos.

Isabelle shrugged. "I only saw them once, but I didn't like them. They yelled at Papa and said nasty things about him in front of everyone." Her lower lip quivered. "They didn't even seem to care that Mama was lying in a box in the ground."

"Did they speak to you?"

"No." Isabelle's eyes narrowed as she recalled their meeting. "They never even looked at me."

"Ugh!" Nina said, expressing her disgust. "And now they want you to live with them?"

Isabelle nodded. "But I'm not going to. I'm not going to give them what they want!"

A steely determination had insinuated itself in Isabelle's eyes. On some level she understood that while this situation seemed to revolve around her, truly it had little to do with her. This was a stratagem in a war being waged between Martín and the Murillos, a war that had started long before her birth and was bitter enough to continue after her father's death. She was not a combatant in this battle, she was the prize, the booty, the ultimate symbol of the Murillos' victory and Martín's defeat.

"I don't get it," Nina said. "What is it that they want?"

"I think if I go to them, it makes Papa look bad."

In a flash of insight extremely mature for one of her years, Isabelle suddenly had realized the prize could be awarded only if it was available. While her opponents were fortified with authority and influence, she possessed the power to deny them what they wanted. And, though being separated from Flora and Alejandro broke whatever was left of her heart, that was precisely what she intended to do.

"Are you afraid? I mean, could they come here and get you?"

Again, Isabelle shrugged.

Nina crawled to the top of the bed and slid under the covers alongside Isabelle. Feeling very grown-up and responsible, she draped her arm around the younger girl and drew her close.

"I won't let them take you," she said in her usual tone of complete and utter confidence.

As Isabelle rested her head on Nina's shoulder, her assuredness faded. Nina was quite adept at bravado, but inside she felt just as nervous as Isabelle. Children were never as well armed as adults. They weren't in possession of such powerful weapons as money and influence and power. Yet, Nina thought with profound respect for the seven-year-old next to her, Isabelle was bent on defying them.

The Murillos believed they had the advantage. Nina believed they had misjudged their granddaughter badly.

Later, after Isabelle went to bed, Luis and Alejandro shared a sherry.

"Did you know that Martín was terminally ill?" Luis asked.

Alejandro nodded, his expression registering surprise that Luis would know something he hadn't learned until recently.

"The summer before last, Martín collapsed. A good friend of ours, Jonas Hoffman, diagnosed him as having cardiomyopathy. Martín swore him to secrecy. It was only when he heard of Martín's death that he explained what had happened."

"Obviously, Martín took the same vow." Alejandro still hadn't figured out why Martín had hidden such a terrible truth. Pride? Fear? The belief that illness was a sign of weakness? "He never said a word. Not even to Althea. The first I heard of his disorder was in the autopsy report."

Alejandro could still feel the hollowness that had formed in the pit of his stomach as he had read of Martín's weakened heart. Worse was the report of a high quantity of digitoxin in his blood. Though the drug was commonly prescribed for heart patients, it did produce side effects: blurred vision, dizziness, headaches. The one that concerned Alejandro most was the possibility of psychotic episodes.

"Discovering that Martín knew he was dying did explain the spate of uncharacteristic quarrels between him and Althea. My guess is that in some byzantine way he was testing her love for him, trying to find out how much she'd miss him when he was gone."

"It's hard to believe he never told her or Flora or you."

Alejandro nodded. Pensive, his thoughts lingering on the inconceivable, he drew smoke from a thin cigar, exhaling it in a long white stream.

"There were signs, I suppose. Flora and I did notice a certain sobriety about him, an odd preoccupation with estate matters and such." He stroked his chin and counted lost opportunities. "I should have pressed the matter."

Luis nodded. The world was full of shoulds. "Jonas felt he should have told Althea himself. If he had, things might have been different."

Alejandro crushed his cigar in the ashtray. "But not for long. From what I understand, there was little that could have been done to extend Martín's life."

"True, but he might have had time to clear his name before he died."

"The chances were slim."

"Too bad. It would have made a big difference to Isabelle," Luis said quietly.

Alejandro nodded and sipped his sherry, somewhat ashamed that his comments had absented her feelings. Luis was right. Isabelle had inherited the burden of her father's presumed guilt. It was a heavy load for someone so young.

"I'm embarrassed to ask this," Luis said, clearly wrestling with his pride, "but I'm not a wealthy man. Did Martín provide any funds for Isabelle?"

Fargas shook his head, as embarrassed by the answer as Luis had been by the question. "He did, but the government has nullified his will. Martín's wishes are irrelevant."

"How can that be?" Luis's face was a portrait of incredulity.

Alejandro patted Luis's knee. "It's hard for Americans to understand the internal workings of a dictatorship. Franco lets the United States build air bases in Spain, gets economic aid, and you assume he's relaxed his grip because Uncle Sam is watching. Yes, he's eased certain restrictions, but believe me, El Caudillo is still very much the dictator and the Falange is still very much in control.

"Martín de Luna was a thorn in the side of Barcelona's ruling faction. They hated him because he was rich, outspoken about maintaining Catalan culture, and openly rebellious about the depravity of the current regime. There was nothing Martín liked better than holding court at one of the cafés on the Ramblas, expounding on the corruption and sin practiced by those holding office. When Althea was murdered, everyone he ever criticized saw a chance to get even. Martín knew it. He knew that even if they had stacks of evidence pointing a finger straight at someone else, he was going to be punished. Not for the crime of murder, but for the crime of speaking his mind."

"He's dead," Luis said. "From what you say, they've succeeded in branding him guilty. What more do they want?"

"The better question is, what don't they want?" Fargas laughed, the sound void of all mirth. "They had been on a campaign to bankrupt him. Each year they increased his tax burden. Believe me, he never would have sold Dragon Textiles unless it was absolutely necessary."

"What about his other interests?"

"The government has confiscated everything else: factories, homes, real estate, bank accounts, everything except for his cars and Althea's jewelry, which in some moment of divine prescience, Althea had bequeathed to Flora."

"How could they do that?"

Fargas's face fell. "May God forgive me, I helped them." Luis was noticeably confused. "Isabelle is Martín's sole heir. By hiding her from the Murillos, we leave the estate vulnerable to escheatage."

"What's that?"

"When a bequest can't be fulfilled because the named survivor is either dead or can't be found, everything in the estate is forfeited to the state. They know we're hiding Isabelle, so they're using this to force our hand. If we bring her back to Barcelona, it's true that she'll inherit whatever's left of Martín's estate—after they tax the hell out of it, of course—but it's also true that she'd be remanded to the custody of the Murillos. If we keep her here with you, away from Javier and Estrella, the state can take every cent Martín had. They've got us and they know it."

Alejandro's jaw had tightened. He was not used to being outmaneuvered when it came to matters of law; he was less accustomed to boxing himself into a corner.

Luis rose from the couch and walked over to the fireplace, stoking the flames absentmindedly. His face was pinched.

"I'm afraid I've been thoughtless, carelessly throwing another mouth onto your table, Luis," Alejandro said, suddenly aware of the consequences of his request. "Neither Flora nor I can house Isabelle right now, but we'll help any way we can." He paused, at once anxious and embarrassed.

"No." Luis had obviously made a decision. "I believe things happen for a reason, Alejandro." He paused, collecting his thoughts. "Miranda and I had a child, a son, who died when he was three years old. We tried to have other children, but couldn't. We thought that was how God wanted it, but then God saw fit to put Nina in our care. Now He has sent Isabelle to us. Why, and for how long, I don't know, but it doesn't matter. Isabelle has a home with us for as long as she wants."

Alejandro almost wept with relief. "May God bless you, Luis Duran."

Luis smiled. "He already has."

Isabelle remained locked in the prison of her grief. Miranda tried every way she knew to coax the bereft child out of the darkness. She talked to her, took her for walks around the town and drives up into the mountains. She sat with her and said nothing, hoping quiet companionship might help. But the determination and resolve Isabelle had called upon during Alejandro's visit had receded, leaving a fragile, hollow shell. Miranda continued to keep a watchful eye.

One afternoon, as she passed through the dining room on her way to the kitchen, she looked out the window and noticed Isabelle sitting on the ground at the edge of the garden behind La Casa. The sun was high, the air was hot. The garden had been abandoned by the guests in favor of cooler sites. Yet there was Isabelle, wearing shorts and a light top, her hair twisted into a knot on top of her head, baking in the midday heat. Miranda slipped outside and proceeded as quietly as she could to the end of the grand porch that hugged the east side of the building. Not wanting to intrude, she tucked herself into the shadows and observed.

Isabelle was drawing in the dirt with a broken twig, sketching what appeared to be flowers and trees. They were scratches made with a primitive instrument on a canvas of dust, but they had form and, in a raw sense, design. Miranda recalled that recently, when she had asked Nina if she and Isabelle spoke when they were alone in their room, Nina had said no.

"She's very quiet, Mama. I try, but she's too sad to speak." Clearly Isabelle's distance disturbed Nina. "But you know how I love to write in my diary?" Miranda nodded. Nina's diary was sacred. "Isabelle doodles. She draws strange faces on scraps of paper and in a notebook she keeps in a drawer alongside her bed."

Thinking farther back, Miranda remembered the last time the de Lunas had visited as a family. Althea had sat in this very garden, sketching the panorama that stretched beyond La Casa's property line. Isabelle, seated next to her mother, a large pad perched in her lap, had done her best to imitate Althea. With her features struck in a serious, artistic pose, she had stared at the landscape and then, moving her pencil slowly across the paper, had created dozens of unsophisticated yet recognizable images. Miranda had been impressed and had said as much.

"She's very talented," Althea had replied with undisguised pride. "Flora and I often argue over whose genes produced Isabelle's gift. Since she seems to have the same eye for line I do and the exceptional sense of color Flora has, I'd have to say she's been lucky enough to get the best of both of us. Of course, she's only six, so who knows."

Who knows indeed, Miranda thought as she retreated into the hotel, an idea blinking in her brain.

That night at dinner Miranda announced that she needed Isabelle's help.

"Things are so busy at the hotel, I need an extra pair of hands in the gallery. Do you think you could help me out?"

Isabelle lifted her face, turned toward Miranda, and nodded. There was no excitement, no resentment, no curiosity. Miranda was certain that if she had asked Isabelle to assist Hercules in cleaning the Augean stables, she would have agreed in the same pliant, obedient manner.

The next day Miranda took Isabelle into the gallery. She had hoped that the brilliantly colored paintings in the current exhibition would have prompted a response, but Isabelle remained withdrawn. After showing her how to clean the paintings with a feather duster, Miranda retired to her office and watched through a window opened onto the gallery.

Isabelle passed the feathers over the first canvas with listless strokes, moving her arm and not her eyes. The second painting also received cursory attention. By the third, however, she was beginning to pause during her task. At the fourth she actually took a step back to observe. Miranda felt her pulse quicken. Isabelle moved forward to dust and stepped back again, this time tilting her head left and then right, narrowing her eyes, then opening them, exposing herself to the sumptuous feast of color and expression laid out before her. Like a starveling at a banquet, she reacted slowly. She was needy, yet fearful. Cautiously she retraced her path, returning to the first three canvases, digesting them bit by bit, finally allowing her senses to taste the full flavor of the art.

Miranda had hoped that Isabelle would want to discuss what she had seen, maybe even what she had felt, but throughout the rest of the day as well as during dinner, Isabelle remained mute. Miranda decided not to push.

Two weeks later Miranda changed the exhibition. This time the work on display was more figurative, depicting life among the Indians in the early days of the American West. Miranda watched as Isabelle studied a picture of a squaw nursing an infant. Backed by lavender-and-pink mountains that rose majestically in the distance, the mother sat in the foreground of the painting, her horse off to the side, grazing in the shadowed grassland. Her hair was dark, plaited into a single braid that hung over her right shoulder. Her face was planed and sculpted, her suede dress beautifully fringed and beaded. Isabelle's focus was not on the softly brushed details, but on the mother's face, which was slightly lowered so she could watch her child suckle at her breast. Her expression was beatific, signifying that this was not simply an act of nature, but an age-old act of continuous connection between ancestors and descendants. The painting made Isabelle cry.

Another one depicted two young Indian braves participating in the Kiowa Fancy Dance. Chubby cheeked with pitch black hair and onyx eyes, they were completely festooned in feathers, from the overwhelming headdresses that rode low on their foreheads to their feather-trimmed vests, pants, and boots. Captured at the peak of the vivacious, spellbinding dance, their faces frozen in a moment of undiluted enjoyment, the painting elicited a smile.

Miranda was certain she had found the key to reaching Isabelle. Now all she had to do was remain patient and trust that she was on the right path.

Next to Isabelle, Nina's best friend was the small leather-bound book that held her most intimate secrets. In it were things she never could have told anyone: how she felt about being adopted, how she wondered why her birth parents had given her away, what they looked like, who they were, and if they ever thought about her. What would happen if Miranda and Luis had another child? Would they stop loving her? Did they love Isabelle as much as they loved her? More?

Nina poured out her heart to the pink-lined pages with religious regularity, venting emotions, airing thoughts, verbalizing dreams. Not only was the process cathartic, but because Nina took great delight in rereading her entries, it was entertaining as well. She fancied herself a writer—one day she intended to pen the great American novel—so it was not unusual for her to embellish and exaggerate daily activities, or to edit her most personal thoughts to make them sound deeper or more lyrical, or to rewrite dialogue, honing it as if her diary were a manuscript she was readying for submission.

Many paragraphs were more fiction than fact, but Nina was a storyteller. She liked living in the world of make-believe. She liked pretending to be someone else or to have something more. To her, any situation could be made more interesting with a little literary embellishment, any person could come off better with an extra bit of verbal polish. She lived life the way it was, but, she reasoned, there was nothing wrong in fantasizing about how life should be.

In real life the Durans struggled to make ends meet, working endless hours to provide the basics, often going without so Nina could have some extras. Nina pitched in as well, helping in the kitchen or with the housekeeping. Yet inside the covers of her pink leather diary, Nina Duran's life took on a completely different aspect. Instead of being poor, she was rich. Instead of being a commoner, she was a princess. Instead of being ten, she was twenty and being courted by the handsomest men in the kingdom. And sometimes, instead of being an adopted child of unknown origins, she was the one in the middle of two sets of parents who wanted her desperately—the Durans and "them."

It used to be that whenever she fantasized about her birth parents, celebrity visages masked the faces in her dreams. Unlikely candidates like James Dean and Clint Eastwood and Robert Wagner competed for the role of her father, with Dorothy Malone and Grace Kelly and Sophia Loren vying for the part of her mother. Once she had met the de Lunas, however, the elegant goddess she imagined was her mother suddenly had brown eyes and deep blond hair—her features were Althea's, her body was Althea's, her manner and temperament were Althea's. Her father became Martín's twin, tall, strapping, imposing, a man men envied and women craved.

It was quite natural for Nina to fix on Isabelle's parents. The de Lunas had flown into town on a day Nina remembered in a once-upon-a-time way, and they had sprinkled fairy dust on a young girl drawn magnetically to those who glittered. They were tall and physically arresting. They were sophisticated and worldly. They were wealthy and romantic. They were all the things the Durans, the Hoffmans, and most everyone else in Santa Fe were not.

After Althea died, Nina grieved. She wept and, for a while, spent a great deal of time alone in her room, staring at a photograph of her and Althea taken that afternoon during the de Lunas' first visit to Santa Fe when they had played dress-up.

Studying the photograph now, seeing Althea festooned with beaded necklaces and a floppy hat with a paper rose hanging over the brim, looking at herself with that delicate fan covering half her face, Nina fought to re-create the giddy closeness of that day and to commune with the spirit of the ebullient woman whose arm was wrapped around her in a warm, protective hug.

The other photograph that never failed to move Nina to tears was of her and Martín, snapped the day he'd taken them skiing at Taos. She could still hear him singing those funny Spanish songs, still feel his strong grip around her waist, still recall how safe she had felt locked in his arms.

Memories like that made Martín's death even more impossible to comprehend than Althea's. He had seemed so invincible, so impervious to the dangers that affected normal mortals. It seemed inconceivable that something as mundane as a heart attack could have felled him. It had been months, yet Nina had not dealt with his passing.

Her need to deny the reality, combined with her penchant for inventing fiction, blocked all avenues of acceptance. She fought the truth by dismissing it as hearsay. After all, she reasoned, there was no firsthand information about anything surrounding Martín's death. He had died alone in a jail cell. Neither Flora nor Alejandro had witnessed his attack. When Alejandro had come to Santa Fe, his visit had been so short and so singularly purposed, there had been no discussion of the funeral, no distribution of detail to paint the scene Nina seemed to need.

Somehow her tangled, nine-year-old reasoning process had managed to twist the facts until she'd reached the bizarre conclusion that Martín was not dead. Rather, he had banished Isabelle to the United States because he was angry with her. After all, her refusal to tell the police what she had seen the night of the murder had led to his arrest. If she had revealed what she knew, she could have spared him the horrors and indignity of imprisonment. But she hadn't, so he had punished her by sending her away. Flora and Alejandro, ashamed of Martín's cruelty, had lied.

Outlandish as it seemed, it made perfect sense to Nina because if she had been in Flora's shoes, she would have done the same thing: she would have protected Isabelle by letting her think her father was dead rather than telling her he simply didn't want her in his life.

Eventually the pain of Martín's death would ease.

The pain of knowing a parent didn't want you never would.

Near the end of November, a senior officer of the Santa Fe National Bank called the Durans and asked if he could come to La Casa for a private meeting. Miranda and Luis agreed, but not without trepidation. The season had been slow for both the hotel and the gallery. The boiler had blown in September, and one of the freezers in the kitchen had decided to quit as well. The resulting cash crunch had forced them to delay payment on some of their bills, but not on their mortgage or the interest on the loan they had taken out to build the pool. While they knew the bank couldn't foreclose because they had been late paying the butcher, to people like the Durans, bankers were rarely bearers of good news.

"I'm sorry I sounded so secretive on the phone," Oscar Yount said when they were seated in Luis's office, "but my instructions were to conduct our business in private." He opened his leather attaché case and extracted a large manila envelope. With carefully manicured fingers, he fussed over the small metal tab, making certain he opened the envelope cleanly, without damaging the tab or his nails.

"May I ask what this is about?" Luis said, nerves mingling with impatience.

"I was told that you were acquainted with a Señor Alejandro Fargas in Barcelona and would understand why this transaction was to be handled with discretion." He removed several large sheets of paper from the envelope and what appeared to be two checks.

Hearing Alejandro's name, Miranda relaxed somewhat. At least he wasn't here to take the hotel. "Yes, we know Señor Fargas."

"Evidently, he was handling the disposition of an estate for . . ." He paused as he searched one of his papers for a name. Miranda helped him out.

"Martín de Luna."

"Right." Yount nodded, checked his notes, and continued. "In our correspondence, Mr. Fargas told me he has already explained what happened to the bulk of the estate."

"It was forfeited to the state." Luis was disappointed. He had hoped that by some legal miracle Alejandro had been able to save Isabelle's inheritance.

"Right," Yount said, his forehead wrinkling with disdain. "Mr. Fargas offered me a brief insight into the situation, and if I might inject a personal note, despite all she's been through, Mr. de Luna's daughter is a lucky girl to have people like you offering her sanctuary."

"We've offered her a home," Miranda said politely. She knew she was arguing semantics, but she couldn't bear to think of Isabelle as a fugitive, even if it was the truth.

"Right." Having punctuated her sentence with his favorite word, he moved on. "According to Señor Fargas, the rest of Mr. de Luna's estate consisted of his wife's jewelry and a collection of antique cars."

Luis nodded, and Yount continued.

"Señorita Pujol has stored the jewelry in a safe place until the child is able to claim it and has sold the cars so that she could pay off her nephew's outstanding debts. Unfortunately, there was not very much left. Be that as it may, Señor Fargas has instructed me to deliver these personally," he said as he handed one check to Luis and the other to Miranda. "The check for ten thousand dollars is to be put into your bank account and used however you wish. Alejandro and Flora want me to tell you that the check comes with love and gratitude from them and from Martín." He paused, giving Miranda time to wipe her eyes and compose herself. "The check for twenty-five thousand dollars is for Isabelle's care. Clothing. Medical bills. Schooling. Whatever. Emotions aside, they know she's an added, unexpected expense. They don't want her to be a burden for you, and although they acknowledge this won't cover everything, they hope it helps."

"I can't," Miranda said. "I don't need to be paid to give Isabelle a home and love and security."

"Right," Yount said, this time with honest sympathy. "I think they know that, Mrs. Duran, but if you don't mind my saying so, I think they did this for themselves as well as for you."

Luis moved behind his wife and patted her shoulder. "Listen to Mr. Yount, Miranda. Alejandro and Flora aren't paying us, they're taking care of Isabelle the only way they can."

"Right!" Yount stood, snapped his case shut, spread his mouth in a satisfied smile, and extended his hand to Luis. "Take a few days to think about what you want to do and then come into the bank and we'll talk. If you need investment advice, I'll be happy to assist in any way I can."

"Right," Luis said, shaking the banker's hand, then turning around to wink at Miranda. "Let me walk you to your car."

Luis and Oscar Yount headed out of the office toward the door, leaving Miranda to stare at the two checks. She had never had so much money in her hands at one time. She hated the fact that it had come to her because of Martín's death. Still, the ten thousand dollars was a godsend. It would allow them to clean up their bills with enough left over for a safety net.

The other check she intended simply to deposit. She believed the Murillos would tire of the fight sooner rather than later and that within a year Isabelle would return to Spain. Luis disagreed. Having discussed the matter at great length with Alejandro, he felt the Murillos were going to behave like bulldogs and that Isabelle would be with them for a very long time.

By Christmas there were signs that Isabelle was emerging from her malaise. She had begun to speak, albeit only when when spoken to, and her teacher had reported an increase in her attention span. Though she wasn't laughing, her prevailing mood had elevated to a softened shade of black.

Still, this would be Isabelle's first Christmas without her parents. Miranda knew all too well that for someone who had experienced a loss, the firsts were the most excruciating. The first Christmas, the first Thanksgiving, the first birthday, the first Easter, the first fiesta—they were days when no drug was strong enough to anesthetize the agony of the grieving soul. But holidays didn't respect the needs of a single person; they catered to the hopes of the many.

Knowing that, Miranda and Luis decided to keep Christmas as they always had. On Christmas Eve the Durans usually invited all the hotel guests and fifty or so neighbors to come sing carols, drink mulled cider, and decorate the tree in the lobby. They had dinner before the festivities and attended midnight mass afterward. The only change Miranda made was to limit her dinner guests to Jonas Hoffman; his wife, Ruth, a journalist who worked for the local newspaper; and their children, Rebecca and Sam. Aside from being their doctor and their closest friends, the Hoffmans were Jewish. Each year at this time, the two families shared holidays. The Hoffmans helped trim the La Casa tree, and the Durans went to the Hoffmans on the first night of Hanukkah to help light the candles on the menorah.

Christmas Eve day, Isabelle kept herself active, offering her services to anyone who needed an extra hand. She completed her chores in the gallery and then helped the dining room staff set the tables for dinner. She helped the housekeepers with the guest rooms. After that she attacked the Durans' private quarters, dusting knickknacks and fluffing pillows until there was nothing left to clean. The one thing she would not do was walk past her mother's painting in the lobby. Althea had given it to the Durans as a gift. Usually it offered Isabelle a connective to the mother she so sorely missed. The idea of seeing it today was simply too painful.

When it came time to change for dinner, Miranda surprised the girls with new holiday dresses she had made. Both were fashioned in bright, holly red velvet. The one Miranda had sewn for Isabelle had a white piqué collar, a big black velvet bow, and crisp white petticoats peeking out from beneath the skirt. Nina's was more sophisticated, with a slimmer skirt and a black velvet collar, cuffs, and sash.

"Merry Christmas!" Miranda said, laying a dress on each bed, her face aglow with happiness and anticipation. What little girl could resist a red velvet dress?

Nina certainly couldn't She squealed with utter delight, grabbed her dress, and ran into the bathroom, holding it against her and preening before the mirror. Isabelle just stared at the bed.

"Don't you like it?" Miranda asked quietly.

For several minutes Isabelle stood over the dress, not moving, not speaking. She appeared disoriented, as if she had never seen a garment like this before and therefore had no idea what to do or say. When she did try to communicate her appreciation, all she could muster was a wobbly curl of her lip and a nod. The alignment of her features, the slump of her shoulders, the veiled look in her eyes—it was a pathetic mosaic of sadness, bewilderment, shattered hopes, and monstrous loss.

"Thank-you, but I—I have a dress," she stammered, looking away from the bed and shutting her eyes as if the sight of something cheerful were a blasphemy.

Miranda wanted to kick herself. She had tried to brighten Isabelle's mood by giving her something special. Instead she had succeeded in reminding the child of all that had been taken away.

"Wear whatever you want," she said lightly as she took the red dress from the bed and hung it in the back of Isabelle's closet.

Isabelle eyed Miranda carefully. "I don't want to hurt your feelings," she said.

"You won't." Miranda stroked Isabelle's cheek, kissed the top of her head, and smiled. "Unless you're late for dinner," she said. "You know how upset I get with cold fajitas!"

When Isabelle's lips turned upward—even for a brief moment—Miranda's heart swelled.

An hour or so later, when the girls joined the Durans and the Hoffmans in the hotel dining room, Nina was resplendent in the vivid red of the season. Isabelle was subdued, shrouded in the navy blue of her mourning, but not quite as unapproachable as she had been.

Miranda thought the rest of the evening proceeded quite well. Luis wisely suggested that they stick to their tradition of enjoying their holiday dinner in the main dining room instead of their private quarters, and this turned out to be a wonderful idea. The noise and chatter and laughter of the guests perfumed the room with the pleasant aroma of revelry, creating an infectious, compelling aura. At the Durans' table, the conversation started out slowly but grew livelier as the evening progressed. No one excluded Isabelle, but neither did anyone press her to participate.

Ruth Hoffman entertained everyone with a story she had been covering for the newspaper about a man who honestly believed he was Santa Claus.

"He had been picked up for shoplifting toys at the mall. When the police questioned him, he claimed he wasn't stealing, he was covering up for his elves. They had gotten confused, he said, and dropped some toys off at the stores that were tagged for children's houses. He didn't want the children to be disappointed, so he came to retrieve the misdelivered items."

Jonas followed up with two terrible Santa jokes that made Rebecca grimace.

"You're a doctor, Daddy, not a comedian. Please try and remember that."

"Did I embarrass you?" Jonas teased.

"When do you not?" Rebecca countered with teenaged pique.

Halfway through the main course, Nina took center stage, regaling her audience with the latest gossip from Hollywood, dispensing details about everything from the steamy Taylor-Burton romance to the storm surrounding the choice of Audrey Hepburn over Julie Andrews to play the lead in *My Fair Lady.*

"Can you imagine?" Nina said as if they were talking about someone down the block. "They shove Andrews aside after she played Eliza Doolittle to standing ovations on Broadway and give it to someone who needs her singing voice dubbed. I mean, Audrey's better looking, but after all, it *is* a musical. Oh, well, that's Hollywood," she said, shrugging like an insider.

Miranda watched in rapt fascination, particularly the way Nina was directing her act toward Sam Hoffman. At just thirteen Sam was a younger version of his good-looking father, blessed with the charm and wit of his journalist mother. More important to a budding adolescent, he was older and in high school and, therefore, extremely desirable. It astounded Miranda to think that her ten-year-old daughter was flirting, but that was precisely what she was doing.

Dessert necessitated an intermission in Nina's performance. While she waited impatiently for the apple pie to be served, Sam, who was sitting in between Nina and Isabelle, decided to take the opportunity to talk to Isabelle. He was upset by the changes he had noticed in her over the past several months. Isabelle had always been a lively sprite, inquisitive and perky, a gamer who was willing to at least dip her toes into the pond of new experiences. From what he had seen, her entire personality had been muted by her dual tragedies. Not that he didn't understand. He had known the de Lunas and knew what had happened to them. He knew how he felt about his parents. He couldn't imagine how she felt without hers. But Sam believed in the power of friendship, that if enough people gave Isabelle enough love and encouragement, she would begin to live again.

"It must have worked," he said, keeping his voice low. "You must be the smartest person in the world."

Isabelle looked at him quizzically.

"You used to ask a million questions. They were real zingers, but now you don't ask any, so I'm guessing you got enough answers to know everything there is to know."

Isabelle started to protest, then saw the twinkle in Sam's eyes and realized he was joking with her. She said nothing, but a smile flickered briefly on her lips.

Feeling rewarded, Sam continued, "Over the years, I did compile my own Isabelle top ten. Would you like hear some of them?"

Curious, she nodded. She never noticed that everyone else at the table was listening as well.

"How does a thermos know what to keep hot and what to keep cold?"

Miranda laughed. She had tried to answer that one.

"Do they only serve western omelets in the West? Why call soda a soft drink when you can't drink something that's hard?"

Rebecca tried to stifle a laugh but couldn't.

"If you lose your mind, do you know that you've lost it?"

Sam paused to see whether or not Isabelle was offended by any of this. She wasn't.

"My personal favorite was when you asked my father how medicine knew where the hurt was. It took you fifteen minutes to answer that one," he said, pointing to Jonas, who chuckled and nodded in response. "He can usually answer anything in sixty seconds or less. I think you set a record, Isabelle."

Nina, wanting to reclaim Sam's attention for herself, stood, raised her water glass, and declared the conversation ended with a loud, "Here's to Isabelle!"

"Here! Here!"

Everyone raised their glasses and toasted the shy girl in the navy blue dress. Though a hesitant smile appeared on her lips, Miranda suspected it did not have a firm hold.

"It's Christmas," she said. "Let's trim the tree!"

Instantly Nina was up and out of her seat. She grabbed Sam's hand, disappointed when he resisted. Bending down so he could speak softly and not embarrass her, he asked Isabelle, "Would you like to help? You don't have to if you don't want."

She looked at him with shy, uncertain eyes. He smiled and tilted his head in the direction of the lobby, as if to say, "Come on. It'll be fun." Rebecca rose and gave Isabelle a gentle nudge. Nina, having swallowed her jealousy, followed suit.

"Sure," Isabelle said.

Miranda watched as Isabelle trailed the others out of the dining room. Her step wasn't leaden, her head wasn't bowed. Luis caught his wife's eye. She smiled and nodded. Isabelle had started on the long road back.

After church, the Durans retired to the family quarters to open presents. The girls changed into their pajamas while Miranda made a pot of cocoa and Luis built a fire. By the time the girls returned, the floor in front of the hearth was crowded with gaily wrapped packages. Nina plowed into the pile, looking for tags with her name on it. She got a fuzzy pink sweater, gloves, a beautifully framed cover of *Life* magazine's special issue on President Kennedy, a small camera, and last, but not least, the latest albums by the Beatles and the true love of her life, Elvis Presley.

Isabelle's packages yielded books, pajamas, a pair of jeans, some pads of paper, and a big wooden box filled with oil paints, watercolors, pencils, and pastel chalks. She, too, was delighted with Santa's leavings.

"These came in the mail last week," Miranda said, lifting two more packages from the pile. She handed the smaller one to Nina and the larger one to Isabelle. "They're from Flora and Alejandro."

Nina hadn't expected a gift from them and certainly not something as exquisite as the gold filigree cross she found inside the box. As she engaged the clasp and felt the delicate cross settle on her neck, her face flushed with guilt.

"Merry Christmas to Isabelle's guardian angel," the card read.

Nina cringed. If Flora and Alejandro only knew how many times she had wished that Isabelle would just pack up and go home, how often she had resented everyone clucking over Isabelle, fussing and fretting about the poor, dear, tragic orphan, how ignored she felt, how annoyed she got. Nina turned away quickly, fearful that someone might read in her face what she knew in her heart: she wasn't the angel Flora and Alejandro thought she was.

Isabelle's package contained a photo album filled with pictures of Martín and Althea, Isabelle, Flora, and Alejandro. As a pictorial summation of their lives together, its impact was ballistic. Snapshots of two lovers in the full swell of romance, pictures of a tiny baby being worshiped by adoring parents, a growing child surrounded by an ever-doting family, birthday parties at the Castell, mementos of vacations and holidays, times spent with Flora and Alejandro, quiet, intimate moments between husband and wife, mother and daughter, father and child.

She turned the pages with tremendous effort, slowly, as if her hand were weighted down by bricks. As the images passed before her eyes, Isabelle retreated visibly into herself. It was as if her mind couldn't deal with the present at the same time it was trying to relive the past. Now and then she winced or shivered or bowed her head, but she didn't cry. She barely noticed Nina standing over her shoulder or Miranda and Luis flanking her sides. She was too absorbed in the enormity of what she was feeling to see anything or anyone else.

The final picture had been taken on Martín's birthday, just before the fateful trip to Majorca. It was the last time they were all together. Isabelle was on Martín's shoulders, Althea was on his lap, Flora and Alejandro stood on either side. They were all mugging shamelessly for the camera, each one making the funniest, goofiest face they could. Isabelle, recalling the incident, started to laugh, but within seconds her laughter turned into uncontrollable, heart-wrenching sobs.

Quickly Miranda took the child in her arms, holding tight in an attempt to still the tremors shaking the small body. All Luis could do was stand by helplessly, able to little more than pray that soon God would find a way to bring her peace. Unobserved by anyone, Nina had taken the album and retreated to the other side of the room.

The more she saw, the stranger she felt. Isabelle was convulsed by an album filled with wonderful family memories. While she sympathized with Isabelle's grief and was incredibly grateful that Miranda and Luis were alive and well, a peculiar feeling nagged at her. It wasn't the first time she had experienced a longing to know the people who had given her life, but this album seemed to underline all that she didn't know. Unable to help herself, Nina looked at shots of Isabelle with Althea and wished she had been there instead. She came across family portraits and felt an inexplicable envy rising in her throat. She found pictures of Martín in all his gigantic splendor and wondered again if perhaps she was right, that he was still alive.

It was then that she tuned in to what Miranda was saying to Isabelle.

"You've suffered a terrible, terrible loss, but you're not alone. You have all these wonderful memories, and you have the constant and continuing love of Tía Flora and Alejandro. You have new friends like Rebecca and Sam. And you have a new family to love you and take care of you."

"Mama's right," Nina said, her own emotions straining. "What happened is behind you. It doesn't matter who did what or who knows the truth about what happened."

"I know the truth," Isabelle said, turning to face Nina, her reaction stunning all who witnessed it.

Suddenly there was color in her cheeks and fire in her voice. Though she was trembling slightly, there were no tears in her eyes, only the glimmer of faith and unshaken belief.

"I know that my father didn't kill my mother. And I know that he loved her, and me, until the day he died!"

CHAPTER 5

1968

Once she had reconciled to being there, adjusting to life in Santa Fe had not been terribly difficult for Isabelle. Customs were different, but she was young and adapted easily. The language was different, but within months her English was flawless. Though she was quiet, she was a congenial child; between her own charm and Nina's insistence that Isabelle go everywhere with her, it didn't take long to build a comfortable circle of friends.

One adjustment that surprised her was money. At La Casa money was usually in short supply, and while the Durans were quite adept at making the most of whatever they had, for Isabelle frugality was a foreign concept. Martín and Althea's lives had defined indulgence; denial and compromise had never been part of the de Luna vocabulary. Circumstances were different now. Isabelle had gone from custom-made clothes to hand-me-downs, from dealing with household servants to doing household chores, from spending long, leisurely vacations in Majorca or on the French Riviera to day trips to the desert or Taos, from being a doted-on, worry-free fairy princess to an orphaned castoff who often fretted she was a burdensome guest in an already burdened home.

In time she not only adjusted, but began to relish her new life. Once her palate adapted to the spices, she learned to enjoy Miranda's cooking. As for the lack of new clothes, eventually Isabelle's artistic aesthetic took over and dressing became a sport. Believing that all colors went with all other colors and that textures were meant to be combined, she mixed and matched with abandon, taking clothing that was somewhat used and creating something quite original by adding a belt here or a vest there.

Having a sibling was new to both girls, but as Nina had predicted, they became sisters. They shared a room, giggles, troubles, confidences, crushes, and accessories, but rarely clothes. At fifteen Nina was a strikingly beautiful young woman. Though she would have been a standout anywhere, in Santa Fe, with its generous mix of Mexican-Americans and Native Americans, she seemed even more unusual. Already five feet nine, with silky straight, flaxen hair, pussy-willow gray eyes, endless legs, and a willowy frame, she was the envy of every short, chubby adolescent in town. At twelve Isabelle was thin and spindly, with a few budding knobs, long, thick brown hair, and nicely turned ankles, but little else to declare in the way of femininity.

Nina became Isabelle's paragon. Whatever Nina did, Isabelle wanted to try: plucking her eyebrows, shaving her legs, wearing makeup. Though she knew those things couldn't compensate for nature's flubs, she assumed they couldn't hurt. Unfortunately, Miranda had set age limits on practices like those, so although it felt unjust to be a tweeze away from looking as wonderful as Nina, Isabelle had to content herself with whatever her genes had produced.

The other thing that impressed Isabelle about Nina was that she knew so much about so many things. Not a movie came to town that Nina didn't see, there wasn't a movie star she didn't have a file on, a singer whose songs she couldn't sing. There wasn't anyone in Santa Fe whose life story she didn't know, nor was there a secret so confidential or a rumor so new she hadn't heard it. Though sometimes Rebecca Hoffman claimed Nina made up half of what she said and embellished the other half beyond recognition, Isabelle remained impressed. Maybe it was because she had never met anyone Nina's age who spoke with such assurance. Nina didn't suggest, she asserted. She didn't beat around the bush or think twice before expressing an opinion. Though often her forthrightness got her into trouble, she said what she had to say—straight out.

After five years of living together, Isabelle knew Nina in a way no one else did. While others believed Nina's confidence stemmed from her enviable exterior package, Isabelle had seen her stare into a mirror when she thought no one was looking and burst into tears because she thought she was too tall and too pale to be of interest to boys accustomed to smaller, brunette beauties. She had watched Nina struggle with her schoolwork, unable to grasp complicated mathematical concepts yet unwilling to stay after school for extra help for fear of being ridiculed. She had spent hours talking to Nina about what she wanted to be when she grew up and knew how fearful Nina was that she would never get to write the book she believed she had within her.

It was also true that Nina knew Isabelle as no one else did. She had been a witness to examples of Isabelle's strength as well as an ear for Isabelle's apprehensions. She had heard the terror in Isabelle's screams during those early nightmares and had listened to the hope in her voice when she described her dream of having a painting hang in a museum. She knew that as aggressive as Isabelle was about her art, that was how shy she was about boys. And she knew that as secure as Isabelle felt with the Durans, she never really felt completely safe.

As for Miranda and Luis, they were so caring that it was only natural for a fondness to develop between Isabelle and her guardians. Luis, the consummate innkeeper, was extremely adept at making people feel wanted. With Isabelle he held out a paternal hand, offering advice and affection and reassurance whenever it was needed, careful never to trespass on the sacred ground of Martín's memory. Miranda was more spiritual and therefore better able to guide the gradual healing of Isabelle's soul. Too, they had much in common: both found the world of color and line and image exciting, and both found comfort in the silence of the desert.

The first time Miranda took Isabelle to the northwestern part of New Mexico, the rugged, flat-topped mesas frightened her. Scanning the vastness from the valley floor, she felt small and insignificant compared to the immenseness of the landscape. It was difficult not to feel threatened and defenseless surrounded by an endless space that seemed to have no entrance and no exit. Yet the longer she stood there, the less intimidated she became. As her anxieties subsided, monumental rock formations and craggy projections became forms and shapes, the vibrant infinity divided into colors and tones.

Though she was awed by the scene laid out before her, this was not the first time she had confronted nature's sculptural ability. Some of her earliest memories were of visits with Althea and Tía Flora to the legendary Montserrat thirty miles west of Barcelona. An eerie, saw-toothed outcrop shaped and chiseled by twenty-five million years of erosion, Montserrat also rose over a valley in a glorious demonstration of cosmic creation. It too boasted gigantic mounds, sensuous bulges, and centuries-old accumulations of stone and earth and dust. But for every striking similarity, there was a sharp difference. Montserrat was painted from a palette of grays and blues, with only occasional strokes of green and black. This palette was a rainbow of reds, ochers, russets, purples, and browns. Montserrat's peaks were rounded, bulging into the sky. These elevations were higher, sharper, steeper. Because Montserrat was believed to be the home of "La Morenta," the Black Virgin, Catalonia's patron saint, and the spot where the knight Parsifal discovered the Holy Grail, it was considered a sacred place and was besieged by a constant invasion of pilgrims. These mountains exuded a hallowed aura as well, but the religion here was not man's, not the miracles of Christianity: it was a primitive spirit that worshiped the marvels of nature.

That first afternoon—like so many that would follow—as she and Miranda picnicked on the desert floor, Miranda told Isabelle about Georgia O'Keeffe. She told her about the incredible woman who had been born in 1887 on a farm in Wisconsin and now lived in a ranch not far from where they were and in a house high atop of cliff in a place called Abiquiu.

"That's where I grew up," Miranda told her.

"Did you know her?"

Miranda laughed. "Abiquiu is a flyspeck village with less than fifty people. Naturally, everyone knew everyone else, especially the famous Miss Georgia."

"Was she nice?"

"Very." A smile of happy reminiscence warmed Miranda's face. "She knew we were very poor, but very proud. Though she wanted to give us money, she knew no one would take charity, so she found other ways to help us."

"Like how?"

"Well, like she heard we had a pretty terrific baseball team, probably the best in the league. The problem was transportation. The school couldn't afford a bus, so the team could only play home games. Miss Georgia changed all that by sending her chauffeur in her big car to drive our baseball team to their away games."

"Did she go to the games?"

"No, but the boys knew she was rooting for them."

"What else did she do?"

"Let's see," Miranda said, ruminating a bit. "She had a huge garden behind her house, which always seemed to produce too many vegetables for her table. She would send bushels of homegrown lettuce and tomatoes and peppers to our houses, begging us to take them, claiming that if we didn't, they would simply rot on the vine. And she hired most of us to work for her."

"Really?" The notion of working for someone as famous as Georgia O'Keeffe utterly titillated Isabelle. "What did you do?"

"I worked as a maid."

"Did you ever get to watch her paint?"

"Not when I was in the house. She used to keep her studio closed when she worked, but I did get to see some of her sketches when it was my turn to walk her home."

"Walk her home?" Isabelle was confused. At the time, Miranda would have been a little girl, Georgia O'Keeffe an old woman.

"As Miss Georgia got on in years, her eyesight began to fail. She was a stubborn woman, completely unwilling to surrender even the smallest expression of her independence, and that included having someone accompany her down into the valley to paint. She'd rise at dawn, pack a lunch, and leave early in the morning. By the time she was ready to leave, it was close to sunset and the shadows made it almost impossible for her to find her way. She was nearly blind by then. So, as a return for her kindness, all of us in Abiquiu would take turns going down into the valley and escorting her home."

"She must have loved that."

Again Miranda laughed. "Yes and no. Deep down, I think she was grateful for the guiding hand, but she, too, had her pride, which was why we used to make up silly excuses as to why we were there."

"Like what?"

"Oh, I don't know. I used to tell her that I needed some rocks for a school project or I was collecting wildflowers for my mother's table. Once or twice I told her I was lost and asked if she could lead me home."

Isabelle giggled. It was a sound Miranda had feared she might never hear again.

"It sounds like a fun game."

"In a way it was, but for me it was an honor. She was a genius, you know."

"Tell me about her paintings," Isabelle said.

Miranda complied, and happily. She told Isabelle about O'Keeffe's flower paintings, how she had rendered a single blossom so large that the tiniest detail became a vital element of the whole, the barest shadow a clue to the very essence of the flower. Every crease, wrinkle, and curve of every petal became a challenge to the beholder, something to look at and ponder, something to marvel at and respect.

"Why did she do that?" Isabelle asked, studying the pictures in the book Miranda had brought, trying to shrink the images in her mind's eye so they would return to a more recognizable likeness.

"She felt that flowers were so small, most people didn't look at them," Miranda said, watching Isabelle narrow her eyes and then open them, expanding and contracting the flower on the page, trying to compare the original object with O'Keeffe's more majestic vision. "It takes a lot of time to really study a flower. She was concerned that we wouldn't take that time, so she made it easier for us by making her flowers so large we would have to look at them."

"I'm glad she did," Isabelle said, tracing the lines of the painting with her fingers, clearly impressed.

On another outing, Miranda showed Isabelle O'Keeffe's paintings of the red hills that distinguished the New Mexico badlands. Again Isabelle was taken with the way O'Keeffe allowed shape to overpower her canvas; the way she allowed color to provide the flow, shadow the depth. It was as if O'Keeffe had sat where Isabelle was sitting and had focused a high-powered lens on the hills in the distance, zooming them close enough to touch, near enough to hear the echoes that rebounded from one canyon wall to another.

Isabelle learned to love the desert, partly because it was time alone with Miranda, but mostly because she had become nature's pupil. With her pencils and crayons at the ready, Isabelle opened her senses to the landscape, allowing it to teach how sunlight affected color, how shadow altered shape, how position created perspective. It fascinated her to discover that in the morning, when the angle of light was lower, the length of a shadow was longer; that by midmorning, when the light angled in on a diagonal, the shadows defined the plane; and that by noon, when the light was directly overhead, no shadows were cast at all.

Most of the time she respected the laws of the color wheel, mixing and blending according to prescribed guidelines: yellow and blue for green, red and blue for purple, etc. Now and then she strayed from the strictures of the spectrum, allowing caprice and inventiveness to take over. She'd blend pink and brown for a gray mountain tinged with warm dust from the desert floor, green and pink and ocher for foliage that thirsted constantly for water but had learned to survive without it. She'd paint a yellow sky hovering over a red hill in a purple desert with pink sagebrush and turquoise tumbleweed. She'd turn a river green, its shoreline red, the mountains purple, the sky black, and the moon orange. What was, didn't matter. It was how she felt about what was that made it onto her canvases or sketch pads. Color became her vocabulary of feeling. The one color she never used was royal blue.

"Why don't you color, too?" Isabelle asked on one of their recent visits to Abiquiu.

Though Miranda had an eye for art and a love for everything creative, she was bereft of actual talent. As she often said, she could barely draw a straight line with a ruler, which was why while Isabelle sketched, Miranda read or simply communed with the spirits that inhabited her surroundings.

"I would love to," Miranda answered, "but I wasn't given the gift you were. I have the eye of the observer. You have the hands and soul of the creator."

"I worry that you're bored," Isabelle said, her forehead knotted.

Miranda laughed. "Quite the contrary. If you didn't paint or draw, then I'd be bored. My eye needs constant stimulation. I need you to give me things to look at."

"And I need you," Isabelle said, grinning at her guardian, "to jump up and down and clap your hands and tell me how good I am."

"For now, maybe," Miranda said, wondering why great talent was so often paired with insecurity, "but you'll see, Isabelle. One of these days, the entire world will tell you how good you are."

Sybil Croft had come to Santa Fe from Dover, Vermont, with a palette of dreams and ambitions. She had discovered her own artistry as a young girl in a small-town school. For someone like Sybil, so plain and shy that she was practically invisible, finding that she could do something no one else in class could do was very special indeed. It was a heady experience to have her pictures on display throughout the school or to be singled out to draw posters for special events. Since there was little else about Sybil that would ever provoke applause, her art became her ego. Acceptance or rejection of what she did became the barometer of who she was and what she was worth.

As an adolescent she experimented with a number of styles in search of her artistic niche. For a while she explored the various avenues of abstraction popular at the time: dripping paint like Jackson Pollock, creating intensely colored landscapelike fields like Mark Rothko, using Rorschach-like configurations like Robert Motherwell. She tried pop art, but found she was too conservative to feel comfortable painting soup cans à la Andy Warhol or flags like Jasper Johns or Lucky Strike packages like Stuart Davis. Ultimately, the group that inspired the strongest feelings of kinship were not her contemporaries, but rather the regionalists of the thirties—Thomas Hart Benton, Edward Hopper, Grant Wood, Charles Burchfield—who used subjects drawn from the regions where they were born to depict the diversity of the American scene.

Convinced that her mission was to capture the heroic essence of New England, Sybil began an intensive study of her neighbors, their surroundings and their habits. She observed them at work, at play, at rest, and at prayer, sketching their expressions and activities. The result was a chronicle of everyday endeavors and ordinary folks—the dawn-to-dusk of reserved, gritty, straightforward people with little or no pretense, a high sense of purpose, and a strict code of morality.

No wonder that when it came time to submit her college senior project—a series of works based on a single theme, executed in the artist's chosen style—Sybil had no difficulty deciding what to paint and how to paint it. She produced five large canvases entitled *Simply Vermont*.

A convenience store on a lonely highway, a young boy pumping gas in the pouring rain, his bright yellow slicker in sharp contrast with the murky black of the night sky.

A white-steepled church on a stormy Sunday, its scanty congregation trudging through the snow—heads bowed, bodies bent—each one visibly resolved that nothing will keep them from their weekly meeting with God.

A child poking out a giggling face from a huge pile of leaves, amusing and dismaying an obliging grandfather, who stands alongside the stack with a rake in his hand, clearly torn between his love of the child and his need to complete his chores.

A ski lift in summer, its chairs still, its motor silent, its fat poles lumbering up the mountain like a lost and lonely climber.

An innkeeper rocking on his porch, a beer in his hand, a dog by his side, a vacant gaze in his eyes that speaks volumes about the tragedy of empty streets, empty rooms, empty pockets, and, often, empty, unfulfilled lives.

Simply Vermont won first prize. Sybil Croft was Best of Class, Bennington College, 1955.

A month after graduation, just as Sybil was ready to leave for New York and the start of her new life, her mother was diagnosed with cancer. For two years Sybil nursed her mother and suffered the consequences of her father's alcoholism, all the while trying to maintain Croft's Landing, the family's small country inn near Mount Snow. When her mother died, Sybil ran as far and as fast as she could.

When she arrived in Santa Fe, her first job was as a waitress-barmaid at La Casa. Over time she and the Durans became friends. Miranda advised her on how and when to show her art; Luis, sensing that working at the hotel revived memories that made it emotionally difficult for Sybil, suggested she take education courses at the university so she could get a teacher's certificate.

"Teaching," he told her, "will give you a decent wage doing something you enjoy and still leave you plenty of time to paint."

That was ten years ago. Now, at nearly thirty-six, Sybil was a respected member of the community, on the board of the Santa Fe Opera, active in an organization of artists working with the Indians to preserve Native American culture, and a frequent judge at prestigious art competitions. While there had been rumors about romances—another teacher, a ski instructor from Taos, a professor from the university—Sybil remained single.

Whether it was a case of personal pragmatism or simply that she had no other choice, in time Sybil reconciled what she had wanted out of life with what life had actually offered her. She relinquished the hope of having a husband and children and reassessed her career. After several disappointing shows—yielding only mediocre reviews and lackluster sales—it became painfully apparent that being the best in one's class did not automatically mean one was destined for national prominence. She might have been devastated if not for the glorious reviews of several of her students, all of whom credited her with bringing out the best in them. It was then that she discovered her real talent lay in teaching.

New Mexico—particularly Taos and Santa Fe—was a mecca for artists and had been since the early 1900s. Names like Will Shuster, Fremont Ellis, Willard Nash, Max Weber, Marsden Hartley, Andrew Dasburg, and, of course, Georgia O'Keeffe made fledging artists believe there was magic in the air that surrounded the Sangre de Cristo Mountains. It wasn't long before Sybil Croft became part of the mystique, drawing painters from all over the country. Some were beginners, others had begun to establish themselves, a few had young but solid reputations. All had decided that Sybil's unique blend of psychological insight and technical mastery could propel them forward. They never worried that she would look to dispose of a style with which they were comfortable or to dilute a message in which they truly believed. Sybil Croft never tampered with personal vision. She simply adjusted the method of communication.

Despite her growing prominence, she continued to teach at both the elementary and the high school, taking great delight in introducing her precious world of art to the young. While many wondered why she bothered teaching cut and paste and color to classes of barely interested children when she could have confined herself to paying customers, Sybil thought the answer was obvious: to mine one perfect diamond from a pile of coal was worth everything.

Isabelle was nine when Miranda asked Sybil to work with her.

"You're not exactly a rank beginner," Sybil said at their first session, "but because you've never had any formal training, I thought we'd start with the basics."

Isabelle considered objecting, reminding Sybil that Flora Pujol was a well-respected artist and had tutored her a great deal when she was young, and that Althea had been a recognized painter and fabric designer who had encouraged and guided Isabelle's early scribblings; but she knew of Sybil's reputation and opted to listen.

"Most objects conform to four basic shapes: the cube, the cylinder, the cone, and the sphere. What I'd like you to do is draw those forms over and over again, varying them a little each time so they begin to look like something we might recognize."

Isabelle enjoyed the game. She turned a tapered cylinder into a tumbler, a tower, and a bottle. An elongated cube became a box and a stick of butter. An indented sphere became an apple; cut in half, it looked like a cup. A truncated cone became a funnel, a rounded cone a wine goblet.

Sybil had Isabelle draw straight lines freehand, frequently turning the paper, changing angle and direction; curved lines demanded a looser arm and a more supple wrist. She drew lines to separate a piece of paper into fourths, asking Isabelle to fill each quadrant with shapes without having one overpower the other. She devised exercises to teach symmetry and balance, rhythm and repetition. From there they moved on to casting shadows, rendering textures and finding the angle of light.

Eventually Isabelle found herself thinking in terms of forms rather than objects, looking at everyday things as constructions or combinations, dissecting them into the four basic geometric shapes, stripping away details and paring them down until nothing was left but form and light and shadow.

By the end of the first year, if Sybil asked her to draw a bowl of fruit on a table with a lamp, Isabelle could produce an accurate still life, her objects recognizable and in relative proportion to each other. If Sybil asked her to draw a landscape, the same was true: the replication of scene was faithful, and there was a sense of scale and unity to the piece. By the end of the second year, during which they explored the endless possibilities of color, Sybil, like Miranda, was convinced that Isabelle had been blessed with the seeds of greatness.

Her only weakness, if at this relatively early stage of her artistic development it was even appropriate to think in terms of deficiency, was portraiture. When Sybil decided to move on to figures, she had asked Isabelle to draw the people at the hotel.

"I'm not asking for full-blown portraits. Just rough sketches."

At first glance, what she got back looked like a stack of half drawings and partial studies. Closer examination showed that although the faces were incomplete, the features chosen for depiction were so distinctive that recognition was easy and immediate: Luis was a mustache over a thin upper lip,

Miranda an almond-shaped eye in a rounded face; Nina was a high-planed cheekbone with deep-smile lines, Sam a wide grin and a square chin. Much to her chagrin, Isabelle had captured Sybil's aquiline nose and pinched expression perfectly.

Some might have called these caricatures; but caricatures, strictly defined, offered ridiculously exaggerated peculiarities or defects. These features were neither exaggerated, nor defects, nor ridiculous. In fact, they were drawn quite deliberately, prompting Sybil to wonder whether the omissions were calculated and conscious—possibly related to a budding personal style—or unconscious deletions prompted by something deeper.

The other thing that concerned her were several sketches of someone Isabelle couldn't identify. While that alone would not have troubled Sybil, it was the agitation his partial image conveyed and Isabelle's brusque, "It's just a face. He's no one I know," that Sybil found unsettling.

When curiosity moved her to discuss the matter with Miranda, she was hustled into the gallery office. From her safe, Miranda took a passel of torn papers, which she laid out on a table for Sybil to see.

"Isabelle did these when she first came to Santa Fe," Miranda said. "Just after her mother was killed."

She confessed that at the time, when she had asked Nina what Isabelle did when alone and Nina had mentioned Isabelle's doodling, Miranda had done something she wasn't proud of but had felt was necessary to understand what was going on inside Isabelle's silent world—she had rummaged through Isabelle's drawers and wastebasket, retrieving scraps of paper that had been crumpled up and thrown away.

"I took these to be self-portraits," Miranda said, separating the faces into piles.

Sybil agreed. There was no question that these drawings were of Isabelle: a small oval face, eyes wide, mouth opened as if ready to scream, scraggly lines alongside the face indicating long hair. There was only one eye, the hair was only on one side, there was no nose, no ears. Yet the emotion was obvious: terror.

"These . . . well . . . I don't know who this is," Miranda said, handing Sybil several wrinkled sketches.

It was the same face as the unidentified man she had done for Sybil: square jaw; large, wide-open eye; mouth caught in a skewered sneer.

"Is this her father?" Sybil asked. Miranda shook her head. "Her uncle?" Again a negative response.

Sybil stared at them, trying to see beyond them into their genesis.

"Even though she only did two or three of them recently, I don't like the fact that she's been drawing this same face the same way for five years and claims she doesn't know who it is."

"I agree."

"Would you mind if I showed these and her other sketches to a friend in Albuquerque?" Sybil said, looking at Isabelle's early self-portraits, shivering at the abject fear displayed before her.

"What kind of friend?" Miranda trusted Sybil, but after all, Isabelle was only in Miranda's care; she wasn't kin.

"He's a psychologist."

Miranda paused, but not for long.

"If Isabelle needs help," she said, slightly embarrassed that she hadn't thought of talking to a professional, "Luis and I need to know how to help her."

Before Sybil unveiled the sketches, Miranda presented Dr. Richards with a summary of Isabelle's history. She felt compelled to add that despite the agitation apparent in some of these drawings, Isabelle was a happy child. She enjoyed being with the family. She laughed often. She had friends. She did her chores willingly. She looked forward to her classes with Sybil and her outings with Miranda. Her grades were good. And according to Nina, she hadn't had one of her nightmares in nearly three years.

When Richards asked if she had any contact with her real family, Miranda told him Isabelle spoke to her aunt in Barcelona once a week and received letters from both Flora and Alejandro several times a month. Though Isabelle yearned to see them, she understood it was not possible at the present time. In the interest of security, Miranda declined to offer a more detailed explanation.

"You must understand that without speaking to the child directly, anything I say is mere observation," the doctor said.

Despite his disclaimer, Miranda's expression remained one of confident anticipation. Her assumption was that his observations had to be better than her guesses.

"Putting together what you've told me and what I observe in these drawings, I can see several possibilities. One is that she prefers landscapes to portraits and is impatient with the tedious process of duplicating the details of physical reality."

The rigid line of Miranda's shoulders softened. That was precisely the type of explanation she had wanted—simple and without odious overtones.

Sybil's posture remained expectant and skeptical. Richards had offered an hors d'oeuvre. She wasn't biting until something more meaty was served.

"Another theory hypothesizes that unconnected lines often reveal a fear of abandonment. In Isabelle's case, that would be more than reasonable."

He studied the early sketches again, then the later sketches. Sybil had also brought several nightscapes Isabelle had done. Though each appeared different, all contained the same elements: a brooding, heavily shadowed, navy blue sky; a full moon hidden behind a dense, rain-dulled cloud; and a harsh, silver bolt of lightning that pierced the blackness yet shed no light.

"Along with doctors and wild animals, fear of storms and darkness are quite common in young children," Richards said. "Considering the horrific memories Isabelle now associates with violent thunderstorms, it's only natural that her fears would be exaggerated."

He pursed his lips as he moved the drawings around, looking at one and then another, selecting several Miranda had told him were of Martín and Althea.

"It could be that as time began to erase her memory of her parents' faces and their images were reduced to separate features rather than a unified whole, her subconscious decided to portray everyone the way she saw her parents. That way, she didn't have to think of them as separate and different."

This prompted Miranda and Sybil to think about their own losses. Each tried to conjure an image of a loved one who had passed on. When they too were able to summon only expressions or quick visions or fleeting glances, they granted the doctor a nod.

"Isabelle and her parents were exceptionally close," he continued, finding himself drawn to the early, pitifully sad self-portraits strewn about his desk. "Think of what's happened to her. Her mother's death was violent and cruel. You said that some believe Isabelle was a witness to that brutality and that it frightened her enough to block the entire event from her mind. Then her father was forced to send her away, was put on trial for a crime he claims he didn't commit, and was thrown into jail, where he died. This poor child's parents were heartlessly ripped out of her life. How could she feel anything but lost and abandoned? How could she see herself as anything but incomplete?"

He looked at the two women seated opposite him. Miranda's eyes were moist.

"I feel so helpless," she murmured.

"Don't. You're doing all you can. You and your husband are providing her with affection and stability. Her aunt and uncle are continuing to give her connection with her past. And her art is providing a much needed outlet."

Miranda wiped her eyes, but inside, tears continued to fall.

"Considering all she's been through," Richards said, wanting to accord Miranda some peace of mind, "Isabelle is doing remarkably well. You and Miss Croft assure me that she's happy and functioning and has not really evidenced any signs of continued trauma in a long time. She's clearly a survivor, Mrs. Duran, and that should give you comfort."

"It does," Miranda admitted. "I just can't bear the thought of her being tormented by the past."

"We're all tormented by our past. It's how well we deal with it that determines our future."

"Is he part of Isabelle's past?" Sybil asked, pointing to the sketches of the unknown man. Richards had avoided them. Sybil wanted to know why.

"Why does she keep drawing his face?" Miranda said, anxiety surfacing all over again. "Who is he?"

Dr. Richards winced. Looking from one to the other, he could tell they knew what he was about to say. That should have made it easier for him. It didn't.

"He's the face she sees in her nightmares," he said quietly. "He's probably the man who killed her mother."

In May Isabelle got the phone call she'd prayed for: Tía Flora and Alejandro felt it was safe for her to come to Barcelona.

"You'll come right after school lets out," Flora said, her voice breaking with emotion. "We'll spend the summer together."

"I can't wait to see you," Isabelle said, longing to know whether she would be going for a visit or if she was going home to stay, experiencing an unexpected rumbling of conflict. "I've missed you, Tía Flora."

"And I've missed you, my darling."

The silence that followed was brief but heavy with sentiment and unspoken words about their forced estrangement. Isabelle had a thousand questions about the Murillos and what was happening with Flora and Alejandro, but she dared not ask them. Her aunt and uncle were certain that the police placed random taps on both their phone lines. Since they never knew exactly when the electronic eavesdropping took place, they were always prudent about what they said, saving details for follow-up letters. So far, the mail hadn't been tampered with.

"Is Teresa Serrat going to be there?" Isabelle asked, remembering Pedro and Consuela's daughter and hoping she was not on the "don't mention" list.

"No. She's going to be spending the summer with relatives in Marbella."

"Oh."

Though only a single syllable, the soft utterance spoke volumes about Isabelle's disappointment.

Suddenly inspired, Flora said, "Would you like to bring Nina with you?"

"Could I? Would it be all right? Do you mean it? Do you mind?"

"Yes, yes, yes, and no, of course not." Flora laughed, delighted with herself and the prospect of having two young girls visiting the Castell.

Several days later two letters arrived from Spain: one for the Durans, instructing them to withdraw enough money from Isabelle's account to cover the expenses for both girls; and one for Isabelle, explaining why they felt the time was right to risk a visit.

During the past five years, Flora frequently had noticed strangers prowling the periphery of the Castell de Les Bruixots. Sometimes they wandered about for a while and left. Other times they lingered for days. Now and then, when she and Pedro drove into town for their weekly shopping, their attention was drawn to a bright spot on the hill just across from them. It glinted sharply, like sunlight hitting the glass of binoculars or a telescope lens.

Flora didn't know whether these intruders were private guards or undercover police, but she had no question about who had instructed them to keep watch on the Castell. With stubborn regularity, Alejandro received long legal documents from the Murillos, demanding Isabelle's return. He responded the same way every time: at present, the whereabouts of Señorita Isabelle de Luna are unknown.

For nearly a year, however, there had been no guards, no spies, and no legal entreaties. Instead of feeling relieved, Flora was unnerved by the unexpected calm. Never one to underestimate the Murillos, Flora exhorted Alejandro to use his contacts to find out whether or not this sudden lack of attention was ruse or reality. When Alejandro got word that indeed the custody suit had been dropped, he and Flora dared to believe that perhaps time had dulled the edge of the Murillos' obsessive quest for possession of their granddaughter.

"So? What do you think?" Luis asked, studying Isabelle's face as she read Flora's letter for the third time. "Are you excited at the thought of going home?"

Even as he said the words, he knew he didn't want Isabelle calling anywhere but La Casa "home." Miranda's expression said that already she too was experiencing pangs of loneliness.

"Well, I'm excited," Nina said, giggling, still not believing that she was going to Europe for the summer.

"I am, too," Isabelle said, smiling for Nina's sake. "I can't wait to show Nina Barcelona. And, of course, I want very much to see Tía Flora again." Even through her smile, her voice wobbled. "I was beginning to feel as if we'd never be together again."

"Just think," Miranda said, trying to generate enthusiasm, "you'll be able to see old friends and visit some of your favorite places. It'll be fun!"

Isabelle widened her smile, but her eyes remained somber.

"What's the matter, darling? Are you afraid to go back to Barcelona?"

Luis moved in front of Isabelle. He too was concerned with her dispassionate reaction. "Alejandro and Flora will protect you," he said. "They won't let your grandparents bother you."

Isabelle looked at him quizzically. The Murillos were so removed from what she had been thinking, it took her a moment to remember who they were and why she might be afraid of them.

"I guess I should worry about them," she said after focusing on the possibility of having to see them or deal with them, "but, well, that's not it."

"Is it me?" Nina asked, confused about Isabelle's sudden attack of the blues, nervous that her dream trip might be called off. "Is it going to be too much for you? I mean, having to show me around and all?"

"No," Isabelle said quickly, annoyed with herself for having created such a negative impression. "I want you to come with me. I need you to be with me."

Miranda could almost see the bands of tension gripping Isabelle. "Does your hesitancy have to do with your parents?" she asked, having guessed that only something very powerful could have given rise to such intense stress.

Isabelle nodded. She lowered her eyes and studied her hands. "I'm nervous," she said.

"About what?" Luis suspected that much as he'd like to, he was not going to be able to do or say anything that would calm her.

"It won't be the same."

"What won't?" Miranda and Luis exchanged worried glances. Nina moved next to Isabelle.

"Going back. It won't be the same." When she looked up, her eyes were veiled with melancholy. "Barcelona means Mama and Papa. It's hard to imagine what it's going to be like without them."

Miranda sighed. She had learned a long time ago that tragedies were like earthquakes: long after the initial devastation, there were constant aftershocks that tested the foundation of even the hardiest soul.

"I know this sounds strange, but I think it will be good for you," Miranda said. "For a long time you've carried around a lot of sadness remembering how life was with them, and a lot of scary memories about how you lost them. What you need is to find the happy memories, because it's those you should carry with you."

A few tears trickled down Isabelle's face. She knew Miranda was right, but she also knew how hard it would be to walk on the Passeig de Gracia and not think of having a hot chocolate with Martín or to walk the hills around the Castell and not think of those lazy afternoons she used to spend with Althea, communing with the clouds and talking to the sun.

Quickly she wiped her face. Another image had arisen, one that made her angry.

"Everyone in Barcelona thinks my father is a murderer," she said, her voice sharply edged.

"Flora and Alejandro don't," Nina said, trying to help.

"Nor do your parents' friends," Luis added. "They all believed in Martín's innocence. And I'll bet there were plenty of others who refused to buy the state's flimsy case against him."

Isabelle shook her head. "Other than Tía Flora and Tío Alejandro, everyone thought Papa killed my mother." Her throat tightened. "And God only knows what they think of me! Maybe they think I deserted Papa? That I didn't stand by him? That I think he's guilty?"

"It doesn't matter what anyone thinks," Miranda lied, knowing that what people thought of a parent always mattered to a child. "In your heart, you know how much your father loved your mother. You know he couldn't have hurt her, and that's all that's important."

Isabelle nodded in agreement, but they all knew that until she actually returned to Barcelona, she wouldn't know how anyone felt, including herself.

In the month that followed, it seemed as if everything revolved around preparations for the girls' trip. After school Isabelle and Miranda shopped for gifts to bring for Flora, Alejandro, and the Serrats. Luis took Isabelle and Nina to the travel agency so they could take part in arranging their itinerary. Several of Isabelle's teachers asked her to lead classroom discussions about Spanish foods and customs. Friends made up lists of mementos for her to bring back, while Sybil created a list of things she wanted Isabelle to do: paint, sketch, take lots of pictures (especially of Antoni Gaudí's extraordinary buildings), experience the different landscapes—beach, waterfront, inner city, country-side—send postcards, and, of course, visit every art museum she could.

"Spain has a rich artistic tradition," she said, her eyes alive with passion, as they always were when she spoke about art. "Think of all the wonderful painters it produced: Velázquez, El Greco, Goya, Picasso, Miró, Dali, Juan Gris. And let us not forget Bartolomé Esteban Murillo," she said slyly. "He may have come hundreds of years before you, but his blood still flows through your veins. And from where I stand, it's not a bad bloodline for a budding artist to have."

Isabelle allowed her mouth to curve upward in a half smile. That was the first time she had ever associated the name *Murillo* with anything positive or pleasant.

Then there was the bon voyage party Miranda and Luis were giving the night before the girls left for Barcelona. Since the Durans had invited most of the town, it was no wonder that everywhere Isabelle went she ran into someone who wanted to wish her a safe journey and a wonderful summer. It was when they said they couldn't wait to hear all about it when she returned that Isabelle realized how many good friends she had made in Santa Fe.

The night of the party, the patio of La Casa was aglow with the yellow haze of dozens of *farolitos,* small paper bags that held candles anchored in sand. Rimming the perimeter of the garden were more lights, tall torches that blazed bright orange against the deep purple of a twilight sky. Crepe-paper ribbons of turquoise and hot pink dangled from the roofline, billowing up and down on the back of a soft breeze like waves in a gentle sea. Top ten records booming from a phonograph added spice to the gusty aroma of meat sizzling on a hot grill. All around there was the sound of felicitous laughter coming from young people excited about friends going off to an exotic place.

There was a lot of talk about what Barcelona was like, about Spain and about Tía Flora's home, the Castell de Les Bruixots. Amazingly, Isabelle had lived in Santa Fe for five years, yet few knew anything about her life in Bar-celona. At first they had been loath to pry into her past; she had been disin-clined to revisit it in any way. Then, as time passed, she became one of them; the fact that she had come from someplace else had become irrelevant. Now it was as if everyone had suddenly remembered that Isabelle de Luna had been born somewhere far, far away from Santa Fe and had questions about everything from time differences to television stations.

Isabelle told them about the various barrios that made up the city, how each quarter seemed to have its own particular flavor: the narrow streets and ancient buildings of the Gothic Quarter known as Barrio Gótico; Barceloneta, the waterfront area where all the fishermen lived; the red-light district of the Barri Xines, or the Chinese Quarter; the fancy shops of the Plaça de Catalunya; the hustle-bustle of the Ramblas. She talked about the people, how strong they were, how valiant. She recalled how beautiful it was to look out at the Mediterranean, even in the summer with its thick, oppressive haze of heat and humidity. She explained that while meat was the centerpiece of most Spanish menus, Catalonia bordered the sea and, naturally, favored fish.

What people were most curious about was the Castell de Les Bruixots, especially after Isabelle explained that the name was Catalan for Castle of Ghosts.

"Was it a real castle?" they asked. "Did it have ghosts?"

"Yes and no, and yes, or so they say," she answered quickly.

Originally the Castell de Les Bruixots had been a real castle, complete with turrets, a great hall, dungeons, even a moat. Built in the tenth century, it may have been small compared to the monumental Alcazar in Segovia, but in its day it had been imposing nonetheless. Over the centuries much of the structure had been destroyed. By the fourteenth century only one tower of the original Castell remained. Instead of tearing that down as well, a group of Franciscan monks looking to build a monastery on that site simply incorporated the tower into their plans.

While the monks dismissed all tales of ghosts, the locals pointed to the inexplicable survival of that one specific tower as proof positive of supernatural powers. It was in that tower that the Lady of the Castell met her destiny.

According to the legend, during the tenth century the Castell was owned by the duke of Cardona. It was a time when Spanish Christians, leery of the followers of Islam, were pushing the Moors southward. While the duke was off doing battle, his daughter announced that she had fallen in love with a Moorish leader and intended to adopt his religion and become his bride. Her brother, then titular head of the family, was appalled. In his father's name, he imprisoned her in the tower. Within a year she died of a broken heart. Some said when the wind whistled around the tower, it was the voice of the Lady of the Castell calling out to her beloved. Others claimed the shrill wailing was a cry of revenge.

"Did you ever go up there?" one of Isabelle's friends asked, her eyes as wide as if she had just encountered the lady herself.

Isabelle laughed. "Many times."

Her eyes darkened for a moment. Now that she thought about it, she had visited the tower only with her father. He used to take her there when the sky was clear and the moon had just appeared over the horizon. He used to say that being de Lunas, they had a special affinity with the moon. She remembered him telling her that she had a direct line to the queen of the night and instead of wishing on a star like other little girls, she could make her wishes on the moon.

"Did you hear her?" one girl asked.

"Were you scared?" said another.

Isabelle shook off her melancholy, noticed how truly entranced her friends were, and smiled. "Only once," she said, pleased to note that her own ghosts had respected her wishes and disappeared. "It was a very dark night. Cold and damp with no moon, no stars." She lowered her voice, compelling her listeners to lean in closer. "I sneaked up the stairs to the tower and opened the door. Errrghh," she squealed, mimicking the sound of creaky hinges. "Slowly, groping the walls to find my way, I tiptoed inside and over to the window. I looked out. It was dark. I turned and looked in. It was darker still. And then, all of a sudden, I felt a presence moving toward me. Closer and closer it came, until finally it was only this far away from me."

With her thumb and index finger, she made a space no wider than an inch. Her audience was spellbound, their faces a breath away from hers. No wonder they shrieked when suddenly Isabelle raised her hands and shouted, "Boo!"

For one stunning instant, the air was still. Then everyone collapsed in laughter. Miranda and Luis smiled and hugged each other. It was wonderful to see Isabelle so animated and so happy. Moreover, it was a moment of great personal satisfaction. Watching her interact with her friends, hearing the sound of her laughter, feeling the aura of camaraderie that infused this entire gathering, assured the Durans that they had been good guardians and had done what they believed Martín had wanted them to do: they had given Isabelle back her childhood.

For much of the party, the other honoree was uncharacteristically quiet. Although she wore a poppy red dress that exuded enthusiasm, Nina's mood was in direct contrast with her costume. She seemed distracted, unable to concentrate. While she mingled with the guests, she never stayed with one person for too long. She listened to Isabelle's story, but with only half an ear. She responded to questions regarding how she felt about going to Spain by expressing excitement, but with only half a heart. She couldn't tell anyone the truth, because they never would have understood. How could they? She didn't understand herself.

For the past week or so, she had felt overwhelmed by an inexplicable depression. Whenever she thought about the journey, instead of bubbling with anticipation, she grew tight and tense, as though she were about to take her college entrance exams rather than her first trip abroad. She thought perhaps she was reacting to Isabelle's nervousness, that her anxiety was more sympathetic than personal. Isabelle was concerned about what awaited her in Barcelona. They were so close, it would be only natural for Nina to be worried for her, but deep down she knew that wasn't it. This malaise was hers. She couldn't explain it, but she couldn't shake it, either.

When Sam Hoffman and Sybil Croft walked in, Nina's mood brightened. She was crazy about Sam, and if the past few weeks were any indication, he was crazy about her. She was about to run over and greet them when she noticed how somber their faces were. Guilt and a blush of shame colored her cheeks. Ruth Hoffman was dying. Though Jonas had a team of nurses tending his wife, Sybil came over every day to spell the nurses and spend time with Ruth. Having been through this with her own mother, she knew how important it was to have someone who cared remain close at hand.

Ruth held a special place in Nina's life: she was a mentor as well as a friend. When Nina had first expressed a desire to be a writer, Ruth had taken it upon herself to help the young girl find her way in the jungle of literary possibilities. As a journalist, Ruth would naturally have encouraged that particular avenue. She urged Nina to work on the school newspaper—which she did—and to take the reporting class offered at the high school—which she did. She also had Nina prepare articles for submission to the local newspaper, which every now and then ran a column written by and directed to the young. When it became clear that Nina's writing wasn't concise enough for the demands of journalism, Ruth helped her test other waters. She had been working with Nina on short stories when cancer engulfed her.

Seeing Sam and Sybil conferencing about Ruth, Nina realized that one of the things weighting her spirit was the thought that Ruth might not be here when she returned from Barcelona.

"I'm sorry we're late," Sybil said, kissing Nina hello. "You look gorgeous, as usual."

"I'll second that." Sam's mouth lifted in a slow smile.

"How's your mother?" Nina said, trying to sound cool and casual even though her face was burning as if she had just come from thirty minutes under a sunlamp.

"The same."

Sam lowered his eyes and shifted his weight. Despite his interest in medicine and his usual ease in discussing illness and injury, his mother's condition and prognosis was a matter separate and apart. His pain was obvious.

"She sent bon voyage gifts for you and Isabelle," Sybil said with deliberate buoyancy as she handed Nina a box. "Open it."

Nina complied, tearing off the wrapping paper and digging within the tissue until she extracted the present. It was a black leather diary with her name, "Barcelona," and the year engraved in gold on the front. Inside was a card that read "Happy Adventure! Love, Ruth."

Nina had to fight not to cry.

"I have to give Isabelle hers." Sybil looked from Nina to Sam, offering them a conspiratorial grin. "You two will excuse me, won't you?"

Sam smiled at Sybil, kissed her cheek, and nudged her off in Isabelle's direction. When she was gone, he put an arm around Nina and steered her away from the party to a dark and quiet corner. "Are you all right?"

She nodded. He was staring at her with such intimacy, she squirmed.

"Sybil really does have an eye."

Nina looked at him quizzically.

"You do look gorgeous."

He slipped his arms around her waist and kissed her. They separated, but only slightly.

"Let's walk," he said, taking her hand.

They had known each other all their lives, but Sam supposed he had really gotten to only know Nina a few weeks before. He had walked into the local ice-cream parlor just after returning from school and had seen her perched on the stool in front of the counter. At first he didn't know who she was—probably because his first sight of her had fallen somewhere around her ankles. Since his eyes had traveled the entire length of her very long legs rather slowly, it took forever until he reached her shorts, which he thought were the shortest he had ever seen. Her midriff was bare. She had cut her T-shirt in half, drawing attention to her chest, which seemed highly developed and, therefore, highly desirable. By the time he reached her face, he didn't care to whom that body belonged. When he realized the body was attached to an extremely attractive face that answered to the name of Nina Duran, he was dumbstruck.

Having been away at school and on a ranch in Colorado the summer before that, he hadn't seen much of Nina. Obviously, while he had been away at college and off playing cowboy, she had been growing up. It felt strange asking her out, but he did, and she accepted. They went to the movies a few times, once to a school dance. Their physical relationship consisted of some deep kissing and a few minor gropes. Lately, however, things had heated up. The attraction was growing stronger, making it nearly impossible for them to be around each other without touching and feeling and testing the limits of their control.

Nina was Sam's escape. When he was with her, she became his solitary focus. Like the brilliant white light of a magnesium flare, her pale beauty blinded him to everything else—the anguish of his mother's illness, the pressure of school, the anxiety over how his father and sister were being affected. Yet, much as he wanted to, he wouldn't make love to Nina. She was only fifteen, the daughter of his parents' best friends. They had grown up together. It wouldn't be right. And what if his passions had more to do with him feeling sorry for himself than feeling something for her? What if he was using her? It wouldn't be fair. Yet as she pulled his head closer to hers and kissed him again, her rounded body pressed against him, the softness of her flesh teasing his, he knew it might not be right or fair, but it would feel wonderful!

Nina sensed the excitement growing in Sam. She felt it inside herself as well but was unsure about what to do. Certainly she had seen enough movies to know the words and gestures of a love scene, but most cinematic love scenes ended at the bedroom door, fading to black or dissolving into something else; the most important part, the part she most wanted to know about, remained a secret.

"I don't want to leave you," she whispered, loving the feel of his arms around her, his mouth on hers, his body near hers, loving the fact that she finally knew what "getting hot" meant.

"I don't want you to go," he said, fighting his hormones, "but in a way, I think it's a good thing."

"How's that?" Nina refused to back off. Though she could tell he wanted to move away from her, she continued to hold him close and to kiss his neck and ears and lips. She had never experienced the power of her sexuality before. She liked it.

"We need to cool off." With that he gently, but definitely, separated from her.

"Why?"

Her blond hair was slightly mussed, her gray eyes soft and mellow, extending an invitation he had to reject.

"Because you're fifteen and because I think we're going too fast and because I don't want to take advantage of you and, well, just because."

Nina laughed. "Eloquently put."

"Hey! I'm going to be a doctor, not a poet." He laughed with her, grateful for her understanding. "Besides, I'll be here when you get back."

"Promise?"

"Promise."

They returned to the party just in time for everyone to wish Nina and Isabelle a bon voyage. As Nina took her place alongside Isabelle, Isabelle whispered, "Where have you been? We've been looking all over for you."

"I was busy."

Isabelle caught the look that passed between Sam and Nina. After the candles had been blown out and the toasts had been given, when Sam kissed her and wished her a terrific trip, she could smell Nina's scent in his hair. A shiver of jealousy ran through her. Isabelle had had a crush on Sam from the first night she met him. She knew she was too young for him to ever look at her as anything more than a friend, and that Nina was too formidable a rival for Isabelle to think about doing anything to change his perspective, but that didn't mean she wasn't covetous.

For the rest of the evening, envy, combined with apprehension about her return to Barcelona, acted like a whisk, stirring together negatives and positives until it was impossible to tell how she felt about anything. Her teachers and Sybil reminded her of things she had said she would do and look up and bring back, and suddenly she felt burdened. Friends patted her on the back, kissed her cheek, offered silly bits of travel advice, warned her they expected at least two postcards, and suddenly she felt fatigued and pressured. Miranda and Luis clucked over her and hugged her every chance they got, and suddenly she felt the vise of conflict. By the time the party began to wind down, Isabelle felt sick.

Nina and Sam were still off to the side, talking. When their guests began to leave, they wished Isabelle bon voyage and waved at Nina. She waved back but never moved from Sam's side. To Isabelle, that was the last straw. Nina's complete lack of participation was annoying, and Isabelle said so later when they were alone in their room.

"What was the matter with you tonight? If you weren't sulking in a corner by yourself, you were off somewhere with Sam or whispering sweet little nothings to him in a corner. Did you forget that this party was for both of us? Me and you?"

"So I wasn't Harriet Hostess. What's the big deal? Why are you so bent out of shape?"

Isabelle wasn't sure. Something was nagging at her, something other than her jealousy about Sam.

"Because your blasé, I-don't-give-a-hoot attitude makes me feel like this trip is a major burden for you and that you don't really want to go. If you'd rather stay here with Sam Hoffman instead of going to Barcelona with me, just say so!"

She blurted it out before she had a chance to think about what she was saying. Yet as she listened to herself, she wondered if perhaps she was the one who didn't really want to go to Spain.

Nina was startled by Isabelle's outburst. It was totally unlike her. "Sam has nothing to do with this," she said. When Isabelle blushed, Nina pressed the matter. "Or does he? Are you pissed off at me because you have a crush on him?"

"No," she said, too quickly. "Okay, maybe a little," she confessed, knowing that her blush had given her away, "but even before he came in, you were kind of hostile, like you'd rather have been anywhere but at our party."

"Was it really *our* party?"

"What's that supposed to mean?"

"It means that this trip and this party are all about you going home. It's not about me. I'm just tagging along for the ride."

It was Isabelle's turn to be startled. "That's not true!" she said, confused and embarrassed.

"Sure it is. I don't belong in Barcelona. I don't come from there. I'm not the princess returning to her castle on the hill. I was only invited so you'd have company on your journey back to your roots."

"Now you sound jealous," Isabelle said, confusion becoming anger.

"Maybe I am," Nina said, surprising both of them with her admission.

"Of what?"

Nina was pacing now, energized by the sensation of feelings rushing to the surface. "I don't know. Maybe it's more fear than jealousy."

"What could you possibly be afraid of?"

"I don't know!" Nina shouted, her voice laden with exasperation. "I guess it's that here, we're the same. We're Miranda and Luis's special children. In Barcelona, we're not the same. You have a family, a history, a place with your name on the door. You're the special child. I'm the odd man out."

"I'm the special child?" Isabelle was aghast. "I can't believe what I'm hearing! My mother was murdered. My father was accused of killing her. Grandparents who wanted no part of my mother and never laid eyes on me suddenly want me to live with them, forcing Tía Flora, the one person I would have wanted to live with, to live alone in Barcelona! What's so special about that?"

For some strange reason, Isabelle's tirade struck Nina as funny. She stopped pacing, sat down on her bed, looked at Isabelle, held up her hands, and laughed. "Not a whole lot. Okay? I admit it. That was stupid," she said, shaking her head. "But believe it or not, I am jealous of your past. You have one," she said with stunning simplicity. "I don't."

Looking beyond the smile, Isabelle saw pain in Nina's eyes. She crossed to Nina's bed. "What do you mean, you don't have a past?"

Nina grew serious again. "I'm adopted, remember? I know where I've grown up, but I don't know who I am. You do. You have a history. You knew your parents. You have living relatives to fill in any blanks you have about your past. I don't. I don't know where I came from or who I came from. I don't have any roots."

"Yes, you do," Isabelle said quietly, taking Nina's hand in hers. "We just have to dig them up."

"And where would you suggest we start?"

The two girls looked at each other. Isabelle squeezed Nina's hand. Nina nodded as if to say, "I love you, too." A sheepish smile insinuated itself on Isabelle's mouth.

"I haven't the foggiest," she said.

"Okay, great," Nina said, formally declaring their squabble over, "let's recap. You're jealous of me because I've got Sam. I'm jealous of you because you knew your parents. Tomorrow we're going to Barcelona to untangle your roots. When we come back we're going to hunt for mine. So, I'm confused. Who's got what?"

Isabelle grinned. Nina started to laugh. Like the two lost souls in the song they had adopted as their personal anthem years before, they put their arms around each other, their heads together, and in unison sang, "We got each other!"

CHAPTER 6

Barcelona, Spain, 1968

Isabelle had warned Nina that Flora would not be greeting them at the airport.

"You've met Tía Flora. She's not the type to stand at the gate waving and shouting."

"Not exactly." Nina recalled the unconventional woman who had brought Isabelle to La Casa.

In her stead, Flora had sent the faithful Pedro Serrat. Positioned off to the side, apart from the enthusiastic throng that had gathered to meet the flight from New York, he was not easy to spot, but when Isabelle did find him, her mouth spread in a delighted grin. Pedro was a humble country man, uncomfortable with city ways, yet in honor of Isabelle's homecoming he had donned a suit and tie. Isabelle was touched by the gesture and by the tearful glistening she noted in his eyes as she ran toward him.

When Isabelle introduced him to Nina, he bowed, charming the young American with her first taste of European gallantry. Her second taste was being ushered onto the backseat of a large, black, slightly battered 1948 Mercedes that Pedro called "the señorita's car." On the way from the airport, the three of them chattered like friends at tea, sharing snippets about Flora and the Serrats, the Durans and Santa Fe, reducing five years of separation to a series of sound bites. In between reminiscences, Isabelle played tour guide, pointing out a few sites on the way to Campíns. Though Isabelle wanted to show Nina everything, Pedro asked that they content themselves with a quick view of the harbor.

Having come from landlocked Santa Fe, Nina was impressed not with the ships or the narrow streets or the ancient buildings, but with the vast blue expanse of the Mediterranean. Stretched before her like an endless carpet, it was a sweep of color so fresh and inviting that she felt like running to the end of the pier and diving in. Gazing enviously at the people sunbathing on a nearby beach, she allowed her eyes to travel out toward the horizon. Never before had she thought about Columbus and his assertion that the world was round. Tracking the infinite straight line that separated sea and sky, she suddenly marveled at his courage. From here, where he'd set sail those hundreds of years before, the world did look confined and small and, yes, flat.

"There he is!" Isabelle turned Nina toward the statue of Christopher Columbus that centered the area around the harbor. "Our link," she said, inviting Nina to take a closer look.

The two of them stood across from the monument, their eyes fixed on Columbus's arm, which was stretched out toward the sea.

"I'm not exactly a sailor," Nina said, "but if he's supposed to be pointing to America, isn't he faced in the wrong direction?"

Isabelle giggled. "Yes, but if he was facing the right way, he'd be pointing inland. I guess the sculptor went for art over accuracy."

Thanks to the crush of traffic on the harborside drive, the noise was so loud that the girls didn't hear Pedro calling them. After a few minutes of yelling, he grew impatient and began leaning on his horn.

"I think he's trying to tell us something," Nina said, finally realizing that the incessant honking was coming from Pedro and the Mercedes.

Isabelle waved to let him know they were coming. As they prepared to dash across the street, she said to Nina, "He's not angry with us. He's terrified of Tía Flora. If we're late, it's his head!"

As quickly as he could, Pedro maneuvered his way out of the city and into the suburbs. Without looking at signs, one could feel the change as they crossed the line from town to country. The air was lighter and cleaner, cooler and more refreshing. As the road began to curve up the hill leading to the Castell, Isabelle asked Pedro to pull over.

"Come," she said to Nina.

Once out of the car, they walked to the edge of a precipice.

"This was always one of my favorite spots," Isabelle said, her voice tinged with reverence. "From here, you can see everything." Looking up, she pointed to a green spot atop a hill. "There's Campíns. The castle and the land around it are our family seat." Looking down, she directed Nina's attention to the city. "But that's where the Pujols and the de Lunas began. They built their fortunes in the factories and foundries down there."

While Nina mused about how casually Isabelle used words like "family seat" and "fortune," Isabelle inhaled the scenery. She had forgotten how bewitching the view was from this graceful bend. A patchwork of rooftops and buildings, asphalt and parkland, what lay before her was a metropolitan abstraction of red, gray, white, black, green, and blue.

The real Barcelona was a vibrant urban sprawl that pushed hard against its boundaries. Squeezed by a semicircle of hills, the sea, and a steady influx of humanity, it had swelled into a populous arena of confrontation between concrete and flesh, a field on which man and infrastructure competed for air and space and prominence. Knowing that, Isabelle supposed, was what made this spot so special. Up high, distance and perspective granted the city a perfection unattainable from down below. Social flaws became invisible. Political strife quieted. Everyday problems disappeared. A churning, bustling megalopolis was reduced to a landscape veiled by an opaline haze.

"It's fabulous, Is. It really takes my breath away."

Nina was honestly awestruck. It wasn't that she took the beauty of New Mexico for granted or thought that it was unequaled anywhere in the world; it was all she knew. Being here was like being introduced to a completely different standard of beauty.

"I can understand why you love it here."

Isabelle nodded. Suddenly she was too overcome to speak. It was warm, yet a chill shivered through her as she looked away from the city, up toward Campíns. Anxious as she was to be with Tía Flora and Tío Alejandro, she delayed. Throughout the long flight, her emotions had yo-yoed between exhilaration and uncertainty. Was she home? Or was she visiting? Was she a stranger? Or family? Was she on holiday? Or in danger?

"Don't be nervous," Nina said, intuiting Isabelle's fears. "Everything's going to be fine, you'll see."

"Right!" Isabelle said, more to herself than to Nina. "I'm here. It's home. I'm twelve years old and I'm a de Luna! I can handle whatever happens!"

She took a deep breath, squared her shoulders, and lifted her chin. Though the gesture was meant to show the firmness of her resolve, her voice betrayed her.

"And if I can't handle what happens . . ."

"I can," Nina said, finishing the thought and taking Isabelle's arm. "Let's go! How much longer do I have to wait to get to this castle?"

With Nina by her side and her courage shored, Isabelle climbed back into the car and set her eyes forward. Within minutes Pedro drove through the gates and up the long gravel path that led to El Castell de Les Bruixots. Nina's breath caught in her throat as she sighted a tower. Isabelle nodded in recognition, her throat also encumbered by a sentimental lump. A soaring turret of ancient stone, solid save for three narrow windows underlining its cupola, it loomed as a symbol of constancy, of survival, of linkage with her nation's history as well as her personal past. Memories hurried back, dashing before her like a rush of film. Faces were blurred, events were clouded, yet with startling clarity she saw and felt every moment she had ever spent in this place.

As the glorious two-story building that had served as her family's home for four generations came over the horizon, a slow, prideful smile eased onto her lips. Glancing at Nina, she saw a face washed with wonder. Notwithstanding the projection of the tower, the Pujol manse was a large, squat structure composed of two wide rectangles united by a series of galleries and an Edenic internal garden. Despite its bulk, the Castell presented itself as a noble edifice. The grounds were luxuriously planted and painstakingly maintained. Gently arched galleries created shade and softness as well as an illusion of height and imponderability. But more than anything else, it was the fanciful character of the facades that distinguished the one-time monastery.

Lavishly embellished with sgraffiti, the ornamentation on the outer walls exuded a look of refined elegance to what otherwise might have appeared to be a cumbersome box. Isabelle had always likened sgraffito to the raised design of a cameo. Achieved by scratching white designs into plaster to reveal the dark ground underneath, the effect was a two-tone, two-dimensional display boasting a delicacy not usually associated with the act of carving. Feathers, cherubs, urns spouting flowers and vines, luxurious garlands, elaborate crests, geometrics with a byzantine flavor, friezes with a quixotic touch—the ornamentation was a veritable banquet of decorative patterning, and all who saw it feasted upon it, just as Isabelle and Nina did now.

Pedro parked the car, and Isabelle's heartbeat quickened. Framed by the portal of the enormous wooden doors was Tía Flora. The last time Isabelle had seen her was in Santa Fe, in the Durans' home. Though she had been too disoriented to notice it then, it struck her now how out of place Flora must have appeared. There, she had been out of context, probably a bit odd to those who didn't know her. Here, she was considered eccentric, but it was part of her charm and the reason for her celebrity. More than her art, it was her unorthodox, unconventional, society-be-damned attitude that had propelled Flora Pujol into a position of significance. In a world that found safety in numbers and comfort in sameness, Flora's allure was her difference.

Nina hung back deliberately, freeing Isabelle to run into her great-aunt's waiting arms. As she came closer, Isabelle couldn't contain the relief she felt about Flora's being just as she remembered. Though her hair was completely white, the style hadn't changed in fifty years. Bobbed and thickly banged, it was like a silver helmet on her head. When she was younger and her hair had been dark, she had powdered her face until it looked chalked, slashed her lips with red, and lined her eyes in black. The one cosmetic she eschewed was rouge. According to Flora, only the meek blushed.

They came together in a desperate embrace, neither one able to part from the other for fear that this moment of closeness might be illusory. Happy tears streamed down Isabelle's face as she burrowed into the older woman's chest. Flora's signature scent of jasmine and violets assailed Isabelle, filling her with an overwhelming nostalgia. When Flora held her at arm's length and asked about her journey, Isabelle's throat was too clogged with emotion for her to speak.

"We had a lovely trip," Nina said quietly.

"Nina, darling." Without letting go of Isabelle, Flora opened her arms, making room for the tall blonde standing there so awkwardly. "I'm delighted you've come."

Nina grinned—inside and out—as Flora hugged her. She couldn't believe she was in Spain, standing outside a genuine castle, being hugged by a woman who was rich and famous and—here, at least—a bona fide celebrity.

They chatted about plane connections and the dreariness of travel and the weather and the drive from the airport and lots of other banalities before Pedro, laden with luggage, offered to show Miss Nina to her room.

Miss Nina. "That would be lovely," she said, having decided that was what Natalie Wood would have said. "Are you coming, Isabelle?"

"Not just yet." She looked from Flora to Nina, seeking approval from both. "Okay?"

"That's fine." Nina offered them both her best Audrey Hepburn offhand yet graceful, over-the-shoulder wave. "Pedro and I can manage."

When Nina and Pedro had gone, Flora took Isabelle's hand and led her away from the house, across the front lawn to a side garden. The minute Isabelle saw the stone bench nestled among the tropical greens, she felt a sense of calm. It was on this bench that she and Flora used to find solutions to most of Isabelle's problems, from simple things like whether or not to wear ribbons in her hair to more complicated matters like why, if everyone belonged to the family of man, people had so many different languages and so many disagreements.

"Nothing in the Castell will frighten you," Flora said, sagely divining that Isabelle might be hesitant about entering the house and confronting the ghosts of her parents.

"I've never been here without them."

"Nothing's changed, except that they're spirits now."

"I don't want them to be spirits, Tía Flora. I want them to be my parents. I want to be their child." Isabelle looked down at her hands, trying to find the words to express her confusion and loss and melancholy. "I miss them," she whispered.

"Then call them!" Flora said in a commanding voice, her dark eyes taking on that peculiar aspect they invariably adopted whenever she waxed metaphysical. "Reach out to them! Bring them home!"

"I don't know how," Isabelle said, wishing she had her aunt's ability to commune with things she couldn't see or touch.

With her customary flourish, Flora spread her arms and looked to the sky, invoking the shadows that lived with the wind to join them in the garden.

"Because they're no longer of the flesh," she said, speaking to Isabelle and whoever else had responded to her call, "the rules that govern the flesh no longer apply. We can summon them when we want. Visit with them as long as we want. Say what we want to them. Feel what we want about them. And do what we want with them. What's even more delightful, no one can chase them away if we don't want them to go, and we don't have to share them. We can keep them all to ourselves."

She wrapped her arms around Isabelle and drew her close, exhorting her to feel the body that was present as a way of giving her confidence to seek the spirits of those who were not.

"Althea and Martín are with us now," she said softly. "They've always been with you, my child. And they always will be."

For a while they remained on the stone bench that was their private refuge, Isabelle cocooned in her aunt's embrace, both of them weeping quietly. After a time Isabelle's angst began to ease. Whether she had been blanketed by an ethereal veil or the power of suggestion wasn't important. What was, was that at last she was ready to go inside the Castell.

She was ready to be home.

Nina felt as if she had been plucked from the real world and dropped into the middle of a fairy tale. Not only had a maid brought her a cool drink and unpacked for her while she showered, she had also been given a lovely suite. High-ceilinged and spacious, it was separated into a boudoir and a sitting room by a gilt-and-beveled-glass partition. The bed was dressed and canopied in red, the damask drapes were red, the chairs in the sitting room were upholstered in red, even the collection of glass perfume flacons displayed on a console were red.

As she got ready for dinner, Nina tiptoed around the suite, almost fearful of making a misstep that would end the wonderful dream she was having. Other than in the movies, she had never seen anything like the Castell. Everything in this room, probably everything in this house, had a history and a pedigree: the paintings, the furniture, the porcelain, the rugs. Along one wall were bookshelves lined with leather-bound volumes of poems and stories by Europe's most famous writers. Many were first editions of classics; others had been given to various members of the family as gifts by the authors.

If she closed her eyes, Nina could imagine another young woman from another time occupying this space, but instead of a pale pink cotton minidress and low-heeled pumps, she would have been wearing a shimmering silk gown and satin slippers ornamented with jewels. She might have worn a coronet or a lace mantilla. She might have carried a fan like the one Althea had given Nina.

A gentle knock on the door interrupted her reverie.

"So?" Isabelle asked, opening the door and peeking inside. "How do you like it?"

Nina looked around and laughed. "One thing's for sure. I'm not in Kansas anymore!"

Isabelle hadn't realized how much she had wanted Nina to like this house. The fact that she did delighted her. "How about a tour?"

Nina grabbed Isabelle's arm and dragged her to the door. "I thought you'd never ask."

Nina was like a four-year-old at Disneyland, astonished at this, amazed at that, finding riches in every corner and on every wall. Downstairs, in the center hall, she marveled at the numerous pointed and vaulted arches that capped every window and doorway. Outlined with thin moldings, creating intriguing shadows and niches, the overall design was Gothic, yet with a warmth and intimacy most Gothic structures lacked.

"The Castell was originally a cloister," Isabelle explained, "so a lot of the architecture is going to feel like a church."

She was right. The long corridors, which were also arched; the stone floors; the statuary ensconced within deep, altarlike niches: it did feel like a cathedral. Yet there was much of the palace in the Castell as well. Paintings in gilded frames lined the walls. Antique carpets were scattered over marble floors. Chandeliers of dark wrought iron competed with those of sparkling Austrian crystal. Wooden beams lined the ceilings in the oldest rooms. Shelves displayed hundreds of leather-bound books and silver artifacts. Every console displayed a jewel, every wall a documented piece of Catalonia's rich cultural history.

As she tried to recite the names of each of the artists or artisans whose works they viewed, Isabelle suddenly realized that two paintings were missing—a pair of small Goyas that had hung opposite the entrance, flanking the stairs leading to the reception rooms.

"They were two of my favorites," she said, scanning the room as if she had overlooked them somehow. "They were thought to have been *modellos* for one of the court portraits Goya had done for Charles the Fourth."

"What's a *modello?*"

"They're paintings an artist does while he's preparing a larger work. You know, like sketches. Only these are done in oil and usually were shown to the patron for approval." Isabelle reviewed the Goyas in her mind, the elaborately costumed women, their daring aspects. "Goya was a gutsy guy," she said, repeating what had been told to her. "Usually court painters flattered the royal family, making even the ugliest person look like Athena or Apollo."

"Makes sense," Nina said. "If the king's paying the bills, the king's gotta look good."

"Right, except one of these portraits was supposed to have been the queen. Instead of showing her as some major beauty, both her pose and her expression made her look kind of gross. The other portrait was of two young girls about our ages. Goya didn't show them as carefree, perfect little princesses. These girls were scared to death, probably of their father."

"Wow! That's fascinating," Nina said, painfully aware of the lapses in her own education. All she knew about Goya was that he was Spanish and had gotten in trouble by painting *The Nude Maja,* a nude portrait of his lover, the duchess of Alba. Nina didn't even know his first name. Isabelle had lived with his work and knew enough about him to discuss him as if he were a neighbor. "I wish I could see them."

"I wish you could see them, too. Unfortunately, I don't know where they are."

Several other important treasures were not in their customary places: an early Velázquez, a large Zurbarán, a Flemish polyptych, a Renoir, a Murillo. While there were still plenty of artistic riches to see, and Isabelle reveled in the joy of showing them to Nina, the feeling that all was not right disturbed her.

"This place is like a museum," Nina whispered, almost afraid to raise her voice for fear of being shushed by an authoritative matron in orthopedic shoes and a shapeless dress.

"In a way, I guess it is. My family has had money for a very long time, and they've always had an eye for good art and a weakness for special collectibles.

My father's mother, Beátriz, loved ceramics. Her father loved Oriental porcelain. His mother collected holy water fonts, of all things."

"What about Flora and her other sisters?"

Isabelle snickered. "The Fates, as my father used to call them—Vina, Ramona, and Flora. Since they were creative beings themselves, they liked the culture of women—books, paintings, music, whatever. Vina was a poet. Ramona was a pianist. Both died before I was born, but Tía Flora told me that the three of them had always been resentful of the fact that they had been expected to produce children, not art, and that they were supposed to stick to the kitchen, not draw attention to themselves."

"From what you've told me, I doubt if any of them knew where the kitchen was," Nina said.

"And why should we?" Flora said, having sneaked up behind them. "Only the cooks had to know where it was. And speaking of cooks, how do you feel about dinner?"

"I'm starving," Isabelle said, accepting a hug from Flora.

"Me too," Nina chimed in.

"Good, because our guests have arrived."

Nina should have been exhausted, but her brain was buzzing. Everything she had seen and heard and experienced during this longest of days demanded her attention. Over and over again she retraced her tour of the Castell and repeated the dinner conversation and recalled the sumptuousness of the feast Flora had arranged in honor of Isabelle and her. Aside from Alejandro, Pedro, and Consuela, she had been introduced to Rafael Avda; his companion, Manuel Cortes; Diego Cadiz, the man who managed Dragon Textiles; and Cadiz's wife. They were terribly elegant and sophisticated, yet exceptionally generous with their affection. While they lavished it on Isabelle, they were not stingy with Nina.

She had never been surrounded by such wealth and obvious rank. Frankly, she found it intoxicating. She was high on the aura of the Castell, exhilarated at the notion of being in the company of true aristocrats. Even Diego Cadiz could lay claim to a historical place in Barcelona. His ancestors may not have been nobility, but he could trace his lineage back to before Columbus's famous sail.

After dinner Flora had taken her into the library and had treated her to a lesson in Pujol/de Luna genealogy, giving her the name and relationship of every person in every photograph, portrait, and engraving. When she had shown Nina a picture of Martín's mother, the eldest of the Pujol sisters, she'd pointed out that Beátriz was wearing a gold filigree cross similar to the one Flora and Alejandro had sent Nina, the one she was wearing now.

Nina was being exposed to a world unavailable to her in Santa Fe. There, everything was laid-back, plain, honest. Even the wealthiest citizens maintained a modicum of humility. These people were different. Rafael Avda, for instance, seemed glossed with a carefully applied patina. He was slicker, more citified, more packaged than anyone she had ever met before, yet she liked him. Despite his affectations, he was courtly and treated her with a chivalric deference that both amused and flattered her. Manuel was equally suave and equally attentive. A marquis who worked as a photographer, he raved about her bone structure and the harmony of her features, eventually extracting a promise that before she left she would allow him to do her portrait.

Do her portrait! Other people had asked to take her picture before, but never had anyone asked to do her portrait.

As she climbed onto the large bed and slid underneath the blanket, she didn't so much look around the room as she surveyed what was to be her domain for the next two months. It was simply too incredible for words. Nina Duran was about to spend her first night in a castle!

I could get used to this, she thought.

Suddenly she thought of how difficult it must have been for Isabelle to adjust to La Casa after living here. She had never focused on that before. How could she have? Her frame of reference wasn't large enough to encompass an environment like this. But having seen it and experienced it, even for one day, was enough to make her wonder how Isabelle really felt about living in Santa Fe. And how she felt now that she was back in Barcelona.

Isabelle, too, had had an extraordinary day. After those first few uncertain moments, she felt as if she had floated through the hours on a champagne bubble. Being home in the Castell, hearing the soft, lyrical sounds of Castilian Spanish, seeing Alejandro and her old friends—it had made her lightheaded and giddy. Everyone had been so loving and so caring, it was hard for her to think of anything except the ebullient sensation of renewal and reconnection.

Yet now, alone in her room, thoughts that had been pricking at her subconscious began to surface. While she would have liked to believe that nothing had changed in the five years since she had been gone, that was not the case. The staff had been drastically cut. The entire upper floor of the west wing had been closed off. Several of the most prized paintings in the Pujol collection were gone. And although she hadn't focused on it at the time, even the formal dining room had changed.

The long, highly polished table fashioned from a tree off the estate still held center court in the coffer-ceilinged room. The Pujols' prized eighteenth-century, delicately gilded Catalan chairs still provided the seating. And an antique Aubusson still covered the floor. But much was missing. Though three wonderfully ornate, eight-light Louis Quinze silver candelabra paraded down the middle of the table, Isabella remembered five. A series of handmade cabinets that ran around all four walls once housed an extensive collection of ceramics from Valencia, Aragon, and Catalonia. Now only the two corner cabinets flanking the back window served as showcases.

With immediate certainty, Isabelle knew that a closer inspection would reveal other subtractions. Had these pieces been stolen? Possible, but unlikely. Given away? Even more unlikely. The missing items had always been considered valuable family treasures. The only logical solution was that whatever was absent had been sold to make up for some financial deficit.

Isabelle had never thought of Tía Flora or any of her relatives in terms of money. Wealth was a given. The Pujols and the de Lunas had it. Those less fortunate didn't. She had known that the Serrats, for instance, weren't as blessed as she, but it wasn't until she had gone to live with the Durans that she had understood exactly what that meant. "Making do." "Getting by." "Saving for a rainy day." Isabelle shook her head in amazement when she realized that she had no idea of the Spanish or Catalan counterparts for those American idioms. The phrases had never been part of her vocabulary.

Determined to figure out what was happening, she went over all that had been said during the day and at dinner, hoping to pick up a clue she might have missed; but there was nothing. Alejandro's spirits had been high, with no shaded glances at Tía Flora, no worried frowns when he thought Isabelle wasn't looking. And Flora had been as effervescent as ever. Her ankle-length, gauzy white gown was as frothy as her mood. She had entertained her guests with amusing anecdotes, a bit of harmless gossip, and the latest political jokes. When everyone was at ease, she had graciously receded from the spotlight, allowing time for the others to ask Isabelle and Nina questions or answer those the girls had asked of them.

The only noticeable change in Flora's behavior was the replacement of her usual public reserve with unabashed displays of affection. Barely a moment went by when she wasn't reaching for her niece, touching her, holding on to her, standing no more than a breath's distance away. It was as if Isabelle's aura had become the source of her oxygen. Flora looked at her and glowed, smiling and laughing for no reason other than the fact that, as she stated no less than fifty times, Isabelle was home where she belonged, and as far as she was concerned, all was right with the world.

But, Isabelle concluded, all wasn't right.

Unable to sleep, she slid out of bed and settled on the window seat that looked out across the front lawn. The moon was high in the sky and nearly full, bathing the land in a wash of palest blue. The air was clear, making it possible to see the full expanse of the Castell's grounds and beyond, into the vastness that was Barcelona by day, a navy infinity by night.

How many hours had she sat in this same spot watching the sky, waiting for the clouds to dance across the moon? Sometimes the shadow of the tower overwhelmed the lawn. Other times it was the distorted shape of a tree or the twisted rectangle of the opposite wing that painted its portrait below her window. The idea that Tía Flora could lose the Castell, that some other young girl could occupy this room and claim rights to this view, both astounded and frightened Isabelle. It was impossible to imagine anyone else living here, but then she had never imagined she'd grow up anywhere but in Barcelona. Clearly, nothing was absolute.

Most twelve-year-olds knew nothing about finances. Isabelle was hardly an expert, but she knew a little. Life had introduced her at an early age to estates and trusts. Living at La Casa had taught her something about budgets and allowances and what it took to maintain property. The Castell incurred expenses in the form of utilities, maintenance of the grounds, upkeep and repairs, staffing, taxes—it was easy to see how lean times could have turned the mansion into an insatiable beast. Add estate taxes and whatever other debts Flora must have been burdened with after Martín and Althea died . . .

"Wait a minute," Isabelle said aloud, struck by an inconsistency.

Flora's financial problems couldn't have stemmed from inheritance taxes. The Castell was not part of the de Luna estate. It was owned by the Pujols. That, too, bothered Isabelle. The Pujols had always been one of the richest families in Barcelona. Tía Flora was the heiress to that fortune. She should have had plenty of money. Flora was eccentric and, Isabelle admitted, had a penchant for excess and overindulgence, but she couldn't have depleted her entire inheritance. No one could squander a fortune living under Franco's flag. Especially in Barcelona.

Again, Isabelle's knowledge of the situation was vague and focused only as much as her tender age would allow, but even as a small child, before she'd moved to Santa Fe, she had been aware of the damage Franco had done to the economy of Catalonia. Her family and most of their friends had been industrialists and bankers, the ones with the most and, therefore, the most to lose. Gatherings at the town house produced incessant grumbling about how Franco hated Catalonia and had imposed particularly strict sanctions against Barcelona, about how he was starving the region of investment opportunities and new industry. She remembered dour expressions and angry whispers about a ruined economy, about once thriving businesses that were merely sputtering along, about those who had been rich suddenly waking up to find themselves poor.

Outside, the sky rumbled. Black clouds blanketed the moon. The trees beneath her window began to bend at the will of the wind. Without warning, a fierce storm had blown in from the sea, inciting the elements until they raged. Huge raindrops pelted the ground, so large that as they passed before her, Isabelle was certain she could count each drop. Suddenly a bolt of lightning cracked the shell of night. As it breached the blackness, it dug deep inside the recesses of Isabelle's soul. Her body trembled.

Fighting for control, Isabelle stared out into the night. Gripping the windowsill, she faced the squall. She didn't need a reminder of why she had left Barcelona, yet here it was—an appropriate, albeit macabre, welcome back. Seeking entry into Flora's world of spirits, Isabelle trained her ear to the wind, listening to the voices of the past, wondering if they had emerged to help her interpret the present.

"Is that what had happened to Tía Flora?" she demanded of the exploding darkness. "Did she go to sleep rich and wake up poor?"

A clap of thunder rattled the window and swallowed her words. Frightened by an unbidden rush of visions she couldn't explain, motivated by forces she didn't understand, Isabelle heard herself verbalizing thoughts she had never voiced before.

"How could you?" she shouted, believing at first she was asking about Flora, stunned when she realized she was asking about herself. "How could you do what you did to me!" she yelled, her voice louder, the sense of release stronger.

The response was another defiant roar. Isabelle shuddered, but she refused to retreat, refused to be cowed by the savage power that had overwhelmed the sky. On another night at another time during another storm, the same force that was behind this violent burst of energy had barged into her life and taken all she had—her parents, her home, her childhood, and her innocence. She had been terrified then. Now, surprisingly, she had no fear. In a move of utter pluck, she opened the window wider, daring the tempest to come inside.

Air currents had shifted the driving rain away from her, pushing the storm farther inland. As she stood and watched this display of raw, untamable strength, Isabelle wondered if nature was Destiny's messenger, if fate rode on the wings of the wind. If it did, if in fact the course of one's life was preordained, then no one could have prevented what had happened that night, especially not a defenseless seven-year-old child.

She closed the shutters, climbed back into bed, and pondered her own destiny. She already knew she was not Fortune's child. But if her past was the guide to her future, she knew with sudden clarity that if she had the will—and just then she was certain she did—she could survive anything.

The next morning Isabelle awoke fired with enthusiasm, eager to reconnect with the people and places and traditions that had always meant so much to her. With a certain amount of impatience, she allowed her body to rouse itself from sleep. She stretched, slowly extending her limbs as far as they would go, toes reaching out toward the end of the bed, fingers straining to touch the ceiling. A rush of blood coursed through her system, chasing both her morning slowness and the sluggishness of jet lag. Feeling fully refreshed, she bounded out of bed and across the room, threw open the shutters, and happily received the sun.

It was a glorious day. The grass glowed with renewed verdancy, glistening green from last evening's rain. The sky was a dome of cerulean blue undisturbed by clouds or industrial smoke, a solid sweep of color that looked as if it had been painted in a single brush stroke. The sun pulsed yellow, shining brilliantly, almost arrogantly, as if to reclaim its dominance over the turbulence that had disrupted the heavens during the night.

As Isabelle drank in the beauty of the landscape, she realized she felt different—transformed, perhaps. She had never heard the word *catharsis*. She had no understanding of what it meant to purge one's soul or to experience emotional purification, yet she willingly accepted this burst of physical energy and spiritual calm as a sign that she had weathered a stormy rite of passage.

The thought made her laugh. She recalled the times she had asked Miranda about growing up, complaining about how she didn't want to be a little girl anymore. Miranda had spoken of patience, of taking things as they came, of allowing life's processes to proceed at their own pace.

"Nothing happens overnight," she'd always said.

Isabelle couldn't wait to tell Miranda that was exactly what had happened.

When the door opened and Isabelle saw Nina and Tía Flora, she flushed, wondering whether or not it was disloyal to be thinking of Miranda while in Flora's home.

"I thought we'd have breakfast together," Flora said, stepping aside so the maid could set down a large tray on the table in front of the window.

"What a lovely idea," Isabelle said, chiding herself for putting thoughts into Flora's head that wouldn't otherwise be there. It wasn't in Flora's nature to be competitive. She was who she was, had what she had, and never coveted anything from anybody else. As long as she was sure of Isabelle's love for her, she would consider Isabelle's affections for another as a bonus for them, not as a threat to her. Besides, Flora had placed her in Miranda's care, Isabelle thought guiltily as she scrambled onto one side of the window seat, making room on the other side for Nina. She would want the two to be close.

"Are you hungry?" Flora asked, curious about the flush and flicker of confusion that had passed over Isabelle's face.

"Starving!" As if to prove her point, Isabelle gulped down her orange juice. When she saw the plate of deep-fried *churros* and smelled the orange-scented hot chocolate, she squealed with delight. "Nina, prepare yourself! You are about to have the treat of your life. Nothing is as delicious as a Spanish breakfast."

She took a *churro* from a plate dusted with sugar and nutmeg, passed it slowly beneath her nose, then stuffed it into her mouth. It was warm and soft and tasted of butter and freshly made dough. The hot chocolate was dark and rich, a frothy mix of coffee and bittersweet chocolate laced with a heavy dose of orange.

"Ummmm." Isabelle closed her eyes and licked her lips.

Nina moaned ecstatically and fell back on the window seat in a feigned faint.

"What do you eat for breakfast in Santa Fe?" Flora asked, imagining the worst.

"Juice, dry cereal, milk, and fruit," Nina said.

"That's in the summer," Isabelle said, laughing at the pained expression on Flora's face. "In the winter it's this awful gluey stuff called oatmeal that even butter and cinnamon can't fix."

"Let's be fair." Nina suddenly felt the need to defend her mother's kitchen. "Sundays are better. We have huevos rancheros, which are eggs doused with hot chili and lots of melted cheese, on top of a tortilla."

"I think Miranda treated me to something like that when I stayed at La Casa."

Nina didn't realize that Flora hadn't ventured an opinion on Miranda's specialty. But Isabelle heard the noncomment and smiled. "I must admit, I didn't like them at first," she said, looking straight at her aunt, "but I've grown to love them." Then, as Flora gave her a tolerant smile, she added, "But nothing beats *churros* and chocolate."

"Don't tell Mama, but I think I agree with you," Nina said, taking the last *churro* and rolling it around in whatever sugar was left on the plate.

Naturally Isabelle and Nina finished long before Flora, who ate with aristocratic deliberation. After a while Nina became impatient. She was eager to explore the grounds.

"Would you mind if I went to get dressed?" she asked.

"Not at all," Flora said, smiling but glad to be left alone with Isabelle.

"Are you having money troubles?" Isabelle asked as soon as Nina was gone.

Her bluntness surprised Flora. She sputtered, placed her cup on its saucer, dabbed a napkin at her lips, and folded her hands in her lap. Her first reaction was to tell Isabelle that she needn't worry about such things, but upon reflection she decided that if Isabelle was mature enough to infer such difficulties and concerned enough to ask about them, she deserved an honest answer, which was just as well. Flora despised lying.

"Yes," she said.

Though it was the response Isabelle expected, it wasn't the one she wanted.

"Oh, don't fret! It's not as bad as you think," Flora said quickly, wanting to dispel all fears of impending financial ruin. "It's just that so many of Barcelona's textile mills have closed or drastically slowed their production that the Pujol foundries and machine shops are hurting. We're still operating, but not as profitably as we once were."

"I thought you owned banks and real estate and things like that."

"I still maintain a controlling interest in the Caixa de Barcelona, but thanks to Señor Franco, even the banks are in trouble."

"Are you going to lose the Castell?" Isabelle asked, her voice not as brave as it had been a moment before.

Flora leaned over and patted her niece's arm. "No, darling. The Castell is safe." Isabelle's relief was so visible, Flora couldn't help but laugh. "You didn't think I'd let them take your inheritance, did you?"

"By 'them,' do you mean the Murillos?" Isabelle hadn't factored her grand-parents into her analysis of Flora's current situation, but there had been something odd about the way Flora had said "them."

Isabelle always knew when Flora was referring to Franco and his subordinates. With them her tone was dismissive and hostile and void of all respect. This time her tone was angry, but edged with enough concern to indicate a reluctant regard for her adversary.

"I can't prove they're behind any of it, but I have been the victim of harassment, both personal and fiscal."

Isabelle's face tightened at the thought of someone trying to hurt Flora. "What do you mean? What have they done to you?"

"Let's say they've been . . . nettlesome."

Flora related a few tales of harmless annoyances, like losing electrical power for no reason, having the water turned off, not receiving mail for several days at a time, having her property taxes raised without cause or explanation. She prayed Isabelle didn't press for more information, because she had no intention of discussing the more serious incidents, like the time the brakes on her car had failed.

It had been the culmination of a series of unsettling events. First the gas tank on Pedro's truck had sprung a mysterious leak. Then he'd almost blown out all the tires on Flora's car by driving over nails that had been sprinkled along a patch of road leading to the Castell. Being cautious by nature, Pedro had become obsessed with safety. Aside from instituting surveillance procedures for the house and installing whatever security measures were available, he had insisted upon checking each of the cars and trucks before anyone put a key into the ignition.

"Why are they doing this?" Isabelle asked, disgusted at the thought of her mother's parents doing battle with her father's guardian. "Is it because of me?"

Flora wished she could spare Isabelle, but like it or not, she was involved. "In a way, yes. The Murillos feel they've been disgraced. And you, my pet, are at the heart of their humiliation."

"I am? How?"

"They wanted to take you away from your father to punish him for killing your mother."

"But . . ." Isabelle was quick to protest her father's innocence.

Flora held up her hand. "We don't have to be defensive. We know the truth," she said with absolute certainty. "What makes me furious is I think they do, too."

"If they know he's not guilty, why don't they say so?"

"Because it benefits them to have people believe in Martín's guilt." Flora spoke through gritted teeth. Even now her maternal instincts were roused, motivating her to protect Martín. "That way they can justify all those years of objecting to him as a suitable husband for their daughter."

No matter how hard Isabelle tried to understand the Murillos, their behavior still seemed stupid and selfish and cruel. "I don't get it," she said, clearly bewildered. "What does any of this have to do with you or me?"

"You weren't here. They couldn't hold you up like a trophy for all the world to see. Naturally they blame me for your disappearance, and so, I suppose, they started this campaign of dirty tricks to wear me down." Flora tilted her head and winked at Isabelle. "Let me assure you, they haven't succeeded."

Isabelle chuckled, but only for a moment. "I'm here now," she said.

"I know, and to answer your next question, Alejandro and I believe that at long last they've given up the game. If we didn't, we never would have had you come to Barcelona."

"Why do you think they dropped the suit?"

"Five years have gone by. Though your mother's murder still horrifies and saddens us, it's old news to everyone else. Frankly, whoever the Murillos wanted to impress don't care anymore. Everyone's lost interest in the case except them and us." Flora reached across the table and took Isabelle's hand. "Besides, with your father gone, I can't imagine what satisfaction they'd derive at this point from winning a custody suit. They wouldn't be taking you away from him. They'd be taking you away from me."

Isabelle was touched by the obvious pain in Tía Flora's eyes at the mere thought of it. "Maybe to them, satisfaction comes more from the winning than from what they've won," she said quietly.

"Maybe." Isabelle's insight brought Flora up short. It made her take a closer look at her grandniece. She supposed that over all these years of separation she had continued to think of Isabelle as a frightened, needy seven-year-old child. Looking at her today, she seemed neither frightened, needy, nor terribly childish. Flora didn't know whether the transformation pleased or bothered her.

"I don't want to talk about them anymore," she said suddenly, bounding to her feet. "Come now! Hurry and get dressed. I promised Nina we would take her into town. I want to introduce her to Barcelona. I want you to see the changes, and"—she leaned down to kiss Isabelle's cheek—"I want Barcelona to see the changes in you!"

* * *

They started in the Plaça de Catalunya on the paved star that marked the center of the Catalonian capital.

"Take a drink," Flora said to Nina, instructing the newcomer to follow Isabelle's lead and drink from the Canaletas Fountain. "According to legend, if you drink from the fountain, you'll never leave Barcelona. As with most legends, it doesn't always work, but it's still a must-do."

They fed a few of the pigeons that flocked to the stone oasis and began their march southeast toward the harbor, Flora shading herself with a white parasol, Isabelle relying on sunglasses to cut the effect of the glare, Nina hiding beneath an L.A. Dodgers baseball cap. For Isabelle, the journey was one of déjà vu. Every Wednesday, weather permitting, Tía Flora, Isabelle, and Althea had paraded down the Ramblas. It was their day to immerse themselves in the city, to visit with their neighbors, to shop at the Boquería, to replenish their mental store of visuals, to touch the vitality that was Barcelona.

It felt strange to walk by the aviary, with its countless cages of squawking birds, without having Althea attempt to teach a macaw or a parrot to say her name; or to pass the newspaper kiosks without having to stop while she browsed through the foreign fashion magazines; or to pass one of the many flower stalls without her buying a rose for her daughter. At first Isabelle struggled with the memories. Her step slowed and her eyes lingered on familiar sights. Flora noticed but kept silent. Nina was too busy photographing everything in sight to see what was happening to Isabelle.

Like pictures in a scrapbook, images began to materialize before Isabelle's eyes. Yet instead of allowing the images to overwhelm her, she let them develop and faced them head on. And she was grateful when they presented themselves plainly, void of excessive sentiment and emotional charge, simply as evidence of experiences she had had with her mother.

It surprised her to realize that time had subdued the impact of the past. Though she still harbored deep pockets of grief, she had returned to Barcelona, confronted her losses, and was still standing, still breathing, still functioning. With sudden clarity Isabelle knew that one of the things she had to do on this trip was rearrange her recollections, to move them to another emotional drawer. If she did, the searing pain she had lived with for so long would continue to diminish.

"Is this too much for you?" Flora asked. "Would you like to go home?"

Isabelle took a deep breath, smiled at Flora, and said, "I am home and I'm fine." She turned and looked at Nina, who was shouting at them to smile into her camera. As they posed for the umpteenth time, Isabelle whispered to

Flora, "And besides, Nina would kill us if we left before she had walked every last inch of Las Ramblas."

The day was hot and humid, yet the streets teemed with humanity: bankers and beggars, artists and vagrants, housewives and aristocrats, tourists and locals, criminals and police. Though Flora cautioned against it, Nina bought a bracelet from one of the dozens of blanket displays. Isabelle bought Nina and Flora roses. Flora bought both girls lace handkerchiefs. Though they passed by several sidewalk musicians, they stopped to study a white-faced street performer. Costumed as a nun, he stood ice still, a living statue with a rosary in his hands, a collection basket at his feet. Other passersby stopped and stared, waiting to catch the statue blinking or moving or sneezing or otherwise breaking faith with his disguise. The longer they stood, the more coins they tossed into the basket. Naturally Nina handed her camera to Isabelle and insisted on having her picture taken with the bogus sister.

Having recorded that special moment, they moved on. Occasionally, as they wandered past the rows of metal chairs that lined both sides of the promenade, Isabelle saw heads bob and fingers pointed in her direction. She heard her name, Flora's name, Martín's name. Flora ignored them, her head high, her eyes straight. Isabelle tried to imitate her aunt's nonchalance, but she couldn't help feeling uncomfortable.

"You're not handling this right, little sister." Nina had looped her arm through Isabelle's. "Wave at them. Flash them a wide screw-you grin and keep walking."

"Like this?" Isabelle looked directly at two biddies who were whispering to each other but staring at Flora and Isabelle, waved, and smiled. The women flushed and looked away.

"Gotcha!" Nina said.

A block or two later the trio arrived at Barcelona's main food market. Actually they could smell it and hear it long before they could see it.

"Ugh!" Nina said. "What do I smell?"

"La Boquería!" Isabelle grabbed Nina's hand and ran the rest of the way.

A cavernous hall filled with the bounty of farmers and fishermen and ranchers, the Boquería broadcast such a wide range of strong, conflicting scents that at first Nina's nose crinkled at the assault. Taking a deep breath, she followed Isabelle and Flora through the high, wrought-iron archway that marked the entrance to the fabled bazaar.

"Tourists," Flora sniffed as they jockeyed through the crowd gathered around the fruit and vegetable stalls that dominated the center aisle.

"What's she talking about?" Nina said, at a loss.

Isabelle giggled. "Though everything in the center aisle looks great, the produce displayed here is meant for the drop-in, not for the regular shopper. It's good, but not the best the market has to offer."

"Sneaky," Nina said, happy to be in on the secret of La Boquería.

When Flora reached the stall she wanted, she took her place at the end of the queue. Señorita Pujol might have been treated like nobility at the other stores she patronized, but the Boquería was not any store. Here, breaking the queue was a serious offense. So was touching the fruit.

While Nina and Isabelle waited for Flora, their eyes wandered from displays of peaches to plums to red cherries to strawberries. Isabelle's mouth began to water. Luscious, succulent looking, at the peak of ripeness, this was temptation in a cardboard box, but Isabelle resisted, piously clasping her hands behind her back. Nina's resistance wasn't as strong. Her fingers had almost closed around a peach when Isabelle grabbed her arm and pulled her back.

"Do not touch the fruit," she said.

"Is it some kind of sin?"

"Close. When I was four years old, I swiped a plum from its container when I thought no one was looking. I had just bitten into it when this hand swooped down and snatched it from my mouth. The woman working the stall held up the stolen piece of fruit and scolded me in a voice loud enough for the entire market to hear. I wanted to die."

"Message received and computed. I will keep my hands to myself."

"Good girl."

"Hey! These women do look like they mean business."

"They are unique."

As Isabelle explained to Nina, the women of the Boquería were a fascinating lot. They could shout down a customer like a barker at a carnival; debone a duck with a flick of the wrist; and behead, descale, and filet a fish or butcher a cow without a cringe or a shudder—yet they came to work dressed like queens, their hair perfectly coiffed, their faces fully made up, their fingernails manicured bright, bright red. Though some dismissed them as mere grocers, fishmongers, or farmer's wives, their bearing defied their station. Perched on wooden risers, reigning over a domain of victuals and viands, they were so stately in manner, their attitude of such noblesse, one could easily believe that numbered among their belongings was a coronet or two.

"Ready to go?"

Having secured a bag of peaches, a loaf of bread, and a wedge of cheese,

Flora guided the girls out onto the Ramblas, where they searched for a vacant table outside one of the many cafés that dotted the walkway. It took a while, but finally they found one. Shortly a waiter brought an iced chocolate each for Isabelle and Nina and a small carafe of chilled white wine for Flora, as well as plates, napkins, and flatware.

As they ate they talked, mostly about life in Santa Fe. Flora winced whenever Isabelle referred to La Casa as "home," but she restrained herself from commenting. It was only natural, she reasoned. The child had lived there for five years. She had made friends, formed attachments, developed schedules and habits.

Suddenly anxious to remind Isabelle of old habits, Flora reached into the large white sack she always carried and pulled out two pads of paper and a box of pastels.

"You remembered!" Isabelle squealed, grabbing a pad and a few pieces of colored chalk.

"Of course I remembered," Flora said, clearly delighted at Isabelle's response. "Now let's see what you've learned in America."

While Nina people watched and snapped off some more photographs, the two artists—one young, one old—began to ply their craft, each filling her pad of paper with a series of colorful images. It was a game Flora used to play with Althea. After lunch they would see who could best re-create the sights they had seen on their walk down the Ramblas. Even when Isabelle was a little girl, Flora and Althea had encouraged her to participate in the game. She had scribbled more than she'd sketched, but they had always found something to praise, something to applaud.

Today Flora couldn't help but be genuinely impressed. Isabelle's vignettes were no longer childish scrawls. They were bold and active, a medley of color and contour. Her settings were easily distinguished—the bird market, the Boquería, the cast-iron Canaletas Fountain—but she had abstracted them until they were more form than fact.

Flora's style emphasized people within a background, relying upon the selection of a few specific details to set tone and demarcate place. Isabelle seemed to prefer creating the illusion of a whole without defining each and every part. Her people were fuzzy silhouettes, figures that moved but lacked precise, recognizable features. Flora's scenes gave off a sense of arbitrary construction; Isabelle's were surprisingly well composed, the obvious result of excellent training.

"These are wonderful!" Flora said with undisguised admiration, laying out several of them on the table so she could look at them again.

"She's great, isn't she," Nina said, her pride evident and sincere.

"That she is."

"Wait till I tell Sybil you liked my work." Isabelle's eyes glistened with satisfaction. Flora's approval meant everything to her.

"Who's Sybil?" Flora hated not knowing the people in Isabelle's life.

"Sybil Croft. I wrote you about her. She's my art teacher and my friend."

"Ah, yes." Isabelle had written about Sybil—dozens of letters, in fact. Shamefacedly Flora admitted that she must have blocked them from her mind out of petty jealousy. She liked to think of herself and Althea as the predominant influences on Isabelle's talent. It was hard to swallow the notion that someone else was molding the young girl's gift.

"She's obviously very good," Flora said. "As for you, you're better than good. You're flirting with greatness, Isabelle de Luna."

Isabelle was so taken with Flora's praise, she went tongue-tied. A wide, proud smile said it all.

"This was my last roll," Nina said, tending to her camera. "I remember seeing a kiosk a block or two back that sold film. Can I go get some?"

"Of course, dear," Flora said. "Just be careful."

"I will."

Isabelle and Flora watched as Nina sauntered away. Though Isabelle knew Nina would have liked to think she looked like a native, there was no way anyone could mistake her for anything but an American. With her long legs and shapely body, her blond ponytail and baseball cap, her insouciant gate and self-assured expression, she was the quintessential American beauty.

"She's great looking, don't you think?" Isabelle said with obvious admiration. "She's so tall and curvy, and she has the softest gray eyes. It's no wonder Sam is nuts about her."

"Who's Sam?" Flora smiled at the blush that pinked Isabelle's cheeks.

"He's the son of Miranda and Luis's friends, the Hoffmans. You remember Dr. Jonas." At Flora's nod Isabelle added, "Sam's his son."

"And I gather you think this Sam is something special."

Again Isabelle flushed. "Yeah, well, but it doesn't matter what I think. Sam's crazy about Nina and barely notices me."

"I'm sure that's not true," Flora said, finding it hard to believe that any young man wouldn't be drawn to her grandniece.

"Trust me, Tía Flora, it is. But how can you blame him? Nina's gorgeous!"

"Don't you think you're pretty?" Flora said.

"No," Isabelle confessed. "Maybe someday I will be, but right now I think I look like a goose."

"You don't look at all like a goose," Flora said, dismissing Isabelle's self-criticism with a wave of her hand. "And because you're so foolish, I'm sending you into the café to get me a glass of cold chocolate."

Isabelle laughed, pushed back her chair, and headed for the café. She had just placed her order when a deep baritone voice sent a chill down her spine.

"Your aunt is right. You don't look anything like a goose. Quite the contrary. You look exactly the way your mother did at your age."

Isabelle turned and found herself staring into a man's chest. He was standing so close to her, she had to crane her neck to look up at him.

Something about his face, his eyes especially, jangled Isabelle's nerves. This man was not a stranger. She had seen him before.

"I'm glad to see that you've returned to Barcelona." His smile was dazzling, but when his ebony eyes fixed on Isabelle's, she saw him in Majorca, at the hotel, at her mother's funeral.

"You're Paco." It wasn't a question. It was an accusation.

"I am."

He smiled again, but Isabelle was not charmed. She was frightened. Quickly she sidestepped around him. He reached for her and grabbed her arm. She wriggled about, trying to loosen his grip, but his fingers were firm on her flesh. From out of nowhere Flora appeared, brandishing her parasol.

"Leave her alone!" Flora's tone was harsh and unyielding.

Paco dropped Isabelle's arm but held his ground. Ignoring Flora, he spoke directly to Isabelle.

"Don't let her fill your head with lies," he said. "I didn't do what she says I did."

"And what is that, Señor Barba? What didn't you do?" Controlled rage underscored Isabelle's words. Hostility outlined every muscle in her body.

Behind them, a small crowd had gathered. Nina was part of it. At first she had thought it was just another street event and had surrendered to the tug of her curiosity. When she saw Isabelle and Flora squaring off against this stranger, she had wanted to run forward and stand by Isabelle, to protect her if necessary; but something held her back. She didn't know what was going on. She didn't know all the players. What if she made things worse? Whatever it was, she stayed back, watching with the same lurid anticipation as everyone else.

Paco fidgeted, clearly uncomfortable speaking before an audience. "I didn't kill your mother," he said in an insistent whisper.

"That's what you say. I don't know any such thing."

"Yes, you do." He leaned closer, his eyes boring into hers. "You were there. You saw and heard everything."

Isabelle's reaction to the charge was instantaneous. Her head jerked to the side as if he had struck her. Flora moved in behind her, torn between anger and curiosity. While she knew Isabelle had heard only denunciation and challenge in Paco's words, she herself thought she had heard something else—a hint of desperation, perhaps.

Was Barba's comment a taunt or a probe? Was he trying to use Isabelle to cast aspersions on Martín or to find out if she might possibly become a witness against him? She was about to ask that very question when she felt Isabelle's back straighten.

The young girl moved away from her protector and faced her accuser. "You're right," she said in a strong, sure voice. "I was there." She paused, but her gaze remained fixed. Barba's nervousness lined his face. "I was asleep in the next room when my mother was murdered, but before that, down in the tearoom, I saw and heard a lot."

Isabelle was determined to maintain control of her dignity. They were not in a courtroom, the crowd encircling them was not a jury, but, clearly, Martín was on trial again.

"I heard you beg my mother to run away with you."

Isabelle spoke with such assuredness, there could be little doubt that what she was saying was not a prepared defense, but the absolute truth.

"I heard her tell you she wouldn't go anywhere with you, because she loved my father and only my father. You said she loved you and that marrying Martín de Luna had been the biggest mistake of her life." Isabelle watched a smug smile slide across his mouth. "My mother laughed." The smile disappeared, replaced by a taut, angry scowl. "She said you were a fool, that there was no romance, that she had never loved you. That's when you got hateful. You kept your voice low, but you were really mad. I saw you grab her wrist under the table and twist it. And I heard you say you'd never forgive her for rejecting you."

A stunned silence canopied the crowd. No one had heard any of this. Even Flora stood mesmerized by the incredible tableau being played out before her.

Isabelle glared at the man opposite her, unwilling to be shaken off by his threatening posture or the fierce intimidation in his eyes. She was only twelve years old, but tragedy had visited her more than once, making her older—and tougher—than her years.

"Did you forgive her, Señor Barba?" Isabelle asked with chilling incisiveness. "Or did you kill her?"

CHAPTER 7

The interior courtyard of the Castell de Les Bruixots was a place of peace, a cloistered garden where long ago men of the cloth had sought solitude and oneness with God. Their devotion must have bequeathed a legacy of tranquillity, because an overwhelming silence pervaded this private oasis, inviting only those willing to respect its contemplative serenity. When Flora visited, as she often did, it was not to admire the beauty of the place—though it was impossible not to—or to entertain guests or chat with friends, but rather, as she did this day, to tap into the innate spirituality of this verdant sanctuary.

As was her ritual when she sought solace, she began by strolling the arcade that bounded the garden, looking out onto it, easing her way into it, as if the scene before her were a painting that needed to be studied to be fully appreciated. Slowly her eyes scanned the landscape. Thick, luxuriant vines crisscrossed the stone walls of the arbored refuge, climbing toward the red-tiled roof like a spider's web. A parade of arches outlined the square, their graceful peaks rising and falling like a scalloped hem. Giant ferns and large-leafed plants crawled alongside flagstone walks and snuggled against patio walls and posts. Four large trees—cypress, olive, palm, and bay—reigned over the interior, as comfortable in the balmy Mediterranean clime as any other native.

Gradually Flora exposed herself, leaving the shelter of the arcade, heading toward the circular bouquet of flowers and greens that marked the center of the cloister. She moved tentatively, burdened by the thoughts that had brought her to this place. Again, following lifelong habits, she busied her hands while she freed her mind, fussing with a browning leaf, pinching a fading blossom, allowing herself to open to an honesty she might otherwise block and avoid.

Alejandro stood in the shadows, watching her, a smile tilting his lips. Garbed in her signature white, a large straw hat shielding her face from the sun, she was the epitome of femininity even in her sixties. Her hands moved with a swan's grace as she tended her plants. When a lock of hair fell forward, she didn't stuff it beneath her hat or slick it back with a clumsy gesture; rather, she curled the disobedient ringlet behind her ear, three fingers poised delicately in a ballerina's fan.

It didn't take long before Alejandro's smile faded. Having loved her for more years than he could count, he could measure the level of her distress simply by the sag of her shoulders. Flora's back was hunched, far more than her task required. As a lifelong student of yoga, her posture had always approached an enviable perfection. Even when she bent over, her chest remained high, her shoulders back, her head even with her spine. Now she was slouched, her head low, her neck off its usual line.

Afraid he might startle her, he approached cautiously, calling her name softly. Her response was instinctive. She turned, opened her arms, and invited him next to her, welcoming the familiar feel of his arms, the familiar scent of his body, the familiar certainty of his devotion. When they parted he expected an exchange of small talk about his week at his country house on the Costa Brava. He would tell her whom he saw, what he did, how his horses were, what the weather was like, etc. Flora would use the time to decide how much, if anything at all, she wanted to discuss with him.

As close as they were, Flora's unyielding independence dictated that she think things through herself. Once she had reached a conclusion, she gladly entertained other opinions, but never before. Only when she was deeply troubled did she ask for, and listen to, advice. Obviously this was one of those times, because it took no prodding at all to get her to describe the explosive meeting on the Ramblas—word for word, gesture for gesture.

"She made him look foolish," Flora said, her agitation visible. "I'm afraid he might want to get even."

Alejandro disagreed. "He might want to, but Isabelle boxed him in."

"How so?"

"I knew about the conversation between Barba and Althea, but during the trial, the court denied me the right to enter it into the record. That's why it wasn't public knowledge."

"It is now," Flora said with no small amount of smugness, unable—and unwilling—to disguise the exquisite pleasure she had derived from watching little Isabelle intimidate the ever-so-suave, always-so-sure Paco Barba.

Alejandro also allowed himself the luxury of a satisfied smile. He remembered how desperately he had wanted Paco brought in for questioning, how devastated he had been when the police's inquiry had been cursory. He remembered, too, Barba's unctuous expression of sympathy when he had heard of Martín's death, and his even more infuriating, "Now that the case is closed, Althea can rest in peace." In Alejandro's mind the case was still open.

"You should have seen him," Flora said, swatting an insect buzzing near her face. "If he could have gagged Isabelle, he would have."

Alejandro grew pensive. His brow wrinkled as he sorted his thoughts. "His intention was to find out what she knew and, if she knew too much, to bully her into remaining silent."

"That's what has me so concerned."

"In her own innocent way, Isabelle neutralized him. This contretemps occurred in front of too many witnesses. If anything happens to her, he becomes the most obvious suspect."

Flora walked toward the olive tree, pausing there to rest her back against its sturdy old trunk. She removed her hat and used it to fan her face. Despite the coolness of the shade, it was hot; she was angry and she felt flushed.

"So he'd be brought in," she said. "He'd be questioned and released, like he was when my Martín's life was on the line."

"Maybe not," Alejandro said, his silver hair glistening in the sunlight, his face a mask of determination.

"Do you think he's guilty?"

"I used to."

"And now?"

Alejandro's shoulders lifted in a shrug, then slumped under the weight of personal disappointment. A heavy curtain fell over his eyes as he removed himself from the present and returned to the past, seeking answers and forgiveness. When finally he spoke, his words tripped over a lump in his throat.

"The only thing I know for certain is that Martín is dead and the real murderer continues to walk the streets." Though he and Flora told each other everything, Alejandro had never been able to confide his questions about the effect of Martín's medicine and his momentary doubts about Martín's innocence.

Flora took his hand, marveling again at how blessed she was to have such a caring man in her life. Despite everything she had said over the years to make him feel otherwise, Alejandro still felt responsible for Martín's incarceration, for the negative, damning tone of the trial, and, yes, even for Martín's death. Though she insisted he had done everything possible, he maintained that he must have missed some vital piece of evidence or testimony that would have freed Martín and cleared his name. Whenever Flora asked if he was suggesting that Isabelle had been an eyewitness to the murder and that if her memory could have been unlocked, her father would have been released, his response was, "That was only one possibility." Alejandro's instincts told him there was something else, some other way of documenting Martín's innocence. What it was, who was hiding it, and why continued to elude him.

"Do you think we have to worry about the real murderer going after Isabelle?" Flora asked, suddenly concerned about taking Isabelle into the city or allowing her to wander about unescorted.

"No," Alejandro said with complete certainty. "She'd become a target only if he thinks she can identify him as Althea's killer."

Flora sighed, the breath trembling out of her mouth. "How do we know she can't?"

"The confrontation on the Ramblas should have told you she's not hiding anything." Flora eyed him quizzically. "She doesn't remember any more today than she did when the crime was committed. If she had, she would have blurted it out in the heat of anger."

"Then you think she was asleep when Althea was murdered."

"It would seem so."

Flora nodded, the gesture an expression of reluctant finality. Much as she hated the idea that Isabelle might have witnessed her mother's death, Flora had always harbored the thought that if Isabelle had, eventually the truth of what had happened that night would be revealed and her beloved Martín would be exonerated. If Alejandro was right, the truth was not Isabelle's to reveal. For Martín's sake, Flora found that difficult to accept.

Alejandro squeezed her hand. He had considered the same set of facts, wrestled with the same conflicting emotions. He had concluded that the matter of what Isabelle saw and how much she knew was moot. Since she wouldn't, or couldn't, shed any light on the case, they had to look elsewhere. Or stop looking altogether.

Nina was having the time of her life. Not only had she fallen in love with Barcelona, but she had begun to feel less like a guest and more like family. Because everyone was helping her with her Spanish, she was nearly fluent, and her accent sounded like theirs. Consuela and Pedro gladly showed her around the Castell and the nearby village. Several times she and Flora had gone shopping without Isabelle. Once or twice Alejandro had sought her out for a private cup of tea and a chat. She even felt as if she had been accepted by Tía Flora's friends.

Rafael Avda had at great length recounted the time he had spent in the Southwest, particularly in New Mexico. He seemed to enjoy telling Nina about when Miranda had come to Barcelona as part of an exhibition at his gallery. And he especially relished re-creating for her the meeting between Miranda and Althea, using the tale as a way of asserting his part in the melding of the two families.

Diego Cadiz had taken her on a tour of one of Dragon's mills. It was a credit to his managerial skills that Paco had kept him on. He had shown Nina the way the cotton was converted into cloth, the way the cloth was dyed and imprinted with designs. Naturally, stories about Althea had permeated the tour.

And Manuel Cortes had come by one afternoon to make good on his promise to photograph her. He had decided to use black-and-white film because he felt she was a young woman whose beauty was all about light and shadow and, therefore, would be better represented without the distraction of color. He'd thought Nina might have been disappointed. She had been delighted.

Though Nina loved all photography, she preferred black-and-white. From the time she was old enough to follow along as Miranda read to her, she had found newspapers and magazines more exciting than story books. They had pictures of real people, while children's books had funny-looking cartoons. At their daily reading sessions, she'd jump onto Miranda's lap and go right for the "page people," as she called them. She'd study their faces and ask Miranda to tell her about them, why they were in the newspaper, what they had done to get their pictures in the magazine. Soon she'd begun making up her own stories, inventing her own scenarios as to what lay behind the smiles or scowls.

Over the years Miranda had tried to expand Nina's interest in portraiture by showing her the work of giants like Sir Joshua Reynolds and John Singer Sargent; but Nina wasn't moved by paintings. She didn't care about color or texture or dimension. She wanted the stark reality that the camera created, not the wishful verity of the canvas. Deciding it didn't matter how one flexed one's imagination, Miranda fed Nina's inquisitiveness with a constant supply of magazines, newspapers, and "picture" books.

One of the first Miranda had given her contained black-and-white photographs taken by a man named Paul Strand. Miranda had said he was very famous and that in the thirties he had taken a lot of pictures in New Mexico, particularly Taos. Nina couldn't have cared less. She could see Taos any time. As always, what she wanted was to get to the faces. That was the part she liked best—looking at people looking into a camera, putting on the face they wanted recorded, the face they wanted the world to see.

Often Nina wondered if the people ever saw the pictures and if they liked what they saw. She doubted it. She had a camera. She was always clicking snapshots of friends and neighbors, and no one ever liked the way they looked. Their noses were too long. Their mouths looked strange. The camera made them too fat, too thin.

Nina, on the other hand, got a kick out of having her picture taken. She liked the idea of posing, of taking a stance, creating an expression or a mood, and freezing it. It was like playing make-believe. She could look angry or sad or happy or curious, whether she felt it or not. She could make a funny face or a serious face or simply sit still. The camera preserved whatever was there at that moment. It captured the surface. It didn't dig beneath. It didn't go where you didn't want it to go.

Candids were different. They caught you unaware, and because of that, Nina liked them even more than portraits. It was amusing to look at people who didn't know they were having their pictures taken. It was like spying, like sneaking up and catching them in a private moment. With the camera as your eyes, you could intrude upon a thought. You could learn a secret. You could uncover a lie.

Miranda had told her that sometimes Paul Strand had set up two cameras when he wanted to take pictures of people on the street—pointing one at the person he had persuaded to pose for him while taking the actual picture with the second camera, thereby catching his subject off guard. Nina thought that was sneaky but great. When she had studied the faces of some of the people he had photographed in New York City, she had speculated about whether they had smiled into the false camera. They weren't smiling in the pictures in the book. They looked frightened and nervous, scared of something other than the box that was recording them. Miranda had said most of them were immigrants who had come to the New World looking for a better life. Studying their expressions, Nina had to wonder: If this was better, what had they left behind?

She had discussed all this with Manuel during their shoot, feeling very sophisticated when he said that he knew Strand's work and was as impressed with him as she was. Encouraged and eager to further his notion of her as someone well versed in his field, she mentioned Alfred Stieglitz and Edward Steichen and Ansel Adams. He knew them as well, but when he asked if she knew his current favorite—another American, this one living in France, with the strange name Man Ray—she had to confess she had never heard of him.

A week later Manuel brought her a book of Man Ray's work, along with a brand-new thirty-five-millimeter camera and a quick lesson in the art of photography. Nina had always enjoyed taking pictures, but before, her equip-

ment had been simple point-and-shoot. This was a camera she could experiment with, and experiment she did. From then on one rarely saw Nina without that camera pressed against her cheek. She photographed every site,
every vista, and nearly every face with which she came into contact.

For Isabelle, Nina's heightened interest in photography became a personal
bonus. Mornings the girls used to spend alone, Nina sleeping in or holed up
in her room scribbling in her diary, Isabelle wandering the land surrounding
the Castell, sketching whatever caught her fancy. Now they explored the
area together. Isabelle painted and sketched. Nina focused and framed.

Even the pleasure of their sight-seeing jaunts increased now that Nina was
looking through a new lens. Watching Nina enthuse about sights Isabelle
used to take for granted made them feel new and exciting: Barcelona landmarks like the harbor, Tibidabo, the Parc Güell, the Sagrada Familia, the
Gothic Quarter, Montserrat. Country vistas that used to glide past her, noticed but unappreciated, gained a fresh gloss thanks to the companionship of
another set of eyes. Even people she might have overlooked suddenly became more interesting.

Yet despite the commonality of their passion for recording what they saw,
there remained a distinct difference—Nina was a spectator looking to capture and collect her observations; Isabelle was an artist seeking to interpret
not only what she saw, but how she felt about what she observed.

Whether it was the passage of time or because Sybil's training had taught
her to see things more keenly, Isabelle discovered that she had become not
only more attentive to particulars, but also more acutely aware of light.
When humidity blanketed the city, as it did so often during the summer, the
light in Barcelona took on a heaviness that was almost palpable. Though she
must have witnessed it before, Isabelle watched in rapt fascination as the
humidity descended like a misty veil. As it enveloped the landscape, it altered
the colors by paling them, by transforming them from primaries to tints.
Rooftops pinked, the sky went from royal to powder, the grass transmuted
from hunter to lime.

On those rare humidity-free occasions, from certain vantage points the
sun seemed to bounce off the shimmer of the sea, warming the light as it
came on shore. On the brightest days, even when the sky appeared unburdened by mists or clouds, Isabelle was certain she detected a faint yellow
tingeing the air. Red leaned toward orange, green flirted with chartreuse,
blue heated to turquoise, purple flamed amethyst.

When she analyzed the difference between what she was painting in Barcelona and what she had been doing in Santa Fe, it boiled down to the power

of light and its effect on color. In New Mexico very little was pale. Beneath the pellucid light that shone in the Southwest sky, nature was a spectacle of vivid chromatics. Colors were intense, almost harsh. Edges were clear, often to the point of sharpness. Sand blistered white. Slate broadcast blue. Sandstone burned red. Everything was primary, chaste, as if a pane of clear glass floated above that unique patch of earth, deflecting distractions and allowing light to come through it with remarkable clarity.

True, the way light insinuated itself onto the landscape was affected by changing weather, revolving seasons, and other natural phenomena like wind currents and lunar phases. Certainly it was influenced by the daily path of the sun as it traveled from dawn's rise to dusk's retreat. Yet somehow, no matter how much or how often color changed, it remained undiluted and pure.

For months before her trip, Isabelle had been working with charcoal and acrylics. Somehow they didn't feel right in Barcelona. Now she understood why. The effects were too strong, too explicit. Responding, she switched to watercolor. By weakening an edge, smudging a line or hushing a color until it became a tint, she could create a soft, hazy, Impressionistic feel. The results were paintings of such quiet delicacy that even the most banal subject was suddenly romanticized, even the simplest vignette about life in the Catalan countryside became a poem: Consuela returning from the market, her arms weighted down by shopping totes. A cow grazing in a neighboring meadow. Nina drying her hair in the noonday sun. Flora snipping flowers from her cutting garden. A fisherman sorting his catch. A vintner tending his grapes. A family burying their dead.

One of Isabelle's most lyrical works captured Pedro outside the Castell's garage, working on his truck. The hood was opened and Pedro was bent over his old friend, studying the exposed engine as a doctor would examine a patient. The truck's body—battered here, dented there—had lost the color and tone of its youth. Once a vivid blue, it bore the scars of age, marred and dulled by deep striations of rust and decay. Its innards also had deteriorated, suffering malfunctions in its fundamental systems, breakdowns of its vital parts. Remembering her father's love of cars, Isabelle was touched in a deep, almost forgotten place to see the affection Pedro lavished on this mechanical object. After finding an unobtrusive spot beneath a nearby tree, she spread out her watercolors, took out her pad, and set about immortalizing the moment.

The massive ten-car garage that had once stabled Thoroughbred horses, the cluster of ancient olive trees planted by monks centuries before, the historic tower of the Castell rising above the roofline—she reproduced all the elements of grandeur, but in a vague and dreamlike way, placing them on the paper as they existed in Pedro's life, as background. Isabelle had never seen Millet's painting *The Gleaners,* yet the same pastoral feel of his great work infused hers. The task and those who performed it dominated the foreground, not as individuals but as symbols. The women in the fields of Barbizon, their kerchiefed heads bowed, their backs arched over their crops, were deliberately anonymous, the expressions on their faces less important than the language of their bodies.

So too in Isabelle's painting. Pedro the person had ceased to be. He had been translated into Everyman, the common man to whom a truck represented survival. With it he was mobile, available for work, capable of providing. Without it he was marooned, dependent upon the mercy of others.

Though her feelings had little to do with trucks or cars or work, Isabelle was highly sensitive to the issue of relying upon others for support. Most days her life at La Casa proceeded on a schedule—school, play, homework, chores, eat, sleep—leaving her little time to think about who was responsible for buying her clothes or providing her food or seeing to her shelter. Yet every now and then she focused on the matter of her sustenance. Was Tía Flora paying for her upkeep? Or were the Durans? Either way she felt guilty about taking, vulnerable because she had no choice.

No wonder she identified so strongly with Pedro and his truck, and her painting exuded so much empathy for her subject. Isabelle related to Pedro's need to protect his independence, to assure himself that he had something of his own on which he could rely, something that would offer him alternatives if his present situation changed or his security was threatened. He cared for his truck because it gave him a sense of having control over his fate. Though he would have been shocked to hear it, Isabelle envied him. His options may have been limited, but just then they seemed more plentiful than hers. She felt as if her life were in the hands of everyone except her.

Perhaps it was the conflux of those feelings, in that place, that prompted Isabelle to risk venturing into the past. Ever since she had arrived in Barcelona she had assiduously avoided painful triggers—the town house on the Passeig de Gracia, her parents' bedroom at the Castell, the Ritz Hotel, the spot on the hill where she and Martín used to hold their private talks, the cemetery, this garage. While she had exposed herself to some raw spots—like the Ramblas—she had maintained a studied distance from anything that would rouse the sleeping giant of her grief. It had taken her too long to silence the nightmares and still the screaming in her head to hazard their return.

Yet after Pedro drove off and she had finished her painting, when she had started toward the Castell, unbidden memories tugged at her, drawing her toward the garage. She approached slowly, somewhat fearfully, as if she were about to enter a mausoleum, which in a way she was. With shaking hands she pulled open one of the enormous doors, dragging it back over the gravel, shivering at the all-too-familiar sound. The moment she looked inside, she was swallowed by regret. Frightened that she couldn't handle whatever haunted the darkness within, she turned away, intending to go, but she was stopped by an aggressive burst of sunlight that rushed past her and il-luminated the cavernous space that had once been filled with the fruits of her father's passion.

It was an enormous expanse, one half a gallery that ran the length, the other half divided into generous stalls. The ceiling was high, the roof peaked, the floor a continuum of concrete, with tall, large-paned windows running along the back wall in a measured sequence. Deliberately blurring her vision, allowing her eyes to see what had been instead of the emptiness that was, Isabelle pursued the trail of sunlight as it wandered about, fondly re-membering the magnificent machines that had been housed in this mam-mouth place.

Martín had collected the finest marques ever made. At one time he had owned two Hispano-Suizas, two Rolls-Royce Phantoms, a Lagonda Vanden Plas roadster, a Duesenberg SJ coupé, a Bentley, a Stutz, a Mercedes touring car, and the most coveted automobile of all, a Bugatti Royale.

Treading lightly, she stepped inside. Barren for years, the garage still smelled of oil and gasoline and leather polish and car wax. Isabelle inhaled the fumes as if they were precious scents, breathing deeply, filling her nose and lungs with the fragrance of her father. How many afternoons had they spent here, Martín buffing and burnishing, she playing among the jewels of the world's automotive crown? She had had no appreciation for the monetary value of the cars, nor for the mechanical milestones they represented. To her they were beautiful toys, elegant carriages in which she could pretend to be a queen or a mythical princess or a movie star or what her father continually reminded her she was—heiress to one of Spain's more significant fortunes.

Tears dampened her cheeks as she toured the ancient stable, going in and out of empty stalls, stepping over forgotten tools, picking her way through the rubble of lost dreams. Martín had told her she would ride to her wedding in the same car in which she had been born. Althea had promised to design her a wedding gown of fabric made at Dragon's mills. She had been told that someday the Castell would be hers, the town house on the Passeig de Gracia would be hers, the glory of the Pujols and the de Lunas would be hers. Her parents had vowed to take care of her. They had used words like "always" and "forever." Yet there were no cars, no fortunes, no queens, and no myths for her to believe in, no guarantees for her to rely on, only cruel echoes rebounding off cold stone walls that sounded like "no one" and "nothing" and "never."

Wanting to escape the feelings of abandonment that threatened to overwhelm her, Isabelle ran toward the far end of the garage. Here—where once a tower had risen above the tree line until it had been destroyed in a fire—the ceiling was lofted higher than in the rest of the building, with huge windows front and back allowing a flood of natural light to fill the deserted stall.

In its original state this structure had been a guest house for the monastery. Located high on a hill in an isolated area, the monastery was often visited by travelers who needed a place to rest before continuing their journey. Since their callers were not always clerics and not always aware of the rigors of religious life, the monks had opted for a separate building. Modest, more dormitory than inn, the guest house had provided basic shelter and few creature comforts so as to encourage brief stays and few returns.

In the fifteenth century the Franciscans were driven away and members of the Catalan aristocracy took possession of the Castell. Being more sociable than their predecessors, they added guest quarters to the main house, freeing this adjunct to shelter the family's personal cavalry. Though the Castell had known many owners since then, the old structure had remained a stable until Martín had converted it to a garage.

Isabelle watched the light play with the dust as it cascaded from its high perch. Microscopic speckles of dirt suddenly became glittery stars dancing before her, teasing her eye, seducing her to join the chase. Up to the window, down to the floor, swirling about in a golden slice of daylight, the twinkling was hypnotic. As she traced the path of the indoor comet, her glance landed on something else that glistened in the sunlight. If she hadn't known it was there, she would have missed it, but years before, Martín had told her about a trap door that led to an underground bunker. Intrigued, suddenly eager to explore, Isabelle wrestled with the rusted door handle, struggling to release it from its carefully crafted niche. It took Herculean effort, but finally she managed to lift the huge wooden square from its bed and shove it off to the side.

The opening was larger than those that covered most hiding places, but Martín had told her this subterranean refuge had been unique in that it had housed horses as well as people. In the days when horses often were valued more highly than humans, it was not uncommon for marauders to slay entire households simply to replenish their own herds. To protect against such an assault, one of the masters of the Castell had constructed this cleverly conceived den, with stairs for himself and his family and a ramp for his horses.

During the Spanish Civil War, fearing that they might have to go into hiding to protect themselves from Franco's bloodthirsty troops, the Pujols had renovated this secret hideaway, installing electricity and plumbing and reopening a tunnel that stretched from the garage to the house.

Isabelle groped around, searching for a light switch. She found it on the wall just under the opening, clicked it on, and started her descent. Suddenly a squeal of utter delight broke through her lips.

Just below her was the Bugatti! Martín's pride and joy. A Royale Type 41. Only seven of them had been built, this one in 1929. Gigantic in its proportions, sinfully luxurious, it was truly the car of kings. She raced down the steps and stared at it as one would a holy icon, marveling in her discovery and in the resourcefulness of whoever had decided to store this treasure here. Slightly stunned, she circled the Bugatti. A thin film of dirt coated its surface, the windows were gray with accumulated dust, spiderwebs filled a few crevices, but the quality of its design was so great that nothing could dull its regal aura. The Bugatti was now what it had been from the day it was made— an enduring emblem of class.

Isabelle undid the bandanna that held her ponytail and began to clean the car. Gently, with great care and love, she slid the rag over the black-and-white body, feeling the wavelike grace of the fender as it arched over the front wheels, sensing the strength that lay beneath the elegantly fitted coach. She polished the proud nose that stretched out from the glamorous chassis, dusting the carefully cut fins that vented the engine, cleaning the glass-eyed, chrome-coated headlights that had guided this noble chariot through the night.

As she worked on the car, she recalled the stories Martín had told her about its eccentric designer, Ettore Arco Isidoro Bugatti. Born in Milan and establishing his factory in Molsheim, a small town in the Alsace, Bugatti had created the legend that surrounded himself and his cars by virtue of his quirky personality. He insisted upon being photographed in riding clothes and a bowler hat. To make his feet more comfortable, he invented a shoe with toes. And because he found the table manners of a Balkan monarch "beyond belief," he reneged on a contract, refusing to sell the boorish king the Royale he had come to buy.

Eventually that Royale had wound up here, in Martín de Luna's garage.

"Tía Flora, would it be all right if I visited Martín's and Althea's graves?"

Nina had been struggling with this for weeks. A day or so after they had arrived in Barcelona, she had asked Isabelle if she wanted to go to the cemetery to see her parents. Isabelle's answer was quick and definite: "No. I don't have to see their graves to know they're dead." Yet something inside Nina demanded visual proof.

"If you'd like." Flora was touched. She knew from Althea that the child had formed an attachment, but she had never considered that she might have lamented their passing. "It's very sweet of you to want to pay your respects, Nina."

"I would have gone with Isabelle, but . . . well . . . I think it's too hard for her."

Flora nodded and sighed. "Though she puts on a brave face, I'm not certain she's completed her mourning." Again she breathed deeply. "But how can I expect her to let go when I'm still hanging on to memories and feelings?"

"I don't think we should ever let go of our memories. If we did, we'd have nothing left."

Flora patted Nina's cheek and smiled. "You're absolutely correct. How very bright and sensitive of you."

Nina blushed at the praise.

Arm in arm the two women walked the length of the property, slowing their gait as they came to the hill of rest.

"They're beneath that tree," Flora said, fatigued from the strain of the walk. "I'll rest here while you have your visit."

Flora seated herself on a stone bench. Nina watched as she closed her eyes, folded her hands in her lap, and began to breathe in a slow, rhythmic pattern. It took a moment for Nina to realize Flora was meditating, calling on those who slept here beneath the stones. Unwilling to disturb her, Nina tiptoed in the direction of the parasol pine, stopping in front of the two headstones that marked the graves of Martín de Luna and Althea Murillo de Luna.

She didn't know what she had expected, but she wasn't satisfied with what she saw: the hardness of the monuments, the cold simplicity of the names and dates of their births and deaths. She supposed she had wanted to see pictures, to read a poem, to hear music, to have something point to the fact that these two people had been exceptional, that they had not passed through this life without leaving a mark.

She was living proof of their imprint. She wasn't a child or a relative or a neighbor. She was a stranger who had been forever changed by having known them. They had brought something special into her life; it was something she couldn't touch or name or define, yet it had been strong enough to make her proud of being tall, of being able to tell a story, of being who and what she was. And for that she would be eternally grateful.

She knelt before them and, instead of praying, drew on every memory she could conjure. She relived every moment she had spent with them, including those horrendous moments when she had heard about their deaths. Slowly, almost fearfully, she opened her eyes, forcing herself to look at Martín's name, absorb what it meant to see it chiseled in stone, and surrender any fantasy she might have about him being alive.

"I know it was selfish of me, but I didn't care if you were angry or sick or in jail," she whispered to the name on the stone. "I needed to believe you were alive because it was easier for me." Despite the fact that no one was there to hear her confession, Nina flushed at her admission of self-indulgence. "Yet seeing you here, lying next to Althea, well, it seems right. Though it's awful for Flora and Isabelle and Alejandro and me, this is better for you."

She closed her eyes again, calmer now, more at peace with herself and her memories of them.

She didn't know how long she stayed, but when she rose to go and looked around, the sun was low in the sky and Flora was gone.

It was late afternoon. Flora, not wanting to have to explain to Isabelle where she and Nina had gone, had returned to the Castell. When Consuela told her no one had seen or heard from Isabelle, Flora began to fret. In the course of checking out some of her favorite haunts, she stumbled over Isabelle's art supply box outside the garage. Seeing the open door, she stepped inside.

Deepening shadows had curtained the area in gray. The air was quiet, but not completely still. Isabelle had been there, Flora was certain of that, but where the child was now remained a question.

Panning slowly, Flora spotted a faint light. Without a moment's hesitation she headed toward the eastern end of the garage. As she suspected, the trap door was askew, the private chambers completely lit. Grabbing hold of her skirt and taking a deep breath, she tiptoed down the stairs, holding on to the walls for balance. When she was down far enough to take in the full view, she paused, needing a moment to gather her thoughts.

Perched behind the wheel in the chauffeur's seat of Martín's Bugatti sat Isabelle, mumbling happily, a faraway look in her eyes, a wistful smile dancing on her lips.

Flora clutched at her heart and bit back a well of tears. Like Isabelle, she had avoided many of the places and objects associated with Martín. It had been five years since she had allowed herself to enter this garage, five years since she had decreed that the Bugatti be hidden away. Though she had told Alejandro and Pedro it was to save the car from the grubby hands of those who had made stealing from her a sport, in truth it was to protect her from the very avalanche of emotion that crashed around her now.

Martín used to say he had four loves in his life: Althea, Isabelle, Flora, and his cars. He also used to say that his order of preference varied according to his mood—and everyone else's behavior. A wobbly smile found its way to Flora's mouth as she recalled the many times she and Althea used to shake their heads and complain that his cars took precedence over everything else in his life. He spent time with them, invested money in them, showed them off in a manner that displayed more pride than arrogance, and loved them with an ardor many men reserved for women. Yet when it was necessary to choose, when he had needed to raise money to keep Dragon Textiles going, he had allowed them to become objects for sale. Flora remembered him grieving openly as pieces of his prized collection had passed into other hands. The only other times she had seen Martín's handsome face contorted with greater anguish was when he had buried Althea and waved good-bye to Isabelle.

Seeing Isabelle now, playing so happily in something Martín had held so dear, filled Flora with particularly bittersweet joy: Isabelle had been born in a Rolls-Royce Phantom I; Martín had wanted her to ride to her wedding in it. If Althea hadn't been present when someone had made him an outrageous offer for it—and hadn't browbeaten him into agreeing—Martín never would have sold it.

Looking at Isabelle now in the Bugatti, recalling her birth thirteen years ago on the backseat of that elegant Rolls-Royce, Flora congratulated herself for her perspicacity and thanked François LeVerre for his generosity.

After Martín had been imprisoned, he had instructed her to follow through on his plans to sell the rest of his collection to François. She was to use the money to pay the heavy taxes imposed on the town house, the foundry, and various other Pujol/de Luna properties so they could not be confiscated by the bureaucratic piranhas he believed were out to bankrupt him. She was not to touch one peso of her own.

"I'm still the man of the family," he had told her the last time she had visited him in jail, the day before he'd died. "I take care of business. You take care of my daughter."

Flora nodded as she had nodded then, holding back tears as she had held them back then. She had done what Martín had asked—to a point. LeVerre had purchased the Hispano-Suiza, the Lagonda, and the Mercedes. Flora had hidden the Bugatti, but she had been able to erase all of Martín's debt, because LeVerre had substantially overpaid for each of the cars. He wasn't a bad businessman, he was a good friend.

Flora watched as Isabelle twisted the steering wheel back and forth, pretending to be driving on an open road. She hated to interrupt the fantasy, but it was getting very late.

"Are you having a nice visit?" she asked.

Isabelle turned toward her aunt, surprised to see her, even more surprised at her greeting. Once again Flora had intuited her deepest thoughts.

"I don't want to be where he's dead," she said softly, answering Flora's unasked question as to why Isabelle hadn't visited Martín's grave. "I'd rather be where he lives."

Flora and Isabelle looked at each other, sharing a long moment of silent understanding. Suddenly Flora assumed an imperious posture, walked past Isabelle, opened the door to the rear cabin of the car, and climbed inside. Leaning forward, rapping her knuckles on the window that separated passenger from driver, she commanded, "Once around the grounds!"

With a broad, delighted smile, Isabelle placed her hands on the wheel and responded with an appropriate tone of obeisance, "As you wish, Señorita Pujol."

By the end of July, escaping the brutality of summer's heat became a priority for Flora and her young charges. Naturally Alejandro came to the rescue with an invitation to spend the next three weeks at his house in Palamos on the Costa Brava. Set on a hill overlooking the jagged coast of northeastern Spain, Alejandro's country retreat was a medieval fortress that, like Flora's Castell, had been a family stronghold for generations.

Well camouflaged by clusters of cork and pine trees, the sprawling estate exuded an unmistakable air of determined survival. An impenetrable box of stone with a commanding view of the sea, it rose high above the red granite cliffs and sandy beaches that distinguished the shoreline, dominating the bluff on which it sat.

Out back, a spacious patio of clay tiles surrounded a modern swimming pool, with two gracefully sculpted sea nymphs at the deepest end enticing visitors to partake of the waters. Wooden chaises covered with canvas cushions faced the sun. Tall, dark green spires of cypress surrounded the area, softening the strict lines and armored look of the sparsely windowed house. Behind high walls, a cobbled courtyard provided another relaxing oasis, this one furnished in wicker and cool white canvas. A magenta splash of bougainvillea against one wall and earthenware pots brimming with pink and white geraniums against another provided a sharp contrast to the severity of the architecture, relaxing the stiff affect of the rigid facade with bold strokes of color and a subtle burst of fragrance.

Inside, the sleek modernity of leather was happily wed to the worn beams and wooden ceilings of another time. A wide mezzanine that overlooked the living room functioned as a small library. Large, heavily cushioned couches, widemouthed fireplaces, paintings by Tàpies, Dali, and Miró, and a vast collection of leather-bound books and classical stone statuary created an atmosphere of intelligent repose. The dining room was stark and simple—a wooden table surrounded by caned-seat chairs, a wrought-iron chandelier—the focus being a series of lit niches that held an array of colorful crystal goblets and decanters befitting the source of the Fargas wealth.

Alejandro's heritage was wine—specifically the sparkling white wine known as cava. Produced according to the méthode champenoise used by Dom Pérignon, cava was an important part of Catalan life, appearing at baptisms, weddings, festivals, even Sunday dinners. As the second son, Alejandro was ineligible to run the vineyard or to inherit the family seat—an enormous Mediterranean villa in San Sadurni, a small town half an hour west of Barcelona in the heart of the Catalan wine region. Instead he had been given this home, an income from the vineyards, and the freedom to do as he wished.

For Alejandro it was an ideal arrangement. He had always preferred working with his mind rather than his hands, and when he needed to get away from the city, he preferred the beach over the forest. His older brother, Milagros, favored the things Alejandro did not, a fact that came as no surprise to those who knew them. Though they shared a physical similarity—both were tall and lean, with a prominent nose, wide, eagle-bright eyes, and a jaw that jutted forward with gritty resoluteness—the differences between them were striking.

Milagros was conservative, a man of tradition. He derived security and comfort from the knowledge that he was doing what was acceptable, what had been done before, what should be revered and perpetuated, because it was right. He had married young, fathered six children, rarely ventured too far from his grapes, and prided himself on producing the finest cava in Catalonia. He had little interest in the cultural arts, a distaste for politics, a fear of anything that would upset his balance sheet, and an innate suspicion of anyone or anything outside his limited circle.

Though he and Alejandro shared a deep affection and respect for each other, they found it difficult to appreciate the conduct of each other's lives. While he never put it into words, Milagros disapproved of Alejandro's relationship with Flora and his lack of progeny, and despite an honest awe of his brother's courtroom skills and reputation for judicial brilliance, he believed that in the larger sense, maintenance of the superior quality of the Fargas label was a far more noble and everlasting goal than trying cases in court.

That had been particularly true when Alejandro went to the bar in Martín's defense. If Milagros could have, he would have forbidden Alejandro to take the case. It was too controversial, too potentially explosive, too public. Having the Fargas name attached to such a tawdry scandal had greatly disturbed Milagros, and he had said so.

"This could do irreparable damage to the family's reputation," he had counseled, his attempts to conceal his anger only moderately successful. "Not to mention the effect it could have on business. Times are hard, Alejandro. The economy is poor. Everyone is struggling to stay afloat. The last thing I need is for you to be associated with a rapist and a murderer!"

Milagros had expected to quarrel with his brother, but in the end he had believed logic would prevail and that Alejandro would put the needs of his family first. What Milagros did not expect was that the family to whom Alejandro would give his loyalty was Flora and Martín and Isabelle. The two brothers had not spoken in five years.

Flora had never been a fan of Milagros Fargas or of his prissy wife, Inez, but despite their dissimilarities Alejandro missed having them in his life. With Isabelle off in Santa Fe, Flora more than understood. For better or worse, Milagros was Alejandro's only sibling, his brood Alejandro's only blood kin. Flora had come from a much larger family, but the years had taken all her relatives from her, including those who should have outlived her. Isabelle was all she had left, and frankly, she feared she was losing her, too.

Flora had listened intently whenever Isabelle discussed the Durans and her life in Santa Fe. She couldn't help but see the closeness between Isabelle and Nina. She had watched Isabelle in the city, noticing her reactions to customs and circumstances Flora—and, at one time, Isabelle—had accepted as commonplace. It was clear that Isabelle had absorbed much that was American, making much of what was current in Catalonia seem foreign and outdated. And she had observed what happened whenever Isabelle and Nina interacted with other young girls their age. The girls she knew in Barcelona or Campíns couldn't hum any of the music from *Hair* or anything by Joan Baez and Bob Dylan. Most had never heard of Elvis Presley or Martin Luther King and didn't care about Robert Kennedy or Vietnam. And while Isabelle empathized with the constant undercurrent of rage against the government of Madrid, Flora suspected that now her beliefs were more conditioned reflex than passionate commitment.

As July turned to August and the date of Isabelle's departure grew nearer, Flora was forced to consider whether it was wise to keep Isabelle in Spain or wiser to return her to Santa Fe. Flora's heart said one thing; her head said another. Unwilling to concede that perhaps the decision was not hers to make, she decided to present Isabelle with a family portrait, a reminder that even without Martín and Althea, Barcelona was home, and that her family circle was wider than just Flora and Alejandro, her world farther reaching than simply to the fences that surrounded the Castell.

Without telling anyone, Flora set about creating a very special weekend. Calling it her Celebration of Summer, she first traveled to San Sadurni to convince Inez and Milagros to end their feud with Alejandro and attend. Getting them to agree was no easy feat, but as stubborn as Milagros was, he had never come up against the likes of Flora Pujol. She allowed him to vent his pique at Alejandro's long and continued silence, listening patiently as he railed about the mulishness of his brother in failing to see that he, Milagros, had wanted only to spare them all—including Flora—from the very pain they were experiencing now; that he had believed his brother shared his pride of name and was both hurt and humiliated by Alejandro's abject refusal to protect its integrity.

When he had finished his tirade and Inez had added her paragraph of personal affronts, Flora faced them both.

"The union between Alejandro and me is not blessed by the church," she said. "Martín de Luna was not of my womb. Yet I challenge anyone, including you, to match my love for both of them. I have been a wife to Alejandro in every single way. I have stood by him in sickness and health, in good times and bad. When he hurts, I hurt. When I bleed, he bleeds. When my son needed help, Alejandro gave it to him, because my son was his son."

Flora's words hung in the air like a dare. Neither Milagros nor Inez had the courage to correct or challenge her.

"Althea was dead. Martín's life was hanging in the balance. Instead of gathering around us during that terrible time and giving us your support, you insulted us by not attending Althea's funeral and, further, by demanding that Alejandro desert a young man he loved as a sign of respect for your family." A gruff, sardonic laugh spewed from Flora's lips. "Not only did you refuse to respect Alejandro's family, you denied its existence. Shame on you!"

Milagros shifted about on his chair, his eyes lowered, unable to return Flora's accusatory gaze. Inez fidgeted with her bracelet. She had always been intimidated by Flora, and this was no exception. Milagros appeared equally intimidated.

"Our grandniece, Isabelle, has returned to Barcelona," Flora continued, "a young woman Alejandro and I have missed terribly. From the day she was born until the day she left us five years ago, Isabelle has been our own personal fountain of youth. She keeps us young and alert. She makes us think and she makes us laugh. She gives us reason to put the past in perspective and look forward to the future. She does for us what your grandchildren do for you."

She paused, forcing them to look at her.

"We would like her to stay here in Spain, but other than us, all she has are terrible memories. I want to change that. I want to show her that even without Martín and Althea, she has connections here, that she has family here."

Again she paused, this time to cap a rising geyser of emotion.

"I want you to make peace with Alejandro."

Milagros's eyes widened, but not with surprise. He had already guessed where Flora was headed. What took him back was the cheekiness of her demand that his be the first hand extended.

"If Alejandro wants peace, let him ask for it." Milagros leaned back on his chair and folded his arms across his chest in a pose Flora assumed he considered appropriate for a dynastic sovereign. Much as she would have enjoyed throwing a well-aimed, sharply pointed barb at his airy pretensions, she had come to San Sadurni in hopes of finding an olive branch.

"In all fairness, Milagros, you were the one who inflicted the wound of betrayal."

"Who do you think you are, coming into my home after all this time and making demands on me?" Milagros said, using bluster to cover his embarrassment at being confronted with the truth.

"I'm a woman who wants to keep her family together, even if certain members seem to be stuck behind high walls of false pride." She narrowed her eyes and fixed them on his, daring him to look away. "Two weeks from now, Alejandro and I are hosting a big party in Palamos for friends and family. You can either be part of it or not. It's up to you."

With that, she rose from her chair and walked to the door. As she was about to leave, she turned, offered Milagros a knowing smile, and said, "The festivities begin Friday at eight."

Apologies between the brothers were brief and private. Alejandro offered no excuses or justifications for his anger or his distance. Once he had recovered from the shock of seeing his brother and his enormous family on his doorstep, he welcomed Milagros to his home, believing that alone was sufficient repair.

Milagros, who had been ruminating about this reunion for two weeks, had thought quite seriously about everything Flora had said. Much as he fought it, his gut told him that she was right—he had been the one to commit the more serious offense.

Despite that secret admission, the most he could verbalize was, "I'm sorry for what happened between us."

Fortunately for both of them, Alejandro's nature was pragmatic and, therefore, more forgiving. He was a realist, with few pretensions. Unlike his brothers, Alejandro's sense of self was not tied up in images of who he *should* be or what he *should* think. He conducted his life according to a very basic philosophy: He was who he was. Accept him or reject him, but don't attempt to change him. What's more, Alejandro practiced what he preached.

"So am I," he said, hugging Milagros and setting aside the hostilities of the past.

Side by side they walked out from Alejandro's study into the courtyard, where everyone was gathered. Flora felt truly rewarded when spontaneous applause greeted their appearance.

She felt even better when Isabelle kissed her cheek and said, "You did a wonderful thing, Tía Flora."

"I'm not so sure Tío Alejandro agrees with you," Flora said, smiling but noting the I'll-talk-to-you-later look on Alejandro's face. "By surprising him this way, I really didn't give him much choice. He had to forgive him."

"Milagros is his brother," Isabelle said with the wide-eyed indignation of the innocent. "Nothing a brother does could be so terrible it couldn't be forgiven."

Flora wanted to agree but couldn't. Sometimes even siblings did unforgivable things to each other.

For the remainder of that evening and most of the weekend, Flora and Alejandro's guests separated according to age: the young played by the pool and on the lawn, the rest kept cool in the courtyard or inside the house, an arrangement that suited Flora just fine. While Isabelle appeared to have made friends among Milagros and Inez's grandchildren, Nina had made a conquest. From the instant Xavier, the eldest of the brood and, without contest, the most handsome, laid eyes on the tempting young blonde from the States, he was in pursuit. Wherever she was, he was. Wherever she went, he went. Though Alejandro expressed concern, Flora, who had spent much more time with Nina than he had, told him not to worry. Nina was eminently capable of handling herself.

What concerned Flora at the moment was not Nina's ability to stave off the heated advances of an adolescent Latin, but Milagros's desire to befriend Isabelle. Whenever the opportunity presented itself, Milagros could be found off to the side, talking to her. At first Flora feared his questions might be intrusive or that he had some secret agenda, but his tone was sincere, his responses genuine. He seemed fascinated by her life in the United States, both its context and the fact that someone as young as she could adjust to a new life-style so quickly. He voiced admiration for the Durans, praising them for being so generous with their home and their hearts. Being a father to so many children, he claimed a special knowledge of the patience required to rear offspring effectively. The fact that they were parenting children not of their blood struck him as especially praiseworthy.

Isabelle seemed taken with him as well. She was curious about the production of cava and listened with rapt attention as he described the process, from the double fermentation to the bottling to the decanting to the corking. She giggled when he organized a taste test for her and some of the other youngsters. Naturally she was the only one who couldn't tell the difference between a brut and a sec, the two dry wines customarily served with food, or between the sweeter dessert wines, *Semisec* and *Dolç*—but she had a lot of fun learning.

Sunday, after the rest of the family had departed—except for Xavier, who had brought his own car and was now giving Nina a personalized tour of the Costa Brava—Milagros, Inez, Alejandro, Flora, and Isabelle convened in the courtyard for a light lunch. The conversation veered onto a discussion of business and family pride. Flora stiffened, expecting Milagros to revert to type and say something that would either demean or antagonize Alejandro. Instead he turned to Isabelle.

"I was very impressed when you showed me your artwork the other day," he said. "You're very talented."

Isabelle blushed, pleased by the compliment.

"I know you come by it naturally, having inherited the combined talents of Flora and your mother, but with all due respect," he said, bowing his head to a surprised Flora, "you're going to outshine them both!"

"Well, Milagros," Flora said, patting Isabelle's hand, "we've finally found something on which we can agree."

"I know I've never told you this, but I think you're a wonderful artist. I'm not sure I understand your paintings, but I like them." Milagros appeared uncomfortable. He wasn't knowledgeable about art, and he knew it. The last thing he wanted to do was say something foolish, especially to Flora.

"The artists who create them and the critics whose job it is to review them are the only ones who have to *understand* paintings. The public is simply asked to react. You've reacted positively, and for that, I thank you." Flora raised her glass of cava and toasted her newest fan.

Encouraged, Milagros continued. "I don't mean to upset anyone, but as long as we're talking about artists, let me say that in my humble opinion, Althea de Luna was the shining light behind Dragon Textiles. Her designs set that company apart, lifting it so far above its competition that it was in a class by itself. I know Dragon had been the pride of the Barcelona textile industry for nearly a century before Althea joined up, but she was its glory."

Alejandro nodded in agreement. Flora sighed, muttering, "Amen," beneath her breath. Isabelle said nothing, but it was clear by the intense look on her face that she was listening and reacting.

"Most of the fabrics in our house were designed by Althea," Inez said quietly, addressing herself to Isabelle. "Your mother had an innate elegance that came through in her work. Her fabrics were always very stylized and unique, but she managed to make them livable. Dragon hasn't been the same without her."

"See, that's what I was talking about," Milagros said, his voice rising a decibel. "When family runs a family business, there's an extra incentive to achieve. Name is involved. Pride is involved. History is involved. Turn a business over to strangers and quality is lost!"

"What are you insinuating, Milagros?" Alejandro said, unable to keep the edge out of his voice.

"I'm not insinuating, little brother, I'm making a comment, that's all. I just didn't understand how Martín could have sold his heritage."

"He had no choice." Alejandro said simply, hoping to end the discussion. An uneasy silence surrounded the table.

"One of these days," Isabelle said, breaking the hush, "I'm going to get Dragon back." Her voice was so even and matter-of-fact, most ignored the fire burning in her eyes. Flora did not.

"Milagros spoke from his heart, darling, but he wasn't in your father's shoes. He doesn't understand the pressures that were being brought to bear." She was careful about her tone, walking a tightrope between offending Milagros and shutting him up. "Besides, none of that matters now. Dragon is part of the past."

"But it was an important part of my parents' past," Isabelle insisted. "It meant a lot to them, so it means a lot to me."

Flora saw it happening but couldn't stop it. A textile mill was being transformed into the symbol of everything that had been torn from Isabelle's life: her mother, her father, her inheritance, her homeland, her ancestry, her peace of mind.

"Someday," Isabelle said, her voice reverberating with passion, "I'm going to take Dragon away from that loathsome man and bring it back to the de Lunas where it belongs."

"That's the spirit!" Milagros said approvingly. "Bring it back to the family, Isabelle."

"I will," she vowed. "I swear it on my parents' graves."

The next day, Flora, Isabelle, and Nina returned to Barcelona. They had spent the entire car ride laughing and exchanging comments about the various people they had met. They were still laughing when they walked into the Castell, but not for long. All vestiges of good humor ended abruptly when they were greeted by two unexpected visitors.

Javier and Estrella Murillo had arrived without notice or fanfare; they'd simply barged into Flora's home, demanding that Isabelle appear before them. When Consuela had told them that the three señoritas were away on holiday, the Murillos had demanded to know when they would return. Consuela had claimed she didn't know. The Murillos were interrogating her when the front door swung open and the trio entered.

"What are you doing here?" Flora said, her voice ringing with indignation.

"They were just leaving," Consuela said, retreating so as not to get caught in the cross fire.

"So this is Isabelle," Estrella said, ignoring Flora and walking past Nina as if she didn't exist. With slow deliberation she stalked her granddaughter, circling her, appraising her as one would a prize heifer. When she had completed her turn, she looked at Nina, who had returned to Isabelle's side and taken her hand. "And who is this?" Estrella said, pointing directly at Nina's nose.

"Not that it's any of your business, but this is Miss Nina Duran. My guest."

There was a flicker of recognition in Estrella's eyes as she connected the name of this blond girl and the people who were boarding Isabelle. After perusing Nina quickly, taking in her height, her unusually well-developed form, and her delicate countenance, she returned her gaze to the shorter, darker girl. At nearly thirteen Isabelle was gawky, her features almost too large for the delicate oval shape of her face, her body stalled somewhere between childhood and womanhood. While the resemblance to her mother was strong—the creaminess of her skin, the feline slant of her eyes, the plumpness of her lips, the slight overbite, Estrella Murillo passed over all that. What she saw were Isabelle's thick eyebrows and strong nose, her high cheekbones and wide forehead. To Estrella's critical, biased eye, Isabelle appeared to have inherited more from Martín than from Althea, a fact Señora Murillo considered a definite liability.

Impatient with what she considered a rude intrusion, Flora boldly insinuated herself between Isabelle and Estrella. "You're not welcome here," she said with cold authority.

"I didn't come for tea. I came for my daughter's daughter."

"Isabelle isn't receiving visitors."

"We're not here for a visit."

"Then what are you doing in my house?"

Estrella looked past Flora, expecting to see a modicum of fear, a small amount of curiosity, and perhaps even a dollop of respect from Isabelle. What greeted her was abject scorn.

Javier Murillo had remained in the background, perfectly content to let the two women square off against each other; but when he realized that something had unnerved Estrella, he stepped forward.

"Isabelle, go upstairs and pack your belongings," he said, clearly issuing an order he expected to be obeyed. "You're coming to Madrid with us."

Flora felt Isabelle stiffen behind her. She reached back and took the child's hand, squeezing it for reassurance. "She's not going anywhere, especially with you!"

"Your views are irrelevant." Javier dismissed Flora and returned his gaze to Isabelle. "I suggest you do as I ask." He was startled by the quiet defiance that stared back at him.

Estrella turned and glowered at Flora, clearly blaming her for Isabelle's disobedience. Estrella was small but formidable, a woman who could be described as attractive but who was far too somber to be called beautiful. Everything about her was severe. Her hair was dark, slicked back, and confined in a tight chignon that hugged the nape of her neck. She was elegantly attired in a well-cut suit with a few carefully selected accessories. She wore little makeup and no fragrance. Her armor was her wealth and her connections, and she wore both with exaggerated pride.

Flora was bohemian in her affect, a definite contrast to others of her station; but no one, including Estrella, could deny that her carriage bore the mark of an aristocratic background. It was difficult to challenge the nobility of a Pujol, even if your name was Murillo. That didn't mean Estrella wouldn't try.

"This matter is not open to debate," she said in her most imperious manner. "Isabelle is our granddaughter, which makes her our responsibility, not yours."

"You're absolutely right. She's not my responsibility. She's my pride and my greatest source of joy."

Estrella had been bested. As she bristled, Javier repeated his instructions to Isabelle, commanding her to gather her things. Isabelle stayed put. Javier turned his attention to Flora. His eyes narrowed. When he spoke there was little civility in his tone.

"We can do this quietly," he said, "or we can do this with the help of the authorities. For Isabelle's sake, I suggest you encourage her to do as I requested."

"Exactly which authorities? You dropped the custody suit a year ago."

"We've changed our minds. Papers were filed this morning."

Flora bent down and placed her mouth next to Isabelle's ear. "I have to get something," she whispered. "You can come with me, stay here with Nina, or, if you'd prefer, go to your room and remain there until they leave."

"I'm fine right where I am," Isabelle said, loudly enough for the Murillos to hear.

Flora headed for her library, leaving Nina and Isabelle on one side of the hall, Javier and Estrella on the other. Like boxers who had gone a few rounds, taken a few punches, and landed a few blows, they took a moment to reassess their opponents and rethink their strategies. Acknowledging that Isabelle was not impressed with his authority and was not going to respond to directives, Javier tried a different approach.

"We don't mean you any harm, Isabelle. We sincerely feel this is in your best interest."

"Martín and Althea didn't agree," Flora said, eliminating the need for Isabelle to respond. She was holding a file folder in one hand, waving an official-looking document in the other. Her glasses were perched on the end of her nose. "According to Martín's will, which is the one in effect since Althea predeceased him, Nina's parents, Miranda and Luis Duran, are Isabelle's official guardians. I am the executrix of Martín's estate. Alejandro is a trustee. I know it won't surprise you to learn that your names are nowhere to be found, in either will."

"Those documents are meaningless." Javier's temper had resurfaced. "The Durans are strangers. We are Isabelle's grandparents, which makes us her next of kin."

"Since when?" Flora asked.

Estrella looked confused. Javier's face was rouged with anger. "What the hell are you talking about?"

"These," Flora said, holding up a sheaf of papers. "In case you've both forgotten, when Althea married Martín, you formally disowned her. You took her name off every one of your bank accounts, rewrote your wills to refuse her access to her inheritance, and barred her from your home. You even went so far as to deny her the use of the Murillo name. Althea had Alejandro subpoena all the documents. She couldn't believe you could reject her as thoroughly as you did. When she saw this"—Flora waved a piece of paper in front of her enemies—"she said she felt as if she were reading her own death certificate."

Nina and Isabelle stood spellbound. The silence in the room grew heavy with anticipation.

"Beneath an order that canceled all her accounts and denied her access to yours, you not only signed your names, but felt compelled to add a sentence that reads 'As of this date, we have no daughter.'"

Flora's words hung in the air like an atomic cloud, menacing and ominous. The Murillos had believed those papers had been destroyed or, at worst, were on permanent file in their bank. They'd never dreamed Althea would have subpoenaed them.

"Alejandro had intended to use these papers in court five years ago, but Martín wouldn't allow it. He didn't want Althea's memory besmirched by making her parents' callous repudiation of her existence public." Flora's eyes clouded. Her face sagged, burdened by sadness. "He believed he would be cleared of his charges. And when he was, he planned to fight you for his daughter." She looked from one to the other, hate blended with pity. "The difference was, he meant to do it without demeaning your daughter in the process."

"It doesn't matter what he intended," Javier said, practically shouting. "He wasn't cleared of his charges and he couldn't fight us for custody. He's dead. Althea is dead. This girl is her child and our heir."

"She's also Martín's child and my grandniece. Now that we've established bloodlines, what's next?" Flora was baiting him.

"Need I remind you that Generalissimo Franco is a close and dear friend of ours?"

"How could I forget? Between the police harassing me and the watchdogs you had stationed outside my house, I know exactly how chummy you are. I suppose it was one of your hired thugs who informed you Isabelle had returned home for a visit."

Estrella's expression turned smug. "We've had passport control on the lookout for Isabelle. We were notified when she entered the country."

"As you can see," Javier added, "if we need the law bent in our favor, it will be." For what he intended to be the last time, he faced Isabelle. "Now. Pack your belongings and say good-bye to your aunt. We'll be leaving in twenty minutes."

"I'm not going anywhere with you. Not in twenty minutes. Not ever!"

Isabelle had decided the time had come to speak for herself. Dropping Nina's hand, she stepped forward and faced the man who insisted on calling himself her grandfather.

"There's no way I'd ever live with you." With chilling directness, she fixed her eyes on Javier. "Mama said you weren't nice to her. She told me you used to lock her in her room if she disobeyed your orders. And you," she said, steering her attention to Estrella. "Mama said you never hugged her or kissed her or tucked her into bed at night or played with her the way Mama did with me. Why would anyone want to live with you?"

The Murillos were visibly stricken.

"I don't want your money or your influence or your name," Isabelle told them. "I have everything I need—Tía Flora's love, Tío Alejandro's love, a wonderful home in Santa Fe with the Durans, the memory of my parents, and the de Luna name. You offer me nothing!"

Taken aback by her forthrightness, Estrella Murillo was speechless. Javier was not.

"You're just like your mother!" he said, spewing the words as if they were laced with vinegar.

What he intended as an insult, Isabelle took as a tribute. "Thank-you," she said, commanding her mouth to smile. "That's the nicest thing you could have said to me."

"This isn't over," Javier said, glaring first at Isabelle, then at Flora. "I know where she lives and I know where you live. What's more, I have the money, the power, and the influence to get what I want. And believe me, whether you like it or not, I will get what I want!"

After the Murillos stormed out the door, Nina seized Isabelle's hands and the two of them whooped around the floor in an exhilarated dance of triumph, ignoring the threat that polluted the air around them.

"You were incredible!" Nina shouted, grabbing Isabelle and hugging her. "The way you stared them down and told them where to get off! Whew! Clint Eastwood couldn't have done it any better!"

Isabelle started to laugh, but the impact of what had just happened stopped her. Suddenly frightened, she looked from Nina to Flora.

"What do you think he meant about knowing where we live? What's he going to do to me? And to you?"

"Nothing, darling." Flora dismissed Isabelle's fears with a wave of her hand. "He was simply making noise. Forget about it."

As she led the girls to the salon where Consuela had iced chocolate waiting for them, Flora felt her heart sink. Even without the custody suit, the Murillos had accomplished one of their objectives: they had taken Isabelle away. She might not be on her way to Madrid to live with them, but they had made it impossible for her to remain in Barcelona.

Bravado aside, Flora didn't take the Murillos' threat lightly. For Isabelle's sake, the sooner she returned to Santa Fe, the better.

CHAPTER 8

1970

From the first, Nina's diaries had overflowed with fantasies: being rich, living in a grand house, wearing fabulous clothes, being surrounded by fabulous people. On page after page, the dreams of a young girl bewitched by the illusional world of movies were spun into hopeful stories that always seemed to begin "Someday . . ."

It wasn't surprising, therefore, that when she wrote about her stay at El Castell de Les Bruixots, she likened it to an audition for the role of leading lady in a film about a life of privilege and pedigree. For two glorious months she had been "Miss Nina," ferrying merrily between sprawling country villas and elegant town houses, waited on, coddled, feted by those for whom "entitled" described not why they should have, but who they were.

Being young and impressionable, Nina was completely overwhelmed by the sumptuousness of the scenery that backdropped their lives. It provided such stark contrast to the humbleness of her own surroundings, she couldn't resist the tug of covetousness. It didn't matter that throughout her stay she had been privy to dozens of conversations about government efforts to humble and humiliate and had overheard many pained discussions about how drastically circumstances had changed under Franco; Nina was an outsider whose nose was pressed against the window of a store too pricey for her purse, so her conclusions were slightly skewed. Instead of assimilating the essence of these Catalans—the profound pride Flora, Alejandro, Milagros, Inez, and their friends had in their heritage—she was impressed by the external blessings of their wealth. Instead of reviling the Murillos and their cruel manipulations, she interpreted their behavior as confirmation of much of what she had learned in the movies: those who had more were respected more, those who could claim a distinguished lineage could expect a certain deference, those who had money had power.

Despite Miranda's caution—"Don't believe everything you read and accept only half of what you see"—Nina's value system began to undergo a subtle reshuffling. Goodness was its own reward, it was better to give than to receive, a full heart was better than a full cup, and, of course, do unto others as we would have others do unto us—all of Miranda and Luis's teachings, which once were accepted without question, suddenly became topics of internal debate.

Nina had known a world of plenty existed, but it always had seemed unattainable. That summer in Barcelona put luxury within her reach and aroused the sense of possibility. It wasn't long before she began to slip into the dangerous habit of comparison, placing a premium on superficialities, equating status with substance, and defining quality by quantity. When she scrubbed bathrooms at La Casa, she thought of Consuela and yearned to be Flora. When she and Isabelle stumbled over each other trying to get dressed for school in their small room, she longed for the suite she'd had at the Castell. When Luis drove her to a school dance in his pickup truck, she wished for Pedro and Señorita's big black Mercedes.

One by-product of this shift was that Nina began to reexamine her relationship with Isabelle. They had been so young when they were put together, and had lived in harmony for so long, she had blocked out their differences, focusing solely on their similarities. They were two young girls brought together by a parallel set of circumstances. Nina had come to the Durans because those who had given her life had given her up. Isabelle had come to live at La Casa because she too had been abandoned.

While Nina had envied Isabelle her time with Martín and Althea and her knowledge of her own past, Isabelle's life before La Casa had been an abstraction and, therefore, easy to handle. Once Nina had been exposed to the reality, however, the distinctions between them became sharper and more obvious. Isabelle was upper-class; Nina was working-class. Isabelle's lineage was distinguished; Nina's was unknown. Isabelle had a small trust fund; Nina had to work for every penny. Isabelle had come from inside that world of plenty; Nina was still standing outside with her nose pressed against the glass.

The only thing Nina had that Isabelle wanted—and that, too, struck her as ironic—was Sam Hoffman. He was the pride of Santa Fe: son of the chief of staff at St. Vincent's Hospital and an award-winning newspaper columnist, valedictorian of his high school class, pitching ace of the baseball team, a senior at Dartmouth College, and rated by all of Nina's friends as *the* catch of the century. She agreed with the consensus that he was extremely good-looking, an obvious achiever, and full of charm. What her friends didn't know was that he was also the perfect sex partner—gentle when it was her first time, aggressive and satisfying after that, always ready and always careful. Nina's feelings for Sam ran very deep, but every now and then, in the middle of the night when no one but the stars could eavesdrop on her musings, she wondered whether or not they actually would wind up with each other.

Again the wedge was that summer in Barcelona. Those few, innocent days on the Costa Brava with Xavier Fargas had proved that fairy tales could indeed come true. Not only was Xavier tall, dark, handsome, and the sexiest dancer she had ever met, not only did he drive a sports car and have a delicious accent, he was also the scion of a prominent European family. He was the prince, heir to an estate, a vineyard, horses, money, and all the other trappings one would expect from the hero of a popular fable.

Sam Hoffman was the son of a doctor. He was going to be a doctor. His dreams were not of castles or cars or mansions and maids. He wanted to be an orthopedic surgeon, a specialty that carried with it years of schooling, internship, and residency. Though he would probably go on to one of the finest medical schools and would probably be able to pick his hospital, he hadn't dismissed the idea of returning to Santa Fe. He was brilliant and provocative and exceptionally caring, but deep down a tiny voice kept telling Nina that Sam was a slice of life. Xavier Fargas represented romance.

Isabelle couldn't have disagreed more, and that stunned Nina. On the few occasions when she had waxed poetic about Xavier, Isabelle had turned up her nose.

"You were in a foreign place. He spoke with an accent. The sun was hot. You were delirious."

When recently Nina ruminated out loud about inviting him to her sweet sixteen party, it was hard for Isabelle to disguise her disapproval.

"I can't understand how you could want Xavier Fargas when you have Sam Hoffman!"

Nina couldn't understand Isabelle's continuing infatuation with Sam and her utter rejection of Alejandro's nephew. According to Nina's script, Isabelle should have been drawn instinctively to the likes of Xavier Fargas. He was her kind. Sam was not. Yet Isabelle couldn't look at Sam without blushing.

Perhaps, Nina thought, when one was born to the purple, one could afford infatuations with those from another class, because inevitably like found like, married, and lived regally ever after. Nina didn't begrudge Isabelle the perquisites of her station, but the ease of it all became another item on her list of things to envy about Isabelle.

Nina's other list—last-minute to-dos for her sweet sixteen party—seemed to grow longer every day. It was only two weeks away, and she still hadn't found the perfect dress or decided how to wear her hair. Though money was tight, with every extra penny earmarked for Nina's college fund, Miranda had agreed to a celebration. It couldn't be on a Saturday night—that would chase away paying customers—and it couldn't run late—there was school on Monday—but she could have music and dancing, a huge cake with sixteen pink roses, and, best of all, a new dress.

She and Isabelle had planned to go shopping that afternoon after school, but it had snowed all night. When Rebecca Hoffman called and said she and a few friends were driving up to Taos, Nina and Isabelle rushed to join them. Neither girl could resist the lure of fresh powder.

"Miranda and Luis won't like it if we cut school," Isabelle said, suddenly wary.

"They won't know." Nina was already wriggling into her long underwear. "I saw them take off a few minutes ago."

"Where are they going?"

Nina shrugged. "Probably on one of their strange outings."

Isabelle nodded, her face growing pensive. Periodically the Durans disappeared for the day, going "nowhere in particular," to do "nothing important."

"Where do you think they go?" Isabelle said, her natural curiosity frustrated by their refusal to talk about these secretive day trips.

"Who knows? I gave up trying to figure it out years ago." Nina tugged at her sweater, glowering at Isabelle, who was still in her nightgown.

"Aren't you dying to know what they do?" Isabelle climbed into her long johns, hopelessly intrigued.

"Maybe they're running guns over the border into Mexico. Or ferrying illegal aliens in from Guatemala." Nina's eyes narrowed. Her voice became a nefarious whisper. "Maybe they're smuggling drugs inside innocent-looking piñatas or taco warmers."

Isabelle giggled and shook her head. "Highly unlikely."

"Or maybe," Nina said with a lascivious laugh, "they're holed up in some sleazy motel having a day of hot and kinky sex!"

"Give me a break!" Isabelle groaned as she grabbed her parka.

"Anything's possible."

"I guess," Isabelle said as she followed Nina out the door. "Still, let's just hope that wherever they're headed, it's not anywhere near Taos."

*   *   *

It was one of those glorious days when skiing seemed to be the only way to fully appreciate nature's beneficence. The snow glistened as if diamonds had been ground into a pristine dust and sprinkled on the mountains with a generous hand. The sun was yellow and high in a bright blue sky. The air was cold and crisp, but clear, with only an occasional breeze. It was the kind of weather the kids loved: no hats, no goggles, just headbands or earmuffs, neck gaiters, and sunglasses.

Nina, Isabelle, and their friends were expert skiers, more than equal to the challenge of trails marked with a black diamond. Steep verticals, ungroomed slopes, fields of treacherous bumps—they skied them hard, exhilarated by their own speed, invigorated by the heady sensation of slicing through the snow and flying down the mountain. It was in the afternoon when they decided to slalom down the tree line.

Isabelle had suggested it. They had come to a narrow trail on the back side. It had been groomed that morning, but there was still plenty of powder close to the pine trees.

"How about skiing in each other's tracks?"

It was something they did all the time: following close behind the leader, matching tracks turn for turn. There were six of them. Rebecca was picked to blaze the trail; Nina volunteered to bring up the rear. Isabelle jumped in behind one of the guys, in front of Nina. Rebecca started out slowly, opting to take the steepest part of the slope on the packed snow, giving everyone a chance to shake off their lunch legs and get the feel of their skis beneath them.

Her pace quickened. The conga line kept up, maintaining distance and speed. Suddenly Rebecca angled sharply toward the tree line, jumping quickly into the powder, then back out onto the packed snow. Three quick, short turns in the powder, two turns out. In, out, deliberately altering the texture of the snow and the radius of her turns, forcing the others to adjust.

As their speed increased, it became harder to stay in Rebecca's tracks. The two directly behind her found themselves increasing the arc of their turns to slow themselves down and avoid bunching. The boy in front of Isabelle lost interest in the game and fell out of line completely. Isabelle, determined not to lag behind, fixed her eyes on the skier just ahead and raced to close the gap. She never saw the twig poking out of the snow.

Suddenly the backs of her skis jerked out from under her. The tips caught the powder and down she went, rolling over in a frightening tumble of skis and poles. Nina had been tight on Isabelle's heels, traveling too fast to stop, too close to the trees to veer away. She tried to edge, but there was no room.

She tried to jump over Isabelle, but it was too late. One of Isabelle's bindings had released. Nina's legs twisted as she tripped over the errant ski. Within seconds, she too was down, falling forward just as Isabelle's legs swung up, slamming the remaining ski into her head.

Rebecca and the others watched in horror as the two girls somersaulted through the snow. Equipment flew through the air, littering the slope with their debris. Several other skiers stopped along the side, fearful of hitting into them and making the situation worse. Despite the speed with which she was falling, Isabelle knew there was nothing she could do now except hope that she wasn't far from a catwalk where the land would flatten out. She looked up. Nina was also free-falling, but her body appeared limp. And she was much too quiet. Sensing that Nina was unable to help herself, Isabelle turned on her side and tried to brace herself against the hill, slowing up just enough to grab Nina's arm, pull her body close, and guide their precipitous slide as best she could.

Finally they stopped. Fortunately someone had had the sense to ski on ahead, get to a phone, and notify the ski patrol.

"Don't move," Rebecca said to the girls, relying on her credentials as a doctor's daughter for authority. "Just lie still until the ski patrol gets here."

Her actual medical knowledge was minuscule, but it didn't take advanced degrees to know that Nina was seriously injured. There was a bulge on her forehead. Her color was gray and chalky. And her left leg seemed to be dangling at a peculiar angle.

Isabelle rejected Rebecca's advice and struggled to her feet. She was badly bruised, and her thumb was jammed and throbbing, but nothing was broken. It was Nina she was concerned about. She was so quiet and motionless, so limp and pale. Isabelle became unnerved.

"What am I going to do?" she cried. "How am I going to tell Miranda and Luis about this?" Tears streamed down her cheeks. Her hands shook. It was all Rebecca could do to keep her from throwing herself on top of Nina. "They think we're at school. I knew we shouldn't have done this." Suddenly Isabelle envisioned the Durans, their faces a collage of hurt and fear and complete disapproval. "Oh, God," she prayed, looking down at Nina, "please let her be all right!"

When the ski patrol arrived, their worried faces and whispered mumblings did little to alleviate Isabelle's fears. She watched in silent horror as they packed Nina's leg and slid a collar around her neck. She winced as they slipped her onto the sled, covered her with a warm blanket, buckled the straps, and prepared her for the delicate ride down the mountain. It was when she heard one of the men in the red jackets call down to the base and order an ambulance that she panicked.

"What's wrong with her? Is she going to be all right?"

"Her leg is broken and she has a concussion, but yes, she's going to be fine." Years of dealing with companions of the injured had taught the mountain medic that quick, honest explanations were best. "Are you a relative?"

"Her sister."

He nodded and patted her arm. Isabelle was so scared, he felt sorry for her. He noticed that several passersby had retrieved the errant skis and poles. "Do you think you can ski down?"

Isabelle nodded.

"Then follow us and you can ride with her to the hospital." He noticed that Isabelle's eyes were wide and somewhat vacant. She seemed totally unaware of tears that continued to fall down her cheeks. "Just take it slow, okay? You look a little shaky yourself, and this sled only has room for one."

The next few days were traumatic. Nina's concussion had been less serious than it had appeared, but her leg had been broken in several places. She was in surgery for hours, on pain medication for days. Though she was able to leave the hospital a week after the accident, that wasn't the end of it. There would be months in a thigh-high cast, a second operation to remove the metal pins the doctors had inserted into the bones, months more of physical therapy. Eventually the leg would heal, but it would require a long time. And a lot of money.

After the cast was off and her health had improved, Nina suffered another shock.

"We had to empty your college fund to pay for your surgeries."

Luis said it quickly, as if once the words had left his mouth, the throbbing pain of inadequacy would subside. "I've spoken to the bank about a loan, but even if they grant it to us, we need a scholarship."

Nina felt as if she had been struck with a club. Her college fund had been a fact of her life for so long, she had begun to believe it was a living entity. Whatever she earned went into the college fund. Whatever extra profits Miranda and Luis made on catered parties or small business conventions went into the college fund. Whatever cash gifts she received went into the college fund. It was something they put into, not something they took out of. Yet here was her father telling her that instead of a full well, there was a void.

Nina sat through the rest of the discussion in a fog. She heard Miranda say that Sybil was certain Nina's grades, plus teacher recommendations, plus a financial statement showing need, would qualify her for a full scholarship. She heard Luis suggest that she apply to the University of New Mexico as insurance. She even heard Isabelle offer to empty her bank account as a way of replacing the monies lost.

"It'll be a few years before I go to college," she said. "We could replenish my fund by then. Why not use that money for Nina?"

"Because it's your money, darling," Miranda said, clearly touched by Isabelle's generosity. "It was left for your schooling and your care. It can't be touched."

"But I feel as if all of this is my fault."

Isabelle's words reverberated inside Nina's head. *My fault. All of this is my fault.* It was as if a button had been pressed and a forbidden thought buried for months in the crypt of Nina's subconscious had risen to the surface. Nina's eyes narrowed and fixed on Isabelle. She recalled Isabelle suggesting the game, Isabelle pushing forward, then falling back, Isabelle tripping, forcing Nina down.

It was an accident, her conscience said. No one was at fault.

Maybe not, but resentment began to boil. Placing blame made her feel better. It gave focus to her anger and provided a repository for her hostility. Suddenly she felt free to ask questions she hadn't dared ask before, such as why was it that Isabelle fell and came away with nothing more than a jammed thumb and some grisly black-and-blue bruises, while she had been left with scars and a weather-sensitive leg, as well as a mountain of debts? Why was Isabelle's future protected and hers suddenly in jeopardy? Why was Isabelle's fund sacrosanct and hers depleted?

Because, she said, giving voice to the blind envy raging within, *life's easier for blue bloods than it is for blue-collars.*

The dignified strains of "Pomp and Circumstance" infused the stadium with an aura of majesty as the graduates filed onto the playing field. Two by two they marched onto the track in a rhythmic cadence, following the dirt path until they came to a cluster of folding chairs. Quietly and with a solemnity suited to the occasion, they filed into the various rows, stopping before their assigned seats and standing uncharacteristically still until José Zaccaro, the last of their class, was in place. Then, responding to a signal by the band director, they sat.

Throughout the benediction and the Pledge of Allegiance, the three band selections, and the various valedictory speeches, Miranda and Luis held hands, their eyes fixed on Nina. This was a momentous day for them, sitting in the stands watching their daughter graduate from high school, knowing that in the fall she would go off to college. Like most parents witnessing this rite of passage, the Durans hoped that Nina's future would be better and brighter than anything either of them had ever known.

As the principal read the name of each graduate, handed them their diplomas, and shook their hands, Miranda waited. When it was Nina's turn, Miranda wept. Luis, too, became a bit teary as the tall blonde he called his daughter returned to her seat. Isabelle and the Hoffmans hooted and applauded, drawing a scowl from the object of their affection. No one was offended. Knowing Nina's love of drama and her predilection for posing, they viewed her sangfroid as part of whatever role she was playing.

"What do you think?" Sybil said. "Anouk Aimée or Jane Fonda?"

Isabelle studied Nina's posture as she left the podium and took her seat. "From the way she's holding her head, flaring her nostrils, and pursing her lips, and considering the number of times she sat through *Love Story,* I'm leaning toward Ali MacGraw."

"Good guess."

When Rebecca Hoffman received her diploma, she was given the same riotous greeting by the same band of fans. Unlike Nina, she didn't know how to act like anyone but herself, so she smiled and waved.

As they watched the recessional, Nina's family mused about her future, wondering where life would take her and what she would become. Miranda believed Nina would follow the stars to Hollywood and find her place within movieland's firmament. Luis imagined Nina a playwright or a best-selling novelist. Isabelle had no thoughts about Nina and a career; she only saw her as Mrs. Sam Hoffman, which, to Isabelle, was more than anyone could possibly want.

That night the Durans and the Hoffmans celebrated with a dinner at the Pink Adobe. For Jonas it was a bittersweet occasion. While he was delighted by the successes of his children and wanted nothing to mar the happiness of the occasion, he couldn't help feeling slightly melancholy. Ruth should have been here. She had lavished so much time and energy and love on her children, she deserved to *kvell* from them. Rebecca had been salutatorian of her high school class and had been accepted at Wellesley. Sam had graduated summa cum laude from Dartmouth and would start Harvard Medical School in the fall. According to Jonas, Ruth deserved all the credit, and it was to her that he offered the first toast of the evening.

Though Ruth was gone, the chair next to Jonas was not empty. He wasn't certain how it happened, or when it happened, but Sybil Croft had eased into the role of companion. She had nursed Ruth for months, standing vigil at her bedside until the end. Then she had ministered to Jonas and the children during their mourning. It was Sybil who maintained the household schedule throughout; Sybil who reminded Rebecca and Sam how important their educations had been to their mother and urged them to channel their grief into something purposeful; Sybil who had insisted Jonas set an example for his children by returning to work.

At some point, Jonas supposed he had—as the song said—grown accustomed to her face. He found himself expecting to see her in the kitchen preparing dinner when he got home and waiting for her daily phone call to find out if there was anything he or Rebecca needed at the store. If several days passed without hearing from her or seeing her, he felt odd, as if he were wearing two different socks or had gone out without a belt. If he read an editorial with which he disagreed or saw something on the news that disturbed him or read a book that raised a point he wanted to debate, he found himself seeking her out. As time went by, the how and when of their relationship began to lose relevance. The fact was, Sybil Croft had become part of his life.

Though she hadn't willed it, nor could ever consciously admit to something so blasphemous, Ruth Hoffman's death was the best thing that could have happened to Sybil. She hadn't planned this. When she'd volunteered to care for Ruth, she had done it out of sheer and honest compassion. She hadn't had any ulterior motives or seductive designs on Jonas. She was as surprised as he when she realized how close they had become, probably more so because attracting the interest of someone as wonderful as Jonas Hoffman fell under the category of "wildest dreams." Men as handsome as Jonas never looked twice at women as plain as she. The miracle was that under these circumstances Jonas hadn't been looking, he had been listening and feeling and accepting help from a warm, outstretched hand. He had gotten to know the soul of Sybil Croft, which was where her real beauty lay.

They didn't live together, and when they slept together, it was always at Sybil's house, and Jonas never stayed the night. Jonas would never sleep with another woman in Ruth's bed and never move another woman into Ruth's house. Sybil understood and respected his feelings. She also understood that until his children's lives were settled, Jonas would remain their father first, her lover second. She never pressed for more because she was overwhelmed by what she had.

Although Sybil and Jonas were a source of some interest to Isabelle on this

occasion, she couldn't help but focus most of her attention on Sam. In her
eyes he got more gorgeous every day. About six feet two, with a deftly planed
face, hooded brown eyes that crinkled when he laughed, a generous mouth,
and a smile that killed, he had a body that seemed designed to make the most
out of a pair of blue jeans and a T-shirt. Sitting across from him as she was
now was pure torture. When he spoke to her, it was a struggle not to blush.
When he spoke to someone else, she hung on his every word, trying to look
nonchalant, praying that her expression was interested rather than wor-
shipful.

Shy and uncomfortable in boy-girl situations, Isabelle didn't have the
vaguest idea how to flirt. Despite the acknowledged expertise of both Martín
and Althea in the attraction of opposites, that talent was not necessarily a
genetic trait, and whatever tricks of the trade Isabelle might have observed,
she had been too young to harvest. At nearly fifteen, too serious to be co-
quettish, too unsophisticated to be a siren, she could do little more than
retreat and wait for some miracle to occur that would get Sam to notice her
without her having to embarrass herself in the process. In the absence of said
miracle, she suffered in silence.

Not only was Nina keenly aware of Isabelle's enduring crush, but secretly
she delighted in it, and had for a long time. Though that made her feel guilty,
since the accident Nina had had a difficult time retuning her emotions. On
one level she recognized that her animosity was irrational, that Isabelle
hadn't been responsible for her injuries or for her precarious financial situation. She also acknowledged how supportive Isabelle had been—insisting
upon contributing her after-school wages to the cause, filling in for Nina at
La Casa whenever necessary, comforting Nina whenever she fretted. Yet
on another level Nina couldn't help feeling stranded and beleaguered and
put upon.

This past year had been hard. Aside from the constant quest for money,
she had studied harder than ever, taking extra honor courses while cramming for her SATs and achievement tests. She'd spent hours filling out college applications, struggling to write the perfect essay. And then she'd spent
months waiting nervously for responses. It was done now, and she had been
an unqualified success. She had been accepted at Boston University, New
York University, the University of New Mexico, and the University of Colorado, with full scholarships offered at each.

So why didn't she feel completely triumphant? Why wasn't she thrilled to
be surrounded by family and friends, all of whom insisted on showering her
with undiluted praise? Why wasn't this evening perfect? Because what she

had achieved had served to remind her of what she lacked. Scholarships were granted on the basis of need, providing money to the have-nots. True, she had proven herself worthy of the investment, but like a glaring error on an exam, being funded seemed to mark Nina down, to brand her as having less than her fellow students. All her life Nina had fought against that notion of being "different from" or "not as good as" everyone else. To think that she had applied for the label struck her as painfully ironic.

Glancing across the table, she caught sight of her reflection in a mirror. Nina had always banked on her looks. Tall, blond, strikingly beautiful—to her, acknowledgment of those facts was not vanity, but rather an accurate accounting of her assets. She had always believed that beauty and personality were all it took to get what she wanted out of life. Applying to college had shattered that perception. All the admissions offices wanted were grades, averages, and a brief essay. No one had asked to see how pretty she was or to find out how bewitching she could be. No one felt it necessary to have her display her sense of fashion or her witty repartee about Hollywood. While obviously she had met their academic standards and fulfilled their requirements, having something as important as her future depend on substance rather than style was a new experience for Nina.

Still, she thought, indulging in a moment of self-admiration, it didn't hurt to have one's statistics wrapped in a glorious package. Especially when competing in that dog-eat-dog, boy-girl arena, where more often than not first impressions were everything.

As if to reassure herself of her superiority, she looked at Rebecca, who was laughing with her father. Dark haired and dark eyed, she was pretty, incredibly brainy, lean of body, and possessed of a certain insouciant charm; but she wasn't the type who would ever be in the final five of any beauty pageant. Isabelle, on the other hand, was wearing a lipstick red sundress that exposed her delicately tanned skin. She looked positively striking. Her long brown hair hung straight down her back, a luxurious cascade of chocolate silk that fell to her waist. Unadorned except for a pair of thin silver hoop earrings and minus all cosmetics save a touch of lip gloss, she exuded a clean, almost primitive beauty.

Again, feeling a bit guilty, Nina admitted she had liked it better when Isabelle played the duckling to her swan. Like it or not, that was changing. Nature was doing an admirable job of correcting itself. Where once Isabelle's nose had jutted from her face and seemed a size too large, it now formed a graceful center, sloping down from those large, enigmatic brown-green eyes to lips that had once looked plump but could now be described as ripe. Isabelle's overbite had made her look funny when she was younger. Lately it had begun to look intriguing, even sexy. Though still shorter than Nina, Isabelle had grown, and her body, once quite spindly, had begun to describe itself in softer, more curvaceous terms. She still had too many youthful overtones to be seductive, but Nina's imagination was keen enough to know that soon Isabelle was going to be stunning.

Not that she needed anything to underline her observation, but suddenly Nina realized that while she had been daydreaming, Sam had engaged Isabelle in an animated conversation about the difference between art and craft. They were smiling and laughing and quite obviously enjoying themselves. In an odd fit of jealousy, Nina deliberately interrupted. Leaning over, she whispered in his ear, "I'm ready. Are you?"

In less than five minutes they were out of the restaurant and on their way to their favorite motel, leaving the adults smiling self-consciously and shrugging their shoulders at the impetuosity of youth, Rebecca griping about their rudeness, and Isabelle wishing she knew what Nina had that she didn't.

In July and August, when the sun was a ball of flame all day, heating one's blood to a near boil, there was nothing Nina liked better than being naked in the wilderness. It was so primitive, so free, so naughty. Everything about it was a turn-on. Working up a sweat getting there, stripping off her clothes, quaffing beer and eating sandwiches in the nude, sunbathing on a rock, and then making love in the great out-of-doors—it was one of the pleasures of living in the Southwest, one she would miss when she moved to the city.

Many times during that summer, she and Sam packed a sleeping bag and a picnic basket into his Jeep and headed north to a clearing on a hilltop just past Tesuque. They had found this spot the year before when they had been out hiking. The climb had taken more than an hour and a half through uncleared forest floor and scraggly brush, but when they'd looked out and seen Santa Fe Baldy in the distance, both had decided the effort had been worth it.

As with much of New Mexico's scenic splendors, there was an unreal quality to the mesa spread before them. Separated by miles of lowland, seeming to spring up from nowhere, it appeared fake, as if a backdrop had been put into place by a crafty photographer who, if the customer wanted, could just as easily have provided a tropical isle or a frozen tundra. Rough hewn yet eerily precise, squat yet majestic, Santa Fe Baldy rose above the flat with an aura of dominance. Thickets of dark green trees and shrubs outlined its base, the timberline thinning dramatically as these monuments of rock rose higher in the sky. Bands of color formed stripes along the wide expanse, making it look like a layered ice-cream cake that had been cut in half, its artistic rainbow proudly displayed.

That day, while the sun continued to dapple the trees around them with yellow, the blue above Baldy had grayed with the onset of a thunderstorm. A bolt of white lightning seared the sky. Nina and Sam waited for the roar of the thunder, but the sound didn't travel the road that led to them. Again electricity pierced the sky. Again there was a soundless response.

Sam slid his arms around Nina's waist, feeling the moistness of her shirt and the warmth of her skin. She leaned against him, pressing her body to his. There was something erotic about standing in a place bathed in unremitting heat, knowing that in the distance that heat was being dispelled by a violent downpour. Intrigued, slightly mesmerized, they watched nature's show in respectful silence.

A sudden breeze intruded on the stillness. Though it cooled their flesh, it reminded each of the other's nearness and inflamed their passion. Without changing positions, Sam unbuttoned Nina's shirt and unhooked her bra. Without removing her clothes, he moved his hands up on her chest and cupped her breasts. His lips sought the back of her neck, licking the tiny beads of sweat that had dampened her skin. Nina wriggled against him. She loved being touched and rubbed and stroked. When Sam's hands were on her, it was probably the only time she allowed herself to relax her hard-edged pose. Sam reveled in the unaccustomed softness, reigning in his own needs while he lost himself in fulfilling hers.

As his fingers slid down into her shorts, Nina closed her eyes and let her body respond to the sensations that were beginning to overwhelm her. Her breath caught in her throat as his tongue followed the curve of her shoulder, up her neck and into the hollow of her ear. Her heart pounded as his hands traced the V of her groin, flickering against her skin in a gentle tease, massaging her lightly yet deliberately as he wended his way to where the throbbing had already begun. Adrenaline coursed through her as she felt the power of his own arousal press against her. Quickly her hands moved behind her and freed him. He was hot and strong and pulsing with needing her, yet still she didn't turn around. They remained standing back to front, touching and playing and tormenting each other until neither had any control left. They fell to the ground, mindless of the twigs and rocks and leaves that lay beneath them, and came together with the same fury as the storm that raged so many miles away.

Afterward, exhausted yet exhilarated, they realized they had made love without a condom. It was the one and only time, yet Nina panicked. The last thing she needed was an unwanted pregnancy. Living through the weeks until her next period were agonizing, but when it came and she and Sam knew they were safe, they returned to that hilltop, claiming it as their private place and nicknaming it the Erogenous Zone.

Naturally it was the setting Nina chose for their farewell party. It was the third week of August. Sam was leaving for medical school the next day. She was leaving the day after that. Because it was the last time they would be alone, she had planned a very special afternoon. Instead of beer, she was going to bring wine and champagne; instead of sandwiches, a basket from the gourmet shop. And instead of Sam's grubby sleeping bag, she had decided on a fluffy down comforter, which she intended to cover with a satin sheet she had stored inside the cooler (something she had read in *Cosmopolitan*).

The one thing she wasn't going to do—couldn't do—was give him what he wanted most—a change of mind about attending New York University in favor of Boston University. As much as she loved him and as tempting as it was to know that in Boston they would be near each other, New York City was where it was happening, and New York City was where she was headed.

Sam kept telling her she didn't know anyone in New York. What she couldn't tell Sam was, that was part of the lure. Though she could never explain it to him in a way he'd understand—she wasn't sure she understood it herself—with Sam she'd have to be who she was. With strangers she could be whoever she wanted to be.

She knew something like that sounded odd, but all summer she had been plagued by conundrums such as that. On the one hand, Sam was her link to who and what she was, yet a part of her had always longed to be someone else. The loyalty he had shown her, the honesty they shared, the experiences—everything that made her feel secure with Sam was everything that suddenly confused her about her relationship with Sam. He had loved her when she was only fifteen, he loved her now, he would love her tomorrow. But was that a positive or a negative? As strong as the pull was to maintain her ties to him, that was how powerful the tug was to cut those strings and run free.

Even today, when she couldn't wait to see him, couldn't wait to wrap her arms around him and make love to him and feel his body all over hers, even today she couldn't wait for the rest of her life to begin.

CHAPTER 9

It was nine o'clock. Nina was about to leave to pick up the basket of food she had ordered when she remembered she had left her camera at Enchantments. Whenever Miranda mounted a new exhibition, Nina photographed each of the paintings in case either an out-of-town customer wanted to see a favorite artist's latest offerings or a buyer wanted a picture of something they had purchased for their insurance files. Seeing that Miranda and Luis had appropriated both La Casa vehicles, Nina set out on foot.

It was a gorgeous morning, sunny and warm, with a cloudless sky and an occasional breeze. She could only imagine how exquisite it was going to be on top of their hill. Smiling with anticipation, she jogged up Canyon Road, enjoying the solitude. Soon cars and pedestrians would fight over who had the right of way and who was going to get to which gallery first, as if there were a limited supply of art and crafts and jewelry and Native American artifacts. She laughed as she made her way up the winding road.

Assuming the front door was still locked, she ran around to the back, letting herself into Miranda's office. Her camera was on Miranda's desk, just where she had left it. She was about to leave when she glanced through the interior window and spotted Isabelle and Sam in the gallery. They were sitting on the floor holding hands and talking, their faces close together, their expressions filled with emotion.

Nina was thunderstruck by the sight of them, especially by the intimacy of their pose. She tiptoed nearer yet hung back, anxious yet reluctant. Why were they here? What were they talking about? Why hadn't either of them called her? Insecurity collided with jealousy. They were so intense. Had they been seeing each other on the side?

"No," Nina whispered with disbelief. "Absolutely not!"

Two days ago she and Sam had made love. The way Sam had touched her and had responded when she touched him . . . It was impossible that the passion she had felt from him was insincere.

Pressing herself against the wall adjacent to the window, she surreptitiously peeked into the other room, just as she had when she was little and her favorite game had been spying on the customers. She had found it fun to listen to those who liked the exhibition discuss how they intended to bargain with Miranda or where they were going to hang their painting when they got it home. It was even more fun to listen to those who hated the show grouse about the prices, wonder aloud who would buy junk like this, and who, in fact, had had the nerve to decide it was art in the first place! But this wasn't fun. This was spying on her sister and her lover.

"I'm telling you that's what I heard. Exactly. Word for word." Though it sounded as if they were gossiping, Isabelle's voice was filled with pain.

Sam kneaded his forehead, something he did only when he was given terrible news. "Tell me again where you were, who they were, what they said."

"I was in the ladies' room at La Fonda. I had gone there to pick something up for Miranda. Two women came in. I recognized the voice of one of them. It was Moira Behart."

Nina curled her upper lip. Moira Behart! Ugh! she thought. I can't stand her.

"She and the other woman had just come from shopping at the Ranch, where they had seen Nina."

Shows how important they are. I never even noticed them, Nina reflected, wondering why Isabelle, who shared her dislike of Moira Behart, was so interested in anything she had to say.

"When they walked in, the other woman was saying, 'First, that horrible beginning. Then, that terrible accident.'

"Moira said, 'It's amazing how well she turned out, considering.' "

How well who turned out? Considering what?

"The other woman said, 'When you think about it, it's a miracle that Luis ever found her. I can't bear to think of what would have happened if he hadn't.' "

Luis found someone? Who? Where?

"What did Moira say?" Sam's voice sounded as if it were coming from the lowest octave in the bass clef.

Isabelle wiped her eyes. Sam reached out and petted her cheek. Nina stared at them through the glass.

" 'What kind of monster could throw a newborn baby away like a piece of garbage?' They were quiet for a minute or two, and then the other one said she thought Nina was a lucky little girl."

Nina didn't feel lucky. She felt sick. Much as she wanted to close her ears and run away, she couldn't. She needed to stay, to hear all there was to hear. Growing more frantic with each passing moment, she pressed tighter against the wall, straining to hear every syllable.

"She could have died in that trash can, Sam." Isabelle was crying. Sam wrapped his arms around her.

Nina felt as if the rope anchoring her to her mooring had just been cut.

"But she didn't die." Sam was stroking Isabelle's hair. "Luis and Miranda found her and adopted her. It's a happy ending to a terrible, terrible story."

Suddenly Isabelle pulled away. "Maybe it's not true. Maybe Moira was making it up."

Sam shook his head. Why was he shaking his head? Nina wondered.

"When I was ten and Nina was seven, I remember eavesdropping on my parents. They were talking about how Nina's adoption had become official and how happy they were for Miranda and Luis, how happy they were for Nina."

"Nina knows she's adopted. That doesn't mean . . ."

Again he rubbed his forehead and shook his head. "My father had been the doctor to examine Nina when Luis brought her in."

Nina felt numb, as if she had been injected with ice. She couldn't move. She couldn't think. Then, suddenly adrenaline shot through her bloodstream and she couldn't do anything but run out the back door, down the hill toward La Casa. As she ran she kept replaying Isabelle and Sam's words over and over again.

Thrown away . . . garbage . . . monster . . . lucky . . . adopt.

Miranda's car was parked out front. Nina ran into the hotel, racing from room to room until she found her mother repotting some plants out by the fountain. Nina's face was flushed, she was dripping with sweat, and her heart was pounding.

"Nina, darling," Miranda said, wondering what had happened. "What's the matter? Are you all right?"

Nina stared at Miranda, as if seeing her for the first time.

"Did Papa find me in a trash can?"

Miranda was too stunned to prevent her body from recoiling.

"Then it's true." Nina's face blanched. The light left her eyes; gray turned to steel.

"Yes," Miranda said, her voice laden with reluctance. "It's true."

"Tell me!" Nina demanded. "Tell me everything!"

Seeing no alternative, Miranda acquiesced.

"Papa and I were going to attend the noon mass. We had brought coffee and doughnuts to the park next to the cathedral. When we finished, Papa went to throw the empty cups and the bag into the garbage when something made him stop." Miranda trembled as the scene replayed itself before her eyes. "He thought he heard a kitten crying."

Miranda's breath caught in her throat as she recalled Luis lifting the mewling infant from its filthy cradle. She could still see the pink sweater in which the child was wrapped, dotted with coffee and chocolate stains. Bits of paper sticky with honey or sugar clinging to the soiled fabric. The baby's hand was in its mouth, and it was sucking at its tiny fingers, whimpering when this produced neither nourishment nor comfort.

"At first we were so shocked at what we had discovered, we simply stood and stared, as if we were waiting for you to explain how you got into that horrible can. I remember how my hands shook when I took you from Papa." Tears dotted Miranda's cheeks, yet she smiled as she had smiled then, with a mix of wonderment and confusion. "Inside that makeshift bunting was a baby girl, naked and soiled, its umbilical cord tied with a shoestring." Miranda tried to gauge Nina's reaction, but the girl's face was as unreadable as stone.

"We rushed you to St. Vincent's where Dr. Jonas examined you. We also called the police." Miranda's voice dropped to a whisper. "It was God's will that we found you," she said, again reviewing that day's events as if she was recounting the miracles of the Bible. "We rarely attended the noon mass. But that day we did. The weather was rarely warm in February. But that day it was. There were other garbage cans around. Papa picked that one. Don't you see, Nina, you cried so Papa would find you. You chose us. And we chose you."

She went to embrace Nina, but her advance was repulsed. Nina didn't want affection, she wanted information.

"What happened next?"

"Jonas kept you in the hospital overnight. The police, after a fairly thorough investigation, concluded that the . . . your . . . mother had given birth to you on her own, probably in the train station. They were fairly certain she skipped town soon after."

Nina winced, but Miranda sensed she wanted to hear all of it and so she complied.

"The police arranged for you to be released in our care while they continued to try and locate your mother." It pained Miranda to refer to anyone else as Nina's mother. "We called you *niña*—little girl—afraid that if we gave you another name, we would be tempting the fates to take you away. While we prayed your mother would come to her senses and claim you, we prayed just as hard that she wouldn't so we could keep you for ourselves. It was nearly a year before Social Services named us as your official foster parents." Miranda looked deep into Nina's eyes, begging her to try and understand. "It was the happiest day of our lives."

A thick curtain of silence hung between them. Miranda didn't know what else to say, and so she waited. Nina didn't speak either, but it was clear that she was growing more and more agitated.

"My real mother threw me away. Like I was nothing. Like I was trash."

"Don't say that."

"Why not? Other people say it."

"Who? What other people?"

People I loved and believed in. People I trusted. People who betrayed me. "It doesn't matter. Why didn't you tell me?"

Nina's voice was rising. Her body was trembling. Miranda moved toward her. Nina shrank back, fending her off.

"I intended to," Miranda said, "someday."

"I don't believe you!" Nina shouted, her face flushed bright crimson.

"It's true." Miranda wanted to defend herself, but she could see that something terrible was happening to Nina. "Papa and I love you," she insisted, hoping to stave off whatever storm was coming. "We never wanted you to be hurt."

"Then why did you lie to me? Why did you tell me I was special? That God sent me to you?"

"That wasn't a lie. You are special. And to Papa and me, you are a gift from God."

"What about the other part? About the garbage can? Is that true?" Nina's color had gone from red to chalk. Her eyes remained fixed on Miranda. Her tremors had grown more pronounced. "Or is that something else you made up?"

Before Miranda could issue a denial, Nina's posture changed, her expression changed. It was as if she had retreated, momentarily losing herself in thought. Her eyes moved off Miranda, roaming the garden, searching for someone or something.

"You did make it up," she said, suddenly pointing a finger at Miranda and raving. "You're getting paid to keep me, just like you're getting paid to keep Isabelle, aren't you? Did my real parents die like Isabelle's or did they go away someplace? Did they leave you money in their wills? Do you get a check every month? Or do I have a trust fund you never told me about?" Miranda let her rave. "Sure, don't answer. I understand. You don't want anyone to know. You want them to think you're this saintlike person. But you're not. You made up the story about the trash can to cover up a secret trust fund, didn't you?" She shook her finger at Miranda. "Sure! I work my ass off and you live off the money my parents left me!"

"No. There is no secret trust fund. No one is paying us to keep you," Miranda said, praying Luis would appear and help her. "You're our daughter. We love you."

"I'm not your daughter. You said so."

"Please," Miranda pleaded. "Don't say that. We're a family."

"No! You made up that awful story and told everybody."

"I didn't."

"Then why did Isabelle and Sam say those things? Are they lying?"

Isabelle and Sam? Miranda was frantic. She wanted to know how they found out, how Nina found out. She wanted to say yes that they were lying just to end this nightmare, to erase what Nina had heard, but she couldn't do that. As bravely as she could, she faced the child she thought of as her own.

"The story is true. Papa and I found you in a trash can next to the cathedral. People know about it because the police asked a lot of questions when they were searching for your mother. They looked for her for a long time, but they couldn't find her." Miranda was crying now. "We loved you from the minute we laid eyes on you. And you loved us, Nina. I'm your mama. Luis is your papa. We're a family. What happened in the past, what was said or wasn't said, it doesn't matter."

Nina heard none of it. All she heard was that everyone knew something about her that she didn't; all she felt was pain and humiliation, two feelings that, from then on she would always associate with truth.

Nina spun on her heels and ran into the house, slamming the door behind her. For a long time, Miranda stood at the fountain, feeling the spray of water against her face, staring at the spot where moments before Nina had stood and demanded the truth. She had no idea why this had happened or what would happen next, but she knew that things would never be the same—for any of them.

Luis found her sitting on her bed, staring vacantly out the window. He approached her slowly, not wanting to startle her. From what Miranda had told him, Nina had been startled enough to last a lifetime.

"Mama told me you had a rough morning." Gently, stroking her hair with his fingertips, he sought to make contact and open discussion. If they didn't talk this out now, the problem would multiply and, like an infestation, grow and spread until it was completely beyond control. "I'm sorry you had to find out this way."

Without turning to face him, Nina said, "Then why didn't you tell me yourself?" Her voice sounded hollow, as if she had just finished sweeping the last of her emotions out of her soul, cleansing herself of anything and everything that had even a remote chance of hurting her.

"I should have." Luis waited for her to agree with him. She said nothing, just stared out the window at the open space beyond the boundaries of La Casa. "I suppose Mama and I felt that how you came to us wasn't as important as what you meant to us. You're our entire world, Nina. In your heart, you have to know that."

Her silence grew louder. Luis clasped his hands in front of him, prayerlike. For several moments he withdrew, trying to find the right words. They could never go back to what they had been before this revelation, he knew that; but he was certain that if he could get past Nina's anger and disbelief and the shock, he would be able to find the path to her heart and open it again.

"You were crying," he said. "When I picked you up, you stopped. You were trembling, sucking on your hand, gulping for air, but when Mama took you in her arms and held you close, your whole body quieted. You knew, Nina. You knew immediately how much we cared. You could feel it. Can't you feel how much I love you now?"

Nina felt nothing. She had come to her room to cry, but there had been no tears. There was no temper tantrum, no screaming, no throwing things across the room. There was nothing. She felt nothing, because she had nothing left. In those few minutes that she had eavesdropped on Isabelle and Sam, her dreams had died, her illusions were spent, and her sense of worth had been trampled. Not only had she discovered that her birth mother had disposed of her like yesterday's trash, but Isabelle, the girl who claimed to be her sister, had discovered this heinous secret and, instead of coming to her, had gone to Sam. Sam, the man who professed to be her lover, had known about this for years and had never said anything. They had betrayed her, and she would never forgive them.

"Nina. Talk to me. Tell me what you're thinking, how you're feeling. Please, baby. Let me help you."

Slowly she faced him. Her eyes were flinty and cold. Her jaw was tight, the veins in her neck strained.

"And how are you going to help me? Are you going to put an ad in the newspaper telling everyone in town to forget what they know and to believe the pretty little lies you've fed me all these years?"

Luis shook his head. "No, but Nina, as upsetting as this was for you to hear and as ugly as it sounds, it's not topic A on everyone's gossip list. People haven't been whispering about this behind your back every single day of your life."

"Well, they sure were doing a great job of it yesterday and today. Yesterday Isabelle overheard Moira Behart talking about it in the ladies' room at La Fonda. Today Isabelle and Sam were talking about it at Enchantments. For all I know, tomorrow there's going to be a town meeting in the plaza to discuss the circumstances of Nina Duran's birth." Sarcasm and disgust outlined her words.

"Okay. So Moira Behart brought it up. Isabelle overheard her and discussed it with Sam. It was talk. That's all. Just talk."

Nina bounded off the bed like a spring that had been held down too long. "Talk! That's all it was? Talk!" She was verging on hysteria, but Luis could do nothing to stem it. "They were talking about me, discussing something I didn't know about me. Something important. Like how I was born and thrown away and plucked out of a garbage can like an unread newspaper. To me, that's not just talk!"

"Do they think that the woman who gave birth to you is awful?" Luis said, raising his voice to a level to match hers, demanding that now she listen to him. "Yes! And well they should. Do they think less of you? No. And why? Because there's no reason to. You're a wonderful, bright, beautiful young woman who's given me, your mother, your sister, and everyone in Santa Fe a thousand reasons to be proud!"

Nina was shaking, her eyes wide and wild. "You don't understand," she said. "This changes everything."

"How? Why? What does it change? You're still the same person you were when you woke up this morning."

Nina shook her head and held out her hands, staving off his onslaught of words, rejecting the reasoning behind them. How could he possibly understand? Luis saw the outer Nina. He had never seen her grand visions or her exalted aspirations. He had never crawled inside her skin and touched her wishes of being a star or a queen or a woman of stature. If he had, he would have known that to realize those dreams, she believed she had to rise above being the daughter of Spanish-American innkeepers, above being working-class, above being adopted. That was mountain enough to climb. To rise above being a trash-can baby as well made even the smallest goal seem hopelessly out of reach.

"I'm not the same person," she said as mournfully as if she were speaking of the dead. "And neither are you."

"Maybe not." The arrow stung, but he accepted the blow.

"You shouldn't have lied to me. You should have told me the truth!"

"You're right. I should have, but I didn't. Now that you know, why won't you discuss it with Mama and me?"

Nina stared at him as if he had demanded she give him a formula to cure cancer on the spot. *You should have told me the truth. Talked about it. Discussed it. Dealt with the truth.* "I wish I'd never heard the truth!" Her chest heaved. Her body was trembling. Her own honesty had shocked her.

"I agree," Luis said. "I wish I could have spared you, but whether we like it or not, the truth has a way of coming out. And like toothpaste in a tube, once it's out, you can't squeeze it back in."

Nina narrowed her eyes, looking at something Luis couldn't see. There, in front of her, were all her plans for the future, lying like kindling on the wreckage of what she had believed had been her past. Suddenly she knew she had a decision to make: either she could pick herself up and move on or she could throw herself on the pyre of what was.

"Maybe so," she said, turning to the window again, readjusting her sights and making new plans, "but I'm sure as hell going to try."

Sam had thought a lot about Nina that summer, what it would mean to lose her, what it would take to keep her. One of the major differences between them—also one of the stronger attractions—had been that he was the scientific type, one who favored structure and the law of probability and control. She was more imaginative, more open to experimentation and the vagaries of chance. She was beautiful and exciting and someone he believed had enormous potential. And while he recognized that she had every right to pursue her own dreams, in whatever city she felt they might be realized, he didn't relinquish ties easily. She had been the main character in an important chapter in his life; he had thought they would write the next chapter together.

As he drove to La Casa to pick her up, awash in a wave of nostalgia, he tried to dismiss his concerns over his early morning conversation with Isabelle. When she had called him the night before and said she had to speak to him about something urgent, he hadn't taken her seriously. He had thought she wanted to talk about his pressuring Nina to go to Boston. If Isabelle was anything, she was fiercely overprotective. When she'd told him it was about Nina's birth, his blood had chilled.

He had known about Nina for years. Aside from the conversation he had overheard between his parents, when he had begun dating Nina in earnest, he had asked his father if what he had heard was true. When Jonas had confirmed it, he'd reminded Sam it was not something that needed ever to be discussed. Sam hadn't, until that morning. And when he and Isabelle had finished, he had told her the same thing Jonas had told him: Leave it be.

Nina seemed more reserved than usual when he picked her up, but he attributed that to the sadness that always accompanied their good-byes. He might have focused on her mood more closely, except that once they reached their mountaintop, he had other things on his mind.

Nina hadn't planned a picnic; she had created a bacchanal, complete with wine from a skin, sugared grapes, and his favorite opera blaring from a tape deck. Against the magnificence of a late summer day, they feasted on buffet culinary treats and each other, neither of them willing to break the sensual spell that enveloped them with something as unsatisfying as talk. They had been lovers for nearly three years yet still managed to invent new ways to arouse and pleasure each other. When finally they were sated, Sam popped the cork on the champagne and offered a toast.

"To us," he said. "And our future."

He drank. Nina didn't. After Luis had left her room, she had debated whether or not to cancel her afternoon with Sam. But if she did, she would have to explain why, which was something she didn't want to do. Why listen to phony excuses about why he had never told her what he knew, why he had been willing to discuss the intimate details of her birth with someone other than her, why he hadn't included her in his discussion? It was obvious—it wasn't important enough, she wasn't important enough. It was okay to take her out and show her off, it was okay to sleep with her, but it wasn't okay to be honest with her. Well, she had decided, one good turn deserved another.

"I'm not going to Boston," she said with a ring of finality.

"That's definite?"

"Yes. I don't know whether I'm going to be an actress or a writer or what, but if I want to be big and important, and I do, New York's the place."

"What about us? I thought you loved me. I thought we had something going here."

With a toss of her long blond hair and a hollow laugh, she said, "You're great, Sam, and it's been fun, but we're history. You're a terrific lay, a good friend, and one hell of a nice guy, but you know what they say about nice guys."

Stunned by her harshness, suddenly angry, Sam stared at her, his face turned suddenly hard. "And you think I'm going to finish last, is that it?"

"Your big goal is to heal the sick of Santa Fe," she said as if that were an absurd idea.

"You could do worse."

"I intend to do better. Much better!"

"Really?"

"Really." She rose to her feet and stared down at him. "You may not think so, but I'm going to be famous."

"Doing what?" he said, coating his voice with incredulity.

"I don't know yet, but one thing's for sure. It'll be something a hell of a lot more exciting than being Mrs. Sam Hoffman, country doctor's wife and humble hausfrau!"

With that, she turned and started down the hill. As she climbed into the car and waited for him to follow, she congratulated herself.

"Now he knows how it feels to be used," she said, her voice blending the sting of resentment and the contentment that came from retaliation. "Now he knows how it feels to be disposable."

When Nina walked into the sitting room of the Durans' private quarters, Miranda, Luis, and Isabelle were waiting for her.

"I was beginning to worry," Miranda said, starting for Nina, then stopping when Nina's expression told her an embrace wouldn't be welcome.

"No need."

Isabelle had been stunned when Miranda had told her that Nina had been at the gallery that morning and had heard every word she and Sam had said. She'd tried to find Nina to explain, to apologize, to do whatever was necessary to make things right, but Nina had gone. The girl at the front desk said she remembered Nina leaving with Sam Hoffman. "How was your afternoon with Sam?" she said now with artificial brightness.

"Hot." Nina underlined the word, making certain Isabelle had understood that she was not giving a weather report.

Isabelle backed away. Nina was hurt and angry. Isabelle wished there was something she could say or do, but Nina had to be willing to listen, and just then she appeared to be fresh out of patience.

"Come," Miranda said, trying to gather them around the table. "Dinner's ready."

"I'm not hungry."

"I made all your favorites." Miranda forced a laugh. "We're having Christmas dinner in August!"

"I'm not eating it now, and I won't be eating it at Christmas."

"Why not?" Luis asked, disturbed by her unequivocal tone.

"Because I'm not coming home for Christmas," Nina said. "When I leave here tomorrow, I'm gone."

"I don't understand." Miranda understood all too well, yet she needed to hear Nina say whatever it was she had to say.

"It's simple. I'm going to New York and I'm starting over. Whatever was, was!"

"And that includes all of us." Isabelle's sympathy was waning. Nina was being awful. She had assumed her Katharine Hepburn pose, neck straight, shoulders square, head high and tilted back ever so slightly. Isabelle wanted to smack her.

"Yes," Nina said. "It does."

"How can you say that?" Miranda asked, hurt and confused. "This is your home. We're your family. We love you. You can't simply cut us out."

Nina started for the door. "Yes, I can."

Miranda and Luis remained in the living room, staring at uneaten dinners and empty chairs. Isabelle followed Nina to their room, slamming the door behind her.

"Look! You want to be angry at someone, be angry at me."

Nina looked at Isabelle with eyes that flamed with hostility. "I'm not angry. I passed angry hours ago. I'm into furious."

"Fine! Be furious, but be furious with me, not them."

"I hadn't realized the church was having a fire sale on halos and wings," Nina said, her tone laced with sarcasm. "First we have the Holy Mother and Father, those God-fearing, selfless souls who plucked the child of a sinner from the jaws of hell. And now we have Holy Sister Do-Good, protector of frauds and impostors. Is everyone in this household, except me, a Vatican-certified saint?"

"How can you be so cruel?"

"Life is cruel."

"They're your parents."

"In name only."

"Stop it, Nina. They're your parents and have been since the day you were born. They've loved you and fed you and cared about you, and instead of thanking them, you just blew them off as if they were complete strangers. You should be ashamed!"

Nina laughed. "Well, I'm not, so get over yourself and spare me your grateful child routine. They're not my parents. And you're not my sister."

"We may not be blood," Isabelle said, softening her tone, "but I love you as if we were sisters."

Nina's eyes hardened. "Sisters don't talk about each other behind each other's backs. Sisters don't try to steal the other one's boyfriend. And sisters don't do *this* to one another!" She raised her knee and thrust her scarred leg at Isabelle.

"It was an accident." Isabelle reeled, stunned by the force of Nina's attack. "I fell. You fell on top of me. I didn't do it on purpose. Why would I? I would never do anything to hurt you. You know that."

"I don't know anything of the sort," Nina hissed.

Isabelle threw up her hands. "Okay, yes, I overheard something terrible about you. Yes, I went to Sam, but only because I was confused and scared and didn't know who else to go to." Nina's face was frozen in a mask of hate. Isabelle feared there was nothing she could say to precipitate a thaw, but she continued to try. "I wasn't chasing Sam. I was talking to him as a friend, mine and yours. And as for that"—Isabelle pointed at Nina's leg—"it was an accident."

"Yeah, right!" She laughed, but it was void of humor. "Like it was an accident of birth that you knew your parents and I didn't . . . that you have a castle in Spain and I live above the store . . . that you have a bank account to pay for your education and I have to scrounge for every stinking dime . . . that you're an heiress with aristocratic relatives and I'm . . . well, I don't know what I am!"

"You're Nina Duran, Miranda and Luis's daughter," Isabelle insisted, annoyed at Nina's display of self-pity. "They love you. Why must you break their hearts? Can't you just kiss them good-bye, tell them you love them, and leave on a high note?"

"It would be a lie, and unlike the rest of this so-called family, I tell it like it is." She threw the last few items from her closet into the open suitcase on her bed and slammed it shut.

Isabelle snorted in disgust. "Gee. All these years I thought I was living with Nina Duran. Now I found out you're really George Washington. Wow! I'm impressed." She snickered.

The sound acted like a detonator on a bomb. "Laugh all you want," Nina seethed, allowing hostilities she had kept buried to erupt in a burst of red hot anger. "But one of these days you will be impressed. Because one of these days—in the not-so-distant future—I'm going to be the big shot and you're going to be the also-ran! I'm going to be someone and you're going to be nothing!"

"Don't hold your breath," Isabelle retorted, her own anger clearly displayed.

"Mark my words," Nina taunted. "It's going to happen. And when it does, Señorita de Luna, we'll see just how noble you really are!"

With that, Nina grabbed her suitcases and stormed out of the house.

Two days later Nina was where she wanted to be—in New York City. She spent her first afternoon exploring her new neighborhood, starting with Washington Square Park and branching out from there. She prowled the funky clothing boutiques on Bleecker Street and the charming antique shops on Twelfth Street. She spent an hour amid the crowded tables and jammed bookshelves of the Strand, studying the attitude and aspect of everyone there, and grabbed coffee at a dingy, smoke-filled luncheonette she was certain had a poet in every booth.

She was on her way back to the dorm when she passed a small store that looked as if it were a cross between an antique shop and a junk wagon. There seemed to be as much merchandise outside the store as in, with everything from a Thonet rocker to a crystal chandelier to a bowl of buttons crammed onto the limited stretch of sidewalk that fronted their window.

Intrigued by the display, Nina scouted the items on top of the table and then rummaged through the boxes under the table. From those boxes she picked out a lovely old cameo tagged at ten dollars, a pair of ecru lace gloves at two dollars, an ivory hair comb for fifty cents, and a silver brush and comb set for twelve fifty. She had gathered everything up and was about to go inside to total her purchases when she spotted a portrait of an elegant blond woman and a large man with dark hair and green eyes tucked between the rocker and the window. Judging by the pose—the begowned and bejeweled woman on a velvet chair, the man in formal attire standing behind her, his hand on her shoulder, her hands folded in her lap—and the gilded frame, it probably had graced the wall above someone's fireplace. If the jewels were real, Nina guessed that the wall might have been one of many in a mansion, either on Long Island or in Newport or on a plantation down south, or maybe even somewhere in England.

She didn't know why, but she felt drawn to the portrait. Carefully she eased it out front, lifted it onto the table, and studied the faces of the couple whose likenesses had been rendered in oil. Who were they? she wondered. Were they wealthy socialites or the figment of some artist's imagination? Had this hung in their home? How had the owner of this store gotten hold of it? Were these people dead, alive, down on their luck, or just on to bigger and better portraits? Giving in to an impulse she couldn't explain and paying a price she couldn't justify, Nina took the portrait and her other goodies back to her room, where she hung the large painting above her bed. That night she sat at the end of her bed for the longest time, staring up at the stiff couple in the portrait, trying to commune with them. It was just before she fell off to sleep that she realized why she had been so taken with them—the resemblance was vague, but in a way they looked like Martín and Althea.

The next day her roommate moved in. When she looked at the painting and asked who the glamorous couple was, Nina answered with a smile and a voice full of conviction.

"My parents."

The rest of her life had begun.

CHAPTER 10

Santa Fe, 1974

If anyone had asked Isabelle when she'd decided to be an artist, she would have answered, "The day I was born." Though she never consciously made the decision to make art her life's work, it had always been the outlet that had allowed her life to work. Filling a blank piece of paper with color or covering a canvas with an image gave her such immense, indefinable pleasure that nothing could compete with it.

Art was her best friend. It provided her with company when she was lonely, entertainment when she was bored, a catharsis when she was troubled. As her most trusted companion, one that accepted ramblings and allowed mistakes, it became an outlet for her psychic musings.

Though she had a curious mind and a keen intellect, Isabelle functioned emotionally; her responses were born of feelings and instincts rather than analysis and introspection. By visualizing her thoughts and giving them dimension, they attained a reality she was able to confront and assess. Often, while her paintings evolved, a subliminal examination was going on, of insecurities or petty jealousies or pockets of doubt or secret delights. The colors would change, the brush strokes would vary, the composition of the painting would shift. Her hand moved according to an inner rhythm tuned to the part of one's soul that existed at a depth beyond the reach of the conscious mind.

Her earliest portfolio showed a child in a clash with her existence, struggling with cataclysmic upheavals. Then her output had consisted mainly of disjointed sketches, thick lines, crowded spaces, deep, dense colors, and a marked absence of light. As she settled into her life in Santa Fe and denial gave way to acceptance, she returned to pastels and began to allow light to insinuate itself. When Miranda introduced her to the badlands, the vistas were so extraordinary and the shadings of nature so remarkable, she copied more than she invented yet, even so, managed to achieve striking originality with her unusual use of color.

In her next phase she moved away from the figurative, relying on abstractions and light and shadow, as well as color, to express herself. This change in style coincided with the time just after Nina left home and Sam and Rebecca went off to school. Though Isabelle had other friends, she was experiencing a new round of feelings, some so deep and intense that they could not be interpreted through objects. She felt somewhat adrift on the sea between childhood and womanhood. Some days her mouth hurt from smiling all day, giggling with the girls about the nonsense only adolescents found funny. Other days weighed so heavily that she couldn't raise a smirk, let alone a smile. She was surrounded by admirers and lonely at the same time, happy with her life yet questioning the meaning of it, looking forward to graduating from high school, panicked at the thought of moving on.

For years people had inferred that Isabelle had been gifted with extraordinary ability. Though she deflected that sort of praise with sincere expressions of modesty, she couldn't help but internalize the notion that she possessed the seeds of greatness. She was not unaware of the quality of her work; in fact, there were times that she was awed by what she was able to produce. Yet the thought nagged at her that she was the big fish in the small pond, the shining star in a limited galaxy. Her work had never been viewed by anyone outside of Santa Fe (Flora didn't count). While she didn't dispute the credentials of the gallery owners along Canyon Road who had juried her work, she feared that their opinions had been influenced by their friendship with Miranda and/or Sybil. The real question was, How would she fare alongside artists who had trained in Europe or New York or Chicago?

It was a point she raised one afternoon in April when she and Miranda were going through their Friday ritual of cleaning the family apartment and preparing the evening meal. It was one of the Duran customs Isabelle enjoyed the most, having an early dinner and then spending a quiet evening at home. With everyone so busy, Miranda and Luis claimed they needed one night with no distractions, one night when they could sit and listen and catch up on what was happening with each of them.

That Wednesday Isabelle had given Miranda a small painting as a birthday gift. Luis had hung it over the fireplace in their living room, across from one of the three paintings Althea had left with them so many years before. It would have been impossible not to have compared the work of mother and daughter; so, detaching themselves as best they could, Isabelle and Miranda did.

Althea's painting, the third in a nativity trilogy, was called *The Holy Ghost* and depicted a moonlit canyon that did indeed look as if it could have been home to sacred spirits.

Blue predominated, ranging from the pale tint of a tear to the eerie pitch of a bottomless well. Geometric shapes transformed themselves into rock formations that spanned the canvas, separating the navy sky from the white desert floor. Squares lay on their sides. Rectangles jutted up toward the blackest part of night. Triangles projected pointy crags into the mysterious vastness. Shaded with burgundy and pink and mauve, the boulders grew darker as they moved farther into the shadow of the moon, a single luminescent circle shining like a perfect pearl in an ebony vault.

Isabelle had harnessed the colors of dawn. A hot sky burned yellow from the sun. Mountains sizzled in the heat, glowing with fuchsia-and-violet-and-crimson peaks. A shallow river sliced through the rock, the water in its bed simmering with livid shades of lavender. Infused with an aura of triumph that radiated from the sultry floor of an awakening earth to the feverish heaven of a rising sun, the painting was just as much a paean to the everyday miracle of a new beginning.

"It excites me," Miranda said, looking up at it, her arms akimbo, her dust cloth momentarily idle. "I can feel my blood racing even now."

Isabelle hugged her. "I'm so glad you like it."

Miranda returned the embrace. "I think your mother was right when she said that Flora had won the battle of the genes. Your use of color is exceptional."

"You're prejudiced."

"No, I'm not."

Isabelle laughed. "Are you going to try to tell me you're objective where my art is concerned? Or that Sybil has an unbiased eye?"

"We try," Miranda said, conceding the point. "But it doesn't take a New York art critic to recognize talent."

Isabelle's forehead wrinkled.

"What's the matter?"

"Who's to say how a New York critic defines talent?"

"That's a good question," Miranda said, watching her ward carefully. "Sybil is coming for dinner tonight, why don't we ask her?"

Isabelle agreed, but as she finished setting the table, she had the feeling that Miranda and Sybil had anticipated the question and had already prepared an answer.

"Many critics believe raw talent is simply the ability to translate one's creative impulses into something visual," Sybil said, pausing in between forkfuls of Miranda's special chicken and rice. "The consensus seems to be that greatness comes only to those whose talents are augmented by intense dedication, a mind open to inspiration, and, most of all, an unquenchable passion to create. You have an abundance of all three, Isabelle."

"So what am I supposed to do? Just keep painting until someone discovers me?"

Luis and Miranda exchanged glances across the table. Isabelle had been correct: this dinner had an agenda.

"Yes and no," Sybil said. "Yes, you should continue painting, but not in a vacuum. As you know, I'm a big believer in technique. When skill becomes second nature, creativity has a free hand."

"I sense a message here." Isabelle eyed her mentor. "What is it you're trying to say?"

Sybil struggled with her emotions, wondering why doing what was right for someone else so often necessitated inflicting pain on oneself.

"The time has come," she said, smothering her personal regret, "for the student to find a new teacher."

"Are you leaving Santa Fe?" Isabelle's face registered shock and dismay and confusion, all at once.

"No," Sybil said with a sly smile. "But we think you should."

Isabelle looked from Sybil to Miranda to Luis.

"We have conspired to make some inquiries on your behalf," Luis said, taking the lead.

"Where and why?"

"Miranda and I thought you seemed to be having trouble deciding what to do after graduation. Since it appears obvious that art is your calling, we asked Sybil about schools and tutors and what course would be the best for you to follow."

"And Sybil said . . . ?"

On her own, Isabelle had investigated colleges known for their fine art departments, like Bennington, Skidmore, and Yale, but they were expensive. The money Oscar Yount had invested for her might not cover four years at schools like those. Moreover, requirements like biology and algebra made her nervous. She had toyed with the idea of attending one of the art academies in Paris and, naturally, had given a great deal of thought to living with Tía Flora and continuing her studies in Barcelona now that she was no longer a minor. The only option she had not considered seriously was the one Sybil presented.

"For an artist," Sybil said matter-of-factly, "New York is the center of the world. It's where the galleries are and so many of the emerging artists are and where the critics are and where all the major exhibitions take place. It's where you have to be, Isabelle."

"New York?"

Despite Isabelle's international background, she thought of herself as a small-town girl, which was one of the reasons she had rejected the notion of moving there. New York frightened her. From the movies she had seen and the books she had read and the magazine articles she had studied, the metropolis loomed as something that needed to be conquered rather than somewhere one chose to live. While some of her fears might have been dispelled by Nina, no one had heard from her since she'd left. For all Isabelle knew, the monster that was New York had swallowed her up.

"There's a wonderful teacher at the Art Students League in New York named Ezra Edward Clark. He's quite insane and will work you until you plead for mercy, but he's a genius at bringing out the genius in others. I think he's the man to take your talent to the next level."

Sybil had just hit upon the second reason Isabelle had dismissed New York—the question of readiness. What level was she on? Where did she fit within the broad spectrum of those defined as having potential? Was she long on talent and short on technique? Or vice vera? Was she truly singular or one of many who simply believed she was? Should she train elsewhere before going to the mecca? Was she prepared for the competitiveness of New York? The cutthroat, all-consuming ambition that seemed to be a requirement for survival there? Isabelle believed in herself, but self-protection had become a way of life, emotional safety her chief consideration.

"Where would I live?" she said, her voice tentative, her body language an essay on uncertainty.

"I called a friend at the league," Sybil said. "They often get requests for information about living arrangements from out-of-town students, so they have a service that helps locate apartments for those who need them and match up roommates."

Isabelle nodded. *Apartment. Roommate. New York City.* Not that she wasn't grateful for Sybil's effort on her behalf, but the words sounded as appealing as *spaceship, alien, Mars.*

"Sounds great," she lied, knowing that what they were saying about why she had to go to New York was true, wishing she liked the idea of leaving home more. "When do I go?"

Miranda saw the fear and heard the sadness. Everything Isabelle was feeling, she was feeling, too, but it was time for *la periquita* to fly.

"After your month in Barcelona, why don't I meet you in New York? We can set up your apartment and meet your roommate together. What do you think?"

Isabelle rose from her chair, walked around the table to Miranda, and wrapped her arms around her. "I think I'm terribly lucky to have you for a mother," she said, hugging Miranda.

Luis's heart was full as he watched Miranda and Isabelle embrace, but not so full that he didn't remember the night their other daughter had left for New York. It had been over three years without a letter, a postcard, or a phone call. Miranda, unwilling to accept what Nina had said that last night as her true feelings, viewed them instead as a natural response to the anxiety of leaving home and going so far away. She had tried to reach Nina, using the address and phone number Nina had given them before the final debacle. Her letters had been returned stamped "Address Unknown," and the person who answered the phone each time she called insisted she had the wrong number. Miranda feared something awful had happened to Nina. Luis believed her disappearance was deliberate and permanent.

As he watched Isabelle and Miranda giggle and hug each other, he considered the differences between the two young women he had raised. Neither was of his blood, but he had loved both Isabelle and Nina as if they were. Moreover, he had tried to love them equally. Though they were from different seeds, he believed he had given them the same amount of water and sunlight and food. Yet one was warm, while the other had turned cold. One appreciated anything that was done for her, the other disparaged all those around her. One behaved like a daughter, the other like an enemy.

When Miranda confided to him the next day that she hoped Isabelle would somehow find Nina, he nodded and agreed, but without conviction. At this point, if they did find Nina, he wasn't sure any of them would like what they found.

The building was on New York's Upper West Side, on the corner of Ninetieth Street and Riverside Drive. Built before World War II, it was a gracious structure of red brick with white stone trim. There was no doorman, and the lobby could have used refurbishing, but, Isabelle told herself, it was across the street from a park, near a downtown bus, and almost affordable in rent. The way she and Luis had figured it, with one decent job or two bearable part-time jobs, plus some careful budgeting, she might have some money left over at the end of the month for a minor indulgence or two.

Miranda had suggested that Isabelle dip into her bank account, the one Flora and Alejandro had funded so many years before, to get her started in New York, but Isabelle had demurred.

"We're taking my tuition out. That's enough. Besides, I don't need very much," she had said. "I'd rather save it for that rainy day you've always told me about."

"But you'll need furniture and art supplies and clothes."

Miranda couldn't bear the thought of Isabelle being denied something her inheritance might have provided. She wanted Isabelle to have whatever she was entitled to as a de Luna, things beyond the reach of the Durans. Isabelle never withdrew anything from the account, except to pay for her plane tickets to Barcelona. To do so would have embarrassed her guardians, and she loved them too much to do that.

In addition, Isabelle still stung from Nina's inference that she was a spoiled heiress. While she knew the words had been said in the heat of anger, they had struck a nerve. Isabelle didn't like being called indolent and self-indulgent. She didn't like being characterized as something she was not. She didn't like feeling less than. Nina had challenged her. Isabelle had accepted the challenge.

Besides, she told herself, she had other plans for that money. One day she hoped to use it to buy Dragon Textiles.

The apartment the Art Students League had found for Isabelle was on the first floor in the back of the building. A small one-bedroom that overlooked an alley, it had a boxy space that served as a combination living room/dining room, a minute bathroom, and a closet someone had audaciously named a kitchen. The apartment was furnished—if one considered two metal beds, a ratty brown corduroy couch, three floor cushions, and a low, quasi-Danish modern cocktail table furnished. Its best feature was a half rail that separated the entrance hall from the living room, creating the illusion of space; its worst was the total lack of daylight. And if complete sunlessness weren't distressful enough, every surface was painted a dark, grotto brown. Isabelle reached the only conclusion possible—the previous tenant had been a cave dweller in a former life. Within minutes she felt claustrophobic.

"What if my roommate likes this?" she asked Miranda, her eyes wide with dismay.

"You'll compromise."

"What if she's not a person who compromises? What if she gets insulted when I tell her I don't like this? What if she insists that things be her way or no way?" Isabelle sputtered, all her anxiety about moving to New York and living with a stranger tumbling out in a nervous rush. "What if I don't like her or she doesn't like me? What if we don't get along?"

"You'll find a way to make it work, the same way you made it work at home." "With Nina," Miranda had wanted to say, but she held herself in check. This was Isabelle's time. "Why don't we get started with our cleaning?" she said, changing the subject.

Without waiting for a reply, she took off her coat and rummaged through the shopping bags they had filled at a nearby supermarket. After three hours of scrubbing, dusting, vacuuming, and polishing whatever they could, the place looked better, but it still fell far short of deserving an enthusiastic description. They were putting the linens on Isabelle's bed when the person who would occupy the other bed appeared.

"Is this the biggest dump you've ever seen, or what?"

Isabelle and Miranda turned toward the door. Framed within the portal was a short, pudgy girl with big blue eyes, pencil-thin brows, dimpled cheeks, huckleberry lips, and a mane of wild, curly black hair. She was wearing bell-bottoms that were too tight across her middle, a patchwork vest that was too long for her frame, a poet's shirt with sleeves that were too overwhelming for her height, and a black newsboy cap that got lost in her hair.

"That old saw about getting what you pay for must be true," said the apparition. "This place has 'cheap' written all over it."

"I'm Isabelle de Luna. This is my mother, Miranda Duran."

"Hey! Far out."

As they shook hands, Isabelle's eyes zeroed in on her roommate's fingernails. They were long and painted a shade that made her think of eggplant. Moreover, each finger carried an assortment of rings, piles of silver and gold bands as well as several that bore symbols like the zodiac ram, the ancient ankh, the Greek symbol for woman, and a Jewish Star of David.

"And your name is . . . ?" Miranda asked, hoping she had managed to smother her shock.

The young woman hesitated. She furrowed her brow and studied her audience, assessing their ability to be trusted with something she considered personally important.

"Okay, here it is. My real name is Hazel Strauss," she said, crinkling her nose as if someone had just burned an egg, "but for obvious reasons, I stopped using it when I was ten. Now I'm called Skye."

"Skye?" The only people Isabelle knew with names like that were Native

Americans, and to them those appellations were out of reverence for nature. Somehow Isabelle doubted reverence had had anything to do with Hazel's selection.

"Why not?" Skye said, answering Isabelle's unasked question. "My eyes are blue. My personality is heaven, and my body is positively divine!"

Her laugh was quick and friendly, her manner loose and easy. "I tried things like Buffie and Binky and Muffie and Kitten, but they just didn't do it for me. Know what I mean?"

Isabelle had no idea what she meant, but she nodded anyway.

Skye could see that neither Miranda nor Isabelle was getting it. They were staring at her as if she were a specimen in a glass case.

"Do I look like a Hazel to you?" she said, splaying out her arms in a way that invited comparison between herself and whatever image the name Hazel conjured.

"Not exactly," Miranda offered, chuckling a bit as she grew more comfortable with the girl called Skye. She was odd but likable. Vastly different from Isabelle, but companionable and, considering Isabelle's innate shyness, probably a good balance.

"So what do we do about this place?" Skye asked, her hands on her waist, her eyes surveying what she clearly thought of as wreckage. "I feel like I'm standing in a box of prunes. This color has got to go!"

She had spoken the magic words. Isabelle's mouth spread into a broad smile.

"I was so afraid you were going to like this," she said, laughing, relief brightening all her features.

"The only creatures who possibly could have liked this make it a habit to hibernate in the winter. I come from Queens, Isabelle, not the Canadian Rockies!"

Miranda stayed the weekend, helping with whatever she could. By Monday morning she felt she could leave without having to worry about Isabelle's living arrangements. The apartment was shaping up, and Isabelle and Skye were getting along. Despite their outward differences, they had connected on another level. Miranda was delighted.

Though she had promised Luis she wouldn't, before she left she asked Isabelle to do her a favor. "Would you keep your eyes and ears open for word of Nina?" she said. "I know I'm asking you to do the impossible, but you never know. You might run into her. Someone might have heard of her or seen her. I just need to know if she's all right."

Isabelle hugged Miranda. "I'll try," she said, but a few days later, during one of those conversations in which biographies were exchanged and she sketched out the situation for Skye, she had to agree with her new friend's conclusion: People who wanted to be lost, stayed lost.

The Art Students League, housed in a Beaux Arts building that claimed a large part of Fifty-seventh Street between Seventh and Eighth avenues, had been part of the New York art scene from before the turn of the century. Georgia O'Keeffe had studied there, as had Burgoyne Diller, David Smith, Irene Rice Pereira, and many other artists whose work hung in museums or decorated the homes of major collectors. Like other cultural institutions, the league had experienced varying waves of popularity and prominence, but each era seemed to spotlight a particular teacher. In O'Keeffe's day it was William Merritt Chase, known as "the American Velázquez," who became rich and famous thanks to his portraits of well-to-do families and his charming commemorations of bourgeois life. In the twenties Richard Lahey and Jan Matulka introduced the modernist aesthetic to their students. In the sixties and seventies it was Ezra Edward Clark.

Isabelle entered his classroom fizzing with excitement and trepidation. Ezra Edward Clark was a most difficult taskmaster, but he had been blessed with an internal divining rod capable of detecting real, raw talent. She had heard he had little patience for dilettantes and, in order to weed out the unworthy and the uncommitted, worked his students until many of them quit. She would not be one of them.

When he walked in, Isabelle was surprised at how striking he was. Though his hairline was receding, what remained was silver-blond and shoulder-length. Like his Scandinavian forebears, his visage spoke of sculpture: a forehead that was broad and intelligent, eyes that were cerulean blue and probing, facial planes that were sharp and chiseled. He was tall, but lank, with fingers so long and graceful they might have belonged to a surgeon or a pianist. Despite the vivid green shirt he wore, Isabelle was certain she detected a negative aura surrounding him, a gray halo that seemed to verify the stories she had heard about a woman he had loved desperately, but had vanished without a trace. Too, there was the matter of his mouth, the thin downturned lips and the complete absence of anything even approaching a smile.

"My name is Ezra Edward Clark, and my job is to help you decide whether or not you were meant to paint. I'm not here to teach you as much as I am here to test your resolve."

Linking his hands behind his back, he strolled the room, looking at each of his students so intently, most felt he was looking through them.

"People like to believe that art requires inspiration." He turned sharply to the young man nearest his arm and pointed to him. "Do you believe that?"

"Yes, sir, I—I suppose I do," the boy stammered, caught off guard.

Ezra grunted in disbelief and shook his head. "Then what do you do when you're not inspired? Pump gas and wait for lightning to strike?"

Skye tittered. He pounced on her. "What is inspiration?"

Her face burned with embarrassment. "Something that makes you want to paint," she said, masking her face with a confidence she didn't feel.

"If I threaten to flunk you if you don't paint, is that inspiration?"

"Of a sort."

Isabelle lowered her head and hid her smile behind her hand. One month of living with Skye had taught her to expect the unexpected and the irreverent.

Ezra loomed over Skye for a moment, clearly trying to decide whether or not to take her on. Choosing to continue along his original path rather than take a combative detour, he asked several other students to define inspiration. He wasn't pleased with the answers.

"A beautiful sunset."

"A luscious body."

"The voice of God."

Practically spinning on his heels in frustration, he turned to Isabelle, who had chosen to remain outside the debate.

"What's wrong with those answers?"

"They're all externals," Isabelle said quietly. "Inspiration is internal."

"There is a God after all," he muttered. Then, sensing he could draw more from this stunning young brunette, he stood alongside her, took note of the name on her drawing pad, and continued their dialogue. "Is it a spark that needs to be ignited by an outside force in order to flame? Or is it something that constantly smolders within?"

Isabelle answered without hesitation. "I think inspiration is another word for creative energy, so to me, it's always there. It just has to be tapped into."

Ezra nodded. He had been asking this same question on the opening day of his course for years. He had elicited the correct answer only twice before. Both students had gone on to achieve a modicum of fame. Maybe this girl would do as well, or better.

"Tapping into one's creative energy is what this class is about," he said, turning away from Isabelle and addressing the class as a whole. "I want you to buy five three-by-four canvases. Each day you are to fill one of those canvases with a painting. Not half a painting. Not an outline or a sketch. But a completely composed, carefully conceived painting. At the end of the week, you will turn them in for evaluation."

"A painting a day?" a young man in the back blurted out. "That's impossible."

Clark fixed his gaze on the heavily bearded skeptic. "If you have real talent, nothing is impossible." As the young man withered, Clark clapped his hands for attention. "For the first week, I want you to do five portraits of the same person."

He had anticipated the groans that would follow his edict. In these days of minimalism and rampant expressionism, fledgling artists wanted to let their spirits fly over the canvas, depositing color and line at will, which was precisely why, for the first few months, he demanded tradition and control.

Naturally Isabelle and Skye selected each other as subjects. Skye's portraits were technically superb but unremarkable. Isabelle appeared as she was, her features correctly drawn, but with little or no imaginative interpretation. Isabelle's portraits of Skye, though casually sketched, were marvels of color and light. Each one had been cast from a different spoke of the wheel, allowing color to create a different mood via tint and shadow and tone.

Since most art students came to the league with some prior training, doing the same face five times may have been tedious, but it was not traumatic. The next week's assignment—portraits of five different people—was more strenuous, but still not a problem. Landscapes in the style of the Impressionists were manageable, as were watercolor seascapes à la Englishman John Turner; but when Clark demanded detailed scenes of domestic life, some of his students began to chafe.

"It takes a long time to do them right," one girl complained.

"When Vermeer needed money, he completed a painting in a matter of hours. So did Rembrandt. And do you know why? Because they relied on a discerning minority of patrons for support. And so will you, my friends."

He waited for his words to sink in. They were young. They believed they were painting for art's sake. Ezra Edward Clark was a realist. He had learned through bitter experience that art was not a hobby. It was a profession, and like other highly trained professionals, the best were paid well, the mediocre were passed over, and the poor were ignored. After his mistress, Sonya, left him, he had slapped together several paintings in hopes of raising the money to launch a search for her. The work was not his best and, therefore, sold well below his previous prices.

When he began to teach, the memory of that humiliation prompted his insistence that, as an exercise, students should put a commercial value on their paintings. Critics called him crass, but in his mind, compelling an artist to attach a monetary evaluation to his or her art gave it a reality that went beyond the work's artistic conception, treated it with the seriousness he felt it deserved, and prepared the student for the real world.

"As the market grows tighter, your skills must be sharper," he said. "You must be able to produce good work quickly, with or without inspiration. If you don't, someone else will."

Isabelle found Clark's class exacting but fun. Skye hated it and him.

"How the hell does he expect me to push out a painting a day, wait tables so I can pay rent, do my other assignments, tend to my laundry, and still have time to hunt down the man of my dreams?"

"Put dream man on hold," Isabelle said, stripping off her waitress uniform, hanging it in the closet, and throwing herself on her bed in an exhausted heap.

"Yeah, sure, easy for you to say," Skye said, twisting her hair into a knot on top of her head. "You're not the sex goddess I am, so you don't know what it is to walk around a seething hotbed of unfulfilled passion."

Isabelle groaned and covered her face with her pillow.

"I think that's Clark's problem," Skye said, slathering cold cream on her face.

"What is?"

"Unfulfilled passion. I think Mr. Impossible is sex starved."

Isabelle peeked out from beneath her pillow. "And how did you reach that conclusion?"

"His whole routine is compulsive. A painting a day. This style this week, something else next week. Do more. Do it better. It's a clear sign of pent-up frustration."

Isabelle tossed the pillow behind her and rested against it. If Isabelle had learned one thing living with Skye, it was that despite her beatnik prose, her instincts were keen.

"Maybe he's love starved," Isabelle said. "I've heard he's still pining away for that woman."

"Yeah. Sonya something."

"Rumor has it she used to go away for long periods of time. Do you think she was having an affair with someone else?"

"Maybe. Or maybe she checked into a sanitarium for an occasional shrink job."

Isabelle thought about that for a moment. "That could be. I mean, after what she lived through with the Nazis. Ugh! I can't imagine surviving something like that." She shivered.

"My parents are survivors." Skye said it quietly, almost as if she felt it were something Isabelle should know but nothing she wanted discussed.

"Your parents were in the Holocaust?" Isabelle's flesh went cold.

"They were both at Auschwitz." Skye busied herself wiping the cold cream off her face, hiding behind a wad of tissue.

"How awful." Isabelle felt foolish saying something so banal, but she was at a loss.

"Actually," Skye said, her manner more somber than Isabelle had ever seen, "I suppose they did what this Sonya did. They disappeared, too. The difference is, my parents disappeared inside themselves."

"What do you mean?"

Skye paused. Isabelle sensed this was a painful subject, one that her friend avidly avoided.

"They refuse to talk about it."

"I've heard a little about what went on in those camps. They probably just want to spare you the horror of even hearing it secondhand."

"I'm their child. I'm a part of them. I have a right to know who they were before and what made them the way they are now." She looked small and vulnerable yet, at the same time, angry and resentful. "Their silence created a wall between us. I'm on one side and they're on the other, barricaded behind some terrible secret that's really nothing but the truth."

"They lived that truth once already," Isabelle said, treading lightly. "Why would you want them to live it again?"

"Because if they don't insist that the world remember what happened," she said, her eyes blazing, her body tight with conviction, "it could happen again."

Isabelle was working two jobs and taking three courses, but she was happy. She loved living in New York, with its drumbeat energy and its exotic populace. She loved living on the West Side, with its ethnic mix and its old buildings and its array of boutiques and bodegas. She loved Skye, with her unique combination of forced eccentricity and down-home honesty. Month by month they had grown closer, as each had discovered in the other a nesting place. Skye needed Isabelle's calm to anchor her when she ventured too far out on a limb. Isabelle needed Skye's protective cover when she felt threatened by a sophistication she didn't yet understand. And while she couldn't deny that the first semester had been little more than an artistic endurance test, she loved Ezra Edward Clark's class.

"That's because you're his pet," Skye insisted whenever Isabelle defended him.

"That's not true."

"Oh, no? I don't see him asking other students if he can save their paintings!"

"He's held a few of yours aside."

"A few. How many of yours has he stashed away in his closet?"

"Maybe a dozen," she admitted.

"Fine. He's held back three of mine."

"That's three more than some of the others," Isabelle said, trying to win Skye over to her side with some left-handed praise.

"By the time the year ends, he'll be lucky if he has anyone other than us in his class, he's such a dictator."

It was true that many who had started the class in September had fallen by the wayside. Most had churned out uninspired, paint-filled canvases. A few had risen to the occasion and, in the process, discovered something very valuable—they were prolific. Isabelle was one of those few. So was Skye.

Once Clark allowed them to paint in their own styles, Skye found it easier to meet his weekly requirement. Considering that hers was such an exceedingly au courant persona, one might have expected her art to be on the cutting edge, yet her work tilted toward the past. Though she employed the simplified, flat colorations of a modernist and abstracted her backgrounds, her signature was psychological portraits. More often than not, her subjects glared out at the viewer or stared into an unsettled space. Some in the class found her art too blunt. Isabelle, knowing Skye's personal history, understood her exploration of life's brutal effect. It was clear by Clark's comments that while he knew nothing of Skye's family background, intimacy with a woman like Sonya had sharpened his awareness of the depths of man's cruelty to man.

"You have an intense gaze, Miss Strauss," he said. "These images are rather disquieting."

"Not everything in life is pretty."

"I agree." He placed all five of her week's canvases next to one another on a shelf. Each was a study of anxiety and frightened isolation. "Your work reminds me of one of my early idols, Ernst Ludwig Kirchner. He, too, preferred brute frankness to idealized beauty. There's also an artist working today,

Lucian Freud, Sigmund's grandson, who seems to share your view that the job of the artist is not to soothe the viewer, but to shock."

"I don't think it's my job to do either," she said, confronting Clark with his own words. "My job is simply to paint how I feel."

Clark's eyes narrowed as he studied the young woman with the wild hair and flamboyant wardrobe. His upper lip curled slightly in a smile of approval.

"Well said."

If Ezra had been surprised by the quality of Skye's work, he was not surprised by Isabelle. Though she appeared much more conservative than her roommate, her art was far more electrifying. Almost from the first, Clark had recognized in her that rare, precious ability to translate feelings into form, just as Kandinsky had transposed sound into color. But in his estimation she didn't go far enough.

"Confront your environment," he insisted, trying to get her to shed the restraints of convention. "All you're doing is transposing nature to a canvas. I want you to move beyond that."

"I want to do that, too," Isabelle said, "but I'm not sure I know how."

"Feel what you see," he implored her. "Let the internal react to the external."

It was difficult at first. Isabelle had never analyzed the way she selected her subjects or why her canvases looked the way they did. She simply painted and others responded. Yes, Sybil had taught her certain skills and had encouraged the development of some visual insightfulness, but, as she had feared, something was still lacking, something that was holding her back.

Ezra gave her some sensitivity exercises.

"Lie down in a darkened room. Close your eyes and sink into the comfort of stillness. Give yourself over to it. Let it cleanse your mind of superfluous thought. And when you've made contact with your soul, paint what you feel.

"Sit on a park bench or stand on a street corner. Plug your ears to eliminate the sounds of the city and concentrate solely on the sights and movements around you. Watch how people move, not where they go. Touch the energy they leave behind. Feel it. React to it. And then paint it!"

Little by little her sensitivity to her surroundings heightened. By blocking out the unnecessary, Isabelle learned how to find and feel the core. Keyed to a point where she felt as if her soul had replaced her skin, she began to feel everything so intensely that the only antidote was to paint or sketch, to somehow translate the sensations within onto a surface.

As always, nature was a favorite subject, except now, instead of the red hills and violet mesas of New Mexico, her vistas were a skyline crammed with jutting architecture and tar-black streets teeming with men and machines in a hurry. Her colors grew dusky, hovering in the charcoal black, smokier ranges of the spectrum. Her shapes turned sharp and geometric, so much so that she had to smile, thinking of Althea, wondering how she would have captured New York.

When she was new to the city, her work displayed her awe. Her landscapes were broad, quick repetitions of what her eyes could see from a street corner or a rooftop or the window of a bus. She painted the factories along the East River, the astounding ascent of the Empire State Building, the skating rink at Rockefeller Center, the moneyed cathedrals of Wall Street. During her second year, having grown more accustomed to the world of glass and cement, she drew her sights in closer, telescoping and enlarging parts of the whole, dousing her images with colors that expressed her response to what she saw.

A cracked tenement window reflecting the skyscraper across from it, all of it drenched in the liberal red of a summer sunset.

A neighborhood stoop, patterned with the black-and-gray shadows of people passing by.

A golden spire reaching up into an azure sky, a nearby chimney exhaling the blackened breath of a factory.

Even Isabelle was excited by the changes. They weren't drastic. She was still using large blocks of color, slightly ambiguous forms, and a skewed rainbow, but they flowed better, they said more, and they spoke louder. Her only disappointment was Ezra Edward Clark. Instead of praising her, he pushed her harder, criticizing nearly everything she did, challenging her to venture off into new directions, demanding that she redo and rethink and repaint.

She was beginning to think she and Sybil and Tía Flora and Miranda had overestimated her talent and that she would never be anything more than ordinary.

He had begun to realize he was midwifing a gift that was nothing short of extraordinary.

CHAPTER 11

I t was hot. As Isabelle rounded the corner of Fifty-seventh Street and Seventh Avenue she could feel her clothes sticking to her skin. Fanning her face with a letter from Miranda, she wished she could snap her fingers and summon a New Mexican mountain breeze. She had returned to Santa Fe for her twentieth birthday, but the week had seemed mercilessly short. She had seen Sybil and Dr. Jonas, several of her high school friends, and, as luck would have it, Rebecca and Sam. Rebecca was off to Yale Law School and promised to try to make it down to the city for a visit. Sam was finishing his last year at Harvard Med and was beginning to think about where he would intern. Isabelle hoped he picked New York.

Seeing him again had revived her crush and a few of her girlish fantasies about riding off into the sunset with the young doctor, but when she returned to Ninetieth Street and mooned over him to Skye, rambling on about how good-looking he was, how bright and kind and wonderful, the voice of truth sliced through her reverie with sharp words and cutting sarcasm.

"You sound like a dog waiting to be petted. He's so kind and decent," she mimicked. "Who cares! What I want to know is, does he make your heart flutter and your thighs go weak?"

"Sort of."

"Sort of? Isabelle, this is not an intellectual question. You shouldn't have to think about whether or not you want to jump this guy's bones."

"It doesn't matter what I want," Isabelle said, growing more uncomfortable by the minute. "He barely notices me, that way, I mean."

"That's because to him you're a family friend. You have the same sex appeal as his sister or his horse!"

"Gee, that makes me feel wonderful," Isabelle said, accustomed to Skye's unflinching honesty, upset by it nonetheless. "Thanks so much."

"Don't mention it."

Skye watched Isabelle pout and shook her head. She would never understand why Isabelle was so skittish about her own sexuality. Even in a paint-stained T-shirt and shorts, Isabelle was an exotic creature with a long, lean body and a face that had been put together by a sculptor with an unusual eye for beauty. To someone like Skye, it seemed wasteful to have such enormous physical appeal and such a narrow vein of confidence.

"The only reason you have a crush on Sam Hoffman, boy next door, is because there is no other person of the masculine gender in your life," Skye said, feeling the need to explain the workings of the world to her friend. "You are a twenty-year-old virgin. That may not be a sin, Sister Isabelle, but it's not a blessing, either."

"Look who's talking!" Isabelle shot back, defending her maidenhood. "You're not exactly beating them off with a stick."

"Hey! That's not from lack of trying. I will admit, I had been hoping that when I took out my lifetime membership in Weight Watchers, along with my calorie counter and fat-free cookbook, I would get a week in paradise with the stud of the month, but no such luck."

Isabelle laughed. "We are pathetic."

"Horny? Yes. Undiscovered and unappreciated? Yes. But pathetic? Isabelle, you make me weep."

Just as she neared the Art Students League, the weather changed. The sky darkened and a breeze kicked up, brushing her face and arms with the portent of a coming storm. Racing for the door, she felt an odd premonition that her life was about to change as well. She welcomed the idea as much as she welcomed this rainy respite from late summer's heat. It was a new school year, after all. She was twenty years old. She had been working nonstop ever since she'd come to New York. Perhaps Skye was right; maybe it was time she had a boyfriend. But Skye, who was full of confidence and pluck, kept emphasizing *when*. For Isabelle the question was *how* and *who*.

She shouldn't have worried. Love was about to find her.

It was a month before she noticed him, but it had taken her that long to get accustomed to being in a life class. She had avoided this course as long as she could, but Clark, who had appointed himself her personal adviser, had demanded that she sign on. Isabelle couldn't explain her reluctance, nor did she understand the tremendous discomfort she felt sketching someone who lay naked on a platform, but she cringed during every session. She had never been at ease with nudity. She supposed a psychiatrist could find something from her childhood that contributed to this phobia, but since she didn't like the idea of psychiatry any more than she liked nude models, she doubted she would ever find the root.

The first few models had been women, which had made it easier for Isabelle. She would look, study the length and weight of the model, and sketch them, using her own body as a prototype, adjusting to the differences she had noted between the other women and herself. If they were heavier, she made the breasts fuller or more pendulous, depending on age and pose. If they were shorter, she adjusted the line and proportions of the torso. Since she never drew complete faces anyway, she didn't bother with anything more than a cursory glance at features such as eyes and noses and mouths. Cheekbones, chins, and necks were all that mattered.

This morning, however, she was confronted by a large, naked male stretched out on a chaise, resting on his side so that his pose was completely frontal, his maleness prominent and unavoidable. Isabelle had never seen a man undressed before, which must have been obvious to anyone who noticed her blush and look away.

"Think of him as a still life with flesh."

The baritone voice belonged to the man at the easel next to her, a man whose smile was so dazzling, it made her forget that he must have noticed her embarrassment.

"Excuse me?"

"He's not the prettiest fella I've ever seen, but I've worked with him before. He's harmless."

"Are you making fun of me?" Isabelle asked, rattled by the stranger in the white T-shirt, well-worn jeans, and cowboy boots.

"Absolutely not!" he said, crossing his heart and disarming her with that unbelievable smile. "I'd never make fun of a lady as pretty as you."

Again Isabelle blushed.

"I'm Cody Jackson."

He put out his hand, and she was almost afraid to take it. Her heart was fluttering, and her thighs were weak. Where was Skye when she needed her?

"I'm Isabelle de Luna."

"Nice name."

"Thanks."

"Where're you from?"

"Santa Fe."

He nodded and gave her a thumbs-up. "I'm from that neck of the woods myself. Durango, Colorado."

He had eyes as blue and inviting as the Mediterranean and hair as light and fine as the sand on the beach at Palma. His chin, however, square and strong and with a deep cleft, had Southwest stamped all over it.

"I guess that makes us neighbors."

"Maybe." He narrowed his eyes; his smile remained intact. "But you don't have the same accent as other folks I know from Santa Fe."

"I'm from Barcelona originally."

"No kidding?"

It was Isabelle's turn to smile. He seemed so unaffected, so open, so friendly. "No kidding."

Their tête-à-tête was interrupted by a scowling instructor.

"If neither of you is in the mood to draw, perhaps you should take an early lunch?" Lucien Fitzsimmon was small and balding, but he had a ferocious mien.

Isabelle was about to turn back to her drawing pad when Cody said, "Great idea, Fitz!"

He grabbed Isabelle's pad and his own, took her arm, and, before Fitzsimmon could stop them, led her out the door and down to the street.

"Are you nuts? He could flunk us for a stunt like that!"

"He could, but he won't. The buzz on you is that you're a star on the rise and Ezra Edward Clark's personal project. I happen to hold the same privileged position with old Fitz. He'll get over it. You'll see. Meantime, let's jump into Wolfie's before everyone in New York decides they absolutely have to have corned beef for lunch."

Cody Jackson was the breath of mountain air Isabelle had wished for. Not only did they share a fondness for the same geographical region and a wistful loneliness for the incredible natural beauty of the land they'd left behind, but their lives and dreams revolved around precisely the same core. To sit and talk with a young man who was absorbed by the same things that consumed her was more than merely intellectually stimulating, it provided validation for the narrow focus of Isabelle's life. To have that same man visually reconnoiter her body every time they were together, to sense that he was plotting a course that would lead to a different kind of sharing, was physically stirring to the point of being almost unendurable.

In class, having him near her while she was supposed to be concentrating on the model on the dais, was torture. She struggled through each session as if it were penance for the sinfulness of her private thoughts, the ones in which the naked male was Cody, unclothed and accessible, and the naked female was herself, waiting and willing. For three hours every day that skylit studio became the site of some powerful psychic foreplay, a visual and visceral exploration of all that was sensual and erogenous. Both of them felt it, and keenly, because after class, though they couldn't stay away from each other, neither could bring themselves close enough to risk contact.

When one Friday afternoon he invited her to have dinner at his loft the next night, she accepted and then spent twenty-four hours in turmoil. She was nervous about exposing herself to love. Though she didn't obsess about Martín and Althea, she couldn't deny that the vicissitudes of their marriage had had an effect on her. Though her memories were vague, her parents had shown her how powerful an emotion love could be; they had also shown her how untrustworthy it could be.

Skye, of course, wasn't interested in anything other than the rendezvous itself.

"Have a couple of glasses of wine. It'll relax you," she instructed with the authority of one who had been deflowered already. "And stop worrying. Cody's cool. He'll be a terrific first time."

Isabelle sighed, her breath leaving her chest in a nervous wave. "Why is it you can talk about things like this so easily and I can barely think about it without agonizing over every pro and con?"

"I'm Jewish," she said, as if it should have been obvious. "We talk first and feel guilty later."

"I feel guilty now and I haven't done anything yet."

"That's because you're Catholic."

"Great," Isabelle said, shaking her head. "According to you, it doesn't matter which side of the Bible I'm on, I'm guilty if I do and guilty if I don't."

"Precisely! Which is why I say go with the flow."

"But I don't know what to do! I don't know what to say! I don't know what to wear!"

"Soft and subtly sexy," Skye said, rummaging through Isabelle's closet and tossing a few things on the bed. "And tie your hair back. Men get off on loosening a women's tresses. It's some throwback to the Middle Ages, I think. And don't forget to dab perfume between your breasts. As for knowing what to do, no problem. Mother Nature has already programmed your computer. All Cody has to do is press the right buttons and you're in for one hell of a night!"

His loft was in SoHo, on Greene Street. Like most downtown lofts, it was one large, high-ceilinged room with big, uncovered windows, a skylight, and a bathroom. The walls were white and bare, the floors hardwood and blond. An easel and several works in progress occupied the corner beneath the skylight. Slim pipes and industrial track lighting crisscrossed the ceiling, reminding all who visited of the building's former incarnation as a factory.

In another corner, a long couch dressed in Indian blankets, an old wooden door balanced on a low pedestal of bricks, and two canvas director's chairs created a small conversational grouping. A bunch of red tulips in a crockery pot, books about John Singer Sargent, Rubens, Fragonard, and Matisse, and a paperweight fashioned like a Rodin sculpture decorated the top of the makeshift coffee table. In the far corner, on top of a raised platform, lay a mattress dressed in plain white bed linen; another Navaho blanket splashed the bed with color. Running along behind, like a three-dimensional head-board, was a collection of cowboy boots, lined up neatly in pairs, their textures and colors a visual poem about Cody's ties to the West.

The kitchen was little more than a string of old appliances across from a counter, the dining room another door, this one raised on wooden trestles, and four flea-market chairs, each one different, each one clearly a bargain. Yet with another bunch of tulips surrounded by a circle of candles, brightly colored napkins, dime-store plates, and big-bellied wine goblets, the overall effect was byzantine and charming. Isabelle was impressed and said so.

"Thanks. It's fill-in-the-blanks decorating, but what the hell? It works for me."

He handed her a glass of wine and invited her to join him by the stove, where he was watching a pot of spaghetti. On the counter in a wooden bowl, a big green salad waited to be dressed. She could smell bread heating in the oven. Patsy Cline was wailing in the background.

Cody noticed her checking things out. "I hope you're not into gourmet cooking. I'm preparing a special feast, but it's a far cry from fancy."

"I come from Santa Fe, remember? The fanciest we ever get at La Casa is fajitas!"

"I also remember you saying something about Barcelona."

"That was a long time ago," Isabelle said. "Besides, this looks great."

"You look great," he said, leaving the spaghetti to boil by itself as he took her face in his hands and kissed her lightly on the lips.

Her stomach lurched. She almost spilled her wine. But she didn't pull away.

"Thanks," she said. "You look pretty good yourself."

And he did, in his denim shirt and ubiquitous jeans, his feet shod in a pair of well-worn black boots.

"Maybe we'll skip dinner and go right for dessert," he said, kissing her again, lingering longer this time.

"And miss out on spaghetti à la Jackson?" She wondered if she sounded as breathless as she felt. "I thought it was your specialty?"

"It's only one of my specialties," he said, his lips still pressed against hers, "but"—reluctantly he released her and returned to his food—"it is something you should have at least once in your lifetime."

"I'm sure," she said, giggling nervously.

Trying to ease the tension building between them, Isabelle wandered off toward the corner where his paintings were. Cody remained by the stove, but his eyes never left her. She was wearing a filmy black floral dress that fitted close at the top, was belted at the waist, then floated gently around her legs. She had pulled her hair into a loose chignon that nestled at the nape of her neck. Soft, stray strands fell from her temples. Long silver earrings dangled alongside her cheeks. Her eyes were dark, her lips stained a berry red. As she moved, the delicate fabric billowed between her legs and against her thighs. She was slim, but far from linear. He wanted to undress her. He wanted to make love to her. He wanted to paint her. But first, he reminded himself, he had promised to feed her.

Isabelle could feel his eyes burning into her flesh. She had expected that such wanton lustfulness would have embarrassed her, but instead it excited her. Even without looking at him, without touching him, without even being near him, she could feel her desire for him growing. Forcing herself to focus on something other than what was bubbling inside her, she opened her eyes to the canvases propped against the wall.

No wonder he was so at ease in the life drawing class, she thought. Judging by these paintings, another of Cody Jackson's specialties was nudes.

There were three of them, each using a different woman, each in a different stage of completion. One was still rough, without definition or clarity. The other two must have been nearly finished, because Isabelle couldn't imagine what he could do to improve them. The backgrounds were plain, primed canvas and nothing more, but the bodies were lush, the flesh tinted and toned as if rays of sunlight strained through a prism had shone down on them as they posed. The facial expression of one conveyed a certain antagonism. The woman was sitting on a chair, her arms resting on her knees, her torso bent so that her breasts hung like empty sacks, casting a dark shadow on the more private regions of her femininity. She was older, out of shape, and angry, maybe about needing money so badly that she had felt compelled to pose nude for a stranger. Her face stared out at Isabelle, daring her to comment.

The other woman was young and fit and clearly eager to display her wares, as nothing was hidden or shaded or covered by a hand or a cloth. She had laid herself out backward on a chaise, her head hanging off the side, her feet raised and resting against the seat back. Her hair was blond and long, its ends hovering just above the floor. Her tongue was licking her upper lip. Her eyes were closed, in ecstasy, perhaps. Isabelle wondered if Cody had slept with this odalisque before he'd painted her, or after, or at all.

"I didn't," he said, reading her thoughts. He slid his arm around her waist.

She leaned against him but continued to stare at the painting, too unnerved by her own reactions to face him. His lips found the soft flesh on the side of her neck.

"One of these days, I'd love to paint you."

She laughed. It was nervous and self-conscious. "You know how squeamish I am about nude models," she said, wriggling out of his grasp, needing to get some distance between them.

"Then I'll just have to do it from memory."

Having declared his intentions for the second time, Cody smiled and held out his hand. For the moment Isabelle didn't know whether they were headed for the table or the bed, nor was she certain she cared. He held the chair for her, refilled her wineglass, and took the chair opposite her. They ate quickly, but once dinner was over, Cody proceeded slowly.

He switched the music from country to classical, lowered the lights, and invited her to join him on the couch. She was feeling mellow and warm, and when he put his arm around her, she snuggled next to him. They talked for a while. He told her what it had been like growing up on a ranch in Durango, playing football for the high school team and then announcing he wanted to be an artist.

"Hadn't you painted or drawn all your life?" she asked, astounded that someone with his talent might have had to suppress it.

"Only in private," he said. For the first time since she had known him, Isabelle caught an edge to his voice. "My folks are real old-fashioned country types. In their minds, men don't paint. They rope cattle. They ride horses. They play football. Maybe they take their boots off and put a suit on for some kind of office job, but they don't dance. They don't design clothes. And they don't paint!"

She turned and looked at him. The pain she had expected to see shadowing his eyes was there. "But you're wonderful," she said. "Have they ever seen your work?"

"They're not interested."

"That's too bad. Maybe if they saw some of your paintings. Maybe if you invited them to New York . . ."

Cody put his finger on her lips, a slow smile waltzing across his. "I have to be honest, Isabelle. Right now, I don't care about anything except you."

He took her in his arms and drew her close, his mouth silencing any response she might have had. Isabelle felt her body go limp as his hands glided up and down her back and their kisses deepened. Inside, she smiled as he unpinned her hair and combed it loose with his fingers. Ever so slowly, his movements tender and considerate, he invited her to join him on the wondrous adventure she had put off until now.

Her breath had begun to shorten, and without even thinking, she moved closer to him, tightening her arms around him, pressing her lips harder against his. His fingers sneaked between their bodies and began to unbutton her dress. She had on a slip, but no bra. He stroked the black silk, softly enticing the flesh underneath to respond. Isabelle had never dreamed that such pleasure could come from the simple act of a man's hand touching a woman's breast. He undid her belt and the rest of the buttons, his eyes locked on her face, watching to see if she was nervous or frightened. She was hesitant, but only for a moment.

Seeing the need in his eyes, feeling the need in her body, she stood, let her dress fall to the floor, removed her hose, and waited. With her mane of brown hair cascading onto her shoulders, her breasts hard beneath her slip, her skin flushed with excitement, she looked like every one of his fantasies. He rose to meet her, smiling as he heard her breath catch in her throat. Crushing her against him, he kissed her and, at the same time, lifted her into his arms and carried her to his bed.

She watched as he undressed, amazed that simply the sight of him could quicken her blood and send it coursing through her veins. He lay down next to her, propped up on one arm, his eyes worshiping the form that lay beneath the sheath of black silk. Instead of removing it, he sketched her body on it, tracing her breasts, the line from her chest to her waist, the V that guarded the entrance to the deepest part of her. She shivered at his touch, fighting to control sensations she had never felt before. He slid the thin straps off her shoulders and down her arms. As the fabric fell away, his lips welcomed her flesh.

Isabelle had never experienced such total physical involvement. There wasn't a part of her, inside or out, that wasn't feeling something new and exquisite. He suckled at her breast, and her thighs trembled. His hands slithered her slip past her hips, and she felt moist and hot. His mouth feasted on her flesh, and her body began to undulate, swaying instinctively as if the music filling the room had awakened something tribal within her. She opened her arms, asking him to cover her. When he did, she reached for him, needing to feel the power behind his virility.

Her fingers closed around him, and he moaned, the sound coming from deep within his throat. She held on to him as she moved beneath him, delighting in the pleasure she was giving him. His mouth covered hers as his hand reached down and stroked the part of her that wanted him most. Instantly she felt a pulsing sensation that seemed to envelop her entire being. Writhing, straining, each aroused the other's gender to a point of excruciating desire. She raised her hips and ground them against him, begging him to complete what he had started. He sheathed himself and entered her, restraining slightly, so as not to hurt her. Isabelle was beyond caution. She reached behind him, pulling him closer, drawing him deeper and deeper. There was no pain, only intense joy, as Cody initiated her into the extraordinary world of carnal passion.

Instead of turning shy or backing away, Isabelle responded to him eagerly, again and again. By morning they lay next to each other completely exhausted and convinced that they were in love.

"Was it good, bad, indifferent, or kinky?"

"It was glorious." Isabelle swooned as she accepted a cup of hot coffee and joined Skye on the couch.

"I take it the cowboy is rather sexy."

Isabelle hugged her knees to her chin and grinned as moments from the previous night passed in front of her eyes. "Rather!"

"Well, good for you!" Skye embraced her roommate, genuinely delighted that things had gone well. She adored Isabelle and would have felt awful if after all her prodding and poking, Cody Jackson had turned out to be a brute. "Are we in love?"

"We are." Again Isabelle's face glowed with thoughts of Cody. "I didn't want to leave him," she confessed.

Skye's smile stalled. "You're not thinking of getting married or moving in with him, are you?"

Isabelle hadn't thought beyond the touch of his hands on her body. Giving it cursory consideration, she shook her head. "I am positively wild about him, but no, I'm not jumping into anything."

"Except his bed," Skye teased.

"Every chance I get!"

Isabelle couldn't remember ever being as happy as she was during those first months of her affair with Cody. She had never felt so totally alive. It was as if he had rubbed an abrasive against her skin, making it raw and overly sensitive, open to every imaginable nuance of feeling. Her painting reflected the potency of her emotions, but not simply in terms of color and form. Suddenly there was a new consciousness about her work, a tender, strictly feminine sensibility that seemed to require a return to the softness of watercolors. Her forms grew rounder, more lyrical, more voluptuous; what was more important, they were exceedingly personal.

Before, Isabelle's work had reflected the influences of those who were teaching or advising her: Tía Flora, Miranda, Sybil, Ezra Edward Clark, even Fitzsimmon. Her new work was her own. Still abstract, still retaining her affinity with nature, she began to evoke its harmony through imperfect rounds like swellings and mounds and buds. It was as if she were equating her emerging sexuality with nature's unfurling, a process at once delicate and powerful. She seemed fixed on the forces that move the natural world, the strength that opens the fragile petals of a flower, the peaceful surge of flowing water, the energy that propels a cloud across the sky. She avoided the severe geometrical forms so intrinsic to modern art. Her circles were never perfectly rounded, her angles were never precise, because while her vocabulary derived from nature, the dynamics of her work drew their power from the lush, rapturous cosmos of female response.

Cody had expected their intimacy to release Isabelle from her lingering puritanism. He had believed that because she was comfortable in bed with him, she would be more relaxed in their life drawing class and more accepting of the notion of posing nude. He discovered that one thing had nothing to do with another. Isabelle still squirmed on her chair at the sight of someone exposing his or her sexuality to a room of strangers. Worse, she thought, was when one of the students disrobed for the benefit of the class. She understood that most artists couldn't wait to capture the human form. She understood that the models were able to detach their personalities from their bodies. What she didn't understand was why her feelings on this subject mattered to anyone but herself. When she asked Cody, he admitted it was difficult to understand how someone so sensual in appearance and manner could be so prudish.

Isabelle's quick answer was, "My strict Catholic upbringing." Seeing how rattled she was by the question, Cody knew not to press. Even if he had, there was no way Isabelle could have explained about the nightmares, those incessant blue blurs of horror that had plagued her as a child. Though they returned only rarely now, they hadn't lost their ferocity or their power to upset her. Sometimes they were nothing but menacing, anonymous shapes slithering around the blue. Other times the shapes became bodies without faces, writhing or struggling, or fighting—she wasn't sure. And then there were those awful nights when her entire being was racked with a terror that defied description. She sweated and twisted and turned and moaned as if she couldn't bare to look at the visions the night had delivered, but when she awakened she had little memory of what she had seen. She sketched whatever slivers she could recall, but all she retained was a facial feature or a body part. Nothing was ever connected. Nothing ever made sense.

Annoyed with himself for distressing her needlessly, Cody took her in his arms, soothed her, and assured her that it was precisely that blend of austere restraint and unfettered sensuality that excited him so.

Unfortunately Lucien Fitzsimmon didn't share Cody's opinion. He was dissatisfied with Isabelle's work and called her into his office to tell her so.

"I see no improvement, Miss de Luna. Is it that you're not trying, or are you totally incapable of replicating the human form?"

Isabelle bristled beneath what she considered unfair criticism. "Neither of those two statements is true, Mr. Fitzsimmon," she said, feeling oddly emboldened. "I am trying, and I am quite capable of drawing naked bodies. I simply find it unpleasant."

"Why are you so offended by nudity?" he asked, with a look on his face that could only be described as a leer.

"I'm not offended by it, sir, but neither is it my first choice as a subject for my art."

Fitzsimmon was so practiced at intimidation, he was taken off stride by her resistance. "One must be flexible," he cautioned with an annoying air of pomposity.

"I agree," Isabelle countered. "Which is why I feel that if you would allow me to interpret what I see in my own style, instead of insisting that I produce rigid anatomical sketches, I think we would both be much happier."

Without a reasonable—and defensible, should he be challenged by the league's board—comeback, Fitzsimmon agreed to allow Isabelle the artistic freedom she requested. What he got in return were some of the loveliest watercolor nudes he had ever seen. While remaining faithful to her style and her habit of incompletion, Isabelle fashioned color studies of the models who appeared in class. Instead of being defined down to the last eyelash, they were anonymous frames energized by color. Some appeared to be silhouettes—pliant black shapes, bending and twisting amid a watery swirl of sunlit colors. Others were solo figures, studies in shading and nuance that used pose and tone so effectively, they spoke more of solitude and aloneness than most detailed portraits.

Fitzsimmon's reaction was so uncharacteristically enthusiastic, Isabelle felt compelled to share her triumph with her mentor. She skipped down the steps from the skylit studio and headed toward Ezra's second-floor office. As she neared the door, she noticed it was slightly ajar. The voices coming from inside were familiar—Ezra's, of course, and Skye's.

"What will you tell them?" she heard Ezra ask.

"I'll think of something," Skye answered.

"I don't see why you have to say anything. You're an adult."

"To you, maybe. Not to them."

Isabelle stood as close to the door as she could without being seen. It was wrong to eavesdrop, she knew that, but she couldn't tear herself away.

"And if they don't grant you permission?"

"It's not a matter of permission, Ezra, it's a matter of consideration. I won't hurt them and I won't worry them."

There was a silence. Isabelle, concerned that she was about to be discovered, began to back away.

"I'm sorry. I guess I still don't understand them."

"Then you have to try harder, because to understand me, you have to understand them."

Isabelle didn't know who "they" were, but she had a pretty good idea about who "us" was. Carefully she tiptoed down the hall, away from Ezra's office, breaking into a run when she thought she was out of earshot. She left the building with her heart pumping and her head racing. She had been so involved with Cody, she supposed she hadn't read the signs; but thinking about it now, she realized they had been there for quite a while. Over the past several months Skye had calmed, both in her manner and her wardrobe. She had lost fifteen pounds. Isabelle had attributed the changes to maturity. Obviously there had been another catalyst, one who never would have entered her mind.

Then again, Ezra too had been different lately—less strident, more positive, less critical, more constructive. Had Skye been right all along? Had Ezra been starved for love or sex or both? And for how long had Skye been the source of his satisfaction?

She was still marveling at this stunning revelation when someone who looked very familiar turned the corner. Tall, blond, a visibly lean body wrapped in a black coat, her eyes covered with sunglasses . . . and something about her gait and bearing that prompted Isabelle to shout, "Nina!"

The woman turned to look at her. It was Nina. Isabelle ran to her, her face filled with a smile, her arms open for an embrace that was not to be. Nina took a step back. Her expression was cold, her manner offputting.

"I can't believe I've run into you! Can you imagine? In the middle of New York City?" Isabelle chattered on, putting her arms at her side yet forcing her smile to remain. "I can't tell you how hard I tried to find you. I called NYU. I called hotels. I called everywhere I could think of." She was breathless, blocking out the complete unresponsiveness of her companion. "But wow! To just run into you on the street like this. It's amazing." Nina was looking at her as if she were mad. "So how are you? You look incredible, but then again—"

"Stop it!" Nina's voice was low and frigid. "Stop prattling on as if this grand reunion is going to result in a chummy little tea party, because it isn't."

"But it's been years. I thought things would have changed."

"Things haven't, but I have." Nina pulled the collar of her coat together, closing herself in, shutting Isabelle out. "I've made a whole new life for myself here in New York, and you are not part of it. Do you understand?"

"No," Isabelle said, rattled, shocked, embarrassed, insulted, and more than a little annoyed. "Frankly, I don't. We lived together as sisters. We shared a past, a lot of good times. We used to care about each other. So we had an argument. So what! Why can't you drop it? Why can't we make peace?"

"Because I don't want to." Her tone was as angry now as it had been then. "I don't want to make peace with you. In fact, I don't ever want to see you again."

She turned on her heel and started to walk away. Isabelle grabbed her arm. "You don't mean that."

Nina jerked free of Isabelle's grasp. "Oh, but I do. When I left Santa Fe, I wiped you, Miranda, and Luis out of my life. I don't miss any of you. I don't think about any of you. And I don't want any of you in my life! So do yourself a favor and forget about me. Believe me, I forgot about you years ago!"

Nina stormed up the block, her shoulders rigid, her stride deliberate. Isabelle felt as if she had been beaten. She started to run after Nina, hoping to convince her how wrong she was to turn her back on her family; then suddenly she stopped. Maybe someday Nina would go back to being who she was. Maybe someday she would see that Miranda and Luis and Isabelle and

Sam had never meant her any harm. Maybe someday she would be ready to love them again.

Maybe someday, Isabelle thought sadly. But not today.

Throughout her shift at the coffee shop, if Isabelle wasn't fretting about her disastrous run-in with Nina, she was debating what to do about Skye. She decided that rather than confess to eavesdropping on a private conversation, she would try to draw the information out of her roommate another way. How, she wasn't certain, but with luck an opening would present itself.

It did, when she ran home to change before heading over to job number two, cocktail waitressing at a local jazz club. Skye was dressed in the black slacks and black shirt the owner required for those working the front room, but she was lying on the bed, gazing at the ceiling.

"Are you okay?" Isabelle asked as she hung up her coat and checked to see if she had enough time to shower.

"Yeah. Fine."

"You don't look fine."

"How would you like to do me a favor?" Skye asked, sitting up and facing Isabelle.

"Sure. What do you want?"

"I need you to lie for me."

"To whom about what?" Isabelle said, trying to sound casual.

"To my parents."

Isabelle could see how conflicted Skye was; she didn't blame her. Isabelle had visited the Strausses on several occasions and had grown quite fond of Skye's parents. They were reserved and not prone to idle banter, but they were kind and intelligent and extremely personable. They were not the kind of people one lied to easily.

"Okay," she said hesitantly, waiting for the other shoe to drop.

"I need you to tell them I'm spending spring break with you."

"Because . . ."

"I'm going to Paris with Ezra."

Isabelle feigned shock. "I thought you hated him. Why would you go to Brooklyn with him, let alone Paris?"

Skye laughed, but only briefly. "I used to hate Ezra," she said.

"Used to?"

"Okay," she said, deciding that coy and subtle was not as effective as her usual frankness. "Don't faint, but I'm having an affair with him."

Though Isabelle had expected that, she was stunned nonetheless. "When? How?"

"About the same time you and Cody narrowed your universe to two."

Six months. Isabelle felt so selfish for not having seen what was going on with Skye.

"He called me in to talk about my painting. Like you, he had grown concerned with the increasingly dark mood he saw taking hold of my portraits. I don't know what possessed me, but I told him about my parents and how I suspected that all the faces I did were people I imagined had been in the camps with them and maybe had died instead of them." Skye fidgeted with her rings. It had been difficult admitting that she had been committing her nightmares to canvas; she still felt shy about discussing them. "That's when he told me about Sonya and what had happened to her family and what he suspected had happened to her."

"Which was?"

"He thinks she was some kind of spy and was killed on assignment."

"How tragic."

Skye nodded. "I thought so, but Ezra seemed to believe she might have welcomed death. He said that sometimes he thought she was courting it."

Isabelle was confused. She had always viewed death as an enemy. She couldn't imagine seeking it out or welcoming it like a friend.

"He said that in retrospect, she was more vacant casing than functioning person, more restless spirit than flesh and blood. He feels that chunks of her soul had been robbed by the deaths of each of her parents and each of her children. He thinks she might have felt guilty about surviving and, though I can't see this, was almost anxious to join them. He said there was a haunted quality about her, a ghostly aura that kept others, including him, away."

Isabelle had no basis for understanding this woman Sonya, but digging deep into her own memory stores, she recalled how withdrawn Martín had seemed after Althea had died. At the time she was too young to analyze it, but over the years she had assumed that his emotional recession had been prompted by the state's false accusation and/or his illness. Now she wondered if guilt and loneliness hadn't been part of the equation.

"Do you get that feeling from your parents?" Isabelle asked. "That they feel guilty?"

"Sometimes," Skye said. "But because they don't talk about anything, I can't be sure." She was silent for a moment, thinking. "Look, they triumphed over an incredible evil, and I think that makes them feel strong and grateful and happy to be alive. But, then, how can you feel good when so many died so horribly?"

Skye sighed. This whole issue was one of those imponderables philosophers liked to gnaw at; she had to live with it.

"Why can't you tell them where you're going?" Isabelle asked, recognizing the need to shift the conversation. "And with whom?"

"Because he's not Jewish, he's too old, and nice girls don't go to Paris with men who aren't their husbands. Other than that? No reason."

Isabelle smiled. It was nice to see the return of Skye's lighter side. "Where are we supposed to be going?"

"Any place where there are no phones for them to call me twenty times a day to find out if I'm wearing a coat and eating right."

"How about trekking in the Himalayas?"

"Schlepping they'd buy," Skye said, shaking her head. "Trekking? I don't think so."

"Okay, how about an artist's retreat? Why not tell them we're going to a cabin in the Rockies, where we're expected to do nothing but eat, sleep, absorb the scenery, and paint."

Skye chuckled mischievously. "You know, Isabelle, for a major Goody Two-shoes, you can be one devious broad when you want to be."

The night Ezra and Skye left for Europe, Isabelle and Cody toured several SoHo galleries, something they did regularly so they could remain abreast of what was happening in the market. For a man who was too in love with the human form to abstract it, and a woman who was too overpowered by the emotional tug of nature to try to tame it, some of what was making art news in the seventies was startling. Conceptual art, which was about ideas rather than objects, confused Isabelle. Though they intrigued her, she had trouble relating to canvases with nothing but words on them. When, in one gallery, she came upon a John Baldessari canvas with nothing but the words *True Beauty* painted in the center of it, she stood before it, dumbfounded yet mesmerized.

"I don't get it," she said to Cody, whispering so as not to attract attention to her ignorance.

He, too, was having difficulty. "Me either. I guess I'm used to images being the subjects of paintings."

Isabelle nodded, but she suspected there was more of it than that. She studied the canvas for a long time. Finally she smiled.

"I've got it," she said, poking Cody. "He's making fun of us."

"Us?"

"The art public, the people who demand that paintings be beautiful. Baldessari is giving us what we want. He's saying, 'You want true beauty in a painting? Here it is!' "

"I think you're right," he said, laughing and shaking his head.

They moved on to another gallery, this one showing graffiti art. Once the province of slums and subways, graffiti had suddenly moved from the streets into the galleries. One artist, who had signed his street art "Samo" but was now being called by his real name, Jean-Michel Basquiat, was creating a buzz. Some critics were very excited about his work. Others dismissed him as a teenage scribbler. Cody agreed with the latter. Isabelle wasn't so sure.

Perhaps his wild, color-drenched canvases spoke to her. Perhaps it was the highly keyed emotional content of his work. Certainly it wasn't the subject matter. Basquiat was a black city kid. She was a sheltered, white, middle-class female. Yet his vivid colors, his use of commercial symbols to express very personal thoughts, struck her as courageous. He wasn't afraid to criticize the majority or to confront them with the anger of the minority. Basquiat spoke as an outsider; he was the voice of the Other. The Catalan in Isabelle understood that.

She and Cody debated Basquiat throughout dinner, reaching no conclusion other than the fact that he must have done something right if they had spent two hours talking about nothing but him. When they returned to Cody's loft, he sought to neutralize the effect of Basquiat's intensity with delicate Chopin études and a bottle of red wine. It wasn't long before the atmosphere had mellowed and the tension between them had become sexual rather than intellectual.

Isabelle was still languishing in the drowsy, soporific haze that followed their lovemaking when Cody surprised her.

"I'd like you to pose for me," he said. "I have to submit six paintings for my final seminar project. I want to paint you."

Isabelle simply stared at him.

"I love you," he said, sensing she needed to be assured of that. "I love your body. All I want to do is to immortalize how I feel."

"But you know how I feel about posing nude." She felt cornered.

"You wouldn't be posing in front of a group of strangers. It would be just me and we'd do it here, where you're comfortable."

Isabelle struggled with her love for Cody, her queasiness about what he was asking her to do, and the awareness that it was almost impossible to protest on the grounds of modesty when, in truth, if she and Cody were alone in this loft, it was rare that her clothes were on.

"I'll do it on one condition," she said, instantly rewarded by Cody's smile. "Anything!"

"You can't paint my face. You can create a face. You can use someone else's face. But you can't use mine."

"If I can't use yours," he said, kissing her cheeks and her eyes and, then, her lips, "I won't use any."

For the rest of their holiday, Isabelle came to Cody's loft after work and posed for him. The result of this collaboration was a series of six, wonderfully mysterious paintings Cody dubbed "The Shy Temptress."

Fitzsimmon, Ezra, and others at the league considered his work worthy of being entered in a contest being run by several Parisian galleries in an attempt to mount a show of emerging American artists. When Cody told Isabelle he had been selected and was going to Paris, her reaction was mixed.

"I'm so proud of you," she said, meaning it, yet wrestling against an odd wave of loneliness.

"Come with me."

"I can't."

"Why not? After all, if not for you and this unbelievable body, I wouldn't be going. It's just for the summer, and besides, think how wonderful it would be living together in Paris."

"Cody, I have to find a job. I don't have the money to go to Paris."

"What about your aunt in Barcelona? Wouldn't she send you the money for a ticket?"

That annoyed Isabelle. "I wouldn't ask her," she snapped.

"Don't get angry," Cody said. "I was only trying to think of a way for us to be together."

Isabelle backed off. "I know, but I can't ask Tía Flora or Luis and Miranda to fund a trip to Paris. I'm old enough to be self-sufficient, and that's what I'm going to be! Besides," she said, smiling, sidling close to him and caressing his cheek, trying to bridge the distance she felt separating them, "didn't you say it was only for the summer?"

He nodded. Her soft floral scent filled his nose.

"It'll be torture, but we can manage three short months apart, can't we?" She began to unbutton her shirt. A slow smile waltzed across his lips.

"I'm not so sure," he said, watching her lift her blouse over her head, feeling the magnetic lure of her flesh.

"You go," she whispered, surrendering to his touch and the demands of her own desire. "I'll be here when you come back."

They made love then at a fevered pitch, as if trying to assure each other that the passion they felt was strong enough to last. But afterward, as they lay in each other's arms, both of them knew that passion was an emotion of the moment. Love was what lasted.

At the beginning of August, Cody called.

"You can't imagine how terrific the exhibition was," he said, his enthusiasm traveling thousands of miles. "We sold four of 'The Shy Temptress' series as well as some of my other work."

"That's fabulous!" Isabelle said, happy about his success, ashamed at how jealous she was.

"My reviews were great, and the people who came to the show had such flattering things to say, the gallery wants me to be part of a spring show. Isn't that amazing?" Cody heard the silence but pressed on, his words coming in a nervous rush. "Paris is everything we always thought it was, Isabelle, but I miss you something fierce." Still, silence. "I have a great flat in Montmartre, and I've got a couple of jobs lined up for the two of us. You'd love it here, Isabelle. I'd love you here. Please. Say you'll come."

"I miss you, too, Cody, but I can't."

"Why not?"

She heard the longing in his voice and it tugged at her, but she resisted. She had to. She had made other plans.

"Ezra wants me to study with Clarence Bowman," she said quickly.

Now it was Cody's turn to be silent. Clarence Bowman was one of the great pedagogues.

"There are a dozen teachers in Paris as good as or better than Clarence Bowman," he said, hoping she wouldn't ask him to name them. "Why can't you study with one of them?"

"Because Ezra thinks Bowman's strict style will balance my tendency for, as he puts it, unfettered expressionism. Plus, Bowman's going to be the artist in residence at the University of Wisconsin. Ezra wants me to sit in on his art history lectures, as well as his master classes."

"What about what I want?" Cody said, his voice petulant and angry. "Why is what Ezra Edward Clark wants more important?"

The words were out of Isabelle's mouth before she had a chance to edit them. "Because what Ezra wants is to further my career. Let's not forget that when you got the chance to further your career, you took it without a second thought!"

"That's not true," he argued. "I begged you to come with me. I love you, Isabelle. I thought you loved me."

"I do," Isabelle said. "And I miss you, but, Cody, please understand, this is a rare opportunity. I can't turn it down. It means too much to me."

"More than being with me."

"This isn't a matter of more than," she replied, explaining it to herself as well as to him. "This is you getting an opportunity to make a name for yourself in Paris and me getting the chance to study with Clarence Bowman."

Later, when she repeated the conversation to Skye, including their awkward good-bye, she wondered if she had done the right thing.

"Hmmm," Skye said, stroking her chin, narrowing her eyes, pretending to ponder the conundrum presented to her. "Madison, Wisconsin, or Paris, France? Take classes at the state university or take up residence in a flat in Montmartre? Fulfill your sexual cravings or your destiny?" She paced the floor in front of Isabelle, taking huge strides à la Groucho Marx. Finally she stopped and faced her friend. "Wisconsin."

"I knew you'd say that."

"It's the only thing to say."

"But what about Cody? What about how I feel about him?"

Skye shook her head. "If you really loved him in a happily-ever-after way," she said, "you wouldn't have asked me a thing. You would have been on a plane to Paris."

Isabelle nodded. It was always hard to hear someone verbalize what one knew to be true but, for various reasons, hesitated to admit. "Did you know Ezra got me a job teaching art at a local high school?"

"That man is a regular Santa Claus," Skye said, with a self-satisfied grin. "But don't feel so special. He got me a job, too. I'm going to be working for Julian Richter."

Isabelle's eyes widened. Richter was the biggest and most highly respected art dealer in the city. His gallery was known for creating reputations and careers.

"What are you going to be doing?"

"Grunt work, I suppose, but Ezra thinks I have *the eye.*"

Isabelle hadn't looked at it that way before, but Skye probably did have the instincts necessary to be a dealer. Throughout their years at the league, she had been able to spot who was or was not going to make it, and why.

"That's great!" Isabelle said, hugging her roommate, overcome by the odd sense that she was going to miss Skye more than she missed Cody.

Skye, feeling the same nostalgia, poured them each a glass of wine. Isabelle was first with a toast.

"To Julian Richter's new right hand. Just make sure you do a good job," she said. "One of these days, I may need the contact."

Then it was Skye's turn.

"Here's to you, Isabelle de Luna," she said. "Someday, I'm going to be able to say 'I knew you when.'"

Isabelle laughed. "Well, don't hold your breath. While you're doing the New York scene, I'm going to be in Madison, Wisconsin, first stop on my road to fame and fortune."

CHAPTER 12

In the six years since Nina had left Santa Fe, she had graduated NYU (communication arts), changed her name (Nina Davis), given up on acting (easy to do once she discovered she had no talent) and modeling (tall enough, not gaunt enough), amassed a résumé of odd jobs (waitress, sales clerk, dog walker, house sitter), furnished a third-floor studio walk-up with remnants of other people's lives, and, after a stint as a secretary in the sales promotion department of *Mademoiselle* magazine, had finally landed a job in the publicity department of Hartwick House (one of New York's leading book publishers).

Since the pay was barely above minimum wage, Nina was forced to become rather creative about supplementing her income. For one thing, she kept her job at Chez Vous, a catering concern that prepared elegant dinner parties for the foie gras–and-caviar set. In spite of the late nights and the resultant puffy, morning-after eyes, she considered it a plum job. During the winter season it was busy during the week, dead on the weekends. In the summer it was the reverse: nothing during the week, crazy every weekend, racing out to the Hamptons and taking care of those to whom "ordering in" was a catered dinner for fifty on the patio.

She had been working for Chez Vous for four years, starting as part of the kitchen cleanup crew and working her way up to bartender and waitress. Though her boss, Lila Tufts, was Lucrezia Borgia in a Saint Laurent tuxedo and a sleek, near crew-cut hairdo, Nina suffered whatever abuse Lila handed out. In her employ, Nina gained entry into the finest apartments in the city and a firsthand education in the care and feeding of the very, very rich.

Another financially beneficial contact was her best friend, Clive Frommer, a contributor to "Page Six," the full-page gossip section of the *New York Post*. Their friendship began two years before when they discovered they were the only two people in their theater class who stood absolutely no chance of ever walking the boards on Broadway. When Nina faced that fact, she returned to what she considered to be her destiny—writing—and with Clive's encouragement began the novel she felt she had been born to write. Clive—admitting that to him the play was not the thing, but rather the players—got a job at *Playbill*. From there he moved over to the *Post*, first as an assistant to the drama critic, then as a "Page Six" grunt, verifying rumors and scandals told to or overheard by the editors of the "Page." Nina helped him advance his own cause—and hers, since Clive paid her—by passing along information she picked up at Hartwick House—about authors, agents, and the like—and by telling him whatever the buzz was at the parties she waitressed.

Her job at Hartwick House was basically long on tedium and short on excitement. Most of her time was spent writing and distributing press releases hyping an about-to-be-published book: arranging author tours, book parties—using Chez Vous as much as possible—readings, signings, and various other get-the-author-out-there events. Occasionally she was sent out on a minitour—Cleveland, Cincinnati, Indianapolis, Toronto, or a similar configuration of cities—with one of the house's newer authors or one who was less experienced in the art of selling *the book*. Twice, however, she had accompanied major authors, one a Vietnam war hero, the other a romance novelist, crisscrossing the country and hitting at least five cities in each of the four major markets.

Though author tours were notoriously grueling, Nina loved them. While the standard city-a-day schedule was numbing, she got to meet radio personalities, attend luncheons and dinners with booksellers and wholesalers, visit places she'd never been before, stay at fine hotels, and dine at some of the country's better eateries. Her biggest kick was being inside the TV studios, both watching how the crew worked and judging how well the guests did, taking notes and absorbing whatever she could for when it was her turn.

On Cleveland's *The Morning Show,* she noticed that the anchorwoman always sat slightly forward, her best side facing the camera, her posture making her look constantly engaged.

On *AM/Northwest* in Portland, Oregon, she switched between watching the live interview with the major and the moderator and watching what came up on the monitor. She was trying to ascertain which was more effective: speaking to the camera or speaking to the moderator and the audience. The answer was painfully obvious. Speaking to the camera, as the major was doing, made him look inexperienced and unprofessional, like a man on the street who at any moment was going to wave and say "Hi, Mom" instead of a man who had survived three years in a prisoner-of-war camp.

In Charlotte, North Carolina, she stood off to the side while her author was interviewed for *Top o' the Day*. Lovey Chiles was a fifty-something, red-headed "beehive"—industry parlance for romance writers with rounded, heavily lacquered hair. While Lovey favored dresses Nina thought were better suited for meetings of the Horticultural Society, on this particular day the author looked wonderful in a simple russet silk dress that showed off her girlish figure. The producer disagreed.

"She's going to be one big red blob."

"Why?" Nina asked.

"Because the camera doesn't distinguish among shades of a color. It's going to zone in on either the red of her hair or the red of her dress and color-adjust to one or the other."

"So what should I tell her to do?"

"Since her hair is such a distinctive feature, get her to wear something light and softly patterned. That way, the main focus will be on her face where you want it."

On *Good Morning, San Francisco* Lovey was supposed to be interviewed by the female anchor, a woman who professed to be a fan. As luck would have it, she was off on a honeymoon, leaving Lovey to a man who clearly had no interest in or respect for romance novels.

"I can see it now," he said, splaying his hand dramatically and winking at the audience. "There you are in a chenille bathrobe and curlers, typing away at the kitchen table while hubby and the kids are tucked away in bed."

Nina was impressed by the way Lovey responded to the man's velvet attack. She smiled graciously, then parried and lunged, mentioning the name of the book ten times in a four-minute segment.

On the road, Nina introduced herself to every producer and director and personality she met. She handed them her business card and made sure to write them a follow-up thank-you. Having watched Lila, she was aware of the importance of networking and had begun to amass a Rolodex of people who might prove helpful in the future.

Whereas Nina had never given up her dreams of being famous, she was determined to be ready when that day arrived. "Ready" meant perfecting a look, polishing her social skills, refining her biography, and mastering the technique of allowing others to believe you've told them everything, when in truth you've told them only what you want them to know. If she had learned anything working at Hartwick and Chez Vous, it was the importance of one's image and the sharpness of one's focus.

In order to construct the perfect image, Nina spent hours poring over fashion magazines, snipping pictures and collecting names of the best hair-cutters, stylists, and makeup artists in the city. She cut out fashion do's and don't's, as well as trendy ins and outs. She was never going to be caught eating an artichoke if asparagus was the vegetable of the moment, or smelling of Shalimar if Chanel No. 5 was the preferred *parfum*.

She also opened a file for Nina Davis. In it were pieces from *Town & Country* on old English families, Boston's Brahmins, San Francisco's Nob Hill elite, and whatever other bloodlines sounded compatible with who she wanted to be. She saved pieces from *The Connoisseur* on porcelain and silver and other collectibles that might have been handed down from generation to generation but, with patience and a trained eye, could be acquired at rummage sales, local antique shows, and country auctions. She read biographies of the rich and famous, as well as the obscure and eccentric, excerpting interesting tips and tales from each. Little by little she was molding the person who would become Nina Davis, but until she had all the pieces put together and memorized to the point of feeling natural, she kept to herself and focused on her passport to celebrity—her novel.

SoHo Cinderella told the story of an orphan raised in a downtown tenement by an evil couple who took in foster children for the money. The youngest and fairest of three, she was the family workhorse, forced to cook and clean while the others enjoyed the benefits of her labors. When she was old enough to be taken out of school, she was made to work alongside her guardians in an overcrowded clothing factory, sewing sleeves into expensive gowns.

She was there almost a year when the designer happened to tour the factory. Despite her kerchiefed head, unmanicured nails, ragged clothes, and dirt-stained skin, he recognized her beauty immediately, plucked her from the sweatshop, and moved her uptown to the showroom. There she functioned as a mannequin, modeling the luscious evening gowns that were the label's signature. If customers pawed her—which they did—she was to say nothing. If they wanted to buy her a drink, she went. If they wanted to go farther than that, well, it wasn't discouraged.

One day a young man came to buy. The son of America's department store king, he fell madly in love with the tall, pale young woman with the sad eyes and languid walk. Cupid's arrow pierced her heart as well, but what chance did she stand with the mercantile? Heartbroken and ashamed, she ran away. He ran after her, found her, and in true fairy-tale fashion, whisked her away to his castle in the sky, a penthouse on Park Avenue and Seventy-second Street.

Every minute she could steal from a day, Nina worked on her novel—in the morning before she left for work, weekends, any night off she had, and every noon. While Hartwick's editors were at their regular tables in the Grill at the Four Seasons and her co-workers were checking the racks at Alexander's or Macy's, Nina was typing away on her manuscript. The only person privileged to see any of it was Clive Frommer and then only because he was helping her write the sex scenes.

"I'm experienced and somewhat inventive," she said over pasta and wine, "but I want kinky, and since I seem to be celibate these days, you are my inside track on what is currently passing for kinky."

"I accept the compliment, but let's not forget, it's boys that make my heart sing, not the luscious, sensuous, ripe-bodied heroines of novels such as yours. I'm into Rhett Butler, darling, not Scarlett."

"So what! I'll just put a 'she' where you've got a 'he.' "

"Why not?" he said, suddenly amused at the idea of being Nina's sexual ghost. "Just don't forget about me when you're chatting it up with Johnny Carson."

Nina leaned over and kissed his cheek. "I never forget my friends."

"That's good," Clive said, draining his glass and affecting a look Nina recognized as his quasi-Bogart mien, "because as my dear departed mommy used to say, 'Friends once forgotten become enemies forever.' "

"Mommy was a very together lady," Nina said, her laughter turning dark as she relived the perfidy of Isabelle and Sam huddled together, talking about her behind her back. "Those are words to live by."

And I do, she thought with renewed vengeance, thinking back to that afternoon and her contretemps with Isabelle. The intensity of her own reaction surprised her. She would have thought five years would have distilled her anger, but it hadn't. She felt as betrayed and abandoned now as she had then. It didn't matter that Isabelle had apologized and pleaded for Nina to understand that she and Sam hadn't meant to hurt her and that she should remember and consider all the wonderful years they had shared. Clive's mother made more sense than all of Isabelle's arguments put together.

Nina had been the friend once forgotten. Now those who had forgotten her were her enemies. Because in Nina's other book, the one in which she kept her accounts, once was one time too many.

Spring always prompted a flurry of parties for Chez Vous. Three weeks in a row Nina worked five sit-down, black-tie dinners. She was exhausted, but she needed the money. Hopefully, she told herself every morning as she dragged her body out of bed, she wouldn't have to do this much longer. At the end of March she had handed *SoHo Cinderella* to Jodi Cutler, Hartwick's editor in chief. Jodi had been surprised to receive a manuscript from a staffer but had assured Nina she would read it.

"I may not be able to get to it right away," she had said apologetically, pointing to the ledge behind her desk, which was stacked end to end with manuscripts.

Nina had nodded compliantly and said, "Fine. Okay. Whenever." But from the moment she had exited Jodi's office, Nina had agonized. "She *has* to like it," she said, repeating it over and over like a mantra, perhaps hoping to telegraph her thoughts and influence a decision. As days lapsed into weeks, she began to wander by Jodi's office. It was silly, she knew. Editors rarely read during daylight hours. It was an after-work, after-dark activity. But Nina couldn't help herself. As if it were a tropism, she was drawn from her chair, down the hall, up the elevator, past the string of windowed cubicles housing lower-echelon editors, and to the corner where Jodi held court. Sometimes she carried memos from her boss so that she could claim purpose. Other times she pretended she needed copies of one book or another to send to various producers or book reviewers. And still other times she simply strolled by as if taking a constitutional and Jodi Cutler's office just happened to be on her route.

Clive told her she was acting like an idiot. "Don't make a pest out of yourself," he said. "All you're doing is creating negative vibrations." She nodded obediently. "Get your mind off the book and concentrate on gathering gossip instead. I don't know about you, *ma cherie,* but the summer season is nearly upon us and I haven't a thing to wear."

"I'm sweating out my future and all you can think about are swim trunks?"

"I don't wear *trunks,*" Clive said as if they were the undisputed cause of syphilis. "And I'm not being insensitive." He put his arm around her and squeezed her shoulders in a buck-up embrace. "But really, Nina, there's nothing more you can do except wait it out."

"Easy for you to say. You're not making a dollar and a quarter a week like I am." Nina crumpled onto the nearest chair, pulling her knees up under her chin. "I'm broke, Clive. I have school loans to pay back, overdue bills, and no light at the end of this grimy, poverty-ridden tunnel. I need that book published."

"Even if Hartwick buys it, they're only going to give you a portion of the advance up front. The rest comes later, when it's published, which you know, could take up to a year."

Nina groaned. "What the hell am I supposed to do in the meantime?"

"I already told you, babe. Stop bitchin' and start snitchin'!"

New York's social scene was like a series of pinwheels, each one swirling around its own center. To the outsider whose only knowledge of the high-powered and deep-pocketed came from paparazzi snapshots and gossip column recaps of who was where with whom, it might have appeared as if the city were divided cleanly and simply into two camps: the traditional haves and have-nots. In reality the haves were divided many times over into myriad sets, each with its own entrance requirements, its own standards of excellence, its own personality, and its own rituals. All that was missing was a secret handshake and a club tie.

There was the inherited wealth, ancestors-over-on-the-*Mayflower* summer in Newport aristocracy, but since they didn't have to prove to anyone how rich they were, they didn't party much. There was the Wall Street/corporate America, blue pinstripe by day, black tie by night set. Those who curried favor with entertainment moguls and anyone with a Hollywood connection. Culture vultures whose charities of choice included the ballet, the Philharmonic, the opera, and the Metropolitan Museum. The art crowd, which never missed a Saturday at the galleries or an event at the Whitney or the Modern. The music crowd, which seasoned their parties with divas, conductors, and the occasional soloist.

There were groups with a decided ethnic cast or political purpose, groups so liberal and daring that they invited athletes to sit next to diplomats and cliques that paraded their government alliances by sprinkling a senator, congressman, or ambassador among the unelected and unappointed. Since outsiders were allowed—as long as they had some kind of cachet—it wasn't unusual to find decorators, fashion designers, TV anchormen, reporters, authors, and an occasional model milling about. They were called "color."

Since each set was like a distinctive little club, it was not uncommon to see some of the same faces night after night. One face Nina was seeing more and more of lately was that of her daytime boss, Anthony Hartwick. Tall, rangy, with black hair and jade-green eyes, Hartwick was silver-spoon elegant and back-street sexy, a combination Nina found impossible to resist. But around the office, the stories about him were legion.

Scion of the Hartwick family, one of Boston's old-money dynasties, he had made the decision to move the headquarters of the venerable publishing house to New York and to actively pursue best-sellers instead of maintaining a list made up almost exclusively of literary fiction, as his predecessors had

done. Thanks to some clever buys and well-thought-out publicity and marketing campaigns, within a relatively short period of time Hartwick House had
become a major player. On the personal front, he was married and divorced
and remarried. Rumor had it that marriage number two was on the rocks.

She couldn't imagine why she hadn't noticed him before, but she certainly
had a fix on him now. He was a stunning figure of a man, about ten years
older than she, whose elegant manners and social grace seemed to define
savoir faire. The man positively oozed breeding, which to Nina was like an
aphrodisiac. Curious, she tried to figure out which of the forty women was
Mrs. Hartwick, but since everyone knew everyone else, they spoke without
addressing each other by name.

When they were seated, however, Nina scanned place cards until she
stopped behind a woman whose dark hair was cut exactly like Nina's: stick
straight, chin length, with a long fringe of bangs. Her features were doll-like,
and beneath her striped silk Ungaro kimono, her body appeared thin and
shapeless. When Nina went to pick up her tray from the kitchen, she asked
Lila for the scoop on Sissy Hartwick.

"Cecilia, only child of Brandon Cromwell, head of Cromwell Investments,
heiress to a fortune!" Lila dished information as quickly and efficiently as she
dished risotto. There were few in this town she didn't know and little she
didn't know about them. "Her first marriage was to Dashell Crowes, one of
the shining lights in Daddy's company. He had been Daddy's choice and,
according to Sissy, an unqualified disaster. It seems poor Dashell couldn't get
it up. Since Daddy was hot for a grandbaby, he agreed to an annulment. Three
years ago, she brought Hartwick home. Word is, Cromwell can't stand him.
Calls him the Beantown Bookpeddler and grumbles about how unsuitable he
is, but hey! Sissy's always got a big smile on her face. The man must be a stud."

"So how many children have they produced?"

"None. How many dinners have you served?"

"On my way."

All evening Nina observed the Hartwicks. They were at different tables, so
it was difficult to tell how they related to each other, but neither one of them
had any problem relating to the people next to them. Mrs. Hartwick seemed
utterly fascinated by her dinner companion, a young, intense, midwestern
congressman who had obviously hypnotized her with his discussion of grain
allotments and farm subsidies.

Mr. Hartwick was engrossed in conversation with Greta Reed, a woman
Nina had seen at numerous other parties. Fortyish, with piercing blue eyes,
blond hair, and big bones, she owned one of New York's better art galleries.

Though Nina knew little about her, whenever she had heard people talk about Greta Reed, the adjectives used most often were powerful, aggressive, tenacious, and, when she had to be, ruthless.

My kind of gal, Nina thought as she studied the large woman holding Anthony Hartwick in thrall.

It surprised her to note that for one who cultivated such a strong, Amazonian aura, Greta's taste was exceedingly feminine. Her dress was a floaty chiffon, her hair was softly coiffed, and her jewelry was delicate, probably antique. Also fascinating was her constant twirling of a sculpted gold band around her finger. One wouldn't associate nervous habits with someone so self-assured.

Nina was intrigued, especially when the discussion turned to the macabre tone of Greta's current exhibition, "Ghosts," which featured works by painters Mark Rothko, Arshile Gorky, and Jackson Pollock and sculptor David Smith. Smith died in 1965 when his pickup truck spun off a country road in Bennington, Vermont. Pollock died nine years earlier in a fatal car crash. Gorky hanged himself in his barn in Sherman, Connecticut, in the summer of 1948. And sometime during the night of February 24, 1970, Mark Rothko gulped down an overdose of barbiturates and then hacked through his elbow veins with a razor.

"Whatever possessed you to mount an exhibition like this?" Anthony said.

"They're all great artists. They all died in their prime. Each death was another tragic subtraction from American art. There's a string there."

"A rather bloody string, don't you think?"

Greta leaned forward, her breasts straining against the confines of her gown, her alto voice dropping to a near whisper. "We may deny it," she said, taking Anthony's hand as if to make certain he didn't run away. "It may make us uncomfortable. But we're all hopelessly captivated by death. Especially the notion of someone daring to usurp God's power by taking a life—more so if it's his own."

"I don't agree," Anthony snapped, pulling away. "You're giving the subject of death too much credit. It's not the draw you think it is."

"No? Then why is the gallery more crowded than McDonald's?"

"Because of the inherent value of the artists on display. You didn't need the hook, Greta."

"Ah, but I like hooks."

"You like to shock and stun."

Her laugh was hearty, more like that of a farmgirl than a Fifty-seventh Street doyenne. "You're right, I do." Her blue eyes fixed on Hartwick. She didn't know why they were fencing, but his moves were interesting. "So, tell me," she said, probing. "Did I shock you?"

"No, but the prices of the paintings did. How do you arrive at such numbers?"

Others at the table turned toward them. Obviously they had been listening with half an ear. Several were collectors. Put money and art in the same sentence, and you had their full attention.

"In art, a fair price is whatever you think you can get."

"That sounds very cynical, Greta. And very self-serving."

"Maybe so, but it's honest. Works of art don't have intrinsic value like a car or a book. Worth is based on pure, irrational desire. If you want it badly enough, you'll pay whatever's asked."

"But if you know that's how the game is played, you can refuse to be manipulated by it."

Greta cocked her head to one side and studied her companion. Clearly it bothered him to think that an external force might be able to insinuate itself inside his psyche and orchestrate his moves. "You seem to be a man who prides himself on his control," she said with unmasked directness, "and that's fine. But don't kid yourself, Anthony. Everyone can be manipulated by their desires."

Nina, who had been hovering in the background, rapt, suddenly looked up and found Lila glaring at her. Without wasting any more time, she cleared the table in preparation for the dessert service. Anxious to escape the kitchen before Lila had a chance to dress her down, she went out a different door from the one she had come in. Finding herself lost in a back hallway, she opened the first door she came to. There, on her knees, engaged in a very personal act with the congressman, was Sissy Hartwick. Both were so heavily involved in their intermezzo, they failed to notice Nina, who sneaked out as quietly as she could.

Just in case someone had spotted her in the back hallway, Nina waited a few days before calling Clive. "Paydirt!" she exclaimed before telling him what she had seen.

The next day, couched in euphemisms that stretched the English language to its limits, the semiblind item about a publisher's wife and a servant of the people appeared on "Page Six." The day after that, she and Clive celebrated their biggest check ever with dinner at Elaine's. Two weeks after that, Jodi Cutler left a message that she wanted to see her.

After some polite preliminaries about the weather and such, Jodi said, "I'm sorry, Nina, but I don't think we can publish *SoHo Cinderella.*"

Nina stared at her as if she were speaking in tongues. The idea that she was rejecting the novel was simply incomprehensible. Jodi, having seen that look of complete bewilderment before, continued.

"Our schedule is very heavy in the area of women's fiction. There's simply no room for this book. I'm sure you understand."

"Actually, no, I don't." Nina had rehearsed at least twenty responses, ranging from controlled rapture and great modesty about Hartwick offering her the highest advance ever paid for a first novel to gracious thanks to incredulity to abject indignation. Under the circumstances, the latter seemed most appropriate.

Exhibiting great patience, Jodi gave Nina a discourse on the difficulties involved in compiling a publishing schedule: budget constraints, production considerations, marketing timetables, author demands, the need to combat the competition. She maintained her smile throughout, but her eyes showed the strain she felt. She had hoped that Nina, being in the business, would have taken the excuse offered and left it at that.

"Schedules can be juggled."

Jodi was getting annoyed. "It's not as easy as it sounds," she said, offering Nina one last chance to save face.

"It is if you want it to be."

Jodi's smile evaporated. "There is no way I could justify juggling a schedule for a refried fairy tale."

"That's insulting."

"I'm sorry, Nina, but that's all *SoHo Cinderella* is. It's trite and predictable and, to get to the heart of it, poorly written." Jodi would never get used to devastating someone's dreams, but over the years she had convinced herself that it was for the best. They could move on to other things, into areas where they might find the success they had wanted to believe writing would bring. "I've read some of your press releases," she said, hoping to soften the blow. "They're good, Nina. Crisp. Pithy. Often with a sense of humor. Why not stick to communications?"

"Thanks for the advice." Nina stood, lifting herself to her full height, keeping her steely eyes trained on Jodi's face. "I'll be sure to remember what you said."

Two months later Nina found herself waitressing at the home of Greta Reed. A spectacular West Side apartment overlooking Central Park, it wasn't large—Greta lived alone—but it was uniquely laid out, with rooms that were spacious and grand. As might be expected, the backgrounds were kept deliberately spare to highlight whatever art Greta was enjoying at the moment. While it was rumored that she had a collection worth millions, she displayed very few pieces at one time, perferring to store the rest or, on occasion, loan out a selection to museums.

Her entrance hall boasted a black, white, and gray diptych by Frank Stella: two squares filled with rigid stripes that created an illusion of protrusion and retraction, teasing the eye into seeing a convexity and concavity that didn't exist. A Dubuffet sculpture of a man seated on a bench looked like a black-and-white cartoon. Three thin, gold metal disks seemed to rise on a wall like bubbles from an elysian bath.

Two sets of stairs with lacy wrought-iron railings went from the back side of the entrance hall into a sunken living room. In one corner was a column by Louise Nevelson, a black monolith that looked like a modern totem made from chunks of charcoal. Next to it, hanging above a sofa, was a Monet from the 1920s, his favorite water pond at Giverny rippling in dusky shades of purple, blue, and dark, moody mauve. There were two attenuated Giacometti heads on a cocktail table, a curvaceous bronze by Jean Arp, a stabile by Alexander Calder. There was a Picasso in the powder room, a Frankenthaler over her bed, and, over her dresser, an Andy Warhol that looked like a double-exposed photograph of Elvis Presley.

A Rothko crowned the fireplace in the library, its somber yet serene field of reds and russets blending with the rich mahogany that paneled the room. Soft leather couches and caramel carpeting attempted to create a den of peace, yet the tone of the room was unsettled, unnerving. On the far wall was the reason: an acutely disturbing painting by the Mexican surrealist Frida Kahlo. Born of the pain she had suffered over her husband's affair with her younger sister, the self-portrait she crafted resonated with the excruciating hollowness of her isolation, an expression of her grief.

The artist stood in the center, unconnected, alienated, a metal rod piercing the hole in her chest where her heart had been plucked out. At the ends of the rod, tiny cupids seesawed. Like her husband, Mexican artist Diego Rivera, they frolicked at her expense, unmindful of the torment love's ups and downs can cause. Alongside her, scrapped like a useless piece of garbage, her heart bled as she wept.

While it was well known that everything in Greta's apartment was for sale, this painting was not. Though many speculated that the reason was personal, since Greta wasn't involved with anyone, had no children or known relatives, it remained an enigma.

Nina couldn't have cared less about Greta's private life; it was her own life she was worried about. For as long as she could remember, she had wanted to be a writer. There was nothing she loved more than reading over something she had written, to see words on a page and know that she had put them there. It was exhilarating when the paragraphs flowed one into the other with a verbal grace that made it all feel right and natural. She had spent years filling diaries, reading magazines and commercial fiction, studying writing styles, experimenting in an effort to find one that best suited her. She had been on her high school newspaper, editor of her high school yearbook, a contributor to her college newspaper. She had a way with words; everyone said so. Ruth Hoffman. Every teacher she ever had. Clive. Flora Pujol. Everyone, it seemed, except Jodi Cutler.

Nina felt like a bank depositor in a failed savings and loan; everything she had invested had been lost through no fault of hers. She believed she was talented. *SoHo Cinderella* might have been flawed—most first novels were—but she would have taken editing gladly. A few days after her meeting with Jodi, she tried to tell her just that, that if Jodi would tell her what was needed, she would do whatever was necessary to make the book work. Jodi's response was a curt, "I'm too busy, and besides, Nina, nothing is going to make this book work. Give it up."

If Nina had been angry before, she was livid now.

"Who does she think she is?" she ranted to Clive, dissecting Jodi Cutler like a frog in a biology lab. "She's nothing but a plain Jane with a title. The woman's lipstick is too pink. She's too skinny to be sexy. She dresses like she thinks *Popular Mechanics* is a fashion magazine. And no matter how wonderful she thinks she is, she's not the only editor in town!"

"Right on," Clive said, applauding. "Forget about her. Just send the manuscript somewhere else."

"I don't know anyone at any other publishing house."

"So what? Just look up 'editor in chief' and send it over."

"Don't be so naive," she said, totally exasperated. "If I send it over without an agent or a recommendation from someone important, it'll wind up on a slush pile, waiting for some fresh-out-of-college reader to pass judgment on it. No! That would be too humiliating."

Instead she began to give herself pep talks, trying to revive a fighting spirit that seemed to be lying dormant.

"You came to New York with nothing," she'd say to the dejected face in the mirror. "No friends. No family. You put yourself through college. No one helped you. You helped you! You found a way then. You'll find a way now!"

At the moment, however, she was agitating, biding her time with the patience of a dog in need of a walk.

Lila wasn't helping. Instead of assigning Nina to Greta's living room, where all the big shots were, she dispensed her to the library. Nina served the smoked trout with crème fraîche and two caviars, grumbling under her breath. In the other room were people like Diane von Furstenberg, Thomas Hoving, Anthony Hartwick, pop artist Roy Lichtenstein, and Rona Barrett. The only luminary at her table, other than her favorite postprandial entertainer Sissy Hartwick, was Julian Richter, another of New York's premier gallery owners.

Nina had enjoyed working these parties when she had felt her dreams were within reach. Now all she felt was envy and resentment. Why were they sitting and she serving? What lucky breaks had they enjoyed that she had been denied? Like this Skye person seated next to Richter. She was younger than Nina and, judging by her clothes, not part of the Saks Fifth Avenue set. Why was she here?

When the conversation shifted from a new movie called *Star Wars* back to art, Nina surmised that Skye assisted Richter. Every now and then, as she leaned over to set down or retrieve a plate, she could overhear Skye talking about wanting Richter to see a new artist she had recommended, not one someone else had championed. The man seated across from Skye, to Sissy's right, hailed from Wisconsin. Eager to join in the conversation, he mentioned that the renowned art pedagogue Clarence Bowman was in residence at the University of Wisconsin.

"I know," Skye said. "My closest friend, Isabelle de Luna, is in Madison now, studying with him."

The gentleman was impressed. "The chancellor lobbied very hard to get him to spend time at the university. He's considered one of the best. Your friend must be very talented."

"She's incredible. Isn't she, Julian?"

Everyone, including Nina, waited for the master's word. It wasn't simply Richter's ability to discern talent that was legendary; it was his genius as an architect of artistic careers that kept the public dazzled. One could almost see Sissy and several other collectors in the room waiting to see whether they should remember the name Isabelle de Luna.

"She has potential," he said simply.

Nina wasn't savvy in the ways of the art world, but judging by the whispers that followed his pronouncement, in this group, at least, Isabelle had just been anointed. It fascinated Nina to see how one stray comment made in the right place by the right people could strike a match and light someone's way. That it was her estranged sister who had been given this serendipitous assist—in her presence, no less—seemed to underline Nina's belief that destiny did indeed have its darlings.

Distressed and in need of a bathroom, Nina left the library and headed toward Greta's room. The corridor leading to the master suite was curved, making it impossible to see inside the bedroom until one was actually in the room. As she approached, she heard a man's voice. Thinking there might be an extracurricular activity taking place, she stopped. And just in case it might be something she could feed to Clive, she listened. Judging by the one-sided conversation, she decided that the person to whom this man was speaking was on the other end of a phone, not the other side of a bed.

"I'm right around the corner. . . . Greta Reed's . . . The usual crew. . . . I told her before we came I had an author in from out of town that I had to see. . . . Who cares what she believes? Our marriage is way beyond having to come up with feasible explanations for our all-night absences. . . . I'll be there by eleven."

Nina recognized the voice as belonging to Anthony Hartwick. Quickly she found a closet, slipped into it, and waited until she heard him leave. After she'd used the bathroom, she went to the kitchen to see Lila.

"I'm think I'm getting sick," she said. Without lipstick and with an extra dusting of powder, she did look wan. Lila studied her as if she had X-ray vision and were looking beyond the flesh for infectious viruses and diseased microbes. "I can handle the next two courses, but if Charlie can cover for me on cleanup, I'd be most grateful."

"You do look like shit," Lila said bluntly, while nodding sympathetically. "You can cut out after you put down the dessert plates. I'll do your coffee."

Nina waited across the street from Greta's building until Hartwick came out. He walked two blocks north, turned onto Sixty-sixth Street, and strode into the second building from the corner. Nina followed at a distance, waited until she was sure he was in the elevator, and then approached the doorman.

"Listen, I need a favor," she said breathlessly, her coat open so he could see her waitress's uniform. "That guy who just came in here? I was working a party he was at, and he dropped his wallet when he was putting on his coat. I've got to give it to him. Can you tell me which apartment he's in?"

"Tell you what," the doorman said, surveying Nina, clearly unused to being confronted by women who met him eye to eye. "You give me the wallet and I'll give it to him."

"Yeah, right. He'll give you a fat reward and I'll get nothing for my trouble."

She shook her head. "Uh-uh. No good." She waved a twenty in front of him. He shook his head. She added a ten. Still nothing. "Last offer," she said, adding another twenty. "Fifty dollars for the apartment number and who lives there."

The man snatched the money from her hand and grinned. "Nineteen B, and I don't know the name of the woman who lives there."

"Now, now, that's not nice." Nina's pleasant manner had taken a definite turn.

"Honest. All I know is the apartment's owned by Hartwick House, whatever that is, and the woman works there."

"And how often does this gentleman visit?"

The doorman hesitated. Nina pulled out another ten. She had just spent a night's earnings.

"At least twice a week," he told her. "Sometimes more. And he doesn't just visit. Most of the time, he stays the night."

The next morning Nina couldn't wait to grab the Hartwick House personnel directory. Quickly she rifled through it, looking for anyone who lived at that address. When she found it, she laughed out loud. Then she called Clive.

The next day this item appeared on "Page Six":

> NICE WORK IF YOU CAN GET IT. *Apparently, one of the perks of being an editor in chief at Hartwick House is an apartment in a tony West Side building. According to our sources, the two-bedroom, high-floor, view-of-the-park apartment is paid for lock, stock, and divan by the company. Add in carfare, lunches, and after-hour visits by the publisher—it's the best deal in town!*

The office buzz was incredible. It was all anyone talked about for days. Jodi Cutler and Anthony Hartwick! Some said they had known all along. Most were shocked. But everyone had something to say. Nina pretended to be as surprised as anyone. She listened to the chatter, sympathized with the grumblings, laughed at the jokes, and wondered along with her co-workers whether it was best-sellers or bedroom tricks that had garnered the fancy West Side digs, and whether a few more of each might get Jodi something bigger and better on the East Side.

The first sign of trouble was a visit from Clive.

"They canned me," he said as he walked past her and headed straight for the refrigerator and the vodka.

"What?"

"Fired. Let go. Released. Thrown out. How many other definitions do you need?" He tossed the clear liquid down his throat as if it were water, pursing his lips as the alcohol scorched his esophagus.

Nina poured herself another glass of white wine. Before Clive had barged in, she had been celebrating Jodi's disgrace. Clearly it was complete, because Jodi had been too embarrassed to come to work. Her secretary had said she was on a business trip, but someone who lived nearby said they had seen her in the supermarket, hidden behind dark glasses and a kerchief. As for Hartwick, he had so many scandals already attached to his name, another one could hardly ruin his reputation. Nina had done her deed and gotten away with it, or so she had believed.

"You didn't tell them where you got your information, did you?"

Clive swished his second shot of vodka around in the glass and scowled at her. "Of course not! I'm a journalist. I never reveal my sources." Before she could comment on the ridiculousness of such a statement, he grinned, raised his glass to her, and said, "It was fun while it lasted, eh, baby?"

Nina laughed and drank with him. "Yup. It was a hell of a ride."

She had been expecting the call inviting her to visit Hartwick's office for days. When it finally came, she was prepared. Wearing her best attitude, she strode late into his office as if she, not he, had asked for the meeting. Her pace was curbed somewhat by the size of his office and the fact that there was no desk. It had taken a short elevator ride to get here, yet she felt as if she had been mysteriously transported uptown to an elegant penthouse.

Large, square, with ten-foot ceilings, the space was dominated by the art that accessorized it, rather than the pieces that furnished it. One painting took up an entire wall, very modern, all color and form, looking like a violent terrestrial explosion. Along another wall, a long, black wooden squiggle that Nina supposed was classified as a sculpture snaked its way from end to end. Two black leather couches formed right angles with each other, a plain acrylic table in front of each. Two Regency-style armchairs upholstered in the same black leather closed the conversational group. There were Oriental jugs, carved Buddhas, and an African drum. A single vase of peach tulips and curly willow twigs provided a touch of softness.

"You wanted to see me?" she said, suddenly a bit unsure of herself. He motioned for her to sit on the chair facing him. She did so, crossing her legs, displaying the length of them, watching as he assessed her.

He took his time before speaking, sipping mineral water from a crystal goblet, studying her as if she were a piece of art brought there for his approval. Those jade-green eyes she had thought were so sexy across a dinner table turned sinister across the divide of his office. Looking out at her from beneath thick brows and a low ridge, he seemed to be willing her discomfort.

"Do you know why you're here?" he asked.

Nina offered him her most innocent smile. "I haven't a clue."

As his lips began the slow ascent toward an insidious smile, Nina noticed how full they were, particularly the lower one. Nice, she thought. Very nice.

"You're fired." He said it calmly, without the slightest sign of anger, yet Nina sensed it was there, simmering just below the surface.

"May I ask why?"

He nodded. "You may."

He was turning this into a cat-and-mouse game. Nina had played many times before, but she had always been the cat. She didn't like being the mouse. "Okay, why are you firing me?"

"Because you're a snitch."

"I beg your pardon!" Nina's tone was properly indignant, but she feared a slight flush might have colored her face.

He placed his water goblet on the table in front of him, rested his arms on his thighs, and leaned forward, bringing his face that much closer to hers. Nina could almost feel the surge of negative vibrations emanating from deep within him. He was straining to control them, but like a magnetic field run amok, they caused the hairs on her arms to crackle from the static given off.

"For a long time, I was disturbed about leaks concerning several of Hartwick's authors and a few of our company practices. I was upset by embarrassing snippets of gossip about friends of mine that never should have found their way into print. And then, Miss Davis, there was the piece about my wife and the congressman." The muscles in his jaw tensed. His eyes darkened. Nina was actually beginning to feel nervous. He looked like a spring that had been coiled way too tight.

"I fail to see what any of this has to do with me," she said in clipped tones, her head high, her chin thrust forward Bette Davis style.

"I didn't see it at first, either. Then, one day, I happened to notice you in the elevator. You are a woman worth noticing," he said with a gracious nod. "But it wasn't your feminine charms that were sticking in my mind. It was something else. It took a while, but finally it came to me. Chez Vous. You were one of their waitresses. You worked here. A coincidence?"

"A coincidence is exactly what it is," Nina said, standing in a huff, her outrage on full display. "And frankly, I resent the implications!"

"You're in no position to resent anything. Now sit down!"

It wasn't a request. Nina obeyed. He stood, circling her chair, making her feel as if she were in a cauldron on top of a roaring fire, about to become cannibal stew.

"I don't believe in coincidences, Miss Davis. I prefer private investigators." When Nina started to rise from her chair, he placed a firm hand on her shoulder, keeping her where he wanted her. "You were at every party that preceded an article about Hartwick House, me, my wife, and my friends. When this last article appeared, I asked Miss Cutler if she knew any reason that you might want to soil her name. She told me she had rejected a manuscript of yours. I asked her to give it to me."

He stopped directly in front of her. Again he took his time. When he spoke, his voice was as hard as flint, his words as hurtful as arrows. "She was right," he said. "It stinks! The only talent you have is for making trouble. But you won't make it here. You have exactly one hour to pick up your paycheck and get the hell out!"

When Nina got home, there was a brief message on her answering machine from Lila: "You stupid bitch!"

For six months Nina pounded the pavement, looking for a job, living off unemployment and what little savings she had. With each passing day her rage toward Anthony Hartwick grew. She wasn't denying what she had done, nor was she contradicting his charges of disloyalty and invasion of privacy. But he had gone too far. He'd fired her from Hartwick House, made certain she lost her job at Chez Vous, and because he was the one who had lobbied for Clive's dismissal—threatening to sue the *Post* for libel—her third source of income had also been eliminated. He hadn't simply let her go; he was out to destroy her.

When Clive landed a job as assistant to the society editor at the *Daily News,* Nina greeted the news with mixed feelings. She was thrilled for him and told him so over dinner, but when she returned to her apartment, the mask came off. She was alone and frightened. Clive's good fortune had served to underscore her desperation. For much of the night she sat in the dark, trying to see through it, wondering what to do and where to go next. At some point an idea came to her. She mulled it over, considered it, debated it, and, finally, decided to implement it.

The next morning she went to the *Post* to see Pete Moynihan, Clive's exboss. They hadn't replaced Clive yet, so she presented herself as a candidate for the position. Moynihan skimmed her résumé, put it down on his desk, and laughed.

"I've had enough trouble with Hartwick House, Miss Davis. You're a nice young woman and I wish you luck, but no thanks."

"If you're worried about the lawsuit, don't be. He's going to drop it."

Moynihan's blue eyes twinkled. He leaned back on his big chair and shifted his cigar to the other side of his mouth. "And why would you think that?"

"He has to. He's charging libel. You printed the truth."

"You know that for sure."

"I should. That whole mess with Anthony Hartwick was my fault." She watched his surprise register before continuing. "Clive Frommer and I were friends. I had a lot of ins, so I fed him everything I could. It got to the point where whatever we talked about he printed," she said, slowly raising the knife over her friend's back, taking careful but deliberate aim. "When I told Clive about Hartwick and his secret honey, I was speaking off the record. I thought he understood that." The blade sliced flesh, and blood began to flow. "But I forgot how ambitious Clive is. Unfortunately, his lack of prudence cost you a lawsuit and me my job."

"I'm sorry to hear that," Pete said, "but that still doesn't tell me why I should hire you."

"I was the one doing Clive's job, and before he screwed up, I was damn good at it. Thanks to me, 'Page Six' got some very hot scoops."

Moynihan nodded. That was true. He'd wondered where Clive had dug up some of the stuff he brought in.

"I've got the sources and the know-how to be a great gossip gatherer. I know how to listen, whom to listen to, what to print, and what to squelch. Frankly, Peter, I don't think you can live another day without me."

She waited a month after being hired before placing a not-so-blind item about "an anonymous, eponymous New York publisher whose black-book list of mistresses was longer than his company's list of best-sellers."

That afternoon she received a telephone call from a man who insisted upon remaining nameless but who strongly suggested she cease and desist in her attempts at slander. She heard anger in the voice she recognized as belonging to Anthony Hartwick, but she heard undertones of nervousness and respect as well. That's when she knew she'd found her calling. Jodi Cutler had been right. She wasn't meant to write novels or even short stories. Her talent was telling tales.

CHAPTER 13

Isabelle looked out over Lake Mendota, wondering when, if ever, it would shed its gray winter coat. She couldn't remember the last time the sun had shone. Since late October the landscape had been an achromatic study in the persistent neutrality of gray, black, and white. While this achieved a certain harmony, like a thumping C below middle C on a keyboard, when incessant the overall effect was depressing.

It had snowed the night before, the thick blanket of white whirling about in the wind. For a long while she had sat in a darkened room, watching the glistening shower. There was something eerie about the silence of snow. Even at its most ferocious it didn't scream or pound or crash like a rainstorm. It didn't assert itself with electronic displays or thunderous pronouncements. It simply fell, as if leaving its witnesses to draw their own conclusions as to its power and beauty.

Isabelle stared out the window of her small apartment on Langdon Street. It had taken time to adjust to this northern clime, but once she had, she had become intrigued with the effects of ice on the landscape, how cold shaped the horizon, how temperature affected light and mood. Snuggling on an easy chair by the window, she picked up a piece of charcoal and sketched what she saw. While it wasn't her favorite vision of dawn, there was a certain mystical aspect to the ascendancy of a silvered morning. There were no yellows, reds, or ochers as in Santa Fe. No blues, lavenders, or pinks as in New York. Here, one didn't watch a sunrise; one observed the evolution of gray, from the dense opacity of granite to the soft, peaceful tones of dove.

Her hands moved quickly, as if trying to ward off the bitter temperatures outside. Sharp lines for tree trunks and limbs. Wider sweeps for the lake: darker close to shore, fading as it moved toward the horizon. Quick, rounded strokes for rocks, blended splotches for puddles and ice patches. Shading. Shadowing. Jagged edges. Barbed projections.

She put down her charcoal, picked up her coffee, and studied the completed sketch. Suddenly she shivered and then smiled, realizing the chill had come not from the air around her, but from the paper in her lap. She had created that moment of cold. Whatever she thought of Clarence Bowman personally, his teachings were taking effect.

He was a little man, short and plump, with such enormous stores of energy that he made Isabelle think of a bombshell. Yet his artistic philosophy was spare and pacific, derived from the principles of Japanese art: organic forms flattened and stylized to fill a shallow space. Her first sessions with him had been painful. She was used to elegant sinuosities and the flamboyant splashing of color. He demanded reduction, control, thoughtful planning.

"Your goal should be simple," he said. "Just fill space in a beautiful way."

It sounded easy, but simplicity was difficult to achieve. He assigned exercises that reminded Isabelle of her first sessions with Sybil, only this time it was Bowman's basics she was learning: enclosing or dividing geometric shapes, eliminating or shifting elements to create a different composition, alternating dark and light forms, contrasting the softness of biomorphic shapes and the hardness of geometrics. He had her study the artistic expressions of children and primitives, looking for the common element.

"Spacing! It's universal and instinctive. Go back to it! Use it!"

He taught her the Japanese principle of balancing dark and light. And he taught her to use music as inspiration.

"Let it stimulate your visual imagination. Listen to the pure, undiluted beauty that is music's essence. Let it flow through you like a life source and then pour it into your art."

Whenever Bowman spoke like that, Isabelle heard Ezra and knew why he had sent her here. Ezra and his devotion to Kandinsky. Ezra and his insistence on planned productivity. Ezra, whose flights of colorful virtuosity always remained enclosed within a defined space. He wanted her to fuse Bowman's highly disciplined aesthetic with her own sense of luxurious extravagance.

Music had helped. In the early stages, when she was trying to learn how to conquer and control space, she played Chopin's nocturnes, making her compositions as precise and controlled as his. Later, when she felt she was beginning to master Bowman's principles, she enlarged her repertoire, tripling the size of her work surfaces, still trying to keep the design in proportion to the space. Grander size demanded grander music: Beethoven's *Eroica,* Tchaikovsky's *1812* Overture, Liszt's Hungarian Rhapsodies.

Without being conscious of what she was doing, she began to dash back and forth like a runner building up speed, stepping back as the music built to a crescendo, bolting forward at the crash of the cymbals to splash color onto the canvas or create texture with a palette knife or squeeze paint from a tube or smudge something with her thumb.

Sometimes she painted so fast and expended so much energy, she was drained and drenched with sweat when she finished. Soon it became a habit to shed her clothes until she was comfortable. In the studio she took to wearing men's undershirts beneath her blouses and sweaters so she could strip and retain a modicum of modesty. At home it wasn't unusual for her to paint in her underwear or in the nude. Often she'd remove all her clothes, pour herself a glass of wine, turn down the lights, and paint long into the night. With the music playing and the snow falling outside, it became an experience charged with an eroticism so intimate and so sensually fulfilling, it was almost orgasmic.

It was the work from those particular sessions that Isabelle mailed to Skye, who had been badgering her to send something she could show Richter.

"They're very hot," Skye said, calling after she had received them. "I don't know who the new man is in your life, but whatever buttons he's pressing, I'd like to know."

Isabelle laughed, wishing she and Skye were in the same room instead of a thousand miles away. "There is no man in my life other than Clarence Bowman, and believe me, you don't want him near your buttons."

"Maybe, but whatever he's doing or saying, Isabelle, this is some of the best work you've ever done. I'm awestruck, and you know I'm not a person given to that sort of thing."

"Did you show them to Richter?"

"I did."

"Well, are you going to keep me in suspense or are you going to tell me what he said?"

"He wants to meet with you the next time you're in New York."

Isabelle flushed: nerves, excitement, caution, fear, all coming together in an instant of emotion. "What does that mean?"

"It means he likes what he sees, you idiot! What do you think it means?"

"What did he say? Tell me everything."

"Calm yourself," Skye said, smiling. "I'm not there, and I know you're scampering around like a puppy looking for its pillow. You're making me nervous just listening to you."

"What did he say?" Isabelle shouted into the phone.

"Okay! He said you had a very sensuous style and an inventive, intriguing vision. Those were his exact words. Are you happy now?"

Isabelle was ecstatic. If she could, she would have flown to New York on the next plane; but it was still March, and her teaching contract ran until the end of June. She was scheduled to visit Tía Flora for a few weeks after that.

"It'll be months before I get to New York," she said. "When I do, do you think Richter will still want to meet with me?"

Skye smiled. She hadn't told Isabelle all of what Richter had said, because she hadn't wanted to brake Isabelle's momentum. "No problem," she said casually.

Isabelle said good-bye, bundled into her coat, scarf, hat, gloves, and boots, and prepared to brave the early morning cold. As always when she hung up after speaking to Skye, she found herself engulfed in a well of loneliness. She let it flood her but didn't wallow in it. She felt the pangs of separation, allowed herself a few moments to miss those she loved, then shook it off and went to work. She wasn't *here* to worry about what was happening *there*. She was here so that she would be accepted there.

Julian Richter was forty-four years old and had been influencing and contouring the art world for nearly twenty years. As the preeminent patron of the New York scene, he had been making and breaking careers with such bold strokes that often his own celebrity threatened to outshine that of his protégés. There were as many articles about him as there were about his artists, as many paparazzi photos of him in the tabloids as there were of the socialites who frequented his gallery. And as many rumors about his personal life as all of them put together.

Something about Julian Richter intrigued. Whether it was his remarkable string of successes or the elevated company he kept or the secrets he refused to reveal, he was a media darling. Together, he and the press had created a persona, a mystique, that Julian wore like a voluminous evening cape. He'd swirl it about himself in a series of dramatic flourishes, draping his privacy with a palpable aura, covering what he didn't want revealed, leaving just enough slack to create a sense of false possibility. The public knew only what Julian wanted them to know.

The biography he authorized told of a young man born to a wealthy family to whom scholarship and culture were as essential as food and water. "One must feed the soul in the same proportion as one feeds the body," his father used to say. Having the money to support such a philosophy, Julian grew up surrounded by fine art. A Renoir did not require a special trip to a museum; it was the small painting in the drawing room near the wing chair. The moldings in the library weren't carpenter-carved crowns, they were the hand-hewn fruits and flowers of the famed eighteenth-century Dutch master

Grinling Gibbons. The walls of the dining room didn't delight with the repet-
itive patterns of wallpaper, they astounded with two phantasmagoric para-
dises painted by Jean Antoine Watteau.

To Henry Richter, however, it wasn't enough simply to appreciate art; one
had to be enlightened by it and educated about it. The Watteau couldn't be
enjoyed for itself; it had to be appreciated, for its place in the history of art as
well as for its beauty.

"Great artists invent things that sound banal," Julian's father had said
when he'd explained that Watteau was the one who had invented the draped
human back. "In his hands, the back became as expressive as a face." Clearly
Henry relished the notion of looking over someone's shoulder, spying on
them, being part of a secret to which only he, the artist, and the subject were
privy. "Other artists try to create something new, but fail."

Sir Joshua Reynolds was a favorite target of Henry's. "Sir Sploshua," he
called him, chortling as he told Julian how commonplace it was for the face
of a Reynolds portrait to fall off if the painting was shaken, thanks to the
mayonnaiselike recipes he'd concocted to add texture to paint: three different varnishes, eggs, oil, wax, turps, asphalt, and resins.

Julian's mother, Hedda, was a feminist long before the term was fashion-
able. She too was a collector, but her fortune was spent on paintings done by
women, particularly those by Impressionists like Mary Cassatt and Berthe
Morisot. Using their works as a blackboard, she lectured Julian on the sup-
pression of women. She pointed out how compressed their pictorial environments were, arguing that those shallow picture spaces were meant to
represent the restricted sphere of movement permitted women in the nine-
teenth century. She grumbled about why Morisot's delicate brushwork and
elegant colors were called "feminine," when her brother-in-law, Edouard
Manet, used exactly the same techniques and no one applied that adjective
to him. And she wondered why Morisot's *Psyche,* a painting of an adolescent
studying herself in a mirror, was said to have validated the belief that vanity
was natural to women.

"Men bathe and dress and gawk at themselves in the mirror, too. It's simply a conspiracy among male artists not to show their kind participating in
acts of narcissism."

What Julian's biography didn't reveal was that while his parents spent time
with him when they were home, they were rarely in residence. His father's
business took him to Europe and the Orient, his mother's causes called her
from all four corners of the globe. Julian and his two younger brothers were
left to the care of servants.

Even in his absence, Henry's strict set of behavioral rules remained in effect. Julian's brothers complied; he did not. To him, Henry's standard of perfection was too difficult to attain. It required too much discipline, too much sacrifice, too much worship of Henry. There was also the fact that father and son had problems other than a clash of personality. Julian was smaller than his father and brothers. He was slight and often sickly, which to a man who gauged masculinity according to the traditional measures of height and brawn made him appear less competent, less capable, less than valuable. That Julian grew up constantly in need of a claque around him and could not bear to be alone was not surprising. That he required a public arena in which to perform and was possessed of an overwhelming need to "show them all" was not unexpected, either.

According to his standard interview line, while Julian's eye for art may have been sired by the advantages of his background, he insisted it was further nurtured by his own talent for photography. Though critics debated that claim—some agreeing, others pointing out that exhibitions of his own work didn't always sell out—no one argued Richter's ability to divine the newest star.

All the great dealers—Alfred Stieglitz, Betty Parsons, Leo Castelli, Ileana Sonnabend, Greta Reed—had a sixth sense about art's next step. All could feel below the surface of today's successes and anticipate tomorrow's triumphs. Yet several times, artists who had been rejected by others had been taken on by Richter and had become stars. So what did Julian see the others didn't? What did he have the others didn't? Unshakable arrogance and a knack for promotion.

While he held the integrity of the artist in high esteem, and never degraded the notion of talent and vision, Julian approached the business of art with unheard-of irreverence.

"A painting's like a box of cereal," he was fond of saying. "The gallery's a supermarket. My job is to convince the consumer that the box of cereal on my shelf is better, more desirable, and more delicious than the hundreds of other boxes of cereal on hundreds of other shelves."

Most times, he succeeded.

When Skye had brought him a portfolio of her friend's work, he had agreed to look at it only because he liked Skye. To be honest, he had expected to find the same mediocrity present in ninety-five percent of all samples sent to him. He was stunned to find himself emotionally moved by the charcoals and watercolors spread out before him. Over and over he studied the work of Isabelle de Luna. What he saw was an extraordinary talent in the secondary stages of bloom. Though young, de Luna had a powerful style and a firm command of space.

Julian would leave the room and return, anxious to see whether the impact lessened upon repeated viewings. It changed, shocking him less than in the initial instance, but still jarred his feelings, still made him look again. He could tell by the variety of styles presented that she was not yet fully developed; she was still experimenting, still finding herself, but if he had a passion for anything, it was for cultivating emerging artists, shaping them, inventing them, fathering them.

He lifted a watercolor nude and stared at it. The body of a woman beckoned to him, her lush form lying on its side. There were no features on the face, no fully described limbs, yet the softly rounded outline of a female excited him. She was modest yet bold, shy yet not unresponsive to sex, demure yet willing. His finger traced the ovoid shape that was a breast, moving down to where the crux of her femininity disappeared behind a shadow. His mouth went dry. His eyes teared with the joy of discovery.

It was the end of August when Isabelle returned to New York. She had stayed longer in Barcelona than she had planned, but Tía Flora hadn't been well. Though she scoffed at Isabelle's fussing over her, she was seventy-six and age was beginning to nibble at her health. Isabelle was conflicted, but Flora was clear about what she should do.

"It's time to go back to New York," she said emphatically. "You were not born to be a nursemaid, Isabelle. You were born to paint. Now, get on with it!"

Isabelle intended to get a place of her own, but until she settled in and had time to look for something suitable, she had accepted Skye's generous offer to stay with her. Six months before, Skye had moved from their old apartment on the West Side, downtown to SoHo. Her Greene Street apartment was airy and spacious and typically Skye. One wall was painted black, the one adjacent to it gray, the others white. Her furniture, a conglomeration of 1950s kitsch and flea market finds, looked like the families at the wedding of a mixed marriage, each side trying to get along with the other while clinging resolutely to its own customs. A red womb chair faced a victorian couch upholstered in black needlepoint. Hanging over the back was a Spanish shawl with six-inch fringe. In front of that imperious piece sat an incongruous turquoise boomerang table bedecked with a collection of candlesticks, each one filled with a tall white taper. A lone palm tree filled one corner, an enormous gilded mirror another.

Her bedroom looked as though it had been taken from a set of a Gloria Swanson movie: a queen-size bed with a black silk headboard, rounded and tufted. Propped against it was an array of satin pillows, each painted with the reedlike elegant ladies popularized by Erté. An art deco mirror looked out over a bureau cluttered with crystal perfume flacons. Another tall palm stood guard by the sole window, draped in luxurious folds of black satin.

What interested Isabelle most about Skye's apartment was the art. A wintry nightscape of Lake Mendota Isabelle had sent Skye for her birthday occupied most of the gray wall in the living room. On the black wall hung another large piece, which was the antithesis of Isabelle's: figurative, ungainly, incorporating broken china plates into its background, it was by a young man named Julian Schnabel. Between the two large windows was another somewhat disturbing piece, this one by David Salle. Scattered about were smaller works by other unknowns Skye had discovered in her travels.

"Richter and I have different sensibilities," she explained later. "In a few cases, I felt something he didn't. He chose not to represent the artist. I chose to buy. Maybe it's a contest between us about whose vision is clearer about where art is headed, I don't know, but I liked them, so I bought them."

If either of them had worried that the year's separation might have put a strain on their friendship, they needn't have wasted the energy. Within moments of their reunion they fell into the familiar rhythm of their relationship, laughing and teasing and talking just as they had when they were living in the cave on Riverside Drive.

"I've noticed a change in your conversation," Isabelle said.

"I was hoping you'd notice." Skye ran her fingers through her long curls and struck a pose. "I was interesting before. I'm endlessly fascinating now."

Isabelle shook her head and smiled. "Yes, you are that, but that's not what I meant. Something is missing from your dialogue."

Skye pondered Isabelle's observation, as if running down a list. "I don't curse as much as I used to," she said.

"Nor do you mention Ezra's name."

Skye picked some dried wax off the side of a candle and whatever had dripped onto the table the last time it had been lit, stalling until she could organize her response. When everything was tidy, she explained that she and Ezra were no longer lovers.

"We both decided we could use some therapy," she said matter-of-factly. "The end result was my therapist told me that what I had wanted from Ezra was the love and affection and closeness I didn't get from my father. His therapist pegged me as a substitute for Sonya. I've accepted the idea that my father does love me. He may not show it the way I want him to, but he shows it as best he can. Ezra's come to terms with the fact that Sonya left because of her needs, not his failures."

"You both sound so healthy," Isabelle said with honest admiration.

"Oh, we are. We're focused and centered and in touch with our inner selves." She laughed at her own psychobabble. "Now he's dating Greta Reed, and I'm diverting my heretofore rapacious sexual energy to my work."

"In other words, he's got a honey and you don't."

"Exactly!"

"So what's Julian Richter like?"

Again Skye measured her words. "He's positively electric, Isabelle. Brilliant. Seductive. Mysterious."

"I don't like to sound pushy, but how soon can I meet with him?"

"You do sound pushy, but I'm going to allow it because I need a bargaining chip."

"Are we about to negotiate my share of the rent?" Isabelle asked, her curiosity aroused by the unusual flush coloring Skye's cheeks.

"How could you even ask such a question! You're here as my guest for as long as you want."

Isabelle narrowed her eyes, leaned forward, and fixed her gaze on her friend. "Now I know you're up to something. Are you going to confess, or do we play inquisition?"

"I think I was presumptuous."

"Because?"

"I showed him some of your work."

"I know," Isabelle said. "The charcoals and watercolors I sent you from Wisconsin."

Skye nodded but looked uncomfortable. "I also showed him some of your watercolor nudes from Fitzsimmon and a few of the paintings you did for Ezra."

Isabelle tried to recall which pieces Ezra had saved, which watercolors Fitzsimmon had held, worried that what had been presented wasn't her best effort. "What was his reaction?"

Again Skye obsessed about the dried wax on her candles. Isabelle waited. The silence grew heavy. "You're part of his opening exhibition."

"What?" Isabelle's heart was pounding, but not from elation. She was furious. "If you didn't know better, he should have," she said, rising from her chair, crossing her arms across her chest, and pacing. "How could you allow him to mount my work without my permission?"

"I thought you'd be pleased." Skye sounded like a four-year-old trying to explain why she had crayoned a doggie on Mommy's wall.

"Well, you thought wrong!"

"He's the most influential dealer in New York. He liked you, Isabelle. He wanted to show you. I didn't want him to think twice about it."

"He should have and so should you!" Isabelle had no qualms about venting her rage; she knew she was right, but she also knew Skye had had her best interests at heart. "When is this show opening?"

"Tomorrow night."

Isabelle could only laugh. "That doesn't even give me enough time to buy a dress!"

"We have all day tomorrow," Skye said meekly, responding to Isabelle's sarcasm.

"What time is it?"

"Time?" Skye bounded off the couch. "Right! It's only four o'clock. The stores are still open late, we could hit—"

"We're not going anywhere," Isabelle said as she grabbed her purse and headed for the door. "I'm going to see Julian Richter. I'll be back later."

"Promise?"

Isabelle didn't answer. She simply shook her head and closed the door behind her. The last thing she wanted Skye to see was the affectionate smile on her face.

The Richter Gallery was on Madison Avenue, between Sixty-sixth and Sixty-seventh streets. Isabelle's hand was already on the doorknob when her eye caught the sign in the window: NEW SEASON/NEW FACES. THE NEW YORK DEBUT OF ISABELLE DE LUNA, FRANK PONS & JAMES CARSTAIRS. She stared at it as if she had never seen her name in print before. Her eyes traveled to the left of the sign and stopped again, this time on one of her charcoals. She remembered the night she had drawn this one. It had been New Year's Eve. Cody had phoned earlier. The aftermath of that call was an unavoidable spell of desolation. She had turned on her favorite Rachmaninoff piano concerto, poured herself some wine, and had a good cry. Afterward she had stripped off her clothes, poured some more wine, and reminisced about what she and Cody had had. As she stared at the drawing now, she blushed. Though the bodies had been distilled to little more than their roundness, there was no denying that the interlocking shapes were a man and woman, nor was there any denying that their joining was intensely passionate.

Rattled by the sight of her own sexual fervor, Isabelle looked away, concentrating instead on getting into the gallery. Unfortunately the door was locked. She knocked loudly, hoping someone would let her in. After several moments an elderly man cracked open the door. When she asked to see Julian Richter, he informed her that Mr. Richter was out, he didn't know when he would return, and she should come back during regular gallery hours.

"I'm Isabelle de Luna," she said, flashing her driver's license so he wouldn't slam the door in her face. "I'm part of the exhibition. I just got into town and Mr. Richter was supposed to give me a preview of the show. Please. It's my first one."

He let her in and stood back, guarding his boss's property, granting her some privacy. When she entered the front room, she froze, overwhelmed by a rush of pride. She had never seen her work displayed like this: oils and acrylics dominated one wall, watercolors another, charcoals a third. It was a clever arrangement, giving her a range she wasn't certain she could claim, grouping pieces so they showed her ability to shift from the most liberated brushwork to the most controlled sketches, from wild, explosive color to constrained, implosive design. The effect was powerful.

She found it humbling to be an observer of her own talent, but no matter how exhilarating it was to see her creations on the walls of this renowned gallery, she was possessive about that talent and unhappy that it had been put on display without her permission. "When will Mr. Richter be here?" she asked.

"Seven or so."

At seven o'clock Isabelle returned. This time the door was open. Slowly she let herself in. The front room was lit like a stage, with carefully placed spots lighting the work on the walls. Two men with their backs to her were standing in front of a large charcoal she had done in Wisconsin. Executed with quintessential Bowman spareness, yet combined with her own instinctual sensuality, it portrayed a face without any feature except a mouth, lush lips slightly parted, the head gently tilted upward, a woman lying back against a pillow of hair. A rounded arch alluded to an arm, a crescent to the curve of a neck, a shadow to someone hovering above. Was she welcoming her lover? Or was she reveling in the aftermath of pleasure?

The two men whispered to each other, neither removing his gaze from the seductive woman on the wall. One was very tall, broad-shouldered and lean, his dark suit bearing all the signs of a custom tailor, his affect one of innate confidence. The other was short, bearded, more studied in his dress and his pose. He stood with one arm bent, his hand resting delicately against his chin, the other arm folded beneath in support. Now and then he nodded, clearly agreeing with his companion's assessment of the piece before them. Isabelle assumed he was Julian Richter, and it was to him she said, "Take down these paintings."

Both men turned. Richter's cobalt eyes narrowed, turning wolfish. His mouth tightened into a wary line. "I beg your pardon?"

"I'm Isabelle de Luna. This is my work, and you don't have my permission to show it."

Richter appraised her with a quick but educated glance. He had fantasized about Isabelle de Luna for a very long time. Looking at her now, with her bronzed skin, glistening brown hair, and snapping hazel eyes, he smiled. She more than met his expectations. And while he might have been shocked by her demand, he was impressed by the courage it took for her to issue it.

"May I introduce you to Philip Medina?" he said, deliberately disregarding her command. "Not only is he the owner and CEO of Cisco Communications and a major art collector, but he was just about to make an offer on this exquisite charcoal. Weren't you, Philip?"

The man next to Richter fixed his stare on Isabelle. His eyes were hooded and black, yet soft, like the charcoal she had used to create the woman who seemed to have captured his interest. "The portrait doesn't do you justice, Miss de Luna." His voice was deep but hushed, giving Isabelle the impression he was accustomed to people listening when he spoke. "You're far more captivating in person."

Isabelle was pleased that he had noticed the resemblance—most people didn't—and flattered by his compliment, but she was there to quarrel with Richter, not to flirt with a stranger. Ignoring him, she repeated her grievance.

"You have no right to negotiate with Mr. Medina. If he wants to purchase this piece, he'll do it from me directly or not at all."

Julian seesawed between pique and excitement. He had dealt with temperamental artists before, but few were this stunning and this talented. Though he resented the awkward position she was putting him in, he capitulated. He was more desirous of signing her than debating her.

"I'm terribly sorry about the confusion, Miss de Luna, but you see, I thought Skye spoke for you."

"I'm perfectly capable of speaking for myself."

"And of creating wonderful art." Once again Philip Medina insinuated himself into the middle of the conversation. "Do you know how gifted you are?" he said.

"Yes, I do." Isabelle's answer was bold and unequivocal.

The corners of Medina's mouth lifted in an admiring smile. This was someone who knew who she was and what she was worth. As a businessman he understood the value of a product; in a field that depended on creativity, he also understood the value of the producer. "As Julian said, I am a collector, and I would like very much to add this piece to my collection."

It was hard to avoid the sincerity in his voice or the magnetic pull of his gaze. For the first time since she had confronted the two men, Isabelle allowed herself to look at the person who wanted to be the first to buy her work. Soft brown hair, a square chin with a subtle cleft, a broad brow that furrowed at a challenge, a sharply planed face that changed completely when he smiled: he was undeniably handsome. In repose he recalled everything she loved about a Rodin sculpture—the sense that beneath a carefully honed surface simmered enormous energy and that the dimensions of his form were indicative of the magnitude of his being.

Isabelle could almost feel the power that pulsed within this man, the intensity with which he conducted his business and probably his life. Yet when he smiled his face became boyish, illuminated by the part of him that loved finding something special, owning something new, being in the company of something beautiful. She guessed him to be in his early thirties, about ten years her senior, yet the shadows she saw reflected in his eyes made her think that like herself, he had experienced more of life than his youth conveyed.

The negotiations were delicate and, as she had wished, direct. Richter had affixed a price of twenty-five hundred dollars to the piece—it was all she could do not to express surprise at the number. She subtracted the sixty percent she felt Richter would have taken for himself and asked for one thousand dollars. Richter would have settled for less, but Isabelle didn't know that. She was too new to the process to know that offering a prime customer a first look and a highly discounted price was common practice. It was a way of creating demand: give a break, get the bonus of using the buyer's name as an incentive for others. Medina, who played the game more adroitly than most, could have bartered but didn't. He wrote a check, promised to be there the following night, and, though he preferred otherwise, left Isabelle and Richter alone.

"Congratulations." Julian folded his arms across his chest and surveyed the young woman before him. "That check makes it official. You're a professional artist."

In spite of herself, Isabelle grinned. Richter took advantage of the thaw.

"We seem to have gotten off to a very bad start. I sincerely apologize for the misunderstanding."

Isabelle had planned to scold him again, but he was being too solicitous for her to go at him.

"You're absolutely within your rights to demand that I knock down this part of the show, but please, Miss de Luna, for both our sakes, I wish you would reconsider."

"I don't like feeling that I'm not in control of my own art," she said, her tone definite but without hostility.

"I don't blame you, but at the risk of offending you, let me give you a quick lesson in the reality of being an artist in New York: you'll never be totally in control of your art."

"And why not?"

"Because regrettably, the value of one's art is determined by price. Price is a function of the market, and the market depends on many things, most of them irrational." Richter watched Isabelle carefully. She was listening. He wished he knew if she was buying what he was selling. "Art runs through cycles and trends. It goes in and out of fashion more often than hemlines. One season painting is au courant, the next season sculpture is the rage. The season after that, art is dead and tapestries are hot. The only two things an artist can control are what she creates and whom she entrusts to represent her."

"Which is where you come in."

Julian smiled. "Precisely. In all due modesty, I run the most prestigious gallery in New York City. By allowing me to exhibit your work, you gain a certain credibility you wouldn't get elsewhere. Like it or not, Miss de Luna, where your art hangs is often more important than what your art is."

Isabelle slipped her hand into her pocket. Her fingers touched Philip Medina's check. The charcoal was wonderful, she knew that, but would it have garnered twenty-five hundred dollars under someone else's banner? Richter did have a reputation for getting top dollar for his artists' work. And she did need the money.

Aside from the obvious reasons, like rent, food, and other living expenses, there was Isabelle's obsession with owning Dragon Textiles, a fixation reinforced during her recent visit to Barcelona. She and Tía Flora had spent a great deal of time talking about the family name: what it had been, what it was now, whether or not it would mean anything in the future. Difficult as it was to believe, even after all these years there were those in the community who continued to whisper about her mother's murder and her father's guilt. When she had asked why the gossip refused to die, Flora explained that unsolved mysteries bothered people, that most wanted conclusions to problems and those left unresolved were like an unhealed sore. Too, she said that whenever there was trouble at the textile plant, the workers liked to use Martín as a scapegoat for their woes. Bitter about Dragon's decline since its sale to Pasqua Barba, they believed that somehow Althea's death was tied to the death of the company and that Martín was responsible for both. To Isabelle, that continued link between her father and Dragon's slide was all the more reason to regain control. To do that, she needed a lot of money. To get it, she decided suddenly, she needed Julian Richter.

"If I do agree to allow you to represent me, what does it involve?"

Julian's pulse quickened. "I handle the sales of all your work, as well as publicity for the shows and public relations concerning the artist."

Isabelle laughed. "Public relations? I don't have a public."

"Ah, but you will." Julian had shifted into his Pgymalion mode, mentally costuming Isabelle for the opening, planning how he would introduce her to the press, deciding on a persona for his newest star. "We're in the business of image, Isabelle. You paint them, I create them." Making a circle with his thumb and index finger and looking through it as one would a lens, he roved her body, surveying, assessing, evaluating. "I don't like clichés, but first impressions are key." He walked around her, pacing like a cattleman before an auction. "There have been dozens of wonderful female artists in this century, but none of them has a face."

"What do you mean?" Isabelle was beginning to feel uncomfortable.

"If you were walking on the street, would you recognize Helen Frankenthaler or Alice Neel or Lee Krasner or Agnes Martin? No! The two whose images are branded permanently into the public consciousness are Georgia O'Keeffe and Louise Nevelson. Why? Because they created dramatic portraits of themselves and never varied from their personal themes. O'Keeffe wore her hair back in a severe knot and dressed like a nun. What a divine contrast she created between her strict, colorless garb and those brilliantly vivid paintings.

"Nevelson was just the opposite. Her work was hard, structured constructions made out of wooden boxes painted flat black or white. Her sculptures are monastic in their simplicity, yet Nevelson the woman was gloriously theatrical, always bedecked in tons of elaborate jewelry and colorful head scarves, to say nothing of her notoriously long false eyelashes.

"They were fabulously famous because they were personalities, women who demanded that the world pay attention to them and their art. That's what I want you to be, Isabelle: a personality."

"I don't want to be anything other than who I am," she said firmly.

Richter blinked. He had been so absorbed by what he was saying, he had assumed she was lapping up every word. "I don't want to change you," he said gently, fearful of frightening her away, "I simply want to make you more of who you are."

"And how do you propose I do that?" Isabelle was wary but curious.

"Your background is Spanish. You speak with a slight accent. You grew up in Santa Fe, a city with a decidedly Spanish cast. Play it up!" He was into the role of impresario, striding across the floor, gesturing, making Isabelle acutely conscious of her red dress and her silver jewelry, the twist of hair that hugged the nape of her neck, the silver comb that held it in place, the jumble of bracelets that dangled at her wrist. "Wear color. Lots of it. Mix it boldly and brashly. Wear bangles and beads. Just do what you did today, only more so."

Isabelle remained unsure. Julian forced himself to remember she was young, probably scared.

"I'll tell you what: Let's not worry about any of this until after the show. I want you to feel comfortable with me and what I do. I want you to trust me." He smiled, his blue eyes glinting. "If, after we've gotten to know each other, you think I'm the one to represent you, I'll take on the task with pleasure. If not, no hard feelings. How's that?"

"Fine."

Richter could see by the relieved look on her face that his instincts had been correct: she should not be rushed. When she left, he stood by the window of the gallery and watched her hunt for a taxi. He was not a man without confidence, and normally he approached new artists with aplomb, certain that they would sign with him. He was going to have to work a little harder to get Isabelle de Luna to submit control over the details of her career to him. But if she did, she would be famous. If she didn't, he believed it would be the biggest mistake of her life.

When Isabelle and Skye walked in, the party was not yet in full swing. The gallery was busy, but according to Skye, most of the players hadn't arrived. People were milling about, holding champagne glasses and nibbling on tidbits like smoked salmon on black bread and cucumber slices dashed with dill, but they were mostly gallery bees. Though they bought occasionally, they were essentially lookers who buzzed around openings more intent upon acquiring social points than art.

"What's he doing here so early?" Skye asked, tilting her head in the direction of Philip Medina. "Not that I'm not glad to see him. The man makes my heart go ba-boom." She fluffed her hair, straightened her shoulders, and threw Medina a casual wave. "Can you imagine being good-looking, brilliant, and rich all at the same time?"

"He bought one of my charcoals," Isabelle said quietly.

"You didn't tell me that!"

"Neither did I tell you that your boss demanded I dress like a flamenco dancer."

Before Skye could respond, Richter entered the room. It was only a moment, but Isabelle saw him pause when he spotted her. His eyes noted the cream-colored dress—spare, loose, unadorned—that her hair was loose and free falling, her only jewelry a delicate Indian *heishi* necklace of dark and light shells, her only detectable cosmetic a dusty rose tint on her lips. To his credit, his face remained expressionless as he approached.

"You look lovely, Isabelle," he said as he took her hand and kissed it like a gallant. "Next time, I'll trust your judgment about things like habiliment. You're clearly much better at dressing you than I am."

They chatted amiably about the positive response of those who were there, and then he introduced her to her fellow exhibitors, several of his regular customers, when they began to arrive, as well as two or three reporters. Isabelle had expected him to barker the works in his gallery, to promote the artists on display via flattery and pronouncements about future greatness. Instead he worked the crowd, playing them against each other. When he noticed four of his biggest buyers clustered together in the front room, he arranged for the *New York Times* photographer to snap Isabelle and Philip Medina in front of the charcoal he had bought. Within half an hour the charcoals had sold out.

When one of the Park Avenue doyennes expressed an interest in a cityscape, he told her someone else—someone he knew she knew—had liked it, too. She bought it instantly. He spoke about Isabelle only when asked, repeating his standard line about new artists: "You have to love it, because you never know. I could be wrong about her." He had been wrong so seldom that by the time the official cocktail party had ended, he had sold over half of Isabelle's work, had reserves on half of what remained, and predicted that within a week everything would be gone.

"You should feel wonderful. Your debut has been an unqualified success." Philip Medina handed her a glass of champagne. "This is the very least you deserve."

He had been hovering on the periphery all evening, observing the scene from a clearly defined distance. Though she hadn't mean to, Isabelle had been keeping track of him out of the corner of her eye, trying to get a sense of who he was and what he was about. He didn't glad-hand or work the room. Rather, people came to him, men eager to talk business, women anxious to engage in flirtation. Isabelle couldn't be certain, but he appeared to do neither. Whenever she had rimmed his circle in her travels, he was talking about art—specifically about her.

"You must have brought me luck," she said, wondering why she felt so relaxed around a man who seemed to inspire the opposite response in most of those with whom he came into contact.

"Talent brings its own luck."

His eyes smiled, yet his mouth remained impassive, prompting Isabelle to muse about which feature she would have selected to convey his essence if she were painting him: the eyes, in which she thought she saw openness and warmth, or the lips, which appeared constrained by an inscrutability designed to keep others away. While she responded to the former, as a woman whose personal philosophy was "Safety first," she understood the latter.

"I'm sure Julian has plans for you this evening, but if you wouldn't mind, I'd like to invite you to dinner some other night."

"I wouldn't mind at all. That would be lovely."

Neither of them noticed Julian Richter standing off to the side, watching, listening. He had just sent James Carstairs and Frank Pons off with Skye to the bistro where he was hosting an après-opening dinner. He hung in the shadows as Medina and Isabelle said their good-nights.

"Did you enjoy your debut?"

Isabelle looked around the room, counted the red "Sold" dots and the blue "Reserved" dots alongside her paintings, and laughed. "I enjoyed it a lot," she said, feeling almost giddy.

"I'm glad. I wanted your first foray into the jungle known as the art world to be a satisfying one."

"To be honest, I'm floating."

"Savor the feeling," Julian said as he smiled and extended his hand. Isabelle took it happily. "But don't float away. We have a party to go to."

When Isabelle and Julian joined the others, the general mood was high.

Pons and Carstairs were pleased with the results of the opening and gladly shared their feelings about being part of Richter's stable with Isabelle.

"He's tough with the press and other gallery owners who might look to shanghai you, but he's been up front and more than fair with us."

Isabelle listened to them as she watched Julian snap pictures like a grand-mother at a christening, arranging group shots, coaxing smiles, encouraging silly poses. The next day, at lunch, when he presented her with a blowup of her and Skye, she was touched.

"I know how close you are. I thought you might like this."

"I do. Very much. Thank-you."

He had taken her to Le Cirque to celebrate her successful baptism into the art world and to plead his case. Isabelle was agog. She wasn't accustomed to fancy lunches with wine on the table, celebrities and socialites on the ban-quettes next to her. Nor was she accustomed to being with a man who at-tracted the kind of attention Julian did. Every few minutes someone came over to say hello, exchange patter, and meet Isabelle. Clearly, being in Julian's company granted immediate status.

When Isabelle asked about the people she had just met or those she had met the night before, he didn't simply list their credentials; he encapsulated them in a light, anecdotal manner, making her laugh about the eccentricities indigenous to New Yorkers—and he did so without making her feel like a bumpkin. She could hardly believe how relaxed she was with him. Julian Richter was a stranger, and a famous, somewhat intimidating stranger at that. Yet throughout lunch, in between the stories, were expressions of con-cern about the pressures of instant fame.

"You've created a splash, which, in turn creates expectation. You can't let that dictate what you do next." He leaned close to her and smiled, his dark blue eyes softening. "Your talent is the only guide you need."

"Other than you, of course," Isabelle teased.

Julian laughed. "I wasn't going to bring it up, but now that you mention it, yes, I think I might be able to figure in the equation of your success."

"Well, so do I." It wasn't Isabelle's nature to play games. She had observed him last night. He was incredible when it came to manipulating the desire to buy and completing the sale. She had seen another side of him at the party afterward and yet another side of him today, over lunch. She had seen enough. "If you would, I'd like you to represent me, Mr. Richter."

Julian bowed his head. "It would be an honor, Miss de Luna."

They were sealing their bargain with a toast when she saw him. She almost dropped her glass. He was talking to Sirio, the owner of Le Cirque, when he saw her. Black eyes framed with thick, arched brows fixed on her, remaining so as he walked the few steps to where she was sitting.

"Señorita de Luna. It's been quite some time. What a pleasure to see you."

Isabelle didn't answer. Nor did she introduce him to Julian, whose expression alternated between curiosity and concern.

"I'm Pasqua Barba," he said, extending his hand to Julian, keeping his gaze on Isabelle. "I'm an old friend of Isabelle's mother."

Julian stood, deliberately placing himself in between the intruder and Isabelle. "Whoever you claim to be, it's clear you're not an old friend of Miss de Luna's, so if you don't mind, we'd like to enjoy our lunch. Good day, Mr. . . ."

"Barba."

"Good day, Mr. Barba." Julian remained standing until Paco was led, reluctantly, to a table on the other side of the room.

"Thank-you," Isabelle said. "He's—"

"You don't have to explain. He upset you. That's all I need to know." He placed his hand on hers. "Don't worry about him. I won't let him bother you."

Isabelle nodded. Before Paco had interrupted them, she and Julian had been discussing how to manage her career. He felt she couldn't be out of the public eye for a long stretch of time and had recommended that she come back with a solo show as soon as she had completed enough paintings. After that, he would hold her back and allow a mystique to build around her. Isabelle had promised to find a loft and get to work.

"How would you feel about returning to Santa Fe to paint?"

Her heart was still pounding, still reacting to the shock of seeing Pasqua Barba in New York. She hated knowing he was here, so close to her.

"It would be fine, I guess." She wished her head would clear. She wasn't thinking straight.

"This should cover your expenses for the next year." Julian handed her a check.

When she looked at the amount, she was stunned. "I can't take this," she protested.

"Yes, you can. And you should." His smile was reassuring in its certainty that he knew what was best for her. "This city is not the place for you. There's energy here, that's true, but it's too agitating, too disturbing, too anxiety-ridden, for your art. The way I see it, your soul is in the hills of Santa Fe, the colorful solitude of the mountains and the peaceful serenity of the desert. I want you to go home, Isabelle, where your muse is most comfortable and your talent can ripen and flourish."

Isabelle's eye was drawn to Pasqua Barba, who continued to stare at her. Her hand held a check that offered her a chance to paint in a safe, secure place. That afternoon she signed a contract binding her to Julian Richter. Two days later she left town.

That same day, the Sunday edition of *The New York Times*'s "Arts & Leisure" section ran a piece on the Richter Gallery show that raved about Isabelle; with it was a picture of Isabelle and her first patron, noted collector Philip Medina.

Philip called Skye's apartment, looking for Isabelle, and learned that she had gone on a work retreat and wouldn't be back in New York for quite some time.

Julian Richter poured a glass of brandy and toasted himself. While he couldn't take all the credit—some of it had to go to the conveniently disturbing presence of that Pasqua Barba—by now Isabelle had arrived in Santa Fe, away from everyone who might want to influence her or date her or befriend her or hurt her.

Across town, Nina Davis read the article and fumed. While her star was stumbling along at "Page Six," Isabelle's was ascending. ". . . an artist to watch . . . one of the brighter lights of the current season . . . now part of the famed Medina collection." Each quote acted like an incendiary, sparking an explosion of anger. Furious, frustrated, she crumpled the newspaper into a ball and pitched it across the room. "Don't you dare think you're better than I am," she said to the crinkled mass. Pacing around it as if the article contained a dangerous poison, Nina tried to rechannel her heat. The paper began to unfold. Isabelle's face began to reappear. Nina stared at it, consumed by the insult that had grown over the years into a monstrous personal challenge.

CHAPTER 14

1978

Bored with "Page Six" and tired of being unknown except to a small group of tabloid gossip faithfuls, Nina began searching the trade papers for openings. Months went by before she spotted a piece about Cisco Communications developing a daily celebrity-oriented television show. To be called *The Insider* and syndicated to a hundred markets, it had "golden opportunity" written all over it.

After four phone calls and four "Mr. Medina is unable to take your call but will get back to you as soon as possible" responses, Nina wondered if the position had been filled.

No, she told herself. If it had, the article would have mentioned who the reporter was. Besides, she'd been such a pest, Medina's secretary would have said the job was taken just to get rid of her.

Knowing that Medina weekended at a house in East Hampton, she called a few of her sources to check on his schedule. Once assured that he would actually be in residence that coming weekend, she called over to the Maidstone Golf Course. By pretending to be one of his secretaries, she requested and received confirmation of his tee-off times as well as the names of the men in his foursome.

It was at times like these that she was grateful to whoever was responsible for her tall genes. After hiding her femininity beneath scruffy jeans and an oversize sweatshirt, she stuffed her blond hair into a grimy baseball cap. Pulling the brim down as far as it would go and telling herself it was all for a good cause, she tromped through the marshes until she found the back entrance of the club and carefully made her way to the caddy shack.

Certain that the starter and the caddy master would have tossed her out if she approached either of them, she opted to rely on the fail-safe method of appealing to man's instinctive sense of greed. Explaining that she was a reporter (true, sort of) out to get an exclusive interview with Philip Medina (true, sort of), she convinced a couple of bag carriers to give her a break and let her substitute for Medina's usual caddy. A fifty here and a fifty there didn't hurt. When they agreed, she slipped into the white cotton jumpsuit that was the caddy uniform, fell in behind Rufus, the second caddy for the group, and followed him to the first tee. Luckily the starter was preoccupied with the next foursome.

Following Rufus's lead, she grabbed Medina's bag and the bag of Philip's playing partner, trying not to grunt when she hoisted them onto her shoulder. Thanks to Rufus, who cued her about where to stand, when to back off, how to spot balls, and which clubs to give Medina and his partner, she managed to do her job for several holes without anyone noticing that she was not a he. When she was certain she was far enough from the clubhouse not to be arrested instantly, she dropped the two golf bags on the tee, took off her cap, and let her blond hair fall to her shoulders.

"Mr. Medina, I'm Nina Davis," she said, holding out her hand. He didn't take it. She hadn't thought he would. "I don't mean to interrupt your game, but I've been trying to get an interview with you about the job on *The Insider*. Your secretary is extremely adept at the runaround, and while I might respect her dodging skills, I couldn't help feeling she was doing you a terrible disservice by keeping you from meeting me."

The other three men were startled, then amused. Medina looked angry. Nina quickened the pace. "I'm the gal you're looking for. I'm ballsy and clever and tenacious. I have an incredible memory for facts and a bloodhound's nose for a trail. I'll track down a story no matter where it is, how hard someone's trying to hide it, or what I have to do to get it. The mere fact that I am standing here talking to you is testimony to my ingenuity."

Medina's face remained infuriatingly inscrutable.

"Okay. You may not be happy with me for interrupting your momentum, although frankly, the way you were playing, I'd think you'd be delighted with a chance to rest and stop the bleeding." She smiled. He didn't. "You have to give me credit for getting here and finding a way to plead my case."

Quickly she recited her résumé, exaggerating here, embellishing there. When still he didn't respond, she began to fear the worst.

"I know I look raggy today, but honestly, Mr. Medina, in real life I'm a pretty good-looking woman, and I photograph extremely well." Suddenly she was exhausted, and her bravura faded. "All I'm asking for is a chance."

Medina turned away, bent down, slid an eight iron out of his golf bag, and teed up a ball. "A chance is all I'm going to give you," he said, taking a practice swing. "You may turn out to be the best reporter in the business, but frankly, you're a rotten caddy. Don't expect a tip."

With that, he hit the ball and watched as it landed on the green of the par three, four feet from the pin. At the end of nine, he replaced her with a regular caddy and handed her a slip of paper.

"Call my secretary on Monday to set up a screen test." He perused her slowly, moving from her sweaty baseball cap to her wrinkled white jumpsuit to her grass-stained sneakers and a slow smile wreathed his mouth. "And a dinner date."

Dining at Le Cirque with Philip Medina was an exquisite experience. Sitting on the front banquette where only the privileged gained entry—having Sirio stop by the table to chat, being introduced to Barbara Walters and Lee Radziwill, the heads of CBS and Revlon, Peter Jennings and Johnny Apple of *The New York Times*—was like being handed a first-class ticket to heaven.

"You've barely touched your food."

"I'm too overwhelmed to eat."

Nina hadn't meant to be quite so honest. She would have preferred that he view her as a sophisticated woman fully acquainted with the playgrounds of the rich and celebrated, but being *here,* with *him,* well, she simply couldn't pull it off.

"I hope your assertion about your talent is as accurate as your appraisal of your looks." Philip smiled as his eyes surveyed the assets of the woman seated across from him: pale blond hair that fell softly onto partially bared shoulders, smoke-gray eyes, cheeks that rounded when she smiled, plush lips that made offers without words.

"You won't be disappointed, Mr. Medina," Nina said, gleefully taking note of his obvious interest.

"Since we're about to become colleagues, I think it's appropriate that you call me Philip, don't you?"

Again she would have preferred to respond more coolly, but as he toasted her with his wineglass and she looked into his onyx eyes, Nina blushed.

"I understand you used to work with Clive Frommer."

Nina's blush faded. How did he know she knew Clive? And how much did he know about her arrangement with him?

"I helped him out when he was at 'Page Six.'" She said it casually, displaying far more interest in an errant stringbean.

"He's quite good, don't you think?"

Clive had a three-minute spot three days a week on a morning talk show. When Nina had called to ask him for help finding a job, he had brushed her off like an unwanted flake of dandruff.

Instead of answering, Nina smiled and sipped her wine, leaving her review of Clive's performance open for interpretation. Medina changed the subject.

As he chatted about the growing fascination with celebrity gossip, Nina listened with half an ear. Lightheaded from the wine and the company, she couldn't help ruminating about what to do with this glorious man at evening's end: should she invite him into her apartment? Go to his apartment if he asked? Should she play coy and virginal? Or was he expecting a reward for his beneficence? While she was more than willing to become intimate with Philip Medina, even through her grape-induced fog, she guessed that sleeping with the boss on a first date probably was a bad idea.

Philip confirmed that when he walked her to her door, returned her keys, thanked her for a lovely evening, wished her luck, and promised to call her the next time he was in Los Angeles.

"Oh, well . . ." She sighed as she closed the door behind her. "I got the job. I guess I'll have to wait to get the man."

The Insider was a low-budget project with a four-person crew that did everything from bookings to research to editing to makeup. During the day Nina worked like a dog, establishing contacts, tracking down stories, following up leads. At night, if she wasn't cruising the restaurants or party hopping, she was glued to her television, tuned in to every celebrity reporter or newscaster she could find, studying technique, analyzing what worked and what didn't. The first thing she did was line up sources. From experience she knew to befriend the toniest caterers, the most popular hairdressers (manicurists and shampoos girls, too), the most successful realtors, drivers from the busiest limousine services, and whichever gardeners were willing to talk to her. She made friends with salesgirls on Rodeo Drive, Mercedes and Rolls-Royce mechanics, and one or two of the clerks who worked the admissions desk at Cedars Sinai and Los Angeles General's emergency rooms. This group formed the spine of her network. She plugged them whenever she could, and they fed her information whenever they could. It wasn't quite as inside as she needed to get, but it was enough to get her started. Ultimately, however, she needed up-front, in-your-face, person-to-person access to the stars. The problem was how to get it. She wangled invitations to whichever parties she could, but they were strictly B list. She was an unknown with no cachet and no power. Until she acquired one or the other, she was doomed to cruising the "also starring" circuit.

The answer came to her one night when she was working the crowd at a completely unnewsworthy barbecue. She was watching would-be studs and starlets stuff their faces with hamburgers and French fries when suddenly she asked, "Is it true Julia Thomas ate herself out of the role of the ballerina in *The Turning Point?"*

Thomas was a dancer with the New York City Ballet who had been touted as Baryshnikov's next partner. Rumor had it he had arranged for her to try out for the part, but it was given to Leslie Browne instead. No reason had ever been given for her rejection. Nina's question was pure pie in the sky, but two days later Julia Thomas called from New York.

"I never auditioned for that role," she said with proper prima ballerina indignation. "Mikhail wanted me to test, but I said no. Why would I leave a solid career in New York for Hollywood?"

"Money is usually a pretty good inducement."

Thomas laughed. "They didn't offer me enough to pay for my plane fare."

"Their loss," Nina said, hearing the effect of the insult in the other woman's voice. "Browne was okay, but I've seen you dance. You would have been fantastic."

"Thank-you." Julia paused. "Why did you say what you did at the party? Had someone said that to you? Is it something that's going around?"

Nina felt guilty, but at the same time an idea was beginning to take shape. "In all honesty, Miss Thomas, I never dreamed someone would repeat it to you. I said it as a joke."

"A word of advice, Miss Davis: There are no jokes in Hollywood."

Maybe so, Nina thought after they had said good-bye. But for every straight line, there's a punch line; for every baited hook, an unsuspecting fish.

The next night, after Nina had plumped up her meager tidbits with a flourish of glib verbiage, she threw out this morsel: "Is it possible that there was more tension and terror on the set of Universal's upcoming *Jaws* 2 than on the screen?" The next morning someone from Universal's public relations office was arranging for Roy Scheider to interview with *The Insider* and tell everyone how chummy the cast and crew were. A rhetorical question about whether or not Jane Fonda considered *Coming Home* penance for her anti-war activities resulted in interviews with Bruce Dern, Jon Voight, and Jane Fonda. A quip about John Travolta in *Saturday Night Fever*—"If John Travolta could do them, how difficult could those dance steps be?"—got her not only an interview with the star, but an on-camera dancing lesson as well.

Nina's ratings began to rise. Her syndication numbers increased. But more important, along with her new, heightened visibility came that most precious of commodities—entry into the community. It didn't hurt that whenever

Philip Medina was in town, he squired her about. Suddenly it was the A list, a better table at Ma Maison, a nicer greeting at Giorgio's. Suddenly, if she wanted to know what was happening between Sondra Locke and Clint Eastwood or why Blake Edwards had signed Bo Derek for *10* or who was stabbing whose back on the Columbia lot, she placed a call.

Nina's next step was to earn the trust of both her sources and those whose lives were the subject of her show. When she received a tip, she checked the facts before reporting them on air. If she interviewed someone, it was a thoroughly researched piece. If she strayed beyond the intended plug—which she did whenever she could—she tried to make the piece personal, insightful, and, above all, memorable.

Having read *Photoplay* and other movie magazines all her life, Nina had dozens of seemingly insignificant facts already stored in her head. She added to that mental file by studying *Variety* and *The Hollywood Reporter* and searching out personal histories in the library. It wasn't long before she became known for drawing her guests out, getting them to reveal something about themselves they had never told anyone before.

One actress who sizzled on screen confessed that she still kept her baby blankets under her pillow. A strapping soap opera star who was usually costumed in leather and chrome surprised his audience by singing an aria from *Tosca.* Rosey Grier, the football star, brought samples of his needlepoint. Dudley Moore played Beethoven. Phyllis Diller talked about her painting.

After the first year, however, Nina decided that being good was not good enough. Every free hour she had, she studied her tapes as well as those of her competition. Many Hollywood reporters fawned over celebrities; others softpedaled their interviews, believing that simply standing next to a famous face on screen was sufficient. To Nina, that was okay if you wanted simply to get by. She wanted to move up. Yet hard as she tried, that single, magical element that would lift her above the fray and distinguish her from everyone else doing the same job eluded her.

Casting herself into the role of Everyfan, she tried to recall what had intrigued her when she was a young girl poring over *Modern Screen* and the celebrity columns in the papers, what had made her read one magazine over another or listen to one reporter rather than his or her counterpart. Remembering how easy it was to find basic biological facts or information about an upcoming project, she dismissed things like that as lures. Shock without substance didn't do it, either. While supermarket scandal sheets teased with outrageous headlines, true gossip junkies knew they were come-ons with no payoff. Nina had always been attracted by news that stunned or changed one's mind about a celebrity or altered one's vision of who or what they were, the intimate stories that let you look behind the facade.

When a star suffered a nervous breakdown and most headlines linked her illness with her career, Nina remembered the reporter who wrote of the hardship the actress endured raising a retarded child. When fans began to deify a teen idol who had died drunk behind the wheel of his car, Nina gave begrudging kudos to the few reporters who felt compelled to tell the more tawdry details of his life as a bar crawler into beating, boots, belts, and bondage. When it was discovered that the son of one star with a reputation for installing "swear boxes" on her sets and fonts of holy water beside each doorway in her home had been arrested for child molestation and was involved in the production of kiddie porn, Nina felt it was only fair to reveal the names of both mother and son. She never went to see that actress's movies again.

In the end, Nina concluded she could trade in innuendo the way Hedda Hopper and Louella Parsons had done (and she had done in the beginning), turn vicious like Walter Winchell and Elsa Maxwell and simply swipe and slash, or elevate the task of talebearing by cloaking gossip in a costume of importance. To do that, she had to create a sense of urgency about the news she was dispensing and ask the questions to which her audience wanted answers, the questions her colleagues labeled "dangerous."

She asked one of the movies' most enduring leading men if he was gay; a TV sitcom star—whose mother had been a famous singer who died from liver failure—plagued with rumors of drug and alcohol problems if she thought chemical dependency was an inherited trait; a rock and roll singer if he had known ahead of time that his Cleveland one-night stand was only fourteen. It wasn't long before Nina Davis had a national reputation and access to anyone and everyone in Hollywood. No one refused her calls. And while most headliners were terrified of talking to her, no one rejected a request for an interview. They couldn't afford not to. Nina had what they feared and what she'd always wanted: power.

"Thank-you for joining us on this edition of *The Insider*. This is Nina Davis inviting you to tune in next time and reminding you: Anyone can tell tales. We tell the truth!"

As she watched her daughter's broadcast, Miranda's expression vacillated between pride and disappointment. One minute her mouth was wreathed in a smile that could only be worn by a blatantly immodest parent; the next minute the crescent turned downward, wobbling slightly as the realization struck her that she was only one of many viewing this show, part of an audience, a stranger to the woman on the small screen.

"She looks wonderful, doesn't she?"

Luis and Isabelle exchanged glances. Miranda's perpetual good nature was inspiring, but in this case both felt it was ill served.

"Yes, she does, but she was always beautiful," Luis said, stating the obvious.

Nina did look stunning, Isabelle thought, her blond hair swooped over her forehead Veronica Lake style, her lids smoked with a shade of eye shadow that intensified the gray of her eyes. And there was something more, an on-air confidence that Isabelle found slightly unnerving. When Nina stared directly into the camera, as she was doing now, Isabelle could almost feel the heat of that stare. Though a practiced smile rested on Nina's lips, Isabelle couldn't get past the steely glint in her eyes. It was that "I dare you to challenge me" look she remembered from their childhood. She had seen it when kids teased Nina for being so tall or Isabelle for having an accent, when she had faced down the Murillos that summer in Barcelona, when she had defied Isabelle to refute what she had seen as a betrayal that morning at Enchantments.

"You have to hand it to her," Isabelle said admiringly, giving her sister her due, wishing she knew how to bridge the ocean between them. "She always said she wanted to go to Hollywood, and there she is!"

All eyes remained fixed on Nina's face as the show ended and her image faded. Miranda and Luis sorted their own private thoughts as the credits rolled. When the Cisco Communications logo appeared, Isabelle was startled to find herself wondering if Nina and Philip Medina knew each other and, if they did, how well. Embarrassed that a thought like that could creep into her consciousness and tweak her ego, she squirmed about on her chair. How could she feel jealous about a man she had met twice? It was silly, but there, the inevitable "Would he prefer her over me?"

With the specter of Nina still hovering above them, Miranda clicked off the television and turned her attention to Isabelle.

"Did I tell you someone from Barcelona stayed here several months ago who claimed to be an old friend of the family?"

Isabelle's skin prickled. "A man with pitch black eyes?"

Luis didn't like the look on her face. "Yes. His name was Barba. Pasqua Barba. Do you know him?"

Isabelle nodded and then rubbed her brow as if a headache were settling in.

"He asked if he could buy one of your mother's paintings. The one that used to hang in the lobby."

"You didn't sell it to him, did you?" Isabelle had sprung up from her chair, her voice practically a shriek.

"Of course not," Miranda said, comforting Isabelle, assuring her that Althea's paintings were hers to do with as she chose.

"Who is this Barba?"

"I think he's the man who murdered my mother."

Miranda and Luis were dumbstruck and frightened. What was he doing in Santa Fe? Why had he come to La Casa? Could he have been looking for Isabelle? Rather than share their concerns with her, they attributed his appearance to coincidence.

"He said he was touring the United States and that Rafael Avda had recommended he stay here."

It sounded reasonable. Paco was a collector. He had dealt with Rafael in the past. Still, Isabelle didn't trust him.

"How many more paintings do you need to complete?" Miranda said after she thought they had exhausted the subject of Pasqua Barba and felt they should return to more pleasant matters.

"Two," Isabelle said, trying to switch gears. "One's half done. I intend to start the other one by the end of the week. Hopefully they'll both be finished by the time Skye goes back to New York. That way she can take them with her."

"When is the opening?"

"Julian hasn't mentioned an exact date. Sometime in September."

"I hope it doesn't conflict with the show at Enchantments."

Miranda's offhand manner didn't cover the undertone in her voice. Something about this exhibition was very important to her, yet when Isabelle asked about it, she would only say it was a special group of Mexican and southwestern artists who had been friends of the Durans for years.

"We'll ask Skye tomorrow when she gets here."

"I can't wait to see her again." Miranda allowed a spontaneous giggle to brighten her face. "You're going to love her, Luis."

Luis smiled and nodded assuringly. If she was half as endearing as Miranda and Isabelle painted her, she was special indeed.

Although, Luis thought as the two women discussed the dinner they were planning to welcome Skye, Julian Richter also had received glowing notices from Miranda and Isabelle, and Luis hadn't found him special.

During each of Richter's three visits to Santa Fe, Luis had tried to like the man who was piloting his ward's career, but Richter was too proprietary for Luis's liking. His was not a protective embrace; it was a trap baited with promises of riches and renown. He felt it when he watched Richter in Isabelle's studio, studying her paintings, pacing back and forth in front of them as if something were not quite right, some infinitesimal flaw that only someone with his incredible eye could see. He told her they were good but made her feel they were not good enough to sell without him. Whatever Isabelle lost in the way of confidence, he gained in terms of her dependency. Luis feared that Richter didn't want to represent Isabelle. He wanted to own her.

Later, after he had locked the doors and checked in with the night clerk, Luis retired to their private quarters. Miranda was curled up on an easy chair in their bedroom. Assessing the look on her face, he knew that she had been there long enough for her thoughts to travel back in time, to places they no longer visited, calling on people with whom they were no longer welcome.

"May I join you?" he said, tapping on the arm of the chair.

Miranda turned toward him and tried to smile, but she was still caught in the tangle of her musings. He sat on the windowsill next to her, holding her hand, letting her decide whether she wanted to stay where she was or return. She lingered for a moment longer, reluctant to end her sojourn with the past. When she did, her face maintained a residual melancholy that clouded her eyes and surrounded her voice with traces of an echo.

"Do you think she'll ever come back?"

He knew she was thinking of Nina. "To live? No. For visits? Maybe. Despite the way she left, she knows our door will always be open to her."

Miranda nodded, a wistful smile replacing the grimace that had occupied her lips just moments before. "She always did have stardust in her eyes, didn't she?"

"That, and an overactive imagination." Luis chuckled, recalling the many times Nina had monopolized the dinner conversation with news of the day. Of course, Nina's bulletins concerned the lives and loves of the stars of her favorite movies or television shows or records, never the goings-on of friends or neighbors. "Don't forget. She's still young, and Hollywood isn't the fairyland she thinks it is."

"Do you think she loves us?"

Luis hadn't expected that. "In her way, yes."

"I'm never sure."

"That's because you want her to love you unconditionally, the way you love her." He shook his head, went to the bed, and sat on the edge, facing his

wife. "Nina can't do that, Miranda. She's struggling with too many unresolved feelings about her birth parents and the truth and why we hid it
from her and God knows what else!"

"Will she ever come to terms with all of this?"

"That depends," Luis said, fixing his eyes on Miranda's, "on whether she's
the kind who needs to live with the truth or prefers to live a lie."

As she always did when she returned to her casita, Isabelle stopped short of
the entrance to her quaint little house and smiled. When she had told
Miranda and Luis she wanted to come home to paint, they had offered her
the casita they had lived in during their first years in Santa Fe.

Naturally Luis had insisted on renovating. He retiled the floor, widened
the windows, reorganized the living space, and added skylights and enough
square footage for a serviceable studio. Never one to scoff at superstition,
Isabelle painted the doors and window frames of the Paint Box, as she had
dubbed the casita, a blue so electric that it was almost blinding.

Inside, the main room was hot pink; biscuit-colored tile and cedar latillas
softened the impact. Two low, steplike walls created a separation between
the living and sleeping areas, as did a violet wall against which Isabelle had
placed an antique wooden bed dressed in a rainbow of bedclothes. Brightly
patterned rugs splashed across the floor. Kachina dolls enlivened tabletops
and shelves. Plants filled every windowsill. Nooks and crannies held black-
and-white pottery from local pueblos.

Isabelle's collection of Indian jewelry was displayed on the bedroom side
of the step walls, each piece dangling from a metal nail in a medley of turquoise, coral, olive shells, melon shells, fetishes, squash blossoms, silver,
and pearl. Over the fireplace hung one of the three paintings in Althea's
series "The Nativity." Next to her bed, lovingly mounted and framed, hung
Isabelle's somewhat-the-worse-for-wear fabric swatch.

Isabelle's studio stood in stark contrast with the rest of the tiny house.
Stark white, void of everything except an easel, a stool, and a wooden table
strewn with supplies, the space was dominated by a pitched roof containing
large, flat skylights. During the day the sun provided all the light she could
possibly want. At night illumination was supplied by a single lamp, sometimes in concert with the moon.

Isabelle never went to bed without visiting this room. It was almost as if
being with her art took the place of saying her prayers. In a way she supposed
it did, because everything she believed in was centered in her art. God. Love.

The miracle of nature. The eternal mystery of man. The spirituality of creation.

As she turned on the light this particular evening, her eyes went immediately to a large canvas propped against a wall. Sitting cross-legged on the floor, she studied the painting. Dominated by dusky shades of violet and gray, a thick white cloud appeared to eddy from a near black vortex. It rose from a central core, pushing its way out and up, using its strength to convey a reverence for the powers beyond human comprehension.

Isabelle had painted it during her last visit to Barcelona, after a day that had been one of the most wonderful of her sojourn and a night that had been one of the most depressing. Tía Flora had been ill and bedridden for much of the time, greatly limiting their activities. When, finally, Flora was able to join Isabelle at the table for dinner, they made it into a gala evening. Though it was just the two of them, they dressed up and lit all the candles in the grand dining room and had the cook prepare something very special. They talked about their favorite things—art, family, and Isabelle's parents. Quite unexpectedly, Tía Flora asked Isabelle if she had ever been in love.

"I thought I was, once," she said, referring to Cody Jackson, the only man in her life to date.

Flora clucked her tongue and shook her head. "If you had to think about it, you weren't!"

"You must be right because I didn't follow him to Paris."

"What would you have done if he had stayed in New York? Would you have married him?"

Isabelle answered honestly. "No. I wasn't ready. Or he wasn't the one. I can't say."

Flora was nodding, as if she had once shared the same feelings.

"Why didn't you ever marry Tío Alejandro?" Isabelle asked, suddenly wondering if there had been someone else in Flora's life. "You claim to love him."

"And I do. Always have. Always will." She sipped her wine, savoring it for a moment in her mouth before letting the juice of the grape glide slowly down her throat. "I never was willing to give up my independence. If I had married, that's what I thought I would have had to do." She grew quiet and reflective. "Back then, Barcelona society had very definite rules about behavior. I wasn't very good at obeying rules that shoved me in the background, insinuating that because I was a woman, I wasn't as interesting or as important or as relevant as a man. I couldn't accept the stupidity that said I shouldn't paint or, if I did, I shouldn't show. I detested words like 'unseemly' and 'unladylike' and 'improper.' "

She laughed at her vehemence, obviously recalling a contretemps or two from her past.

"When Alejandro stayed with me despite my refusal to marry him, and escorted me all over town, declaring his love for me whenever and wherever he chose, I thought my heart would burst at the love and devotion and courage such an act displayed."

"Maybe one day I'll find my Alejandro," Isabelle said, touched by her great-aunt's words.

Flora looked at Isabelle. A somber smile tugged at her lips. "I wouldn't trade what Alejandro and I have shared over these many years for anything, but what you should look for, Isabelle, is what your father and your mother had.

"Certainly they had passion, which is what most young people mistake for love. Beyond that, they had two things everyone needs and few get: they trusted each other, and they made each other feel safe." Her voice softened as she looked at her grandniece. "When you find a man who can not only arouse your passion, but can inspire your trust and make you feel completely safe, marry him!"

Unable to sleep after their discussion, Isabelle had climbed up into the tower of the Castell. Outside, on the terrace that surrounded the Gothic peak, she sat and communed with the darkness. Before she knew it, the night had passed. Exhausted, both physically and emotionally, she watched in awed silence as, gradually, the veil of night lifted.

The pace was slow, almost hesitant, like the body when it begins to waken after a deep sleep, stirring, yet not completely willing to abandon the shelter of slumber's cocoon. The clouds lightened in the east. The sun climbed over the surrounding mountaintops. Morning unfolded in an exquisite and triumphant burst of color.

And a young woman, certain that this particular dawning had been staged to deliver her a spiritual message, found the inspiration she needed to embark on her own climb.

Isabelle returned to New Mexico eager to begin a series of abstract landscapes. Venturing into the frightening emptiness of Death Valley, the echo-filled craters of the Grand Canyon, the rainbowed spires of Bryce Canyon, the gullies and buttes of the Badlands, Isabelle tracked the dawn. She camped out for days in each location, acquainting herself with the land, sleeping beneath the stars, waking just before the curtain of day was raised.

It was both astounding and, at the same time, reassuring to realize that while sunup adopted a different aspect depending on the contour and context of the ground over which it rose, the act of daily creation remained a constant. No matter what man did, whether it was a noble sacrifice or an evil deed, he was powerless to stop the morning.

The forty paintings to be put on display at the Richter Gallery in September were Isabelle de Luna's anthem to dawn: "Ode to Eos."

It was as if Skye and the Durans had known each other all their lives. Within hours of Skye's arrival they were chatting and laughing like old friends, talking about everything from lighting a gallery to chili recipes. Jonas and Sybil, who had married the year before, stopped by after dinner and almost didn't leave.

Sybil asked Skye what it was like to work for the renowned Julian Richter.

Skye rolled her eyes. "Difficult! He's a genius, I'll give him that, but believe me, the man has a serious ego problem. Not only does he think he's the greatest thing since Botticelli, but he actually looks upon me as a lesser being. Can you imagine that?"

Egged on by their laughter, she imitated him addressing her: slouched shoulders, one arm resting on the other, fingers stroking an imaginary beard, his voice straining with patience. "Skye, I have something to say. It's important, so pay attention. I'm only going to tell you this once." She paused as he paused, adding weight to his words: "Good morning."

She entertained them with hilarious stories about the goings-on at the gallery, recounting Julian's hysteria over minutiae like how many flowers filled the vase on the front desk or his insistence that she count how many lines he got in Hilton Kramer's column in the *New York Observer* compared to Greta Reed or Leo Castelli.

When the subject of Julian Richter had been exhausted, they moved on to the differences between being Jewish in New York and being Jewish in Santa Fe.

"Delis," Skye said emphatically. "With all due respect, there isn't a decent kosher delicatessen within a fifty-mile radius of this burg."

Jonas laughed. "No argument there. Even in Albuquerque, I can't say that you'd find cold cuts or smoked fish or kosher franks like you get in New York. The Jewish population just isn't big enough."

"It's bigger than you think," Skye said, her expression shifting suddenly.

"Have you suddenly become a census taker?" Isabelle asked, her mouth curled in an amused smile.

"No. But . . ." It was clear that Skye's thoughts had strayed. "Has anyone ever heard the term hidden or crypto-Jews?"

"I'm lost!" Isabelle said, throwing up her hands in a gesture of confusion. "We've gone from dissecting Julian's peccadillos to critiquing colds cuts to debating the number of Jews living in and around Santa Fe. Skye, darling, what the hell are you talking about?"

"When I was on the plane coming in from Dallas, I read an article about a recent incident in El Paso. A bunch of stores were vandalized. Windows were smashed and swastikas were painted on the walls. The article said the owners of the stores were crypto-Jews. I'd never heard the term before. It intrigued me."

The room suddenly turned quiet. Jonas's face was stony. Isabelle and Sybil both appeared curious. Miranda's and Luis's expressions were harder to read. Skye was beginning to wish she had never raised the matter. Nonetheless, she continued.

"The article said they were descendants of the Jews who went to Mexico after they were expelled from Spain during the Inquisition."

"So why were their stores attacked?" Isabelle still didn't understand.

"Something about them living like Catholics, but really being Jews. They were found out, and some of their fellow townsfolk went ballistic."

"Was anyone hurt?"

Skye's face hardened. "Two people were killed. Several were injured. Most of the businesses were destroyed."

"That's outrageous!" Sybil said. "Do you know anything about this group?" she asked her husband.

"A little."

"According to the reporter's sources, there are clusters of crypto-Jews throughout the Southwest. They say that some families have been hiding their Judaism for five hundred years."

"Is that true?" Isabelle asked Jonas.

He shrugged. "I don't know. Here and there I've heard stories, but without personal testimony, it's hard to know what's true and what isn't."

"You think they exist, don't you," Isabelle said.

Jonas nodded.

"Maybe this was an isolated incident," Sybil said, still straining to understand.

Skye shook her head. "We like to think the world has grown tolerant, but it hasn't. No matter how much we might like it to be otherwise, each generation seems to produce its own brand of Crusaders." Skye's voice was even, but it rumbled with anger. "The Nazis may have been the worst. But they were not the first. And they won't be the last."

It was nearly two in the morning when Skye and Isabelle retreated to the Paint Box.

"You have to be the luckiest human being on the planet," Skye said as they rolled out the convertible bed in the living room and made it ready for sleep. "Not only did you have Señor and Señora Perfecto as parents, and Flora, the fabulous eccentric, as your guardian angel, but when the shit hit the fan, you landed here in Southwest heaven with people like the Durans. Cinderella must hate you."

"They're great, aren't they?" Isabelle's filial pride was in full evidence. "And how about Jonas and Sybil? Aren't they fabulous?"

Skye nodded, but her thoughts were on something else. "I think I upset Miranda and Luis with that El Paso stuff."

"Of course it upset them," Isabelle said. "It upset everyone. It was a terrible incident."

"I know, but they got real quiet. Maybe they thought I was pissed off because the bad guys were Mexican-Americans. I wouldn't want them to think I was buying into that brown-bias thing."

"They would never think that," Isabelle reassured her. "Besides, Miranda adores you."

"From the first day I met her," Skye said, grateful for the change of mood, "I knew she was a woman of extraordinary taste!"

The bed made, Skye cuddled into one corner, Isabelle into the other. "She's going to take me on a tour of Canyon Road and the other galleries in town," Skye said.

Isabelle nodded. "There's no better guide to the art market in Santa Fe."

"She seems really keen on the artists in her season opener. 'The Eighteen' is an intriguing name for a show."

"There are eighteen artists exhibiting," Isabelle said, wondering why Skye thought the title was so unique.

"I know, but giving a bunch of exhibitors a name invites the conclusion that they're a group with something in common. Besides, numbers are mystical."

" 'The Eight' had something in common," Isabelle said, referring to a group of American painters popular in the early 1900s, "but they were far from mystical. They were eight artists who chose to exhibit together when the National Academy of Design rejected their paintings of slums."

"What about 'the Blue Four'?"

"I never thought of Kandinsky, Jawlensky, Klee, and Lyonel Feininger as a group," Isabelle said. "Nor did I ever consider them mystical."

"That's because they gained greater recognition as individuals and because you're a Philistine and not as tuned in to art mumbo-jumbo as I am."

"Is that a fact?" Isabelle stifled a smile.

"It is," Skye asserted firmly. "The German woman who brought them together and repped them in the States named them 'the Blue Four' because she believed deep royal blue was a spiritual color."

"I hate that blue." It came out of her mouth so quickly, Isabelle shocked herself, to say nothing of Skye. "I'm sorry, I didn't mean to . . ."

Skye held up her hand; explanations were unnecessary. She knew all about Isabelle's nightmares, those journeys into a deep blue void where there was nothing but noise and half memories and features with no face. She had thought they were gone, but Isabelle's reaction said otherwise.

"Are you having those headaches again?" she asked.

Isabelle shrugged, as if to say "Now and then." "The weather hasn't been great. We've had a lot of rain, and as you know, I don't take well to rain."

Thunderstorms were the worst. They made Isabelle's head throb unmercifully. Though she had been to a number of doctors, she had been told nothing could be done. One, however, seemed particularly taken with the fact that her name was de Luna. He suggested she might be one of those rare individuals who was impacted physically by the gravitational pull of the moon. He urged her to track her nightmares and headaches carefully, checking to see if they related to storms and high tides and the various phases of the moon. She didn't do that, but she did continue to sketch whatever she saw during the nightmares, keeping them in a file for some future time when perhaps their meaning would become clear.

"One of these days, Is, the nightmares and the headaches are just going to disappear. You'll see."

Isabelle tried to smile, but the effort was wasted. "I hope you're right. The problem is, I keep thinking they're trying to tell me something, something important. Maybe about the night my mother was killed."

"Having put in a fair amount of time on a shrink's couch, I can tell you that if there is something hiding in the darkest depths of your gray matter, it will come out when you're ready to deal with it and not a millisecond sooner. So, relax. It'll happen when it happens."

"Thank-you, Madame Freud," Isabelle said, crawling over and wrapping Skye in a grateful embrace. "I feel much better now."

"There's no need to thank me," Skye said, returning Isabelle's hug, "but since I am a member of the working poor, I would appreciate it if you would consider these keen psychological insights as exchange for my room and board."

"Done!" Isabelle said with a much needed laugh.

Over the next several weeks, while Isabelle worked on her last two paintings, Skye spent a great deal of time with Miranda. Not only did they visit every gallery in Santa Fe, but Miranda took Skye outside the city to the various pueblos, introducing her to potters, jewelers, weavers, and other Indian craftspeople who made the Southwest such an artistically rich region.

Skye also spent a great deal of time talking to Miranda about Enchantments: how she had managed in the beginning when money was tight, why she thought she was successful, what her focus was, how had it changed over the years, and how she found new artists.

"Do you want to open your own gallery?" Miranda asked.

Skye shrugged. "I don't know. I'm still trying to decide whether I'm more effective as an artist or a dealer."

"Which gives you more pleasure?"

Skye mulled over Miranda's question. "Each feeds a different need," she said. "For me, painting is an emotional release, so I don't always consider it a pleasurable experience. It's also a very solitary profession, lonely sometimes. As a dealer, I can be part of both the art world and the outside world. I like that."

Miranda nodded. She felt the same way. "Do you think you'd want to deal with established artists or seek out the brave young souls who are breaking new ground?"

"Both," Skye said, shaking her head. "When I see something new, something that seems to be pushing art forward even in the smallest way, I get an unbelievable, almost uncontrollable rush! Time might prove me wrong about some of the judgments I've made, but to me, the excitement is in having the guts to make the judgment in the first place.

"Watching an artist like Isabelle develop and mature gives me a thrill. What's changed? How far has she come? How much farther can she go? Is her work timely? Or timeless? It's like trying to define the limits of creativity. Some grow and stop. For others, there are no boundaries."

"You see a different kind of art in New York," Miranda said.

"True," Skye said, intuiting Miranda's fears for Isabelle. "But don't you worry about our girl. It doesn't matter whom you stack her up against, she shines. Trust me. Isabelle de Luna is going to be one of the greats."

Each week since Isabelle had come to Santa Fe, she had received a call or a letter from Julian Richter. Aside from inquiring about her progress, Julian used the occasions to increase his familiarity with her. After a visit, he'd ingratiate himself by raving about her family and New Mexico. He'd ask about her health and the weather and other inconsequential matters. Then he'd ask how she was feeling about the work she was doing or about her solo debut. He was always solicitous and encouraging, always knitting kindness with an implication of strength—his was a reliable shoulder, lean on it when needed—always talking about the kind of wonderful future he foresaw for *them.*

It wasn't long before his letters were colored with an air of intimacy. Certainly Isabelle was flattered by his attention and, if pressed, would admit that she was drawn to him. Yet despite the seductive aura of his power and his ardent pursuit, caution dammed the flow of her feelings.

The second week in August he called to say he had scheduled her opening for September 18.

Isabelle girded herself for an explosive response. "I can't be there."

"What? You have to be there!"

"I know. It's just . . . I don't know how to explain it."

"Try," Julian said, clearly agitated.

"Miranda and Luis are hosting an exhibit at Enchantments that night."

It was unusual for Isabelle to be conflicted when it came to her art— usually it came first, everything else came second. But it was unusual for the Durans to ask her for anything. They had, and she didn't see how she could refuse.

"I know it's unprofessional of me and impossible for you to understand, but I have to be here." The silence on the other end of the phone screamed at her. "I'll see if I can get them to reschedule," she said meekly, wondering how she was going to accomplish that.

"No. Don't." Julian's voice was calm and surprisingly sympathetic. "Nothing important has gone to the press yet. I'll move it up two days. No harm done."

Isabelle practically swooned at his generosity. "I don't know how to thank you."

"Having you by my side will be thanks enough. Wish Miranda good luck with her show."

Julian Richter had just punched a hole in the dam.

The opening night of Miranda's exhibit was unlike anything she'd ever done before. None of the artists of "The Eighteen" were going to be present. Their names would not appear on the program. The gallery was to remain locked until Miranda led everyone inside. Isabelle thought shrouding the show in such secrecy was a stroke of promotional genius. Miranda claimed it was necessary.

Instead of holding the cocktail party for the press and a selected group of invited guests inside the gallery, as she usually did, the party was held out-side in Enchantments' garden. It was a lovely evening, warm and sweet with the fragrance of summer's last blooms perfuming the air. The moon was high and bright, floating above the gaily lanterned garden as if part of a set. Isa-belle mixed and mingled, accepting the best wishes of those who knew she was having her own show in New York, enjoying the spirit of anticipation that buzzed through the crowd.

Last night she had viewed the show. She wished Skye could have been there to see it, but she had returned to the city two weeks before. As Miranda had predicted, Isabelle found the works striking and disturbing.

Stylistically they were varied: several traditional pieces, many abstract paintings and sculptures, surreal accounts of nightmares filled with symbols Isabelle couldn't read, brilliant landscapes, haunting portraits—a full pano-ply of artistic expression. Precisely what they were expressing—anger, fear, rage, passion, hope—Isabelle wasn't sure, but Skye had been right about one thing: This group was united by something larger than aesthetics.

When it was time, Miranda opened the doors and invited her guests in-side. At that same moment the wail of a fire engine's siren pierced the con-vivial atmosphere in the garden. A vivid orange haze rose in the distance. People turned, looked, commented on the horror of fire, and then turned away, eager to follow Miranda and return to more pleasant diversions.

Miranda's shriek chilled the air, swallowing the easy laughter and idle chatter of those behind her. Luis elbowed his way to his wife's side. Isabelle followed. When those at the head of the crowd entered the gallery, they too froze, paralyzed by the same assault of fear and horror that had felled Miranda.

The paintings in the front room had been slashed. Pieces of canvas hung like dead skin. Two large sculptures had been smashed, once powerful forms reduced to a pile of dust. In the center of the floor, stuck in one of Miranda's terra-cotta planters, was a wooden cross soaked in blood. It was a monstrous display of hatred and senseless devastation, but horrid as it was, the nightmare was not over.

Less than an hour later Miranda and Luis learned that the vicious fire they had seen illuminating the sky had devoured La Casa. The once proud inn had been reduced to little more than a pile of gray ash. Here and there one could make out metal objects like bedsteads, andirons, a few of Miranda's pots and pans. Everything else, except Isabelle's Paint Box, had been burned beyond repair.

Isabelle and the Durans spent what was left of the night at the Hoffmans, returning to the wreckage at dawn. Charred black fragments created a morbid silhouette against the brightness of the morning sky. An acrid smell assaulted their noses. Smoke stung their eyes.

Miranda wept as she tiptoed among the rubble. Luis stood by the gate, transfixed.

"Gone," he whispered. "Everything we worked for is gone."

Isabelle ached for them. La Casa was more than their home. They had come here as newlyweds. They had worked as handyman and cook to earn their keep. They had risked everything to take it over, to build it up, to make it their own. It had taken years of sacrifice and work and dedication, but they had succeeded. La Casa was well known, well respected. Yet in one mad moment everything they had worked for had been burned to the ground.

Isabelle draped her arm around his shoulders. She, too, was feeling the staggering pain of loss. Somewhere in the blistering waste were the bed she had slept in, the window seat where she used to dream about her future, the back room off the kitchen where she and Nina used to play.

"Memories don't burn," Isabelle said to Luis, hoping to comfort herself as well as him.

He nodded, but both of them knew that scattered among those ashes were a host of irreplaceables: two of Althea's paintings, the family's collection of Christmas tree ornaments, scrapbooks and photo albums, a box of Nina's baby things, pictures of their son, Gabriel.

"We'll rebuild La Casa." It was a strain to find a positive face for this tragedy, but Isabelle tried anyway. "For years you and Miranda have talked about redoing the place, updating it and all. Now's your chance!"

It was a struggle for Luis to speak. "We don't have the money."

"We'll find it."

"Where?" he said, his voice choked with grief and despair. "In there?" Struggling to dam his tears, he ventured into the cinders, poking at the incinerated debris that had been his life. Isabelle remained at the gate, watching as the Durans held each other and cried.

Later, when Sybil arrived with coffee and muffins, Miranda realized Isabelle was scheduled to leave for New York later that morning.

"I'm staying," Isabelle said.

"No," Miranda argued, "you're not."

"There's nothing you can do here." Luis's voice was hollow.

"I can help with the cleanup. I can lend moral support. I can take care of you." As difficult as it was to look at the seared remains of La Casa, it was harder to look into their eyes. "Where will you stay? What will you do?"

Miranda hugged Isabelle and commanded a smile to her lips. "If you go to New York, there'll be room for us in the Paint Box. We'll figure out where to go from there."

After a lengthy—and futile—period of protestation and an excruciating good-bye, Isabelle left, but before going to the airport she paid a visit to Oscar Yount.

"It may not be my place to ask, but would you know whether or not La Casa was adequately insured?"

Yount hemmed and hawed about procedures and privacy, but, like everyone else in town, he had heard about the show and the fire. The Durans were a well-liked couple. If he could help, he would.

After a few phone calls he said, "I'm afraid your instincts were correct, Isabelle. La Casa was terribly underinsured. At today's rates, the policy will never cover reconstruction."

"How much is in my account?" Years before, Isabelle had turned her money over to Yount to invest. She had intended to use it to buy Dragon Textiles. Suddenly it had another, more immediate purpose.

"We've done quite well," he said, unable to keep a proud smile off his lips. "We've worked it back up to its original worth. Twenty-five thousand dollars."

Isabelle nodded sadly, wondering why dreams were always so much larger than the bankrolls needed to make them come true. Twenty-five thousand dollars was a lot of money, but not enough to cover the rebuilding of La Casa.

"Tomorrow night, an exhibition of my work opens in New York. I don't know how much I'll earn from that show, but whatever it is, I'm going to send it to you. Combine it with my trust fund and give it to the Durans. I don't want them to know where it came from. Do you understand?"

Yount was touched. When he had taken over management of the account, he and Isabelle had discussed her goals. He knew how much that fund meant to her.

"They have a copy of their policy. They're going to know what they were supposed to receive," he said.

"Make something up. Tell them the previous owner had a policy on it that was still active. Tell them it's a landmark and Santa Fe had a policy on it. Tell them whatever you want, but don't tell them it came from me."

By the time Isabelle landed at La Guardia, she was exhausted. She was in no mood to meet Julian at the gallery, but she couldn't cancel, not after all he had done. She dropped off her luggage at Skye's—who was scouting the opening of a competitor—showered, changed, and headed uptown. She stepped out of the taxi and stopped outside the gallery door, suddenly nervous, suddenly fearful that she would walk in and find the cruel vandalism Miranda and Luis had found, that her paintings would be slashed and ruined. With moist palms she turned the doorknob and walked in.

The front room was dim, the only lights a few deftly placed spots that illuminated six of her exquisite matins. In the center of the bare wooden floor was a table set for two. Elegantly laid with gleaming silver, sparkling crystal, fine damask, and plain bone china, the low, lush all white bouquet of lilies, roses, freesia, and tulips created a still life in shades of pale. One of Bach's Brandenburg concerti played in the background.

Julian stood at the archway leading to the second gallery, his all-black ensemble in stark contrast with the setting. His arms were crossed, his eyes studying her with an intensity that put her off balance.

"Before the hoopla begins," he said, holding out his hand, inviting her to join him on a tour of the gallery, "I wanted you to have a private viewing of your own genius."

Isabelle's paintings were different from much of the work of the late 1970s. She was not a minimalist like Agnes Martin or Brice Marden, painting sleek grids and stripped-down surfaces with near machine precision. Nor was she part of the emerging Neo-Expressionist school of emotive, often violent, art. Francesco Clemente, David Salle, Sandro Chia, Ed Paschke, Julian Schnabel, Anselm Kiefer—these artists created a stir by presenting work that evoked thoughts of power rather than ideals of beauty.

Isabelle's landscapes startled in the manner achieved by a well-trained public speaker, who captured attention not by raising her voice and screaming louder than the loudest voice there, but by lowering her voice and delivering her message with quiet confidence. Both powerful and beautiful, they reminded the viewer that despite the cataclysmic changes being thrust on society, despite drugs and inner-city violence, environmental decay and dangerous geopolitical wrestling matches, nature still provided a refuge.

"How do you think I'll fare with the critics?" she said, displaying the protective apprehension of a mother before her child's first school play.

"You're the calm in the storm," he said, guiding her toward the front room.

"Somehow I don't think Hilton Kramer or Robert Hughes will leave it at that."

He held out her chair, helped her get seated, and then seated himself. As if summoned by a silent buzzer, two formally attired butlers entered the room, one to pour wine, the other to serve a delicate first course of smoked trout.

"To the success of the 'Ode to Eos' exhibition," Richter said, raising his wineglass, moving it toward hers, "and the dawn of a magnificent career."

Isabelle's response was not what Julian had expected. Instead of a smile, his toast was greeted by quiet tears.

"Did I say something wrong?"

Isabelle shook her head, steadied her emotions, and told him about Enchantments and La Casa. His face registered honest shock and dismay.

"When I walked in here tonight, I was carrying a suitcase of unreasonable fears. This dinner, this viewing, your reassurances—they mean a lot to me."

Julian reached across the table and enfolded Isabelle's hand in his. "You mean a lot to me," he said softly. "And you needn't ever worry. I won't let anything hurtful happen to you or your art. You're safe with me."

The next evening Isabelle shook hands and answered questions and received praise with muted disbelief. As she accommodated photographers and stood beside her paintings, she looked far more serene than she felt. In her ivory ankle-length sheath, her hair unfettered, her neck dressed with a double strand of turquoise and silver, she was a vision of calm. Yet anyone attuned to detail would have noticed how often her fingers touched the turquoise beads, how desperately she was trying to access the good luck Navahos believed were inherent in the ancient stone.

She needn't have worried. Midway through the party Julian told her she had sold out. He held her as she wept with joy.

Later, at a celebratory midnight supper at Richter's town house, her emotions spiked again when he read her reviews:

"Isabelle de Luna's paintings hark back to earlier times, while at the same time tilt art forward with astounding force" *The New York Times.*

"Throughout Isabelle de Luna's solo debut, one is treated to a very ambitious dialogue with art both past and present" *ARTnews.*

"Isabelle de Luna's world is an emotional, protean heaven of brush strokes and texture, a place where ambiguities exist and change provokes anxiety" The *New York Observer.*

Isabelle listened to the words in a haze of candlelight and champagne. All her life she had dreamed about this moment. It was hard to believe it had become a reality, yet it had, thanks to the man who had put down the newspaper and taken her in his arms. As Isabelle felt his lips graze hers, the power she had sensed in him became intoxicating. She had seen how potent he was in one arena, which was why she was willing to experience his might in a more private venue.

Julian took her to his bedroom, an exquisite lair of elegant woods, luxurious fabrics, and fabulous paintings. Treating her like an icon, he undressed her with near reverential silence. Isabelle could have sworn there was music playing when they had first walked in, but it was gone now. There was no sound other than clothes dropping to the floor, bedcovers being tossed aside, and bodies sliding onto crisply ironed sheets.

Julian said nothing, preferring to let his hands communicate his admiration, caressing her body with an urgency only slightly tamed. And while his hands roved, his eyes watched. He seemed to need to see her breasts harden and her eyes close, to see her hips sway as his fingers whispered across her skin and his lips grazed her flesh. He needed to hear her gasp as he probed the mystery of her sex, to hear her moan as he pressed his own desire against her. And when he felt her quake at the mighty thrust of his virility, his exhilaration was complete. She had been a fantasy for so long, the reality was almost more than he could bear.

For Isabelle, the night loomed in her consciousness as an enigma. How could it be that this man, who had made her feel as sheltered as a child and as desirable as a woman, could at the same time have made her think about the need to protect herself?

Why would she need to protect herself against him? She had trusted him with her career and had succeeded beyond her wildest dreams. She had trusted him with her body and had not been disappointed. Yet something about the way he made love to her had set off a velvet alarm.

The next morning he aroused her again, and again she was troubled. Julian didn't make love to her as much as he took her. Though he satisfied her, her pleasure seemed a by-product of his own. It was at the height of his passion, however, when Julian blurted out, "Finally, you're mine! No one else's. Just mine," that Isabelle knew: this was the last time she would lie in his bed.

She would give him her art. But her body and her soul, she intended to keep for herself.

CHAPTER 15

1982

For the international set, the wedding of Pilar Padillo and Philip Medina's father, Nelson, was the social event of the year. For Nina Davis, it was her long overdue coming-out. She refused to consider that her name might have been put on the guest list because she had once worked for Philip Medina, that now she was a reporter for the *New York Daily* as well as the celebrity commentator on the *Today* show, and that by accepting, she was expected to cover the festivities with a favorable eye.

In her view she deserved to be invited. She was, after all, one of the reigning queens of the society pages. She was giving Cindy Adams, Suzy, and Liz Smith a run for their money as to whose crown contained the largest and shiniest jewels. Of course she'd be invited! Having Nina Davis there was as much a coup for the Medinas as being there was for her.

Naturally the invitation precipitated a flurry of activity. This was not your average New York wedding. This was a long weekend in Majorca at Philip's villa, with everything from transportation to toothbrushes paid for by Nelson Medina. Unwilling to leave anything to chance, Nina buried her staff in assignments: guest accommodations, travel arrangements, complete background briefings on protocol, bride, groom, immediate family, previous husbands and wives, possible long-lost children, any attendees whose names they could get hold of, and, most important of all, what was expected in the way of wardrobe. Being invited to attend such a gathering was akin to being asked to appear at court. The last thing Nina wanted was to attract negative attention because of a lack of gloves, a hatless head, or an improper hem length.

The morning she was scheduled to leave, a limousine picked her up at her apartment and drove her to Kennedy Airport, where she was greeted by a bevy of special attendants; one saw to her luggage, another took her passport, and yet a third escorted her into a private lounge, where she and forty-nine other guests would await the departure of the jet Nelson had chartered to fly his American friends to the wedding. Nina's confidence flagged a bit when she reconnoitered the lounge. Though she recognized over half the New

York contingent, they were people whom she had mentioned in her column, not people she had interviewed up close and personal.

This was a group who didn't care if they were talked about in Nina's nationally syndicated *Pandora's Box;* they were discussed in *Forbes*'s "America's Richest Four Hundred." They were socialites, and socialites were different from celebrities. Celebrities—which were Nina's bread and butter—craved fame, at almost any cost. Recognition was the reason they went into show business in the first place, though to be fair, courting publicity wasn't always a matter of ego. The measure of one's fame often decided the length of one's career: the better one was known, the greater the draw at the box office, the meatier the roles, the louder the applause, the better one was known, et cetera.

Socialites preferred their fame sanitized. They cared what was said about them. The men didn't mind talk about their business successes or their charitable impulses or their civic-mindedness. They did, however, object to words like "ruthless," "heartless," "philandering," and "exploitative." The women enjoyed flattering coverage of their intercontinental shopping sprees and spartan diets, their good taste, good works, and good looks. What they didn't want to read about were failed face lifts, unbecoming hairdos, disgruntled help, unhappy spouses, or women who were younger, thinner, richer, and more involved than they.

While Four Hundred fame might have been harder to attain, it was much simpler to maintain than Hollywood fame. The Four Hundred was based on money: as long as one made it and held on to it, one was assured of acclamation. In Hollywood, if talent was all that went into the creation of a star, Nina Davis would have been out of a job. The star machine was fueled by what Nina called the Mighty Four: scandal, sensation, shame, and slander. Success without any of the preceding was possible, but the hill was steeper, the climb more difficult, the perch much narrower.

As Nina scanned the lounge looking for an opening among the various clusters, she spotted an empty chair next to none other than Anthony Hartwick. Having shed wife number two a while back and having tired of his most recent paramours, the handsome Mr. Hartwick appeared decidedly available.

"I hope this isn't taken," she said, folding herself onto a vinyl club chair with an attitude that said "Too bad if it is."

Hartwick's face remained blank for half a second. Then a name attached itself to the blond hair and endless legs seated next to him: "Nina Davis."

Nina nodded, smothering her relief that his response had been cordial.

"From caterer's snoop to syndicated columnist. Congratulations. That's quite a leap."

"I've got long legs," she said, letting him know she had noticed his once-over.

He laughed and then, as if she had granted him permission, proceeded to travel the length of her body again, this time much more slowly. She felt as if she were being measured for something.

"Success becomes you," he said finally.

"And it feels as good as it looks."

His upper lip curled in a half smile; the other half was a deliberate leer. Unable to control her habitual glibness, Nina had tossed out the come-on without thinking. The fact that he picked up on it so quickly made her blush. Fortunately she was spared further embarrassment by the announcement that the plane was ready.

Hartwick escorted her on board, settled her on the seat next to him, and spent the entire flight engaging her in conversation. By the time they landed in Palma, Nina had the distinct impression that Anthony Hartwick, a man who had fired her and threatened her, had designs on her.

After checking into their hotel in Deyá, a tiny village outside Palma, and taking a much needed siesta, they were picked up in a caravan of limousines and driven to Philip Medina's villa for a prenuptial dinner. Throughout the ride Nina found herself confronted with feelings she thought she had expunged. It had been many years since that summer in Barcelona, yet in spite of herself, the driver's Catalan accent, combined with the delicious scent of nearby orange and lemon orchards, prompted a longing for things familial: times spent at the Castell with Tía Flora and Tío Alejandro, her life at La Casa with Mama and Papa, the closeness she had shared with Isabelle.

The cliffs surrounding Deyá suddenly became the Sangre de Cristo Mountains of Santa Fe; the road they were traveling, the road from Barcelona to Campíns. The soft, early evening air, redolent with the perfume of almond and olive groves, intensified in her mind, growing stronger and more pungent, like the smells coming from Miranda's kitchen or Luis's famous barbecues. Her eyes pooled, and she swallowed hard. She missed all of it but would retrieve none of it. That life, and everyone associated with it, was gone, relegated to pages in a mental scrapbook taken out only on holidays or occasions like this, when a scent or a view or a name triggered a recollection of a past she was determined to forget.

Suddenly she wondered whether Tía Flora would be at the wedding. It was possible. Flora Pujol was one of the pillars of Barcelona society, she thought. For a moment the prospect of seeing Flora again delighted Nina; then it terrified her. She couldn't afford a public reunion. Her biography didn't include Isabelle de Luna or her relatives.

According to the script, Nina was the only child of Hale and Leslie Davis, a wealthy couple of English/Scottish heritage who had died when their private plane crashed and burned in a lowland field while paying a visit to the family distillery. She had been fourteen, sent off to Scotland to finish her primary schooling, returned to the United States to attend college, and been on her own ever since. Those were the basic facts of her fiction, to be embellished only when necessary.

Early on, Nina had thought she might have to create an entire dossier, but time reaffirmed something she had known all along—most people were self-centered. If you asked questions about them, they preferred answering to asking about you. By always asking first, Nina had managed to reveal little about herself. As far as anyone knew, her life story was brief, slightly tragic, yet at its core a tale of bravery and self-reliance. In effect, Nina had condensed her life to the length of one of her columns.

"Have you ever been to Majorca before?" Anthony asked, leaning close, inhaling the delicate Oriental overtones of Nina's perfume.

"No," she said, offering him a companionable smile. "Have you?"

He nodded. "Often. I have a few authors who live here."

"Is that how you know Nelson Medina? Through business?"

"Yes and no," he said. "Nelson and I are both in the book publishing business, but we met because Philip and I were at Wharton together."

That didn't surprise Nina. One of the many sociological theories she espoused was that the world was a lot smaller when you were rich. Another was: Those who "had it" knew how to spend it. Philip Medina's villa proved her point.

Perched high on a steep promontory on the Formentor Peninsula, it was truly spectacular. A compound consisting of a main house (entrance hall, gallery, living room, dining room, kitchen, staff quarters), the master suite (a separate structure with an enormous bedroom, bathroom, sitting area, and patio), and two generously sized guest houses, it had been built into cliffs that overlooked a secluded cove of turquoise water.

Their driver had explained that Señor Medina had hired one of Spain's most avant-garde architects to design his retreat.

"Señor Philip loves the land," said his employee/admirer. "He wanted a home that blended into the landscape, not one that eclipsed it."

Nina was no connoisseur, but to her he had succeeded brilliantly. Constructed primarily of rock excavated from the site and huge walls of glass that looked to the sea, the entire compound was so cleverly integrated with its surrounding, it appeared at one with cliffs on which it stood.

One entered through a turn-of-the-century watchtower that had been incorporated into the main house, its soaring height crowned by a grid of skylights. Two large abstracts in gray and blue—one by Georges Braque, the other by Picasso—mirrored the uneven lines and erratic shapes of the aging stones on which they hung. Minus any other adornment, the utter austerity of the space created an aura of drama that made Nina's knees buckle. As she followed the others through a skylighted gallery into the large, irregularly shaped living room, she gratefully accepted a proffered glass of cava.

The furnishings were contemporary and comfortable, no hard edges, no fussy accoutrements, everything simple and luxuriously spare. Decorated with passive tones meant to echo the soft colors of the land beyond the glass, the interior emphasized the striking canvases that dominated every wall. Modern masters like Fernand Léger, Kandinsky, Chagall, and Cézanne stood shoulder to shoulder with contemporary giants like Helen Frankenthaler, Morris Louis, Arshile Gorky, and Willem de Kooning. Sculpture by Jean Arp, Rodin, and Henry Moore sat on consoles and tabletops and in carefully selected corners.

On the plane she had asked several people if they knew why the wedding wasn't being held at Nelson's villa at Lake Lugano. Standing here in Philip's Majorcan manse, she found it hard to believe, but the Lugano villa was supposed to put this to shame. One woman's guess was that since three of Nelson's other weddings had been held there, the soon-to-be fourth Mrs. Medina was feeling a bit superstitious. As a cynical newswoman, Nina also suspected that the former Miss Spain wanted her nuptials reported in the Spanish press so that all who had looked down at her before would know they had to look up to her now.

While circulating among the celebrated in an attempt to get a fix on the dozen or so subplots she should be tracking, Nina picked up two interesting rumors: Pilar and Medina *fils* were not what one would describe as "close," and *père et fils* didn't get along real well, either. Nina was left to wonder whether the elder Medina had pressured his son to host the wedding as a peace offering to the bride or if Philip had offered his home to his father as a gesture of family harmony. Either way, Nina's eyes and ears were open.

Anthony Hartwick proved to be the perfect escort. Not only did he look devilishly handsome, but he was exceedingly gracious about introducing her to anyone she didn't know—which was the entire European contingent. It didn't hurt that he was outspoken in his admiration for the way she looked. Sheathed in a spare black dress with an illusion back that gently embraced her figure, accessorized with nothing more than gold earrings, Nina provided a much needed oasis in a room filled with opulent silks and mammoth jewels.

"You're quite remarkable looking," he said, taking another glass of cava from a waiter's tray and handing it to her. "I can't imagine why I didn't notice before."

"Frankly, neither can I," Nina said, thoroughly enjoying herself.

Taking her arm, he led her outside onto an immense stone terrace, one of an elaborate network of terraces, stone paths, patios, and gardens filled with cactuses, cypress trees, and bunches of lavender. They were not alone. A cluster of French-speaking guests were seated at a table near the pool. A group of Italians had commandeered two tables near one of the gardens. A troop of Americans were being led on a tour of the grounds by Philip Medina. And toward the far wall, surrounded by a circle of Spaniards, the bride and groom were holding court.

Nelson, sixty-one and still a vibrant and handsome man, was one of San Francisco's most famous sons: architect of the Medina Publishing fortune, renowned art collector, even more renowned ladies' man. His first wife—and Philip's mother—Olivia Tarquin, had hailed from a socially prominent family of ship builders, which made her 1943 nuptials with Nelson the talk of the town. When they divorced after ten years of what everyone knew had been a horrible marriage, that too had been the talk of the town.

After Olivia, Nelson had married two other women in semirapid succession, spending no more than three years with either of them. The scuttlebutt was that he couldn't go more than a week without being unfaithful. After his third divorce he decided to do the honorable thing: he would avoid infidelity by avoiding marriage.

For years Nelson was a blissful bachelor, flitting from one flower to another like a bee in the spring. When he began courting Pilar Padillo, no one paid much attention. Blond, beautiful, slightly older than most of the women who had populated his harem, yet substantially younger than Nelson, Pilar was greatly underestimated by the odds makers who handicapped society's marital sweepstakes. They knew she had come from a family of extremely modest means from a small city outside Madrid. They knew she had been married twice before, once to a bullfighter, once to a nightclub owner, that she had borne a son out of wedlock by a father she refused to name, that her mother behaved more like a manager than a mom, and that she was a painter of no renown. What they didn't know was that Pilar Padillo was the first woman in Nelson's life to make him laugh. Even now, surrounded by a group straining to find the humor in Pilar's story, he was chortling.

Though Nina had been out with Philip Medina a dozen times, he had remained a mystery. Researching Nelson Medina had given her an excuse to dig farther and research Philip. It frustrated her that despite her best efforts she had found more on the father than on the son.

On the surface the two appeared very much alike. Both were in the communications industry (Nelson published books and magazines, Philip newspapers and TV), both highly successful (though Nelson was higher on the Forbes Four Hundred, Philip wasn't far behind), both avid art collectors (Nelson old masters, Philip twentieth century), but while Nelson was about to embark on marriage number four, at thirty-six years old Philip was still single: no weddings, no engagements, no long liaisons, no outward signs of any desire to settle down.

Nina was musing about that when bells summoned everyone to dinner. As she and Anthony made their way back to the house, they caught up with the group Nelson and Pilar had been entertaining. A trio just ahead caused Nina's breath to catch in her throat: it had been fourteen years, but she was certain the couple was none other than Javier and Estrella Murillo and the third party, Pasqua Barba.

What if they recognize me? she thought. What if they make a scene?

Someone called to Estrella. As she turned around to respond, Nina coughed, covering her face with her hand. Relieved hardly went far enough to describe how she felt when Anthony led her to a chair several tables away from Isabelle's grandparents and that horrible, horrible man. Her seat faced them.

While the Murillos were still a fearsome pair, still proud and severely elegant, they looked older, even weary. Nina wondered if they still harbored their senseless hatred of Martín and still insisted on Paco's innocence. She wondered, too, whether they were still bent on avenging Althea's death through Isabelle. But most of all, she wondered why she cared and why the past kept insinuating itself into her present.

Though she tried not to, she couldn't help staring. She supposed she was testing, waiting for one of them to look at her, wanting to know if they remembered her. Paco had never really seen her up close, so she was safe around him. The Murillos were different. She had been face to face with them. But she had been a child then. She was a woman now. They had seen her once. They had been focused on Isabelle and Tía Flora. They couldn't possibly recognize her. *But she had recognized them.*

Philip was visiting his guests, stopping at each table, talking a bit, and then moving on. Presently he was standing over Estrella, chatting with her and Javier. What about? Nina wondered. What could Philip Medina have in common with the Murillos? Art, perhaps? Horses?

As he proceeded toward her table, Nina tried to view him objectively, not as her once-and-possibly-future boss, or as a once-and-hopefully-future escort. One could see he was polished and charming and at ease with everyone, no matter what the age or nationality. One could feel the dimensions of his reach by watching the high and mighty defer to him. And unless one was blind, one could also view him as extremely sexy. The strong outline of his face, the hooded, watchful eyes that took everything in yet revealed little, the well-exercised physique, the long fingers—women trampled over one another in an effort to impress him.

Not for the first time, Nina wondered why he had never taken her to bed. Certainly she had hinted rather broadly at her willingness to change the tenor of their relationship, yet despite her efforts it had remained stuck on a strictly professional, purely platonic, infuriatingly celibate level.

He had moved only three places when the man across from Nina, a Barcelona publisher, asked, "Who's the new artist, Philip?" Nina followed his hand as he pointed to a large painting commanding most of the long wall of the dining area.

"A native of your fair city," Philip said. Nina's stomach lurched. "An unbelievably talented young woman named Isabelle de Luna."

At the next table, Paco didn't seem at all surprised, but Javier and Estrella Murillo were. Eyes widened, they turned in unison toward the painting, staring at it as if it were some kind of spectral revelation.

"In fact," Philip continued, "this painting is entitled *Dawn in Barcelona.*"

The man studied the painting and nodded his approval. "You wouldn't happen to know if she's related to Martín and Althea de Luna, would you?"

Nina's eyes remained glued to the Murillos, her heart pounding. Estrella's face reddened as if her blood pressure had spiked to a dangerous level. Javier looked deathly pale.

"I have no idea. Why?"

"No particular reason. Althea was an artist and a friend. I was just curious if this young woman might be her daughter."

"Whoever she is, she's a major talent, Lluis."

After Philip left, several people at the table began discussing Isabelle's

painting and her parentage. Though Nina was listening carefully to every
word, her eyes were trained on the Murillos, who were making their excuses
to Nelson and Pilar. As she watched them leave, she saw two old people
bowed by the fallout of something that had happened nearly twenty years
before. Nina couldn't decide which burden was heavier, their grief over Althea or their hatred of Martín.

". . . absolutely revitalized Dragon Textiles."

Nina had missed something. "I'm sorry," she said. "I was distracted. What
were you saying about Dragon Textiles?"

"I was talking about my friend Althea," Lluis said, clearly delighted to
retell his tale. "When she married Martín de Luna, Dragon had been in the
doldrums for quite some time. Being an artist, she naturally took an interest
in the mill, which was good, because while the production facilities needed a
bit of modernization, the real problem was design.

"At her urging, Martín shut down production while he retooled the plant
and she revitalized the product." He smiled, his face caught in the remembrance of something past and pleasant.

Inside, Nina was caught up in her own recollections of the de Lunas.
Outside, her expression was one of polite interest.

"They were gutsy!" Lluis said. "In the midst of Franco's repression, she
and Martín invited fabric buyers to a cocktail party at their town house to
unveil a special line called 'Paintbrush Patterns.' " He paused, gauging the
level of interest. Seeing he had their attention, he went on. "She had enticed
several well-known artists to give her paintings that could be transposed onto
elegant fabrics. For the premiere collection, the one they showed that day in
their town house, Althea's paintings stood side by side with their silken counterparts. It was fabulous!"

While Lluis went on to boast about Dragon's subsequent success, Nina
turned to Anthony, whose eyes were riveted on Isabelle's painting.

"Do you like it?" she asked, annoyed that he was so intrigued.

"I rarely agree with Philip, but this time he's right. She's going to be one of
the greats!" Suddenly he turned to Nina. "Do you know her?" He sounded
like an adolescent who had just discovered someone who might actually have
met his favorite rock star.

"I've heard of her."

"But do you know her?"

Nina didn't like the tone in his voice. It was too cloying, too admiring.
Worse, she realized that several others at the table had heard his question
and were anxiously awaiting her answer. Nina tensed. It was one thing to

reminisce about Althea and Martín. It was something else to have Isabelle de Luna intrude on her life. The last thing she wanted to do was to have to praise, explain, or defend a woman she wanted to best.

Hartwick repeated himself. "Do you know her?"

Nina's response betrayed none of the emotion she was feeling. Instead she issued a cool statement of fact. "As I said, I've heard of her. If you're asking why I never pursued her for one of my special interviews, the answer is simple. I deal with media celebrities and society swells. Isabelle de Luna is neither."

The wedding was lovely. Beneath the bluest sky Nina had ever seen, the bride—in a soft, ivory silk suit by Givenchy—and the groom—in a dark suit, gray vest, black silk tie—recited vows they had written themselves. Pilar's bouquet was a simple spray of orange blossoms. Nelson's boutonniere was a white rose. Pilar's mother stood up for her daughter. Philip was his father's best man. At the end of the short, oddly moving ceremony, Pilar's teenage son held up a bird cage. Both bride and groom reached in and took out a white dove. They kissed each other, kissed the birds of peace, and then, to the accompaniment of enthusiastic applause, let them fly.

Afterward, during cocktails, Nina worked the crowd, chatting with this one, listening to that one, questioning, grilling, asking, examining. It was a wedding, of course, and not a mass interview session arranged for her convenience, but her job was to report on society doings, so she would. Still peeved about Anthony Hartwick's badgering, she deliberately had driven up in a different limousine and so far had managed to avoid him.

Aside from all the other gossip she was gathering, one of the most interesting aspects of these festivities was to note the restrained animosity between the Medina men. While it might have appeared to others that Philip was following in his father's footsteps, Nina guessed they were engaged in a fierce competition. Her first assumption was that their problems were left over from Nelson and Olivia's divorce; but according to several people who claimed to know, the men weren't battling for Olivia's affection. Word was Philip had as little to do with his mother as his father did.

On her way to the powder room, Nina was mulling over whether or not to pursue the matter. She was walking through one of the galleries when she came face to face with Estrella Murillo. The gallery was narrow. They couldn't avoid looking at each other. Fortunately, no one else was around. Just in case.

"Good afternoon," Nina said, offering the sour old woman a megawatt smile. "Lovely wedding, don't you think?"

Estrella's eyes narrowed. Nina's smile wavered. "Yes," she said. "Lovely." She perused Nina's face. "You look very familiar. Have we met before? I'm Estrella Murillo."

"Señora Murillo." Nina pondered the name. "No. I don't think I've ever had the pleasure." She bowed her head modestly. "I am on American television. Perhaps that's where you've seen me?"

"I've never been to the States," she said with a haughty sniff. "I must be mistaken." Estrella continued on her way, leaving Nina to wonder whether or not she was convinced.

Later, on the main patio, she noticed Estrella pointing at her and whispering to Javier. Nina had never cared before, but suddenly she hoped her ersatz sister was a reader of *Pandora's Box*. Upon her return, she intended to write a lengthy, juicy piece about being in Majorca with Philip Medina and Spain's influential Señor and Señora Javier Murillo. Let Isabelle wonder what was going on between her and Philip; let her worry about what was being said behind her back.

Fueled by an ancient anger, she spun around, and hit smack into Philip Medina.

"Are you having a good time?" he asked, holding her arms, steadying her.

"Aside from this minor collision? Yes." The smile was in place, the mask was back, calm was restored. "But how could I not be having a fabulous time? This place is spectacular. The people are fascinating. The food is four star. And the host is not only extremely gracious, but, if you don't mind my saying so, Your Excellency, looking mighty hot."

His smile was slow and confined to his mouth. His eyes remained fixed. "Have you toured the villa?"

"Not all of it."

"Come," he said, taking her hand. "I insist."

The paths and stairways that connected the various parts of the compound wound up and around the main house, one fork leading onto its roof. From there, as Philip pointed out, they could view the cove in its entirety. Though an opening to the sea existed, it wasn't visible. All one saw was turquoise water, a stretch of white sand, scattered islands of rock, the tail of the peninsula, and, here and there, a small sailboat bobbing on the gentle ebb and flow.

By following the path that curved around the house, they walked up toward the guest houses. Built into the side of the mountain, they were integrated so completely, if the blue sky hadn't been reflected on the glass it would have been possible to have missed them altogether.

"If you took a boat out to the middle of the cove, and looked back, you'd be hard-pressed to tell that there's a house here at all."

"Is this the wave of the future or a hideout?" Nina asked.

Philip didn't blink; neither did he smile. "Everyone needs a place to hide," he said.

On their way back Nina changed the subject, moving to lighter things, like Pilar and her infamous mother. "I hear she's a mother-in-law joke come true."

"Since she's not my mother-in-law, I don't have to worry about it. My father does."

Nina was certain she detected a certain element of glee.

"Have you spoken to Pilar?" he asked.

"Briefly."

"What do you think?"

Nina couldn't believe he was asking her opinion. "She's fun." Philip cocked his head, as though curious. She elaborated. "That may not be on anyone's list of essential qualifications for becoming a Medina, but between you and me, I think that's what hooked your father."

Philip nodded but said nothing. They walked in silence for a few minutes, her arm linked through his. Nina couldn't help grinning inside at the looks on people's faces as they spotted them. If one was judged by the company they kept, her numbers had just jumped a notch.

As they rounded the corner onto the main terrace, Anthony Hartwick came over to chat. "I've been looking for you," he said, taking Nina's hand and kissing it.

"And for me?" Philip said, offering his hand.

"Sorry, Medina. You've never been my type."

As they sparred, exchanging quips that hugged the edge of socially acceptable sniping, Nina found herself amused and intrigued by their quasi rivalry. Clearly they knew each other well, but in their case longevity hadn't translated into fondness.

"How's Hartwick House doing?"

"Very well, thank-you," Anthony said with a certain pique. "And you?"

"Ekeing out a profit."

Nina almost laughed. Cisco Communications was a giant and getting bigger every day.

"Thanks in no small measure to the talents of people like the beautiful Miss Davis," Philip said with a gallant bow.

When he smiled, he dazzled. Nina wondered if that was why he smiled so rarely—to save the impact for when he needed it.

"How kind you are, sir," she said, fluttering her eyelashes to match her Vivien Leigh/Scarlett O'Hara accent.

"That's not being kind. That's being honest." He squeezed her hand, granted her another smile, and then excused himself. "Much as I hate to leave you, I have to see to my other guests." Turning to Hartwick, he said, "Be nice."

"I'm going to take that as my cue to apologize," Anthony said. "I was rude last night and I'm sorry."

Since there was nothing to gain by remaining angry and everything to gain by being accommodating, Nina forgave him. To seal their truce, Anthony called for more champagne. "Here's to us," he said.

Nina wasn't expecting the kiss, so when he slid his arm around her waist and pulled her to him, she didn't think, she responded.

From then on Anthony refused to leave her side, even when Philip returned to hover around her, which was often. At one point, listening to their banter, she worried that she was the pawn in a game they had been playing since college. Nonetheless, if the truth were told, she was enjoying the game.

At the end of the evening, however, only one invited her to share his bed. While she didn't hesitate to accept, she was troubled by the little voice inside her head that kept insisting he was her second choice.

And that she was his.

When Anthony and Nina entered his room, a decanter of brandy and two snifters were sitting on a silver tray, waiting for them. A small fire burned in the fireplace, joining with a single lamp and a few candles to bathe the room in a gentle orange haze. Anthony poured some brandy for her and some for himself, closing his eyes as he inhaled the smoky vapors that wafted up from the belly of the crystal balloon. He swirled the amber liquid about and then, in a single swallow, poured it down his throat.

Nina sipped hers, watching him from a wing chair facing the bed, feeling an unmistakable excitement brewing inside her. They hadn't spoken since they'd left the limousine. He had led, she had followed. Somehow she'd guessed that was how he liked it: him controlling, she acquiescing. She wasn't really the acquiescent type, but she had decided she wanted this man. If it had to be on his terms, this time, so be it.

He poured himself a refill and downed it as quickly as he had the first. When his glass was emptied, he walked over to her, placed his hands on the arms of her chair, leaned over, and outlined the shape of her mouth with his tongue. She could smell the brandy on his breath, as well as the scent of arousal. Again he traced the line of her lips, never pressing against them, never intruding beyond them.

Nina remained passive; she did nothing but receive, reveling in the unexpected freedom to luxuriate in her own feelings. Her eyes closed as his lips grazed the skin of her cheek, her eyelids, her nose. She tensed as his tongue moved lower and explored the curve of her neck. His teeth gnawed at her ear and the soft flesh beneath her chin. He hadn't touched her with his hands, yet she could feel her body growing needy and demanding. Suddenly he backed away.

"Take off your clothes."

His voice was husky, coming from the place where desire was born. She did as he asked, turning around so that he could unzip her dress. When it was loose, she faced him and, very slowly, let her taupe chiffon tea gown fall to the floor. His eyes held hers; she reached back and undid her bra. He watched without comment as she freed her breasts and then removed her hose.

"Now me."

She complied happily, sliding his jacket off his shoulders and down his arms, undoing his tie and his buttons, one by one. As he had done with her, she kept her eyes trained on his face as she stripped off his shirt. She pressed against him, pleased by the gasp that greeted the meeting of their skin. Moving even closer, she got rid of his belt, unzipped his pants, and slid her hand inside. She was glad to feel that his excitement matched hers, that even without words it was obvious he approved of what he saw.

She knew he wanted her to undress him completely, but for the moment she was in control. Still holding him, she rubbed her breasts against his chest and, with her free hand, pulled his mouth toward hers. She kissed him, hard and long. Then she pulled back and leaned back, bringing his head down to her breasts, making him taste her, making him do what she wanted.

Suddenly needing to have more of her, Anthony rid himself of the rest of his clothes, picked Nina up, and carried her to the bed. She lay back, more than ready to receive him, but instead he lifted her on top of him, welcoming one of her breasts in his mouth, courting the rest of her with his hands. His intensity was contagious. Nina felt herself straining to rein her passion, to master her impulses the way he mastered his; but she couldn't. He touched her, and raw, unchecked sensations raged, every nerve ending wired to his fingers. She wanted him to recede so she could pleasure him the way he was pleasuring her, but he left no room for her to move. He was the one doing, she was at his mercy.

Afterward Nina lay by his side, spent but satisfied. A warm sensuousness suffused the air around her, carrying with it a desire for closeness. She wanted him to hold her, to tell her how good they were together. Instead he lit a cigarette and lay there smoking, not speaking, not touching, not allowing her near him. Angry, Nina left his bed and threw on her dress.

"What are you doing?" He sat up and stared at her, clearly shocked by her behavior.

"What does it look like I'm doing? I'm leaving."

"So soon?" He leered at her. "What if I want you again?"

"Then you'll get up off your ass and come find me," Nina said, slamming the door behind her.

As she walked down the hall to her room, she wondered if she should have stayed. Some men needed distance after such intense intimacy. Then again, maybe for him this was a simple slam-bam-thank-you-ma'am lay. No, she told herself. Anthony Hartwick had wanted her. He had campaigned for her and enjoyed her. He would want her again. She was certain of it.

Nina spent the rest of the night waiting.

CHAPTER 16

October 1983

Julian Richter appraised himself in the mirror, grimly noting a few harbingers of impending antiquity. His hairline was receding. That displeased him, but keeping his beard and mustache in proportion helped camouflage the extent of the loss. Age had deepened the lines alongside his nose and had creased the skin at the corners of his eyes. That, too, distressed him, but rather than have them surgically removed, he accepted them as signs of maturation and character. His body, he was pleased to say, was relatively fit. While he didn't deny himself his gustatory indulgences, they were occasional. Now and then, he exercised.

As always, he had dressed predominantly in black. How a noncolor had become the signature of chic in a world defined by color, he didn't know, but it had. Of course, he never dressed completely in black. That would be too conforming. This evening he had accessorized his black suit with a charcoal-gray silk shirt, a gray paisley ascot, and a gray silk pocket square, which he adjusted again, making certain the soft peaks fell precisely the way he wanted.

Satisfied at last, he exited his office and began his preshow stroll through the gallery. His practiced eye checked the lighting, the alignment of the paintings, the stacks of pamphlets and postcards, the positioning of the guest book, and the bar. He stopped short at the front desk. Instead of five white calla lilies in a round-bottomed black vase, there were six in a glass cylinder.

Skye never would have committed such a visual atrocity! Even numbers didn't look right. They were too balanced. The straight lines of the lilies needed the roundness of a globe. The black and white echoed him and Isabelle. This new girl was an idiot!

On cue, his young assistant walked in. Allowing his impatience to surface, he shot a barrage of orders at her. With admirable calm, she nodded and went about fulfilling them. Julian's temper was legendary. Skye had told her to ignore it; most of the time she did.

Julian checked his watch: five-thirty. In half an hour the doors would open to "Moon over Manhattan." Feeling quite smug, he looked over the guest list. Everyone had said he was foolish to hold an opening on a Friday night. No one would come, they said. Since the sixties when Leo Castelli had made the switch from gala, extravagantly catered Tuesday night openings to no frills, no alcohol, Saturday walk-throughs, this was the way it had been done. Don't buck tradition, they cautioned. Stick to the standard Saturday event. But that was precisely the point: Isabelle de Luna was anything but standard fare. And this series of New York nightscapes was extraordinary enough to warrant a break with the norm. Besides, reorganizing the calendar of the art world was a bold strike, and these days bold was not only in, it was de rigueur.

The good news about the 1980s was that it was proving a boom for contemporary art. The number of private collectors had multiplied. Corporations had entered the buying arena. And there was a growing excitement about the art being produced. After the languid 1970s, a decade that according to many had produced no major new artists, the sudden and almost hysterical interest in Schnabel, Borofsky, Clemente, Chia, and de Luna portended well for artists and dealers alike.

The bad news was the 1982 Wall Street bonanza. Suddenly there were dozens of new millionaires, each anxious to hang his wealth on his walls. Auction houses were competing with galleries for the big art dollars. SoHo was challenging Fifty-seventh Street. And as the number of galleries increased, the ability to lure and promote new artists, while keeping and retaining the price levels of established artists, was becoming an everyday concern. Wherever Julian looked, he faced a challenge. Mary Boone had made a splash with Schnabel and Salle. Arne Glimcher had debuted Lucas Samaras at Pace. Paula Cooper had brought the world Jonathan Borofsky. Europeans, eager to cash in on America's buying frenzy, were opening galleries to represent their compatriots. The pond was getting crowded.

Losing Skye had been a blow. While he had respect for her eye, he had grown to depend on her ear. She heard things he didn't. She felt vibrations he didn't. She had an uncanny sense of what was about to become a trend, what was about to become passé. Once, Julian had been as sensitive as she, able to spot movements when they were beginning to emerge, able to pick the best practitioners of that style. Now there were whispers that he was losing his edge. Though he disagreed vehemently, he did admit—only to himself, of course—that he had missed a few he should have corralled. He blamed it on the rapidity of the changes. On the number of new warriors on the street. On the intensity of the competition.

Skye blamed his misses on something else: she had warned him that self-involvement was blinding his judgment. So often deciding to represent an artist was the result of how a dealer felt about the personality of that artist: if there was substance in the person, the likelihood was there was substance to the work. Skye accused Julian of having trouble seeing past his nose.

His response to her quitting seemed to make her case. Not only was he stunned, he was indignant. In his mind she should have been grateful for her experiences with him. When instead he was confronted with anger, he re-coiled. She reminded him that he had taken credit for most, if not all, of her discoveries, had refused to increase her salary despite her contribution to the gallery's profits, had mistreated many of her finds—deliberately, she thought—and had taken to demeaning her in public. When she heard that he had bad-mouthed her to the press, she resigned.

Several of his artists had defected recently. Two had followed Skye to Pace. One, whom he had nurtured for five years, had bolted and gone to Greta Reed. Another was opening tomorrow at Blum-Helman. Though he still commanded an envious roster, his reputation had been soiled by those desertions. He had gone from being the grand seigneur of the art world to, as one of the so-called pundits had said, "a man with questionable business tactics and a tendency for slick tricks."

What angered him most was that he wasn't doing anything his competitors weren't. Was he hyping artists as if they were rock stars? Yes. So were they. Was he bidding at auctions to maintain price levels on certain artists? Yes. So were they. Was he buying back work of his artists to keep them out of the market, thereby creating greater demand and higher prices? Yes. Were they? And then some! Yet he was the target of all the negative attention.

Chalking it up to America's macabre tendency to delight in slashing the points off its brightest stars, he brushed aside his pique and checked the time. Ten minutes. His nervousness mounted. He wondered if he had made a mistake not preselling the show as he usually did. Certainly the buyers were there. He had been getting calls for weeks from collectors eager to spend between fifty and seventy-five thousand dollars for the privilege of owning an Isabelle de Luna. The only one permitted a private audience was Philip Medina. As expected, he had selected the best of the collection.

By seven o'clock Hilton Kramer, Jed Perl, Calvin Tompkins, and several other art critics had arrived. So too had a gossip columnist, Nina Davis, from the *New York Daily*. To Julian her presence symbolized what was wrong with art in the 1980s. The art itself was only a small part of the scene. Who was buying, what they were wearing, whom they spoke to, and whom they left with had suddenly gained equal footing with the works on display. Julian was outraged. It was enough to have to deal with the idiosyncratic visions of legitimate art critics. When had a tabloid byline qualified someone to judge art or empowered them to make or break a reputation?

She didn't matter, Julian told himself as he watched her chat it up, her back to the paintings, her eyes on the door. The only woman who mattered tonight was Isabelle de Luna.

As he waited for her to arrive, he anguished again about his inability to secure an intimate relationship between them. He didn't like to fail at anything, especially in areas attributable to his manhood. Rebuffs like that became instantly magnified, because they echoed his father's disapproval. When Isabelle said she "didn't want to complicate things," Julian heard, "You're not man enough for her." When she said, "I need to keep my professional life separate from my private life," Julian heard, "If you weren't such a poor excuse for a man, she wouldn't have to make excuses not to sleep with you."

Henry Richter was the standard against whom Julian measured himself. At home, Henry had sermonized about the importance of morality; away, he had debauched without guilt. He had bragged about the stability of his marriage out of one side of his mouth, while whispering crude jokes into the ears of his mistresses with the other. He had demanded that his sons be honest, yet he cheated his partners with impunity. While Julian's brothers might have taken Henry's teachings to heart and lived according to what their father said, Julian's life mimicked what Henry did.

In his youth, promiscuity had been the rule. The more women he could bed, the more notches on his belt, the prouder he thought his father would be. Then Henry passed a comment about anyone being able to lay with pigs. Stung, Julian immediately shifted his sights upward, to the women he imagined his father would pursue. Unwilling to risk ridicule on his performance, Julian hired one of New York's most expensive call girls to teach him everything she knew about the art of sexual gratification. Confident in his ability to excite and satisfy, he threw himself into the competition, seeking out the most beautiful, most voluptuous, most sensuous females he could find and chasing them with the avidity of a hunter. Each conquest was a victory, each satisfied lover a rebuke to Henry's charges of inferiority.

Maturity, Henry's death, and the frightening prospect of disease had changed the rules of battle. Instead of viewing each date as a potential X in his win column, Julian began to discriminate. Acknowledging that in his social strata reputations were built not on what a man did, but with whom, he began to sacrifice quantity for quality. Isabelle de Luna was prime, yet despite his best efforts she refused to repeat their one night of passion. It bothered him. In a strange way it excited him. But most of all it challenged him.

Once before, a woman had denied him his pleasure. Eventually he had had his way with her. Eventually he would have his way with Isabelle.

Isabelle hated watching people accept or reject her. She would have preferred to stay home, but of course, that was not allowed. She arrived on schedule—seven-fifteen—and was immediately shuttled into Julian's office for private interviews with the art press. She answered questions about the theme of her show: "I moved from dawn to dark because those are the frames of our daily existence. I moved from landscapes to cityscapes, because those are the parameters of my existence."

Why she wore white: "Its most important property is that it reflects light. At these shows, I prefer to stand to the side and let my work dominate. If it reflects me, then I reflect it."

What was she saying with the highly saturated fields of color in the background and the lighter, friskier brush strokes that she had used to imply the city's landmarks: "The skyline is secondary to the sky itself. No matter how stunning our progress seems, our world is ephemeral. These buildings of steel and concrete, these structures which were made to withstand the forces of nature are illusory, a mere sketch in the portrait of time."

Her personal life: "Is personal."

Isabelle knew people thought she and Julian were lovers. She knew that an answer like the one she had just given perpetuated those rumors, but that was the way she wanted it. It protected her from overlustful predators and spared Julian's ego. Skye, who lately didn't have one good word to say about her former employer, couldn't have cared less about Julian's pride. She loathed the fact that there was anyone in this universe who might believe that her friend Isabelle could be involved with the likes of Julian Richter and said so, frequently. Just the other night, they had argued about him.

"It's time to move on," Skye had said.

"Why? Julian's gallery is one of the best. My prices are high and holding and he's responsible for that."

"Maybe, but he's not responsible for you."

"I don't know what you're talking about."

"Oh, please! The man positively runs your life. He tells you when to get up in the morning, when to paint, what to eat and when to go to sleep. Thank God you don't let him tell you whom you're allowed to sleep with." She stopped storming around Isabelle's loft and glared at her. "You don't, do you? Ugh! Please tell me you haven't . . ." She grimaced, grunted, and held her stomach, visualizing exactly how she felt about having sex with Julian Richter.

"Only that once," Isabelle said meekly. It was hard to defend against Skye's accusations, because fear of her dependency on him and the extent of his control over her were the two reasons she had distanced herself from Julian in the first place.

"One time too many, if you ask me," Skye mumbled, too agitated to drop the subject. "I'm the one who set you up with him, but now I'm telling you it's time to get away from him."

"But why should I go to another gallery? I'm doing just fine where I am."

"Don't you feel the hold that man has on you?"

"No. I don't."

"I don't care if you lie to me," Skye said, plopping onto a chair directly across from Isabelle, "but don't lie to yourself. He has his claws wrapped so tightly around your self-esteem, he has you believing he's the only one who can give you the success you want. Trust me, he's not."

"He's good to me, Skye."

"Of course he's good to you. You're his meal ticket! And he's your Ezra, your father substitute. You latched on to him when you were young and scared, hoping he would take care of you and keep you safe. Well, I have a hot flash for you, Is. You're all grown up. You don't need Julian anymore."

Isabelle's silence didn't deter Skye from raging on. "I don't trust him, and neither should you."

"You used to be his most ardent acolyte."

Skye nodded. "True. But familiarity bred contempt." She knitted her hands together as she weighed how much farther she should go. Arguing with Isabelle was one thing; frightening her was another. "Over the years, I saw him do things that were very wrong and very ugly."

"Like what?"

"Like deliberately underpricing an artist he was displeased with and wanted to be rid of. Like berating young artists he wanted to cow into submission. Like watching him wangle certain pieces out of his superstars for his own collection."

Isabelle cringed. Still, she resisted. "He's never done any of these things to me."

"Maybe not," Skye said, "but if the occasion arose, Isabelle, he would."

Skye's words were ringing in Isabelle's ears when she spotted Philip Medina. Momentarily sequestered in a corner, she took advantage of her invisibility to observe him. It surprised her to see people shy away from him, shrinking as if in fear. She knew from the nightly news that he was in the midst of negotiating for one of New York's newspapers (the *New York Daily*), and that neither side was happy with him: present ownership viewed him as an interloper, labor management viewed him as a threat to their power, portraying him to their flock as an ogre who insisted on maintaining the bottom line no matter what the cost. Only the workers saw him as a savior.

From what Isabelle had read, Philip had gathered them together and spoken to them without filters, without people interpreting his words according to their own agendas. The workers heard a man who told them in plain language, they had a choice: they could meet him halfway by trimming the unreasonable fat from their contract demands and becoming more efficient, or they could watch a New York tradition disappear, and their jobs along with it.

What she read in the papers, what she was witnessing now, didn't jibe with her memory of the man. Granted, their meeting had lasted only a few minutes and he had been trying to charm her into giving him what he wanted, but nonetheless her instincts hadn't read what these reports were saying. She had found him strong, yes; insistent, perhaps; but hardly brutish. Seconds later he turned and noticed her staring at him. His features, which had been locked in a thoughtful pose, rearranged themselves into a portrait of gladness. Maneuvering through the crowd, he quickly made his way to her side.

"Not only does your work get better and better," he said, shaking her hand, holding it a moment longer, letting it go reluctantly, "but you get more exquisite all the time."

Wearing a slim ivory tunic over pants, her hair restrained in a twisted braid that hugged the nape of her neck, her ivory skin virtually bare of makeup, her only adornment a necklace of delicate Biwa pearls, she was strikingly, simply beautiful.

She thanked him; they exchanged social preliminaries—how have you been, what have you been doing, etc.—talked about nonsense—the weather, the show, the quality of the wine—smiled, and even shared a laugh or two; yet Isabelle sensed they were reciting lines, that the real conversation was running beneath the words. She had felt it the first time she'd met him, a connection, a chemistry that invited a greater, more intense involvement.

"If memory serves, I invited you to dinner a while back. I think you accepted. So what happened?" He was standing very close to her. His scent, his eyes, his gentle, insouciant manner, worked like gravity, pulling Isabelle deeper into his aura.

"I don't know," she said, returning his smile. "I think I disappeared."

"Unless I'm completely delusional," he said, leaning even closer, "you're here now, in the flesh."

"That I am."

"How's tomorrow night?"

Julian had planned a dinner with several of his most important patrons. "I can't."

"Sunday brunch?"

The evening might run late. "How about Sunday dinner?" she said. Julian never planned anything for Sundays. He hated them.

"I love Sunday dinners," Philip said, clearly delighted. "I'll call you early afternoon. Okay?"

When Julian's arm slipped around Isabelle's waist, it startled her. She rebounded, as if he had splashed cold water in her face. His grip tightened. "If you're talking about the show, it's doing more than okay," he said, facing Medina, drawing lines. "It's completely sold out!"

"I should hope so," Philip said, having heard the slap of the gauntlet but refusing to back off. "Then again, when you have genius to hang, it's easy to be a success." He looked past Julian at Isabelle.

"Success is never easy," Julian retaliated, his tone ringing with pomposity. "I would think someone with battle scars as fresh as yours would know that."

"If that's your left-handed way of offering encouragement in my current negotiations with the *Daily,* thank-you." Philip's eyes had turned dark, glinting like shards of obsidian.

"If you want my advice," Julian continued, unable to stop, "what you need to do is gain the trust of the workers. Prove to them you don't want to own them, that you simply want to share in their success." He squeezed Isabelle's waist and planted a kiss on her cheek. "It's worked for us."

Isabelle winced at the proprietary tone—more than that, at the message being delivered to Philip Medina: Julian Richter was in control of the enterprise known as Isabelle de Luna. No interlopers allowed.

Having been given little choice, Philip congratulated Isabelle, mumbled something deliberately insincere to Julian, and moved on. Off to her left, Isabelle saw Skye shaking her head.

*   *   *

"Why do I feel a lecture coming on?" Isabelle said a few minutes later.

"Not from me." Skye feigned complete innocence. "Tonight is a triumph. Why spoil it with inconsequentials like the fact that the man treats you like a pet? I wouldn't dream of discussing any of that with you now."

"You're too kind."

"I know." Skye bowed her head modestly. When she looked up, her eyes widened. "Who is this stunning male person barreling toward us?"

Isabelle didn't answer. Instead she threw herself into the open arms of a tall, handsome man in a sports jacket, shirt, tie, and cowboy boots. "Sam Hoffman! What a fabulous surprise!"

"Some surprise," he said, speaking to Skye. "An invitation would have been sufficient, but no. I got phone calls from her parents, my father, my stepmother, my sister, and four cousins I didn't even know I had. I probably got a call from your parents, too. Well," he said, turning back to Isabelle, "you got your way. I'm here. Are you happy?"

"You bet I am!" She hugged him again and then introduced him to Skye.

"So you're the one my father's been raving about. The nice Jewish girl with one name, a quick tongue, great hair, and fabulous eyes."

"You forgot incredibly sensuous body, keen intellect, and dermatologist-approved skin."

"Dad must have wanted to leave me a few things to discover on my own."

"Smart man, your dad." Skye crossed her arms and blatantly surveyed the exterior of Sam Hoffman.

"Would you like me to pirouette for you?"

"It might be helpful, but if I said yes, Isabelle would kill me."

"In an instant." Isabelle felt as if she were trapped in a Neil Simon play.

"Jonas had quite a bit to say about you, too," Skye continued. "Yale. Harvard. Big-time bone doctor. It's impressive." Sam accepted her compliment with a gracious smile. "So how come we never met before?"

"Bad karma?"

Skye grinned and nodded. "Yup. That must be it."

"Sam was in Europe with the United States ski team, getting them ready for the 1980 Olympics, when La Casa reopened," Isabelle explained, wondering if either of her two friends was listening.

"I was sorry I missed the reopening," Sam said, looking directly at Skye. "Now, I'm even sorrier."

Isabelle couldn't believe Skye was blushing. "It was wonderful," she said, filling Sam in while Skye regained her equilibrium. "The whole town showed up."

Isabelle grew misty just thinking about it. All of Santa Fe had turned out to share that night with the Durans. They had toasted them and applauded them, giving them a standing ovation when the mayor awarded them each a distinguished citizen medal.

"The place is truly spectacular."

"I've seen it," Sam said. "What's really great is that despite its new luxuriousness, at its heart it's still La Casa."

"Did they ever find out who started the fire?" Skye asked.

Sam's expression grew troubled and angry. "No, but they suspect a group of religious fanatics."

Isabelle was stunned, but, recalling the cross, she supposed she shouldn't have been.

"What was in that show that would have upset a group like that?" she asked, disturbed that she was hearing this from Sam and not from Miranda.

More than once, she had asked the Durans about the police investigation—if they had any clues, if they had turned up any evidence, etc. Each time Miranda dismissed the incident as a random attack, horrible but without explanation. Luis also avoided a discussion of the fire by simply bemoaning it as a symptom of the growing penchant in our society for senseless violence. Isabelle found their reluctance to find and punish the people who had wreaked such havoc strange.

"At first," Sam said, his thoughts paralleling hers, "no one could figure that out. Mainly because Miranda was vague about the details and far too accepting of the consequences. Her attitude was like, Okay, the damage is done, let's get it cleaned up and move on. The police knew she was holding back, but it was only when they threatened to interrogate each of the artists that Miranda came clean and revealed that the exhibition was *converso* art."

"Like the crypto-Jews in El Paso." Quickly Isabelle explained about the article Skye had read.

"She was afraid the same thing would happen to them," Sam said. "So she kept quiet."

"No wonder they called themselves the Eighteen," Skye said, practically to herself.

Isabelle saw Sam nod in agreement. "Why? What is it about the number eighteen?"

"It's *chai.*" Sam's jaw was tight. "It means life, and it's supposed to be lucky."

"Not that time, it wasn't." Skye, too, was grim.

"The people who trashed the show and set the fire were sending a very pointed message: If we find you, we'll hurt you!" Sam shook his head.

Isabelle commiserated, suddenly nervous about the possibility of further recriminations against Miranda and Luis, perplexed at how things like this happened, and annoyed that they did.

Skye was all of those things. But most of all, she was curious.

Nina was standing in the doorway between viewing rooms when she saw Sam Hoffman stride into the gallery and wrap Isabelle in a huge embrace. She should have retreated immediately, but she couldn't. She was frozen there, unable to keep from staring. Though she fought it, an old hurt gripped her. She watched them hug and grin at each other, noticed how easily they talked, how smoothly they interacted. Had they been seeing each other all this time? Or was this touching scene a reunion? What would happen if she ambled over? she wondered. Would Sam welcome her with the same warmth? Did she care?

Telling herself she was beyond cowboys like Sam Hoffman, Nina slinked into the other room, dismayed by this second stroke of bad luck. The first had been seeing Philip Medina and Isabelle so engrossed in each other. If Medina bought the *Daily,* he would be her boss again. The last thing she wanted was for her boss getting cozy with her past. Actually it was in anticipation of his purchase of the *Daily* that Nina had decided to make an appearance this evening.

Other than their run-in on the street, Nina had assiduously—and successfully—avoided her "sister." With Isabelle's star on the rise and *Pandora's Box* gaining in popularity, however, she had begun to believe that a face-to-face was inevitable. If so, she intended to orchestrate it.

Until Isabelle's friend Skye and Sam left, Nina restricted herself to the rear gallery. Once they had gone, she strode into the front room. Isabelle was standing dead center, talking to three admirers. When she saw Nina, her eyes widened and her mouth spread in a welcoming smile. Before Isabelle could embrace her, Nina stuck out her hand and said, "Miss de Luna. It's a pleasure to meet you. I'm Nina Davis. I write a column for the *Daily.*"

After the others excused themselves, Isabelle said, "What's going on? Why couldn't I acknowledge that I know you?"

"It's better that way."

"Better? How?"

"It avoids questions I don't want to answer."

Nina might have looked different, Isabelle noticed, very citified and savvy—but she waved her hand and jutted her chin and rolled her eyes the same way she always had when she wanted to dismiss subjects she considered invasive and unpleasant.

"What about the questions I want answered?" Isabelle asked. "Like why you were so obnoxious that time we met? And why no one has heard from you? And why you won't even drop Miranda and Luis a card telling them you're alive and well and living wherever the hell you're living!"

Nina shifted her weight from one foot to the other, embarrassed because she was certain people were staring at them, impatient because she wanted to get on with her agenda. Isabelle wasn't letting up.

"It's been years. You could have contacted one of us."

Nina lowered her eyes and wrung her hands, straining to find the right words. When she spoke, her voice was soft yet reverberating with echoes of difficult times and difficult decisions.

"When I came to New York, no one cared who I was or where I came from."

Isabelle nodded. To her, anonymity was one of the city's most appealing qualities.

"For a long time I lived in limbo, neither here nor there. Then, I got into the newspaper business. My job was to ask questions. But every now and then, someone would ask me about me. I, well . . . I created a past. I invented a family so no one would know the truth." Her fingers tugged at her hair. "I know what you're thinking, but try to understand. One fact could have opened the door to a story I didn't want told." Her gray eyes fixed on Isabelle's face. "I'm sure your press releases don't divulge the real reason you resettled in Santa Fe."

Isabelle had told Julian her parents had died when she was seven years old, that she had been raised by the Durans, and that she had an aging aunt in Barcelona, but nothing more. Fortunately he was a man who didn't care much for delving into one's past. His attitude was, Don't ask about mine, I won't ask about yours.

"You're right," Isabelle said, "they don't."

"Now that we understand each other," Nina said, brightening, "let's catch up. Let's reconnect."

"I'd like that," Isabelle said, a familiar feeling of intimacy washing over her. "Tell me how you got to be the famous Pandora!"

Nina summarized her rise to prominence, editing all references to Philip Medina. Here and there she threw in an anecdote about Elizabeth Taylor or a quip about Cher or the hot rumor making the rounds in Hollywood about Sylvester Stallone. When she had brought them up to the present, she said, "Enough about me. Other than producing these incredible paintings, what's been happening with you?"

Isabelle should have feinted. She never saw the punch coming.

The next day *Pandora's Box* was dedicated to one item: beneath the headline AFFAIRS OF THE ART, Isabelle read that she was having an affair with Julian Richter. When she stormed into Nina's office at the *Daily,* waving the paper in her hand, Nina simply laughed.

"Invasion of privacy? Distortion of the facts? Give me a break! Thanks to me, everyone in New York is talking about you."

"That's not the point and you know it!" Isabelle fumed. "I never said anything about Julian and me except that we were close friends."

"Close friends. Lovers. Same thing." An arrogant, self-satisfied smile defined her lips. "Besides, when I spoke to Julian, he more or less corroborated the story."

"More or less?" Isabelle was practically shouting. "Is that anything like yes and no?"

"Close enough."

"How could you?"

"It's easy," Nina said.

Isabelle's eyes flamed. Fury, hurt, disillusionment, and resentment churned inside her, rising toward the surface in a red rage. "You've become a real parasite, Nina. How could you lie and betray me that way?"

Nina's smile faded. She planted her arms on her desk, leaned forward, and glared at Isabelle, her face a mask of contempt. "Betrayal? You don't know the meaning of the word."

Isabelle was about to counter when she realized Nina was baiting her. Refusing to be drawn into her web a second time, she turned and walked out.

"You ought to be kissing my ass!" Nina shouted, angry that Isabelle wasn't going to stay and go a few more rounds, angry that she had been dismissed. "I've done you a favor, Señorita de Luna. I've made you a star!"

As she watched Isabelle storm out of the newsroom, Nina seethed. She had so much more to say, so many slights to avenge, so many wounds to heal. But, she reminded herself, spinning her chair around so no one could see the expression on her face, this match had just begun.

CHAPTER 17

Paris, 1985

For months afterward Isabelle brooded about the slanderous piece in the pages of the *New York Daily*. After leaving Nina's office, she had gone straight to Julian's apartment. When she'd showed him the paper and repeated her conversation with Nina, his reaction had been one of complete sangfroid.

"She's right," he had said, dismissing her indignation with a blasé wave of his hand. "She's made you a star. I see nothing wrong with that."

"What did you tell her?"

"Nothing that isn't so. I said we had a special relationship that transcended the standard patron/artist alliance. When she asked if we had any plans for the future, I said that we intended to remain together."

"You deliberately made it sound as if we were having an affair. Why?"

"Why not? Romance sells newspapers . . . and paintings. Besides," he said, opening his arms and inviting her into his embrace, "now that everyone believes we're lovers, maybe you'll surrender to your true feelings and make that fiction fact."

Isabelle didn't bother to respond. She simply left.

While she might not have forgiven Nina, on some level she understood Nina's actions. She didn't understand Julian's. His nonchalance about his part in Nina's treachery and his crass indifference to her feelings angered Isabelle almost as much as the negative media blitz Nina's piece had created. Like it or not, she had been pitched directly into the middle of the feeding frenzy that was the 1980s art hype. Wherever she looked there was a follow-up piece in one paper or another or a television tabloid show speculating on her love life. Since Isabelle's ambition never had included being a celebrity at any cost, this sudden, unbidden notoriety greatly disturbed her. And while she couldn't blame Julian for Nina's chicanery, neither could she forgive him for applauding it.

*   *   *

Julian had messed up, and he knew it. Not only had he not taken Isabelle's sense of propriety as seriously as he should have, but he had misjudged the intensity of her response. She hadn't bounced back as he had anticipated she would. Though she might not have withdrawn from him completely, she wasn't as available as she used to be, nor was she as tolerant. She found excuses not to accompany him to a dinner or social event. When they did go out in public, she rejected any overtures that might be misinterpreted as gestures of intimacy. She found reasons to skip what he called "his evening with friends": a monthly gathering of disciples to review a book or movie he had suggested, debate something he deemed of political importance, or join in a round-table discussion on a subject of his choosing. She grew impatient with eccentricities she used to countenance and argumentative about pronouncements she used to accept.

As Julian began to realize the depth of Isabelle's retreat, he increased the fervor of his defense. Her show had been a stellar success, he reminded her. She had made lots of money. Her name was everywhere. So what if people thought they were lovers? He told her it added to their mystique—the painter and the dealer, Stieglitz and O'Keeffe, Pygmalion and Galatea. He told her how much he cared for her, that he hadn't meant to hurt her, that he had thought being mentioned in *Pandora's Box* would have helped her career.

Another reason he had encouraged Nina's suspicions: the insinuation of a romance between himself and Isabelle would keep the wolves at bay. Philip Medina, for instance, had called to verify the article. Julian hadn't hesitated for a moment before telling him that yes, he and Isabelle had been lovers for years. "We've talked about marriage," he lied, "but nothing's definite."

Eager to recapture her affection, Julian mounted a campaign to bridge the distance between them. The first step was to divert the blame for their problems. Skye became his primary target. He accused her of saying terrible things about him, of trying to discredit his abilities as a dealer, of trying to besmirch his character. When Isabelle didn't refute his indictment, he knew he had hit his mark. For once, however, being right terrified him. Skye wasn't simply sniping. She was laboring on behalf of her new employer to steal Isabelle, and Julian couldn't allow that to happen. Isabelle's departure could ruin him.

To counter Skye's efforts, Julian went about trying to regain Isabelle's trust, hoping that her affection would follow. He moved slowly and cautiously, unwilling to press her. When it became apparent that although her temper had calmed, there was not one romantic ember left to kindle, he reverted to a tactic he had used in the past: he suggested that Isabelle seek inspiration outside New York. It was a recommendation that would come back to haunt him.

The French Art Council was hosting a special showing of works by American artists at the Palais-Royal. Called, naturally, "Americans in Paris," it was being touted as the most important exhibition of the year.

"It's a complete waste of time," Julian said, viewing the invitation as another piece of chum thrown in the water to tempt Isabelle away from him. "Paris hasn't been the center of the art world for fifty years."

"The invitation was sent to me, Julian, not you. And I have responded yes."

Julian paced, one hand stroking his beard, his jaw tight with barely controlled pique. "And what paintings do you plan on exhibiting?"

"I've been asked to bring ten. If you'd like, you may select the ones you think would be best."

He stopped and faced her. His complexion, kept slightly tan by carefully controlled sunlamp treatments, paled. His voice rumbled. "What if I don't want you to take any? What if I say that if you do, you'll dilute the impact of your next New York show?"

Isabelle never blinked. "The best artists in America have been asked to show there, Julian. If I'm not among them, it's as good as saying we don't think I belong. And you and I both know I do!"

Nina was strolling down the Faubourg Saint-Honoré, happily swinging a passel of shopping bags with designer logos, when she spotted Anthony Hartwick coming out of Hermès. She wanted to ignore him, to snub him the way he had snubbed her in Majorca, but he had seen her and was headed in her direction.

"Nina! What a pleasant surprise!" He put his arms on hers and kissed her on both cheeks. They separated, but he continued to hold her. "I almost forgot what a fabulously gorgeous woman you are."

"Fuck you, Hartwick!"

He laughed heartily. "I've missed you, too."

"I could tell by all the phone messages I got. And the flowers. And the candy. And the notes begging my forgiveness."

"Okay! You're one hundred percent right. I'm . . ."

"A heartless shit? Yes, you are."

"Would you believe me if I told you I found you so exciting it frightened me?"

"No."

"That's too bad, because it's the truth."

If his emerald eyes hadn't smoldered the way they did, and if those plush, softly arched, magnificently ripe lips hadn't formed that irresistible little-boy pout, and if his expensive cologne hadn't made her think of palaces and princes, she would have blown him off and gone on her way. But she found him as exciting as he claimed he found her, which was how she found herself dining with him later that evening at Le Grand Véfour and, later still, naked in his suite at the Plaza-Athénée.

His appetite for her was ravenous and insatiable. He took her again and again, varying their position, often getting rougher than she liked. But listening to him groan with pleasure as he grabbed at her flesh, hearing him almost sob as she brought him to climax, then weep as she aroused him once again, she rejoiced in the oddly satisfying sensation of brute passion. By morning Nina ached, but as she dozed off in his arms, she was convinced she was in love.

Paris was everything Isabelle knew it would be. There wasn't a street that didn't boast magnificent buildings. There wasn't a park that didn't entice, a market that didn't beckon, a shop that didn't tantalize. She had arrived a week before the show, giving herself time to wander and absorb the wonders of the City of Light. She went everywhere with a sketch book, stopping, scribbling, creating a diary as only an artist could, using the language of line and space, shadow and light.

When she wasn't drawing she was in a museum, feasting on the banquet of masterpieces Paris offered. Despite its intimidating size, Isabelle felt at home walking through the Louvre, perhaps because reconnecting with the history of art felt like a reunion with ancestors. Strolling the dimly lit, high-ceilinged corridors, listening to the wooden floorboards creak as she went, she was suffused by a sense of humility.

She believed art was a continuum, a visual chronology that recorded not only the doings of society, but their thoughts and sentiments as well. Sometimes, isolated in her studio, absorbed in the work before her, it was easy to lose perspective, to forget there was a world outside her loft and that she was a product of that world, reflecting its culture, its advances, its sense of frustration and failure; it was easy to forget she was part of a line.

As she went from floor to floor, room to room, she tried to place everything in context, reflecting not only on technique or motif, but also on the relationship of each movement to its time. What fascinated Isabelle was the steady track of art's evolution. Styles developed and ran a course. At certain junctures, just when it appeared art had dead-ended and didn't know where to go, scientific discoveries were made, philosophies changed, visions altered, and art lurched forward again.

In order to get the most of her visits, Isabelle segmented her days, viewing only as much as she could absorb. Starting at the beginning, she followed the line from the Middle Ages, when creativity was in the service of the papacy, to the Renaissance, when artists like Michelangelo and da Vinci added dimension to flat surfaces and the illusion of flesh to sculpture.

It astounded her to realize that when, in the 1600s, the largely Protestant north countries moved art into the household, the whole business of art changed. Instead of predominantly religious themes hanging in churches or palaces, domestic scenes became the norm and ordinary people became collectors. Pictures became commodities. Names like Van Dyck, Rembrandt, and Rubens became commonplace.

Isabelle devoted an entire morning to the delicious pleasure of losing herself in the playful sensuousness of Watteau, Fragonard, and Boucher. Plump, rosy-cheeked women on swings; men in powdered wigs, ruffled shirts, and shiny silk knickers; cherubic children romping about in an Elysium—they were scenes from a pastel paradise that could only have been created in France, she thought, and only when Louis XIV and XV reigned over their flamboyant courts. Rococo wasn't as intellectual as the Renaissance or as dramatic as the Baroque, but neither was it as dark or as serious.

The day of her own opening, Isabelle eschewed the Louvre and headed for the Tuileries and the smaller Jeu de Paume museum, which housed the Impressionists. Perhaps it was Isabelle's love of landscape that drew her to this movement or her romance with color and light. Whatever the connection, as she wandered through the dim, poorly lit museum, she had to fight to control the urge to remove the canvases and set them up outside in sunlit gardens or sidewalk cafés or the seaside, which was where she felt they belonged.

Instead of struggling with faithful representations of fact, artists like Claude Monet examined "how we see," how things like sunrises, or water lilies on a pond, or the reflections of sunlight on the Seine "impressed" us. Renoir offered fleeting glances at flirting couples, pretty women, and happy children. Degas, whose own eyes were weak and myopic, allowed the public to peek through a curtain of pastels at bathers and ballet dancers. Cézanne simplified forms and distorted reality. Van Gogh colored the fields of Arles with the primal intensity of his emotions.

Isabelle left the Jeu de Paume weak with awe, yet certain that had she lived then, she too would have answered the call of change. In a way, she thought, ambling back to her hotel, she and her contemporaries had also been challenged by the specifics of their time. Europe and the United States had suffered two world wars. Countries had been torn apart, borders had been redefined, nuclear weapons became a threat. Psychiatry had forced men and women to face their nightmares and their sexuality. Technology had exploded. Television had thrust the world into people's homes. The canvas and the photograph were no longer the only means of visual communication. With reality confronting from every side, it was no wonder that abstraction became the logical outlet for expression. Sculptors sought new materials, new molds, new ways to configure their feelings. Painters experimented with color and form. They created styles dubbed pop and op and neo and post.

Now, like Isabelle, many were combining the abstract with the figurative. Some used their work to make political statements and to issue social commentary. Some challenged the definition of taste. All demanded involvement and response. Had she and her fellow practitioners reached out for the figurative because they feared society was losing sight of its humanity? Was it because abstraction no longer relieved their angst? Was it ego? A way of re-creating themselves? Or was it simply the next step?

Isabelle was still musing about things metaphysical when she walked into the Palais-Royal. The cocktail party was in full swing, with flashbulbs popping and waiters scurrying to fill each outstretched hand with a flute of champagne or a miniature vol-au-vent. The men, looking debonair and polished in their tuxedos, formed an elegant sea of black. Most of the American women were also in black, preferring the secure chic of no-frills fashion.

Les femmes françaises, on the other hand, were a veritable garden of riotous silks and frenzied florals. There was nothing subtle about them. They rejoiced in their national obsession with style, shouting femininity from their hair to their makeup to their jewelry to their excessive use of perfume.

Isabelle, while remaining true to her trademark white, succumbed to the temptation of French fashion and wore an Yves Saint Laurent gown of ivory crepe. Sleeveless, spare, with an underlayer that gently caressed her body and two long panels that fell from her shoulders like a Roman tunic, it was a triumph of understated design. As always, her jewelry was American Indian, her necklace a series of textured gold triangles, carved like an Anasazi zigzag and set tip to base. One triangle, like her earrings, had been filled with chunks of red coral.

From the minute she entered the grand hall, several of the event's sponsors descended on her, escorting her from one group to another, introducing her, raving about her work, delighting in her ability to converse in French. In the course of her wandering, she was stopped by a familiar face.

"Cody!" Isabelle recognized him immediately. How could she ever forget that dazzling smile? He hugged her, oohed and aahed about the way she looked, and then, with obvious awe, congratulated her on her success.

"The buzz around the old palais is that Isabelle de Luna is far and away the best of the show." He chuckled, yet his face was clouded with disappointment. "If only you had come with me, I might have been able to bask in your reflected glory."

"You don't need to bask in anyone's reflection, Cody. You're a wonderful painter."

"That makes an audience of one. Things have been so bad, even I have my doubts."

Isabelle stroked his cheek, trying to coax another smile. He still had the softest skin she had ever felt on a man and the bluest eyes.

"Maybe it's simply a matter of representation. Art is the thing, but a good agent helps. I was lucky. Julian Richter represents me, and he's the best." She said it as a matter of rote. There was a time she'd believed it wholeheartedly. "Have you thought about moving back to the States? This exhibition is fabulous, but at the risk of insulting everyone here, Paris is not the epicenter of the world."

"I've thought about it a lot." His mind flashed on an image of a young, insecure girl clinging to him. He didn't know what bothered him more, the fact that now she was successful and self-assured and he wasn't or that he needed her and couldn't think of any reason she might need him. "But you know how it is. I know everyone here. I don't know anyone in New York. It would be like starting over, and that's hard to do."

"You know me," Isabelle said softly.

Cody wanted to continue the conversation, but it was time for the exhibition to open. Though she promised to get in touch before leaving Paris, he doubted that she would. After tonight she would be an international celebrity. He would still be a nobody.

Nina had observed Isabelle and Cody Jackson's reunion with great interest. She had no idea who he was, but their body language spoke volumes about what they had once meant to each other. She would have dashed right over to the anonymous blond, but Anthony was being so attentive, she didn't want to break the spell. They had spent three days together, taking in the sights, dining, and then ravishing each other's bodies. Nina was exhausted but elated. Where she had worried that outside of the bedroom he might be more circumspect about their relationship, he wasn't. At restaurants, on the street, at his hotel, here at the palais, he introduced her in a way that clearly implied she was more than a date. Nina had never had a man of his stature claim her. The feeling of acceptance produced a definite glow.

In fact, this entire evening was a coup. Not only was she being viewed as the inamorata of an impressive man, but she was there representing ABC television, the *Daily,* which was now New York's largest daily newspaper, and her syndication group. People recognized her. They wanted to be interviewed by her. She was *the* Nina Davis. She was big time.

Also, she thought, looking around, she more than held her own among the hoi polloi of the fashion world. Having correctly assumed that her country-women would opt for black, she had spent more than she could afford on an exquisite gold lamé evening suit by Bill Blass. Though she had tormented herself trying to estimate the number of times it had to be worn to be worth the expenditure, standing next to Anthony in the Palais-Royal, receiving admiring glances from the haute monde, she didn't regret a single cent.

She was scouting the room for likely interview subjects when she noticed Philip Medina approaching. Over the years their friendship had continued to grow more familiar but had never crossed the line into intimacy. He seemed content to keep it as it was. He was her boss, so she was loath to push.

"Philip! How good to see you!" she cried, feeling ever so Grace Kelly.

Hartwick's greeting was less enthusiastic. "All things are relative," he said, shaking Medina's hand and forgoing even a socially correct smile.

"It's always a pleasure to see you, Anthony. I think it's your unremitting charm that delights me so."

"Must be."

"Now, now, boys," Nina said, laughing nervously. The last thing she wanted was to referee a battle between her lover and her employer. Fortunately her antennae had picked up the Trumps—Donald and Ivana—and the Steinbergs—Saul and Gayfryd. Claiming her need to earn her salary, she left.

Medina and Hartwick eyed each other. Anthony was about to walk away when Philip stopped him. "I'd like to buy Hartwick House," he said without preamble.

"It's not for sale."

"Not yet, perhaps, but word is it's in trouble, Anthony. Big trouble."

"We expanded our printing facilities. That's all. It was a huge expense. It's taken a toll on our bottom line. It's not the first time a business suffered a slump after upgrading." His eyes narrowed, his mouth curled with sarcasm. "But gee, thanks for asking," he said as he turned to leave.

Philip took hold of his arm. "Rumor has it you've been using company funds to pay off your gambling debts." His voice was low and, if Hartwick had elected to listen, laced with concern.

"That's bullshit!"

"Is it?" Philip noticed the tiny droplets of sweat that beaded Hartwick's hairline. "Let's not forget, Anthony, we go way back. I've seen your addiction to gambling up close and personal."

Hartwick pulled his arm from Philip's grasp. His mouth twisted into a snarl. "So, I like to play cards! Big deal! That doesn't mean I'm embezzling company funds. You have a lot of nerve making an accusation like that, Medina."

"If I'm wrong, I apologize," Philip said. "If I'm not, when you're in deep enough and you're ready to sell, call me."

"Don't hold your breath," Anthony mumbled as he mopped his brow and watched Medina walk away. "I'll save my own ass, thank-you. I've done it before and I'll do it again."

It rankled Nina that Isabelle was the center of things. More, because she deserved to be. Before she'd inspected the exhibition, that fierce competitiveness that consistently simmered below Nina's surface had bubbled upward, bringing with it an all-too-familiar resentment that she played second banana to Isabelle's starring role. Then she'd accompanied Anthony on a tour of the various booths. At each one Nina anticipated being struck by that bolt of lightning that said, "This is genius!" Several came close, but when she stood in front of Isabelle's canvases, her breath caught in her throat. They were astounding. The raves were justified, which meant there was no way Nina could avoid making Isabelle the centerpiece of her coverage. Understanding that Isabelle might be harboring some leftover hostility, Nina approached cautiously, using Anthony as her shield.

"Brava!" she said, clapping her hands, brazening her way through an admiring throng as Bette Davis might have done, all affectation and attitude. "You have taken the city of Paris, and, dare I say, the entire art world, by storm!" It took unbelievable muscle control to keep her smile in place, especially when she saw the animosity that filled Isabelle's eyes. "We are all so overwhelmed by your work and so proud to be able to claim you as one of our own."

Nina applauded again and looked around, encouraging the Americans in the crowd to join in. Isabelle inhaled deeply. Nina's posturing was trying her patience.

"May I introduce you to your newest fan," Nina said, moving right along. "Mr. Anthony Hartwick, head of Hartwick House publishers. Anthony, Isabelle de Luna."

Instinctively she turned toward Anthony as she made the introduction. What she saw startled her. His face was rapt. As he shook Isabelle's hand, he appeared almost dumbfounded.

"It's a pleasure to meet you," Isabelle said with remarkable grace, considering the circumstances.

"The pleasure is all mine." He offered a courtly bow of his head. "You are a remarkable painter, Miss de Luna." Isabelle responded with a nod and a thankful smile. "I saw another piece of yours once before."

"Oh, right," Nina butted in, wanting to remind both of them of her presence. "We were at Philip Medina's villa in Majorca for the wedding of his father, Nelson. What was the name of the piece, Anthony?"

His eyes never left Isabelle's face. *"Dawn in Barcelona."*

Isabelle's eyes refused to stray anywhere near Nina. "I'm glad you liked it."

"It was extraordinary. The colors and the mood were so, well, perfect."

It seemed odd that he should speak of color just when Isabelle had fixed on the color of his eyes. They were the same deep, wondrous green of Martín's, that rich, luxurious shade of emerald that every now and then glistened with sparks of yellow.

"I take it you've been to Barcelona," she said.

"Several times."

"If it was during Franco's reign, please go back. We weren't ourselves then, but the Catalan spirit is in full bloom now. The city is vital and alive and, I suppose, making up for lost time."

Her smile was one of pride and relief that such a bleak period in her birthplace's history was truly over.

"Did you grow up in Barcelona?"

"No, I grew up in the United States, but I have a great-aunt who lives in Barcelona, so I visit as often as I can."

"That must be why you've managed to retain that wonderfully soft Castilian accent. It's enchanting."

Again Isabelle thanked him, noting that he was as handsome as he was likable. It was no wonder that Nina had linked her arm through his possessively. Secretly it delighted Isabelle to see how uncomfortable Anthony's attentiveness made Nina. She deserved it.

As if he had read her thoughts, Anthony asked, "Do you have any siblings?"

Isabelle's answer was swift. "No." Nina was surprised to find herself disappointed by the response. "And now, if you'll excuse me, Mr. Hartwick, I have some other people I must see. It's been a pleasure."

While she had enjoyed her conversation with Anthony Hartwick, Nina's presence had begun to stifle. Isabelle left the booth and disappeared quickly into the crowd, leaving Hartwick confused and Nina more than a little upset.

"Why didn't you just come right out and ask for her phone number? Better yet, why didn't you just ask her if she wanted to go to bed with you? It would have saved a lot of wear and tear."

Hartwick's expression turned sour. "Women who whine bore me. When you've gotten over your jealous snit, you know where I'll be."

With that he too walked away, leaving Nina standing all alone in Isabelle's world.

Agitated by Nina, Isabelle headed out of the exhibition area in search of fresh air. As she turned the corner, she hit smack into Philip Medina.

"I'm so sorry," she said, blushing the minute she identified her victim.

"I'm not." Philip still had his hands on her arms. "At least this time you've run into me and not away from me. We're making progress."

Her laugh was immediate. "I suppose it does look as if I've gone out of my way to avoid you." He nodded and pursed his lips. His expression was stern. His eyes were gentle. "Please don't take it personally."

"How should I take it?" His gaze remained fixed.

Isabelle felt bewitched. There was something magnetic about Philip Medina. She had seen this man twice in her life before tonight, each meeting separated by years, yet the attraction hadn't waned. "I think it's more poor timing than anything else," she said, wondering why this man's presence was so titillating.

"If I invited you to join me for dinner tonight, how would my timing be?"

"Perfect." He smiled; she wanted to giggle. "I do have to stay until the end."

"I'll wait."

*   *   *

Nina's evening was beginning to feel like a balloon with a pinprick—there was still some float in it, but it was rapidly losing air. Though she had managed to snag some important interviews, including one with Princess Caroline, who was still coping with the tragic death of her mother three years before, she was minus her anchor piece. Though Anthony had offered a weak apology, he couldn't seem to stay out of Isabelle's orbit. Several times Nina had meandered by the de Luna booth, scouting an opportunity to make her pitch to Isabelle. There was Anthony, hovering, staring, gawking like a stage-door Johnny.

It was nearly ten o'clock. Finally Nina felt the circumstances were right. She didn't want a crowd; neither did she want to be alone. Several people were milling about. Isabelle was off to the side. She looked tired.

"Stardom can be such a strain," Nina said, keeping her voice low. Isabelle didn't answer. "Better get used to it. After tonight, your wheels are on the fast track." Isabelle still didn't respond. "Okay," Nina said, her tone turning brusque and no-nonsense. "I'll get right to the point. I want an exclusive interview. I can guarantee national coverage in the press and on TV." She paused for emphasis. "I can also guarantee it will be favorable."

Isabelle laughed, but instead of pealing with gaiety, it had the hollow sound of cynicism. "First of all, your guarantee is worthless. Second, I've been approached by dozens of reporters representing the international press. Why would I give an exclusive to a gossip columnist?"

Nina bristled at the put-down. "Because I'm the gossip columnist doing the asking," she said, throwing their past onto the negotiating table.

Isabelle threw it right back. "All the more reason to say no."

"Where is your loyalty?" Nina demanded, stung, but waving her sense of outraged self-righteousness like a freedom fighter's flag.

"How dare you even let the word *loyalty* pass over your tongue?" Isabelle's voice was almost a hiss. "Where was your vaunted sense of loyalty when you concocted an affair between me and Julian Richter? Where is your loyalty to Miranda and Luis? Have you called them? Sent them a card? Done anything that's right and decent where they're concerned? No! The only person you're loyal to is yourself. Well, guess what, Nina *Davis*. You get what you give. You've given nothing to me. You'll get nothing from me!"

Nina started to follow Isabelle, eager to continue their battle, but within seconds after storming away from her, Isabelle was met by Philip Medina. Nina watched them smile at each other, watched Isabelle's arm slide through his, watched their bodies touch as they strolled toward the exit.

Nina moved closer, waiting for one of them to see her, for one of them to look back. Neither did. Isabelle glided down the steps and into the night as if nothing had happened. Nina had been forgotten.

Embarrassed, unnerved, Nina hurried down the steps, unsure about where to go. Anthony was expecting her. Just then she wasn't certain he was the answer. But being alone wasn't appealing, either.

"Do you mind if we share that cab?" a voice said as a taxi pulled up to the curb.

Nina looked at the face attached to the voice and smiled. "Not at all," she said as she slid in alongside Cody Jackson.

Isabelle should have paid more attention to her food—Taillevent was one of Paris's finest restaurants—but she had been hypnotized by the man seated across from her. As Philip talked about the differences between his father's collection and his—"Nelson remains devoted to the old masters. I prefer modern art"—Isabelle watched the reflection from the small table lamp play with his features. Shadows shaved the plane of his cheekbones and hollowed the flesh beneath. A slice of light chiseled a sharp edge to his nose, the line softening as it bumped over his lips and chin. His eyes, locked on hers, flamed like black opals, glinting with sparks of green and blue.

As she sipped her wine, growing lightheaded from both the grape and the company, she listened as he described the Villa Fortuna, Nelson's home-cum-museum on Lake Lugano. Displaying the nonchalance of one who had grown up with extraordinary wealth, he detailed the private dock, the massive seventeenth-century villa that boasted an astounding art inventory: Rembrandts, Pissarros, Manets, Canalettos, Bonnards, El Grecos, Titians, Goyas, Tintorettos.

"Did you learn about collecting from him?" Isabelle asked, completely agape, unable to imagine a private residence containing so much precious art.

"By osmosis, I suppose. My father collects everything—art, people, businesses, women. As a child I couldn't avoid learning how to amass." On the surface his words granted his father credit for passing on a certain knowledge; the bitter edge to his tone, however, made it clear he resented any comparison.

"I, too, come from a family of collectors. Art, books, musical scores, religious pieces, ceramics, everything except butterflies."

Philip laughed. He reached across the table and took her hand. "And what do you collect?"

"Indian jewelry and Indian pottery, when I can afford it." Philip looked quizzical. "My parents died when I was very young. For various reasons, I didn't benefit from their estate. I did benefit from their prescience, though, because they sent me to be raised by people who had little money but gave me everything love had to offer."

"Take it from me. You were lucky. Love beats money every time."

Isabelle was certain she saw him wince. Instinctively she squeezed his hand. He smiled, but she sensed he was burdened with memories nothing could salve. Having her own private store of painful recollections, she understood.

Segueing onto something else, she said, "While I agree in principle, it would be nice not to have to worry about money."

"Has it been difficult for you?"

"I haven't starved or anything like that, but my life-style is hardly luxurious."

"Doesn't Julian take care of you?" Was there a tinge of annoyance underlining his words? Or was she imagining it?

"He gives me a monthly stipend, which he credits against the profits from my shows. Lots of gallery owners do that with their artists."

"I thought Julian was more to you than simply an agent."

Isabelle blushed, partly out of irritation. The last thing she wanted was for Julian Richter to insinuate himself on her evening. "He's not, but even if he were, that doesn't make him my benefactor."

"Forgive me. If I've stepped over a line, I didn't mean to. I'm forever curious about how an artistic soul manages to survive in a commercial world."

"It's difficult," Isabelle said, grateful to have abandoned Julian. "Remaining faithful to an inner vision when the rent is three months overdue isn't always easy."

Philip surprised her by confessing that aside from the generous sums he contributed to museums, he funded a number of art scholarships for talented children and acted as a patron to artists whose work he deemed important.

"Artists are poor by nature, but to me, the world would be so much poorer without art that whatever money I spend on them is well spent indeed."

Something in his voice told Isabelle that this passion was not a paternal hand-me-down; it was intensely personal. "Did you want to be a painter?" she probed. "Is that why you love it so?"

Philip had anticipated the question; he wasn't sure he was prepared to supply the answer. "No. And yes." A tentative smile wobbled on his lips, then tightened. He gulped his wine, still debating.

"Now I've stepped over a line," Isabelle said. "It's my turn to say I'm sorry."

Philip shook his head, took her hand, and looked deep into her eyes. "I'm a fiercely private man by nature," he said, "but from the moment I met you, I've wanted to know everything about you. Were you a happy baby? Do you look like your mother? Or your father? Did you have braces on your teeth? Did you ever have bad dreams? Who was your first boyfriend? What's your favorite color?" His boyish smile brightened his face, albeit briefly. "If I'm going to butt into the corners of your life, you have a right to know something about mine.

"When I was eight years old, I contracted polio. Fortunately, the degree of paralysis wasn't severe. My legs and arms were affected, but the doctors assured my parents that with bed rest, the application of hot bandages, and constant muscle massage, I could expect to regain almost total use of my limbs.

"My mother, Olivia, became obsessed with my recovery. Aside from the prescribed methods of cure, she added two others. While I was confined to bed, she entertained me with art books and slides. Then she gave me dozens of drawing pads and crayons and paints so that I could work my fingers and wrists and arms." Philip laughed, recalling his efforts. "Picasso didn't have to stay awake nights worrying about me," he said. "I didn't produce one single drawing that was worth saving, but the experience taught me to appreciate those who did."

"What a horrible time that must have been," Isabelle said, reeling from his revelation. Philip's silence confirmed her assessment. "Thank God you came through it."

"I do thank God, but most of all," he said, his voice oddly distant, "I thank my mother. My left side had been left terribly weakened. To help rebuild my muscles, Olivia decided on golf as a supplement to all my other therapy. As a righty, I had to build my left side in order to play the game."

Again that boyish smile flickered across his mouth. "My mother was a terrific golfer. She loved taking me to the driving range, arranging instruction, taking me onto the golf course—it was something she felt was good for my health and good for our relationship."

"Are you and your mother still close?"

Philip's eyes darkened. His mood did a complete about-face. "No. When push came to shove, my mother sold me out!"

His anger must have been hovering, because it exploded quickly. Isabelle didn't expect him to continue. He did pause, clearly struggling with old hurts.

"When I was eleven years old, my parents divorced. My mother accepted a settlement in exchange for custody."

What he didn't say was that his mother left him to live with a father who withheld both affection and approval, conducting his own life in a manner that every single day of Philip's life managed to reinforce the boy's feeling that he was a burden and an inconvenience. Nelson cavorted with, married, and—mercifully—divorced two showgirls in rapid succession. While they were part of Nelson's life, they were part of Philip's life—like it or not. Shallow, acquisitive, insensitive to anything except Nelson's sexual needs, one of them simply ignored Philip. The other, attuned to his hostility, retaliated by lying to Nelson, claiming an insult or offense, thereby incurring Nelson's wrath and pushing father and son further and further apart. Philip longed for his mother, but Olivia remained mysteriously absent from his life.

"She married a stockbroker who had been a friend of the family and moved to New York."

"Do you ever see her?"

"No." Suddenly he called for the check, and shortly after they left, Philip's dark cloud of anger following them back to Isabelle's hotel. When they reached the door to her room, he appeared chagrined.

"I've been the world's most tedious date. If you aren't totally disgusted with me, would you let me make it up to you by taking you to Majorca for the weekend?"

"I had planned to visit my great-aunt in Barcelona."

"What if we stop there on the way? Do you think your aunt would mind?"

"I think she'd be delighted," Isabelle said.

"And you?" His lips caressed hers. It was a gentle kiss, one that carried no demands yet felt full of promise.

Isabelle hadn't been to Majorca since she was seven years old. Looking up at Philip, his eyes still clouded by the phantoms of his past, she felt certain that he was the perfect escort for this long delayed journey back to the island of turquoise water and white sand and disturbing ghosts.

Cody Jackson's apartment was a garret on a narrow, cobblestone street in Montmartre. Climbing five flights of stairs in high heels wasn't exactly what Nina had in mind when she invited herself for a nightcap, but like a hound on a scent, she was following a hunch. When finally they reached their destination, Nina's first reaction was: A loft is a loft is a loft. Whether in Paris or New York, the artist's need for open space dominated. As Cody uncorked a bottle of chilled white wine, Nina enthroned herself on an easy chair at the far end of the room and looked around.

The building was old, so the roof was gabled but—this was obviously what had appealed to Cody—had been modernized with a large skylight. The wooden floors were bare except for several Navaho rugs strewn here and there. The furniture, of the no-consequence flea market variety, didn't warrant description, but the paintings did. Mr. Jackson was a man with an eye for the human form. His nudes were provocative, almost to the point of arousal, yet Nina could see why they hadn't created a public stir. They were too beautiful, too sultry, too reminiscent of Matisse's odalisques. The current rage was to present the human body without censure, wrinkled, flabby, and, more often than not, boldly anatomical. Jackson's nudes weren't daring enough; they didn't confront, they didn't embarrass, they didn't demand that the viewer explain why he looked away or laughed or blushed or lusted at the image on the canvas.

"Do you like them?" Cody asked, handing her a wineglass and taking a seat on the couch.

Nina was too involved with his paintings to answer. She envied his women. She imagined them coming to him filled with trust, disrobing without fear of derision or violence or thoughts of conquest. The flesh of these women had been stroked with a hand that glorified all that was female about them, a hand that was capable of patience and tenderness and immeasurable giving.

Nina yearned to be treated like that, to be cherished and prized. Sam Hoffman had come close, he had loved her in his way, but he had been young. She had experienced other men, but they had been casual relationships, void of the emotion that might have made up for a lack of technique. Anthony was different from all the others. He was exciting and exotic and fluent in the vocabulary of sex. He made her hot and wild and weak with wanting; he made her believe she loved him and hungered for him; but he never made her feel treasured or valued or unique.

"They're quite wonderful," she said, finally tearing herself away from the paintings, zeroing in on the painter. "A woman could fall in love with a man who reveres femininity the way you do."

His laugh was modest. "Some have. Most haven't."

"Silly girls." Nina slid her feet out of her shoes, curled her legs under her, and sipped her wine. "When did you come to Paris? And why?"

Cody offered a brief biography. Since Nina's interest in him had turned decidedly lustful, she was watching more than she was listening. She almost missed it when he mentioned he was at the Art Students League at the same time as Isabelle de Luna. What had his eyes said? What had his tone indicated? She could have kicked herself for having wandered into the middle distance! On and on he droned, talking about the success of that first show, his two others, and the drought that followed.

Soon Nina was bored. When he asked if she wanted to see some of his other paintings, she considered pleading fatigue, but he looked so needy, she followed him about the loft, her libido still craving fulfillment. If, after the tour, he didn't take her to bed, she was going to take a taxi directly to Anthony's hotel.

At the far end, partially hidden by a table laden with supplies and several works in progress, hung two large paintings in the shadows. Tiptoeing over dropcloths, brushes soaking in cans of turpentine, and used-up tubes of paint, Nina winnowed in for a closer look.

On a background of raw, untreated canvas, haloed by a thickly textured nimbus of pastel tones, were two faceless nudes. As before, the bodies were tenderly portrayed, but there was an added element here, something that grabbed Nina's attention. Was it the idealization of the model, the overwhelming sense that the artist had been madly in love with his subject? Was it the certainty that he knew her body intimately? Was it the recognition that in one pose he had captured a moment of exquisite passion—and, in the other, the moment that followed the consummation of that passion?

"Who is she?" Nina asked, her eyes riveted to the languid woman with the long dark hair.

"The Shy Temptress." He looked at the two paintings wistfully. "They're part of the series I told you about, the one that brought me to Paris."

"Was she your lover?"

"She was a model."

"What was her name?"

"I don't reveal the names of my models," he said, hoping to close the subject by walking away.

But the subject wasn't closed. Nina remained where she was, eyeing the paintings, studying the Shy Temptress carefully. With growing confidence and her reporter's instinct, she put together times and places, the fact that he had chosen to mention Isabelle's name over others who had come from the league, the way he had looked at the paintings, the way he had looked at Isabelle during their meeting earlier that evening.

Cody Jackson didn't have to reveal the name of his model. Nina knew exactly who she was.

CHAPTER 18

In his early days, before he owned newspapers and television stations, Philip had worked as an investigative reporter. He often thought that was the best time, when he was out in the field, tracking a lead, covering a story, unearthing facts that might otherwise have remained buried. Understandably, even after he had surrendered his beat for a corporate desk, gathering information remained a habit. In business he preferred to be forewarned and forearmed. In his personal life he sought protection against enemies who pretended to be friends. Also, he had an endless fascination with puzzles.

Whether they were world emergencies or personal dreams, Philip believed most puzzles could be solved. He didn't accept the notion of a perfect crime. There were always clues; sometimes it took years of hard work to ferret them out, sometimes they remained unfound, but they were there. His theory: Most puzzles fit a pattern. History provided the guide for international crises, human nature the frame for the other. The trick, if there was one, was to establish the pattern, track it, note the point of departure, and investigate the deviation. There was always a reason for stepping off the line or breaking the code or not sticking to a pattern. Order provided comfort and security. To venture outside was a risk. It took either great courage or utter desperation to motivate a movement away from the fold.

When a major news event was breaking, or a story that engaged human interest was being written, it was difficult for Philip to remain an observer. The sidelines was not his favorite venue. It was not unusual for one of his staff reporters to find the boss on the scene of some local tragedy, or in the morgue researching an issue currently making news, or sitting in on a brainstorming conference on national issues.

By the time Philip had run into Isabelle at the Palais-Royal, he already had a dossier on her. He had started the folder after that first night, in Julian's gallery. Her painting, her feistiness, and yes, her beauty had intrigued him. The dossier wasn't complete; it contained only what he was able to glean from Spanish newspaper files—Althea's murder, the suspicion that Martín was her killer, his subsequent death—and the little Julian had told him—Isabelle's move to Santa Fe, the Durans. He had followed up by reading sketches on the history of the Pujols and the de Lunas, particularly Beátriz, whose astute stewardship of the family empire had been documented outside of Spain. But nothing prepared him for the majesty of the Castell and the dignity of Isabelle's great-aunt.

When they arrived, Pedro said "the Señorita" was in Isabelle's garden. Isabelle led Philip around the side of the mansion to the green oasis that had always been her special place. There they found Flora in full, white Zouave pants and a white tunic, seated on the ground, her legs crossed in a lotus position, her back straight, her hands holding a string of beads. Her eyes were closed, the expression on her face beatific.

"She's meditating," Isabelle whispered to Philip. They had stopped, unwilling to intrude. "Knowing Tía Flora, I'm sure she's already done an hour of yoga. She claims it keeps her young."

"It must work," Philip said, noting the love in Isabelle's eyes as she watched her aunt. "It's hard to believe she's eighty-four years old."

"Wait until you get to know her." Isabelle chuckled as if at a private joke.

When Flora opened her eyes and spied Isabelle and her handsome friend, she broke into a huge grin and beckoned them to join her. The introductions began and ended the formalities. As Flora said, "At my age, I don't have time to waste on convention. Come. Sit next to me. Tell me who you are and what you're about."

Philip wasn't used to being on the opposite side of an interrogation, but he respected directness. He had grown up with so many lies and secrets, honesty had become a priority. He answered Flora as best he could, giving her a synopsis of his life. She was more impressed by his art patronage than his business acumen. He was impressed with her. At eighty-four, Flora was a marvel. Her hair was shock white, her body was slim to the point of frailty, but her skin remained smooth, her eyes sharp, her tongue even sharper.

When Isabelle described her stay in Paris, Flora sniped, "When I was your age, women were expected to remain shackled to the house. I remember the shock on my father's face when I asked if I could visit Paris. You would have thought I'd asked to parade down La Ramblas stark naked."

"Yet you speak several languages," Philip said, repeating what Isabelle had told him.

"Our house was always filled with guests from abroad, and I have a good ear for languages. I listened and I learned. And I did get to travel some," she said, reminiscing about trips with Alejandro and Martín. "But I had obligations here, so I had to rely on my spiritual travels for insight and sophistication."

She shielded her eyes from an unwelcome slice of sunlight and studied Philip. She liked his face, the wide brow that reminded her of Martín, the brooding eyes that softened when he looked at Isabelle but appeared curtained when he spoke of himself. It was a strong face, one that communicated confidence and a certain dispassion, but on his forehead, just above the bridge of his nose, faint lines wrote a different story.

"Do you meditate? Or are you one of those caught-in-the-rat-race American corporate types who scoff at things like that?"

"Tía Flora!"

"It's okay." Philip laid his hand gently over Isabelle's, assuring her he wasn't insulted. Flora liked the way he touched her niece. "I don't scoff," he said, "but I suppose I am skeptical of things like yoga and meditation."

"It creates a wonderful path to inner peace." Something in Philip's eyes told her serenity was a stranger to him. "Yoga connects the mind and the body and the spirit. It helps us heal our worldly wounds."

Philip could feel Flora rummaging around inside his soul. How she had found the entrance, he wasn't sure, but the fact that she had impressed him.

"It's all in the breathing," she said, illustrating her point by inhaling and exhaling through her nose.

"Do you meditate?" he asked Isabelle. She and Flora exchanged looks.

"I've tried. I'm not very good at it. I do the postures, though." There was an edge to Isabelle's voice. For whatever reason, the subject upset her. Philip didn't press.

"It's not easy to still your mind," Flora said. "Eliminating the everyday clatter makes us susceptible to unbidden thoughts or frightening visions. Not everyone has the emotional stamina to face the void."

Isabelle bounded to her feet. "Enough of this! I want to take Philip on a tour of the Castell, and then I want to have lunch."

El Castell de Les Bruixots charmed Philip. He was entranced with its history, its architectural splendor, its gardens, and the magnificence of its content. His eye was trained to divine excellence, and here it abounded. After viewing the Goyas, the Mirós, the Zubarán, and the like, Flora's paintings startled him—mostly because they were so defiantly different from anything in her home.

Feminine, floral, familial, the iconography was completely personal in its references. Knowing some of the family history, he was able to pick out Vina and Ramona, Martín, and, in one or two, even Isabelle. Vina was often shown with a pen or a book, Ramona with piano keys, sheet music, or some other musical symbol. A recurring symbol—sometimes subtly placed, other times predominant—was a bouquet, three flowers in full bloom, with one partially opened bud he presumed was Beátriz.

Though her paintings were snapshots of the social scene of her day, Philip detected a lurking social consciousness. He also sensed the paradox of Flora's unique situation: she was both an insider and an outsider, extremely wealthy, an accomplished hostess, a friend to many interesting and famous people, but a woman and an artist and an extremely determined feminist.

"So, what do you think?" Isabelle asked, unable to interpret his long silence.

"Her paintings are idiosyncratic, to say the least. Slightly outrageous. And totally Flora!"

Isabelle laughed. "Tía Flora's both a snob and a social activist. It's one of her greatest contradictions. She glories in artifice, but despises phoniness."

"A girl after my own heart!" Philip was finding the aunt as captivating as the niece. "She does have an eye for the defining characteristics of class and milieu," he said, pointing to scenes of lavish parties and fancy dress balls.

Isabelle nodded. "They're stage sets. That's why her paintings made her friends uncomfortable. She exposed the theatricality of the upper classes, putting it out there for all of them to see. They preferred the reflections they saw in their own mirrors."

"Was she a big influence on your painting? I see a similar extravagance with color, but little else."

"Come," Isabelle said. "I'll show you my other font."

Four of Althea's paintings hung in the formal rooms of the Castell. Several others decorated the corridor leading to the south loggia. The rest were in what used to be Martín and Althea's bedroom. Philip noticed Isabelle hesitate before stepping inside. He took her hand. His parents may have been alive, but he, too, felt as if he had lost them at a very early age.

Together they entered a lavish suite, all dark Spanish wood and white Spanish lace. Philip noticed several vases filled with flowers. There was no musty smell, no maudlin aura of a maintained shrine. He wondered if Flora had spruced up the room for Isabelle's visit or kept it fresh for the many times she visited here.

Shifting from Flora's work to Althea's was a strain on his sensibilities. Where Flora was delicate, Althea was bold. Where Flora was figurative, Althea was abstract. Yet it was clear that both these women—Flora with her love of the rainbow and Althea with her power of expression and dramatic use of line—had seeded Isabelle's genius.

"She was a very talented woman," he said quietly. His eye caught a picture of Martín and Althea on a dresser. "And a very beautiful one as well."

He lifted up the photograph so he could take a better look at Isabelle's parents. They were undeniably stunning, but more than that, even to a stranger's eye it was clear that these two people were indisputably, irrevocably crazy about each other. He felt Isabelle alongside him.

Without looking at her, he slid his arm around her waist. "You inherited the best of each of them," he said. "They certainly were handsome."

"So's your father," Flora's voice intruded.

Philip dropped his arm from Isabelle's waist and returned the picture to the dresser. Both turned to look at Flora, who was standing in the doorway with a smug smile.

"I didn't connect the face with the name before. You must look like your mother."

"You know Philip's father?" Isabelle was startled. Philip was surprised and wary.

"I've known Nelson for years. Though I didn't know your mother, I've had the somewhat dubious pleasure of meeting the other Mrs. Medinas." She looked from Philip to Isabelle, amused by their expressions. "Your father knew him," she said, enjoying her little revelation.

"Papa?"

"Nelson collects antique cars, doesn't he?"

"Among other things," Philip said. It was an effort to erase the sarcasm from his voice.

"So did Martín. When the economy plunged and Martín needed to raise money, he sold off some of his cars. Nelson bought the his and hers Rothschild Hispano-Suizas."

"What incredible beauties they were!" Philip said, able to recall every curve and every line.

A matched pair of exceedingly aristocratic automobiles built in 1934, they were as black, as elegant, as sleek, and as powerful as panthers.

"Of all the classics my father owns, those are the most luxurious. Unfortunately, wife number two demanded Yvonne de Rothschild's coupe as part of her buyout. The mate, Anthony de Rothschild's J12, is stored in a huge warehouse in San Francisco with the rest of Nelson's collection."

"Are you a classics aficionado?" Flora asked.

"I don't collect them, but I am a fan."

"I'd show you Papa's garage, but it's empty now," Isabelle said, and she and Flora shared a smile. Both remembered the day they had taken an imaginary drive in the Bugatti.

"I'd like to see it anyway."

"After lunch," Flora said, linking her arm through Philip's, sending Isabelle ahead to tell the cook they were ready. As they ambled down the stairs, Flora stopped. "You're a nice man, Philip Medina. I like you."

Philip felt like a schoolboy. He actually blushed. "Thank-you. Your opinion means a lot to me."

"Isabelle means a lot to me."

Philip nodded but didn't know what else to say. He and Isabelle barely knew each other. They had met a few times, shared a dinner, some conversation, nothing more. Yet if he were honest with himself, there was more. Flora probably would say he and Isabelle were old souls who had been together in a past life. While that might not have been part of his vocabulary, he didn't dismiss the notion. Odd as it sounded, that was how he felt.

"Take your time," Flora said, as if divining his thoughts. "She needs time, too."

After lunch, Isabelle had given Philip a quick tour of the garage, including the secret cellar.

"Why is the Bugatti still down here?" he asked.

It was a reasonable question. Isabelle knew her answer wasn't, but it was the truth.

"Neither Flora nor I has the heart to move it. One of these days, I suppose I'll either bring it to the United States or sell it. For now, it's where my father would want it to be."

When it came time to leave, Isabelle wasn't sure who had the more difficult time—she, Flora, or Philip. Flora extracted a promise that whenever Philip was in Barcelona he would visit. Philip raved about Flora and the Castell throughout the plane trip to Palma, as well as on the car ride to Formentor. When they arrived at the villa, however, it was Isabelle's turn to rave.

Philip's home was overwhelming: the watchtower, the angled layout of the public rooms, the decor, the art, the walls of glass that looked out on a panorama that startled. When Philip slid aside one of the doors, Isabelle practically raced onto the terrace that jutted out over the cove, eager to confront the scenery. Once there, she froze.

Her entire being was engulfed by the incessant blue of the bay and the sky that covered it. She felt dizzy. Blue frightened her. Gripping the wall to steady herself, she closed her eyes and waited. When the visions didn't come, she opened her eyes slowly, hesitantly. There were no hobgoblins, no half faces or featureless forms. Only a glorious, gleaming, invigorating blue. Suddenly it felt joyous and nonthreatening, life-affirming and not ominous. Isabelle decided to embrace it.

At first Philip couldn't imagine what had happened. He had ambled on ahead, talking about excavating rock and moving sand, when he felt an emptiness beside him. He looked back, saw her stagger and hold on to the wall. He had started toward her when, with her eyes fixed on the craggy strip that sliced the gently rippled water, Isabelle reached into the large canvas tote on her shoulder, extracted a pad and a box of pastels, and began committing the cove to paper.

Philip felt Isabelle was the most exciting woman he had ever met. Certainly her physical beauty attracted him, but he had known too many beautiful women to grant externals a priority. Rather, it was her essence that electrified him—watching her respond to nature's canvas, seeing her translate scenery into images, feeling the intensity of her drive and her need to express herself. He understood much of it; his own ambition was intense. What he didn't understand—her ability to isolate herself without detachment, her willingness to subject herself to criticism, the reckless honesty with which she infused her work—he admired and envied.

Later, after they had rested and changed, she met him in the living room, wearing softly tailored slacks and a sleek, one-shouldered top, both in bright carnation red. Her hair floated to her shoulders. Her eyes were dark and smoky, her lips red and glossed. Thick silver cuffs glistened from her wrists, thin silver hoops dangled from her ears. Everything about her was simple and uncomplicated, everything except the way she made Philip feel.

"I've never seen you in a color," he said, joining her by the window. "At your shows you wear white. Today you wore black. Both flatter you, but in case you didn't know, you're exquisite in red." His lips grazed her cheek. Her scent was fragile and green, a blend of patchouli and ylang-ylang.

They chatted and drank cava and continued their exploration of each other. They talked about music and politics, San Francisco and Santa Fe. Philip talked about the joy his paintings gave him; Isabelle was honored by the prominent placement of *Dawn in Barcelona* and told him so.

"Your charcoal hangs over my bed in New York," he said with a sly grin.

"I hope it doesn't interfere with anything important."

Philip laughed. For the moment he couldn't think of anything more important than being with her.

Over dinner Isabelle encouraged Philip to talk about Cisco Communications. As he described his vast network of newspapers and television channels, she found herself drifting, engaged in a second, separate conversation with herself. She was trying to silence her inner voice, which insisted upon making comparisons between Philip and Julian. In truth she was aggravated that Julian was even in her consciousness.

Perhaps the dialogue had been triggered by the fact that Philip was wearing all black—and didn't look studied. His silk shirt was open, his jacket was unstructured, his slacks were easy. There was no artifice about him, no sense that he needed a costume in order to be who he was. He presented himself. Julian acted out who he wanted to be. Even when they were alone, Julian performed, playing the role of the commander, the one in control, and, yes, the father. Philip exhibited the same personal assuredness, the same decisiveness, the same ability to manage, but he didn't seem to require applause or to demand constant murmurings of approval or to need confirmation of her appreciation.

After dinner they took Catalan sweet wine onto the terrace. The night was heavenly. Soft music drifted out from hidden speakers, wafting over them and onto the bay. The air was cool. Philip draped his jacket over Isabelle's shoulders. As she bent over to lean on the seawall, wisps of hair played on her skin, a lambent wash of moonlight illuminated her face. Philip thought he had never seen anything so lovely.

"I don't know what to do with you," he said, stunning both of them with his candor. "I'm not used to feeling so disarmed."

"Do I make you uncomfortable?" she asked, rising, her eyes meeting his.

He laughed and raised his hands, as if surrendering. "Quite the opposite. You make me too comfortable. I smile and laugh more than is my custom. I've told you things I've never shared with a woman before. I feel things I've never felt before."

"Like what?"

"Like contented and relaxed and excited and intrigued and nervous and protective and—"

Isabelle took his face in her hands and kissed him. His arms wrapped around her, pressing her next to him. The kiss deepened, his grasp tightened, but then she pulled away.

"You confuse me, too," she said, slightly breathless, "which is why I'm going to sleep. Now. Alone."

In the middle of the night Philip grew restless. Wandering out of his quarters, he was drawn to a dim light on the main terrace. There, before a large canvas on a wooden easel, was Isabelle, her body wrapped in a light robe, a palette of oil paints hooked around her left thumb, a thick brush flickering across the surface, leaving waves of color in its wake. She was a veritable fireball of activity, dabbing, swiping, slashing, smoothing. Even from a distance he could see the night emerging on her canvas: the moon, a royal blue crescent suspended in a navy sky broken now and then by pale gray clouds. He watched in silence, not wanting to intrude, too hypnotized to leave.

Suddenly she stopped. He expected her to step back, to examine the work, to add or subtract; but no. She was finished. Showing signs of fatigue, she returned her palette to a box that was sitting on the floor, closed it, stretched her arms and legs, and walked to the seawall. Her face turned toward the sky. Whether she was looking for further inspiration or for approval was unclear. Philip called her name softly, so as not to startle her.

"Why are you working in the dark?" he asked, standing alongside her.

"Van Gogh often went out at night to paint when he had a need for a mystical union with something larger than himself."

"Is that what you needed?" Philip asked, trying to look beyond the veil clouding her eyes.

Again she glanced up at the sky, drawing from it, holding close whatever spirits she found there. When she looked at him, her eyes were wistful.

"My father always told me that because of our name, the moon was special to us, like a relative or something. Many times when I was little, on nights like this when the sky was black and the moon was blue, he used to bring me to a window in the tower of the Castell. He said the reason the moon was blue was because it missed me. Tonight, I missed him."

Philip held out his arms. Wordlessly they came together. For a while they stood holding each other, surrendering to the seductive whispers of darkness. Then they walked to his room. Philip closed the glass doors, but the moon followed them inside. With its pale cerulean light surrounding them, he untied her robe, watching as it drifted open. She was wearing a silk negligee, delicately patterned, spare in its coverage. Isabelle never moved as his eyes traveled the length of her femininity. He was enjoying the journey; she allowed him to stare. More than anyone, she understood the erotic pleasure that could be derived from mere observation; sight was a powerful sense.

So was touch, which was why she let her robe fall from her shoulders. Philip read the invitation and accepted, sliding his hands around her back, bringing her within a breath of him. She shivered as his cold fingers touched her flesh, but then his mouth covered hers and she felt suffused with a nascent heat. Her hands laced around his neck, tasting him as he sampled her. His hands prospected, gliding over her negligee, under her negligee, seeking and then finding her breasts.

The seductive rapture of silk against skin rushed to her brain like a drug. She began to lose herself in the wonder of his touch, the way he caressed her, where he caressed her. Her hands hurried to push aside his robe. Eagerly they slid down his chest until they couldn't slide anymore. She thought she heard him groan, but her ears were filled with the sound of her own blood coursing through her veins. She had never felt so needy, so grasping, so completely avaricious. Quite clearly his wanting was just as intense.

He stripped her of her nightgown, stepped out of his robe, and led her to his bed, where they fell on each other with a passion that bordered on desperation. He couldn't get enough of her. What his hands didn't explore, his mouth did. He exulted in the magnificence of her body, the soft folds of her roundness, the sinuous curves of her waist and neck, the tautness of her belly. He inhaled her as if her perfume were an aphrodisiac, yet all the while he knew it wasn't a scent that had him so aroused, it was an aura, an essence, perhaps even an awareness of destiny.

Her hands guided him near the heat, but instead of entering, he hovered like a pendulum, tantalizing, tempting, bringing them both to a point near madness. When neither could stand the separateness, he filled her and she clung to him. It was as if all that had gone before—the day in Barcelona, the evening, their other encounters, perhaps even their other lovers—had been merely a prelude to this one exquisite, volcanic moment.

It was the moments that followed that signaled a sea change in their lives, however—those quiet, satisfied moments they spent in each other's arms, during which each experienced the delicious contentment that resulted from a combining of the physical and the emotional. It didn't matter whether Philip was ready or Isabelle was prepared. It didn't matter whether they had moved too fast or gone too far or said too much. It was too late for afterthoughts.

In the blue light of Majorca's moon something very special had occurred.

Philip's eyes weren't fully opened when he felt the void. His hand touched the sheet where she had lain. It was still warm, but it was vacant. Squinting to avoid the first light of day, he rose, washed up, slipped into trunks and a robe, and went to look for Isabelle. At her guest house, the curtains were open, the door was unlocked. Stepping inside, he called to her. No one answered. He checked the closet and breathed a sigh of relief. Her clothes were still there. She hadn't left. Startled by his own response, he stopped and took his emotional pulse.

For Philip, the profundity of the feelings that had flooded him last night had been a first and, therefore, were troubling. He was not a man who trusted intimate relationships. He hadn't witnessed many successes in his lifetime, so he had little faith in the likelihood. His parents' marriage had been a fiasco, as had Nelson's subsequent unions. As for his parents' relationship to him, there, too, naught inspired confidence. The term *father/son* had never held any lure for Nelson. Though they had common interests, they never shared anything. They didn't go to ball games or museums or car shows together. They rarely ate a meal together. While he did remember his mother being wonderful and doting when he was a boy, that umbilical connection seemed to have been severed easily, if not painlessly.

The natural conclusion to draw was that the only safe attachment was to things. Experience had taught him that while people provided pleasure, they made demands, created obligations, and sometimes caused great suffering. As Nelson proved again and again, objects were far more desirable. They didn't break unless he broke them, they didn't disappear unless he threw them away. Philip's lesson: It was better to have things that belonged to him than to allow himself to belong to someone else.

Armored in a suit of oft repeated, self-protective rhetoric, he continued his search through the main house and out onto the terrace. When finally he spotted her on the beach below the villa, the rhetoric vanished. Dressed in a skimpy bikini, her hair in a ponytail, a twisted bandanna tied around her forehead, Isabelle was doing yoga on the sand. He watched as she moved from posture to posture with the suppleness of a dancer, turning each pose into an effortless sketch of symmetry and line, a careful composition of strength and style, agility and grace.

Slowly he descended the stairway that led to the beach, his eyes trained on the woman he had come to think of as a poem. Beautiful, lyrical, possessed of an expressiveness that astounded him. Everything she did wrote a verse about how she felt: the way she was posing now, the way she made love, the way she painted, the way she spoke. Last night he had been swept away by their similarities, their love of art, their lonely childhoods, their fierce independence, their intensity.

This morning he seemed focused on their differences. If she was a poem, he was prose, all description and exposition, unimaginative and matter-of-fact. He headed a communications conglomerate, yet he found it difficult to convey emotion. He hid behind efficiency and power, always keeping his hand close to his chest, never allowing sentiment to interfere with the pursuit of a goal. Other women he had been with had accused him of being cold, steel plated, and fervently private. With them he was. With Isabelle every pore felt open, every surface exposed.

"I missed you this morning," he said as he bent down and tenderly kissed the back of her neck. She was sitting with her legs tucked under her, hands together, palms flat, eyes closed. She completed her breath and turned to look at him. Her smile was intimate and reassuring. When she raised her hand, he took it and joined her on the blanket. "I couldn't imagine where you'd gone."

"The dawn was so breathtaking, I couldn't resist."

The morning sun bathed her in a pale yellow that seemed to gild her skin. Philip thought she looked like a goddess. "I can't resist you," he said.

"Then don't."

Reaching behind her back, she untied the top of her bathing suit and removed it. She slipped off her headband, loosened her hair, and untied the two knots that held the other small strip of fabric to her body.

As they made love on the beach in the early hours of an emerging day, Isabelle felt consumed by a rage of fiery sensations. Every cell in her body was alive and responsive, raw and eager to take what was being given and to give back in kind. She had been attracted to Philip from the start and probably, in her subconscious, had fantasized what it might be like to make love with him; but she never could have imagined she would feel as she did. He had only to look at her and she wanted him. He had only to touch her and she wanted him never to stop.

Yet afterward, as they lay next to each other in the sand, she knew there was more between them than just sex. She loved talking to him, listening to him, laughing with him, being quiet with him. Obviously the question that nagged was, did she love him? More to the point, did she know what love was?

They spent most of the day on the beach. After lunch they encamped on lounges beneath two large umbrellas. Isabelle brought a sketch pad and began to draw Philip. At first she was too engrossed in what she was doing to notice, but when he shifted positions for the third time, she began to realize she was making him uncomfortable.

"Is my sketching upsetting you?"

"Yes."

"Why?"

"For the same reason I don't like photographs taken of me."

"Because you don't like looking at your body?"

Philip smiled. There was that reckless honesty of hers. "Exactly."

"In case you didn't notice," Isabelle said with a salacious grin, "I think your body's quite wonderful."

Philip laughed and returned to reading his book. Isabelle continued with her drawing. Suddenly he put down the book.

"How did you feel about your father?" he asked.

Her answer was simple. "I loved him."

"Even after he was accused of murdering your mother?"

"Even then," she said, making it clear that she had always and would always believe in his innocence.

"See this?" he said, pointing to his left leg.

She nodded, guessing what was next. Though his calf muscle was strong, his left thigh muscle was thin. The same was true of his left arm: the forearm was as strong as the right forearm, the left bicep was lean. After he had told her about the polio, she had detected a barely noticeable limp. Her eye for proportion told her that the left leg was probably slightly shorter than the right; the same was probably true of his arm.

"To my father, this made me permanently, irrevocably imperfect. He never forgave me."

"Have you ever forgiven him for feeling that way?" Isabelle asked.

Philip was taken aback by the question. "No, I guess I haven't. I compete with him in every conceivable way. If he buys one painting, I buy two. If his company shows a five percent profit, I shoot for ten."

"What's the point?"

Philip sighed. How did one condense a lifetime of unresolved rage? "I want to prove him wrong."

"What you want is to prove to him that you're as good as the other kids." Isabelle's voice was soft, padded with understanding.

"Right again."

"We all carry baggage from our childhoods, Philip," she said, recalling the nasty whispers about Martín's guilt. "What you have to learn to do is to lighten the load."

"Have you?"

"A little," she said honestly, "but I still have a long way to go before I'm free of all my burdens."

"What's holding you back?" he asked, endlessly intrigued with her.

Isabelle didn't answer right away. Philip watched her face, wondering if she was deciding how much she could trust him with. Though she was forth-right about most things, on family matters he suspected she wasn't completely open.

"I'd like to restore my family's good name," she said.

"Is that why you want to buy Dragon Textiles?"

Isabelle laughed. "Tía Flora's been telling tales out of school."

"She wasn't snitching," he said, defending his new friend. "We were talking about your mother. Flora told me how Althea had revitalized the company."

Isabelle shrugged, her frustration evident. "I'd love to be able to get it back, but right now it appears unlikely. The company's not for sale, and even if it were, I don't have the money."

Philip's instincts warned him not to make an offer. She had made a statement, not a request.

"Do you really think that after all these years, people still gossip about your family?"

"Probably not, but clearing my father's name is important to me."

"Do you have any idea who might have done it? Or why?"

"I have suspicions, but no evidence. I was seven years old. I don't remember anything of that night. I fell asleep in the other room. For all I know, it was a random attack by a stranger."

Philip moved over to her lounge and cradled her in his arms. She was trembling. As he held her close, he sympathized. Like her, he was haunted by an unsolved puzzle. Why had his mother abandoned him? Had he pushed her away? Or had someone else pulled her? Like Isabelle, he knew the answer was lurking somewhere just beyond his grasp. But, he admitted, he was luckier than she was. If he chose, he could confront his mother and demand answers. Isabelle had no one to confront, no one to ask. If her puzzle was ever to be solved, she was going to have to solve it alone.

The next morning Philip gave Isabelle a golf lesson at a driving range. Afterward they drove into Palma, where they lunched at a little bistro in the Portela Quarter. They were lingering over their wine when Isabelle noticed a small group of people gathering in the square. She watched for a few moments and then grinned, her eyes sparkling like those of a child anticipating her favorite party game.

"They're going to dance the sardana!" She grabbed Philip's hand and led him into the square, prodding him to join in.

In minutes the circle had formed, one person taking the hand of whoever was near. Philip, who wound up on the other side of the round, had heard of the sardana but had never taken part before. He knew it was the national dance of Catalonia and a source of immense pride to its people.

Catalans didn't care that it was mocked in the rest of Spain because it was so slow and unathletic; they boasted of its democracy, its spirit of inclusion. Under Franco the sardana had been banned. Exercising a perverse logic, Catalans bragged of the ban: the sardana was a dance of unity, of Catalan unity, of pride in their heritage and not in the heritage of Spain.

Because it was a dance of community and sharing, tradition demanded that everyone put something of theirs in the middle of the circle. Philip took off his jacket and threw it on top of a jumble of coats and bags and hats. Isabelle offered her straw hat. As if from nowhere, an instrumental group materialized—tenor and soprano oboes, a drum, and a long flute—and the music started. The circle began to move, gracefully, slowly, as was the style of the sardana. Tourists gathered to watch. Some cut in, separating Philip and Isabelle even more.

The tempo quickened. One man, who had appointed himself the leader, shouted, "*¡Amunt!*" instructing everyone to move up and down. Isabelle raised her arms, then lowered them, bowing as she did so, then up again, her head high and proud. Across the way, Philip watched as she kept pace with the lively beat, unable to concentrate on anything except the litheness of her body and the exhilarated expression on her face. Since he wasn't familiar with the steps, he stumbled over his own feet, but it didn't matter. His heart was keeping time with another rhythm altogether.

They spent the ride back to Formentor and the rest of the evening laughing at Isabelle's golf and Philip's dancing, each promising to practice and do better the next time. Fortunately neither needed lessons pleasing the other in bed.

The following day Julian called and demanded that Isabelle return to the States immediately.

"You insisted this was a grand opportunity. I disagreed, but it appears I was wrong. Your success has traveled across the ocean. I'm being besieged by demands to mount a de Luna show as quickly as possible. This is your moment, Isabelle. I suggest you grab it."

"I have to leave," she told Philip, who was sitting beside her.

"So soon? We had planned to stay another day or two."

"I know, but I have to get back to work. Julian's arranged a show for October. That leaves me less than four months to complete a series."

She looked to Philip for sympathy. What she saw was vexation.

"Julian's pulling your strings, Isabelle."

She turned, sliding into the corner of the couch. Already he could feel a distance.

"Why would you say that?"

"He didn't have to plan a show for October. He could have waited to discuss this with you when you got back to New York. This isn't about your career. Don't you see? This is about us."

"That may be, but he's booked a show, which means I have to leave." Even to her own ear she sounded like a child repeating what a parent had told her.

"Are you going because you want to paint or are you going because you want to be with Julian?"

"My leaving has nothing to do with Julian." She struggled for a moment. "Or you. I don't know if I can make you understand this, Philip, but the core of my life is my art. It's who I am."

"And what attracted me to you in the first place," he said, reminding her of where they met, why they continued to run into each other. "I would never ask you to change that."

"I know." She wanted to add, "That's why I love you," but didn't.

"Julian's acting like he owns you."

"He doesn't own me. He represents me." Her answer was crisp, almost curt. She didn't like having her pride or her independence trampled.

Philip backed off, softened his tone. "You're a fifty-percenter, Isabelle. That makes you his partner in your shows, not his employee. He's supposed to consult you on things like the timing of an exhibition."

"But I'm not a fifty-percenter," she said, shocked by the burst of fire in Philip's eyes. "Julian still gets sixty percent of whatever I do."

In a sudden eruption of energy, Philip bounded out of his seat, pacing the room like an enraged tiger. "That isn't right!" he growled.

"Maybe not, but that's the way it is." Isabelle thought he was overreacting, but she didn't want to pursue the matter. Her relationship with Julian was more complicated than simply numbers. Both of them knew it, but it was her problem to work out, not his.

"Forget Julian's motives and methods. I was a success in Paris. That's a fact. A window of opportunity has opened for me, Philip. That's another fact. I have to take advantage of it." Her eyes pleaded with him to understand.

He tried. He took her in his arms and held her and told her he understood, but two things troubled him: every time he and Isabelle danced, Julian cut in; more disturbing, Isabelle allowed the interference.

That night their lovemaking was passionate, but different. Isabelle sensed a reserve that hadn't been there before Julian's call. It was as if Philip were holding back, testing her, testing his ability to trust his feelings for her. Philip, who only hours before had believed she was falling for him as quickly as he was for her, felt space where there had been closeness.

A second thought had crept in between them.

CHAPTER 19

Santa Fe

Isabelle bypassed New York and went straight from Spain to New Mexico. For the first few weeks she was so torn between missing Philip and avoiding Julian, she was unable to paint. Instead she rode with Luis early in the morning and then accompanied him on his chores as she had when she was younger. It had taken her entire trust fund and most of the profits from two exhibitions, but as she surveyed the remarkable changes between the old La Casa and the new, she secretly crowed at the results.

Architecturally, La Casa cleaved to adobe tradition—eagle corbels portaled the hand-carved entrance doors, lintels were electric blue, edges were rounded, angles softened, interiors integrated viga and latillas ceilings with kiva hearths and tiled floors—but it no longer looked like an expanded house with one level jutting out from another. The fountain remained, as did several of the old cottonwood trees and the stone drive, but the miradors were gone, as were the two giant elms by the front gate.

The kitchen had doubled in size and was no longer the sole province of Miranda and her assistants. The restaurant at La Casa, under the guidance of a chef who had created a cuisine he called "Nouvelle Southwest," had become a Santa Fe hot spot, the bar an elegant place even for locals to spend an hour or two. The pool was modest, but quiet and Edenic, set off to the side in a richly planted garden. Indian crafts decorated niches and hollows. Paintings and sculpture by well-known southwestern artists distinguished the lobby, library, restaurant, and bar. Each guest room boasted a fireplace and a small seating area. At night, in addition to turning down the beds and leaving a chocolate mint on each pillow, La Casa maids left a folded note that told a bedtime story taken from Indian lore. Luis and Miranda truly had earned their four stars.

Afternoons Isabelle spent with Miranda at Enchantments, catching up, talking about life in Santa Fe, Tía Flora and Alejandro, Isabelle's run-ins with Nina, the budding romance between Skye and Sam Hoffman, Rebecca's first child, Jonas and Sybil, the changing patterns of the art world, the increased popularity of craft, everything except Philip and Julian.

Julian called three times a day. After a series of awkward conversations, he surprised her with a visit. When Isabelle showed him to his room, he hinted that he'd prefer staying at her casita.

"I came here to be with you, not to visit the state capital."

"I understand that and I'm delighted to see you, but I think this is a better arrangement."

"Better for whom? Philip Medina?"

Isabelle's hazel eyes crackled as she reacted to Julian's jab. "He has nothing to do with us."

"Us? What an interesting concept," Julian said with deliberate sarcasm, hoping to bait her into an argument. He wanted to know about her stay in Majorca, her involvement with Medina. "Tell me, Isabelle, can there ever be an us? Was there ever an us?"

She faced him squarely. She knew this game and had decided not to play. "No. Not in the way you mean."

Julian bristled at the rejection. Still, he plodded on.

"I don't understand why. We had been so good together," he said. He took her hands in his, raised one to his lips, and bussed it softly.

Isabelle's response was a suspicious smile, one a child might have offered a parent who, in trying to warn away further disobedience, had wrapped guilt and menace around the innocuous question "Are you going to be my good little girl?" Her body language was even less receptive. She retracted her hands and stepped back.

Her rebuff felt like a slap, but Julian still refused to retreat. Instead, in a last-ditch effort to restore harmony, he returned to one of his favorite roles, that of the caretaker.

"Tell me what you need," he said expansively. "I'll get it or do it or make it! Whatever you want. Just tell me."

Isabelle saw the trap being laid. He would give, she would take, she would owe. "Right now," she said, adroitly sidestepping his heavily laden generosity, "I need to paint. And to do that, I need space."

Julian's eyes widened with respect. By raising the flag of her art, their one sure common denominator, she had given him no choice but to accede to her wishes.

"Then space it is," he said, bowing gallantly.

After a few moments of clumsy, meaningless chatter, Isabelle suggested he rest while she completed some chores. They would meet again at dinner.

Julian agreed, walked her to the door, and for the moment, at least, let her go.

He stayed for three days. Isabelle tried not to make the inevitable comparisons, but watching Julian with Miranda and Luis prompted memories of Philip and Tía Flora. Where Philip had been open and accepting, dealing with Flora's directness with good humor and tolerance, Julian's attitude toward the Durans and their friends was one of blanketed condescension. It wasn't that he disliked any of them, it was simply that he seemed unable to adapt to any changes in his environment.

He was a Manhattan man and behaved as if he had been kidnapped and was being held hostage in the burgs of New Mexico. He was used to deciding between a Margaux and a Médoc. Here his choices were margaritas or sangria. Instead of smoked salmon and delicately sauced veal, he was served nachos and chicken flavored with peppers and cilantro. Instead of Bobby Short and Karen Akers, the prevalent sound was Randy Travis and the Judds. Julian was a fish in the desert. When he left, everyone breathed a sigh of relief.

Julian's departure increased Isabelle's awareness that she hadn't heard from Philip in nearly a month. While she dismissed her moodiness as stress, Miranda knew better. One night after dinner she came to the Paint Box and found Isabelle alone in her studio, staring at a blank canvas spread out on the floor in front of her. She handed Isabelle a steaming cup of herbal tea spiked with a cinnamon stick, found a vacant spot on which to sit, and said bluntly, "Tell me about Philip Medina."

It was as if Isabelle had been waiting for a button to be pushed. She poured out her heart, confiding how wonderful their weekend together had been, her ambivalence about making any kind of a commitment, her frustration with Julian, her seeming inability to let go of one phase of her life and move on to another. Miranda advised Isabelle to put her career on hold and take the time to explore her feelings for Philip.

Isabelle's shoulders slumped with rejection. "Even if I wanted to do that, I haven't heard from him since I left Majorca." Her eyes glowed for a moment, stoked by warm, fulfilling memories, then faded as the emptiness of the present reasserted itself. "Maybe I misinterpreted everything. Maybe it was a fling and nothing more."

Miranda had no way of knowing whether Isabelle was right or wrong. Neither was she certain that it was wise for her to side with a man she'd never met, but when Isabelle had arrived in Santa Fe, she had been cloaked in a mood of such contentment, it was hard for Miranda to think ill of Philip Medina.

"Maybe he thinks you're too locked in to Julian and is giving you time to make a choice."

"What choice? Philip isn't a dealer. And Julian isn't my lover. Why must I choose between them?"

"Because Julian is not the type to share you with anyone."

"That's what Philip said." Isabelle's voice was quiet.

"Smart man." Miranda felt reassured. Medina's instincts matched hers. "Do you love him?"

"I don't know." Isabelle's words described uncertainty. Her face, flushed pink with enchantment, expressed another opinion. Suddenly her features stiffened. "Even if I do, that has nothing to do with my career. Julian made me famous."

"So what?" Miranda didn't like the robotic cadence of Isabelle's speech. "You can always find someone to sell your paintings. You can't always find someone to fill your heart."

"Julian's the best in the business."

"That was important in the beginning. You're established now."

Isabelle shook her head. Miranda sounded just like Skye. She looked as if she wanted to cover her ears with her hands.

Miranda persisted. "You're the talent, Isabelle. Julian's a dealer. You're a rarity. He's one of many."

"I can't leave him! It would be a terrible betrayal." She was agitated, edgy. Her tone said she wanted the conversation ended.

"Why?" Miranda said. Isabelle looked away. "Because it would be like leaving your father?"

Isabelle, visibly rattled, spun around to face Miranda. She argued about this with Skye all the time. "Maybe." Her voice was a whisper of surrender.

"Don't confuse Julian with Martín," Miranda said, treading lightly. "And don't beat yourself with an old stick. You didn't leave Martín, he sent you to us. And even if you had stayed, you couldn't have changed the course of history."

Isabelle may have acknowledged Miranda's assessment with an assenting nod, but her retreat into a reflective silence said something Miranda had always suspected—Isabelle would never fully accept the mantle of complete innocence; she would always believe she could have helped her father.

"Philip is ten years older than I am," she said after a while. It sounded like an idle statement, but really it was a summary of questions Isabelle was asking herself: Was she always going to be looking for a replacement for

Martín? Was she defending her dependency on Julian? Or was she making the same mistake all over again?

"It's not age we're talking about, Isabelle, it's attitude." Miranda decided to counter Isabelle's vacillation with frankness. "Julian Richter wants to keep you permanently under his thumb. That's not paternal caring or even romantic love; it's possession."

"How do I know Philip isn't more of the same?"

Miranda smiled at the lovely woman she thought of as her daughter. "I suspect your head has told you already that he's different, from Julian and every other man you've known. If your heart needs reassurance, okay, but remember, that takes time."

While Isabelle spent her nights grappling with emotions, her days were devoted to painting. Despite the continued silence from Philip, her conversation with Miranda had served as a potent cleanser, enabling her to produce work that exhilarated. Each painting was a glorious recollection of the scenic splendor of the villa by the bay, each a passionate tribute to the man inside the villa. Whether she saw him again or not, the velvet shawl of security in which Philip had wrapped her during her stay in Majorca had had a profound influence.

Where once she had refused to use blue, now she appeared unable to use anything else. Cobalt, royal, gentian, azure, sky, sea, lapis, indigo. Blue became her elected language of expression, each variation in tone a syllabic point of emphasis, each shading an accent. It bled through the pores of the canvas and created a field. Brushed, stroked, daubed, or washed, it probed Isabelle's incessant romance with nature as well as her infatuation with Philip.

In the past, Isabelle's landscapes had been painted from a spiritual perch. She had viewed the world from an awed distance, so far away that reality blurred. Being with Philip had inspired her to confront her subjects and the feelings they aroused, to burrow deeper into her being in search of a core. Instead of being the detached observer, she became intricately involved, eliminating outlines and magnifying visions until they pressed so hard against one's consciousness, they pounded.

In one painting Isabelle plunged headlong into an implosive blue so intense and brilliant, it felt like the center of a Kashmiri sapphire. Against a cobalt ground, a cornflower blue flame raged, challenging the viewer to think about whatever or whoever they associated with blue.

In another she immersed herself in a sensuous bath of turquoise and ultramarine. Without boundaries to define its shores, the water became measureless, evoking the sensation of suspension, of floating on an aqueous rainbow of shimmering color.

Another vision dove deeper, hazarding bottom. Without light, the spectrum darkened. Navy and steel hinted at shadows and craggy rock. Lapis and smoke presented obstacles and hurdles. Here there were no soft tones, no light bubbles rising to a surface blessed with the yellow of the sun. Here were only stark reminders of the inescapable depth of one's reality.

From the bay Isabelle moved to the heavens, painting the Majorcan sky at dawn, at dusk, midday, late afternoon, zooming in on a cloud, an incoming storm, a rainbow, a sunset, each study a profound paean to the chorus of color that accompanied the earth's rotation.

While all the paintings were spectacular, the most powerful was *Blue Moon,* the nightscape she had started on Philip's terrace. It was the one she intended to keep for herself, perhaps someday to give to Philip.

Entitled "Visions in Blue," this series, Isabelle was convinced, was her best work ever.

In September she returned to New York and displayed the paintings for Richter. She had expected Julian's reaction to be nothing short of euphoria. Instead he ripped them apart, calling them commercial wall hangings, van Gogh wannabes, and so forth. Isabelle was stunned. She reeled from the cruelty of Julian's commentary and then shot back, accusing him of being vengeful and striking back because she continued to refuse to share his bed.

"My personal access to your body is not the issue. My opinion concerning this body of work is." He looked at the paintings as if they exuded a noxious odor. "Under no circumstances will I exhibit them."

Unnerved, yet prodded by pride, Isabelle stood firm, refusing to avert her eyes, meeting his anger with equal rage. "If you refuse to show these paintings, I'll bring them to a dealer who will."

"You can't." Julian's eyes glossed with victory. "In case you've forgotten, we have a contract. *I* own these paintings. I own everything you've done or ever will do. And that, my darling Isabelle, makes me the one with the power to decide what is salable."

"Don't do this, Julian." At that moment she loathed him. "Either show 'Visions in Blue' or give them back to me."

"I won't show them and I won't return them."

"Why not?" Isabelle was practically screaming. "If you don't want them, why not let someone else exhibit them?"

"Because I have too much invested in you, and they could devalue the rest of your work," he said with a snort of utter disgust. "They're that bad."

For weeks after their showdown, Isabelle wrestled with a hydra of fury. If her anger at Julian quieted, frustration over her contract surfaced. If she stilled her anxieties over the reach of Julian's control, doubts about the quality of her work eddied. If she wasn't fantasizing about extracting vengeance on him, she was beating up on herself for signing such a self-destructive document.

Not only did Isabelle feel that she had been completely inept in the way she'd handled the business aspect of her career, but her sense of artistic worth had been tied to Julian's approval for so long, his venal criticism crippled her creatively. She felt incapable of painting or even sketching. To make matters worse, in November Julian mounted a de Luna show of odd pieces, paintings taken from different series, having no connection, no message other than artistic disarray. It was a show designed to humiliate her. And it did.

Skye tried to console her. "He can't ruin you. You're too good."

"Read my reviews." Isabelle tossed a stack of newspaper clippings onto the table between them. "Jed Perl is wondering whether I've lost my direction. *The New York Times* thinks I've let my former successes go to my head. *The Washington Post* has decided I was a nova, shining brightly for an instant, then fading." She looked at Skye, her hazel eyes dimmed, her face lined with the pain of what she perceived as failure. "He may not have ruined me, but he sure managed to kick the shit out of me."

Skye soothed her friend as best she could. "I've been keeping my ear pretty close to the ground. From what I hear, most of the cognoscenti have guessed that this show was some kind of gotcha!"

Isabelle looked confused.

"It happens all the time. You had a fight. He gets pissed off and mounts a 'fuck you' show. Forget it, Isabelle. It's a crack in the sidewalk, not a cavern."

Isabelle remained unconvinced.

One evening three weeks later, Isabelle opened the door of her loft and found Philip Medina standing there. A picture of sartorial splendor, he was wearing a cashmere coat, a tweed sport jacket and slacks, and a silk shirt.

She looked disheveled, her hair in an undisciplined ponytail, her face and hands dotted with paint, her sweatsuit so splattered, it looked as if it had been designed by Jackson Pollock.

"Am I too late for dinner?" he asked as if they had spoken that morning.

"About six months."

He inclined his head and tapped his index finger against his lips. "It must be cold by now."

"Very cold."

"Hmm. I was afraid of that."

He stepped aside and stretched his arm in front of Isabelle, compelling her to do the same. At the snap of his fingers, a staff of three paraded into her apartment; set up a table and chairs, complete with silver, crystal, napery, and flowers; laid out an elegant buffet on her kitchen counter; placed a California Fumé Blanc in a silver ice bucket; slipped a disk of Pablo Casals performing Bach in her stereo; and left.

Philip walked over to the counter and lifted the tops of the silver chafing dishes, letting out puffs of steam. "See? Everything's nice and hot."

"Including me." She was trying to convey her vexation via a glare. Judging by the curl of his lips, she decided it wasn't very effective. "I'm angry with you, Philip."

He nodded. "I know. You have every right to be."

"Well, thanks so much."

"You're welcome." He opened the bottle of wine, poured some into a glass, sipped, and smacked his lips. "Superb! Care for some?"

Isabelle planted her hands on her lips. Her face flamed with pique. "No! What I want is an explanation."

"The food's getting cold."

"Now!"

Despite her refusal, he handed her a glass of wine, encouraged her to sit, and took the chair opposite her. "I told you in Majorca, Isabelle, you make me crazy. You affect me in ways no one ever has before." He laughed at himself. "I've never been at a loss for words, but when you left, I didn't know what to say. I must have picked up the phone a hundred times."

"Funny," she said, fighting the tidal pull of his eyes. "Not one of those calls got through."

"I was a jerk. I admit it. I just couldn't get past the fact that Julian whistled and you ran."

"I did not run! I had a commitment to fulfill. I thought you understood that."

"Honestly? I thought I did, too, but somewhere in the back of my brain, I saw your leaving as confirmation of a commitment to Julian Richter, not to the Julian Richter Gallery."

"You saw it wrong."

The hostility in her voice confused him. Was she angry with him for making things difficult between her and Julian? Or was she angry with Julian for interfering with them? In fact, he never had been certain exactly what Isabelle's relationship with Julian was. He had accepted what Julian had told him after the *Pandora's Box* piece—that they were lovers and had planned to marry—because he had had no reason not to. Thinking about it now, he realized, Isabelle had never said anything that confirmed it.

Opting to let the matter lie, he reached across the table for her hand. She let him take it. It felt so good to have him touch her.

"I heard what happened," he said. Her face paled. "In fact, I went to see the show."

Tears welled in Isabelle's eyes, but she fought them back. She hated the feeling of defeat that washed over her every time she thought about that debacle.

"I should have been there for you."

"Why weren't you?"

He held up his hands and sighed, reflecting his own stupefaction. "Ego? Jealousy? An honest decision to let you decide the fate of your relationship with Richter without any complications from me? I don't know."

He couldn't stand the hurt in her eyes, more, the thought that he had helped put it there. The lines on his forehead creased. His mouth hardened. "Had I known Julian would respond so cruelly, I never would have let you deal with him alone."

"What difference could you have made? He hated the series and refused to show it."

"Perhaps I could have persuaded him to take another look."

"Julian doesn't believe in second opinions. His word is final."

"Not always."

There was an unmistakable edge to Philip's tone. Isabelle was intrigued. When she asked him to elaborate, he danced around the question. She sensed he was holding back.

"That's enough about Julian," he said suddenly, slapping his hands on the table for emphasis. "Let's get back to us. I've admitted to being a heartless cad. I've apologized. I've brought a three-course bribe. Can I please be forgiven? Or do I have to run down to the car and get my hairshirt?"

Isabelle granted him the faintest of smiles. "No hairshirt. The last thing I need is for you to shed on my paintings."

"Nothing like a practical woman to put a damper on a man's romantic enthusiasms."

Philip sighed. Isabelle shrugged. Philip stroked his chin. Suddenly his face brightened. He wiggled his eyebrows and leered at her suggestively.

"There must be something I can do to earn Her Ladyship's forgiveness."

Isabelle stifled a grin, turned imperious, and handed him her plate. "You can serve dinner before it gets cold. Again!"

By tacit agreement Isabelle and Philip conducted their courtship slowly and privately. Rather than dining at Le Cirque or La Côte Basque, where they would be chewed up quicker than the plat du jour, they ate downtown in restaurants where the uniform was black, the lights were dim, and the talk was sotto voce. Though occasionally she ran into other artists at these haunts, after a quick hello and a sympathetic look, it was over. They understood. She was down. They were up. Next week it could be reversed. None would cast a stone.

Skye was elated to hear about Isabelle's romance with Philip. After a terrific evening of takeout Italian and too much red wine, Skye and Sam declared Philip eminently suitable. Thereafter Skye arranged a couple of other dinners, a Sunday afternoon jaunt through the Museum of Modern Art, a bagels-and-lox brunch at her apartment.

Believing she would be backed up by both Sam and Philip, Skye continued to plug her boss, Glimcher, repeating his desire to represent Isabelle. When that didn't garner a positive response, she mentioned others—Boone, Emmerich, Cooper, Reed, even Castelli. Isabelle insisted she wasn't ready to make another commitment.

"Besides," she reminded them, "I have to get out of my contract with Julian before I can negotiate with anyone else."

Right before Christmas, Philip invited Isabelle to attend a special opening at Greta Reed's gallery.

"No way."

"The worst thing you can do is hide," he said. "This show is being touted as the event of the gallery season. Everyone will be there. You should be, too."

He handed her the invitation, entitled "Art and Soul: The Unveiling of a Genius." She studied it and rejected it. "It sounds like a circus. I'm not in the mood for clowns."

"You'll be with me. No one will hurt you."

Isabelle recoiled. Julian had said almost the same thing to her once. Philip continued to insist that by not going she was handing Richter an uncontested victory.

"The first time I ever saw you, you put Julian Richter in his place without breaking a sweat. And in case you've forgotten, you weren't exactly shy about telling me where to get off. Since when are you the retiring violet type?"

She shook her head, clearly as confused as he. "You're right. It's not my style, but he got to me. That show got to me."

"So you've been beaten up." Philip put his arm around her. She leaned against him. "You come from tough stock. I know. I've met the indomitable Flora Pujol!"

Isabelle chuckled. "I should send her in against Julian."

Philip turned her around so that she faced him. With his hands firmly on her shoulders and his expression stony, he said, "You don't need anyone to fight your battles for you, Isabelle." She looked uncertain. He softened. "If, however, you'd like someone in your corner, I'm ready. Just say the word."

Isabelle disengaged herself from him and paced, weighing her options. She balanced one down against her many ups, a bruised ego against a career revival, a victory for Julian versus a victory for herself. Recalling Julian's arrogance, revisiting the triumph in his eyes as he'd punctured her dignity, the satisfaction in his voice as he'd demeaned her work, she felt something stir deep inside her. Pride began to bubble and rise. Anger redirected itself out instead of in. She didn't need anyone to tell her she had talent. She didn't need anyone to inspire her to paint. She had been born an artist. And yes, she came from tough stock.

"Let's do it!" she said, startling Philip with her enthusiasm.

As they toasted her decision, Philip grinned. She was beginning to trust him. He was beginning to believe they had a future.

The Reed Gallery on Spring Street in SoHo was jammed with press, collectors, art groupies, and anyone who was anything in the New York art world. Despite the December cold, the crowd had spilled out onto the street, making it feel more like a holiday open house than an art opening. Spectators gathered across the street to gawk at the beautiful people and play "find the celebrity." Steve Martin, a funny man with a serious art collection, was there, as were Robert De Niro, Joan Rivers, Mary Tyler Moore, Calvin Klein, and, according to rumor, Madonna.

As Isabelle and Philip stepped out of their taxi, Isabelle spotted Julian standing in front of the window to the gallery—assuring himself of a flattering backlit photograph—talking to someone from *ARTnews.* She was grateful his back was turned. She would deal with him, but later was better than sooner. Philip held her arm as they jockeyed their way into the entry, a relatively small space created by two three-quarter walls meant to separate the street from the show. To one side, Isabelle noticed a crowd gathered around Cody Jackson. He was being interviewed by the art critic of *The New York Times.*

"What's he doing here?" she said, more to herself than Philip. "And why is he being interviewed by *The Times?*"

"Who is he?"

"Someone I used to know. An artist. I saw him in Paris. He was crying about what a failure he was."

"He must have succeeded at something," Philip said, concerned about the look on Isabelle's face.

This man's presence was bothering her. Suddenly it bothered him, too. Why would *The Times* care what a down-and-out artist had to say? Unless he was saying something scandalous about someone better known? Instinct warned Philip to take Isabelle and leave, but it was too late. The crush pushed them forward, into the large rectangular vastness that was the main room of the gallery.

At first Isabelle didn't fully absorb what she was seeing. On the two long walls facing each other were six nudes that looked hauntingly familiar. Filling the short wall that centered the room was *Blue Moon,* its cyanine brilliance illuminated by a series of spotlights. It looked spectacular, and for a moment Isabelle forgot herself and simply reveled in the sight of it. She was too preoccupied to notice that the huge crowd had ebbed, pushing everyone, including Philip, out of the way to make room for celebrity reporter Nina Davis and her crew.

Finding a camera pressed close to her nose, a microphone shoved under her mouth, and flashbulbs blinding her eyes, Isabelle felt trapped and helpless.

"Ladies and gentlemen," Nina said, speaking to the camera, "Isabelle de Luna, artist and artist's model."

She turned back to Isabelle, her eyes those of a predator. "How does it feel to see yourself so literally exposed?" she asked, watching Isabelle cower in the glare of the spotlight.

When Isabelle didn't answer, Nina directed the camera to pan the nudes and then continued.

"Cody Jackson told us that when you two met at the Art Students League, you hated drawing nudes, that it embarrassed you. I guess that depends which side of the easel you're sitting on." She laughed. A few in the audience joined her.

Julian Richter stood near the back, his arms folded across his chest nonchalantly, his face blank as he watched the public flaying of Isabelle de Luna. Only if one got close enough to look past the mask into his eyes would his glee be noticeable. Philip got that close.

"How could you?" he said, deliberately standing in front of the smaller man to block his view. "This is low, Julian, even for you."

"I don't know what you're talking about." Julian stepped to the side, but Philip parried. "This isn't my gallery. Cody Jackson isn't my artist. And frankly, this is none of your business."

"I think it is."

Julian laughed. It was a mean sound, one of unmistakable contempt. "Why, because you're fucking her?"

Philip lunged for Julian's neck, then stopped himself. "No," he said, leaning down so his face was only inches from his adversary. "Because you fucked me!"

Julian's face flushed crimson. He was fuming. He didn't like being threatened, particularly by someone who could hurt him.

"We had an agreement," Philip said. "You didn't stick to it. Yet you're holding Isabelle to some bullshit contract she probably signed under duress."

"The difference, my friend, is that a contract is binding by law. A gentleman's agreement is only binding if the two parties involved are gentlemen. I'm not. And neither are you." With that he slithered away, like a snake in the grass.

Cody Jackson had mixed feelings about what was happening. He was riding the crest of an unprecedented high. He had been interviewed and photographed and filmed until he was growing tired of his own biography. His paintings were hanging in one of New York's hottest galleries, creating news. His name would be in bold type in the morning columns. But so would Isabelle's. She was the other half of this golden coin, but she would be tarnished, the subject of a seamy scandal, disgraced and dishonored because of his naiveté. Cody honestly felt bad about that. Isabelle had never done anything to warrant an act of vengeance, which was how he suspected she viewed this. He would have liked to explain it to her, to tell her it wasn't the way it looked, that he hadn't intended to use their past to bring her down like this. Judging by the mortification he read in her face, however, he doubted she'd ever forgive him.

This wasn't the way it was supposed to be. Nina had told him she thought he was an astounding artist, one whose talent obviously had slipped through the cracks and deserved to see the light of day. After they had made love, she had encouraged him to talk about his dreams, baring his ambition with the same finesse she had used to remove his clothes. Pretending sympathy, she had promised to help him, to set it up so he could return to the States a hero instead of a goat. Her suggestion, which had seemed to come to her out of the blue, had been to gather the entire "Shy Temptress" series and mount that as his first show. She had assured him of a good gallery connection and quality representation, national coverage and critical exposure. She never said a word about Isabelle.

The day before, when he had come to the gallery and realized what this exhibition was all about, he'd confronted Nina. She'd shown a different face from the one that had looked up at him from beneath his sheets. Then it had been soft and pliant, eager to please and be pleased. Yesterday it had been flinty and impassive, impervious to anything as childish as second thoughts or guilt feelings.

"Should I tell Greta to take down the show?" she had said. "Would that make you happy? Do you want to crawl back to your sleazy garret and return to being a nothing? Or do you want to be a someone? It's up to you."

Cody never professed to be noble. He never claimed to be altruistic or selfless. He was a country boy who all his life had hungered for one thing: recognition as an artist. Nina offered that to him. And he took it.

"According to reviews, your last show at the Richter Gallery was a disaster," Nina said, furrowing her brow, trying to look as if she weren't enjoying this. "Do you have a comment?"

Isabelle's ability to absorb abuse had reached its limit. Looking straight at Julian, who was peering at her from the second row, she said, "It was a poorly mounted, extremely amateurish exhibition, done without my knowledge or my consent. As was this carnival." She directed her next words to Nina. "Frankly, I'm surprised at Greta Reed. She doesn't usually allow herself to be suckered."

Greta, who was standing near enough to hear Nina's interview, was not happy. She thought she had conceived a brilliant show, one that would honor both the talent and the woman who was Isabelle de Luna. It was to be the kickoff for a year of homage to women artists. Instead it was turning into something that approximated a mud-wrestling match.

Why, she asked herself, hadn't she trusted her instincts and tossed out Nina Davis on her designer-clad butt?

When Nina had brought in the slides of Jackson's nudes, Greta hadn't been terribly impressed. They were lovely; he had a fine hand and a lush eroticism that reminded her of Courbet. But her gallery didn't cater to that audience. Her clients would find Jackson's temptresses too derivative, too clichéd, too mainstream. She had been prepared to reject the series when suddenly she was gifted with the opportunity to take possession of Isabelle's "Visions in Blue." It was then that the notion of the dual show came to her. Until this very minute when she heard Isabelle accuse her of being suckered, she had believed the idea had been her own, and quite original at that. Now she was forced to wonder.

Isabelle had had enough. She called an end to the interview by simply walking away. Nina remained unfazed. Standing alone, surrounded by an audience eager for a big finish, she splayed her hand, drawing attention to the paintings. The camera panned the nudes slowly, like a voyeur reluctant to look away. Finally it came to rest on *Blue Moon.*

"This show is a portrait of an exceptional painter: Isabelle de Luna. Acknowledged as one of the few stars in the contemporary field, she has managed to remain a mystery, until now. Tonight, through her work and the work of Cody Jackson, both her body and her soul have been bared. Thanks to Greta Reed, who had the courage to unveil a myth, we've been shown what de Luna wants us to see . . . and what she doesn't.

"She's a paradox, this Isabelle de Luna. A woman who hated nude drawing class and then eagerly posed nude for her lover. A woman who expressed her gratitude to the man who discovered her and nurtured her by accusing him of selling her out. A woman who asserts her independence to everyone except the man she allowed to buy her." She counted to ten, allowing the impact of the explosion to subside. "Stay tuned for interviews with the three most important men in Isabelle de Luna's life."

Nina ran her finger in front of her neck, signaling her cameraman to cut tape. Handing the mike to her assistant, she was positively aglow. When Isabelle grabbed her arm and pulled her to the side, Nina was momentarily stunned.

"Let go of me," she commanded, tugging unsuccessfully against Isabelle's grip.

"What did you mean about a man who bought me?"

Nina had been waiting all night for this. "You mean you don't know?"

"Know what?" Isabelle demanded.

"Julian Richter hasn't been paying your little monthly stipend all these years. Philip Medina has. I don't know if the man loves you, but one thing's for sure, sweetheart, he owns you."

Isabelle's mouth fell open. She released her grip on Nina's arm. "You're lying!"

"Wouldn't you like to think so."

"Where would you hear something like this?"

"Philip told me." Actually Julian had told her. "He and I have a history, you know." She watched as Isabelle turned ashen. "Oh, dear. Obviously you didn't know that, either." She clucked her tongue in sympathy. "We met years ago. In fact, Philip gave me my first break." She smiled as if remembering a treasured moment. "To be perfectly honest, we were attracted immediately and became close, close friends. We worked together and dined together and went to premieres together and . . . well, did lots of scrumptious things together—if you catch my drift."

She positively savored Isabelle's devastation, but it wasn't complete enough.

"Our *amour de coeur* isn't quite as intense now, but even a little of the best is better than nothing at all. Wouldn't you agree?"

"I—I don't believe you," Isabelle stammered, fighting back tears.

Ah, but you do, Nina thought delightedly.

"Whether you do or you don't is of no concern to me," she said aloud. "I know what I know."

Having accomplished all that she wanted, Nina flashed a triumphant grin at her victim, tossed her hair, straightened her shoulders, and sashayed into the crowd to interview Julian and Greta Reed and the glittering array of celebrities who were simply buzzing about the public humbling of Isabelle de Luna.

When Philip got to Isabelle, she was in a corner, alone, numb, and bewildered. Her face was chalky. Her mouth was slack. Her eyes appeared vacant, as if the shell were in place but the instruments of sight were looking elsewhere. He assumed it was the overall trauma of the evening she was reacting to, nothing specific, certainly nothing concerning them. When she confronted him with what Nina had said, his heart thundered to his feet.

"Nothing is the way she made it sound."

He attempted to lead her to the door, to take her home, where they could discuss this quietly. She refused to move.

"Then how is it? Did you date her or didn't you?"

"Occasionally, but . . ."

Images of Philip in bed with Nina assaulted Isabelle. Sickened by the sight, she blinked them away. "Did you buy me or didn't you?"

"Please stop using that phrase."

"Why? Does it bother you?"

"Of course it bothers me, because it's not true. Nina used it because it's explosive. It creates headlines."

"Then you haven't been funding my living expenses."

Philip shifted his weight from one foot to another. If only he could shift responsibility as easily.

"From the first time I saw your work, I thought you were brilliant. You know that. I bought a charcoal. The one that hangs in my bedroom. Remember?" No response, just large hazel eyes that stared at him in a way that made him sweat. "I told you I've often acted as a patron to new artists. After I bought the charcoal, Richter came to me and asked if I would be willing to help launch you. I was."

"Why didn't you tell me this yourself?"

"I would have, eventually."

Isabelle nodded, her expression openly doubtful. "You had a problem telling me, but no problem telling Nina."

"I didn't tell Nina anything about you. She's lying."

"She's lying, but what she said is true."

Isabelle wanted to ask when they had discussed her: over dinner, in bed, before or after they made love? Suddenly a thought intruded.

"Is this why you thought you could persuade Julian to take another look at 'Visions in Blue'? Because he had taken your money?"

Philip's silence was an uncomfortable one because it was an admission.

"In Majorca, were you angry that Julian was acting as if he owned me because *you* owned me?"

"Don't knock this whole thing out of shape, Isabelle. Yes, I paid your expenses in exchange for your work. I've done it with other artists I believed in. It's what being a patron is all about."

"I thought we were lovers. Now you tell me we're simply artist and patron."

"That's not what I—"

She held up her hand. Her face had blanked. She had shut him out. He could see it; worse, he could feel it.

"I thank you for your support," she said woodenly, coldly, "but I'm self-supporting now. I don't need your money. And I don't need you."

She started for the door, but when she saw Greta Reed, she took a sharp detour. Without polite niceties or preamble, she broke into the circle around the dealer, shooed everyone away, and demanded to know where Reed had gotten the nudes and how she had gotten her hands on *Blue Moon*.

Greta, conscious of the press, kept her voice low and controlled. "Someone brokered the nudes and suggested that they might make an interesting show. As for *Blue Moon*, I obtained it and several other paintings from the 'Visions in Blue' series in lieu of payment on a debt."

For Isabelle, confusion momentarily replaced rage. "What debt does Julian Richter owe you?"

Greta wanted to laugh. No one would ever know the extent of his obligation. "I'm Julian's partner in the Richter Gallery. Silent, but substantial. It's my money that gave him his start and my money that bails him out whenever he takes one flier too many."

"He told me he hated those paintings."

"Julian's a liar as well as an inept businessman. They're wonderful, darling. You know that. And I know that. Fortunately for me, Julian's male ego had been sufficiently trampled by you, so that when I demanded he pay off several of his overdue notes, I was able to barter the paintings instead."

Something was missing from this equation. Isabelle could feel a gap between Greta's explanation and what was logical.

"I understand bartering paintings. It's done all the time. What I don't get is why you stick with Julian if he's such a bad risk."

"It's simple," Greta said, knowing it wasn't simple at all. "He's my husband."

CHAPTER 20

It was true, Nina decided. Vengeance was sweet. In Paris, when she'd asked Isabelle for an exclusive, that self-righteous, self-styled O'Keeffe had dismissed her like a piece of trash. Simple gossip columnist indeed! Now she knew how much power Nina had, how canny she was. Perhaps now the bitch would show her the proper respect.

As Nina reviewed the tape in Greta's office before it was taken to the studio for the eleven o'clock news, she couldn't help gloating. Finally the planets had aligned. Her universe was in order. She was on top. Isabelle was somewhere else.

The night had not been perfect, however. There had been one or two bad moments, like when that Skye person had threatened her.

"I know who you are and what you're hiding," she had said, that wild mane of curly hair adding to her menace. "Either you erase Isabelle de Luna from your personal hit list, or I'll have to feed your competitors some personal data on you."

Nina had scoffed, turning up her nose and terminating the conversation with a patronizing wave of her hand, but she took the threat seriously; it would be foolish not to. Later, when she'd had time to reflect on what Skye had said and analyze the possibility, she concluded that Skye would never go public without Isabelle's permission. And whatever their differences, Isabelle was too devoted to Miranda and Luis to allow them to be dragged through the press.

The other nasty moment had been a brief run-in with Philip Medina. More accurately, a snub. He was leaving, she was heading for Greta's office. They nearly collided. Uncertain as to how much Isabelle had told him, and finding it impossible to avoid him, she simply smiled. The ice in his stare erased it immediately. Without even acknowledging her presence, he swept past her, leaving her to wonder whether she had shot herself in the foot or between the eyes.

As she headed home in a taxi, she cleared her mind of such nettlesome trivia and concentrated on what waited for her at the end of the ride. In anticipation of her victory, she had arranged an après-opening supper at her apartment. Arriving less than thirty minutes before her guests, she ran through a quick check of the floral arrangements and the organization of the buffet table. She instructed the help about how she wanted the service to proceed, which guests needed their alcohol intake monitored, and what music to provide as background, including what decibel level to keep it at and when to shut it off. Then they were to make certain all her candles were lit, her cushions were fluffed, and her silver picture frames were immaculately polished.

Retreating to her bedroom for a swift change of costume, she scanned the apartment, congratulating herself on its quiet elegance. When Jodi Cutler had lived here, it had been dark and drab, not unlike its occupant. In little more than six months Nina had effected a complete metamorphosis. One would never know that the woman who lived here was not to the manner born.

Gone were the heavy woods and dark fabrications, the beefy chairs and thick cloistral drapery. Everything was creamy, light, and feminine without being frothy, much like Nina: vanilla walls and blond wood, low-pile Berber carpet and delicately gilded consoles, ivory linens and pearl white marble. The few antiques she had acquired over the years—those she counted as her inheritance—fit in nicely: a painted *fauteuil en cabriolet* freshly upholstered in a bone and beige stripe, a bureau plat that held an array of personal photographs, a few small end tables, a bedroom armoire and pier glass. Over the fireplace hung the portrait of her mythical parents, the one she had bought in the Village the day she'd arrived in New York. Old pen-and-ink drawings framed in gold tattooed the walls in the living room. In the den, her collection of black-and-white photographs dominated, shaking the stillness of the overwhelmingly pristine decor.

Racing into her dressing room, tearing into one of her closets, she smiled, recalling the evening Anthony had offered her this place. It was shortly after they had returned from Paris. (The wanton—yet profitable—night she had spent with Cody Jackson had indeed sparked Anthony's jealousy. He had been waiting in her hotel room when she returned the next morning. Obviously her no-show had been a turn-on.) They had been at her old apartment getting ready for a charity dinner. Anthony, still wet and excited from their shower together, had wanted to watch Nina dry off. It titillated him to see her towel her body, dabbing places he had just visited, pressing against flesh he had just savaged. But her bathroom was too small for such indulgences. Annoyed, he went to the bedroom closet, where he kept a few suits. He removed a navy blue Armani from the hanger and was about to lay it on the bed when he sniffed a faint floral scent. He thought Nina had sneaked up behind him. She hadn't. He thought it was her potpourri or a fragrance candle. It wasn't. Then he lifted his jacket to his face, and his nose affirmed what he had feared. His clothes smelled like a Victorian sachet.

"That does it!" he said, slamming closet doors, thundering between the bedroom and the bathroom. "This place is too damn small!"

Not only did Nina agree, but she already had an alternative in mind. Jodi Cutler had moved out of the Sixty-sixth Street apartment right after the scandal; it had been vacant ever since. To Anthony the solution felt easy and immediate. To Nina it seemed just. And to make sure she didn't repeat Jodi's mistakes, she had her lawyer draw up a two-year sublet agreement.

"If we have a bad night in bed," she had told him, "I don't want to wake up the next morning in the street."

Now she had a marble bath and an honest-to-goodness dressing room with mirrored closets (Anthony had two of his own in the bedroom), a vanity table, and a chandelier. Built-in shelves housed her collections of perfume flacons, silver boxes, and fans, the centerpiece the one Althea de Luna had given her. An orchid plant in a celadon bowl garnished a bureau. Next to it was a lead-glass box to hold her Chanel chains and earrings, and a scallop-edged crystal dish overflowed with her favorite Agraria potpourri.

Normally Nina took her time dressing. She enjoyed savoring her surroundings, but tonight she was late. Hurrying, she refreshed her makeup and perfume, slid her legs into a pair of black silk pants, topped them with a black chiffon peasant blouse, and stepped into high, sling-back heels. With practiced fingers she twisted her hair up into a rakish topknot and secured it with pins. Pulling here and there, she freed a few tendrils to languish alongside her face and atop her shoulders. Around her neck she fastened a five-strand antique choker of pearls she claimed had been left by her mother. She had haunted a downtown shop noted for estate jewelry for months until she'd found the right piece. Assessing it in the mirror, she tilted her head and nodded. Yes, it looked like something Leslie Walker Davis, may she rest in peace, would have bequeathed to her beloved daughter.

As she greeted her guests, Nina struggled to suppress her delirium. Filing past her were people with bold-faced cachet: Isabella Rossellini; Blaine and Robert Trump; Greta Reed; Phil Donahue and Marlo Thomas; Susan Lucci; Dominick Dunne; Duane and Mark Hampton (the designer behind her soigné apartment); Clive Frommer and his *amour du jour*; Joan Lunden; Regis and Joy Philbin. In a corner near the bar stood her devastatingly handsome inamorata, Anthony Hartwick, deeply engrossed in a conversation with Julian Richter. Her guest of honor, Cody Jackson, was being swarmed by the couture-gowned, coiffure-lacquered, surgically enhanced social bees who simply adored the young and suddenly famous.

Naturally Nina's photographer was ubiquitous, capturing every air kiss, every cheek-to-cheek hug, every careful-don't-spread-the-collagen smile. As Nina moved among them, chatting gaily about the opening, feeding their insatiable appetite for gossip by dropping juicy tidbits here and there, she accepted compliments for her family heirlooms graciously and without pause. It had been so many years that she had been spinning the tale, she had almost begun to believe her own fiction about the proud and noble Davis clan, their aristocratic roots, their tragic end. She barely thought about the Durans. They had been consigned to history—someone else's history.

The only contacts she had with her past—other than her contretemps with Isabelle—were the ads she compulsively placed in newspapers around the country looking for the woman who had borne her and discarded her.

The day after she left La Casa, before heading to the airport, she had gone to the largest newspaper in Albuquerque and placed the first ad:

> *Found in a trash can February 22, 1954. Santa Fe, New Mexico. To my long-lost mom: All is forgiven. Please get in touch.*

From then on, according to what she could afford, she'd buy a month's worth of ads in the personal columns in the most read newspaper of a particular city. The cities varied, some big, some small, most of them in the West. She always ran the same message, along with a New York post office box number. Every few years she repeated the cycle, enlarging her list of cities, increasing the frequency of the ads. She had never received a reply. She wasn't certain what she would do if she did.

Anthony Hartwick sipped his Glenlivet appreciatively. There was nothing like a single-malt Scotch. Relishing the voluptuous sensation of the smooth whiskey gliding down his throat, he caught sight of Nina—laughing, chatting it up, that obscenely sensuous body wafting through the room like a provocative scent. He was aroused simply thinking about what they would do after everyone had gone. Feeling the heat of his gaze, Nina turned toward him. He raised his glass and smiled. Just last night she had teased him about the myopia of his tastes. "You like Scotch in your glass and a Scot in your bed."

He couldn't deny either statement, especially the part about enjoying Nina in his bed. She was able to bring him to a point of such mindless excitation that, as he had told her in Paris, it frightened him. Anthony felt it was dangerous to let sex dominate one's senses and determine one's behavior. At first, reacting to what he perceived as a threat, he had turned away, both literally and figuratively. Then, when he ran into her serendipitously, he decided that fate had intervened. The gambler in him decided to roll the dice.

Something about Nina Davis tantalized, something beyond those long, sinuous legs and incredibly responsive breasts. He supposed it was that he recognized traits in her he had been forced to acknowledge in himself. A loner who tended toward secrecy and exaggerated self-protection, he had been drawn to the insistently solitary side of the public Miss Davis, the side that guarded her past, constructed walls around her heart, and trusted no one but herself.

Too, was her love of the game. Like him, Nina enjoyed competing and winning. Like him, she could be ruthless and completely void of mercy. Tonight, watching her joust with Isabelle de Luna, had been exhilarating, particularly when he noticed the bereft look on Philip Medina's face. Anthony had never liked Medina. From the day they first met, he felt as if he and Philip were locked in a battle of betters. Who was the better card player? The better student? The better businessman? The better lover? Over the years Anthony reckoned they had competed in almost every arena. Unfortunately Philip had won more rounds than he had lost.

Cisco Communications made Hartwick House look like a financial pygmy. His art collection dwarfed Anthony's in both size and scope. His network of associates outnumbered Anthony's Rolodex. But, Hartwick thought with some satisfaction, when it came to women, Philip Medina ran a distant second.

More than once both men had dated the same woman. Each time Anthony had been the one to put the notch on his belt. Certainly that had been true with Nina. He had seen Medina display an interest in her at his father's wedding; whether or not he had pursued her, Anthony didn't know, but it didn't matter. Ultimately he had lost out. Isabelle de Luna was hardly a conciliation prize, however. In fact, Hartwick thought, suddenly inspired, it might be interesting if he got to know her better. It would certainly up the stakes in the game between him and Nina and in the one between him and Medina.

"Tell me about Isabelle de Luna."

Anthony and Julian Richter had been discussing Alfred Taubman's stewardship of Sotheby's. Julian had been ranting about Taubman's latest offense: giving advances to people who planned to sell their art through Sotheby's. When Anthony interrupted, Julian was taken aback. He tried to return to the subject of art, but Anthony persisted, nearly to the point of rudeness. He wanted to know everything about Julian and Isabelle—how they had met, how long they had been together, why they had separated, where she lived, with whom.

When Julian demanded to know why Hartwick was so interested, Anthony's reply was simple. "I'm a fan. Also, I suppose the publisher in me is always interested in the biographical details of those in the public eye."

"After tonight, I doubt if you could drum up much interest in a book about the once heralded de Luna." Julian's mouth, normally quite dispassionate, lifted in a brief, spontaneous spasm of delight. His eyes remained implacable and hard.

Hartwick rushed to Isabelle's defense. "I think you underestimate her talent, Richter, and overestimate the public's reaction. You and Miss de Luna have a history that didn't end happily, so it's understandable that to you, tonight may have seemed like a deserved comeuppance. But let me remind you of a painful truth: to the rest of the world, tonight was simply another art show."

For Cody Jackson, it had been anything but. The two remaining paintings in the series had sold—one to Anthony Hartwick, one to Cisco CEO Philip Medina—for amounts that staggered. In less than an hour he would appear on every news show in the metropolitan area. Morning newspapers all across the country would carry articles about him and his work and his connection to Isabelle. Greta Reed had agreed to take him on. He was drinking Veuve Clicquot champagne, nibbling toast triangles black with beluga caviar, hobnobbing with people he once would have asked for autographs, laughing at jokes he didn't get.

Seeing Nina walk toward the kitchen, he followed, stopping her in the entry foyer. His head was light from the champagne, a condition that tended to stimulate certain other bodily reflexes. Pressing his hand against the wall so his arm created a barrier, he leaned in and leered.

"You're one hell of a woman, Nina."

"I'm glad you think so, Cody." She tried to move, but he had her blocked.

"I know I gave you a hard time the other day, but, hey. You were right and I was wrong and I'm big enough to admit it."

"Damn gracious of you." Peering over his arm, she looked to see who was watching this horse opera.

"I can't tell you what this night has meant to me." His mouth fell on hers. She turned her head so quickly, he almost stumbled.

"Just enjoy it."

"I intend to."

He smiled, clearly unaffected by her rebuff. Nina wondered how that crooked grin could be so devastatingly appealing one minute, so crude and backwater the next.

"Later, after everyone leaves, I'm going to show you how much I appreciate what you've done," he murmured seductively.

Nina put both hands on his chest and heaved. "No, you're not!" Her voice was low but commanding. "Let's get something straight, Jackson. Our Parisian tryst was an aberration, a one-night stand, a never to be repeated or talked about incident. Am I making myself clear?"

Cody appeared dazed. When he'd first approached her, he had been teetering between mildly high and drunk. Suddenly he was stone sober. "I guess so."

"I don't want you to guess. I want you to be very, very sure about this. I helped you get what you wanted. You owe me big time, and you're going to pay me back with your complete and utter silence."

The last thing she needed was for this lonesome cowboy to start shooting off his mouth. Anthony's reaction was part of her concern, but there was more. Up to now her only public involvement with Greta's show had been tonight's interview. Otherwise she had managed to remain anonymous. No one knew of her relationship to Isabelle. Besides Greta and Cody, no one knew she had agented the paintings. Greta had signed an agreement to honor that confidentiality; Nina regretted she hadn't demanded the same of Jackson.

"Do we understand each other, Cody?"

He snorted and nodded his head. Either he complied or, as quickly as she made him, she would ruin him. "I get the message."

"Good." She smiled and patted his cheek. "Now go back inside and mingle with your fans."

As he watched her sweep into the kitchen and out of his life, he wondered why he suddenly felt dirty.

"You are the most vicious harridan I've ever known!" Julian said, shepherding Greta into Nina's bedroom for a private chat.

"I love you, too, my darling." Greta appeared unmoved by his anger.

"Telling Isabelle we were married was completely unnecessary."

Greta's fingers twirled the intricately carved gold band on her right hand. Unnerved, Julian grabbed her wrist. His eyes appeared transfixed on her ring. "Why do you still wear that?"

"Why not?" she asked, jerking free from his grasp. "It's a lovely piece of jewelry." She studied the ring, then returned her attention to Julian. "Did it make your lovers uncomfortable? Did it diminish their passion? Is that why you took yours off?"

Julian sneered. At one time Greta had spoken to him with respect. Now her tone was laced with scorn. "I want a divorce."

"We've been happily separated for years. What's changed?"

"Everything! We have no relationship. In fact, we can barely stand the sight of each other. So what's the point? I want out."

"Okay." Her mouth spread in a slow, malicious smile.

Julian had expected resistance, a moment of flustered opposition. Instead she seemed to be enjoying herself.

"I'll be generous and let you keep the apartment, even though it's still in my family's name, but I want your debts repaid in full."

Though he tried to disguise it, Julian's expression reflected the panic he felt. "Unfortunately, my cash reserves are a little low at the moment."

"Fine. If you can't come up with the cash, I'll take the gallery and my pick of your inventory."

Julian exploded. "Absolutely not! I've built a reputation. Made a name for myself. Why should I hand it all over to you?"

"Because the only thing you've built is a pile of debt."

"And a stable of some of the world's finest contemporary artists!"

"You have an eye for talent, I'll grant you that, but you have no head for business, Julian. If not for my money, your precious little gallery would have folded years ago."

"For God's sake, Greta, I gave you Isabelle's *Blue Moon* and offered you the rest of the paintings in that series," Julian hissed, his temper beginning to rage. "Why don't you take them and be done with it? Surely the profit on 'Visions in Blue' will clear up any outstanding debts I might have."

She shook her head. "First of all, your obligations amount to several millions of dollars. Second, my guess is that Isabelle is going to sue for release from her contract. Until that litigation is over, I won't touch her work. And last, Julian, you owe me more than money. Much, much more."

His frustration evidenced itself in a near wail. "What is it that you want from me?"

"Blood," Greta said in a voice that chilled the air. "Your blood."

He pounded his fist on a nearby table. "Why do you do that? Why do you insist on accusing me of a crime I didn't commit?"

"Which crime are you talking about, Julian? Since we were married at the time, your affair with my sister was adulterous? Or is it the charge of murder to which you so strenuously object?"

"She killed herself," he asserted, sweat beading his brow.

"Over you and the pain you caused her, the shame you inflicted on her."

"How was I supposed to know she'd do something so extreme?" His hand tugged at his beard nervously.

"It might have occurred to you, but you never think about anyone or anything except yourself."

"I didn't go after her. She seduced me."

Greta raised her hands, moved toward him, and then suddenly clenched her fists, as if only divine intervention had prevented her from strangling him.

"She was seventeen, Julian, a mere child. She didn't know the meaning of the word *seduction*. You lured her into your bed to prove what a big, important man you were. But you didn't just sleep with her, you told her you loved her over and over again until she believed it. And when you finished using her, you dumped her like a dirty tissue. She pleaded with you to take her back. She was desperate. Anyone could see that. But instead of being kind and leaving her with some shred of pride, you laughed at her. She may have hanged herself, but you were responsible."

Julian protested, "It wasn't something I wanted to happen. I felt terrible about it, still do. Over the years, I've suffered as much as anyone."

"I disagree. I don't think you've suffered nearly enough." Greta's voice sizzled with unresolved fury. "The day I found my sister dangling from that rope, I vowed that if I did nothing else in my life, I would make you pay for what you did to her."

"I didn't *do* anything!" He heard the shrillness in his voice and hated himself for allowing her to rattle him.

Greta could smell his fear. Her eyes sparkled as she circled him like a vulture over carrion. "You can deny it all you want, but we both know what you did. And what you deserve."

"Since when are you judge and jury?"

"Since the day I decided that I was the only one who could extract justice." Suddenly her look turned almost quizzical. "The funny part is, you helped me set the trap. Another man would have wondered why his wife walked out on him, yet never asked for a divorce; why a woman who hated him continued to lend him money. But you were so blinded by ego and arrogance and greed, you played right into my hands. You asked, I gave. Again and again and again, until you succeeded in creating a mountain of debt you can't possibly satisfy."

She laughed, but this time it was the triumphant laugh of someone who finally felt revenge within her grasp.

"Since Isabelle's paintings are such a large part of your portfolio, I'll wait until your legal wranglings with her are finished. Then, I'll file for divorce." Her expression became positively gleeful. "Every paper in town is going to jump on this story and ride it to death. They're going to put our marriage and each of our respective affairs under a microscope, including your murderous relationship with my sister. The best part is that all your sneaky manipulations and questionable business practices will be made public. There won't be an artist or a collector within a thousand miles who'll have anything to do with you."

Greta licked her lips as if the moment were delicious. "By the time this is over, Julian, I will have taken your money, ruined your business, and destroyed your name. You see, my sweet, I've given you just enough rope to hang yourself!"

Nina's den bulged with people eager to share her moment. Along with her own furniture, she had provided rows of folding chairs and had rented two additional televisions to stand beside her own, all for a three-minute spot. Although she would have loved everyone to watch *Nightline*—focused that night on what it was like to be an artist in the high-stakes, high-visibility 1980s—since she hadn't been interviewed for the show, she could find no reason to suggest watching. She had, however, spotted Jeff Greenfield at the gallery and immediately assumed the de Luna *scandale* would provide the nucleus of his introductory report. Her VCR was programmed and ready.

She heard the lead-in for her piece. Her heart began to thump, her mouth went dry. It was the same nervousness she used to experience before stepping onto the stage for her high school plays, that adrenaline-raging sensation of standing on a dangerous precipice. Do it right: success and praise. Do it wrong: failure and humiliating barbs.

The camera zoomed in on Nina as she intro'd the interview. *Face looks good. A touch too pale. Bump up the blush. Hair's fine. Voice sounds steady.* Cut to Isabelle. *Should have insisted on a full shot. She looks too angelic, too vulnerable. It's those eyes, that puffy, pouty mouth. Damn!* Midview. Face to face. Question after question. Isabelle's defiant silence. The silence of the audience at the gallery, the matching stillness in her apartment. Nina cringed. Watching herself go after Isabelle with such unharnessed ferocity was humbling. She had felt so powerful at the moment, so on top of the issue. It looked different now. She had punched too hard, battered too long. She should have backed off and let Isabelle react. She had wanted to come off a crusader. Instead she had shown herself to be a bully.

When it was over, no one applauded. No one came over to congratulate her. Instead there seemed to be a rush for the powder room and the bar. Within minutes she and Clive Frommer appeared to be the only ones left in the den.

"Nice job, Lizzie Borden." Clive shook his head, his polished, attenuated features skewed into a look of bemused disbelief.

"I beg your pardon?" Nina treated his comment as a tease. She battered her eyelashes and fanned herself, partly for effect, partly because he had splashed on a bit too much Vetivier. When he didn't laugh at her makeshift Scarlett O'Hara, she regrouped. "You didn't like my interview?"

"No, I didn't," he said bluntly. "That was a major hatchet job. I'm surprised your clothes weren't splattered with the poor woman's blood."

Uncomfortable, Nina quickly thumbed through a mental file of rationalizations, justifying her behavior, excusing that of her guests: jealousy, ignorance, timidity, a lack of understanding about and a level of discomfort with disseminators of the truth. She could levy any or all of those labels on everyone there, except Clive.

"That's how some might perceive it," she said, cloaking herself in a crust of hauteur. "I saw it as a carefully planned, in-depth interview."

"In-depth my ass!" He fixed her in his sight, holding her attention as only one who knew you when could. "I don't know what Isabelle de Luna ever did to you, but that was a payback if I ever saw one."

"Clive, darling, we each have our own modus operandi. My style happens to be a bit sharper than yours."

"Is that a defense or your subtle way of saying my columns are dull?" His lips twisted into a wry smile. He was a regular on a morning talk show and a local nighttime news program and was in line for a spot on CNN. His column appeared in two New York papers, and his readership was even with hers. They both knew he was anything but dull.

"I don't need a defense."

"You never do, do you?"

"What's that supposed to mean?"

" 'A girl's got to do what a girl's got to do.' Isn't that your motto?"

His eyes had turned dark. Once, they had served as beacons guiding her to the safe haven of his friendship. No longer.

"Clive, you're getting tedious."

"And you're getting carried away with yourself, Nina. One of these days, someone's going to grab that knife you wield so skillfully and stuff it in the middle of your back. And you know what," he said, shoving his champagne glass in her hand, "you're going to deserve it!"

He left slowly, lingering in the living room, demanding that she watch as he chummed it up with her guests, smiling, glad-handing, making friends who would confide in him whenever he asked. Nina following at a distance, shivered, holding herself as if someone had opened the window and invited the December chill inside. Still clutching Clive's glass, she took a quick, sedative sip of the champagne, but like her mood, the bubbles had gone flat.

Nina stared at the underside of the canopy that umbrellaed her bed. Anthony lay beside her, spent from their lovemaking. He had been particularly barbaric tonight, lunging at her the minute they were alone, taking her first on the living room floor, unmindful of the roughness of the carpet on her back. He had ground his body into hers, pumping so hard and so fast, she thought he would rip her open.

Exhausted and sore, she had longed for sleep, but he wasn't finished with her. Taking another Scotch into a scalding hot shower, he drank while Nina satisfied him. He made no attempt to satisfy her. This was not meant to be an event of mutual fulfillment. Never verbalized, but nonetheless true, this was a service rendered, an act of obeisance owed him for his financial generosity. Nina convinced herself she indeed had a choice, that pleasuring him in whatever way he wanted was equally enjoyable to her, that each expressed giving and taking in his own way.

It was later, during the dark hours, that Nina questioned the fit of this relationship. So much seemed so right. She found him as ravishingly handsome as he found her beautiful. While his sex was rough and aggressive, passive, gentle lovers bored her. She and Anthony shared a love of books, enjoyed rainy Sundays at the movies, preferred dining out at New York's four stars to eating in, relished political debates—while he was a Republican and she a Democrat, each was moderate enough to avoid serious clashes. She dabbled at tennis, he feared skiing, both loathed golf. His love of dancing and their frequent postprandial visits to Doubles had surprised her, but because he was so good and it intoxicated them both sensually, it quickly became a habit.

There was also the matter of family. Nina worried about becoming seriously involved. If she were, the man might demand elaboration of her biography, a family album, a trip to her ancestral home in Scotland, the house she had lived in before her parents died, a relative or two. Anthony was as close-mouthed about family as she was. The most he would say was that he was an only child who had loved his mother and hated his father. His parents had died when he was young, and he had been raised by boarding school prefects, a benevolent grandmother and the head of the clan, his grandfather, Alston Hartwick, an exceedingly unpleasant man who was also now deceased. According to Anthony, there wasn't anyone left to talk about.

This should have elated Nina. It was, after all, the answer to a prayer. Rather, she felt disappointed, disenfranchised, denied the perquisites of pedigree. When she had fantasized about matching up with a man like Anthony, her dreams had been accessorized with holidays at the family mansion, a wedding attended by Brahmins, in-laws who would welcome her to the bosom of their family by opening hearth and vault to her, who would marvel at the gracious home she would make for their son, dote on the grandchildren she would produce. If she ever married Anthony—and to date neither had shown an inclination to march to Mendelssohn—there would be a void.

So what, she thought as she looked at him asleep beside her. With him she would gain automatic status and instant acceptance. She would be Mrs. Anthony Hartwick. Why worry about family when, given the chance, she could create a dynasty?

The next morning Nina arrived at the *Daily* around eleven. Strolling toward her office, she gladly accepted the kudos of those who had seen her ABC piece and couldn't wait to read her afternoon column for the next installment of the saga of Isabelle de Luna.

She was still beaming as she eyed her desk. Telegrams in one pile. Phone messages in another. A bunch of flowers from her camera crew. Her mouth swelled into a broad grin and then quickly faded when she saw an envelope taped to her computer. Inside was a letter written on Philip Medina's stationery. Short and to the point, it read "You're fired!"

By one o'clock she had cleared out her desk at the *Daily*, been notified that her syndication deal was under review, and had been axed from ABC. All thanks to Philip Medina.

And Isabelle.

CHAPTER 21

Barcelona, 1987

I sabelle tried to rise above the fallout from the Reed show, but in the end she surrendered to the reality that until those hungry for gossip about her had been sated, she was food for the media. Her mood was low. Christmas was approaching, yet she felt no goodwill; she felt betrayed by a cadre of those she had trusted. Cody, Nina, Julian, Philip—she had been intimate with the men, familiar in a different way with Nina, allowed each of them unedited access to her soul. For reasons she would never fully comprehend, they had turned that closeness against her.

Initially she barricaded herself in her apartment, refusing to answer the phone or the incessant pounding on her door. Lonely, frightened, and in need of a friend, she sneaked over to Skye's apartment. Soon it became clear she had exchanged one cell for another.

"I can understand wanting to get away," Skye said when Isabelle announced she was suffering from cabin fever. "Why not come to Santa Fe with Sam and me? You've got the Paint Box. Miranda and Luis would kill before they'd let anyone get near you, and if they missed, Jonas and Sybil and Dr. Sam would be maybe a step behind."

Suddenly Skye stood, her feet spread, her eyes narrowed to an intimidating glower. She mimed pulling a hat down on her brow, placed her hands on her hips, and faked a double draw. "I can see it now. High noon in Santa Fe. Reporters on one side of the Plaza. The Hoffmans, that fabled gang of Jewish cowboys, on the other." With fingers pointed, her hands jerked downward several times in quick succession. "Bang! Bang!" Her fingers raised to her mouth, she blew off the imaginary smoke, then stuffed the imaginary pistols back in her holsters and moseyed on back to her chair. "Them varmints wouldn't stand a chance!"

Isabelle laughed, marveling at how good it felt. She hadn't laughed in weeks.

"Come on, Is. It's the holidays. You can't stay in New York. Only tourists spend Christmas in the city."

"I'm not going to stay in New York. I'm going to Barcelona."

"Hey! Great!" Privately Skye was disappointed. "Flora and Alejandro must be ecstatic! When will you come back? After New Year's?"

"No."

"Okay," Skye said, suddenly realizing there was more to this trip than simply visiting aging relatives. "When?"

"It depends."

"On what? Or should I say whom?" Philip had been relentless in his efforts to speak to Isabelle. She had been equally stubborn in her refusal to do so. Skye had been an unwilling middleman.

"What," Isabelle said emphatically, wanting to deemphasize Philip's importance. "I've hired a lawyer to get me out of my contract with Julian." Skye applauded. Her face telegraphed complete approval. "It could be nasty."

"Will be," Skye said, wondering if Isabelle knew how truly vicious Julian Richter could be.

"I know, but it doesn't matter. Until I can get free of him, I can't sell through anyone else. And without an outlet for my work, I have no way of earning an income. He has me boxed into a corner."

Skye groaned. Isabelle had some money put away; she lived frugally, but still . . . Knowing Richter, she realized this could drag on for a very long time.

"Besides," Isabelle said, refusing to allow Julian to dominate her thoughts, "I need to withdraw from the world for a while."

"You've been hurt, Isabelle, I know that, but running away is not a healthy form of exercise. It doesn't burn up any calories, and it doesn't change anything."

Isabelle hoped she could unite the myriad ramblings that had brought her to this conclusion, offer a reasonable explanation.

"I'm not running away. Hopefully, I'm running toward something," she said. "Lately I've felt a lull in my creative energy. I could lay it off on depression and lots of other negative feelings that are overwhelming me right now, but it's more than that. It's as if my muse is tired and needs her battery charged.

"Look at me," she said, drawing Skye's attention to the hollows under her eyes, the sallowness of her skin, the downcast turn of her mouth. "These days I'm a stranger to myself. I rarely laugh anymore. I can't go out. I can't bear to stay inside. I can't stand being with people, but I can't stand being alone." She threw up her hands, shrugged her shoulders, and attempted a smile. "I'm having a crisis."

"Big time," Skye said, having no choice but to agree.

"This is going to sound odd."

"Try me. I've always been big on odd."

"The Castell is overrun with creative ghosts. My mother's spirit. The specter of Flora's imagination. Vina. Ramona. Even the phantoms of my own youthful scribblings float in the air there. I need to breathe that atmosphere, Skye. I need a retreat that will allow my creativity to incubate and reassert itself.

"And I need sanctuary for my soul while it goes through this upheaval." Again she struggled to arrange her thoughts. "My first years were spent on that hilltop in Campíns. I have deep roots there, and despite the ugliness that brought me here, I remain tangled in those roots." The shadows in her eyes deepened. "I feel safe in the Castell and with Tía Flora. I love you, Skye, and I love Miranda and Luis. I know you would do anything to help me and protect me, but right now I don't feel safe anywhere else."

Despite Tía Flora's best efforts, Isabelle ate very little, slept even less, and wouldn't see or speak to anyone, particularly Philip. She did, however, unburden herself with Flora. The more they talked about what had happened, about Isabelle's past relationships with Cody and Julian and Philip, the more Flora noticed a trend that struck her as familiar.

Isabelle disappointed men in the way men usually disappointed women: she held back, never granting full empowerment over her will; giving some but not all, leaving only a part ever truly committed. Many times Alejandro had accused Flora of the same resistance, the same reluctance to give of herself fully. In the early years he hadn't understood and had viewed her aversion to traditional roles as an idiosyncratic assertion of independence. Flora considered it a valid objection to man's age-old, one-sided habit of demanding a woman's sacrifice of self. Eventually Alejandro had come to respect Flora's right of self-sovereignty and to understand that it was not disloyal to love him without enslaving herself to him. When Flora had met Philip, she had intuited he was a man capable of that same latitude.

"You didn't give him a chance," Flora said during one of their conversations.

"To do what? Cheat on me with the likes of Nina? Tell me things he should have told me before? Or wait until someone else humiliated me with one of his other secrets?" Her emotions were so raw, every subject chafed; Philip's dissembling galled.

"I've spoken to him. He's heartsick, Isabelle. He loves you, don't you see that?"

"I don't care."

"Yes, you do."

Isabelle retreated to the window seat in her room, pressed her back against the wall, hugged her knees, and stared out at the horizon, beyond which was the world she had forsaken. She saw no reason for this particular debate because she saw no future with Philip. From the beginning, even before the contretemps at the Reed Gallery, they were a questionable item. As much as pulled them together, pulled them apart: the chemistry they couldn't deny, the feelings they wouldn't admit, the commitment neither of them seemed able to make.

"It doesn't matter whether I care or I don't," she said with finality. "Before I can deal with Philip Medina, I have to make peace with Isabelle de Luna."

Flora would have liked to argue that point but couldn't.

Six months went by. Flora, helpless to do anything other than watch and worry, stood by as her niece plummeted to an emotional nadir. Having taken this slide several times in her eighty-six years, she knew that along with the pain came new insights; along with the recrimination, knowledge.

Whenever she could, Flora attempted to provide Isabelle with the tools to move on. When Isabelle became overwrought, she encouraged meditation, reminding her, "The mind should be your servant, not your master." When she appeared bent on grousing, Flora guided her toward the positive, blocking the negative energy that threatened to enfeeble her spirit. And when, finally, she sensed the bottom had come, she pointed out that Isabelle's life had imitated the mountains that had backgrounded her childhood: she had risen to glorious peaks, but once arrived at the zenith, she had but one destination—descent. The only alternative now was another struggle upward.

Slowly, as spring gave way to summer, Isabelle began to emerge from her spiritual chrysalis. The purgatory process had been ruthless, but suddenly she felt eager to return to work. Eschewing both horse and car in favor of a bicycle, she took off in search of new venues. She returned each day with a sketch book filled with drawings, but none of them satisfied. When an invitation came from the Reys—longtime friends of Flora's—to vacation at their villa on the Côte d'Azur, the opportunity appeared heaven sent.

Reinaldo and Sofia Rey, whose fortune had multiplied tenfold during the post-Franco construction boom, considered Barcelona their home base; ski season took them to their chalet in Zurich, summer to this villa in Juan-les-Pins. On a hill overlooking Angel's Bay, the swath of sea between Nice and

Cannes, their manse was grand in proportion, Spanish colonial in style. With the Mediterranean as a lure, every seaside bedroom had a balcony of its own, every window a view, every door an opening onto a massive expanse of terrace that traced the length of the frontage.

Inside, the focal point was a two-story skylighted atrium that at one time had been an open-air courtyard and was now a sun-filled entry/sitting room. Radiating off this center were spacious rooms, lavishly furnished, replete with art treasures that ranged from eighteenth- and nineteenth-century architectural studies to contemporary works by young Spanish artists, including a painting from the "Ode to Eos" series Isabelle had given them as a house gift.

Isabelle had been granted use of a vacant garage as a studio, one that remained separated from the house and, therefore, was not beset by the fumes of the Reys' five automobiles. Free to spread canvas on the floor or tack it to sturdy frames that rested against twelve-foot-high walls, Isabelle reveled in the space.

Each day she awoke before dawn and moved out to her balcony to witness nature's renewal, welcoming it with the same unbridled enthusiasm with which she greeted her own artistic renaissance. Then, after doing yoga on the lawn, she would enter the garage, where she stayed until dusk, attempting to narrate her recent psychic journey via a series of enormous, color-intense canvases, each of which described a single emotion.

Sometimes night called her to the balcony as well. Usually it was peaceful in the ebony hours. The palm trees swished back and forth in the gentle breeze that wafted in off the water, their sound one of whispers and the soft murmurings lovers might favor. Now and then the moon illuminated the docile waves that somersaulted onto the beach, capping their lapis crests with bubbling white foam.

One evening Isabelle sat on the balcony, bundled in her robe, watching a storm rage far out at sea. There were occasional harsh gusts of wind and an unusual bite to the air, but it wasn't raining on shore, nor was the quiescence of night interrupted by any thunderous rumblings. There was nothing between her and the tempest but a navy vastness. Lightning flashed—first in one place, then in another, a brilliant zigzag that cracked the sky like an eggshell. Mesmerized, she felt as if the drama before her had been scripted by Poseidon. Set on a watery stage, the play of sea and sky bewitched, charged as it was with an electrifying energy. Isabelle listened but heard only unintelligible dialogue. She watched but saw only indefinable images. Nothing was clear except the sobering feeling that she had dreamed scenes from this drama many times before but never had seen the finale.

Each year the Reys hosted an anniversary party, inviting family, most of their neighbors, a large contingent from Spain and other countries on the Continent, and a group of business associates and friends from the States. Finding it impossible on the night of the party not to get caught up in the preparations, Isabelle and Flora joined their hosts on the terrace, eager for the celebration to begin.

Isabelle greeted Sofia warmly, kissing the older woman's cheeks and thanking her again for her healing hospitality.

"It's been my honor to have you." Sofia, a tall, slender woman with green Catalan eyes and hair that, despite her age, still held some of its original brunette color, patted Isabelle's hand, surveying the ripe body and tanned skin of the magnificent young woman before her. "Reinaldo and I have invited a mix of people, many of whom are as young and attractive as you. Perhaps someone will catch your eye tonight?"

"I doubt it." Isabelle's imagination pictured Sofia raising Cupid's bow and aiming arrows at any available male between the ages of eighteen and eighty. "But," she said, noting the woman's disappointment, "you never know."

As the sun set, the Reys' guests arrived, by launch from yachts moored in the bay, by chauffeured Rolls-Royces or Mercedes limousines, by hotel cars from all over the Riviera. Glamorous, well-tended women in chiffon and lightweight silks and the new Christian Lacroix poufs painted the lawn with soft flutters of color. The men arrived garbed like variations on a theme: white pants, an open-neck silk shirt, an easy jacket or, in the case of some, a nautical navy blazer, the occasional ascot, the rare tie, hair carefully slicked, nails neatly manicured, skin buffed.

Because this was an international crowd, languages and accents abounded, as did opinions and senses of humor. Since many of the guests knew each other, or were acquainted with a friend of a friend, there was a great deal of intermingling. After being introduced to several dozen people, Isabelle found herself on the poolside loggia with Flora and some old friends of Martín's, François LeVerre and his wife, Eunice.

"I satisfy Reinaldo's passion for classic cars," François said, explaining his presence.

"Is that how you met my father?" Isabelle asked. "Did you sell him a car?"

"No." François looked as if he were about to say something, but his wife's expression stopped him. "My father manufactured clothing in the south of France. He bought most of his fabric from Dragon Textiles and, because of that, got to know the Pujol sisters quite well. When your father was ready to attend university, Flora sent him to Aix-en-Provence. He lived with my family for four years." He looked wistful. "He was my best friend."

It was rare for Isabelle to meet people she did not know who had known her father, especially in the years before he had met Althea. She could have spent the entire evening listening to Eunice and François reminisce about the young Martín de Luna.

"Actually, it was my father who introduced Martín to classic cars," François said, delighting Isabelle with tales about the many days his father, Daniel, and Martín had spent working on the Bentley roadster and the Duesenberg coupé and the Stutz. "At one time my father had an extraordinary collection."

"What happened to it?"

"World War Two." François said it casually, but Isabelle felt stupid and insensitive. Sensing her embarrassment, François reached over and patted her hand. "When the Germans moved in, my father bribed several of the officers running the city by giving them priceless automobiles." His eyes darkened as he retreated into his memories. "He thought he was protecting us. Terrible rumors had begun to filter back about people being herded into cattle cars and transported to ghastly death camps. By then, we were the only Jews left in Aix. My parents begged your father to return to Barcelona, but he wouldn't go. It seems he had grown quite attached to us."

"I can see why," Isabelle said softly, warming to the Frenchman. Eager to learn more about her father's friendship with the LeVerres, she prodded François to continue.

"Eventually we abandoned our house and hid out in the basement of my father's factory. One day, Martín and I returned from town and my parents were gone. Windows had been smashed. Blood stained the concrete near where they had slept. One of my mother's shoes lay on the stairs.

"We searched every inch of the factory. I wanted to search every building in Aix. And if they weren't there, I wanted to track them down, all the way to Germany if I had to. I was out of control. Martín convinced me that if the Germans had come for my parents, it wouldn't be long before they came back for me. He insisted the only way we could help my parents was to stay alive and try to locate them through diplomatic channels." François sighed, his breath trembling like a soundless sob. "Admitting I couldn't rescue my parents singlehandedly was the hardest thing I ever had to do.

"We left Aix-en-Provence that very night, heading west on narrow, country roads in a 1923 Mercedes Model K." He laughed at the foolishness of attempting to escape in a slow-moving, wildly conspicuous car.

"Where were you headed?" Isabelle asked, completely entranced.

"Barcelona." Again he laughed. "I remember throwing my hands up in frustration and reminding Martín that Hannibal had tried to cross the Pyrenees and failed. He argued that the Model K may have been slow, but was a definite step up from elephants. He also reminded me it was the only chance we had.

"The way was hazardous enough, but Martín made it more so by insisting that we drive without headlights much of the time. During the day, we hid the car as best we could—in forests, deserted barns, back roads, whatever. I'd stand guard. Martín would go for supplies.

"In Montpellier, I tried to find several relatives and family friends. Their homes were empty, their names erased from the minds of all I asked. I tried again in Sète. Same results. Each vacant house, each unrecalled name, intensified our apprehension about the fate of my parents.

"It was at that point Martín decided we had to brazen our way through to the border."

"But that was so dangerous. You were a wanted man. What if they had caught you?" Isabelle shivered at the might-have-beens.

For years, François had had nightmares about that very question. "I knew a little about cars, so I reworked the Model K. I created a cubby in a small space between the back of the rear seat and the trunk. It was bumpy and uncomfortable and, after an hour or so, quite painful. Breathing the exhaust fumes made me nauseated, and there were times when I wondered which would burst first, my bladder or my lungs. But it didn't matter. I knew that whatever I was suffering was minor compared to what my parents were being forced to endure."

"Were you ever stopped?"

"Twice, once in Narbonne and once in Sigean. Both times Martín's fluent German saved us. He showed them some old papers we had found in my father's garage file and told them he was ferrying the car on orders from an officer in Aix. Doors were opened and closed, windows rolled up and down. The hood was lifted, the tires were kicked. But once the trunk had been opened and closed without incident, we both felt free to breathe."

François's brow knotted. "We were headed toward Prades, a small community close to the Spanish border that had become a refuge for escaping Catalans. We were almost there when the road forked. The shoreline was perilously open. Our only other choice was the mountains, but the brakes of the Model K were unreliable. Again, we felt we had no choice.

"The road was steep, winding up and around the Pyrenees. A mule would have been the appropriate vehicle, not an expensive, outmoded touring car. But Martín felt the trees would provide cover and the difficulty of the route would discourage traffic. It was hours before we reached the crown of a deserted peak. After Martín had scouted the area and assured himself we were alone, he opened the trap door and helped me out. I was certain my legs were permanently bent," François said, grimacing now as he must have then.

"Martín went to reconnoiter a quicker way down. I used the time to stretch my limbs and relieve myself."

François's face tightened. His hand clenched into fists. "They were on me in a minute. I knew they were there when I felt a gun in my back and the hot breath of a German soldier on my neck. They were the two who had stopped us in Sigean. They hog-tied me, beat me until I was nearly unconscious, and then dragged me to a spot no more than ten feet in front of the Model K. One of them had a gun trained on my head. The other had jumped into the car and started the motor.

"He was examining the dashboard, trying to figure out which switch did what, when Martín crept up behind the first soldier and wrestled his gun free. The car was rolling. The German was laughing, shouting anti-Semitic slogans as he prepared to drive the big Mercedes over my body. Martín fired. The bullet hit the back of the German's head. The car swerved to the right, ran over my leg, and then headed for the cliff. We could hear the car bouncing off the rocks as it plummeted downward. Then, all we heard was silence."

François's eyes were vacant. His color was pale, his breathing shallow. He had returned to another time; it had been a lifetime ago, yet the pain and fear of that old moment remained fresh. Isabelle moved next to him and wrapped her arm around his shoulders. Still enmeshed in the story, she asked, "What happened to the other soldier?"

François answered without thinking. "He was dead. Martín had crushed his larynx and killed him."

Isabelle was stunned. Suddenly her brain felt too tight for her skull. Her head throbbed, blinding her momentarily. She covered her eyes with her hands. François comforted her. His voice was soft but certain.

"Your father saved my life, Isabelle. He did what he had to do."

Isabelle nodded her head slowly. Then she turned to Flora. "You knew about this?"

"Yes."

"Yet you never said anything. Why?"

Flora returned her niece's stare boldly and confidently. "I thought it was best, under the circumstances."

Before Isabelle could comment, Sofia Rey approached, accompanied by Javier and Estrella Murillo, Paco Barba, and an attractive dark-haired woman. Isabelle, her thoughts too muddled and raw to deal with any of them, rose to leave, but she was too late.

"Can you imagine my surprise when your grandparents walked in?" Sofia said with forced gaiety, her voice teetering on a decibel level that could have shattered glass.

As an old friend of Flora's she knew the Murillos and the de Lunas had been estranged for years. She was simply trying to put the best face on an awkward situation.

"Javier and Estrella are guests on the yacht belonging to my niece's husband, Paco Barba."

Sofia made the introductions hastily, as if the faster she performed the task, the less uncomfortable she would be. After mumbling several inanities about how small the world was, she excused herself, leaving everyone staring at one another. Estrella was the first to speak.

"I'm delighted to have this chance to see you, my dear." Nervous as to how it would be received, she smiled, her mouth wobbling. When Isabelle didn't respond, she tilted toward Javier, leaning on him for support.

"We're old," he said quietly, directing his words only to Isabelle. "We don't have time to dwell on ancient angers." His eyes were rheumy, his skin drooped with age. "We are blood, Isabelle. Must we behave like enemies for the rest of our lives?"

Isabelle had a dozen answers, none pleasant. If Flora hadn't nudged her, she might have refused Javier's hand. Instead she took it. She did not, however, shake Paco's hand. Some gestures, no matter how benign, were impossible.

Paco, undeterred by Isabelle's slight, introduced his wife. "Anna, Isabelle de Luna and her great-aunt, the venerable Señorita Pujol." Flora nodded at Paco's wife and, as graciously as she could, introduced the Le-Verres.

Anna greeted them politely and then turned to Isabelle, a genuine smile gracing her lips. "Paco's a great admirer of yours, Señorita de Luna. In fact, we own several of your paintings."

Isabelle couldn't respond. All she could do was stare at those dark, haunting eyes.

"While I adore *Dawn in the Canyon,*" Anna continued, somewhat rattled by Isabelle's unshaded hostility, "your nightscape of Manhattan's harbor is utterly bewitching."

Isabelle tried to thank her, but politeness was impossible. Seeing these particular people now, before she had had time to digest François's story, irked her beyond measure. It was as if their appearance were meant to underscore a coincidence she wasn't willing to concede. Instead of being pleased by Anna's enthusiasm, she dismissed it without response. Paco, recognizing that there was no way to salvage the situation, mumbled something inconsequential, took his wife's arm, and went off to find more receptive company.

Isabelle would have preferred to see the Murillos leave with the Barbas, but they remained. The ensuing conversation was so superficial, it was painful—the weather, the Reys, the lovely party, the food. Other guests drifted over. Isabelle was desperate to get away, but she was the center of attention, her fame the light attracting the social moths. For reasons she couldn't explain, Isabelle didn't protest when the Murillos encouraged their friends to meet their talented grandchild.

It felt odd to listen as they praised her work, odder still to hear them laud her *Dawn in Barcelona,* the painting that hung in Philip's Majorcan villa. Isabelle was at a loss to explain why she was participating in this charade. Perhaps she needed to know that she had won their respect. Or perhaps she felt obliged to accept their accolades on behalf of her mother. Flora was not as generous. When the LeVerres excused themselves, she went with them out onto the terrace for a badly needed breath of fresh air.

A few moments later Javier became involved in a debate with an old friend about the effect of pesticides on their horses' feed. Left alone, the two women endured a strained silence. Estrella, subdued by age and time, was obviously humbled by Isabelle's success and emotionally cowed by her physical resemblance to Althea. She hadn't seen Isabelle since she was a child. Then the likeness had been muddled; now it was clear. The pouty mouth, the height of the cheekbones, the length of her legs, the sensuousness of her body—all were unequivocal gifts from Althea.

"You're as beautiful as your mother was," she said softly, her words climbing over a lump in her throat. "And from what I've seen and heard, you've taken her talent a giant step forward. She would be very proud of you, Isabelle."

Isabelle wanted to challenge Estrella, to ask her how she possibly could know what Althea would have thought, and since when did she care, but something in the old woman's voice touched her. Instead of venting rage, she looked at her mother's mother and said, "Thank-you."

Encouraged, Estrella pressed on. "I would like to think that we might be able to have a relationship. To speak occasionally. Perhaps for you to visit our home." She paused. Whatever she wanted to say next required effort. "When you were born and for years after, your mother begged me to come see you, to enjoy the privileges of being a grandmother. Pride kept me away. It's taken me many lonely years to concede how wrong I was."

"You were wrong about my father, too," Isabelle said. Her voice was controlled and void of rancor, but there was no denying the underlying passion. "My mother loved him, and he made her very happy. You didn't think so, but he was a wonderful husband and a wonderful father."

She waited for Estrella to disagree or question Isabelle's judgment. Neither occurred.

"He didn't kill her, Señora Murillo, because he couldn't. As for us, I can't have a relationship with you as long as you remain friends with the man I believe may have taken my mother's life."

Estrella nodded. She had expected that. "Paco was with us that night. That's the truth."

Isabelle shook her head. She had witnessed his rage that very day. She could still feel the heat of his anger. Alejandro had hypothesized that the Murillos had paid off the police. Isabelle had believed it then, and she believed it now.

Estrella laced her fingers together and stared at them as if somewhere within that web were solutions to unanswerable questions. "I'm willing to accept your assertion that Martín was incapable of murder," she said with obvious difficulty.

Isabelle swooned slightly and then shook her head, trying to slough off a torrent of unbidden thoughts.

Estrella, interpreting Isabelle's response as disbelief, continued. "I'd like you to take my word that Paco is also innocent. I may be many things, Isabelle, but I'm not so loathsome that I would knowingly harbor my daughter's killer. However it appears to you, I loved Althea."

"Then who?" Isabelle could have kicked herself. How could she have asked that of this woman?

"A stranger, perhaps. A hotel employee. Someone Althea knew and none of us did." Estrella shook her head, her shoulders heaving as if she carried the weight of the world. "I don't think we'll ever know. But to be honest, I'm not certain that after all these years it matters."

Estrella might have been right about never knowing for certain who killed Althea, but she was wrong about the effect of time: it still mattered a great deal to Isabelle. Now more than ever.

After her conversation with Estrella, Isabelle left the loggia and was seeking Tía Flora when Sofia, eager to compensate for whatever embarrassment she might have caused, grabbed Isabelle and brought her to meet people she described as two of her dearest friends.

"They're simply dying to meet you, my dear," she oozed. "He's one of the world's great collectors, and she's, well, she's one of the world's great spenders." She was still laughing at her own joke when she introduced Isabelle to Nelson and Pilar Medina.

Nelson's eyebrows lifted in admiration as he surveyed Sofia's houseguest. Pilar watched her husband carefully as he bowed and gallantly kissed the hand of the long-legged young woman in the scooped-neck, body-hugging vanilla sheath. When it was her turn to extend a hand in greeting, she made certain her twenty-five-carat diamond was visible.

"I'm an old friend of your aunt's," he said, his face looking as boyish as Philip's when he smiled.

"So she's told me."

"What a pity she wasn't well and couldn't attend our wedding," Pilar said, linking her arm through Nelson's.

"She was sorry she missed it."

"Actually, our nuptials were held at my son's villa on Majorca, where he has a magnificent painting he attributes to you. *Dawn in Barcelona.*" Isabelle nodded, acknowledging the painting, not her relationship with Philip. "You're extremely talented, Señorita de Luna."

"Thank-you. From a collector as renowned as you, that's high praise indeed."

"Nelson collects old masters."

Nelson looked at his wife as if she had just recited a nursery rhyme, which would have made as much sense as what she actually said. "What does that have to do with Isabelle?"

Pilar was flustered. Her face pinked and she retrieved her arm, shrinking beneath Nelson's critical gaze. "I only meant she's a contemporary artist and you don't collect them. Philip does."

"And a fine collection he has," Nelson said, turning away from Pilar.

"So I've heard."

"He has an extraordinary eye. I'd like to think he learned something from watching me, but one is either born with the eye or not. Just as one is born with talent or intelligence, or not."

"Do you buy on impulse or do you buy on the basis of knowledge about the period?" Isabelle asked, forever fascinated by the different methods employed by collectors.

"Knowledge." He paused, clearly wanting to give her the fullest answer possible. "I love the energy and color and freedom of expression in contemporary art, but collecting old masters was my way of continuing my education. It's one of the reasons I love my paintings so. I know how they fit into their times. What the political circumstances were, the fashions, the philosophies, the musical preferences, the popular novels. Context! That's the key to understanding art. Context! Because art is never created in a vacuum."

It fascinated Isabelle to note the similarity between father and son: the passion, the intensity, the insistence on quality, the thought behind the decision to buy.

"I would love for you to meet Philip," Nelson said, suddenly inspired.

"We've already met."

"Really?" Pilar asked. Obviously she had decided to rejoin the party. "Where?"

"At the Richter Gallery. He was at several of my shows."

Nelson chuckled. "If he didn't make a move on you, he's losing his touch." He laughed a little harder and wagged his finger at Isabelle. "Watch out for him. He's a ladies' man just like his old man. The more the merrier, I always said. Until I met you, that is," he said, grinning at Pilar in a manner meant to imply that he had never really abandoned his philandering ways, although rumor was that since Pilar, he had.

Pilar allowed Nelson to nuzzle her. She knew he was apologizing for being short with her. It was a sign of savvy that inspired admiration from Isabelle. Whatever Pilar was—and in truth Isabelle didn't know enough about her to judge—she was adept at handling her man. Isabelle realized she could learn a thing or two from a woman like Pilar.

"I'm not sure Philip would recognize the right woman if she was staring him in the face," Pilar said suddenly.

"My wife is not my son's number one fan," Nelson explained.

"He's too competitive." She meant with her for his father's attention. Nelson, whether deliberately or not, reacted to a different take on the word.

"You can never be too competitive, especially in business. Look what Philip's doing. He's cornering the cable industry, buying one cable system after another." He smiled and shook his head, clearly impressed by his son's accomplishments. "I'm a captain of industry, but Philip is a veritable giant!"

Isabelle wondered if Philip had ever heard praise like this from his father's mouth. If what he had told her was true, she doubted it.

Several minutes later, when Nelson went to replenish his drink, Pilar, like a child who had been holding her breath far too long, exploded, blurting out much of her pent-up hostility.

"If Philip Medina ever does make a move on you," she said, spouting in Spanish, her voice resonant with warning, "run the other way. He's cold and ruthless and selfish. And, might I add, he has a very low opinion of women. He doesn't trust anyone in a skirt. Probably some throwback to whatever went on between him and Nelson and his mother." She fumed for a moment and then continued her tirade. "When it became apparent that Nelson and I were headed for a permanent relationship, he came to my home and interrogated me. Can you imagine the nerve of him? Asking me what I was looking to gain? I'm convinced that Nelson made me sign a prenuptial because Philip wouldn't have given him a minute's peace if he didn't.

"Nelson's male ego would like to believe that Philip could never settle with one woman. My female instinct says the only reason he hasn't married is he hasn't found anyone who would want him!"

Isabelle listened politely and said nothing, but in her heart she disagreed. The Philip she knew wasn't cold and ruthless and selfish. The Philip who had interrogated Pilar sounded like a concerned son, not a bully. And despite Pilar's warnings, despite everything that had gone wrong between them, she wanted him.

The stress of the evening was beginning to take its toll. Tired, feeling slightly out of sorts, Isabelle decided to retreat to her room. She was about to mount the stairs when Paco stopped her.

"Please," he said, his hand touching her arm. "Don't run away from me."

"We have nothing to say to each other."

"Isabelle, why can't we at least be civil?"

His eyes were still coal black and lively, but his hair had grayed and his skin had begun to slacken. He was nearing sixty, yet, she realized with a start, she still thought of him as the young, swashbuckling Romeo she had encountered on the beach at Palma. Had she frozen him in time? Was she trapped in the same capsule?

"You know why, Señor Barba." Her voice was surprisingly void of venom.

Isabelle wondered whether it was because she was tired of repeating the same accusations or because she was beginning to have doubts.

"I loved your mother." His voice was vigorous. He never seemed to tire of asserting his affection for Althea. "I was angry that she didn't return that love, but never, ever, would I have hurt her."

"But you would have done anything to hurt my father. The same day you took his company, you sat in the tea room at the Ritz and lobbied to take his wife and child away from him. That night, someone did take my mother from my father. Why shouldn't I believe it was you?"

"Because it wasn't." He spoke with annoying assurance.

"If you're so certain of your own innocence, why do you care what I think?"

"You're Althea's daughter. You're all that's left of a woman I cherished."

"Ah, but I'm not all that's left. Dragon Textiles was hers. You own it, and I don't think you should."

"Why not?"

"One, because you only bought it to spite my father and impress my mother. Two, because you're doing a lousy job running it! And three, because it belongs to the Pujols and the de Lunas, not with you." She paused, but only for a moment. "I want to buy Dragon Textiles, Señor Barba. And I want you to sell it to me."

He was about to answer when they heard a bloodcurdling shriek. Isabelle turned in the direction of the howl and saw Pilar Medina hurl herself to the ground where Nelson lay in a lifeless heap.

The next few minutes were a blur of people bustling about trying to help. By the time the medics arrived, Nelson was dead.

Later that night, alone in their rooms, Isabelle and Flora discussed the evening's tragic events.

"Pilar is taking him back to Lake Lugano," Flora said, dabbing at her eyes. "He always said it was where he wanted to spend eternity."

"Do you plan to attend? It's a big trip to Lugano."

"Nelson was a dear friend."

"Then I'll go with you."

"Seeing Philip will be difficult, especially under these circumstances."

Inside, Isabelle smiled at the endless paradoxes that were her aunt. There, in the middle of a grieving face, were eyes filled with hope.

"It's all right, Tía Flora. I can deal with it."

It took Isabelle a long while to fall asleep that night. When she did, her rest was fitful, disturbed by nightmares steeped in unremitting blue. She saw herself, not as she was, but as she had been when she was young, with a little girl's face and little girl's clothes. Other people drifted in and out, few stayed, none were recognizable. Disjointed faces pressed against the dark side of her eyelids. Lips moved without words. Features floated in a midnight pool. A raised eyebrow. A mouth caught in a sneer. Voices made no sense. Images didn't connect. She saw herself howling into the void, demanding clarity. She felt as if she had been blindfolded and tossed into the centrifuge, spinning aimlessly, fighting the continuous onslaught of hallucination. She resisted, but it was too strong, too powerful. Deeper and deeper she sank, into the blue.

She woke with a start, bolting upright, her body covered in sweat, her mind still trapped in the dream. She hadn't realized she was screaming until Flora came to her side and held her tight.

After she had calmed, she quickly sketched what little she could remember. They told her nothing, yet she tried as best she could to explain what she thought had triggered the return of her nightmares.

"It was hearing that story about Papa. And seeing Paco Barba again." She studied the drawings, searching for answers that always seemed beyond her grasp. "Estrella swears he was with them that night in the restaurant."

"Alejandro checked that story many times," Flora said, wary about the effect of her next words. "There were others who substantiated that alibi."

"They paid everyone off!"

"Not everyone has a price, Isabelle."

Isabelle's breathing quickened. She stared at Flora. "Are you saying you don't think Paco killed my mother?"

"I'm saying I don't know."

Isabelle recalled Flora's face when François blurted out how Martín had killed the German soldier. "You don't think Papa killed her, do you?"

Flora hesitated for only a second before saying, "No. Never."

But for Isabelle, that second challenged a lifetime of implacable conviction. "Am I the only one who's absolutely certain of my father's innocence?"

"You're not certain, Isabelle, because you can't be. No one can be. Without a witness, or some hard evidence to pinpoint who was in that room that night, everyone, including your father, is innocent or potentially guilty."

"Estrella doesn't think we'll ever know the truth."

"Perhaps that's for the best," Flora said.

CHAPTER 22

Lake Lugano, Switzerland

The grounds of Villa Fortuna swarmed with mourners. One after another, launches motored across the lake from Lugano's city center to the villa's private dock, bobbing patiently in the water as their passengers disembarked, then turning around to repeat the trip.

For Isabelle, the day was a trial. She found funerals, even for strangers, difficult. As she took her place alongside Flora and Alejandro, her black straw hat straining sunlight from her face, she watched Philip walk slowly from the house down the long aisle separating the mourners toward a small, flower-strewn stage. Pilar was on his arm, her head bowed and pressed against him, her face veiled in black. Philip whispered to her throughout the length of their journey, prompting occasional nods, a few whimpers. Her seat was in the front, between her mother and her son, facing the view Nelson had declared "the reason for eyesight."

Across the lake—a deep, cool, azurite blue that glistened as if it had been sprinkled with the dust of a million pearls—a gentle ridge rose from the depths, standing like a symbolic barrier between the solidity of earth and the ethereal world that lay beyond. The sun was high, few clouds marred the sky, yet a lavender haze draped the horizon like a widow's veil, tingeing the distant hills with shades of lilac and mauve. As a light breeze blew softly across the lawn, Philip mounted the podium from which he would deliver the eulogy for his father.

His face was drawn, his eyes covered with tinted glasses. Isabelle noticed a tremor in his jaw muscles; he was gritting his teeth in dread of the task ahead. He stood tall, his body looked strong, but to Isabelle's eyes his left side seemed to list. She guessed that his father's death had hit him harder than he had imagined it would, that his body had become an arena for a battle between love and hate, grief and guilt, revenge and remorse.

Before he began the eulogy, he looked down at Pilar and then scanned the crowd. His eyes stopped twice: once when he spotted Isabelle, and again on an elegant woman in a finely cut suit. His gaze lingered on her, and the lines

of his forehead furrowed, then he returned to Isabelle. He looked but made
no gesture of acknowledgment. It wasn't necessary. She knew he had seen
her. He knew she was there.

"Nelson Medina was a man of many worlds. He published magazines and
books. He owned and raced horses. He collected classic cars and old masters. He was a shrewd investor and a daring gambler. He was a friend to
many, an enemy of some, a heartless cad in the eyes of others. In his last
years, perhaps because he had finally found someone who had the courage to
say no to him as often as she said yes, he found a happiness I don't think he
had known before."

Philip looked at the woman who had rarely said anything nice about him,
a woman with whom, that morning, he finally had made peace by saying
privately what he now said publicly.

"You taught him to see life's limitations and accept them. You encouraged
him to acknowledge his own shortcomings and accept imperfection in others. You taught him to laugh, most importantly at himself. By doing all that,
you not only made him a happy man. You made him a better man."

Pilar's head bobbed as she wept into her hands. Philip continued.

"Nelson Medina squeezed the juice out of life. He twisted the cloth of
human possibility, wringing from it everything he could. He never waited for
life to come to him, because he was afraid he'd miss something, that there
wouldn't be time for him to do all he wanted to do, or see all he wanted to
see. He attacked life, grabbing whatever he wanted, whether it was a woman,
a car, a painting, or a business. Some, including myself, faulted him for his
single-minded aggressiveness. But he got what he wanted, and he enjoyed
what he had. Counting the numbers who have come here today to pay their
respects, assessing the accumulations of his lifetime, recalling the pleasure
he took from each person and everything he met or acquired along the path,
I feel a certain envy. He took the risks and reaped the rewards.

"Nelson Medina was my father. We weren't close in the conventional
sense of the word. We didn't play ball or pal around like some fathers and
sons. We argued more than we talked. We debated more than we discussed.
We were estranged for more years than we were together. And we competed
with each other more than we confided in each other.

"Yesterday, as I was preparing this eulogy, a note was delivered to me from
someone who had spoken to my father the night he died. She thought it was
important for me to know that he was proud of what I had achieved and who
I had become. It was."

Flora squeezed Isabelle's hand.

"I wish he had said those things to me, it might have changed the conduct of our lives, but to be fair, there are things I should have said to him. I'd like to say them now.

"I learned much of what gives me pleasure from my father. Though he didn't introduce me to art, he showed me how to enjoy it, how to learn from it and live with it. He taught me to respect those who created beauty, just as he taught me to respect those who competed with me in business. He insisted I be strong, even when I thought I was destined to be weak. He forced me to use the brain I had, in place of the brawn I lacked. There were times when he pushed me too hard, yelled too loud, demanded too much. There were times when I wanted to push back and complain about impossible expectations and untenable demands. But if not for those expectations and demands, if not for him pushing me, I might not have become what I am today, a man who made his father proud."

He paused, looked down, fought for control.

"If I'm honest," he said quietly, "I would have to say I won't miss much of what was. But I will miss what might have been."

The silence was deafening as Philip left the stage and headed for Pilar, who collapsed in his arms, sobbing. He steadied her, and together they walked down to the dock and boarded a launch. As stipulated by his will, Nelson had been cremated. The launch prowled the shoreline, hovering close to his "private garden of Eden." When they reached a spot that pleased her, Pilar opened the cinerary urn and let the wind disperse the ashes of Nelson Medina.

Listening to Philip deliver a eulogy for his father, hearing the pain and sense of loss in his voice, struck a chord too deep inside Isabelle to ignore. Rattled, she sought a quiet place. As she wandered around the lawn toward the patio, she bumped into a tall blonde in a short black dress. Despite the large dark sunglasses, Isabelle recognized Nina immediately.

"What are *you* doing here?" The mere sight of her had pushed a button releasing a storm of repressed fury.

Nina remained defiant. "In case you're having a lapse, aside from our personal entanglements, Philip was my boss. Until you pressured him to ruin my career, that is."

"I did no such thing."

"Like hell you didn't!"

"Placing the blame on me would make it easy for you, wouldn't it? Then you'd be the victim. That's your favorite role, isn't it, Nina? The poor victim. The innocent scapegoat." Isabelle's voice was taunting.

Nina clenched and unclenched her fists, straining against an erupting anger that threatened to overwhelm her. "It was my professional duty to report the news no matter who it involved, especially when it was the truth."

She had fed that same line to Philip several times in phone calls and, when he would no longer accept her calls, in letters.

"Okay. If that's how it is." Isabelle's eyes were wide and mocking. "Do unto others."

"What does that mean?" Nina demanded.

Isabelle's eyes narrowed. Her face loomed as close to Nina's as she could without touching. Her voice was low and ominous. "The next time you print so much as a syllable about me or my family, I'll make certain the press knows the truth about you. The whole truth and nothing but the truth!"

Having said her piece, she left Nina alone on the lawn, her threat hovering in the air like a bomb homing in on its mark.

Nina wouldn't give Isabelle the satisfaction of showing her distress, but inside she was in turmoil. It had taken months of humiliating interviews and explanations to secure another syndication deal—smaller coverage, less significant papers—and a slot on a local morning show. She was working, but her prestige had plummeted. The last thing she needed was to be exposed as a personal fraud.

Throughout the years Nina had been concocting a past, inventing parents and schools and degrees and credentials, she knew that while there might have been others who knew the truth—Sam, Skye, neighbors from Santa Fe—only three could have denounced her with any credibility: Isabelle, Miranda, and Luis. Miranda and Luis probably would remain silent forever; it wasn't in their nature to strike back. But Isabelle meant what she said.

Suddenly, by upping the stakes, Isabelle had changed the game. She had gone from being an adversary Nina wanted to trump to a liability Nina had to defuse.

As Isabelle made her way through the throng, she realized that Nelson's ex-wives were in attendance. The only one who interested her was Olivia. Slim and urbane in a black Chanel suit, her hair cropped short, her elegant, still youthful features boldly displayed, she stood in stark contrast with her successors, who could only be described in varying degrees of flamboyance.

Isabelle had taken note of her when Philip sighted her during the ceremony. Afterward, Olivia discreetly had reunited with old acquaintances and one-time relatives, maintaining a respectful distance from both Pilar and Philip. Her companion, whom Isabelle assumed was her husband, was a debonair, silver-haired man suffused with an aura of personal confidence. Yet his eyes kept watch as if he weren't comfortable in these surroundings, as if he expected to encounter something exceedingly unpleasant during his stay here. His discomfort was understandable: this home, these grounds, these people, belonged to Nelson Medina, a man who had hurt Olivia in the past.

In a small study, Olivia and Philip faced each other. Philip's body language was stiff, wary, completely ill at ease. Olivia's posture showed a degree of sadness, but mostly determination.

"I'm surprised you came," Philip said, looking into dark eyes that matched his own, eyes he hadn't gazed upon in years.

"I didn't come for him. I hated him. I came for you."

Philip shifted from one foot to another, feeling like a small child, resenting her for making him feel that way. "You didn't hate his money. You took that rather than me." It felt funny saying what he had always wanted to say, but he supposed she had caught him with his guard down.

"I had no choice, and despite how it seemed, I didn't take his money for me. I invested it, and when you needed it, I gave it to you."

Philip was confused. "What money? Needed it for what?"

"The Towne-Crier chain."

Philip was visibly shaken. When he had graduated Wharton, he had gone to his father for a job. Nelson had told him the only way he was going to prove himself a man was to go out and make his own way in the world. It was the last time Philip had ever asked Nelson for anything.

He left San Francisco and got a job on a small newspaper in St. Louis, where no one had ever heard of Nelson Medina. After several years, talent and hard work rewarded him with investigative assignments, several of which gained national attention. But no matter how much Philip enjoyed what he was doing, his nature—whether genetically inherited or competitively inspired—was acquisitive. Not only did he want to write for the *St. Louis Reporter,* he wanted to own it.

In college Philip had been part of a group that was into gambling in a big way. Like the father he loathed, he was good at cards, with a gambler's instinct that rarely deserted him. It hadn't taken long for him to discover that cards could earn him a lot of money. By the time he graduated, having gambled part of his winnings in the stock market, he had managed to accumulate one hundred and fifty thousand dollars.

Using that as seed money and his last name (banks believing Nelson was a better, more supportive father than he was) as collateral, Philip bought the *St. Louis Reporter.* Several years later, when he wanted to turn his profits around and buy a chain of newspapers in the Midwest, he found himself short the amount the bank required. Within days of his meeting with the bank, John Harms, the family lawyer, had come to him with a certified check for half a million dollars. Philip had assumed the money came from Nelson. Instead it seemed his mother had funded his dynasty.

"I don't know what to say."

"Actually," Olivia said, a smile gracing her face, "I would prefer that you not say anything. I'd rather you let me speak. You listen."

Philip agreed, closing the door to the study, offering her a seat on the couch and a brandy. As she settled against the cushions, crossing her long, sinuous legs, Philip assayed her. The picture he had carried of her in his head was a little boy's view of his mother, favorable and, he had assumed, prejudiced. The grown man surveyed the woman without bias and still appreciated what he saw. She was quite attractive. He was glad.

"There's an old saying that 'absolute power corrupts absolutely,' " Olivia began. "I think that was true of your father. When I met him, he was charming, bright, handsome, curious, and fun to be with. He was the man you described as Pilar's husband." She smiled at the irony. "But when we married, he was young, just starting out. Then, he began to accumulate money and power. The more he got, the more he had, the worse he behaved.

"Nelson became abusive, both physically and emotionally." She looked squarely at Philip. "It wasn't unusual for him to slap me around when I displeased him, which was any time I disagreed with him or denied him. Nor was it unusual for him to humiliate me by cavorting with other women at parties given in our home."

She paused, swirled the amber liquid in its glass, and took a hefty swallow. Some memories never lost their sting.

"I stayed because of you." She paused again, as if she were debating how far to go, how much to tell. "When you were seven years old, I began having an affair with Jay Piersall. He was gentle and kind, and frankly, Philip, he loved me at a time I needed desperately to be loved.

"When you contracted polio, it was Jay who held me when I cried and massaged my muscles after I had spent hours massaging yours. It was Jay who gave me the strength to persevere and search for anything that would help you. Your father was too caught up in how your polio affected him to notice how it was impacting you or me.

"When I decided that life with him had become intolerable for both of us, I asked for a divorce, assuming there would be no question about custody."

Her mouth screwed into a contemptuous sneer. Nelson was dead. She had watched his ashes scatter less than two hours before, yet she couldn't stop hating him.

"Oh, he was more than happy to give me a divorce, but he wasn't going to give me anything else, especially my son."

Philip's agitation matched Olivia's, but for different reasons. She was reliving a lifetime of painful experiences in an effort to reach out to her only child, reciting unpleasant facts she felt he needed to know. Philip was listening, but the information was too shocking, coming too fast, for him to put it all together into a comprehensible whole. He needed time to absorb what he was hearing. For too many years he had lived according to a set of conclusions that suddenly was being declared invalid.

"California's a community property state," Philip said, ending the pregnant silence that had fallen between them.

Olivia nodded. "Unbeknownst to me, Nelson had been stockpiling an arsenal to counter that. As you know, Jay is a stockbroker. What you don't know, is that early in his career he had used insider information in deals that profited his customers and himself. Nelson, having been one of those customers, had a dossier on Jay which he threatened to bring to the SEC." She issued a mirthless laugh. "As if that weren't enough, the very same man who brought strange women into my bed was so outraged that I was leaving him for someone else, he vowed to go public with every seamy detail of my affair with Jay, scandalizing me, my family, and most of all you. My lawyer told me I had no other choice but to settle out of court."

Olivia downed the remains of her brandy. Philip fought to erase the images flitting before his eyes, images of his father shouting at her, threatening her, laughing at her inability to fight back. It wasn't that he didn't believe his father capable of such bullying; he had seen it as a child, been victim of it as an adult. But he wasn't ready to sympathize with Olivia.

"Nelson gave me a number of valuable paintings, all of which had been bought in my name, plus a cash settlement equivalent to my share of the house. That was it. No custody. No alimony. No visitation rights. Just my freedom."

She rolled her wedding band around on her finger, knowing it was the symbol of a love gained, a love lost. Her eyes were moist when she looked at Philip. While there was a sense of her having made peace with her decision, there was also deep regret.

"I took what I could and left. After Jay and I married and moved to New York, I initiated a custody suit. Nelson was married again. I thought surely he would have a change of heart, but his need for revenge was greater than I had anticipated."

She put her glass down on a nearby table and faced Philip. "But all that's in the past. Nelson's gone. We're here, and I would like us to try to start fresh, to have some sort of relationship." Her eyes softened and a familiar half smile danced on her lips. "I'm still your mother. And I still love you."

Philip, rattled by a rush of memories, just shook his head. "Maybe. We'll see. I don't know."

"Well, at least you didn't turn me down flat," Olivia said, reaching over to caress his cheek. "That's good enough for now."

Nina was beginning to question the wisdom of attending this funeral. It had been one of those spur-of-the-moment decisions. When Anthony had called to tell her what had happened, she had expressed her shock and, of course, her deep sorrow at the passing of Nelson Medina. When he'd said he was heading to Switzerland for the funeral, she'd announced she was going along.

Her plan had been to use the occasion to worm her way back into Philip's good graces, but it wasn't working out that way. When she had gone through the receiving line and it was her turn to pay her respects, he had been polite, but nothing more. Then she'd had her set-to with Isabelle. Then the unexpected appearance of Sissy Cromwell Crowes Hartwick Van Clef had put Anthony in a nasty mood. And now she had spotted Tía Flora and Alejandro on the other side of the living room. Was there no end to her bad luck?

Fortunately Anthony had decided that being in the same room with his ex-wife and her latest husband was so distasteful, he had gone in search of a bar. Nina was left to contemplate her next move. As unobtrusively as she could, she studied Flora and Alejandro. They were still a handsome couple: Flora with her silver helmet of hair, pale face, and flowing white dress; Alejandro with his avian features and reed-thin frame. Did she approach them? Pretend she didn't see them? Avoid them? (After all, how would she explain knowing them to Anthony?) In the end, her affection for the elderly Catalans won out.

"Flora Pujol!" she said, striding across the room, a broad, expectant grin on her face. "Alejandro Fargas! What a surprise!" Flora's expression remained blank, Alejandro's suspicious. "Tía Flora," she said quietly, hoping no one could overhear, "it's me, Nina. Don't you recognize me?"

Flora looked her straight in the eye, letting Nina see that her vision was clear and precise and unclouded by age. "No, I don't recognize you at all."

"I spent a summer with you at the Castell. Of course it was many years ago and I was only a teenager and I guess I've changed a lot." She tittered nervously. "You haven't changed at all. You look great. Both of you." Neither Flora nor Alejandro responded. "I still remember that fabulous party at your country home, Alejandro. What a great time that was."

"What did you say your name was?" Flora asked, cutting Nina short.

"Nina."

"Nina what?"

She should have known not to match wits with Flora. "It's Nina Davis now," she replied in a voice barely above a whisper.

"I knew a Nina Duran once," Flora mused, her eyes fixed on the younger woman's face. "She and my grandniece, Isabelle, were like sisters. As I recall, Nina Duran was a nice girl, sweet and honest, with a real sense of family. Unfortunately, that girl seems to have disappeared."

Flora's tone was even, without harshness or obvious criticism, but Nina heard the disappointment, the dismay, the hope that perhaps Nina would cease her charade and return to her old skin. Nina scolded herself for her naiveté. How could she not have known that Flora and Alejandro would side with Isabelle? She was kin. Nina was an outsider.

"Obviously I've made a mistake." Nina's defenses had kicked in, giving her voice an edge. "I'm not who you thought I was. And you're not the people I remember." She turned, but Flora caught her arm.

"Family is a powerful connective, Nina. But the power is not in the blood, it's in the heart."

Nina wanted to go, yet something inside her needed to hear what Flora had to say.

"Those who love you first, love you without condition. It doesn't matter how wide the breach or how much time has passed, it's still there for you if you want it."

"I have everything I want!"

"Perhaps you believe that," Flora said, "but I don't. One of these days you may be called upon to make a choice. Don't make the mistake of choosing pride over family. You'll regret it."

*   *   *

"Your presence is exceedingly disturbing, Miss de Luna."

"And why is that, Mr. Hartwick?"

"This is a funeral. I've known Nelson Medina most of my life. I flew thousands of miles to pay my respects. I'm supposed to feel sad. Yet, standing here with you, I confess, I'm not sad at all. You're exquisite."

Isabelle laughed. "And you have a very smooth routine."

Hartwick looked aghast. "Are you questioning my sincerity? I'm cut to the quick."

Isabelle laughed again. "I don't know how sincere you are, but you are charming."

His green eyes filled with invitation. "Does that mean if I called you for dinner you would accept?"

Hartwick was Nina's significant other. Why was he coming on to her? Isabelle wondered.

"Perhaps," she said, remaining deliberately vague.

"I can be very persistent."

"And I can be equally resistant."

With mock gallantry, he bowed from the waist. When he stood he took her hand, raised it to his lips, and kissed it. "It is with an open mind and a full heart that I accept the challenge, my lady."

Nina could barely control her rage. After Flora and Alejandro had left her, she had gone looking for Anthony. She found him on the terrace, deep in conversation with Isabelle. Though she hadn't heard a word of their conversation, watching them laugh and flirt with each other had infuriated her almost to the point of hysteria. Had Isabelle approached Anthony, targeted him deliberately to vex her? Or had Anthony put the moves on Isabelle? There were rumors that several times, when she had been out of town, he had been seen with other women; but she had dismissed them. She had told herself they were probably authors or publicists or agents. After all, publishing was filled with women.

Still, she worried. Secretly she had expected he would have proposed to her by now. They were practically living together. While she hadn't pushed it, neither had she ever discounted her interest in the notion of marriage. Was it possible he was growing tired of her? Longevity was not one of Anthony's strengths. Neither was loyalty.

But, she vowed, positively seething at the sight of her lover kissing her enemy's hand, if he's going to leave me, it's not going to be for Isabelle!

*   *   *

It didn't take long for Nina to decide on the quickest, easiest way to strike back. Despite her insistence that they were finished, she was certain Isabelle loved Philip. Despite his protestations to the contrary, Anthony competed with him on every playing field he could find. Neither would be happy to see Nina with him. For a while Nina thought she'd never be able to activate her plan. Whenever two were in place, the third was not. Finally she noticed all three on the lawn. Isabelle was introducing Anthony to Flora and Alejandro. Philip was being attacked by Hollywood's newest crush, a stunning redhead named Bettina Marlowe.

Bettina fixed the collar on Philip's shirt and stroked his cheek. Philip nodded as the screen star with the pre-Raphaelite hair spoke and appeared to be giving her his full attention, but Nina could see he wanted desperately to be rescued. After whispering to Bettina that Martin Scorsese was inside the house looking for her, she watched the eager actress cut and run, then turned to Philip. He didn't look thrilled to see her.

"I know I'm not your favorite person," she said with proper humility, "but when I heard about your father's sudden death, I wasn't about to let our past disagreements keep me from coming here to express my sincere condolences."

He didn't look as though he were buying this. Truthfully, Nina didn't care, as long as he didn't walk away from her. She wasn't looking to create a relationship, she was creating an illusion.

"Having lost both my parents, I know how devastating a quick, unexpected passing can be." She reached out, clasped his arms, and looked deep into his eyes. "Death is always difficult, but when you're unprepared for it, well, it's . . ." She shook her head from side to side, slowly, mournfully. "I can't tell you how moved I was by your eulogy. I wish I had been capable of such eloquence when my parents were memorialized. Unfortunately, I was too young."

Her voice caught in her throat. Philip—bless his compassionate soul—put his arm around her and reassured her. Nina found it difficult not to smile.

Isabelle had watched Nina's one-act play and had made the mistake of believing her eyes. It hurt to see Philip with her, to see them talk and touch; to imagine them making love. Yes, it made her jealous and angry and bitter. Yes, she was eager to get away from the sight of them. But she had come to Lugano to offer her condolences, and that's what she intended to do.

It was late when the crowd of sympathizers finally thinned. Philip was conversing with someone when she approached to pay her respects. He continued talking, but his hand found hers and held it firmly.

"Thank-you for your note," he said when the man to whom he had been speaking departed.

"I thought you should know how he felt."

"It made a difference." His onyx eyes bored into hers, making it difficult to look away.

"I'm sorry about Nelson," she said, not knowing where else to go.

"I'm sorry about us." He looked at her face, so ivory and demure beneath her broad-brimmed hat, her body lush and inviting even in her tailored black suit. "Can't you forgive me? Can't we put all of that extraneous stuff behind us?" He lifted her chin, demanding that she look directly at him. "Yes, there are things I should have told you, but I wasn't deliberately hiding anything. It just didn't come up. Can't we move past that?"

"I don't know." Had he moved past his affair with Nina? Could she ever move past that? "It's not that easy."

He forced a laugh. "Sure it is. Just say 'You're forgiven' and it's over."

His tone was too offhand, too breezy, too nonchalant. Suddenly he sounded like a man who was used to getting his way, and she didn't like it. She wondered if she had been the flavor of the month for May, if Nina was the flavor for July, and who knew, if maybe Bettina Marlowe was already lined up for August. All at once she was angry.

"I noticed you talking to your mother in the study earlier today. Is that what happened between the two of you? She said 'I'm sorry for abandoning you; I thought you'd understand'? You said 'Sure, okay, you're forgiven' and the hurt just disappeared? I don't think so."

"This isn't the same, Isabelle."

"Not the circumstances, perhaps, but the principle is the same. You can't take anyone's feelings for granted, especially those who trust you. And people who are supposed to love each other can't have secrets."

"Do we love each other?"

Neither one had ever spoken that word before. Philip leaped on the opportunity. Isabelle demurred. She was embarrassed. She hadn't meant to reveal so much of herself.

"Do we?" he repeated.

Isabelle wished she could have said yes, but he hadn't affirmed his affection for her, he had asked a question of her. Moreover, his voice had been shaded with hesitation. Isabelle needed certainty.

"Once, we may have been headed that way," she said, refusing to force what he seemed unwilling to give. "Now, I'm not so sure."

She walked away without giving him a chance to respond. He let her go without taking the initiative to stop her. Strong, independent, envied by much of the world, they were a man and a woman scarred by their child-hoods, both emotionally damaged by their parents—she by their deaths, he by their lives.

Isabelle needed to feel safe. Philip needed to be sure. The chasm between them widened.

CHAPTER 23

Hazel Strauss had grown up in a first-floor apartment in Kew Gardens, Queens. It was a nice building, with a garden courtyard and airy rooms, near a park that had lots of swings, a sandbox, and a jungle gym that other children were allowed to climb. Hazel couldn't play on it because her mother was afraid her daughter might fall and hurt herself. Hazel couldn't walk to school with her friends; her mother was afraid something might happen on the way. She couldn't have a puppy; her parents were afraid the dog might attack her.

Murray and Pearl Strauss were immigrants who, like most immigrants, had come to America with language problems, customs that differed from their neighbors, and hopes for a better life; they had come with dilapidated suitcases and ragged bundles, filled with the same apprehension as any newcomer to a foreign land; but they had arrived with something other refugees didn't have—a string of numbers tattooed on their arms. Murray and Pearl Strauss had survived the Holocaust.

At thirty-two, Hazel Strauss, now known as Skye, was afraid of planes, trains, dogs, and cars. She flew only when absolutely necessary—and then only with a tranquilizer—never took trains, avoided anything canine, and refused to drive on city streets or crowded highways. Having grown up with no grandparents, no siblings, no aunts, only one uncle, two cousins, and an extended family of people linked by horrific experiences rather than comforting genes, Skye looked with undisguised envy upon those who had stacks of family albums and cousins clubs meetings and backyard barbecues. She had trouble with the notion of casual friendships and distant relatives. People were categorized as either acquaintances or "like family"; she either loved them and would do anything for them or could take them or leave them; would defend them to the death or couldn't care less. There was no middle ground.

She was openly neurotic, had logged an inordinate number of hours on a psychiatrist's couch, and was, by her own admission, "nuts." Yet she was an extremely accomplished, very attractive, supremely confident woman who could claim the respect of her peers, financial success, and a handsome, well-educated orthopedic surgeon as a suitor. But then, anything less would have disappointed Murray and Pearl. And Skye couldn't do that.

Pleasing her parents was the cornerstone of her life; she had to make certain that their dreams for her were fulfilled, regardless of whether or not they coincided with her dreams for herself. Growing up, she couldn't tell her mother she'd been in a fight with one of her friends, or felt fat and ugly, or wished she didn't have to take piano lessons, or would have liked it better if her father had been warmer and less rigid, her mother quieter and less smothering.

"You don't know how lucky you are," was the constant retort. It wasn't said as criticism; it was uttered in hushed tones usually reserved for prayer—in this case a prayer that their child would never witness what they had, would never suffer as they had.

Whenever Skye thought about her parents, their relatives and friends, the image she conjured was one of sad faces. They partied hard at bar mitzvahs and weddings, laughed loudly at jokes only they understood, enjoyed meals with near desperate gusto, danced the hora with a zeal that left others exhausted. But she knew they had secrets they couldn't—or wouldn't—share.

It was that sense of exclusion that left Skye feeling distanced. It was seeing those numbers on their arms every day that erased the notion other children entertained that the world was perfect and told her she was different. It was that feeling of having to make up for her parents' torturous youth, of having to offset their pain, that had Skye throwing up every day before she went to school, fearful that she might do something to let them down. It was the undeviating, unremitting, overwhelming guilt—about surviving when others had died, succeeding while others failed, eating while others starved, having more, feeling better—plus an ever-present aura of premonition, that made it impossible for them, or for Skye, to have a sustained good time without worrying that something bad might happen.

She understood. One minute her parents were living a normal life, being kids, celebrating holidays, falling in love, going to school, doing whatever young people in Poland did. The next minute they were ripped from their homes, locked inside a railroad car, taken to a terrible place where families were separated from each other, where they had to sleep in drafty, disease-ridden, overcrowded, filthy wooden bunks, were given barely any food, and were forced to do backbreaking labor, where their parents disappeared into a big building that made an awful noise and created a gruesome stench.

She understood the motivation behind the mantra "The less anyone knows, the better," as well as their refusal to accept illness or inadequacy or to discuss things outside the home that might cast aspersions or lead others to believe something, anything, was wrong. Hitler had taken the weak and imperfect first. Hitler had encouraged neighbors to betray neighbors. Hitler had tried to wipe out an entire people simply because they were Jewish. The silence and the secrecy had been necessary. They were the tools of survival.

For much of her adult life, Skye had tried to loosen the strings that bound her to her parents' past. Instead of being a teacher in a safe, suburban school, as they would have liked, she dove headfirst into the bohemian art world, living in that strange place called SoHo and associating with those strange people. She rebelled against their hopes for an early marriage and instant grandchildren by becoming involved with unacceptables: older men like Ezra Edward Clark, a Wall Street type who either had never heard the word *faithful* or simply didn't understand it, a ravishing Italian sculptor who thought his sexual prowess made up for his lack of talent, and a string of others who never could have qualified as suitable husband material.

Then she met Sam Hoffman. The Prince. Her parents' dream come true: Jewish, a successful doctor, bright, handsome, devoted to his family, and madly in love with their daughter. Though Skye had been taken with him immediately, it was the total rightness of Sam that bothered her. Was she in love with him because she had been programmed to fall in love with him? Was she in love with him because he would make her parents happy? Or because he made her happy? For five years she played with their relationship like a yo-yo. She'd allow them to grow close and then she'd push away; she'd let things get really good, then pull back. She wasn't teasing. She was testing the gods.

Sam had been as patient as a saint, but finally he had had enough.

"Miss Hazel," he had said one night in her apartment, "I am asking for your hand in marriage. Now this is a simple question, Miss Hazel, one that requires a simple answer. No long-winded excuses about building a career or not being sure or needing more time. It's either 'Yes, I love you and want to spend the rest of my life with you.' Or 'No, I don't love you, it's been fun, see you around.'"

When Skye came to Santa Fe in June of 1988, she came with two questions for Isabelle: Would she be Skye's maid of honor at her wedding to Sam in December? and Would she be the solo artist at the opening of Skye's gallery in October?

Isabelle was thrilled about both. "Some maid of honor," she said, hugging Skye and giggling about her upcoming thirty-second birthday.

"The rabbi's not checking proof of age, Isabelle. All you have to do is look gorgeous, walk down the aisle, hold my bouquet, weep a little so my mother's not the only one bawling under the *chupa,* and assure me every thirty seconds between now and then that I'm doing the right thing."

"You don't need me for that," Isabelle said, suddenly envying her friend. "Sam's the best, which is exactly what you deserve."

Skye's eyes watered, but her mouth was wreathed in a smile. "When I think of all those years I kept him dangling. Whew! Am I lucky he didn't take a hike." She sighed at the might-have-beens. "Early on, he had tuned in to my neurosis about believing that nothing good was permanent. My shrink says it's typical of children of survivors. He calls it the here-today-gone-tomorrow syndrome."

Isabelle nodded. She had survived a different tragedy, but she suffered from the same syndrome. "Now what's this about a gallery?"

"Can you believe it? I'm opening my own place! Me! Fat little Hazel Strauss from Queens." Skye fell back on the couch and guffawed.

"If you'll pardon me for saying so, it's about time."

"Yeah, I guess. But better late than never, eh?"

Skye studied her friend. Isabelle was trying to conceal it, but she was having a hard time absorbing all this good news. Understandable, since in Skye's opinion, Isabelle's life-enjoyment meter was teetering on empty. In New York she worked twenty hours a day and went out rarely. Here, Miranda reported it was pretty much the same. Isabelle was hiding: from the art world, from Julian, from life, but most especially from Philip.

"So, now that your suit with Julian has been settled and you're free to relocate, how about coming with me and being my opening act?"

"I'd be insulted if you asked anyone else."

"I glad you feel that way." She paused, pretending to polish her engagement ring, which was considerable (after all, Murray was a diamond merchant). "Would you feel differently if I told you Philip Medina is financing the project?"

Isabelle was torn. Skye was her best friend. She trusted her. It was Philip she couldn't be sure of.

Skye had anticipated the conflicted look on Isabelle's face. "Listen, Is. It's your call. If it really bums you out, we'll forget it, no hard feelings. If you can handle it, I'll have a contract drawn up and sent to you. You have your lawyer look it over. That way there can be no surprises, no secrets, and no hidden strings."

Isabelle knew how important this was to Skye. In truth, it was a good move for her as well. The suit with Julian had just been settled. He got to keep whatever she had done while under contract to him—including the "Visions in Blue" series—but not the paintings she had withheld for herself. If he showed her works and they sold, he had to give her fifty percent of the sale. Best of all, she was free to sign with someone else. Skye's timing was perfect.

"I do need to exhibit," she said, pretending to think out loud even though her decision was already made. "And you are well-known to both the press and the big collectors. You'll probably be a great success in spite of yourself. So yes. I would be happy to have you represent me. Have your lawyer call mine in the morning."

A week later Skye informed Isabelle that Philip was coming to New Mexico on business and that she had invited him to stay for the engagement party Jonas and Sybil were throwing for her and Sam. Isabelle hadn't seen him in a year. She had read his name in the columns, at openings, at charity dinners, at auctions, with a different woman every time. It had been rumored that he had been one of those bidding on van Gogh's *Sunflowers* when it sold in London at Christie's to a Japanese corporation for $39.9 million, and on van Gogh's *Irises* at Sotheby's New York auction when it sold to an Australian tycoon for $49 million. She had dismissed the stories because Philip's collection was primarily contemporary, but then she read that Nelson's will had decreed that Villa Fortuna was to be turned into a museum and that Philip was to take charge of managing his art collection. *Sunflowers* and/or *Irises* would have fit perfectly with what she had seen at the villa.

While Isabelle tended to downplay Philip's appearance, Miranda and Luis could hardly contain their excitement. First Skye and Sam were engaged. That alone was enough to set their pulses racing. Jonas and Sybil were throwing a huge party at La Casa in honor of their betrothal. And now Philip Medina was coming to Santa Fe and staying at their hotel. Though Luis warned Miranda not to play cupid, he had to admit he was anxious to meet the man his wife claimed was the love of Isabelle's heart.

It was awkward at first. Isabelle had been polite, had taken him on a tour of the grounds, but had kept a tight rein on her enthusiasm. To his credit, Philip followed her lead, waltzing at a respectful distance, never crossing the line and asking anything personal. That night Miranda had arranged a family dinner as a welcome for their guest, with Jonas and Sybil, Sam and Skye, Rebecca and her husband, Mack, joining them.

Philip charmed them as easily as he had charmed Flora. He exchanged golf stories with Jonas—promising to play with him, Sam, and Mack before leaving town—discussed the surge in popularity of Southwestern art with Sybil and Miranda, politics with Mack (a first-term congressman from Massachusetts), and the changing face of the tourist business with Luis. Mack was curious about Philip's burgeoning cable business and how he thought it would affect the future of television. Philip thought cable would make TV better through competition. Miranda wanted to know what he was doing with Nelson's collection.

"I've hired a team of curators to inventory and evaluate everything. The collection is extensive, to say the least, but it's lacking organization. The bulk of it will remain at Villa Fortuna, but I am entertaining requests to have segments travel to selected museums."

Sam, conveying anxiety about Skye's new venture, asked whether Philip believed the skyrocketing prices of art at auction would continue to influence gallery prices.

"If anything, the auctions have stirred the pot. Prices for contemporary artists are ballooning." He turned to Isabelle. "You're going to be astounded at what a de Luna is going to fetch when your next show opens."

"I hope so," she said, smiling self-consciously. She feared she had been out of the market too long, that whatever audience she had built up had moved on to adopt other favorites.

After dinner Sam suggested a drink at El Farol, a bar and tapas restaurant at the top of Canyon Road. The Durans and the elder Hoffmans begged off, as did Rebecca and Mack, who had to tend to the children.

The house, a landmark building that had been there since Santa Fe's early days, was a warren of small rooms, and this evening it was packed. The front room stretched long and narrow, with the band and the bar on one side, a string of tables filled with people who took their beer and their country music seriously on the other.

As they were led to a small table in the far corner, eyes peeked out from under cowboy hats and cigarette smoke and followed them. This was a locals bar, so no one paid much attention to Isabelle and Sam. They were authentic, and it showed in their well-worn boots, Sam's Navaho bolo and leather vest, Isabelle's conch belt and Zuni earrings. It was people like Skye, in her downtown New York black, and Philip in his uptown sports jacket, silk shirt, and slacks, who provoked curious looks and under-the-breath commentary.

Once they were seated, they ordered tequila shots for the men, margaritas-no-salt for the women. When the waiter brought their drinks, Philip offered a toast to the newly afianced couple. When Sam ordered a second round, Philip toasted their mutual venture: Skye's gallery and her debut artist. Isabelle nodded her appreciation and smiled as she watched Philip slug down the tequila and keep time to the music. She had been fighting her attraction for this man, but seeing how easily he blended into an environment she had considered out of his realm, she sensed she was losing the battle.

"You're very adaptable," she said.

"To what?"

"Philip, you're an international kind of guy. This is down-home western, and yet you're into it."

"Surprised?"

She laughed. "Yes! I picture you doing the bossa nova, not the tush-push."

"There's a lot about me you don't know, Isabelle."

"I suppose so." She looked away. That boyish smile still had the power to excite her.

"Though I'm delighted to celebrate with Skye and Sam and to formalize your association with Skye's gallery, I came to Santa Fe for a completely different reason. Tomorrow I'm going to visit a very special foundation. How would you like to accompany me?"

He had leaned closer so she could hear him over the music. His sandalwood scent triggered memories that sent her blood racing.

"Sure. Why not?"

They left before breakfast with a basket provided by Miranda and filled with muffins, a thermos of coffee, and fruit. When Philip headed northwest from Santa Fe, Isabelle assumed he was headed toward Bandelier, the remains of a large Anasazi farming village now a national monument. As she laid her head back on the seat of Philip's rented convertible and raised her face to the rising sun, she smiled. She hadn't been to Bandelier in ages. It would be fun walking the grounds and climbing the cliff houses.

The air turned cooler, prompting Isabelle to open her eyes. Philip handed her a mug of coffee, which she accepted gratefully.

"Where are we?" They were high in the hills, surrounded by the rich green of a lush forest.

"Near Los Alamos."

"I didn't know you had interests in scientific foundations," she said, again making assumptions.

Los Alamos was the site that had been chosen for the laboratories that produced the world's first atomic weapons. During World War II the community had been isolated from the rest of the state and cloaked in secrecy, because of its national security task force known as the Manhattan Project. Though the city had been opened in 1957 and the original laboratories had been transformed into research labs, Los Alamos remained a top-secret facility.

"I don't," Philip said, turning onto a curving mountain road that led away from the city and up onto a mesa top that boasted the Jemez mountains on one side and the Sangre de Cristo range on the other.

"Where are we going?" Isabelle was confused. "I feel like a child playing blind man's buff."

"A very apt sentiment," he said as he drove beneath a wooden archway that announced the entrance to Boys' Ranch.

They drove slowly down a dirt road flanked by rustic wooden cabins on one side, assorted sports fields and tennis courts on the other. Ahead of them was a cluster of clapboard buildings and a large vegetable patch that looked like an old victory garden. Beyond, Isabelle saw a waterfront with a dock and rowboats on what must have been a man-made lake. Philip parked the car and escorted Isabelle to the main building.

"Okay," she said. "This is a camp."

"Very good."

"You own it."

"Right again."

"You went here as a little boy?"

"No, but somewhere just like it."

When he opened the doors to the dining room, Isabelle couldn't believe what she saw. This was not an ordinary camp. The children were not tanned, healthy, physically fit specimens of American youth. These were sickly children with pale complexions, withered limbs, and curved spines, accident victims, children enfeebled by muscular deficiencies or the residual effects from debilitating diseases, asthmatics laboring to breathe, their inhalators on the table in front of them.

Philip introduced her to the staff, but Isabelle's attention remained focused on the children. As she and Philip visited each table, she saw no tired eyes or self-pitying looks. Their faces lit up as Philip greeted each one by name. Hands were raised to give him a high-five, challenges were levied, gibes were tossed, and promises were made, including one that put Isabelle in the outfield during a softball game.

"Before we do anything else," he said to her when breakfast was over and the boys filed out, "we have to change. The rules are for everyone." He handed her a pair of khaki shorts and a white shirt with a red Boys' Ranch logo and showed her to a place where she could dress.

As he guided her around the camp, she noticed how hard the boys played—or worked, to put it more accurately. She noticed too that despite the slight chill in the air, everyone wore shorts, no one wore a sweater.

"The goal of Boys' Ranch is to toughen these kids up so they can get on with their lives," Philip said, seeing her distress. "It may look harsh, but honestly, it's not."

"It's cold."

"No, it's merely cool, and they can handle it. Just as they can handle having people see them without coverings."

Isabelle looked at him. They were both thinking of their conversation on the beach. "You never stop feeling self-conscious, but you do stop feeling ashamed."

They stopped by the tennis courts. On one court, four nine-year-olds were playing. They hit the ball fairly well, but two of them had trouble running after their shots. One had difficulty serving. But all of them kept at it, shouting encouragement to each other. From the sidelines Philip egged them on. At their insistence he joined them on the court. One at a time he volleyed with them, making them move about, running down even their most errant returns, making them feel strong and able and good about themselves.

Isabelle sat on the wooden bleachers and watched. The legacy of Philip's polio was as visible as the boys' various weaknesses. He was one of them and they knew it, which gave them incentive and hope and the drive to succeed. It amazed Isabelle when she thought that she had made love to this man and had never thought about what others, his father included, might term his imperfection. Was it her artist's eye that rejected the conventional need for symmetry and saw beauty in irregularity? Was it her belief that no one was perfect, nothing was absolute? Or in Philip's case, was it that she loved the man beneath too much to care about the shell without?

"I was nine and a half and fresh out of a rehabilitation hospital when my father sent me to a camp similar to this one," Philip said, taking her to see the stables and the gymnastics center, stopping every few minutes to speak to a counselor or to throw a ball to an eager child. "At first, it was truly the summer from hell. I didn't think it was possible to hate anyone as much as I hated him then. But as the summer wore on and I got stronger and learned to fend for myself, I thanked him. Begrudgingly, of course. I left that camp knowing I was never going to be Arnold Schwarzenegger, but, more important, I left knowing I didn't have to be to survive and succeed."

There was no arts and crafts center at Boys' Ranch, no theater for putting on plays, no camp sing. There was, however, rock climbing, day-long hikes, kayaking, and wilderness weekends. They learned boxing and karate and other martial arts. They lifted weights and jogged and rode mountain bikes and swam in an ice-cold lake. Everything they did was a challenge. Everything they did was difficult and sometimes painful. But every day it got easier.

Before lunch, Philip took Isabelle to the driving range and handed her a golf club. "Let's see if you remember what I taught you."

"Must I?" she said, conscious of the snickering going on among the boys using the range.

"Yes. You must."

Snarling at Philip, Isabelle placed her left hand on the grip, two knuckles showing, the V between her thumb and index finger pointing down, closed her right hand over her left, planted her feet, and swung. Three times she whiffed the ball, missing it completely, nearly throwing herself off balance.

"I'm not a happy camper," she mumbled under her breath.

"Keep your eye on the ball," said the boy next to her.

"Head down," another one contributed.

"Bend your knees." Another county heard from.

Isabelle concentrated as hard as she could. Slowly she drew the club away from the ball, shifted her weight, rotated her hips, cocked her wrists, and came down and through, lifting the ball off the tee and into the air. Her eyes widened as it flew straight and high and long, forming the loveliest arc she'd ever seen. She acknowledged the applause of the crowd with a deep, exaggerated bow.

"Not bad," Philip said, chuckling.

"What's next?" she asked, pretending exasperation but unable to hide the fun she was having.

"Softball."

She groaned, but when they reached the field she gladly took a glove and cap and her place in left field. She surprised them all with her ability to catch and throw. She stunned them when she hit a triple. Philip almost fainted when she slid home on a bunt.

"Luis loves baseball," she explained, brushing dirt off her knees. "So do

Sam and Rebecca." So did Nina, she recalled. "As kids we played all the time."

"Is there no end to your talents?" Philip draped his arm around her shoulders. She automatically slid hers around his waist.

They watched some swimming meets, a riding exhibition, and a wrestling match. When they were getting ready to leave, a few of the younger boys, the ones void of any inhibition, followed them to the car, taunting Philip unmercifully.

"Is she your girlfriend?"

"She's got great legs!"

"Yeah!"

"Are you two in love?" This boy's nose was pinched, as if he couldn't imagine anything more disgusting.

Philip raised both his hands, silencing the chorus. "I don't know, guys."

"Need a few tips?" Lots of giggles followed that remark.

"We like her."

"Me too." Philip grinned at them and winked at Isabelle, who just smiled and shook her head.

"So what's the problem?"

"Let's just say I'm working on it."

They jumped all over him, eager for an embrace or a handshake or a high-five from the man they viewed as their hero. When they drove away, Isabelle thought she saw a few tears.

"I had a wonderful day," she said as they eased onto the highway back to Santa Fe.

"I'm glad."

"You were right last night when you said there was a lot I didn't know about you." Philip's eyes stayed on the road. Isabelle's eyes traced his profile, the straight nose, the strong jaw, the muscular shoulders. "You're a pretty terrific guy."

"That's what I've been trying to tell you." His lips curled. "If only you'd listen."

She smiled, put her head back on the seat, tilted the brim of her Boys' Ranch baseball cap over her eyes, and said, "I'm working on it."

Skye had nothing to do. Sam had driven up to Vail to examine a few members of the United States ski team who needed a clean bill of health from their surgeon before they could start training for the upcoming season. Philip was off at that camp Isabelle had told her about. Jonas was working. Isabelle and

Sybil had gone to Taos for the day. They had asked Skye to go with them, but she planned to go over the guest list Sybil had given her to make sure all the addresses were complete. When she grew bored, she decided to visit Miranda at Enchantments.

She had barely gotten a foot in the door before she ran into Miranda, who was walking out.

"Hi! I thought I'd come by and pick your brain for some advice about managing a gallery."

"I can't today, Skye. Some other time."

"Oh, sure." Skye thought Miranda looked uncomfortable. "Is something wrong?"

"No. Not at all. It's just, I have somewhere to go." She was rushing Skye, eager to get her out of the gallery so she could be on her way. "If you don't mind, I'd like to close up."

Skye mumbled some hurried good-byes, then walked down the steps and across the street to her car. She had just closed the door when Luis pulled up; Miranda got in his car and they left, rather quickly, Skye thought. She'd never know what prompted her to follow them—caprice, curiosity, a feeling that continued to nag at her—but she swallowed her vehicular fears, jumped into her car, and raced to catch them. Lagging two car lengths behind, she kept them in sight as they drove along Highway 68, the main route to Taos.

As she drove, she recalled that the Durans had seemed a bit melancholy the other night. When she had mentioned it to Sam, he'd told her their son had died sometime in June. They always turned morose around the anniversary of his death. Maybe that's what she saw in their faces, Skye thought. Certainly she had seen that look a dozen times on her parents' faces, each time they lit a *yahrzeit* candle for a parent or a sibling or a grandparent who had perished.

When the Durans exited the highway at Espanola onto a smaller, less congested road, Skye was delighted. Now she could drive at a slower, more comfortable pace. For a long while they followed a dull road through a lot of vacant flatland that seemed bound for nowhere. Suddenly they made a sharp turn up a hill that dead-ended at a small, nearly invisible mesa. Skye, realizing she could watch their comings and goings from down below, drove past, turned around, and, from a distant but reasonable vantage point, waited. They stayed for nearly an hour and then, much more slowly than they'd come, left.

When she was certain they were gone, Skye made her way up the hill they had just descended. Atop the mesa she found what she had suspected: a cemetery. Quietly, respectfully, she got out of her car and walked through the wrought-iron gate that defined this isolated burial place. It was an old cemetery, with many tilted gravestones and weather-worn inscriptions, yet something about its overall appearance looked oddly familiar. The markings, the symbols, the small rocks placed on top of several headstones, all accosted her in a rush of disconcerting visions. Something was wrong; something didn't fit. Nervously she approached the nearest tombstone. Her heart pounded as she studied the epitaph. Shaking slightly, she moved to the next one and the next, overwhelmed by the uncomfortable knowledge that she had uncovered a deeply held, desperately protected secret.

The Durans were Catholic, yet she could find few signs of Christian affiliation in this cemetery. There were no huge crosses, no angels, no statues of saints or the Holy Mother, no quotations of Holy Scripture from the New Testament. Instead she recognized Hebrew writing, the braided havdalah candle used on the Jewish Sabbath, a six-petaled flower that looked suspiciously like the six-pointed Star of David, the lamp that symbolized the Eternal Light. There were headstones shaped like the ark that traditionally held a Torah and, on many, a rose, which to the Sephardim, those descended from the Jews of Spain, stood for the celebration of Moses receiving the Ten Commandments from God.

Some symbols were easy for Skye to place. They were forthright and obvious, chiseled with pride in a heritage they may have kept hidden in life but couldn't continue to hide after death. Others were more subtle, possibly reflecting the fear of the fallout from revelation. Knowing that the number seven held a mystical significance in Judaism helped Skye decode several stones. Being able to read the Hebrew phrases taken from the Twenty-third Psalm, also important in Judaism, helped identify others.

The few gravestones that did bear the sign of the cross had a six-pointed star engraved inside it. That disturbed Skye because she interpreted that as the crux of the dilemma faced by the people buried here: they didn't know which religion to embrace; drawn to both, part of both, practitioners of both, yet unable to commit totally to either one.

Swooping across the top of one stone, Skye saw a carving of a *chupa*, the Jewish marriage canopy beneath which the bride and groom stood while taking their vows. On another she recognized the closed scroll that represented the Torah, the open scroll that symbolized the megillah, the book that told the story of Queen Esther. And along three sides of the gravestone she found bearing the name of Gabriel Abelino Duran was a beautifully carved tallith, the fringed prayer shawl worn by men in the synagogue.

Skye's eyes pooled as she saw the name of the child Miranda and Luis had lost so many years before. Teardrops fell as she read the dates that showed how brief his time on earth had been, the names of his parents who had grieved for more years than he had lived, and the Hebrew recitation of the psalm that said, "Yea, though I walk through the valley of the shadow of Death, I shall fear no evil."

But they had feared evil. If they hadn't, they wouldn't have kept this part of their lives undisclosed. They wouldn't have felt the need to pretend to be something they were not. Skye shook her head and wiped her eyes. Now she understood. Now she knew what it was about the Durans that had nagged at her from the first day she had met them. They wore the same familiar, sad mask her parents wore, the one behind which they hid secrets too dangerous to reveal.

Suddenly she recalled Miranda and Luis's odd silence when she had brought up the vandalism in El Paso. How the title of Miranda's special show—"The Eighteen"—had aroused her curiosity. Sam saying the police had suspected a group of religious fanatics of setting the fire and destroying the paintings. Isabelle remarking when she had come to Shabbat dinner at the Strausses' how Miranda often lit candles on Friday nights, that they went to mass on Saturday instead of Sunday, that they never ate shellfish or pork because of allergies.

She had sensed it but hadn't been able to put her finger on it. Now she knew why she had been drawn to them, why she had been so curious about them. She and the Durans had something very powerful in common: they were children of survivors. Her parents had survived the Nazi Holocaust. Their ancestors had survived the Spanish Inquisition. Her parents had fled Europe after being liberated from death camps. Their ancestors had fled Spain to comply with the Edict of Expulsion.

The differences were that Skye's parents had emigrated to America, where they were free to practice Judaism. The Durans' ancestors had landed in New Spain, where they had discovered religious oppression as dogged and tyrannical as it had been in Queen Isabella's Spain. The Strausses lived openly as Jews. The Durans' ancestors had been forced into a life of deception. Yet for five hundred years, beneath the dark cloak of secrecy, they had passed the vestiges of Judaism from one generation to the next.

Skye searched the ground for a rock. When she found one she placed it on top of Gabriel's tombstone, alongside the two left by his parents. As her fingers released the shiny stone, Skye envisioned the Durans standing where she stood now. She guessed that for a while they had stood in silence, staring at the memorial that marked the final resting place of their only child. Perhaps they had shared a memory or two of happy times spent with a delicious little baby, keeping the darker memories of the baby's decline and death locked inside that special vault for the unfathomable. She was certain Luis had said Kaddish for their son and that Miranda had wept as the ancient Hebrew prayer for the dead spilled from Luis's lips.

Grazing her hand across the carved name of Gabriel Abelino Duran, Skye recited the Kaddish, for Gabriel, for members of her family who had died too soon, and for all the martyrs who had died because of the way they worshiped God. Then she left the clandestine cemetery the way she had come, silently and respectfully.

Throughout the drive back to Santa Fe, Skye debated the pros and cons of confronting Miranda and Luis. In the end she decided to discuss what she had discovered with Sam before saying anything to anyone else, including Isabelle. If Sam suggested they say nothing, she would honor that decision.

Hazel Strauss knew all about keeping secrets.

CHAPTER 24

New York City

Nina was at her desk, drinking her third cup of coffee and reading about the upcoming election. More than anyone she appreciated the value of negativity, but even she thought this was one of the nastiest campaigns in history. Between ads about Willie Horton and speeches about the "L-word," it was beginning to seem as if, in the contest between George Bush and Michael Dukakis, the last one standing would be elected president, not whoever garnered the most votes at the polls.

Scanning the rest of the news, she noticed a small squib opposite the book reviews announcing the opening of Skye Gallery.

"Just what the world needs," she muttered, taking a chomp out of a bagel. "Another art gallery run by another know-nothing, superaffected, ego-inflated bitch!" A groan followed the sentence informing that the premiere exhibition was to be of paintings by Isabelle de Luna. "What a surprise!"

A bigger surprise followed a few minutes later when her secretary buzzed to say her mother was on the phone. Nina froze. She hadn't spoken to Miranda in years. What could she possibly be calling about?

"Skye and Sam Hoffman!" she exclaimed out loud.

A month before, she had read their engagement announcement in *The New York Times*. It had ruined her week. She had taken it as a personal affront that a woman who had threatened her and a man who had betrayed her were betrothed.

So, what could Miranda want? For Nina to call Sam and congratulate him? Fat chance! They probably were coming into town for the gala event. Did she and Luis want to meet with her? Have dinner? Talk over old times? She paused to ruminate about the possibility.

Curiosity having gotten the better of her, she swallowed hard and picked up the phone. Instead of Miranda, however, the voice on the other end belonged to a woman named Brynna Jones. The name sounded familiar. It took Nina a moment to remember that this woman had seen her ad, written to the post office box, and claimed to be her natural mother.

As she had done with other respondents, Nina had sent back a form letter requesting personal information about them as pertained to the child they were coming forward to claim. Few took the second step. Some who did referred to the child in question as a male. Those who got the sex right were mailed another letter giving Nina's office phone number and telling them to call if they were still interested. Many lost interest either when they realized they had to pay for the long-distance call themselves or when they placed the call and heard the operator recite the call letters of the television station where Nina worked. The last thing people running a scam wanted was publicity. This woman had not been frightened off.

As she had done with other respondents, she asked several pertinent questions: When was her child born? *February 22, 1954.* Where had she left her? *In a trash can on the side of the Cathedral of St. Francis.* And how had she left her? *Clean and washed, wrapped in a pink sweater with her umbilical cord tied with a shoestring.* Nina's hands began to shake. Only the woman who had birthed her could have known about the shoestring and the color of the sweater. They were the two facts the newspapers had never printed.

With a mix of trepidation and excitement, she arranged to fly to San Diego the next day to meet Brynna Jones.

On the plane, Nina's mood alternated between the skittish hope that the real Brynna was equal to or better than the fantasy of Leslie Walker Davis and the paralyzing fear that she was not. She couldn't afford another mother she didn't want the world to know about. Especially now.

Nina had tired of being Anthony's mistress and had begun a campaign to become the fourth and final Mrs. Hartwick. Their romance was hardly the stuff of love stories, yet in an odd way it worked for them. Each enjoyed emotional torment—both the giving and receiving. Each needed a partner with enough secrets to eschew prying into anyone else's private places. And each had a problem with sustained loyalty. She knew he cheated on her. She made certain he knew when she cheated on him. Once or twice he had humiliated her in public. She had retaliated by taunting him in her column. The way Nina saw it, if they had survived all that, marriage was the next logical step.

The only thing that could prevent her happily-ever-after was her past.

Brynna Jones was fifty-three years old, and almost every day of that had been spent scraping out an existence. She had worked as a waitress, a barmaid, a counter girl, a gas station attendant, a dishwasher, a cleaning lady—whatever didn't require a résumé or a degree. She had never lived anywhere long enough to set down roots, had never spent enough time with anyone to be able to claim a friend. Once or twice she had been involved with the same man long enough for their relationship to qualify as an affair. But mostly she had had strings of one-night stands or group bedfests she had been too drunk to remember.

She had come to San Diego two years before, having tired of the raw cold of Portland winters. It was months before she landed a job as a cleaning lady at the local television station, and then it had happened only because some local minister had dedicated himself to saving her soul. The work wasn't hard. Aside from one or two who thought it was an oversight that they were here instead of in Hollywood and that any day the *call* would come, the people were okay. And every now and then someone exciting came to the studio for an interview on *Sunup San Diego* or one of the other talk shows.

On her breaks she liked to sneak into the green room, watch the TV, partake of the free Danish and coffee made available to guests of the station, and rummage through the newspapers. After skimming the headlines—just in case the world was coming to an end within the next day or so—and checking the job listings—just in case she got booted from here—she turned to the personals.

When she first saw Nina's ad, she was so rattled, she ripped it out of the paper, hid it in her bra, and quickly retreated to a stall in the ladies' room, where she read it again. Was it a ruse? Had this been placed by some fanatic policeman who had been on her trail for thirty-five years? Why not? Look at that show *The Fugitive* or some of the other made-for-TV movies that portrayed dedicated bloodhounds who got their teeth into a case and didn't let go until either they dropped dead or they found the perpetrator.

Later that night, after a few shots of tequila had calmed her nerves, she decided it was not a trap, but the genuine article. The child she had borne and forgotten was looking for her.

Did she know who Brynna was? Had she tracked her to San Diego? Or was this a stab in the dark? One of many ads placed in many newspapers in many cities? Suddenly Brynna's rheumy eyes brightened. You needed money to place all those ads.

After another tequila she decided that maybe her Bible-toting minister friend was right: God gave everyone a second chance. Of course, why God would bother with her after what she said about Him was beyond her, but she was not about to turn her back on providence.

Brynna recognized Nina Davis's name immediately; the station had a television in every room. Davis emceed a show called *Behind the Scenes,* a talk-fest that gave all the inside skinny on the entertainment industry. As it happened, it was one of Brynna's favorite shows. She laughed out loud just thinking about it.

"It makes a mother proud," she said.

Nothing could be wrong about a black Armani suit, Nina told herself as she pirouetted in front of the mirror for the tenth time, checking her hem, her stockings, her hair, her makeup, even her manicure.

Was the white blouse too stark against the black?

Unsure, she changed into a black blouse. Too funereal. A red blouse? Too garish. Back to the white blouse.

Nina couldn't believe how nervous she was. She had been fussing over her wardrobe all morning. Most likely this woman was a fake, a con artist or a deadbeat. After all, disposing of an infant in a trash can hardly seemed like something a socialite would do. Still, one never knew. Even socialites made mistakes.

Nina checked her outfit again, making certain everything was perfect. If this woman was her birth mother, the little girl in Nina desperately wanted instant, unqualified approval. That same little girl hoped this woman warranted Nina's approval. If she did, Nina believed she finally could be at peace with where she'd come from and who she was.

Nina arrived early enough to select the right table. As planned, she had left a message at the concierge desk as to time and place. After reconnoitering the room, she decided on something overlooking the harbor, yet off to the side so they could talk. After telling the maître d' to escort her guest to their table when she arrived, she sequestered herself at the end of the bar so she could watch the door.

A tall, slim blonde in a stunning red suit strode confidently from the lobby to the maître d's desk. As she leaned over and spoke to the young man in charge, Nina's heart thumped so loudly that she was certain the entire room could hear her. Alas, the woman was meeting a silver-haired gentleman. Two other blondes, either of whom would have met Nina's expectations, disappointed her by joining friends.

She wouldn't have paid any attention to the tall, un–made-up woman in the plain cotton dress if she hadn't noticed the maître d' leading her toward the corner table. Nina's stomach lurched. Her first thought was to cut and run and pretend she had never started this foolish search.

Okay, so she doesn't look like Jackie Onassis. Don't judge a book by its cover, she told herself. Maybe she's had a hard life. She looks nervous. Maybe she's afraid you won't forgive her.

It took every ounce of courage Nina possessed to walk out from behind the bar and cross that room, but after a lifetime of speculating and dreaming and wondering about the woman who had borne her, she couldn't leave without finding out the truth.

"What a kick this is," the woman said as Nina sat down. "Whew! You sure did turn out good-looking!" She tilted her head from one side to another, squinting as she surveyed Nina's features.

Nina was conducting her own survey. Brynna's hair was threaded with gray; it was lifeless, shapeless, and minus anything even remotely resembling sheen, but it was pale blond. Her eyes, puffy, watery, and streaked with thin red lines that spoke of either too little sleep or too much alcohol, were the same soft gray as Nina's. Her mouth was different—thinner lips, not as defined. Her jaw was slack, making it difficult to compare chins, but if Nina erased the fleshiness of age and self-abuse, the high-planed cheekbones echoed her own.

"How about a drink to celebrate our finding each other?" Brynna said, already waving to a waiter. "What'll you have?"

"Just a glass of white wine," Nina said weakly, drowning in a wave of disappointment.

"Because it's a special day, I think I'll splurge and have an extra-dry martini. You know the kind I mean," she said, grinning at the waiter. "Just sort of a whisper of vermouth."

At a loss for anything to say, Nina permitted Brynna to prattle on about how often she watched *Behind the Scenes* and how much she loved the show and how excited she was when she realized that the hostess was her very own flesh. It was all Nina could do not to cry.

When the drinks came, she tried to hurry the process. "Over the phone, you said you had some kind of proof that you were in Santa Fe in February 1954."

"What's the rush?" Brynna motioned to the waiter that she needed a refill.

"I'm anxious to see whatever it is."

Brynna's eyes turned dark, and her mouth tightened. "It's kept for thirty-five years. It'll keep a little longer." She stretched her mouth into a smile. "Now, let's hear what happened to you. I mean, you look like you made out okay. Tell me about the people who took you in."

Nina couldn't believe the sudden rush of affection for Miranda and Luis that flooded her at that moment, the gratitude she felt toward them for saving her from dying or, worse, from a life with this woman. She couldn't imagine spending a day with her, let alone a childhood.

"They were very kind. They raised me as their own." She wasn't about to give out any more information. She might not be on good terms with the Durans, but they didn't deserve to be shaken down by the likes of Brynna Jones.

"Do they still live in Santa Fe?" She was so obvious, it hurt.

"Tell me about you," Nina said, being just as obvious about ignoring her question. "Have you lived in San Diego long? Are you married? Do you have a family?"

Brynna waited until her second drink was put in front of her. While the waiter recited the day's specials, she downed her martini as if it were water. Nina ordered a chef's salad. Brynna ordered a shrimp cocktail, a salad with blue cheese dressing, a sirloin steak, a double order of French fries, and another martini.

"But I'd like a big glass of your best red wine with my meat." Her voice was beginning to slur. People at neighboring tables were beginning to stare. Nina was beginning to feel sick.

"So you want to know about my life? Well, here's the long and short of it. I'm not married. You're the only kid I've got. And though I've been in San Diego awhile, I'm the town-to-town type, if you know what I mean."

She wolfed down her shrimp cocktail and her martini, slathered a roll with butter, stuffed it in her mouth, and continued her autobiography.

"I was born in a backwater town in Texas to real God-fearing, law-abiding folk. By the time I was six, I could rattle off Scripture better than other kids did Mother Goose. I went to church every Sunday, said grace at every meal, and prayed before I went to sleep every night." She plunked her elbows on the table, rested her body on her arms, and leaned toward Nina. "Know what I was praying for?" Nina shook her head helplessly. "That my daddy would stop fucking me in the woodshed."

Brynna laughed at the shock on Nina's face. She gulped down yet another drink and then, much to Nina's dismay, continued her sordid tale.

"Every Sunday he'd tromp on up the aisle and receive communion like he was a man without sin. He'd shake hands with the preacher, chat it up with the neighbors, and take his family home for a proper Sunday dinner. He'd stuff his face with Momma's cooking, and then take me out back."

Nina felt sick. She couldn't stand being with this woman another moment.

Glancing at her watch, she said, "I can't believe it's so late. Not that I haven't enjoyed meeting you, but I have an interview—" She started to rise.

Brynna grabbed her hand and squeezed. "Sit down, sweetie. We're not finished."

Eyeballing Nina to make sure she didn't leave, she reached into her pocketbook, took out a picture, and slapped it on the table. It was a wrinkled black-and-white photo of a very young, very pregnant girl with blond braids in a dress not dissimilar to the one she had on now. A sweater hung out from under what was clearly a man's leather jacket. Nina was certain it was the pink one in which she had been swaddled.

Standing next to Brynna, his arm draped around her shoulder, was a jacketless guy in boots and jeans and a flannel shirt, a cigarette dangling from the side of his mouth. They were standing in front of the old movie theater in Santa Fe, beneath a marquee that announced the feature of the week, *The Glenn Miller Story,* starring June Allyson and Jimmy Stewart.

Nina didn't want to, but she was compelled to ask, "Is he my father?"

"How the hell would I know?" Brynna exclaimed, again laughing so loudly that no one could resist looking their way.

"What do you mean, how the hell would you know?" Nina had passed upset and inconsolable and embarrassed. She was on the way to all-out rage. "Were you some kind of hooker?"

"Wish I had been. If I had a ten-spot for every guy I've bedded down in my life, including my old man, I'd be wearing something just like that."

She pointed her knife at Nina, who recoiled immediately from the supposed threat as well as from the repugnant thought that she was the child of a one-night stand. Disgusted and depressed beyond measure, she motioned for the check.

Brynna put down her fork and knife. "You planning on going somewhere?"

"Yes," Nina said, her anger evident. "I am."

"Don't you want to hear my terms before you go?"

"Terms? What the hell are you talking about?"

"I'm talking about how much it's going to cost you to keep my mouth shut."

"Cost me?" Nina was outraged. "Lunch and cab fare, lady. That's it!"

Brynna leaned forward, her face menacing.

"Listen, girlie, I didn't come looking for you. Frankly, I never gave a shit about whether you lived or died. But as long as you lived, and as long as you've done so well, I think I ought to be rewarded."

"For what?"

"For lugging you around for nine months. For birthing you. And for leaving you where you could be found by people who gave you the cushy life. From the looks of you, you did fine. It's my turn now."

"Your turn my ass." Nina's eyes flamed. "I'm not paying you one cent."

"Oh, yes, you are. Because if you don't, I'll go to the head of the TV station where I work and tell him all about my kid, the hostess of *Behind the Scenes*. Or maybe I'll call the *Enquirer*. I hear they pay big for stuff like this."

She leaned back on her chair, folded her arms across her chest, fixed her inebriated gaze on Nina, and smirked.

"The media's going to love this story: an eighteen-year-old, penniless young woman gives up her baby because she can't afford to feed her. That daughter grows up to be a big TV star who's been looking for her mama all her life. But when the lady isn't what she ordered, she tosses her aside like an underdone piece of meat." For emphasis, she shoved a piece of steak in her mouth. "Juicy, don't you think?"

The worst part: it was the truth. As Nina sat, held hostage by the success of her search, Brynna Jones made her demands. And Nina agreed, because as Brynna reminded her, she really had no other choice.

CHAPTER 25

Skye Gallery opened in October 1988 with an exhibition of Isabelle de Luna's latest works: "The Emotional Rainbow." Taking a page from Julian Richter's book, Skye held her premiere on a Thursday night instead of a Saturday and opted not to presell the show. If she had learned anything from him, it was that anticipation was the most effective marketing tool. And judging by the number of people crowding the gallery only moments after she opened her doors, anticipation was at its peak.

Isabelle had feared that being out of the public eye might have dimmed her star; in fact, her self-imposed exile had created an aura of mystery, inspiring an almost frantic desire among art aficionados to own one of her canvases. Fortunately these pieces did not disappoint. Huge splurges of extraordinary color with a nimbly sketched form and sparsely drawn face, each one represented a different emotion.

Isabelle had not used figures in her previous works. She had refrained from incorporating the human form, concentrating instead on the infinite variety of nature's landscape. These paintings, as she told her interviewers, signaled a new openness on her part, a willingness to share the fruits of her introspection and, together with the viewer, to explore the inner landscape. Also marking a change was her dramatic use of white space as a vehicle "to define the vast, uncharted territory that surrounds our feelings . . . to describe the space that waits to be experienced."

Since this series had been born of Isabelle's spiritual pilgrimage, the paintings pulsed with an indefinable, yet immediately identifiable reality. These were basic emotions, universal responses that rang true regardless of language, nationality, or individual circumstance. These were the sentiments and sensations human beings felt every day, spewed forth with such intensive bursts of energy that the only way to look at them was to experience them.

It was not only the visceral reactions evoked by Isabelle's paintings that assured the success of the show, but *who* was reacting. Skye's opening had attracted the major collectors of contemporary art: Ronald Lauder, S. I. Newhouse, Charles Saatchi, the Rubells, the Broads, the Meyerhoffs, and Peter Brandt, to name a few. Even some whose collections were culled from other periods, like the Kravises and the Steinbergs, came to wish Skye well, to assess de Luna's latest output, and, because it was New York, simply to be part of the scene.

Much to Isabelle's dismay, Paco Barba and his wife, Anna, were among the throng. Though she managed to avoid talking to them, she couldn't tear herself away from watching Paco hover in front of *Blue:* a disturbing, dark painting, in which the face of a child was drawn with one eye wide with fright, the body shying away, the fingers on a raised hand spread as if fending off an attack. The painting represented Death.

Isabelle practically dared him to buy it. He didn't. Later Skye said Paco and his wife had argued about it, but in the end Anna had preferred *Yellow,* Isabelle's ode to Joy. An anonymous buyer had put a reserve on *Blue.*

Anthony Hartwick, who had come to the opening alone, surprised both Skye and Isabelle with his purchase. Done in varying shades of purple, the painting conveyed Loneliness, the separateness one often felt even in a crowd, the isolation it was possible to feel in one's own skin. The eyes were the only facial feature portrayed, and they were undeniably sad, searching for someone, something, anything that would add light to the livid darkness of friendless seclusion.

Philip, previewing the exhibit before the show opened, had been thunderstruck when he saw *Red,* the painting representing Passion. Against eddying veils of motile color that swirled from shades of fiery red to sultry burgundy to simmering corals and pinks, lay a woman—head back, hair flowing, her mouth caught in a moment of ecstasy that was achingly familiar. It was the Isabelle he knew in bed. He bought it instantly.

The other paintings—representing Hate, Envy, Sorrow, Anger, Relish, Apathy, Agitation, Serenity, and Grace—sold within the first hour. One journalist couldn't resist asking the artist why there was no depiction of what was considered man's most powerful emotion: Love. Her answer was honest.

"I'm not exactly sure how that feels."

Opening that same week at the Richter Gallery was a group exhibition of gallery artists, including works from "Visions in Blue." Julian had hoped to dilute both Isabelle's and Skye's success. Instead he fanned the flames of what quickly became known in New York as "de Luna fever." Suddenly Isabelle wasn't simply a well-respected artist, she was a hot property! Her paintings commanded six figures, her name was in every column. *Vogue* asked her to model for them. She was on the cover of *Vanity Fair*, the subject of a big piece in *New York* magazine, a favorite on every important socialite's invitation list, and a featured guest on *Larry King Live*.

Though celebrity was a heady experience, part of Isabelle felt choked by her own success. She wasn't naive, nor was she opposed to prosperity. She understood the importance of public relations and accepted those invitations and interviews that were clearly designed to further her career as an artist. Those that were gratuitous and meant to capitalize on her sudden renown rather than her talent, she refused. She had seen what happened to other artists who had allowed the media to paint an image of them—they sacrificed their essence on the altar of fame and ultimately met with disaster. Isabelle was not about to let that happen to her.

Miranda and Luis arrived in New York a week before Skye and Sam's wedding. On the Thursday night before the wedding, Isabelle invited Skye, Sam, Jonas, and Sybil over for dinner. It seemed like the perfect occasion to christen her new home. Though it was unlike her to splurge, she had used some of her new affluence to buy an apartment in one of the grand old buildings on Central Park West. Thanks to the lingering fallout from Black Monday, it had come on the market at an irresistible price.

Despite Isabelle's protests, Miranda had cooked most of the meal, invading Isabelle's modern kitchen like an army occupying a town. Demonstrating skills she had learned from her nouvelle chef, Miranda served a rich vegetable soup thickened with corn flour, warm corn sticks, spicy veal tacos, and a cabbage, peanut, and mango salad. With Luis making sure no one's wineglass stayed empty for long, conversation remained upbeat and convivial.

Later, after coffee and dessert, when they were lolling around Isabelle's all white living room sated and relaxed, Skye invited the Durans to join her and Sam and their families at temple on Friday night. The request sounded innocent enough, but something in Skye's voice, as well as a visible nervousness on the faces of the others, told Luis it was anything but.

"That's very nice," he said cautiously, "and of course, we'd be honored, but why would you think to invite us?"

Skye took a deep breath. "I did a terrible thing," she said softly. "I invaded your privacy." Miranda and Luis looked quizzical and apprehensive. "When I was in Santa Fe, I followed you when you visited your son's grave."

A startled cry escaped Miranda's lips. Luis took her hand, but his eyes never left Skye's face.

"I know it was a breach of confidence, and I apologize for that, but I can't deny I'm glad I went." Skye paused, clearly measuring her words. "I love you both very much. Being in that cemetery, seeing the Hebrew carved on your son's tombstone, moved me more than I can say. I felt proud to say Kaddish for Gabriel and to place a rock next to yours to let his spirit know we had been there."

A dense, nervous silence canopied the room.

"I invited you to temple because I think you've been practicing your faith in a basement. I thought you might like to worship in public."

Miranda and Luis didn't know how to react. They stared at Jonas, their eyes asking if he had betrayed them.

"I never said a word," he answered.

"Is that where you went on those days when you used to disappear?" Isabelle asked. "Did you go to visit Gabriel?"

Miranda nodded, her eyes wide and watery.

"I didn't mean to pry," Skye said, hating herself for making Miranda cry. "And I didn't bring this up to hurt you. I thought it might be comforting for you to know that people who love you, know the truth and still love you."

Luis turned to Isabelle, his face creased with concern.

"I'd love you if you worshiped starfish," she said, kissing him on the cheek to underscore her point, "but I admit, I don't completely understand."

After a long, tortuous silence, Luis explained.

"Jews had been in Spain for more than a millennium, but in that famous year of 1492, two hundred and fifty thousand people were forced into exile. I suppose, because that was the most dramatic moment in the eight-hundred-year crusade to drive the infidel from Spain, people tend to think the Inquisition ended with the Edict of Expulsion. It didn't. Unfortunately, it continued for four hundred years, in Spain and in New Spain, which was Mexico and many of the territories in the region we now call the Southwest.

"For a while, fleeing to the New World appeared to be a smart decision. The customs were familiar, the language was the same, and because the governors of New Spain needed settlers and businessmen to create revenue for the state, the converted immigrants were welcomed into the community. Though no questions were asked, it was understood that to maintain their status as respected citizens, they were expected to profess their Christianity in public. They did, but in the privacy of their homes, many remained Jews.

"Generations went by without incident, but once or twice a century the holy offices would decide to purge the populace with bogus trials and massive executions. To escape, many of the *conversos* moved north."

Luis turned to Miranda, who appeared shaky and distressed. Tenderly he took her hand.

"It was the women who kept Judaism alive. The men went to work among the Christians, so they lived like the Christians. They ate nonkosher food, participated in church rituals, and voiced approval of opinions that were contrary to their real beliefs. They did what they had to do not to expose their families to the dangers that came with discovery.

"But in the home, the women observed the ritual fasts, found ways to celebrate the various feasts, and, when they could, observed some of the religious dietary customs. They taught their daughters about the Sabbath and their sons whatever passages they remembered from the Bible. They helped arrange marriages and tended to the rituals of burial. It was the women who were the guardians of the Jewish identity."

"How did you find out your ancestors were Jewish?" Isabelle was fascinated.

"There were lots of clues. My mother's and grandmother's houses were the only ones without saints' pictures or crucifixes, which as you know, Isabelle, is unusual for a Catholic home. My grandmother used to go into the bathroom every Friday night to light candles. Often, I saw my grandfather put a shawl over his head and pray. All the men in my family were circumcised. And," he said, looking at Skye, "there was the cemetery. But since I didn't know any Anglo Jews or anything about Jewish practices, I never put any of those clues together."

Luis paused, allowing a memory to linger. "One day, when I was about sixteen, my grandfather took me into a field and told me we were Jewish. He told me the history of the *conversos* and showed me documents that proved several of his ancestors had helped found Santa Fe." He smiled at the stunned expressions on the faces of his audience. "He also told me that as a way of protecting themselves, many families offered a son or daughter to the church. Having a priest or a nun in the family was a way of making their Catholicism evident and unquestionable. I have an uncle who is an archbishop."

Obviously even Jonas didn't know that, because he gasped in astonishment.

"Do all the descendants of the *conversos* know their ancestry?" Skye asked.

"No. Some simply repeat things they saw done in their homes. They light candles, slaughter animals according to Jewish practices, and refuse to eat pork without knowing why. Others know and still stay in that carefully guarded closet."

"I can understand hiding when the territories were under Spanish control," Sam said, "but after the frontier became part of the United States, why couldn't they practice their religion openly?"

"It's complicated. After centuries of believing revelation led to torture or death, secrecy became a habit that history continued to reinforce. If it wasn't threats from the Inquisition, there were stories about pogroms, the Holocaust, frequent visits by the Ku Klux Klan and their ilk, and lots of scattered acts of hate to remind us how vicious anti-Semitism can be. Like the devastation at Enchantments and the fire at La Casa."

Luis lowered his eyes, laced his fingers together, and studied them before facing his audience again.

"Too, there's the matter of identity. While we humans may stomp our feet and demand to be treated as individuals, in reality, we take comfort in packs, just like animals. Because we need to belong to something larger, we cling to the group that looks like we do, speaks like we do, eats like we do, and thinks like we do. The problem is, you can only be a member of one group.

"If we say we're Hispanics, it's assumed we're Catholic. If we suddenly announced we were Jewish, we'd no longer be Hispanic, we'd be Sephardic. Not only wouldn't we belong, but we could appear duplicitous."

"Only to the narrow-minded!" Isabelle's anger was instantaneous and personal. She knew all about labels, the impressions they created, the pain they caused: Catalan. Orphan. Ward. Murderer. Victim.

"Maybe so," Luis said, "but if your family was part of a community that thought a certain way, how do you think it would be received if they found out you were not who and what they thought you were?"

"Does this have anything to do with the fact that neither of you speak to your parents?" Isabelle asked.

She had never been able to understand how people as family conscious as Miranda and Luis could be so disconnected from their own relatives.

Miranda lifted her face and looked at Isabelle. "It was my fault," she said. Luis started to protest, but she raised her hand to hush him. "When Gabriel's condition turned terminal, my parents and Luis's parents were frantic at the thought of their young grandson dying. We told them the doctors had done everything medically possible, but they refused to accept the finality of that diagnosis. They insisted we take Gabriel to the Santuario de Chimayo and rub him with the blessed earth."

"What's the Santuario de Chimayo?" Skye asked.

Sam answered. "It's the Lourdes of the Southwest. The ground on which the chapel is built is reputed to have miraculous healing powers. Many consider the dirt holy."

"Did you take Gabriel there?" Isabelle asked Miranda.

Miranda's eyes filled with tears. "I had been a practicing Catholic all my life," she said softly. "I thought maybe . . ." She shook her head, as if she had just recognized the futility in such a hope. "I carried him in my arms. He was so thin, so weak, he was like a feather. Everyone was there. My family. Luis's family. Their neighbors. Their priests. They watched as I carried Gabriel down the aisle of the chapel. They lit candles and said prayers for us as I went to the small room behind the sacristy.

"They waited next door, in a room filled with dozens of discarded crutches and canes, religious medals, photographs, and letters about children who had been healed, lives that had been saved.

"Holding Gabriel on my lap, I dug into the pit, took the miraculous earth in my hands, and rubbed it on Gabriel's frail body, begging God to spare him. Then Gabriel and I prayed, weeping together as we waited for God's magic to take away his illness and give him back his life."

She buried her face in her hands, issuing a heart-rending sob. "But miracles only come to true believers," she said. "I was not a true believer, so the soil of the Santuario did not heal my son."

She wiped her eyes, anger replacing grief. "No one understood. They had come expecting to witness a miracle, yet none had taken place." Miranda's voice turned hard. "When my Gabriel died, no one came to the mass in his honor. No one accompanied us to the cemetery to say good-bye. No one helped us mourn our baby's death."

"Jonas was there," Luis said, turning to his friend.

Miranda nodded solemnly. "Yes, he was."

"What about your parents?" Isabelle couldn't bear the pain on Miranda's face. "How could they not show up for their grandson's funeral?"

Miranda shrugged, as if her family's behavior would remain forever inexplicable and unpardonable.

"For them, Gabriel's death was an embarrassment. Their friends and neighbors had witnessed God's rejection of me and my son. For a few, that forsaking was a condemnation and an excuse to raise other things."

"What other things?" Skye asked the question, knowing the answer.

"Like the fact that my grandmother's name was Rebecca, my grandfather's name Abelino. That my parents went to mass on Saturday, not Sunday. That our surname, Real, though quite common in New Mexico, was thought to mean 'descendant of Israel.'

"They burned my father's store and painted anti-Semitic slogans on Luis's parents' house. They taunted our families on the street and defamed them in church. They literally chased them out of town. My parents had warned me never to reveal the secret. They felt I had.

"Though Luis's parents said they didn't blame us, Luis's sisters were so humiliated and angry at having to start their lives all over again, they pressured their parents to disown us. We haven't seen or spoken to any of them in nearly thirty years. We don't even know if they're alive."

Tears streamed down Isabelle's face as she reached for Miranda, embracing her with new understanding and heightened affection.

"I didn't mean to open old wounds," Skye said as she walked over to the Durans and took the hand of each of them, her face a portrait of grief. "I only meant to offer you a chance to be who you are. And the offer stands. Please. Come to temple with us."

"You'll be among friends," Jonas said.

Skye folded their hands into hers. "And family."

For Miranda and Luis, being welcomed to a temple as Jews felt extraordinarily strange, almost bizarre. They had been to temple with Jonas many times, but then they had been visitors. This night, even though they were Sephardim, Spanish Jews, and Skye's family were Ashkenazi, or European Jews, they had been greeted with a spirit of commonality. As he and Miranda took their seats, Luis donned a yarmulke out of respect but shied away from draping a tallith over his shoulders. Though he wanted to pray as his grandfather had, he had not been bar mitzvahed, nor had his Jewishness been sanctioned by anyone in authority. The last thing he wanted to do was offend.

The Durans followed the service as best they could, reading the English while the cantor and the rabbi chanted in Hebrew. Luis was astonished to realize that he had heard certain prayers before, probably from his grandfather. Miranda, unsure about what all of this meant, how it would affect their lives, if it would, absorbed herself in the art of the temple, the artifacts of the ritual and the people. She admired the fervent worship of Skye's relatives. Surely they had reason to question God's mercy and compassion, yet they offered their thanks and recited the prayers with moving sincerity.

Afterward, Murray and Pearl insisted upon taking them around, introducing them as part of Sam's family. Though Miranda detected a certain curiosity—they were, after all, Hispanic looking—women with accented English chattered about the upcoming nuptials. Several women warned Miranda not to eat another thing from that moment until the wedding.

"Pearl really knows how to put on a spread!"

The men suggested Luis take a nap. "These things last forever!"

But the best advice came from Pearl, who, when bidding them good night, said, "Just come. Relax. Eat. And enjoy!"

The wedding ceremony was beautiful. A string quartet played a delicate Bach fugue as Mack walked down the aisle and stood under the lavishly embowered canopy, taking the place set aside for the best man. Miranda wept as Jonas escorted his son, walking alongside the man she remembered as a little boy stealing cookies from her cooling racks, making a sad little girl feel part of Christmas, and taking her adopted daughter to his senior prom. As much as Miranda loved Sybil, at that moment she missed Ruth.

Luis nudged her as Rebecca's three-year-old daughter walked down the aisle. Looking like a doll in her long floral print dress, her brown hair pulled back in a softly ribboned braid, her face locked in an expression of extreme seriousness, she plucked rose petals from a painted basket and scattered them along the path to the altar. Rebecca followed her daughter, her pale salmon chiffon gown billowing gently as she walked. Behind her came Isabelle, also an ethereal vision in a delicately draped gown tinted the same coralline as the roses she carried.

Miranda watched Philip as he followed Isabelle's walk. His eyes embraced her, speaking volumes about how he felt. It upset Miranda to see it because she knew Isabelle was equally smitten but was bound by grasping ghosts to a past that refused to let her pursue a future.

"Maybe someday we'll get to see Isabelle as a bride," Luis whispered, he too wishing that Isabelle could free herself from her demons.

Skye, her face heavily veiled, was escorted to the *chupa* by her parents, neither of whom attempted to hide their tears of joy. Miranda sighed audibly as Sam saw his bride for the first time. The love in his eyes, the reverence for this woman he was about to wed, was so powerful, it staggered her. As Skye's parents kissed her and gave her hand to Sam, Miranda leaned against Luis. Seeing these two young people brought back memories of her own wedding. She smiled at her husband, communicating without words, knowing he understood what she wanted to say. Despite all that had happened, *they* were not a mistake.

At the end of the ceremony the rabbi placed a glass on the floor, which Sam purposefully crushed with his foot. The Durans had seen this at Rebecca's wedding, but then, when the guests had applauded and yelled "Mazel tov!" they had remained silent. Now they joined voices with those who shouted the Yiddish congratulation with liberated enthusiasm.

When the bride and groom made their way back up the aisle, Skye sought out the Durans. As she passed their row, she looked at Miranda with a flicker of uncertainty. Miranda blew her a kiss and mouthed, "Thank-you."

It was the best wedding gift Skye and Sam received.

Isabelle was having a wonderful time. Her best friend had married one of her oldest friends. People from her life in Santa Fe were mingling with people from her life in New York. The ceremony had touched her. Seeing Miranda and Luis so upbeat was rewarding. And she was able to use this gathering to chat with dealers like Glimcher, Cooper, Castelli, Boone, and Emmerich, as well as catch up with old friends like Ezra Edward Clark.

"I do hope when you pen your memoirs, you will remember that I was your first mentor," he said with familiar pomposity.

"That you were."

"I was afraid my having exiled you to Wisconsin might have lowered my stock."

"Only during the winter months," she said. Both of them laughed at the old saw about Wisconsin having only two seasons: Fourth of July and winter.

Naturally they talked about the van Gogh sales and the flurry surrounding several upcoming auctions featuring a number of important Picassos.

"Why do you think they've aroused such passion in the buying public?" Isabelle asked.

"Personally, I think their lives intrigue more than their art. They represent everyone's romantic notion of what an artist is. Van Gogh is tragic. His story is one of solitude and madness and misunderstandings and misfortune. Picasso's tale is exactly opposite. He's the poor man who made good, the colorful and romantic figure who was both sexually and artistically prolific, the nobody who became the most important artist of the twentieth century."

It was a thrill introducing Miranda and Luis to Ezra, watching their eyes boggle as he treated them to one of his more bombastic lectures about the importance of New Mexico to the art world. It was only because he was so gallant with them that Isabelle allowed herself to be gracious with his companion, Greta Reed.

"Your new work is superb," she said to Isabelle, trying to relegate their differences to the past. "I'm delighted to see you getting proper recognition for your talent, which, by the way, in my opinion, is considerable."

For several minutes they attempted conversation, but both were relieved when everyone was summoned into the ballroom. Immediately after the bride and groom entered and a blessing was said over the bread, the band struck up a hora.

Isabelle marveled at how quickly the floor filled with exuberant participants, each linking hands with the person next to them, executing the steps with lightning speed as they danced around in a large, undisciplined circle. With Luis on one side, Miranda on the other, all of them sandwiched between Jonas and Sybil, they attempted to keep up. The steps were easy enough, but what carried Isabelle along was the buoyant spirit that seemed to propel everyone there. This was a dance of triumph, of survival, of defiance, even, of faith in the continuance of a family line.

Isabelle couldn't help but compare the hora to her sardana: the same personal physical connection, the same overwhelming sense of pride in one's heritage that it evoked, the same symbolic circle of unity. As she raised her arms in unison with her neighbors, danced into and out of the circle, and watched as Skye and Sam were hoisted above the crowd on chairs, she caught sight of Philip. He was on the opposite side of the circle, just as he had been when they had danced the sardana in Majorca. His eyes locked on her, and her heart filled with nostalgia for what was, what might have been, and what still might be possible.

Suddenly Skye grabbed Luis and dragged him into the middle of the circle, linking arms with him and twirling madly. Murray spun Miranda about, while Jonas danced with Pearl. When Sam fetched Isabelle and took her into the circle, she hesitated, but only for a second. Sam grinned at her, daring her to keep up. Accepting the challenge, she surrendered to the spirit of the moment, spinning, twirling, moving as if her feet were weightless.

When the dance ended, however, she felt oddly deflated. Was this what it would always be for her? A magical high that came from closeness to those she loved and was assured loved her in return, followed by a hollow sense of being alone and adrift?

Skye had placed Isabelle, Philip, Rebecca, and Mack at the newlyweds' table. Being near Philip, Isabelle felt a tug. When he asked her to dance, she wanted to refuse, frightened of the feelings he might awaken when she was in his arms; but she couldn't. As he held her and they moved slowly to the music, she couldn't deny how right it felt to be next to him, how good it felt to have her face against his and to hear him humming in her ear.

"I'm so glad to have you all to myself," he said as they danced among three hundred and fifty guests, "because I have something very important to say."

Isabelle stepped back so she could see him. Those dark, hooded eyes begged her to block out everything but them.

"Ever since Majorca, my life has been empty. No woman has ever excited me the way you do, Isabelle. No woman has ever crawled inside my heart the way you have." His arm drew her body next to his. "I've never said this to anyone, but I love you. I wish you would let yourself love me."

Isabelle wanted to run off the floor, but he wouldn't let her. He held her and continued to dance with her, forcing her to deal with how she felt.

"I don't know how to explain this to you," she said, her conflict obvious. "I don't understand it completely myself, but even if somewhere in my heart I do love you, Philip, it's not enough."

"What's holding you back? Why can't I help?"

"No one can help me. There are things I have to put to rest. Until I do, I won't feel safe, and until I feel safe, I can't allow myself to commit to any man, including you."

Though she read pain and disappointment in Philip's eyes, he didn't challenge or abandon her. Instead he pulled her closer. "I'm willing to help, and I'm willing to wait."

As she let herself sink into his embrace, she wondered when, if ever, she would feel free to love.

Maybe when the nightmares stopped. Maybe when the headaches eased. *Maybe when I don't feel so blue.*

CHAPTER 26

1989

After more than a year of constant demands and an outlay of thousands of dollars, Nina was feeling the pinch of Brynna's blackmail. Aside from the fact that the woman was bleeding her bank account, there was the matter of her stability, which was questionable at best. While she seemed content in San Diego (with a fully furnished beachfront apartment, a brand-new car, and a generous monthly allowance, there was little to complain about), what guarantee did Nina have that she wouldn't suddenly decide to give Los Angeles a try? Or Paris? Or New York?

It was bad enough that she called Nina's office a couple of times a week to chat. Fortunately the assistant who had taken the first call from Brynna had left to have a baby, leaving Nina free to claim that Brynna was a completely delusional woman who thought she was Nina's mother. When others suggested alerting the police, Nina made a show of fluffing off their concerns. While her reputation precluded sainthood, taking time to talk to a "harmless kook" was not out of the realm of possibility.

Brynna's phone calls were only part of the problem. Their deal was based on Brynna's complete silence, but it was hard to cork a drunk. When she was in her cups, there was no telling what she might divulge and to whom. Then, too, Isabelle's name was all over the media. There wasn't a newsmagazine or talk show that hadn't run a feature on the Athena of the art world, not a fashion issue that didn't have her face in it, not a radio commentator who hadn't suddenly become an art expert. Any day Nina expected to walk into Bloomingdale's and be spritzed with the newest celebrity scent: de Luna.

Previously she would have seethed with jealousy, perhaps even worked herself into a vengeful snit; but she couldn't afford to indulge in anything spiteful. With troops of reporters eager to unearth anything and everything they could on New York's newest phenom, and a time bomb ticking out on the West Coast, the last thing Nina wanted to do was draw attention to herself. She was becoming paranoid about being exposed.

At first she assuaged her fears by reminding herself that she had been appearing on national television for years without anyone coming forward with potentially scandalous tales; that there were hundreds of people in Santa Fe who knew her name wasn't Davis and had never said anything. People in show business changed their names all the time. That wouldn't bring the wolves to her door. She could only be hurt by someone who knew the extent of her lies.

The question was: How many were there? And for how long could she count on their silence?

When Robert Burns wrote "The best-laid schemes o' mice and men / Gang aft a-gley," he must have had this particular night in mind. Nothing had gone the way Nina had planned. It was Anthony's forty-sixth birthday. To celebrate, she had taken over L'Orangerie, the private room at Le Cirque, and thrown him a surprise party. First the weather disappointed, providing a raw, November rain that dampened spirits as well as hairdos. Her dress, a clingy de la Renta, didn't look quite as fabulous as it had when she'd bought it. Her guests wouldn't stop talking about Barbara Walters's interview with Isabelle de Luna. And Anthony showed up an hour late, in a foul mood.

His disposition improved after a few drinks, but Nina couldn't be certain whether the alcohol had eliminated his distemper or simply masked it. Throughout dinner she watched him, measuring his humor and his receptivity. His frame of mind, as well as his physical alertness, was vitally important for the success of the second part of this evening.

Tonight was to be the denouement of her campaign to bring Anthony Hartwick to the altar and to enable her to avail herself of the many benefits incumbent in such a match. Having her own financial resources, she wasn't marrying just the money—although two fortunes were certainly better than one—it was the cover and protection intrinsic to Brahmin respectability she craved. Social standing like Anthony's sent out waves of power that intimidated those who might otherwise make frivolous allegations. Accusing Nina Davis of fraud might provoke tabloid headlines, create a momentary scandal, and give the plaintiff her fifteen minutes of fame, but accusing Nina Hartwick of the same offense would invite a retaliatory barrage of lawsuits most ordinary citizens couldn't afford to fight. Yes, she reasoned, the best way to protect her reputation was to hide it behind Anthony's reputation; the best way to do that was to propose marriage. Before she did, however, she planned to remind him of what had kept them together over all these years.

While they had been at the party, a scenic design crew had converted her den into a seraglio fit for a pasha. There was no furniture, only panels of white gauze fluttering from gilded, beribboned poles, creating a diaphanous tent replete with cushions, satin throws, baskets of grapes and figs, a brass tray displaying feathers, golden sashes, and cruets of body oils, one of which bubbled enticingly on a warmer. Candles and incense burned, filling the air with a musky odor that spoke of exotic places and erotic practices. Music with a Middle Eastern accent wafted throughout, heightening the aphrodisia. While Anthony helped himself to another Scotch and studied the fantasia she had created, Nina changed, emerging in an intricately arranged rainbow of transparent chiffon veils.

Knowing his preferences, she undressed him silently, staring into his eyes as she removed his clothes, letting him wonder what she was thinking behind the pale blue veil that covered her face. Though he could have consummated their evening immediately, she encouraged him to wait, to lie back on the cushions and let her seduce him. She watched his excitement grow as she stood over him and played with the sheer strips of fabric that covered her, bending down, allowing the cool chiffon to glance his calescent flesh.

Slowly she began to undulate, moving her hips sinuously, turning sensuously, raising her arms to allow a peek at the possibilities that lay ahead. One by one she shed her veils, all except the one on her face. Then, like an odalisque, she enslaved herself to his passions, rubbing hot scented oil on him, letting him watch as she rubbed herself. When he couldn't stand it anymore, he ripped the veil from her face and launched into her, tearing into her flesh, possessing her with a ferocity that both frightened and exhilarated.

But she didn't let it end there. This was a night in which she intended to present him with a surfeit of sexual delights. There was little she didn't do to him or allow him to do to her. Yet while the premise of the evening appeared to be master-slave, it was Nina who was in control. She was the aggressor, she was the one who had prepared the agenda. For once, Anthony followed. Nina hoped he was equally acquiescent when she changed the subject.

They had showered and were lounging around her living room in their robes, drinking coffee, slowly coming down. It was late. Their moods were mellow. Nina adjudged the time propitious.

"Anthony, I want you to marry me."

Each of the dozen times she had rehearsed this scene, she had envisioned a different response, ranging from outrage to ridicule. Instead her proposal was received with a slow, curious smile.

"I've been down the aisle several times, Nina. It's not the yellow brick road you think it is."

"Perhaps it was your previous brides." Supine, her back resting against the corner of the couch, her legs spread before her, she crossed her ankles, causing her robe to open slightly. "Might I remind you, you've been with me longer than you were married to both of them put together."

He laughed and nodded his acknowledgment. His glance strayed to the spot where her legs stopped and her robe began. "True. So why ruin a good thing?"

"Because I'm thirty-five and tired of being Miss Significant Other. I want to be Mrs. Anthony Hartwick."

He laughed again. "Nina Davis being so provincial? Who would have thought it?"

"You're evading the issue."

"Maybe just a bit."

"Why? You know damn well you love me, as much as you're capable of loving anyone, that is. And in case you've suddenly gone brain dead and can't remember back farther than fifteen minutes, sexually we're unbelievably compatible. So what the hell is the problem?"

"I don't have a problem with us, Nina." When her face brightened he held up a hand, stemming her enthusiasm. "I do, however, have major business problems. Hartwick House is sinking so deep into the red, I'm not sure I'm going to be able to pull it out."

Nina was aware that he was having difficulty meeting his bottom line, but she hadn't expected that to interfere with the conduct of his private life. She supposed she had forgotten how different it was when the name on the letterhead was the same as the name on the company logo.

"What will it take?"

"A socko-boffo blockbusting best-seller," he said with exaggerated pomposity. "Have you any lying around?"

"How about *SoHo Cinderella?*" she joked, too cocky about the success of her private orgy and too involved in her own program to notice that she hadn't evoked even the flicker of a smile. When finally she realized he'd offered no response, she grew petulant. "It's not that I don't care about the future of Hartwick House, Anthony, I do. But right now I care a lot more about creating a future for us."

Anthony's brow furrowed. His jaw tightened. His eyes had an odd cast. "And I suppose you're going to want a big wedding?"

Nina tittered nervously. While she liked the direction in which he seemed to be headed, his tone was unsettling.

"How big can it be? Neither of us has any family."

"I have some cousins I could invite. And some friends and old school chums. How about your relatives in Scotland? Or friends from your prep school?"

He fixed his gaze on her face. Nina suddenly felt quite naked, despite her oversize terry-cloth robe.

"And how about some of your classmates from Wellesley?"

Nina fought off a blush. "I would be happy with just the two of us and a justice of the peace. Why are you looking to invite everyone in our respective yearbooks?"

"Because you don't have any yearbooks, Nina. Nor do you have any relatives in Scotland!"

"What?" Nina sat up straight, clenching her fists so her hands wouldn't shake. "What are you talking about?"

"You. Your so-called family history. It's bunk, Nina. Pure, unadulterated bunk!"

He rose from his end of the couch and walked with agonizing slowness to the fireplace.

"Hale and Leslie Walker Davis," he said solemnly, pointing to the handsome couple in Nina's prized portrait. "I've made a few inquiries. They don't really exist, do they?" He turned to Nina, his eyes mocking. "If they do, neither one of them ever had anything to do with a distillery in Scotland, nor did they ever die in a plane crash anywhere on Scottish soil. The Edinburgh prep school you claim you attended never heard of you. Neither did anyone at Wellesley."

He walked toward her, his eyes glued to her face. At the couch he leaned over, reached beneath her robe, and, in an arrogant display of proprietary rights, grabbed her.

"If I'm going to marry you, Nina, and I haven't said yea or nay, I have a right to know just who the hell you are!"

Nina's mind was racing. She couldn't believe he had investigated her background, but he had, and quite thoroughly at that! Pulling back, holding her robe tighter around her body, she considered her options: she could argue with him and—since they both would know she was lying—lose everything, or she could tell the truth—within limits—and come out a major winner.

"I have a proposition for you," she said, still working out the specifics.

"I thought you already did that."

"I proposed marriage. Unfortunately, you weren't as interested in that as I might have hoped." Her face hardened into a mask of detached indifference.

"This proposition will be more to your liking because it offers not only the confession you appear to be demanding, but the possibility of a huge profit as well."

He went to the bar and poured himself Glenlivet, neat. He offered her one. She declined. She needed a clear head. He sat opposite her, sipped his drink, and nodded.

"Do go on."

Girding herself, she plunged headlong into uncharted waters. "I'll only tell you my story if you buy the rights to it."

"And why should I do that?"

"Because my story is included in a celebrity tell-all I've begun writing called *True Colors: The Real Story of Isabelle de Luna.*" His eyes boggled, just as she had known they would. "In it, I tell the story of Isabelle's parents, their scandalous marriage, their shameful deaths, as well as the details of Isabelle's private life as only someone who has known her intimately could."

"And how intimately do you know Isabelle de Luna?"

"I was raised as her sister," Nina said, triumph ringing in her voice. "Is that intimate enough for you?"

"I'd say so. Go on."

She confessed that instead of being orphaned at fourteen, she had been orphaned as an infant and raised by the Durans, the same people who raised Isabelle. She did cling to Hale and Leslie Davis, the pretend parents she had espoused for so many years, but relinquished the distillery and the Scottish ancestry in favor of a more modest background. She decided that in this case, part truth was definitely better than the whole truth.

"Are you interested?"

"Perhaps."

Nina found that reaction curious. Each time she'd seen him in Isabelle's presence, his fascination with her had been intense. Nina knew he had taken her out to dinner several times, but she was fairly certain that's where it had ended.

"She's the hottest thing out there. A biography of her would be the socko-boffo blockbuster you need to get Hartwick House on its feet again. And I'm here to give it to you."

"For a price."

"Why not? I offered myself to you for free and you turned it down. From now on, honey, everything is going to have a price tag attached to it, including this!" she said as she flashed her nudity in his face.

"Well, well, well. Quite the little negotiator, aren't we?" He gulped his drink, staring at her over the rim of his glass. "What makes you think anyone would buy a biography of an artist? The world doesn't revolve around the intrigues of the New York art scene."

"But the world does want to know everything about Isabelle de Luna." She looked smug because she felt smug. "If they're grabbing magazines and newspapers off the stands to find out everything from her perfume to her shoe size, I think they would love to know that her father was accused of raping and murdering her mother."

She could see by the expression on his face that he agreed. His reluctance, therefore, had nothing to do with the concept and everything to do with punishing her for lying. Nina didn't like being punished.

"This book will have sex, violence, mystery, and a famous name, all in one hot package." Her upper lip curled into a sneer. "I can't imagine a down-at-the-mouth, on-his-ass publisher turning down a chance like this."

Anthony didn't parry her insult. Rather, he dismissed her with patrician sangfroid. "That murder happened years ago in Barcelona. When Martín de Luna died, the case was closed."

"Pardon the pun, but you're dead wrong. Quite the opposite, Martín's death left everything up in the air. No one knows whether he did it or he didn't. Except, perhaps, Isabelle."

"Why would you think she knows?" Anthony's interest sharpened suddenly.

Nina's hopes spiked. "She was in the suite. She claims she was asleep in another room. There are those, myself included, who believe she witnessed the crime and either repressed the memory or was too frightened to come forward."

"If she didn't come forward then, she's not going to say anything now, especially to you."

"So what! I don't need her to write this book. I'm conducting my own investigation. I'll lay out my findings and let the reader draw his own conclusion. It's done all the time."

"Maybe so, but not with my money! The case is old and shrouded in doubt. People aren't going to shell out their hard-earned dollars for rehashed gossip and pie-in-the-sky speculation."

"I disagree," Nina said emphatically. "She's a celebrity. This is a murder, and like it or not, she's smack dab in the middle of it. This book will sell big, Anthony dear. As you've taught me so well, people pay for their thrills."

Anthony put down his drink, rose from his chair, and laughed. "You flatter yourself, Nina, in more ways than one. Why would I pay for what you give so willingly? Why would anyone care about your life or your relationship to Isabelle de Luna? And what madness would make you think that *True Colors,* based on little more than rumor and conjecture, could ever be perceived as more than an extended gossip column? Books like that are high risk," he said, "especially when written by tabloid scribes with phony credentials."

For hours after he left, Nina fumed. She was angry at his lack of support, stung by his insults and the humiliation of being revealed as a fraud. But all that paled before the grinding sense of degradation and rejection that clung to her like gum to a shoe. A familiar nausea rose in her throat, threatening to spill out of her mouth in a bilious flux. Choking it back, convincing herself she had fought too hard and come too far to allow anyone to make her feel like trash, she forced herself to rally.

When the idea for *True Colors* had been born several months before, she had seen it as an insurance policy of sorts: rather than have her lies uncovered by the likes of Brynna Jones and her reputation ruined, she would reveal the truth about herself, the truth about Isabelle, and make a fortune in the process. Now, quite unexpectedly, she had Anthony looking into her past.

Suddenly *True Colors* was more than a backup plan. It was the only hope she had for making certain her future wasn't a dead end.

"Happy birthday, Tía Flora!" Isabelle pressed the telephone against her ear, as if by doing so she could take her great-aunt's pulse and heartbeat and blood pressure and otherwise gauge the declining state of her health. Six months before, when she had visited, Flora had looked so fragile that it had frightened Isabelle. She couldn't imagine a world without her. "I can't believe you're eighty-nine years old."

A surprisingly hearty laugh traveled the miles. "It seems like just yesterday that I was eighty-eight," she joked. "How was the opening?"

Isabelle was amazed Flora had remembered. The evening before, the suddenly extremely prestigious Skye Gallery had exhibited Isabelle's newest paintings, "Mind Travels."

"We sold out before we opened, so I guess it was fine."

Months after completing this series, the end products continued to disturb Isabelle. Poetic but dark, they were reminiscences of troubling thoughts and unnerving visions painted on tall slender surfaces made of aluminum and wood.

"I sent you the catalog," she said, trying to shake off the residual gloom in which this project had enshrouded her. "Can you imagine? It was written by Susan Sontag."

One of Skye's most successful innovations—the public loved it, reviewers hated it—was to enlist celebrities to write the catalogs for her shows.

"How were the reviews?"

"They still hate the fact that I insist upon giving my shows a literary title."

"Tell them that's your aunt Vina's influence." Flora chuckled.

"I have told them, Tía Flora. For some reason, they remain unimpressed with that segment of my lineage."

"How about this part of your lineage? What did they say about your painting?"

Isabelle could almost see the color rushing into Flora's cheeks. She derived such vicarious pleasure from Isabelle's success, Isabelle made a point of photographing all of her paintings and blowing them up so her great-aunt could study them and comment. Even at her advanced age, Isabelle felt, Flora's criticisms were constructive and valid.

"In the exalted words of those who know," Isabelle said, reading from a few of the notices she had cut from various newspapers, "I've taken another surprising turn . . . my images are provocatively hypnotic . . . and, oh, you're especially going to love this: according to Calvin Tompkins, 'The dreamy precision of the shapes suggests an artist for whom painting is a form of meditation.' "

"I do love that," Flora said in a way that let Isabelle know she was smiling. "Was Philip at the show?"

Now it was Isabelle's turn to smile. Flora never gave up. "Yes, he was there. We spoke. That's all."

"Too bad. He's the one, Isabelle. I know it."

"You do."

"Yes, and I told him as much when he visited me last month."

Isabelle was taken aback. "What was he doing in Barcelona?"

"Visiting me," Flora said almost girlishly. "He was on his way to Lugano." She paused, letting Isabelle absorb her news. "But this isn't the first time he's made a detour to have tea with an old lady. He's been here several times. Honestly, Isabelle, he's a joy to be with. We walk. We discuss what's happening in the world at large, as well as what's happening in our own private universes. He's a sensitive man, and I like him."

"You two sound very chummy." Isabelle wondered how she could feel jealous about Philip and her eighty-nine-year-old aunt, but she did.

"We are." On her side of the Atlantic, Flora nodded. She could hear it in Isabelle's voice: there was hope for her and Philip. Now she could move on. "By the way, Alejandro told me he heard Dragon Textiles is for sale."

"Really!" Isabelle was reluctant to leave the discussion about Philip, but this intrigued her. "For how much?"

"I don't know any of the details. I'm not sure Alejandro does, either, but if you wish, he could look into it for you."

Isabelle's mind clicked at a furious pace. She recalled her brief conversation with Paco about Dragon at the Reys'. If only he'd answered her, she'd know whether to go to him in person or go around his back.

"Thanks, but no. I think it's better if he doesn't suspect anyone's making inquiries on my behalf."

After promising to keep Flora informed, chatting about the Durans and Alejandro and how annoying she found it to be old, Isabelle hung up the phone and immediately called her lawyer. She told him what Flora had said and asked him to check it out, albeit very discreetly. Several days later he reported back. Dragon Textiles had been losing money for a long time. Reportedly, their losses had become so heavy, they were beginning to affect the holding company's bottom line. Isabelle's lawyer thought the time was right to go after Dragon. She authorized him to make a bid.

Three weeks later he called to tell her Dragon Textiles had been taken off the market.

"Why? Did someone come up with a higher bid?"

"No. They claim the company is no longer for sale. My guess is that they had a sudden and rather large infusion of cash, because instead of grinding down, our sources in Barcelona tell me the company's gearing up."

"For what?"

"They're entering the International Frankfurt Fabric Competition, a contest held every two years at the Frankfurt Fabric Fair. Evidently the prize is prestigious enough to ensure that the winning mill will be inundated with enough work to guarantee enormous profits for several years."

"And they think they have a chance?"

"According to my contact, they're certain of victory!"

To Isabelle, none of this made sense. After years of hovering near oblivion, why would Paco suddenly boast that they would walk away with the textile industry's most coveted prize?

What's happened? she asked herself, feeling inexplicably threatened. What's changed?

*   *   *

Olivia took advantage of the maid's invitation to make herself comfortable by wandering through her son's apartment. Though she had been there several times before, it had been with Jay and Philip, never alone. She welcomed the opportunity to explore.

Occupying a high floor of a Park Avenue building, the apartment was an elegant man's lair. The black marble floor of the entrance hall was cross-banded in narrow teak strips that seemed to echo the warm café au lait of the walls. Dramatic abstracts by artists from the New York School encircled the entry, providing a visual lecture on the innovation and individuality of the Abstract Expressionists who worked in New York during the 1940s and 1950s: Adolph Gottlieb, who used a household sponge mop to apply large areas of color; Franz Kline, who found housepainter's brushes most effective in creating his wide swaths of paint; Willem de Kooning, who used a fine sign painter's liner to create his briskly drawn arabesques; Robert Motherwell's Freudian images; Mark Rothko's tranquil rectangles; and Clyfford Still's seething primordial landscapes.

The living room, with an eighteenth-century pine mantelpiece set into an alcove finished with a matte black iron finish, was stunning in its contrasts: leather and silk, iron and wood, marble and glass. Here, too, the quality of the art staggered, but the mood turned softer, less confrontational: Jules Olitski, Agnes Martin, Helen Frankenthaler, and Richard Diebenkorn provided colorful oases of calm. The dining room, a masculine surround of marble-inlaid teak walls, had only one painting: a searing black, tan, and white expression of political outrage by Spain's Antoní Tàpies.

Though there were arresting canvases everywhere, it was Philip's bedroom that held Olivia's interest. On the large wall facing his bed was an almost embarrassingly erotic painting done in shades of red. Over his bed, flanked by gouaches by Miró, was a charcoal sketch in a style reminiscent of the figure in the painting on the opposite wall. Olivia recognized the deft hand of Isabelle de Luna in both works. It was when she glanced at the photograph of Philip and a young woman in a baseball cap—arms entwined, grinning into the camera—that Olivia realized the depth of her son's attraction to this woman. Philip never allowed pictures of himself in shorts, yet this one sat out in plain view, on the table next to his bed.

Olivia recalled Nelson's funeral. She had noticed Philip talking to a stunning woman whose name she hadn't known at the time. She remembered asking and being told she was the grandniece of Flora Pujol, an artist named Isabelle de Luna. Olivia had observed them speaking to each other. She had seen the look on Philip's face when Isabelle had walked away. Once before

she had seen that look, that painful portrait of a broken heart—the day she
had told him she was leaving.

Olivia was having wine in the library when Philip raced in.

"I'm sorry I'm late. Since Nelson died, I feel as if all I do is work."

Olivia poured him a glass of cabernet and gave him a few moments to
settle down. As he loosened his tie and removed his jacket, she marveled at
how handsome he was. She had missed watching him grow from a boy to a
man; often, when she looked at him, she was startled by what she saw. At
forty-four, he had tiny lines by his eyes that crinkled when he smiled, which
Olivia didn't think was often enough. His hair remained dark and full, but
she guessed there probably were a few strands of silver lurking. It also awed
her to think that with his own fortune and all that he had inherited from
Nelson's immense estate, her son was one of the most eligible bachelors in
the world. Yet thinking about that picture next to his bed and the expression
she had seen on his face in Lugano, her guess was he would be more than
willing to cede that title to someone else.

"Your collection is astounding, Philip." Because Olivia was an avid and
knowledgeable collector herself, the compliment carried weight. "And so
vast."

"With you and Nelson as parents, I would have felt like a complete dolt if
I hadn't amassed something of value."

He smiled, enjoying the fact that he felt so relaxed around her. It had
taken some doing, but they were on their way to a real relationship. To help
it along, he had appointed her curator of Nelson's collection. She was more
than qualified, and though it felt funny to say, he knew he could trust her.

"Recently, I went to catalog what I own." He chuckled and tilted his glass
at her in a gesture of tribute. "It's an impressive lot, but I could have used
your guidance."

"That's nice to say, but in what way?"

"I bought impulsively. Like Nelson. If it was modern, I liked it, and if it was
available, I bought it. Had I followed your pattern, I would have narrowed my
focus more and concentrated on one particular period."

"While it's true your collection is eclectic, your eye and your taste level are
so superb, Philip, it doesn't matter that you haven't focused on a particular
movement. You've captured an era." She answered his previous gesture by
raising her glass to him. He smiled appreciatively. "How's your new venture
working out?"

"Great! Skye's unbelievable!" His eyes widened with honest admiration.

"Of course, she trained under Richter and Glimcher, two of the best, but she came to the deal with a mix very few have." He paused, prioritizing. "Aside from her instincts about trends, which are right on, she understands a subtlety about the art world many do not: a dealer must be comfortable doing business with the rich. Skye is. She never allows herself to be bullied or to lose her self-respect. She's confident in who she is, what she knows, and what she does, which is why she's making a success out of the gallery."

"You're lucky. I've heard of several closings."

Philip sipped his wine, turning introspective. "The sale of *Sunflowers* was a defining moment," he said almost mournfully. "It set off the recent art boom, at the same time pushing the marketplace out of range of most collectors."

"Me, for one." Olivia's tone was rueful. "Jay and I used to go to a gallery, see something we liked, and buy it. Not anymore! We can barely afford the insurance on what we have, let alone the prices on what we want. We are, as they say, art poor."

Philip shook his head. "I see it happening all over. The bottom is beginning to fall out of the contemporary market, which had been soaring."

Olivia's laugh was sarcastic and envious. She loved art: buying it, living with it, talking about it, searching for it, funding it. It bothered her to feel shut out of a club to which she had belonged for so much of her life.

"When a Jasper Johns goes for $17.7 million and a de Kooning for $20.9 million, something's got to give!"

"That's why I give Skye so much credit. She knew the market was headed for a tough time and that opening a new gallery might be risky, but she had done her homework. Over the years, she had cultivated a group of dedicated collectors who followed her when she left Pace."

"The List," Olivia said with heraldic pomposity, referring to the names of preferred customers who were called by dealers before a show opened or when they heard of a piece for sale that would enhance their collection.

"You can't succeed without it. A dealer's livelihood depends on the care and feeding of spoiled, avaricious art groupies like me."

"You have a lot of faith in her."

Philip nodded. "I had observed her at Richter's gallery, but I really got to know her when she moved over to Pace. She sold me the Agnes Martin in the other room and introduced me to Jim Dine. She also insisted that I buy that box by Lucas Samaras."

Olivia studied the lucite cube on the cocktail table. Protruding from the front were pencils and pens and straws and toothpicks and whatever else one might put into one's mouth. Inside were images overlayed on images, symbols within symbols, colors and textures, text and subtext.

"It's a masterly mass of confusion," Philip said. "Which is why I love it. I can look at it every day and see something else."

Olivia looked, tried to find a point of interest for herself, then decided Samaras wasn't for her.

Philip continued unperturbed. "Before I agreed to invest, however, I asked her what she thought made a good dealer. She told me, 'You have to love the art, not the profits,' and then quoted Andre Emmerich: 'Good art dealers don't sell art; they allow people to acquire it.' That sounded right to me."

Olivia was pleased to note that Philip hadn't become so hardened by his own experiences or so blasé with his success that he had closed his mind to everything other than debits and credits.

"Skye seems to have a special affinity for Isabelle de Luna," Olivia said slyly. "As do you."

Philip laughed. "For a woman who, until recently, hadn't had much experience mothering, you catch on fast."

"Thank-you, dear. Now stop tap-dancing and tell me what's going on between you and that remarkable-looking woman."

"Absolutely nothing." Philip smiled wanly, his eyes sad.

"Do you love her?"

"Yes."

"Does she love you?"

"I think so."

"Problem?"

"She doesn't trust me."

"Does she have a reason?"

"I made a mistake. I apologized and I've tried to prove to her that she can trust me, but there's something else." His forehead creased. It was that puzzle he hadn't been able to solve. Olivia cocked her head quizzically. "She keeps saying that love isn't enough, that she has to feel safe." Frustration lined his mouth. "If I don't know what she's afraid of, how can I make her feel safe?"

Olivia rose from the couch and paced. Philip fell into the perplexed silence of one lost in a riddle. Suddenly she stopped and faced Philip, her expression anguished.

"When I left you, it was because I needed to feel safe. I had been beaten and abused and threatened so often, I felt as if I were in constant peril. But my leaving had nothing to do with loving you. I loved you every minute of every day from then until now. It wasn't enough. I needed to feel safe. Can you ever understand that?"

Philip stared at the distressed woman before him. Fear outlined her eyes, and it startled him: it was the same fear he had seen in Isabelle's eyes, the same fear he had seen years before on his mother's face but had never recognized. He stood and, for a while, held Olivia quietly.

"The child in me can never understand his mother's choosing to go," he said when they had resettled on the couch, "but the adult in me can and does."

"Thank-you." Olivia smiled and took his hand. "I feel for Isabelle, but I know from my own experience, she has to confront whatever it is that's threatening her."

"I'm not sure she knows what it is." He and Flora had talked about Isabelle's demons during their last visit. She too had asked him to be sympathetic with Isabelle's need for time and space. But she had had no answers and no suggestions about how to find them. "All I know is she won't let me help."

"Don't ask," Olivia said. "Just do. Just be there for her whenever you can. One day she'll see through her fears, recognize the love you're offering, and trust you enough to accept it. You did with me. She will with you."

Nina left Philip Medina's office with a big grin on her face. As she had known he would, he had made her an incredible offer for *True Colors:* five hundred thousand dollars! She had told him she would think about it. Just recalling the insouciant way she had let those words trip off her tongue made her giggle. Nina hadn't forgotten the callous way he had fired her. She hadn't forgotten that he had put the squeeze on ABC and her syndication group. She hadn't forgotten that she had entertained fleeting thoughts of a romance with him, egged on by some serious flirting on his part, only to learn that he had fallen for the one woman in the world of whom she would be jealous. Nina hadn't forgotten. And she hadn't forgiven him for anything.

Their meeting had been chillingly cordial, polite, respectful, and wary. They were programmed robots speaking lines, refusing to vary from the impersonal nature of the script. Though she knew he was shocked to learn about her relationship to Isabelle, he had hidden it well. Probably all those years of breeding. While she was certain he yearned to throttle her for wanting to drag his precious Isabelle through the mud, he didn't. Nor did he accuse her of writing the book for revenge. He was a complete gentleman, which was why she didn't wonder aloud if he was offering to buy it so he could squelch it, which was exactly what she suspected he would do.

It didn't matter. Philip taking over Medina Publishing had given Nina the edge she sought. Anthony might not react to an offer from any another house, but he would respond to Medina. Whatever had caused it, there was bad blood between those two, and Nina intended to use it to her advantage. Her only problem was that she needed to conclude this deal as quickly as possible. Brynna was becoming impossible. A couple of weeks ago the thieving wench had called and demanded more money. When Nina had refused, Brynna had repeated her now familiar threat about calling Phil Donahue or Oprah Winfrey.

"Call Geraldo, for all I care," Nina said, having decided to call her bluff. "One word out of you and the gravy train comes to a grinding halt. Got that?"

Obviously she had, because Nina hadn't heard any more from her, nor had she heard a promo about "Nina Davis's long-lost mother" for any of the afternoon talkathons. The Endless Money Pit was content. For now.

When Anthony unmasked Nina's charade, he accomplished two things: he reclassified himself from friend to foe, and he became the focus of a research expedition to Boston. For a man who had gone digging into her past, he'd raised an awful lot of unanswered questions about his own history. Using fast talk and an old credential, Nina gained access to the morgue at Cisco Communications' *Boston Herald,* spending hours in a basement carrel, bent over a microfilm machine to study the social pages from the late thirties and early forties.

She found dozens of pictures of Anthony's grandparents cutting ribbons, attending charity dinners, hosting dignitaries, receiving various medals and awards from grateful citizens. Anthony's father, Albert, had seen his share of newsprint, but he was usually pictured alone or in the company of an "unnamed female companion."

In 1942 Albert Hartwick married Jocelyn Kennelon. He was forty-seven years old, she was twenty. He was the scion of one of Boston's most prominent families. She was one of five children born to a middle-class Irishman who owned a company that published books on gardening, decorating, and cooking.

"She was certainly beautiful," Nina mused, studying the solemn but attractive brunette in the wedding portrait. "Too beautiful to marry someone so ordinary looking and so much older. Unless, of course, the operative words in this marriage ceremony were 'for richer.' "

Searching further, Nina went back and studied everything she could find on Albert Hartwick. Over the years several attempts had been made to link him to one socialite or another, but each seemed a stretch. Clearly he had had no serious, long-term relationships, prompting more than one columnist to tiptoe over the question of his bachelorhood. It didn't appear that he had an extended courtship with Jocelyn Kennelon, either. There wasn't any mention of them other than their engagement—which had taken Boston by surprise—and their wedding.

Curious, Nina rolled the microfilm backward, then forward again, focusing now on the business section. As she had suspected, tucked onto the back page was an article about several small businesses on the verge of bankruptcy; Kennelon Publishing was one of those listed. One month after the nuptials, the company was sold to Hartwick House for "an undisclosed, but substantial sum." Two years later there was a small piece announcing the birth of Anthony Hartwick.

Considering their social prominence, Nina would have expected more. In fact, thinking about it, she realized there should have been lots more, but Jocelyn and Albert Hartwick seemed to be conspicuously absent from every major social function. Jocelyn headed no committees, attended no luncheons, adopted no charitable causes, appeared at no ribbon cuttings, garden club meetings, war bond drives, weddings, or debutante parties. It seemed as if, from the day she'd married Albert until the day she'd buried him, she had disappeared.

What had she been doing all those years? Judging by the picture of her at Albert's funeral, she hadn't been having fun. The once beautiful Jocelyn was now haggard, drawn, aged. Anthony had said both his parents had died when he was young. He'd been ten years old when his father had died. From the looks of her, Jocelyn probably hadn't survived Albert for very long.

Just to be sure, Nina left the morgue and headed over to the Bureau of Records. She looked but could find no obituary for Jocelyn Hartwick. Nor did she find any indication that the woman had remarried or been institutionalized. For all intents and purposes, Jocelyn Kennelon Hartwick seemed to have disappeared.

Seemed to . . .

On a hunch, Nina rifled through every telephone directory for Boston and its surrounding area until she found a listing for Sean Kennelon, Longmeadow, Massachusetts. The next morning she paid a visit to Anthony Hartwick's maternal grandfather.

*   *   *

Telling Isabelle that Hartwick House intended to publish a biography of her written by Nina Davis had not been easy, but Philip didn't want her to hear it from anyone else. She had accepted the news with remarkable equanimity.

"I'm not happy about my life or my parents' lives being laid out for all the world to see and dissect, but Nina and I have been on a collision course for years. I'm only surprised she's willing to admit we were raised as sisters. She's spent most of her adult life hiding that fact."

"People only reveal secrets when it becomes evident that it's more dangerous not to. Something must have pushed her into doing this."

"She never needed much of a push before. Simple revenge has always been motive enough."

"I know, but believe it or not, I think this has more to do with Anthony Hartwick than it does with you."

Philip had thought a great deal about this. Nina coming to him fit only if her purpose was to degrade Isabelle in his eyes while upgrading herself, or to elicit an offer she could use as a negotiating tool. Since he believed she knew the former wasn't going to happen, he opted for the latter explanation and made her an offer she could—and would—refuse.

"Hartwick is in deep financial trouble. If this book hits, it could save his bottom line and turn his business around. Nina must envision a happy ending for herself in that scenario."

"And all I see is disaster. This book could turn my life around."

Isabelle couldn't hide her anger. Long ago she had ceased to feel sympathy for Nina. Whatever had happened to her and between them had happened years before. It was time Nina got over it.

"I tried to stop her."

"I know, and believe me, I appreciate it."

"Enough to have dinner with me?"

She laughed. "Yes, but I can't. Skye's coop'd a show of my watercolors with Miranda at Enchantments. I'm leaving for Santa Fe tomorrow."

"Isn't this where I came in?"

They concluded their conversation amiably, but for Philip it remained unsatisfying. Aside from wanting to be with her, he was worried about her. He had heard the nervousness in her voice when he had told her about the book, how it chronicled her mother's murder and her father's arrest. It had hurt him to read the manuscript. Nina had outlined her past for him, but reading the details had been painful and he had read them over and over again. Not only did he need to know and understand what she had lived through, but he was searching for clues. Isabelle felt threatened by something or someone. He was certain of that. It wasn't the book; that was merely a symptom, not the source of her fear.

Flora maintained it was the ghost of the past, Isabelle's unresolved guilt about not being able to come to her father's aid. While he agreed that was possible, he believed it was more than that. What or who it was, he didn't know, but somehow, he intended to find out. As he had told Olivia, until he knew what was frightening her, he couldn't help her feel safe.

"How dare you look down your nose at me and make me feel like some worthless piece of shit when you've been lying about your family since the day we met!"

Nina had burst into his office, storming past secretaries and receptionists and whomever else had tried to block her way. Anthony's cool usually impressed her. Today, it annoyed her.

"Lying? About what?" He infuriated her further by stretching out on his black leather couch.

"You told me both of your parents had died. *Au contraire!* Your mother is alive and well and living in the south of France with some Spanish writer."

"So she is." He gave her one of those upper class laughs she despised: more sniffling than mirthful. "What of it?"

"And she was never the socialite you made her out to be. She was Irish and middle class."

"And you were raised by Latinos. Don't be a snob, Nina. It doesn't become you." His tone was glib, but his eyes betrayed a nervousness that excited her.

"She only married your father because your grandfather paid big bucks for a bride. Her daddy's business was about to go under. Grandpa Alston was getting desperate for an heir to his dynasty, so he made Sean Kennelon a deal he didn't refuse.

"Obviously, your mother wasn't thrilled with the match. At some point she found alcohol far more fulfilling than her life as Mrs. Albert Hartwick. When your father died, Grandpa wasted no time shipping her off to Europe to dry out. Since she hasn't returned, I assume he settled a small fortune on her, probably with the condition that she never show her face on this side of the Atlantic again." She couldn't contain her triumph. "How am I doing?"

"Quite well." He had straightened his posture, his shoulders squared in a pose of utter confidence. "I suppose you have more?"

"Just a little, but I think it's the best part."

He bowed his head, like a king granting a subject permission to speak. Nina strolled over to the acrylic table before the couch, sat on the edge, and leaned forward, coming to within inches of Anthony.

"Jocelyn was sent away so she couldn't spill the nasty Hartwick secret that Albert was gay and couldn't get it up with a woman. Before she had been traded away by her father, she had been madly in love with a guy from her neighborhood. The day she was dragged down the aisle, that poor, heart-broken schnook signed up for the RAF and left for England. Fortunately for Jocelyn, he came home on furlough, which was when she became pregnant with you. I don't know what happened to him."

"How come? Didn't you dig deep enough or try hard enough?" Anthony's anger broke free of its restraints. His skin was flushed and his eyes flamed with indignation. "He died when his plane crashed over Germany."

Nina backed down. "I'm sorry."

"Somehow, I doubt that."

"Look," she said, regrouping. "You turned your nose up at me as if I were beneath you. What's worse, I believed that I was. I believed that you were part of America's aristocracy and I was some unimportant orphan. Now I find out you're not a Hartwick at all. You're Conan Donnelly's son, and your whole life has been a lie. Just like mine."

"What's the point?"

Nina seated herself on the opposite couch and smiled. "The point is that I was right all along. We're perfect together. And to prove it, I'm going to give you another chance at that manuscript I told you I was going to write. That exposé on Isabelle de Luna. I've finished it, and it's good, Anthony." She paused. She could tell he was interested. She wanted that interest to build. "So good, in fact, that I've received an offer of eight hundred thousand dol-lars for it from Philip Medina."

She knew Anthony would never call Philip and check on the price. What was another three hundred thousand between friends?

"Obviously you didn't sign a deal with him or you wouldn't be presenting it to me."

"I'd rather you publish it." Her eyes softened, her smile shifted from self-satisfied to beguiling. "After all, I've always been extremely happy in your hands."

Hartwick rose and faced the wall. For several minutes he remained with his back to her. When finally he turned around, she held her breath.

"I'll match Medina's offer." She was about to negotiate when he held up his hand. "And I'll accept your marriage proposal."

"What?" Nina hadn't expected that.

"It's the end of June. If the manuscript is in order, I can turn it around and have it in the stores by November, in time for Christmas. We can be married New Year's Eve. How's that sound?"

" 'Auld Lang Syne' has always been number one on my top ten."

He went to his private bar, popped a bottle of champagne, poured some into crystal flutes, and toasted his bride-to-be: "Here's to *True Colors* and true love. May our expectations of each be fulfilled."

As Nina grinned at Anthony and drank the celebratory champagne, she marveled at what had just taken place. In a matter of months she would have a husband in her life—and Isabelle and Brynna out of it. She should have been ecstatic.

So why did she feel as if she had bought the dress of her dreams, only to put it on and find out it was too tight?

CHAPTER 27

Barcelona, 1990

Throughout the long journey to Barcelona, Isabelle barely slept. She was still rattled by what had happened at her birthday party: in the midst of the merriment at La Casa, she had felt an unwelcome presence. Miranda had tried to assure her it was a case of nerves, a matter of having to confront an unwelcome passing. Isabelle couldn't deny that possibility, but neither could she deny the feeling that she was another person's prey.

There was no reason for anyone to be stalking her, yet in recent months the aura of menace had become inescapable. It was a feeling that in a restaurant or at a benefit or an opening, one pair of eyes lingered on her too long. On the street, footsteps behind her were too in step with her own. Hangups on her answering machine were deliberate and frequent. She had tried to escape the silent phone calls and the anonymous stares and the sensation of evil lurking by leaving New York and retreating to Santa Fe, but the threat had followed her to the mountains.

She rented a car and sped all the way to Campíns. As much as she needed to be with Tía Flora in her last moments, she needed to feel the humid wind running its sticky fingers through her hair, to feel in control of the car and the road. She needed to feel the strong thump-thump-thump of her own heartbeat assuring her that despite the call of impending doom that seemed to hold her in its grip, she was alive and well.

When she walked into Tía Flora's room, however, that heartbeat slowed considerably at the sight of the frail, fading woman in the cellophane-canopied bed. Alejandro, weakened by grief and the toll of his own advanced age, sat by Flora's side, her hand resting comfortably in his. Isabelle smiled wanly at him as she approached her great-aunt from the other side of the bed. As she leaned down to kiss Flora's ashen cheek, her nose sniffed the faint scent of jasmine and violets; she smiled. How like Flora to continue the rituals of her life even as she prepared for death.

"I'm glad you waited for me," Isabelle said, taking the chair offered by Flora's nurse.

Flora's mouth twitched and her eyes moistened as she looked at the face of the woman she had brought into this world. It was the one face she wanted to gaze upon before she exited.

"We have things to discuss." Flora's voice was a whisper, yet her eyes appeared to burn. Her mind raced with a youthful energy her body no longer possessed.

"Save your strength." Isabelle stroked Flora's cheek with the back of her hand. It was surprisingly cool.

"I don't have anything to save it for." Her lips wobbled as she smiled at her own joke.

Though Alejandro smiled along with her, his eyes pooled. His pain was evident. They had loved each other and been together nearly seventy years. Isabelle feared Alejandro wouldn't live long without his Flora.

Flora closed her eyes and gasped for breath. The nurse rushed over and placed an oxygen mask over her mouth and nose. Isabelle hadn't even noticed the tank alongside the bed. When Flora's breathing rallied and the mask was removed, she moved her head slowly toward Alejandro. He kissed her gently and patted her hand. For a second or two Flora allowed her eyes to linger on the face of her soul mate, the man to whom she believed she had been linked by destiny. Then she looked away. She couldn't bear the thought of leaving him. It wrenched too much. But, she thought, comforting herself, their separation wouldn't last long. They were going to spend eternity together.

Forcing herself to focus, she redirected her attention to Isabelle. She needed to use whatever time remained to set things straight so Isabelle could be free of her ghosts and find the contentment she had sought for so long. If Flora had a dying wish, it was that the rest of Isabelle's time on earth be jubilant and filled with the kind of love she herself had known with Alejandro, that Martín had known with Althea, that she believed Isabelle could know with Philip.

"There's so much I want for you . . . should have made it easier . . . should have fought to keep you here . . ."

Flora's eyes closed. Isabelle sprang from her chair and hovered over her aunt, too afraid to check for a pulse. Flora's eyes fluttered. To Isabelle's relief, they were open—slack, but open.

"I should have taken on Estrella and Javier."

Isabelle placed her finger on Flora's lips, hushing her, begging her to rest. Someone tapped on the door. The nurse opened it, admitting Philip. Isabelle was stunned. She looked from him to Flora.

"I don't want you to be alone," she said simply.

Flora followed Philip with her eyes as he came to her side, kissed her on the forehead, and then quietly took his place behind Isabelle, who didn't bother to hide the fact that she was glad he was there. Satisfied, Flora allowed herself to slide into a deep sleep. Her breathing grew shallow and irregular.

"Did you call for a priest?" Isabelle whispered to Alejandro.

He nodded, his eyes still fixed on Flora's face. "But before he administers the last rites, she said she wanted you to recite the mantra for her. She said you would know."

Once again Flora's idiosyncratic personality prompted a smile from Isabelle. All her life Flora had juggled Catholicism and yoga, balancing them skillfully enough to insure that she could take from each everything that was positive, while eschewing whatever she found negative. She wanted the priest to bless her, and she had consented to a mass in the cathedral, but before her soul began its journey, she wanted a joyful send-off, one that was peaceful and encouraging, not tear-filled, anguished, and regretful.

Isabelle stood and rapidly rubbed her hands back and forth to create heat. Holding them over Flora's eyes so she could feel the warmth, she shut her own eyes and chanted softly in Hindi. Mantra and yantra. Sound and light, colorful patterns—they were the guides to the place of everlasting peace.

Focusing solely on her great-aunt, Isabelle didn't see the priest enter the room, nor did she see him anoint Flora with oil or hear him as he absolved Flora from her earthly sins in preparation for her ascendancy to heaven. Silently Isabelle continued to recite the mantra, her eyes still closed, her energy totally concentrated on easing the separation of body and soul.

When she opened her eyes, the priest was gone. And so was Flora.

Inside the cathedral, Isabelle sat with Philip on one side, Alejandro on the other. Milagros had passed away five years before, but Inez was there on the arm of her son, Xavier. The rest of the Fargas clan filled the front three pews. Teresa Serrat, her husband, and five children were there as well. Seeing her made Isabelle realize how much she missed Consuela and Pedro. They too had died.

Many of those who had come to bid farewell to Señorita Flora Pujol had come more out of respect for the name than from an attachment to the person. They had not known her, yet the distances they had traveled, the various reasons that had drawn them there, the very diversity of the crowd, served to define the complexity of the woman. Spanish aristocracy and European nobility occupied many of the front seats, along with every important politician from Catalonia. The Pujols, being mercantile giants, were woven into the historical fabric of the region and the nation. King Juan Carlos had sent his son to represent the Crown. Jordi Pujol, president of the provincial government—and a distant relation—was there, as well as the mayor of Barcelona, Pasqual Maragall. Farmers and vintners stood shoulder to shoulder with bankers and manufacturers. International opera singers, classical musicians, novelists, philosophers, and journalists shared pews with pop balladeers, flamenco guitarists, and coffeehouse poets.

But it was Flora's beloved artists who stood as her honor guard. Rafael Avda, Antoni Tàpies, Eduardo Chillida, Jorge Catillo, Luis Feitó, Antonio Saura, Javier Corberó, Miquel Barceló: one by one they walked down the long aisle of the ancient cathedral. Each wore a fresh white rose in his lapel as an expression of sadness. Each stopped to offer his condolences to Isabelle and Alejandro, knelt in front of Flora's coffin, and then took his place flanking the gleaming mahogany burial box.

Lesser-known artists, students, every dealer in Barcelona as well as many from Madrid and Seville, all made the long walk to offer their respects. To the art community of Spain, Flora Pujol was a heroine. She had patronized painters and sculptors, offering food and shelter and money, and had put herself at risk protecting their right to create during the dark, culturally oppressive years of Franco's reign. She had supported them. They remembered her.

Isabelle, wearing white, as she knew her aunt would have wanted, studied the floral blanket she had ordered to cover the casket: red and yellow roses arranged in stripes, as in the flag of Catalonia. Tía Flora was so proud of her heritage, it seemed only right to treat her like the patriot she was. Judging by the floral tributes that crowded the bier, Isabelle was not the only one who viewed Flora in that light. Many arrangements contained red and yellow flowers or bore ribbons imitative of the Catalonian flag. Many, sent by those who knew it as Flora's signature, were pure white. Isabelle hadn't read the accompanying cards, so she didn't know, but one of them was signed "*Nina Duran.*"

As the service proceeded, Isabelle noted with pride the number of illustrious people who offered eulogies. She tried to listen, but in truth her mind was elsewhere. She was wandering around the past, gathering her own memories of her precious Tía Flora. She didn't cling to specifics but let individual instances meld into a vague but powerful manifestation. Flora's wisdom about people, her insights into situations, her ability to distill the largest of life's complications into small manageable packets—all coalesced into a warm presence Isabelle could almost feel.

In accordance with Flora's will, her casket took the same route from the cathedral in the Gothic Quarter to Campíns as her father's had: north through the city, with a special detour past La Sagrada Família, the startling, sand-castle-like cathedral that was Antoni Gaudí's most celebrated work. When the procession slowed in front of the towering, still unfinished cathedral, Isabelle recalled coming here as a little girl.

As part of her contribution to her grandniece's education, Flora had taken Isabelle to visit every one of Gaudí's structures, filling the young child's head with stories about the man who had autographed Barcelona's skyline with his unique and singular vision and inspired the none-too-complimentary English word *gaudy.*

When she took Isabelle to Güell Park, Isabelle could hardly contain her excitement. It was like nothing she'd ever seen before: broad expanses lined with palm trees, sinuous staircases, viaducts, serpentine benches encrusted with glorious mosaics of broken tiles. She had gaped at the zoomorphic sculptures that populated the park, finding them capricious and colorful and, to her eye, childlike.

"How did Gaudí think these things up?" Isabelle had asked, wishing she could take home one of the amusing dragons.

"They're dreams carved in stone," Flora had said.

"I hope all your dreams were fulfilled, my darling *tía,*" Isabelle whispered as the cortege moved away from Gaudí's soaring monument and headed toward the small hillside where Flora would be laid to rest.

It helped to feel Philip's shoulder next to hers, to feel his hand wrapped around hers, to be able to rest her head against him. Still, nothing could protect her from the dread she felt about entering the small family graveyard. Not only was Flora being buried one month to the day after Althea had been buried twenty-seven years before, but this would be the first time Isabelle had been there since, the first time she would lay eyes on her father's grave.

When she stepped out of the car, she was pleased to see how many people had come to Campíns. Rafael, of course. Diego Cadiz. Teresa. Their families. The Reys. Pilar Medina. François and Eunice LeVerre. Alejandro's entire family. What jarred her was to count Estrella and Javier Murillo among the mourners.

"They're here for you," Alejandro said quietly. Leaning on Isabelle for support, he had felt her body jerk, and his eyes had sought and found the source of her discomfort. "They need to show you they care about someone you cared so deeply about." Isabelle started to speak, but Alejandro shook his head. "Their days are limited. They need to make peace with you, Isabelle. Try to find it in your heart to grant it to them."

As Isabelle made the small climb to the hill where she had first seen them, she knew that until she was certain the Murillos had forgiven Martín, she couldn't forgive them.

Philip and Xavier tended to Alejandro as he struggled to reach Flora's freshly dug grave. Isabelle detoured, stopping under the parasol pine at the headstones that marked the spot where her parents lay. Kneeling, she laid a bouquet of pink roses on Althea's grave.

"I still miss you, Mama," she whispered, kissing her finger, then pressing it against the cold stone. "Every single day."

For Martín she had brought a single white rose. There weren't enough of them in the universe to symbolize the sadness that enveloped her when she thought of him.

"It's not finished yet, Papa," she muttered, staring at the ground that held his remains, a little stunned by her own words. They had come out of her mouth before her mind had recorded them.

As she ran her fingers across the carving of his name, Martín Josep Ildefons de Luna, she wondered what had prompted such a thought. Seeing this stone for the first time? Visiting her mother? Seeing the Murillos? Having to relive that awful day, see those terrible images, hear that hideous sound of dirt from her own hand skittering across the wooden box that held her mother?

"Isabelle." She turned toward the voice. Philip bent down, dabbed her tears tenderly, and held out his hand. "It's time to say good-bye to Flora."

Isabelle nodded and allowed him to help her to her feet. His arm slipped around her waist and steadied her as they walked to the crest. Off to the side was the timeworn marking for Antoní Pujol, the founder of the clan. His wife and his son, Ramón, lay nearby, as did Ramón's wife and children. Then there were Josep and Rosa Pujol and their progeny. Joan and Pau, sons who had died too young. Vina, the poet. Ramona, the musician. Beátriz, the entrepreneur and protector of the family fortune. And now, Flora.

Isabelle survived the service by again immersing herself in her own memories of the extraordinary woman who was now entering that spirit world with which she'd always seemed so keenly attuned. The worst moment was watching Alejandro lower himself to his knees, clutch soil in his arthritic hands, bring it to his lips, kiss it, and toss it onto Flora's casket. Sobs racked his body. If Philip and the priest hadn't held him, Isabelle was certain he would have fallen in.

Afterward Xavier and Inez assured her they would see Alejandro home and make certain he was all right. Isabelle knew he'd never be all right again.

It was dusk by the time everyone left. Isabelle had been as gracious to the Murillos as she could, reminding herself they were her grandparents, they were old, and that if Alejandro had negotiated on their behalf, perhaps she should mellow just a bit. But when the last guest had departed and only Philip remained, Isabelle's facade crumbled.

"I can't stay here tonight," she said, suddenly fearful of being alone in the Castell.

"I have a suite at a hotel in Barcelona. Stay with me."

She nodded meekly. Philip left her in the salon while he asked the maid to pack a bag. When it was ready he led Isabelle toward the door. Outside, it had begun to rain. Typical of late-day summer storms, the sky had turned completely black. Despite the heat and humidity that clogged the air, Isabelle shivered as she waited for Philip to bring around the car. As they drove down the hill that led away from the Castell and toward Barcelona, she asked him at which hotel he was staying.

"The Ritz."

Though she claimed she wasn't hungry, Philip insisted they have something to eat. Since it was only nine-thirty, and most Spaniards preferred to dine around ten, the restaurant was just beginning to fill up. The large, wonderfully elegant room with its pale yellow walls and ivory moldings, patterned rug, and crystal chandeliers was relatively quiet. Soon, when all the tables were filled, the noise would increase to a cultivated buzz of glasses tinkling, silverware clattering against plates, and people chattering about their day's activities. Philip hoped to be gone by then.

"It's been a long, sad day," he said as he handed her a glass of red wine.

Isabelle sipped the rioja slowly. She appeared distracted. Philip let her be. Their table was next to a set of towering French doors that allowed them to look out on a patio and garden illuminated by lights from the hotel. Owing to the assault of the storm, a verdant oasis had been transformed into an eerie landscape. Philip looked away. Isabelle seemed transfixed.

Trees were being tossed about by a heartless wind that ripped leaves from branches and flung them to the ground. Flowers were beaten down by the fierce pelting of the raindrops. Isabelle viewed them as powerless prisoners, rooted in place yet straining to free themselves so they could flee the terror being inflicted upon them. The sight of their helplessness made her edgy.

She picked at her food and drank her wine, but there was little that could revive her spirit. Philip, understanding, suggested they retire.

The suite was large, and though she wasn't in a mood to care about details, she couldn't help but notice the eighteenth-century tapestry, a crystal chandelier, shaded wall sconces, gilded mirrors and consoles, delicately carved furniture upholstered in fine silks. Philip showed her to an inviting boudoir decorated in soothing shades of coral. A luxuriously tufted headboard, lush fabrics, finely carved moldings, delicate lamps, smoothly laundered sheets—everything had been designed to soothe and pamper. Next to her bed was a vase with peach roses. Isabelle was certain that particular nicety had been arranged by Philip.

"It's lovely," she said. "Thank-you."

Hearing a knock on the door, Philip excused himself. Isabelle, bothered by the rain, went to close the drapes. A bolt of lightning split the blackness, appearing to shoot from the sky into the street directly in front of her. Completely startled by the image, Isabelle staggered, catching herself on the sill. The thunder that followed shook the room. When Philip returned, Isabelle was trembling.

"I think I'm just in time," he said, handing her a brandy, wondering what had triggered her obvious panic. "It'll calm your nerves."

He closed the drapes, lit the lamp on the nightstand, and encouraged her to ready herself for bed. "More than anything, you need sleep."

After kissing her cheek and reminding her that if she needed him he was close by, he bade her good night.

Following his suggestion, Isabelle went to the bathroom, changed into nightclothes, and climbed into bed. She was completely exhausted. Philip had left her brandy and a few magazines. Sipping the amber liquid, flipping pages of endless fashion photos, listening to the steady pounding of the rain, she grew drowsy. Her eyelids felt heavy. Suddenly the lights flickered. There was a crash of thunder. The windows rattled. The lights flickered again and then went out. Isabelle's heart began to pound.

Nervous, frightened, she slid out of bed. Keeping her hands out in front of her, she treaded carefully toward the door. She was groping about when again thunder pealed so loudly, it felt as if it had come from within the room instead of without. She froze, her fingers clutching the brass doorknob that led to the drawing room. An odd, tingling sensation oozed through her body, making her feel as if a narcotic had been introduced into her bloodstream and was slowly taking hold of her system. She shook her head, trying to clear it. Just then she heard a crash in the other room. Something made of glass shattered. Then she heard a thud. Without thinking, she turned the knob and opened the door.

Lightning flashed. For a second the sky exploded, filling the space before her with light. It was blue. *That* blue. That awful, familiar, terrifying blue. Ahead of her, looking up at her from the floor, she saw a face. A hand reached toward her. She heard her name. She froze, her breath caught in her throat. She knew the voice. But the face. It was *his!* She saw it just as plainly as she had seen it that night so many years before. Those eyes glaring at her, stunned by the unexpected sight of her. That mouth, with its lip upturned in a snarl. How could she have forgotten that face!

She never heard herself scream. She never felt her body hit the floor.

She awoke in Philip's bed, safely cocooned in his arms. The electricity was still out, but a candle glowed from the table next to his bed. The drapes were open. The rain had stopped and the clouds had disappeared, allowing the moon to diffuse its gentle light on the city.

"What happened?"

"You had a nightmare," Philip said, smoothing her hair off her face. "The storm frightened you."

Isabelle snuggled closer to him. As he held her, her mind recalled the moments before she'd fainted. Mercifully, the visions returned slowly.

When she had reviewed them, she sat up and looked at Philip. "I saw him," she said quietly. "I saw the man who killed my mother."

"When the light went out, I ran to get to you," Philip said, unnerved by the spectral look on her face. "I couldn't see. I tripped over an end table, knocked over a lamp, and fell. You opened the door and looked directly at me."

Isabelle nodded. "But I saw *him.*"

"Is he someone you know?"

"Yes. No." Isabelle shrugged. "I'm not sure, but," she said, tears of relief streaming down her cheeks, "it's there, Philip. All these years I believed I had been asleep. I told the police I didn't see anything because I couldn't remember anything. But I wasn't asleep. I saw it. I was in that room." She sobbed, regret tumbling over relief. "What happened that night. It's there, and it's coming back."

Philip held her close. Her body was quaking. He spoke softly. "You shouldn't try to retrieve those memories alone, Isabelle."

"I know." Wiping her eyes on the sheet, she lay in his arms, contemplating what had happened, what should happen next. Philip allowed her the privacy of uninterrupted thought. "Tomorrow morning, I'm going to call Alejandro's nephew, Xavier," she said after several minutes had passed. "He's a psychiatrist and, according to Alejandro, quite good. Besides, I know him, and . . ."

"You'll feel safe with him," Philip said, completing her sentence.

Isabelle pulled away and looked at him, a sudden realization overwhelming her. "I feel safe with you."

Philip's expression displayed both shock and pleasure. "When did you conclude that?"

Though his tone was light, Isabelle didn't smile. Instead she turned reflective. "I must have felt that way for quite some time. If I hadn't, I wouldn't have come here with you. Not on this day, to this hotel." She massaged her temples, as if that would help her think. "My subconscious must have trusted you to protect me from whatever's locked inside my brain."

"That's because your subconscious knows how much I love you." His voice was gentle, as if it had been filtered through a smile, but his eyes were intense and fixed.

"In here," she said, patting her hand against her chest, "I've always known that I love you. I guess my mind had to catch up with my heart." Her voice caught as emotion rose in her throat.

"None of that matters now. What we have to do is plan our future, not worry about the past."

As he said it, they both knew that not worrying about the past was impossible. Only an hour before, the past had thundered back into Isabelle's life.

"Do you remember the other day, when you came to the Castell?" she asked Philip, tentatively beginning to retrace all that had occurred. "Tía Flora said she didn't want me to be alone. Do you think she knew this would happen? That I would get my memory back?"

"I think she believed it would happen someday, but whether it did or not, Isabelle, she didn't want you to be alone."

"I know. She loved you, too."

Her eyes caressed him, but even in the candlelight he could see fear lurking.

"This could take a long time," she said, suddenly uneasy.

"And," Philip added, believing forewarned was forearmed, "there's no guarantee you'll get everything back. These memories have been repressed for years."

"Still, I have to do it."

Philip put his arm around her, drawing her next to him. "But you don't have to do it alone."

Isabelle told him how grateful she was for his love, his patience, his strength, and, especially, his support, but after he had fallen asleep, she stared into the darkness and faced the truth: the next morning she intended to embark on a journey to a place where she had kept devastating memories stored for twenty-seven years. This voyage would be harrowing, and probably there would be many times along the way she would want to stop. But it was a journey that had to be taken. And despite Philip's good intentions, it had to be taken alone.

Xavier's practice was in Pedralbes, a well-to-do suburb of Barcelona. On the Diagonal, near the university, his office overlooked the Parc del Palau Reial de Pedralbes, an Italiante palace used by the royal family on their visits to the Catalonian capital. Isabelle had been seeing Xavier several times a week for two months. Each time she insisted the most pleasant part was looking out the window.

Looking inside her subconscious had proved difficult. Rather than use drugs or hypnosis, Xavier preferred to let the mind open at its own pace. Not only was it healthier, but in the end, he believed it was more accurate. And in a case like this, where ultimately someone might be charged with murder, reliability was essential.

"You're an artist, Isabelle," Xavier had said in their second session, the first having been taken up with preliminaries. "Use your visualization skills to take you back and paint the scenes we need to see."

Seated on a chair behind the couch where she lay, speaking in a soft, even voice, Xavier assisted Isabelle in her return to her childhood. Out of deference to her years in America, Xavier initially had spoken to her in English. When she began to regress, however, she reverted to Spanish, the language she had spoken as a young girl.

They moved quickly from her uncomplicated, happy life in the town house on the Passeig de Gracia and her visits to the Castell de Les Bruixots to that last vacation in Majorca. There, Isabelle's memories became shadowed with anxiety. While her conscious mind claimed ignorance, her subconscious knew what was coming. That knowledge frightened her.

Their progress stalled. Fear acted like an emergency brake, holding them to a single time and place. Slowly, carefully, Xavier rerouted her brain, sliding time frames back and forth in a gentle, oscillating way, tricking her mind into believing she was in one of the key places, but at another time, with people other than those who made up the cast of the tragedy they were there to explore.

Isabelle recalled how much she always looked forward to their summer vacation in Majorca.

"I had made lots of friends. We had such a good time playing in the sand and splashing around in the water."

Her forehead creased as if disturbed by a headache. Her voice dropped. "That year, I wanted more than fun. I had hoped a change of scene might help my parents' marriage. Things weren't right between them."

"Is that where you met Pasqua Barba?" Xavier asked.

Isabelle nodded. Even now she could remember how he had affected her. "He was very handsome, the kind of man women paid attention to." She sighed. "Even married women like my mother.

"He hung around her like a shadow. While my father was able to chase away most of my mother's admirers, Barba didn't chase easily."

The heated conversation between Paco and Martín replayed in her mind. She frowned as she repeated it for Xavier, embarrassed at having to portray her father in such a bad light.

"Was your father equally upset with your mother?"

Isabelle turned her head to the side, avoiding. She hadn't positively identified "the face" as yet. She was fairly certain it wasn't Martín; nonetheless, she hated when something came up that pointed to him as a credible suspect.

"Was he?"

"He was furious with her."

Another day she told Xavier about having her fifth birthday party in the dining room at the Ritz, having lunch with Althea on the patio, having tea with Tía Flora and Tío Alejandro in the lounge off the lobby. She recalled the towering columns, groupings of high-backed chairs around wooden tables, blue-patterned ceramic tubs holding large plants, music being played. Eventually she grew comfortable enough in the setting to face that fateful afternoon when Martín had come upon Althea and Isabelle and Pasqua Barba. Again she had been forced to admit that Martín's rage had equaled, and perhaps exceeded, Barba's.

When they approached the night of the murder, Xavier warned her that because it was the root of her trauma, she wouldn't be able to recall those hours in sequence, nor would she be able to re-create an entire scenario.

"You've kept that night buried for a lifetime, Isabelle. To do that, you had to break it up into little pieces and store it away in a number of different compartments. Our job is to open each drawer, patiently retract whatever is hidden there, and then, when all the pieces are on the table, solve the puzzle."

Xavier was right. Each session produced only parts, never the whole. Althea: naked on the floor, the towel that had covered her freshly bathed body scrunched beneath her. A lamp, smashed, its shade tilted at a funny angle. Althea's hair, wet, in thick, matted strands. An overturned table. The man's jacket: blue with gold buttons. Althea's face: turned to the side, her eyes closed, her lips partially open, her right cheek bloodied. His face: some of the same pieces—the angry glare, the upturned lip; some new—a cut on his cheek, a gold ring on his left hand, the one that was raised toward her.

Their last session took three hours, Xavier deftly guiding Isabelle through the entire night, from the moment she and Althea returned to the suite after Althea's argument with Martín and Paco, to Isabelle hiding in the closet and holding her breath so that the man wouldn't find her and hurt her the way he had hurt her mama.

Everything came back to her, but because it had returned piecemeal, she continued to feel unsure about what the man looked like.

"When you awoke from those blue nightmares," Xavier asked, "did you remember details?"

"Sometimes."

"Did you write them down?"

"I sketched them."

"Did you save those sketches?"

"Some." Isabelle used to feel foolish about saving her doodles. Now she was grateful she had. "Miranda has some, too."

Xavier nodded. He didn't want to show the excitement he felt. "Why not gather them up, study the features, and try to put them together into a portrait. If you can't, we'll give them to a police artist. They do that sort of thing all the time."

Overnight, Miranda sent the drawings Isabelle requested. Once she received them, she spread everything out on the floor of her room at the Castell. For a while she walked around them, circling them as if they were an infectious virus. At one point she left the room. She had begun to feel claustrophobic, short of breath, just the way she had that night when she had buried herself in the back of that closet. She had avoided him then. She was avoiding him now.

She wandered into Flora's study and telephoned Philip. Shortly after their night at the Ritz, she had convinced him to return to New York.

"Xavier and Alejandro will take care of me. And you'll be just a phone call away. Please. The sooner I finish with this, the sooner we can concentrate on us."

Though they spoke every day, twice a day, she missed him. Just then she needed him to bolster her courage. She called his office, his apartment, even his plane, but he was temporarily out of reach. Jittery, she continued to roam the Castell. When she knew she couldn't avoid it any longer, she returned to her room.

For hours she sat amid a pile of paper scraps, some of which she had produced when she was seven years old. She arranged them and rearranged them, working long into the night. She put a nose with a chin with a left eye, then a right. She added a mouth, searched for the shape of the face, a hairline, a jawline, a neck. By morning she had several different pictures of several different men.

When she showed the sketches to Xavier the next day, she told him how discouraged she was.

"We ripped my brain apart and I still don't know who he is."

"These are preliminary drawings, Isabelle. And clearly this man did not carry any strikingly unusual features, like a broken nose or bulging eyes or an easily discernible scar."

Xavier laid out all the sketches. He studied them, pointing out certain features that were repeated in each: thick eyebrows that tended to vee toward the nose, full lips, a nose that seemed to broaden at the tip.

"Paco has a cleft in his chin," Isabelle said, disappointed that her initial recollections didn't point to him with absolute certainty. "The man in these sketches doesn't."

"Perhaps that didn't stick in your memory," Xavier said. "It's a small detail. You only saw him for a second."

Isabelle nodded but remained disheartened.

"Do you recall the color of his eyes?"

Isabelle shook her head. The only color she could recall was blue: the blue of his jacket, the blue of the carpet, the unremitting blue light that suffused the room.

"It is possible, Isabelle, that this man is a stranger and the crime was one of random violence."

Frustration overwhelmed Isabelle, and she began to weep. "After coming this far, I couldn't bear not knowing."

"You've jumped the first and most difficult hurdle," Xavier said. "You've unlocked the door to your mind. Now that it's freed itself of the most upsetting memories, it will be easier to restore the details. And then perhaps you'll be able to put a name to this face."

Isabelle had been too preoccupied to notice, but *True Colors* had hit the stands and the best-seller lists. Nina's timing couldn't have been better. The art market was in a state of rapid decline. Collectors were furious at the runaway prices of the past several years and frantic about the sudden devaluation of their purchases. Galleries were closing. Insurance companies were raising prices and rethinking policies. The glory days were over. But the excitement, the glitter, the names, that had pushed the doings of the art world onto the front pages of every major newspaper in the world still fascinated the mainstream.

They had been on the sidelines watching the roller coaster. They couldn't afford to do more than press their noses against the windows of the salesrooms or the galleries on Madison Avenue and SoHo in New York, or Cork Street and Bond in London, or the rue de Seine and Faubourg Saint-Honoré in Paris. But they could afford a book that dished the dirt on one of the biggest names of the art-crazed 1980s.

Nina became the queen of the talk shows. She became quite expert at revealing her relationship to Isabelle in a way that maximized sympathy and minimized further interrogation. She had even managed to twist the fact that her adoptive mother owned a gallery into a credential qualifying her to comment on the talent of Isabelle and her fellow artists.

Brynna remained a problem. She was furious that she wasn't mentioned anywhere in the book. Nina conveniently had neglected to name her birth mother, just as she had omitted the fact that she had been found in a trash can. Brynna, however, had decided she was an integral part of this saga and threatened to call Oprah personally.

Nina's answer was short, succinct, and to the point: "You so much as breathe your name and mine in the same sentence and I'll have you arrested for extortion. Is that clear?"

A long, angry silence followed. Eventually Brynna responded, "Perfectly."

"Good," Nina said. "Now say good-bye like you mean it, because when I hang up, you're going to forget we ever met."

"What the hell are you talking about?" shouted the voice on the other end. "I'm not through with you yet."

"That's too bad, because I'm through with you. It's been fun, but it's over, Brynna. Have a good life."

*   *   *

In Barcelona the publication of Isabelle's unauthorized biography reopened speculation about the still unsolved murder of Althea de Luna. In tapas bars and cafés up and down the Ramblas, people buzzed about the book and the articles in which the author, Nina Davis, conjectured about Martín de Luna's guilt. In dubbed replays of American talk shows, people listened raptly as she reiterated old police reports enumerating all the witnesses to Martín's rage. She placed Martín at the hotel at the time of the murder, claimed that although he was seen leaving the hotel in a fit of rage several hours before the crime was supposedly committed, there were witnesses to his return.

"It had to be Martín de Luna," she proclaimed with authority. "He was the only one who went into that room."

Someone watching Nina knew that wasn't so—someone who had not only seen a man other than Martín de Luna go into that room, but had seen that same man drop something when he came out, something she had picked up and hidden away. She had intended to turn it in, but then she'd heard how anxious the police were to convict Señor de Luna. According to a friend at headquarters, they were intent on building a case against him. She had been afraid to tell them they were wrong.

All these years she had carried the burden of her cowardly silence. She had allowed an innocent man to be accused and, in the public's mind, convicted. Now he was being accused again. She could clear things up for Martín de Luna, but she had withheld evidence. She could be punished for that.

Maybe she should think about it some more.

As if unraveling her nightmares weren't enough, Isabelle was jolted by one surprise after another. Her lawyer told her that although it was being kept very quiet, Dragon Textiles had been put back onto the market. He also told her that Dragon had won first prize at the Frankfurt International Fabric Fair.

"They must have wanted to pump up the sale price," he told Isabelle. "And quite frankly, they have."

Headlines and pictures trumpeted the local company's triumph across the front pages of every newspaper in Barcelona. Wherever Isabelle looked, there were articles about the coveted prize and the men behind it. One night she turned on the television and found herself confronted with an interview of Dragon Textiles' owner, Pasqua Barba, and his American partner, Julian Richter.

"With all due respect, Señor Barba, over the past several years Dragon has been a rather lackluster company. Did you really believe you could win at Frankfurt?"

Paco grinned into the camera. "There was never any doubt."

"How so?"

"The winning designs were based on a fabulous series of paintings by a world-renowned, Barcelona-born artist—Isabelle de Luna. How could we lose?"

Isabelle clenched and unclenched her fists as bolts of fabric billowed in front of her, the camera moving from one winning design to the next, each an adaptation of one of her "Visions in Blue." She was seething.

"How did you and Mr. Richter meet?"

"Julian Richter owns one of New York's most prestigious art galleries. As you know, I'm a collector. I've been dealing with Julian for years."

The camera panned the living room of an apartment Isabelle recognized immediately as Julian's. And there he was, sitting on the couch that centered the room, garbed in his usual black, his legs crossed, his arm resting on the side of the sofa. Suddenly Isabelle's eyes were drawn to something behind the couch. It was one of her paintings from the "Emotional Rainbow" series. Adrenaline coursed through her, making her tremble with rage. Her eyes narrowed, focusing carefully, making certain there was no mistake about what she was seeing. There wasn't. Dominating the television screen was Julian Richter and, in all its mysterious splendor, her painting *Blue,* representing Death.

"And how did you become acquainted with Dragon?" the interviewer was saying. "Through Señor Barba?"

"No," Julian said. "I've known about Dragon for years. I once had the pleasure of touring the mill with the owner and head designer, Althea de Luna."

Isabelle gasped. Her mouth went dry as the interviewer asked, "And when was that?"

"When I visited Barcelona during the summer of 1963."

CHAPTER 28

You are cordially invited to attend
a reception celebrating the formation of
THE DE LUNA FOUNDATION FOR THE ARTS
hosted by Señorita Isabelle de Luna.
The tenth of December, Nineteen Hundred Ninety,
at the Castell de Les Bruixots, Campíns, Spain.
Half after seven in the evening. Formal attire.

The invitations, issued to a very select "inner circle," were hand-delivered. Several received accompanying letters inviting them to be members of the foundation's board of directors. The messenger had been instructed to wait for a response.

Nina was unnerved by the elegantly liveried, stern-faced man standing before her desk. She didn't like being observed as she read the engraved invitation or Isabelle's letter. She would have preferred to mull it over in private, assessing Isabelle's sincerity at her own pace.

"As the author of the book that has aroused so much interest in the de Luna family, it's only fitting that you attend. As my sister, it's only right that you sit on the board of a foundation honoring my parents and your friends, Martín and Althea."

Nina had to hand it to Isabelle. She sure knew how to aim the artillery; her idol worship of the de Lunas was well-known, especially to their daughter. But what about Isabelle's comment on the book? That had to be sarcasm. Isabelle couldn't be pleased that Nina had revived speculation about Martín's guilt. Yet Isabelle's response or, to be more accurate, lack of response to *True Colors* was quite remarkable. And a bit unsettling. Isabelle could have sued Nina for some of what had been printed in *True Colors*. At the very least, she could have filled in the seamy details Nina had chosen to omit about herself or gone on record as refuting much of what had been written. She hadn't. Instead she was offering an olive branch and a chance for Nina to sit on a board that had instant prestige. Was this the real thing? Or was there a catch?

"And what might I tell Señorita de Luna?" Obviously Jeeves was growing impatient. "Will Miss Davis attend?"

Nina eyed the invitation carefully. On the surface, all that was asked was that she dress up in fancy clothes and come to a party. But underneath the fancy engraving were questions she had been asking all her life: Did she want to be on the inside or the outside? Was she going to join in or be left out? Was Isabelle better than she? Or did Nina's star shine just as brightly?

"Tell Señorita de Luna Miss Davis would be delighted."

Julian was suspicious. Then again, he was always suspicious of nice gestures made by people he had wronged. Isabelle had to have seen the news about Dragon Textiles. She had to be furious that he had marketed her work in such a commercial way. It was demeaning. He had turned her art into merchandise, à la LeRoy Neiman, whose paintings of sports figures and events had been converted into everything from posters to T-shirts to coffee mugs to barbecue aprons.

Too, he doubted she had forgiven him for the cruel things he had said about "Visions in Blue," or for giving Greta Reed *Blue Moon,* or for the nasty, prolonged negotiations over her contract, or for the way he had treated her when she had refused to be his lover. He hadn't exhibited a great deal of caring, he admitted that; still, she shouldn't have left him. He had made her what she was today.

Instead of remembering that and being grateful, she had abandoned him and joined forces with Skye Hoffman, another traitor. Worse, the success of Isabelle's show had granted Skye immediate status, prompting several other artists he represented to jump ship and follow her downtown.

Things were bad. Greta had sued for divorce and, as promised, had petitioned the court for full reimbursement of monies loaned him; in lieu of that, she had requested control of his gallery, his collection, his future earnings, everything except the clothes he wore and the oxygen he breathed. Fortunately court dockets were clogged, giving him time to raise enough cash to satisfy his debts and protect his business. If not for Paco Barba's fortuitous deal, he didn't know what he would have done. Just then, Dragon Textiles was his only source of profit.

The eighties boom had created a nineties bust. He'd been forced to lower the prices on several of his artists. His shows weren't drawing. Collectors were keeping a tight watch on their wallets. He had been so pressed for customers that he had begun to canvass corporations—the only collectors buying these days—going door to door like a Fuller brush salesman. And he had begun to court the art advisers who lectured and gave gallery tours.

Julian snorted in disgust. To have sunk to a level where he was wooing suburban housewives sickened him. But, like it or not, they were out there buying avant-garde art. Their budgets were small, but their interest was keen. And he had to pay the rent.

All around him galleries with less history than his were closing. Dealers were squabbling over collectors, who belonged to whom, who had the right to sell what to whom, etc. He had thought he was holding his own, but then there had been an article in *The New York Times Magazine* examining shifts in the way the business of art was now being conducted. In it, he had been labeled "a casualty of the declining art market." The fact that the following paragraphs touted Skye's savvy and Isabelle de Luna's staying power, naming her one of the few contemporary artists whose prices were holding steady, made him sick.

Now Isabelle had sent him an invitation to a reception in Spain and a flattering, solicitous letter asking if he would serve on the board of directors.

"Having someone with your unique qualifications and your reputation for seeking excellence above all else would be an enormous asset to our foundation. Given that it has been established in memory of my parents, you must know how important its success is to me. I would consider it an honor if you would agree to join us, both at the reception and on the board."

The messenger, who was still waiting for a response, had informed Julian that Mr. Medina had requested the pleasure of his company on his private jet. Such generosity underlined Julian's misgivings. Medina's animosity was anything but subtle. Not only had he stopped buying from the Richter Gallery, but he had gone so far as to sell several paintings he had bought from Julian through Skye, thereby breaking one of the art world's unwritten rules of selling back through the original dealer.

This event had to be a cover for something else. These days Isabelle de Luna didn't need him for anything, and Philip Medina wouldn't offer him a ride on a scooter. An alarm clanged, warning him to decline. Then again, if his suspicions were correct, it was better to look down the barrel of a shotgun than to wait for a knife in the back.

And why pay for an airline ticket if you didn't have to?

*   *   *

Javier had been expecting Paco's phone call.

"Why would she invite me? She hates me," he said with obvious agitation.

"Perhaps it's her way of extending a hand and making amends."

"Do you think that after all these years she's finally decided I'm not guilty of Althea's murder?" He sounded incredulous.

"I would hope so," Javier said quietly. He still hated discussing this topic. "Estrella and I have taken every opportunity to convince her that you were with us that night, just as you said."

"She's never believed you before. Why now?"

"Why not ask her yourself?"

Paco had expected an expression of alliance, not something that resembled a dare. "Are you and Estrella going?"

"Yes. Isabelle called, and believe it or not, we've made peace."

Paco fell silent. Javier gave him time to consider his alternatives.

"I'll go, but I'm not going to take Anna."

"That's too bad." Javier enjoyed Paco's wife. She was bright and witty and an excellent dinner companion. "Why not?"

"Because you never know what's going to be said," Paco replied, his voice strained. "And, as I'm sure you can imagine, there are certain things I'd rather she didn't hear."

Anthony was having a very good day. The figures on *True Colors* were meeting their projections—and then some. Hartwick House was out of the red. He had signed three "designer name authors" who would boost that bottom line considerably. And that evening he had a date with an exceedingly luscious, deliciously young woman. He was daydreaming about her when Nina burst into his office and tossed an invitation on his desk. She was practically chirping.

"How fabulous this is! I get to gloat over my success, announce our wedding plans, and watch Isabelle try to restore her good name, all in one fell swoop!"

She prattled on about booking flights and hotels and taking a possible side trip to the Riviera so she could meet his mother, when suddenly Anthony walked out from behind his desk and put a halt to her exultation.

"I'm not going with you," he said.

"What do you mean? Of course you're going."

Anthony shook his head. He wouldn't have chosen this place, but clearly it was time to do what had to be done.

"This is very difficult for me, Nina, but . . . well . . ."

He wrung his hands and lowered his head, rocking it from side to side as if praying for divine intervention. When he looked at her again, his eyes were blank.

"I can't marry you," he said.

Nina felt as if a brick had struck her chest. It was all she could do not to stagger. "Why not?"

"It would be a tragic mistake. You're a wonderful woman and I care for you deeply, but alas, I'm simply not cut out to be a husband."

His expression was solemn, but Nina's antennae heard him laughing at her. "You were cut out for it twice before," she said, hating herself for sounding so hurt and so desperate.

"And I've been divorced twice." His tone had turned patronizing. He was speaking to her as if she were a stranger, not a woman he had courted and bedded for years. "For me, marriage would be a mistake."

"No," she said, feeling ill as the pieces clicked into place. "The mistake is mine. I should have known. That day when you did that about-face. I wanted happily ever after. You wanted to bolster your bottom line. I handed you *True Colors,* and you fed me a crock of shit."

"That's not so," he said. He tried to sound credible but failed.

Dazed by his callousness, Nina stood amid the debris of their romance, seething yet feeling helpless, wishing she had a way to hurt him the way he had just hurt her. Anthony, eager to be done with this unpleasantness, shuffled his feet and pretended embarrassment. Nina expected him to recant or apologize or at the very least confess to being a louse.

"One other thing. The lease on your apartment is up this month. I won't be renewing it."

"I don't know how I'll get you back for this, Hartwick, but I will. Someday, somehow, I will."

How she managed to hold her head up as she walked out of his office she would never know. It was a performance worthy of Joan Crawford. But, she realized as she wiped her eyes and climbed into a taxi, it was nothing compared to the act she was going to have to put on at the Castell de Les Bruixots.

As Isabelle wended her way through the narrow streets of the Gothic Quarter, she wondered whether she was walking into a trap. Over the phone the woman had offered no information except that she had something Isabelle might want, something that had been found outside Althea's room the night of the murder.

That insidious feeling of being followed clamped on to Isabelle like a barnacle. She tried to shake it off, telling herself the cramped atmosphere of the quarter always induced claustrophobia, that she was being spooked by slender alleyways and malevolent shadows rather than a stalker resolved to do her harm. As she turned off the crowded Ramblas and entered the maze that was the old city, however, she was overwhelmed by nerves. Leaning against the ancient stone walls, she breathed slowly, rhythmically, taking a minute to compose herself.

When she had calmed, she continued on toward their meeting place. She didn't have to look for numbers or ask directions. Els Quatre Gats—the Four Cats—was legendary. She had been there many times, mostly with Tía Flora. This had been one of her favorite haunts. Whenever they came, she lectured Isabelle on the genius of Puig i Cadafalch, one of Barcelona's finest architects, pointing out that this café had been his first commission. She talked about how she and her sisters used to flaunt convention by coming there for poetry readings and shadow-puppet theater. She regaled Isabelle with stories about the many artists who used to gather there, to think and discuss and sketch. She took pride in the fact that it was in this bar that Picasso first exhibited his work. Today, however, Isabelle was alone, being led to a small table where she was to meet a stranger who claimed to have a crucial piece of evidence in the case against her father.

The bar was crowded and noisy, conversations and laughter rebounding off the tile floor and wooden chairs. Sequestered in a corner, Isabelle tried to remain inconspicuous as she kept one eye on the door and the other on her watch. The woman was late. Again Isabelle suspected that the call had been a fake. Hoping to distract herself, she perused the paintings and photographs that chronicled the establishment's illustrious past.

She hadn't even noticed the woman. She must have entered from the back. When she was planted on the seat directly opposite Isabelle, she tapped the table for attention. Short, stocky, with clipped gray hair, wire spectacles, and a red sweater over a black-and-white-flowered dress, she certainly didn't seem sinister. Though she was nervous, her mien was more grandmother than gangster. Immediately Isabelle ordered two glasses of sherry.

"I should have given this to the police when it happened, but I was afraid," the woman said without preamble, her eyes trained on the table, avoiding any contact with Isabelle. Clearly she couldn't wait to be done with this matter.

The waiter brought their drinks. Isabelle sipped hers. Her companion appeared too nervous to lift the glass.

"What is it?" Isabelle asked, looking to move the dialogue along.

The woman glanced around and then dug deep into the bowels of an enormous handbag. Her hand was curled around a lumpy handkerchief, which she pushed across the table. Isabelle opened the cloth ball. Tucked inside was a wide gold band, extravagantly carved.

"Where did you find this?" Isabelle asked, examining the ring. It looked oddly familiar.

According to Alejandro's files, the police had combed the suite and had come up with no physical evidence linking anyone other than Martín to the crime.

For the first time, the woman looked at Isabelle. Her eyes were calf brown, large and frightened. Gripping the glass, she downed her sherry, fortifying herself.

"I was a maid at the Ritz," she said in the same timorous voice she might have used in a confessional. "That night, when the electricity failed, we were given flashlights and told to deliver candles to the guest rooms. I was pulling my cart along the hall when I heard a door open. It was only a few feet from me. I shined my flashlight in the direction of the noise. A man turned and looked at me. He was angry. He demanded to know what I was doing and to get the light out of his face. I was nervous. I guess I stammered a bit. He got even angrier. He rushed toward me, cursing, insisting that I give him my flashlight. I told him I couldn't, that I needed it, but I had candles for his room. He grabbed my hand and wrestled with me for the flashlight. I remember his hand was moist, probably with sweat. He pulled at the flashlight. I pulled back, and when I did, his ring came off. Just then another door opened. A man wanted to know what was going on. The man near me ran. I fumbled about, trying to find a match and light a candle. By the time I did, he was gone."

"But you had his ring."

The woman nodded. "I know it's hard for you to believe, Señorita de Luna, but I wanted to come forward. I wanted to present this to the police." Decades of guilt formed beads of sweat on her forehead.

"What stopped you?"

"One of my friends worked the front desk. He told me that when the police questioned him, he mentioned that a man other than your father had asked which room your mother was in. When he went down to headquarters, they kept him there for hours, twisting his story into so many knots, he couldn't remember who had asked him what. All he remembered was feeling that the police were determined to convict Señor de Luna and they weren't about to let anyone interfere with their investigation. I was young and scared. I had a family.

"When I heard about your father's death, I knew it was my fault." The older woman wept softly, each tear an act of penance.

Isabelle spoke softly, but there was no mistaking the intensity underscoring her words. "There were many people who could have helped my father, me included, but there was only one person at fault: the man who killed my mother and walked away." She clutched the ring in her hand. "It's taken a long time, but we're going to get him, señora. That man is going to pay for what he did!"

"I've got the ring, and I'm checking it out."

"A week isn't much time."

"It's enough," Philip said. "Don't worry."

"These days the only thing I do other than worry is miss you." Isabelle smiled at her own understatement. She positively ached for him, but priorities demanded that she focus her energies elsewhere.

"How are things going with Xavier?"

"He says I'm making progress. I'm beginning to think I'm on a mental goose chase."

"Do you want to cancel the party?"

"No. Xavier says we're close." She paused, as if taking her pulse. "I think so, too."

Philip could hear the strain in her voice. "All you have to do is say the word, and I can be in Barcelona tomorrow."

She was tempted. "No. Let's leave everything the way we planned it. You take care of things there. I'll take care of everything here."

"Including security?"

"Xavier has some friends on the Barcelona police force. They'll be here to guard the grounds. The caterer's staff has been screened. The florist's crew also has been cleared."

Isabelle was trying to minimize the danger to herself, but Philip feared she hadn't hired nearly enough protection. She said she didn't want the Castell to look like a military compound. He had to respect that, but for his own peace of mind he planned to hire two bodyguards just for her. As far as he was concerned, there was no such thing as too safe.

When Isabelle asked Alejandro for his files on Martín's case, she hadn't expected them to be delivered in boxes, but there they sat, five of them, on the floor next to her desk. In between her sessions with Xavier, she spent hours poring over them, trying to extrapolate the basic facts. Philip had told her that conducting an investigation was the same as solving a jigsaw puzzle: the first step was to build the frame; next lay out all the pieces, no matter how small or oddly shaped; and then fit them together within the frame.

Isabelle had constructed the frame by going over testimony of those who had witnessed her parents' antagonism on Majorca and in Barcelona, as well as her own recollections of the tensions that existed between them. She factored in Pasqua Barba's unresolved passion for Althea, the Murillos' public encouragement of his dogged quest for their daughter's hand, the police's refusal to look elsewhere for suspects, and something no one other than Martín and Jonas had known then—the deteriorating condition of Martín's health.

She considered the story François and Eunice LeVerre had told her about Martín and the surprising news that Julian Richter had been in Barcelona in 1963 and had known Althea. As her memory of that returned, she dismissed the notion of a random stranger. She recalled hearing her mother speaking to the man. Althea never would have opened the door to a complete stranger. Unfortunately, for now, the man continued to remain a stranger to Isabelle.

Xavier continued to probe her subconscious, helping her re-create as much of that fateful day as possible. At each session she sat with a sketch pad in her lap, drawing the pictures that played inside her head. As he had promised, incidentals rose to the surface, helping her inner eye focus on the core moment of their therapy. She was like a decorator furnishing a set, each small memory adding to the background, making her comfortable about returning to that place. Once it became completely familiar, Xavier was certain she would relax enough to fully recall the instant when she and that man had locked eyes.

When, finally, it happened, it startled both of them. They had been reliving the minutes before she opened the door to the living room. Isabelle's eyes were focused more on the past than on the page, yet she drew as she spoke.

"I'm scared," she said. "Very scared. It's dark and I want my mama, but she's in the other room talking to someone."

Isabelle stopped drawing. For a moment she held her breath. "Something broke. I don't know what it is. Something glass. There's a thud. Someone fell down. Maybe it's Mama. Maybe she needs help."

Her breathing quickened. Her eyelids pressed together. Beads of sweat dotted her brow.

"I can't find the doorknob. Please, God," she sobbed, lost in the moment, "help me find the doorknob."

She was gnawing at her lip, but she was sketching again, feverishly now. When she spoke she was whispering.

"Shhh! I have to keep quiet. It's naughty to interrupt grown-ups. But, wait. I know someone fell. I have to . . . Oh! What's that? Someone's grunting. No. It's a slap. What's happening?"

Isabelle's head twisted from side to side, and her eyes narrowed as if she were straining to see. Suddenly her body stiffened.

"The light. It's blue, and it's coming from everywhere, filling the room like ink. Everything's blue. Everything." Terror masked her face, but her hand continued to draw. Her pencil flew over the pad, but when it stopped she lay back against the couch, exhausted and emotionally spent. Xavier comforted her as she wept. When she had calmed they both looked at her sketch pad. Isabelle gasped. Staring back at her was the man who had murdered her mother.

It felt queer to look at him, almost as if she were holding a tarantula in her fingers. She felt startled and curious and frightened and fascinated, all at the same time.

"Do you know him?" Xavier asked, fighting to control his own emotions.

"I do, but I don't," Isabelle said, completely forlorn. "I can see him there in that room, on that night, but nowhere else." Futility washed her face like a veil.

"Don't beat yourself, Isabelle. You saw this face for a single instant twenty-seven years ago. You were a child. A very frightened child, whose memory holds only this expression because that's all you saw."

"Xavier," Isabelle said, her voice so soft he could barely hear her. "This face could be my father's."

Xavier knew that for Isabelle, that was the worst possible scenario, but he had to be honest with her.

"Yes, it could be, but before we come to any conclusions, let's bring this sketch to the police. Their computers can show us how this face would look with different expressions. More important, the computer can age it and show us what he looks like today."

"How long will that take?" Isabelle asked, obviously weary. "I don't know if I can handle much more."

"We've come this far," Xavier said, giving her a reassuring hug. "Just hang in a little longer. In a day or two it'll all be over."

The Castell looked glorious. Outside, torches illuminated the path leading to the huge wooden doors emblazoned with the Pujol crest. Inside, candles proliferated, with tapers glowing from candelabra and votaries flickering inside small glass cylinders that dotted nearly every shelf and tabletop. Enormous explosions of flowers burst from vases positioned throughout the public rooms: white lilies, mums, French tulips, and roses mixed with pine boughs and twigs of holly that hinted at the season. Waitresses armed with tapas, and a tuxedoed waiter, in his hands a silver tray filled with flutes of the finest cava from the Fargas vineyards, stood at the ready. In the larger drawing room a chamber music trio could be heard tuning their instruments.

Miranda and Luis had arrived on Philip's plane the day before, along with Sam, Skye, Jonas, Sybil, and Julian Richter. Though Isabelle had taken them on a thorough tour, Miranda, Sybil, and Skye couldn't seem to absorb it all. While the men joined Alejandro in the smaller drawing room, the women continued to explore the Castell. In the center hall, Isabelle and Philip found themselves with a moment alone.

"You leave me breathless, Señorita de Luna," Philip said, watching her cross the room.

Encased in a simple, strapless red gown of knife-pleated silk, her hair swept into a French knot, her skin as soft and white as a calla lily, she was a vision. Sparkling at her neck and dangling from her ears were an antique ruby-and-diamond suite of jewels Martín had given Althea on their wedding day. Flora had kept it in a secret vault; she had hoped to give them to Isabelle on her wedding day. The overall look was one of such luscious elegance that Philip had difficulty controlling his impulses. As he took her in his arms, he told her so.

"You may not ravage me now," Isabelle teased, luxuriating in the relaxed atmosphere of this brief interlude.

"If not now, when?" His lips grazed the soft curve of her neck.

"Perhaps in between dessert and brandy."

"Ah," he said, nibbling at her ear, "my favorite time to ravage." He squeezed her gently and then held her at arm's length, trying to look beyond the smile and gauge the level of her anxiety. "How are you doing?"

"To quote my doctor: As well as can be expected."

That morning Xavier had come by with printouts from the police computer, although by then Isabelle didn't need them for verification. She was certain who Althea's killer was. In the two days following her last session with Xavier, the blue that had distorted her nightmares had disappeared, unmasking once and for all the face that had haunted her for most of her life.

"While I'm sure your testimony would be enough for a conviction, I'm glad we have substantiating proof."

"Me too." She caressed his cheek. "I don't think I would have been able to do any of this without you."

He laughed as he took her in his arms. "You could have, but I'm glad you chose not to."

Just as she wrapped her arms around his neck, the doorbell chimed. Philip could feel Isabelle's heart pounding against his chest. He kissed her. "For luck."

As the door opened and she saw Julian Richter striding across the threshold of her home, she muttered, "We're going to need it."

Within half an hour everyone had arrived: Olivia and Jay Piersall, who had flown in from Switzerland that morning; Estrella and Javier Murillo; Paco Barba; Xavier Fargas; Rafael Avda; François and Eunice LeVerre; and, minus her fiancé, Nina. Despite the sumptuous surroundings, an aura of agitation pervaded. People mingled, but cautiously. Nina stood alone and out of sorts.

In the days before and during the long flight over, she had agonized over this party, exaggerating its significance beyond reasonable proportion. It wasn't simply a social event, it was the main event, the final round between herself and Isabelle. She didn't know why she felt that way, but somehow she knew that good or bad, win or lose, something cataclysmic was going to happen.

Knowing the Castell's capacity, recalling the stories about how lavishly the Pujol sisters used to entertain, she had expected a few hundred exceedingly glamorous, titled, and prestigious guests from both sides of the Atlantic. A marquis here, a duke there, an industrialist here, an heiress there. A few artists, of course. Some European celebrities, perhaps. A playboy or two.

She had shopped for days, seeking a gown that would present her as a highly successful public figure and as one betrothed to the scion of one of Boston's finest families. Ultimately she'd decided upon a kitten-soft black velvet, with a neckline that plunged deep and revealed plenty. It was a gown that announced its wearer was the most confident of women. Nina had convinced herself she was that, until she entered the Castell and greeted its mistress. One look at Isabelle and she felt suddenly and painfully inadequate, like a pretender to a crown.

When she walked into the drawing room and eyed the assemblage of guests, Nina's mood fell even lower. Not only wasn't there a royal in the group, but attendance at this soiree was small, denying her the cover of a crowd. Too, there was the matter of the Durans. She hadn't seen them since that night in 1971 when she had stormed out of their home. Seeing them now rattled her.

Eyeing them surreptitiously from across the room, Nina couldn't help but note—with an odd rush of regret—the passage of time. The twenty years showed. They had aged. Miranda's hair, still sleek and shiny, now gleamed with silver. Her face was lined, her posture was slightly stooped, and her knuckles showed evidence of arthritis. Nina's memory had cataloged her father under "ordinary," so it surprised her to see that on Luis age had begat a look of distinction. Where she had recalled him as slight of frame, tan of color, and indistinguishable in feature, now, in his black tuxedo with his sterling hair and lean form, he appeared to have been cut from far nobler cloth.

As she watched him move among the Spaniards, chatting easily in their common language, she recalled a night several weeks before Anthony had dumped her, when she had been rummaging through an old box of photographs. He had picked up one of Miranda and Luis standing with Jonas and Sybil and several other neighbors. When he'd asked if the people who had raised her were in the picture, she'd said yes.

"Are they the brown ones?"

Even now Nina winced at his description. It sounded so narrow and intolerant and patronizing, so like things she herself had thought. Suddenly an unbidden vision of Brynna Jones and a faceless stranger superimposed itself on Miranda and Luis, mocking Nina for the years she had spent fantasizing about parents who were better, more acceptable, less ethnic, richer, less working class. She saw the portrait that hung in a place of pride in her apartment, a sidewalk purchase, a painting of people she had never met yet had invested with all the respect and dignity usually accorded one's guardians. And she felt ashamed.

"Where's Hartwick?" Philip's voice startled her. She looked at him quizzically, as if she didn't know whom he was talking about. "Anthony Hartwick. My old school chum. Your fiancé."

"Oh, that Hartwick." She sounded casual enough, but segueing from the

Durans to Anthony made her feel as if she were running down a checklist of her more colossal mistakes in judgment. "He couldn't make it."

Philip nodded. "What a shame."

Nina couldn't miss the sarcasm. "I gather you don't approve."

He shook his head. "You can do better."

A slow smile graced her lips as she looked him squarely in the eye. "I tried."

He laughed. She grew serious.

"What is it about Anthony you dislike?"

Philip weighed his words. "It's not a matter of liking him or not. He's a screwed-up guy with a major chip on his shoulder."

"What kind of chip?"

Again Philip considered what, and how much, to say. "Life is far from perfect. Some get a better deal than others. Some who get the raw end learn to compensate. Others hold on to their anger and continue to lash out at anyone and everyone they meet."

Nina squirmed. She couldn't help feeling Philip had included her in the latter group.

"And what would Anthony have to be angry about?" she asked, instinctively deflecting his criticism. "The man's a member of the lucky sperm club, for goodness' sake. He was born with a silver pacifier in his mouth, a family tree with a lot of green, and a name that opens doors. From where I sit, he doesn't have a whole lot to complain about."

"That's because you're not sitting in his chair."

Philip's defense of Anthony surprised her. "I know all about Anthony," she said quietly, deciding to reveal her hand. "I did some research in the morgue of the *Boston Herald.*"

"And what did you find?"

"Enough to prompt a visit to his mother. I went there before I came here."

Philip's brow furrowed. He looked sad, almost regretful, as if he believed some secrets were better left hidden.

"She told me all about how Albert Hartwick had tried to abuse Anthony." Nina's eyes darkened. She may have been mad at Anthony, but her heart hadn't hardened so much that she couldn't feel sorry for what he had lived through. "She said the only reason he stopped was because she threatened the old man: if Albert didn't leave her son alone, she'd go public about his homosexuality and the fact that he wasn't Anthony's biological father.

"According to the reports I read, Albert died as the result of a mugging. Jocelyn said he had tried to molest a teenage boy and the kid had pulled a knife on him. Good old Alston reverted to type. In order to avoid a scandal for the Hartwicks and a jail term for the boy, he bought the family off."

Philip's expression was sober but inscrutable. Nina wished she could read behind those black eyes.

"All that may explain Anthony's insanity, but it doesn't explain why the two of you became rivals. The way I see it, you should have been friends. Neither one of you would have ever listed father-son banquets as your favorite social activity. What was it?"

"The truth," Philip said simply. Nina was confused. "One night when Anthony and I were in college, he got roaring drunk and in a moment of weakness told me his darkest secrets. Though I swore I'd never tell a soul—and haven't—he's never forgotten how much I know, nor has he stopped trying to prove that he's better than his résumé." Philip eyed Nina carefully. "You and he have that in common."

Nina flushed. "Takes one to know one, I guess." Her voice was tinged with self-pity.

"He's never going to change, Nina. And if he remains true to his pattern, he's going to hurt you. If I were you, I'd get out while the getting's good."

"And if you were me, Philip, where would you go?"

Philip took her by the arm, turned her around, and pointed to the other side of the room where Miranda and Luis were.

"There," he said.

"I didn't realize you knew my mother," Isabelle said with a staged smile. "Why didn't you ever say anything?"

"I was quite young when I met her and, if you'll forgive me—I don't mean to degrade her memory—it was such a nonevent, I simply forgot."

Julian issued an offhand shrug accompanied by a brief chuckle. Isabelle was not amused or impressed by his nonchalance.

"Being the clairvoyant that I am, I did expect you to bring that up, however, so I brought you something." He headed for the hall.

When he returned, he handed her a manila envelope. Inside was an eight-by-ten black-and-white photograph of her mother. It appeared to have been taken outside somewhere. Althea's hair was loose. She was in a long-sleeved silk shirt with an open collar and slacks. She was laughing. Her head was thrown back. Her hair was tousled. Her smile lit up the page. Isabelle had seen that pose dozens of times. Her mother never snickered or tittered or giggled. Either something wasn't funny or Althea laughed heartily, just as she was doing in this picture. What fascinated Isabelle, however, was not her mother's visage, but the tone of the photograph. The eyes that had looked at her through the lens had been filled with love, making everything Julian had said a lie.

"I forgot how you answered the interviewer. Why were you in Barcelona?"

"Sight-seeing."

"It must have been a very unique trip. I mean, why would a tourist want to go through a textile mill?"

"In case you've forgotten, my dear, I have an eye for art." There was no mistaking the malice in his voice. "Your mother's mill was producing textiles that were the rage of Europe. I simply wanted to meet the artist behind that success. I was in the area and stopped in." His lips curled in that supercilious smile she loathed.

"Gee, that's funny. Rafael Avda said you met her at an exhibition of your photographs at the Gaspar Gallery." The Gaspars were Rafael Avda's biggest competitors.

Julian's smile faded. "It was such a mediocre show, I blocked it out."

"Really? According to Greta, that show was very important to you. She said you were in Europe soliciting investors for the Richter Gallery and were hoping to use whatever success you had at Gaspars as a lure." Isabelle relished his discomfort. "Word was you were desperate."

"I beg your pardon?" He pulled at his beard. His eyes darted about as if in search of shelter.

"Since you had already squandered your own inheritance, your only livelihood at the time was Greta's largesse." His lips pressed against his teeth. Isabelle's smile broadened. "She says she knows you only married her for her money, but poor thing, at the time she loved you." Isabelle's smile evaporated. "Actually it was in 1963 that she stopped loving you. You had just come off a rather tragic affair. Greta, distraught over her sister's death and your part in it, cut you off. You went out looking for other backers. My mother was one of your prospects."

Isabelle watched Julian attempt to recover from the blows she had landed. It was obvious from his expression that he was stunned by the information she had laid before him, unnerved by the knowledge that she and Greta had spoken, eager to know what other details had been exchanged.

"I do recall asking Althea if she was interested in investing in my gallery."

"And what was her response?"

The scene must have been replaying itself before Julian's eyes, because his demeanor changed. He grew defensive and petulant, forgetting for the moment that the woman to whom he was speaking was the daughter of the woman in question.

"She said she was totally uninterested! Can you believe that? I showed her my work. I talked to her about my plans for the gallery. I told her of my background. And still she turned me down." Julian's expression ranged from simple rejection to a complicated medley of anger and outrage, damaged credibility and bruised ego. "She shouldn't have done that," he said darkly. "It was a big mistake."

Isabelle longed to challenge him, but for the moment she remained silent.

Paco Barba appeared to have appointed himself guardian of the flame. According to Philip's watch, Paco hadn't stepped away from the fireplace in over forty minutes. Occasionally his eyes wandered up to the gilded candelabra and antique Louis XV clock that resided on the white marble mantel or, above that, to the seventeenth-century tapestry depicting the hunting skills of the mythical Orion. Once or twice he had allowed his gaze to linger on the delicately painted floral wall decorations, or the three elaborate crystal chandeliers that illuminated the long rectangular space, or the gold velvet drapes that hung from upholstered valances, or the assortment of Charles IV furniture that filled the formally decorated room. But mostly he watched the flames.

Philip approached him warily. Something in those dark, brooding eyes bespoke a man on the edge.

"You look like you could use something stronger than cava. Can I get you a Scotch or a brandy?"

"No! You can get to the point."

"And what point is that?"

"Why the hell we're here. What this night is all about."

"Isabelle has established a foundation—"

"Stop the bullshit, Medina! Isabelle de Luna wouldn't invite me to the opening of her refrigerator, let alone to celebrate a foundation named for her parents." He was trying to keep his voice down, but it was difficult, as the turgid veins in his neck attested. "I loathed her father and coveted her mother. For most of her life, Isabelle has believed that I raped and killed Althea, something I have denied in the past and will continue to deny."

"Maybe she invited you here to show you all is forgiven." Philip's voice was light and casual. His expression was not.

"And maybe this is all a carefully contrived sham with some hidden agenda."

"Could be." Philip sipped his drink and peered over the rim of his glass at Althea's spurned suitor. "I guess we'll just have to wait and see. Won't we?"

"I hope that velvet feels good against your skin," Skye said, commanding her mouth to smile at Nina. "I wouldn't want you to hurt yourself when you get on your knees and beg Isabelle's forgiveness."

"Don't hold your breath. It'll make your skin turn blue, and you have enough cosmetic problems without adding that to the list."

Skye laughed. "Sam's told me a lot about you, but he never mentioned a sense of humor. It must have been an oversight."

"Must have been." Uncomfortable, Nina had slipped into one of her favorite costumes, the one she usually used to combat a bout of insecurity: arrogant pomposity.

"How come Hartwick didn't come? Was it something you said?"

"No, dear, it's something I wrote." Finally Skye had given her an opening she liked. "Thanks to the incredible sales of *True Colors,* he was too busy to take any time off. I told him not to bother. For me, this is an obligation. For him, it's a nuisance."

Before Skye could shoot back, Isabelle interrupted, cued Skye to leave them alone, and welcomed Nina to the Castell.

"I can't tell you how much I appreciate your traveling all this way," she said graciously.

"I'm sure it'll be worth the trip."

"I hope you'll think so at the end of the evening."

"Is that when the excitement will start?" Nina sniffed. "So far, the party's a bit dull."

Isabelle ignored the critique. "Have you spoken to Miranda and Luis?"

Nina rolled her eyes and examined her manicure. "Not yet."

"Have you spoken to Sam?"

"What is this, some kind of quiz? If I don't pass I don't eat?"

"You and Sam used to be so close, I thought you'd be glad to see him."

"I'm thrilled beyond words."

Over Isabelle's shoulder, Nina sneaked a peek at him. Sam did look quite devastating. He was talking to Philip's mother and stepfather; his arm was around Skye. Nina recognized the gentleness of his touch, the protective curve of his body. Even from a distance she could sense the love within which he had wrapped the woman who had taken his name. A wave of envy washed over her.

Before turning back to Isabelle, she noticed Skye talking animatedly with a seethingly stunning man who looked vaguely familiar.

"Who's that?" Nina asked, nodding in his direction.

"Alejandro's grandson, Xavier Fargas. Don't you remember him?"

Not only did she remember, but suddenly she was reliving that vacation on the Costa Brava, that weekend with the swarthy, sexy heir to the Fargas fortune.

"Where's his wife?"

Isabelle bit back a smile. "He's divorced," she said, wondering how a woman who was supposed to be blissfully happy with one man could be so intrigued with the marital status of another.

"So what's he doing these days? Picking grapes?" Nina had sensed how unseemly her interest in Xavier appeared and quickly adjusted the tone of her questions.

"If that's your charming way of asking if Xavier has taken over the Fargas vineyards, the answer is no, Nina dear. Xavier is a psychiatrist. Perhaps you should avail yourself of his services."

"Perhaps I should," she muttered as Isabelle walked away and Xavier's gaze found hers.

A maître d' ushered everyone into the dining room. A staff of footmen assisted the women with their chairs. Isabelle hosted at one end of the table— flanked by Luis and Alejandro—Philip at the other, in between Estrella and Olivia. Next to Olivia were Miranda, Sam, Eunice LeVerre, Xavier, Skye, Jonas, Javier Murillo, and then Luis. Next to Estrella: Paco, Nina, Rafael, Sybil, Julian, Jay Piersall, François LeVerre, Alejandro.

Isabelle waited while another round of cava was poured, inhaling the splendor of the setting. As she watched the candles flicker in the sterling-silver candelabra that stood like sentries amid a garden of white roses, holly, and pine, she drew courage from the heritage that surrounded her. When everyone was settled, she stood.

She surveyed her guests, knowing that once begun, this play could not stop until it had reached its final curtain. This was to be a night of accusations, announcements, and apologies, a night that would shock some, disturb most, but, if all went well, bring harm only to one. She supposed she could have done this another, safer way, but it was too late for second thoughts. Drawing a deep breath, she took center stage.

"Ladies and gentlemen, I'd like to welcome you to El Castell de Les Bruixots. This is a special night for me. It commemorates the establishment of the De Luna Foundation for the Arts, an organization created in memory of my beloved parents.

"It's also an opportunity to publicly thank a most wonderful man, Philip Medina." She raised her glass and smiled at him. "Not only am I grateful for his financial generosity, which provided the initial funding for the foundation, but also for his willingness to give of himself, even to those who haven't always been willing to take what he's offered." He chuckled. She flushed. "He's made a difference in my life.

"I'd also like to salute a most extraordinary woman, my aunt Flora, whose memory is still fresh and whose spirit will always be felt throughout this incredible house."

Isabelle tilted her glass at Alejandro, who, with tears in his eyes, simply nodded in agreement. Isabelle, too, grew weepy; it showed in the uneven cadence of her voice.

"I cannot stand here without paying tribute to my parents, Martín and Althea de Luna. I didn't have them for very long, but they left behind a legacy that lives to this day, in my heart and in my painting." She swallowed hard. This was not the time for grieving or reminiscing. "It is in their honor that I called you here and to their memory that I ask you to drink."

Silently she sipped from her glass, watching as her guests did the same.

"I would also like to toast the success of *True Colors,* the completely *unauthorized,* not totally factual, but nonetheless best-selling story of my life. The author, as you all know, is Nina Duran, a woman who, after years of running away, has finally admitted—in print, anyway—that she has a sister named Isabelle and parents named Miranda and Luis."

Isabelle's eyes fixed on Nina. Nina stared back. She opted to ignore the use of her real name as well as Isabelle's implied criticism.

"Let's hope this story has a happy ending," Isabelle said as she tipped her glass in Nina's direction. "Now, please, everyone. Enjoy your dinner."

Easier said than done. Throughout the first course the atmosphere remained somewhat strained. After Isabelle's toast, Nina, Miranda, and Luis had exchanged self-conscious looks. They were seated too far apart for meaningful conversation but seemed to strike an unspoken agreement to talk later. Skye was busy befriending Xavier, knowing how much he had done for Isabelle. Sam and Eunice LeVerre debated which area had the best snow: the Swiss Alps or the American Rockies. Luis was talking horses with Javier. Miranda was fascinated by Olivia's description of Nelson's collection. Jay was telling François about a 1943 Lincoln Continental he had just bought. Julian was trying to impress Sybil.

Nina remained the outsider, eavesdropping on several conversations, participating in none. She was disgruntled at having her feud with Isabelle made public; she was also unhappy with her seat. Across from her was some Frenchwoman she didn't know sitting next to an old boyfriend who knew her too well. On her left was Rafael Avda, an old man more interested in talking art to Skye and Sybil than listening to tales of Nina in Movieland; on her right was the Black Prince. The only bright spot in this washout of an evening was that on the other side of Eunice Whatever sat Xavier Fargas.

On any other night, in any other place, Nina would have dived into the middle of his conversation, doing or saying whatever was required to extricate him from Skye's verbal clutches. But this night, despite a best-seller, her own television show, a syndicated column, and an army of fans on both sides of the Atlantic, she was the enemy, not the star. This night everyone else had arrived with a friend or a mate; she had come alone. Worse, this night she and her rival were not battling on an even playing field. She was a guest in Isabelle's ancestral home, surrounded by Isabelle's family, her friends, and a man who clearly adored her. Though Nina battled to maintain it, her usual cocksure veneer melted in the glare of the stunning contrast between what Isabelle had and what she had lost.

Paco was uncomfortable, and it showed. He picked at his food, rebuffed attempts at conversation, and adopted a scowling expression that made it clear he preferred to be left alone. In truth, fear of being left alone was what had caused this black mood. He and Anna had been squabbling for months. Recently she had threatened to leave him.

They had been married for five years—his first, her second—and for most of that time it had been blissful. Then *True Colors* was published. The gossip started all over again. The whispering, the pointing fingers, the curious looks, as he passed through a room. Aside from the tedium of defending himself all over again, he was beset by old memories and feelings. Suddenly it was as if Althea were in bed with him and Anna. She was offended by the intrusion and said so. He tried to explain, but his arguments sounded weak, flawed, and insincere, making a bad situation worse.

He truly loved Anna. Aside from her beauty, which was considerable, he had been attracted to her stability, her intellect, and her enormous capacity to accept him as he was. At fifty-five he had come to the marriage a longtime bachelor with ingrained habits and definite attitudes. She hadn't attempted to change him; rather, she had ignored the bad and encouraged the good. But as she told him: "I vowed to love, honor, and respect you. I didn't promise to wet-nurse your obsession with a woman who's been dead nearly thirty years!"

Paco's mistake was in assuming that because Anna's first husband had been her childhood sweetheart, she understood that Althea had been his passion, his first love, the one love that never died. Quite the contrary. When the invitation to this dinner had arrived, he had demurred. Anna had insisted that he go, with the proviso that "you don't come home until you've exorcised your ghosts."

His eyes wandered down the length of the table to Althea's daughter. Again he wondered why Isabelle had invited him here. As he studied her face, puzzling about what was going on inside her head, he saw her shouting at him on the Ramblas, sneering at him in a restaurant, snarling at him at the Reys'. Tonight, though she had been charming and polite at every turn, he couldn't forget that this woman had hated him for most of her life. Behind her easy smile and practiced grace, Paco was certain a bomb was ticking.

By the time the main course was served, Julian could not contain himself any longer. Donning his gracious benefactor mask and standing so that all eyes were on him, he raised his wine goblet, glanced around the table, and said, "I'm sure you're all aware of Dragon Textiles' triumph at the Frankfurt Fair." He smiled and turned toward Isabelle. "In honor of that marvelous accolade and as a gesture of personal reconciliation, I'd like to return the 'Visions in Blue' series to you."

He paused, anticipating a burst of applause that never came. Isabelle offered him the faintest of smiles.

"It was your artistic genius, after all," he continued, his blue eyes glinting, "that pumped life into the old mill. From the projections I've seen, within six months Dragon will be back on top. All because of you." He tipped his head toward her in a patronizing bow. "Like mother, like daughter!"

Isabelle delayed her response long enough to make him squirm.

"Thank-you, Julian," she said finally. "Even though my paintings have been greatly devalued due to your crass marketing approach, they are rightfully mine and I will receive them with pleasure." She wanted to poke out his eyes with a fork! "Speaking of Dragon . . ."

She stood. Julian, unhappy with her dismissive reply to his largesse, reseated himself.

"As most of you know, the Pujols and the de Lunas made their fortunes from cloth. They were cotton merchants who helped build the nation of

Catalonia and helped write the history of Barcelona. For a long time, a vital part of that history was held in other hands. Tonight, I'm thrilled to announce that Dragon Textiles has returned to the de Lunas."

Enthusiastic applause greeted Isabelle's announcement. Julian's mouth fell open. Paco Barba appeared confused.

"What are you talking about?" he asked.

"That's what I'd like to know," Julian said, looking from Isabelle to Paco. "What is she talking about?"

Isabelle ignored Julian and spoke directly to Paco.

"I've wanted to buy Dragon since I was a young girl. To me, the company symbolized what my family was all about: art, cloth, pride in Catalonia. I saved and saved, but somehow never seemed to be able to accumulate the money I needed. When I did, and I heard Dragon was for sale, my lawyer made an offer, but it was rejected. Dragon had been taken off the market.

"I wondered why, after all those years of letting the company languish, you had entered Dragon in the Frankfurt Fair. My lawyer suggested that perhaps you thought a win would boost your asking price. Clearly he was correct, because shortly after your victory was announced, you let it be known you were looking for a buyer." She glanced at Philip, then returned her attention to Paco. "Fortunately, I had backers who encouraged me to bid whatever was necessary to obtain control.

"Several weeks ago, you finalized a deal with Crescent Industries. I'm Crescent Industries."

Julian's face had turned an unnatural red. Paco's expression was shrouded. A wary silence descended on the room.

"What the hell are you trying to pull?" Julian was on his feet, shouting at Paco, his face crimson with rage. "We're partners! Why didn't I know anything about this?"

Paco looked at Julian as if he were scrutinizing an insect. "You're a minority partner, Julian. When we made our agreement, I retained controlling interest and the right to negotiate any acquisitions or divisional sell-offs." He turned to Isabelle, his face solemn. "I hated selling Dragon, and you know why. But the company was floundering, and besides, it was time to move on. You may not believe me, but I'm glad it went to you."

"Where does that leave me?" Julian blustered, confounded by this rotten turn of events. His cash cow had just been taken away from him. True, he would recover some funds from his share of the sale, but he doubted it would be enough to save him. He could almost hear Greta laughing in the background.

"You always have your gallery," Isabelle said, aware that her effort to sound solicitous hadn't worked.

Julian seethed. His fists clenched as he glowered at Isabelle. At the other end of the table, Philip began to rise.

"We're not finished yet, Isabelle," Julian said. "Not by a long shot."

As he stormed out of the dining room, Philip motioned to one of the security men to follow. Suddenly he noticed that Paco had also left the room.

"Where did he go?" Philip asked Skye.

"I don't know," she answered, upset that she hadn't paid closer attention. "He slipped away rather quietly."

"Nina?"

"Probably to the little boys' room," Nina replied.

Philip scowled. Obviously he wasn't in any mood to appreciate her humor.

"Should I have gone with him?" Nina asked, suddenly defensive.

"Yes, maybe you should have!"

With that he left, leaving Nina chagrined, embarrassed, and wishing she had somewhere to go. Isabelle provided her with an opportunity when she invited everyone to enjoy the music in the large drawing room.

"Afterward, coffee and dessert will be served in the smaller drawing room."

Grateful for any excuse to get away, Nina pushed back her chair. Hoping to avoid Miranda, Luis, and Sam, she quickly started toward the door. She was stopped by Xavier Fargas.

"It's been a long time," he said. His voice was the same resonant baritone she remembered. She still found his accent hypnotic. "You're even more beautiful now than you were as a girl."

He smiled, and for a moment she felt like a girl, young and carefree, unburdened by horrible truths, awkward missteps, and miscalculations.

"It's wonderful to see you again, Xavier. Truly wonderful." An awkward pause followed. All around her people were pairing off. Anxious to have an escort, and even more anxious to cozy up to Xavier, she asked if he was headed inside.

"I am, but I'll be a minute. I'm waiting for Alejandro. Unfortunately he's a lot slower than he used to be. Would you care to join us?"

Three's a crowd, she thought. Especially when it's two friends and a stranger. "Maybe later," she said with an offhandedness she didn't feel. "I think I'll powder my nose first." Taking off with a head-held-high pose that would have made Bette Davis proud, she breezed past a cluster of guests, headed someplace where she could lose herself for a while.

At the other end of the room, Luis cornered Isabelle.

"How are you?"

She said she was fine, but he took her hands in his as if verbal assurances were insufficient.

"I hate to bother you, señorita." A white-jacketed waiter stood at Isabelle's elbow, speaking in a deferential whisper. "One of your guests is not feeling well and has requested some kind of stomach medication. Where would I find that?"

"I'll get it for you." She kissed Luis on the cheek and patted his arm reassuringly. "Go enjoy the music."

She watched him meander reluctantly toward the drawing room, and she smiled, ever thankful that she had him in her life. She started for the front hall but realized everyone would gather there before going into the drawing room. Just then she didn't feel like rehashing or explaining the purchase of Dragon. She had to save her strength for what was to come.

Having decided against using the front stairs, she headed toward the back hallway. At the door, Dallas Crawford, one of the bodyguards Philip had hired, stopped her.

"Where are you going, Miss de Luna?" He was so beefy, the seams of his tuxedo looked as though they were about to burst.

"I need to get something from my bathroom. It'll only take a minute."

"Thompson's watching the upper hall. I'll let him know you're coming up."

As he whispered into the radio attached to his wrist, Isabelle smiled. She had scolded Philip when he'd insisted upon adding these two guard dogs to the four-man security squad she had watching the grounds. She had argued that it wasn't necessary, but just then she wished he were there for her to thank. Having one hulk down here and another stationed upstairs made her feel as safe as she could . . . considering.

CHAPTER 29

Julian was lost, angry, and queasy. Slightly nauseated, he had asked one of the waiters for the nearest bathroom. He could have sworn the man pointed in this direction, but as far as he could tell, this was a hallway to nowhere. Either the waiter didn't know what he was talking about or Julian had taken a wrong turn.

"That's the trouble with old castles," he mumbled, annoyed that he hadn't paid closer attention. "You need a frigging map to find a toilet!"

His first instinct was to retrace his steps, but he had been too annoyed at Isabelle to remember at which corner he had turned left, which one right. Recalling that the Castell was essentially a square, he reasoned that if he continued straight ahead, eventually he would wend his way back to the center hall. It might take a while, but he was in no hurry to return to the party anyway.

Judging by the vaulted ceiling, graceful arches, and elaborate stone carvings, Julian suspected this wing had been part of the original Castell. Cracks in the plaster and a slight slant to the floor seemed to confirm his conclusion. Age notwithstanding, it was an elegant hallway, harking back to a time when architecture was the source of both support and decoration. Soaring triangles and gentle arcs created a sensation of height and motion. Thick columns with solid bases provided a feeling of comfort and solidity.

Lining the walls was an impressive assemblage of family portraits boasting brass plaques engraved with the basic facts of each ancestor: name, date of birth, and death. At various intervals the hallway was divided by portals. Flanking them were slender columns and deep niches, each containing a marble bust of a Pujol forebear resting on waist-high, heavily veined white marble blocks inset with malachite.

Julian adored the feel of marble, so cold and smooth and unyielding. Like a child, he ran his hands along the surfaces, letting his fingers dance onto the graffiti that lined the sides. Now and then he stopped to caress the statuary, admiring as he always did the genius of the sculptor who'd been able to draw power and grace from a chunk of stone.

It surprised him to come upon a narrow winding staircase that appeared to have been cut into a corner. The ones in the main part of the house were wide and gracious, apparently designed to accommodate long gowns and flaring coats. Curious, he followed it up several flights to a tower. It had been constructed as a hexagon: six windows framed within parabolic arches marked the centers of each of the stone walls; three faced front, three faced what he assumed was the rear.

Above him loomed a unique colored-glass cupola. Along the lower edge was a string of men and women dancing the sardana against a background of Mediterranean blue. Rising up from there, moving gracefully toward the crown of the cupola, was a field of small blue and white squares interrupted by a burst of golden feathers.

The moon, tonight full and resplendent, insinuated itself into the ancient space via a series of colorful patterns that stenciled the plain stone floor and walls. For a delightful moment Julian felt as if he were standing inside a kaleidoscope, watching the colors change and the designs redraft themselves. A cloud must have passed by, because suddenly the room dimmed. Patterns faded and shadows emerged. What had been a pleasant experience only seconds before quickly turned eerie. Julian felt uncomfortable, almost unwelcome, as if a hostile presence had taken its place alongside him.

As the light waned, gray became charcoal, blue became black. Julian edged toward the door, holding his arms outstretched, his fingers groping for the banister. Below him he heard the echo of high heels clicking on a stone floor. Because his attention had been diverted, when he went to set his foot on the first stair, he misstepped, twisted his ankle, and yelped in pain.

"Who's there?"

With everyone occupied in the large drawing room, Nina embarked on a nostalgic tour of the Castell. Assuming she was free to roam at will, she headed up the central staircase. When a human behemoth named Thompson stopped her on the landing and questioned where she was going, she challenged him with a well-practiced Barbara Stanwyck snarl.

"Excuse me, my good man. I am a guest in this house."

"I understand, ma'am, and I'm sorry, but Mr. Medina has requested that we restrict everyone to the main floor."

"Mr. Medina could not have been referring to me. I'm Miss de Luna's sister, and there is something I need from my bedroom. It's the large red suite at the end of the western corridor. Now please, step aside."

Knowing there was a large red suite where Nina said there was, recalling that Philip had mentioned that family was attending, Thompson capitulated. Nina pardoned him and sauntered down the hall. When she was out of his line of sight, she proceeded to open doors and revisit places she associated with happier times.

Ramona's room, done in varying shades of beige, ivory, and gold, still had an enormous harp in one corner, a gilded chair and antique music stand in another. Checking the dressing table and finding a plastic box filled with gray hairpins and no makeup containers other than a single, dark red lipstick, a black eye pencil, and a nearly empty compact, Nina concluded that this was where Miranda and Luis were staying. The child inside her wanted to linger; the adult wanted to avoid the memories such an extended stay would evoke.

Flora's bedroom truly upset her. She had flung open the door expecting to see shards of light slicing the air like lasers and prisms of color dancing through the cellophane drapes like mischievous elves. But there was no light in this room, only the somber veil of mourning. She hadn't realized it until that moment, but she hadn't wanted to think of Tía Flora as gone. She had sent flowers to her funeral, but in her heart she had chosen to keep her alive. This dark, silent room confronted her with that lie. Depressed, yet respectful of the woman who had lived and died here, Nina did not walk inside. Instead she stood at the door just as she might have stood at an altar—head bowed, hands clasped—and allowed herself to grieve.

When she came to the next room, she walked to the center, took a deep breath, and tried to recapture the sensation of awe and excitement that she had felt when she'd entered the suite for the first time. This, Nina knew, had been Vina's room. Red and vibrant, the spirit of the room enveloped her once again, reminding her of who she had been then: "Miss Nina," the honored guest. Closing her eyes, she summoned images of that special time: hot chocolate brought to her on a silver tray, having her nightclothes laid out, the drapes drawn, bathwater run, her blankets turned down. Tonight, however, the negligee on the bed appeared to be Skye's. Tonight she and Sam were the honored guests. Nina was an afterthought, if that.

Vacillating between insult and indignation, she left, reluctantly closing the door behind her. She proceeded down the hall slowly, weighted down with thoughts she wasn't prepared to deal with. Reflection was not her strong suit; she didn't like delving or analyzing or contemplating. Mental exercises such as those demanded honesty and self-criticism, two activities she had avoided most of her life. She was much more comfortable with denial and superficiality. They didn't hurt as much.

Deciding to bypass Thompson, she descended one of the rear staircases. Still not eager to join the others, she opted for the longer route along the back end of the house. As she made her way, she marveled at how quiet it was. There might have been a party going on in the northern wing, but there wasn't any hint of it in this corridor. It was too isolated, too far away.

Isabelle found Julian sprawled on the floor just inside the tower.

"What are you doing here?"

"Would you believe I was looking for the bathroom?"

"This isn't it."

"I gathered as much," he said as he struggled to his feet and moved farther back into the tower, which was once again filled with light. "Remind me to thank that idiot servant of yours for sending me on this delightful safari."

"If you'd like, I'll be happy to show you the way to the powder room."

She turned to go, but he didn't follow. Instead he said, "You sure do know how to liven up a party, Isabelle. Spicing up your dinner with the news that you had bought Dragon was very entertaining."

"I'm glad you thought so."

"What other surprises do you have in store? Have you hired a gorilla to sing during dessert? Is a scantily clad chorus girl going to jump out of a cake?"

"Not exactly."

"Ah, but there is something else on your agenda." Her silence disturbed him. He stroked his beard and narrowed his eyes. "Are you still angry because I never told you I knew your mother?"

"It is a rather large oversight, don't you think?"

"I told you, it was a nonevent."

Rage bubbled inside her. "No, Julian, it was anything but."

This wasn't the plan. She wasn't supposed to be in an unprotected place. She was supposed to confront him where help was instantly available. But emotion got the better of her.

"After I heard you in that TV interview, I called Diego Cadiz and Rafael Avda so that the three of us could chat about your visit. They remembered your being in Barcelona then, but I guess you must not have made a big impression, because neither one thought much about it at the time. After we spoke, we all realized they should have paid more attention."

"What are you blithering about?"

"According to them, you fell in love with my mother and pursued her like a lovesick puppy. You used your relationship with Rafael and the Gaspars to ingratiate yourself with her. You asked for a tour of the mill and a chance to photograph her. When she permitted those indulgences, you pushed further, misinterpreting graciousness for attraction. You asked her to dinner. She declined. You persisted. When she asked you to stop bothering her, you were offended. Needless to say, that comes as no surprise." Her gaze fixed on his face. "Anyone who knows you, knows you don't handle rejection well."

He laughed, but the sound rang hollow.

"When I wouldn't have an affair with you, you refused to let it drop. I thought you were just a man who couldn't take no for an answer, but it wasn't a matter of pride or love or even sex, was it, Julian? It was perversion, pure and simple. You couldn't have the mother, so you went after the daughter!" Her eyes blazed with the fire of hate. "When we slept together, was it me in bed with you or my mother?" She grimaced and held her stomach. "I can't believe I allowed you near me. The thought of you even touching me makes me sick!"

"It didn't make you sick then!" Julian retorted. "You loved it!"

"Quite the contrary!" Isabelle recalled that night, those moments after sex, that instant when she knew she would never submit to him again. "Something about you wasn't right. I didn't know then what it was. But I know now." Her voice lowered to a near hiss. "I know it all, Julian."

He rolled his eyes and sighed, as if she were insane. "You're almost as good a storyteller as you are an artist," he said, trying to bluff his way through this ugly confrontation, "but quite frankly, this fairy tale is beginning to annoy me."

Undaunted, she continued. The truth was, she couldn't stop. She had waited a lifetime for this.

"Greta said when you returned from Europe after that summer, she noticed a major change in you." Even in the murky darkness Isabelle could smell his anger. "In fact, she said you were never the same again. I guess murder can do that to a man."

He was breathing like a bull, snorting hot air through his nose. "That sounds like something Greta would say." He shook his head, his face rouging crimson. "Ever since her lunatic sister hanged herself, Greta has delighted in casting me in the role of the felonious villain." His blue eyes dimmed, eclipsed by angry shadows. "It's true I found your mother attractive. It's also true that she didn't return my admiration. But that doesn't mean I killed her."

"You did, and I have proof that you did."

"What kind of proof could you possibly have?"

"Where should I begin?" Her hazel eyes crackled, but her voice remained steady. "One of the waitresses serving tonight had been a chambermaid on duty the night of the murder. After the blackout, she was bringing candles around and saw you come out of my mother's room. You yelled at her and then assaulted her for her flashlight. During the scuffle, she grabbed a ring from your finger. It was your wedding ring, Julian, a duplicate of the one Greta wears. Imagine that!"

Julian was sweating. "I was there, so what? I was staying at the hotel, as were hundreds of other people. I went to her room to continue our discussion about backing my gallery, not to murder her."

"Did you forget that there was an eyewitness to the attack?" She was trembling, fighting to stave off an explosion of outrage and pent-up grief. "I was the eyewitness, Julian. I was there, in that room. I saw you."

Julian stared at her.

"I saw you," she said again, tempestuous fury amplifying her voice.

"No." He was shaking his head from side to side. His eyes were glassy. "No. You're not going to do this to me."

"Oh, but I am, Julian. I'm going to have you arrested and brought to trial, and I'm going to get on that witness stand and tell them what I saw!"

"No one's going to believe you."

"We have the ring with your initials on it and the woman who took it from you outside my mother's room. We have Greta's account of your behavior, Xavier's testimony, and the sketch I made for the police of the man I saw murder my mother."

Julian laughed. The sound of it frightened Isabelle more than his anger.

"Your lover, a lowly chambermaid who glimpsed someone twenty-seven years ago in the dark, a cuckolded wife, and a shrink who's practically a first cousin. Very believable, Isabelle. Who could possibly doubt them?"

"Everyone, because you've got guilt written all over your face."

"And you've got fear written all over yours."

With that he lunged at her, grabbed her arm, and twisted it behind her back. His alcohol-laced breath felt hot and threatening against her face. Remarkably, Isabelle maintained a facade of calm. She twisted free of him. He charged at her and missed. Isabelle screamed, but even as she heard her voice echo inside the tower room, she knew no one else could hear her.

Determined to get help, she raced toward the stairs. Julian caught her arm and jerked her backward. She tripped on the hem of her gown, lost her balance, and fell onto the cold stone floor.

He was on her in a heartbeat, hunkering over her, smothering her mouth with his hand, reducing her cries to whimpers.

Nina could have sworn she heard a noise. Unsure what it was or precisely where it had come from, she chased the sound down the length of the western corridor to the corner where the north hallway began. Standing at the base of a stairwell, she stopped and listened. A second later she heard it again. It was a scream, and it was coming from the old tower. Propelled by curiosity, she tiptoed up the stairs, careful to cloak herself in the shadows.

More than once she had scooped her fellow gossipers by following her nose and sticking it in where it didn't belong. This could be nothing more than a chambermaid or another wandering guest being frightened by a mouse. But if it was something juicy, like an illicit assignation, she wanted names and details.

When first she looked inside, she thought her journalistic instincts had been correct: a man was on top of a woman who seemed to be writhing. Suddenly the woman screamed, not in passion, but in pain. The man slapped her. Nina retreated deeper into the darkness.

"You're not going to say anything to anybody," he said.

"I don't have to. They know, they—"

Even with his hand smothering her response, Nina recognized Isabelle's voice. The man turned his head, presenting Nina with his profile. Stunned, she stifled a gasp. Her heart began to pound. The man assaulting Isabelle was Julian Richter!

Nina's head flooded with a hundred incongruous thoughts, ranging from the inquisitive (What was Julian worried Isabelle would say?) to the self-preserving (Why was this happening to her?) to the crux of the matter. What the hell was she going to do?

It was not Nina's style to barge in where only fools would tread. She was hardly the heroic type. Yet Julian was beating up Isabelle right before her eyes. Confused and more than a little frightened, she raced through a string of possibilities.

She could tiptoe down the steps, head back to the party, and pretend she hadn't seen anything, but there was always the chance that she would run into someone on her way. Besides, even she couldn't pull off a charade as heartless and diabolical as that.

She could run and find Philip, tell him what was happening, and throw it in his lap. But, her conscience said, by the time she got to Philip and they got back here, Isabelle could be dead.

She could try to stop Julian herself, but that would put her at tremendous risk. Listening to him spewing evil threats at Isabelle, it was evident that something had snapped and he was out of control. What was to say that if she defended Isabelle, he wouldn't turn his madness on her?

Suddenly Isabelle cried out. The sound startled Nina, jolting her back to the present and the harsh reality that if she didn't do something quickly, Isabelle was going to die.

Philip's gut was roiling. Something was off. Leaving the others to listen to the music, he asked each of the servants if they had seen either Julian or Isabelle. One of the kitchen men told him Julian had asked about the men's room.

"He said his stomach was upset. He asked if I had some medicine. I asked Señorita de Luna. She said she would get it for me."

"How long ago was that?"

The man shrugged, flustered. "I can't be sure, señor. Maybe ten minutes. Maybe more."

Philip left the kitchen and headed for Dallas Crawford, who was still stationed just off the center hall, in the south corridor.

"Have you seen Señorita de Luna?"

"She's upstairs, Mr. Medina. Went to get some medicine." Noting the concern lining Philip's face, Crawford checked his watch. "It has been a while, though."

"Call Thompson!"

Crawford radioed his partner, pressing against his earpiece so he could hear the answer more clearly.

"She never came up. Thompson assumed she changed her mind. I assumed she was powdering her nose."

It was all Philip could do to control himself. "Did she use this staircase?" he asked, pointing to the one in the center hall.

"No, sir. She said she wanted to avoid the crowd. She went through here."

Philip looked beyond Crawford, through the portal. About twenty yards down, the hallway separated. "Which way did she turn?"

"Frankly, sir," Crawford said, "I don't know."

*   *   *

The clouds shifted away from the moon. An eerie, inky blueness suffused the tower. A sense of urgency gripped Nina, bringing with it a stunning clarity. The woman fighting for her life inside that room was neither a stranger nor an enemy. She was Isabelle de Luna, Nina's sister. Though she had fought the bond between them, denied it, demeaned it, and in fact had done everything she could to destroy it, it had persisted and survived.

All at once the years slipped away, taking with them the perceived hurts and contrived betrayals, the exaggerated jealousies and self-invented rivalry. What remained were fond memories of a shared childhood. In that moment of incredible clearheadedness, Nina knew with absolute certainty that if positions were reversed, Isabelle would have done for her what she was about to do now.

"Julian!" she shouted as she invaded his theater of battle. "What the hell are you doing?"

Distracted, Julian moved his arm. Isabelle gasped for breath. She squirmed beneath him, trying desperately to free herself, but she was too weak to throw him off.

"Get out!" Julian shouted, his voice echoing the insanity Nina saw in his eyes.

Even if she had wanted to, however, she couldn't have moved from that spot. She was frozen there in a state of disbelief. As bizarre as it sounded, Nina realized she was standing in the middle of Isabelle's nightmare. The incessant, unrelenting blue. The man hovering over a barely conscious woman, his legs pinning hers to the floor, his arm bearing down on her throat.

"You killed Althea, didn't you, you bastard!"

He growled at her like a savage poised to attack, but still he refused to relinquish his hold on Isabelle.

Nina's initial plan was to make him come at her. Bending down so her face was level with his, she confronted him with a loud, taunting burst of laughter.

"I always said you were a girl's worst nightmare, Julian." She stalked him, moving to his left, then back to his right. When his gaze followed her, she laughed again. His face was getting redder and redder. "Isabelle knows, doesn't she? That's what tonight is all about. It's not a party. It's a lynching! And I thought Isabelle didn't know how to have fun!"

"Shut up!" he yelled. "Get out or I'll kill her!" Julian was manic. His eyes darted about without seeing. He issued commands and shouted threats, shooting them like bullets into the air, not caring where they fell or what damage they did. On the surface Nina remained infuriatingly cool.

"Even if I left, which I have no intention of doing, nothing's going to save your ass, Julian," she said, raising her voice, praying that someone, anyone, was looking for Isabelle and would get here soon. "I'm not some little seven-year-old who's going to forget what I see. Uh-uh! I'm going remember every filthy detail of this. And when I get back to New York, I'm going to print it in my column and talk about it on my television show. I'm going to tell the world about the big important art dealer who can't get it up unless he's got a woman nailed to the floor. 'Sex on the Richter scale.' Not a bad headline, if I do say so myself."

Isabelle's body went limp. Nina's panic intensified. She thought about hurling herself on top of Julian, of taking off one of her high heels and beating him with it, of kicking him in the back or, better yet, the groin. But what if she made things worse? One look at Isabelle told her things couldn't get any worse.

Forsaking caution, she bulldozed Julian off Isabelle and onto the floor, all the while scratching at his face, chewing at his hair, screaming at the top of her lungs.

"I'll kill you for this!" he said as he curled his hand into a tight fist.

Nina's retort was an elbow to his kidney, accompanied by a swift, a smart-mouthed, "Not if I get you first."

Julian's response was to launch a deadly punch.

It took Philip three minutes to gather his forces and organize teams to search the house and the grounds. When they were set, he took off on his own. The first thing he checked was the door next to the kitchen that led outside to the rear courtyard. Relieved to find it securely locked, he ran through the small corridor that led to the courtyard garden. He unlocked that door, looked and listened, his senses on full alert. After hearing no sounds, seeing no movement, he came back inside and headed off in another direction.

Suddenly it dawned on him that this old hallway led to the tower. Though he couldn't imagine what would have brought the two of them together in this isolated passageway, nor could he picture Julian accosting Isabelle somewhere in the house and dragging her up there by himself, he was leaving nothing to chance. He bounded down toward the door that led to the medieval turret. As he vaulted up the three flights of stairs, he shouted for Isabelle, terrified by the deafening silence that was his only response.

When he reached the small room atop the tower, his heart stopped. There on the floor were Isabelle and Nina, lying side by side, both bleeding, both very, very still.

Paco was sitting in his car, debating whether or not to leave, when he saw Julian running around the side of the house toward the driveway. Behaving suspiciously, Julian opened one car door after another, his manner becoming more and more frantic as he searched for one car with the key still in the ignition.

Moving quietly and carefully, Paco crawled onto the backseat and dropped out of sight. When Julian got to Paco's Mercedes, he must have thought he'd hit paydirt. He slid onto the driver's seat, closed the door, and leaned forward. Paco's arm was around Julian's neck before his hand ever touched the key.

Paco jerked him back against the seat, blocking his windpipe. Then he brought his mouth next to Julian's ear. His breath was hot, his words were harsh. "This is how Althea felt when you killed her."

Julian struggled to wrench himself free of Paco's suffocating stranglehold. He flailed his arms and kicked his legs, hitting the horn, slamming into the dashboard. Still Paco refused to let him go.

"How does it feel to choke to death?" he said as he watched Julian's skin turn white.

Paco didn't think he could have killed him, but when Dallas Crawford opened the door and pulled Julian out of the car, he was glad to be relieved of the opportunity.

Once Jonas had completed his preliminary examination and given his permission, Thompson and Crawford carried the two badly battered women out of the tower. Isabelle was taken to her suite, Nina to Ramona's room, where Miranda and Luis stood off to the side while Jonas tended to Nina's injuries.

The flesh around her left eye was black and blue, the inside corner red from several broken blood vessels. A few teeth had been loosened. A nasty gash on her cheek had required stitches. Her elbows were badly scraped, but no bones had been broken, and as far as he could tell, there was no internal bleeding.

"You should be very proud of what you did tonight," Jonas said. "I shudder to think what would have happened if you hadn't come along when you did."

"Timing is everything, they say." Despite Nina's attempt to sound casual, she was touched by Jonas's tribute.

"You're being far too modest. What you did took enormous courage."

"I second that," Luis said emphatically, moving closer to the bed.

"Thanks, but I don't deserve all this praise," Nina said, recalling how her first instinct had been to cut and run.

"Of course you do!" Luis insisted. "Julian Richter murdered Althea, and there's no doubt in my mind he would have killed Isabelle if you hadn't stopped him."

"Speaking of Isabelle," Jonas said, snapping his medical bag shut, "if you'll excuse me, I have to check on her."

He tapped the bandage on Nina's cheek, making certain it was secure, squeezed her hand affectionately, and left. Luis, having broken the ice, continued the thaw by pulling a chair next to Nina. Miranda wasn't as bold as her husband.

"Mama?" Nina craned her neck so she could see her mother. As she did, pain shot through her head. She winced and lay back against the pillows.

Miranda rushed to her side. "Are you all right? Should we call Jonas back?"

Nina shook her head, keeping her eyes closed until the pain subsided. When it had, she opened her eyes to find both Durans standing by her, fretting over her almost as if the intervening years hadn't occurred. But all three of them knew they had.

"If I hadn't written that stupid book," Nina said, opening the door to the closet where the past was stored, "none of this would have happened."

Miranda shook her head. "This isn't your fault, Nina."

"Yes, it is. I brought it all up again. It was buried, but I couldn't let it be. I couldn't let it rest."

"The book had nothing to do with it," Luis said. "Right after Flora's funeral, there was a bad electrical storm. The two events produced a memory flash in which Isabelle relived that horrible night so many years before." His expression turned reflective. "She learned the way we learned, *niña*. No matter how hard you try, the truth won't stay buried forever."

"We should have told you the truth when you were a child." Miranda said it quickly, as if the words tasted too bitter to hold inside any longer. "It was my fault. I never thought the time was right to tell you how we found you. I didn't want you to be hurt by what that woman did. Yet by not telling you, I was the one who inflicted the most hurt."

"I had a right to know." Nina's voice was soft, but there was no mistaking how she felt about being lied to.

"We were wrong to keep it from you," Luis admitted. "Not a day has gone by since that we haven't felt sorry, but if you had given us a chance, we would have done anything and everything to make it up to you."

Nina fiddled with the blanket, buying the time she needed to organize her thoughts. When she looked at Miranda and Luis, her eyes were moist, but her gaze was steady and sure.

"I was cruel to you," she said. "Worse, I meant to be. I didn't realize it for a long time"—she chuckled, but it was clear she was laughing at herself— "maybe not until this very evening, but I lashed out at you because in my heart I believed you loved me and that no matter what I said or did, you would never stop loving me."

"Your heart was right," Miranda said, taking her daughter's hand and folding it between her own. "We never did."

An uncharacteristically shy flush pinked Nina's cheeks. "You're not just saying that because I took a few punches that were meant for Isabelle, are you?"

Luis laughed. Miranda, being the more emotional of the two, could muster only a wobbly smile. Nina felt suddenly joyous.

"So what do you think?" she said, straining to keep her voice light, her eyes betraying a chronic fear of rejection. "Can we ever be a family again?"

Miranda caressed Nina's cheek and nodded. "It's certainly worth a try, don't you think, Luis?"

"From day one," he said to Nina, "I always thought you were worth the effort."

Isabelle lay against a pile of pillows, Philip at her side. Her neck bore Julian's fingerprints. Her voice box had been bruised, making it difficult for her to speak. She was suffering from a slight concussion, but in light of what might have been, her injuries seemed minor.

There was a soft rapping on the door. It was Paco. Isabelle was weak, but eager to see him. He walked to her side, lifted her hand, and kissed it.

"I'm so relieved to see you're all right."

Isabelle squeezed his hand. "I owe you an apology," she said, her voice catching on a lump in her throat. "All these years . . ."

He touched a finger to her lips to silence her. "Apology accepted." He paused, measuring his words. "I'm only glad that Althea's killer was caught and finally will be brought to justice."

"What were you doing in the driveway?" Philip asked.

"It took a while until I figured out that this party was nothing but an elaborate trap. When I realized that the man who had raped and murdered Althea was in the room, eating and drinking as if he had done nothing wrong, I felt ill. I wanted to leave."

"I'm sorry we had to use you as a foil," Isabelle said.

"It was necessary. I understand that."

"How did you know it was Richter?" Philip asked.

"Process of elimination. Once I caught on, I looked around the table for likely suspects. It could only be him or me, and I knew I was innocent." Confusion lined his face. "But why bring him here?"

"Because the crime took place in Barcelona," Isabelle said. "If he was arrested in the United States, extraditing him to Spain would have taken too long. I wanted it over." She smiled. "Thanks to you, it is."

Paco laughed. "After all these years of being the accused, it seemed only right that I be in on the capture."

When Paco opened the door to leave, Philip was surprised to see Nina waiting just outside.

"Would you mind if I spoke to Isabelle alone?" she asked.

"Not at all," he said. He wanted to thank her, but she seemed anxious, as if her resolve were on a timer and she would lose her nerve if she didn't speak to Isabelle instantly. He escorted her inside and left.

Isabelle took note of Nina's purple eye, the bandage covering her cheek, her swollen lower lip. She noticed too that her dress was torn and her hair was a mess.

"You look like you went extra innings," she said, suddenly reminded of how they used to look after they finished playing ball in the field adjacent to La Casa.

"You don't look so *Vogue* yourself." Nina's tone was easy, but there was an underlying edge of apprehension.

The smile faded from Isabelle's lips. "If not for you, I wouldn't be here. I'm grateful."

Nina sat next to Isabelle's bed. "I figured I owed you one."

"Who's counting?"

"Who isn't?" Nina's eyes rolled. Her smile was shaky and self-conscious. "In case you've misplaced the list of my sins, ask any one of your guests. They'll tell you: I haven't exactly been a saint where you're concerned."

"No. You haven't."

Nina paused. "I'm not very good at confessions or apologies, but I've been a royal pain, and I'm sorry."

Nina expected anger or recrimination. What she received was absolution. "We all make mistakes," Isabelle said. "Believe me, I've got my own list of foul-ups."

Nina's gray eyes pooled. "Maybe so, but you haven't chased everyone away from you. You're not alone." Again she paused, weighing her desire to be honest against the need not to embarrass herself. "I'm not engaged any-more." She shrugged and forced a laugh. "Anthony found his company's bottom line was more attractive than mine. He took my book and gave me the boot!"

Isabelle was moved by the sight of Nina's pain. "You don't have to be alone. We could try to put all this behind us and start over."

"I'm not certain I know how," Nina said. "More to the point, I don't know how you can ever forgive me for all I've done to you."

Isabelle looked at her squarely. "You risked your life to save mine. That makes up for a lot."

Tears trickled down Nina's cheeks, yet her eyes remained firmly fixed on Isabelle. "I blamed you for everything that was wrong in my life. It was so much easier than fixing what was wrong with me. Tonight, in that tower, when I saw your body go limp and I thought you were dead, I realized just how important you were to me. I didn't want to lose you, Isabelle. I still don't."

Isabelle reached out for Nina's hand. Tears blurred her vision, but the smile that graced her mouth was sure. "The most important thing that happened tonight was that you and I found each other again."

Nina could do nothing but nod in agreement.

"I'll tell you what," Isabelle said, covering the awkwardness of the moment. "Tomorrow, come for breakfast. We'll sit over there on the window seat and have hot chocolate and *churros* and a long talk. Just the two of us. Like we used to. Sound okay to you?"

"More than okay." Nina squeezed Isabelle's hand and smiled.

Suddenly the idea of starting over didn't seem as daunting as it had when she had stood outside Isabelle's door. Probably because now she was inside. And she wasn't alone.

Much later, after the evening had been thoroughly dissected and the others had gone or retired, Isabelle asked Philip to take her to the courtyard garden. There, leaning against Flora's ancient olive tree, they looked up past the tower onto a sky that was midnight black, clouds that were cottony white, and a moon that was clear and blue and full.

"Even though the moon is blue," Philip said, "I think your parents are smiling down on you."

"I think they are, too," Isabelle said softly.

"I can't imagine that General Patton is too thrilled with you, however. Your orders were to stay close to the base." He scowled. "Disobedience is a serious offense, soldier!"

Isabelle offered him a quick salute and a gentle kiss. "If I promise to obey from now on, will you forgive me?"

"Maybe," he said with a sly grin, "but first, I have to know how you feel about love and honor."

"What are you talking about?"

Moonlight dappled her skin, reminding him of that first night in Majorca. "I was going to give you this after you made your revelation about Julian," Philip said as he reached into his pocket and presented Isabelle with a small black box.

Isabelle opened the box. A large oval diamond winked back at her.

"Somehow the words 'Better late than never' sound particularly poignant right now." Philip couldn't shake the memory of calling out to her and not getting a response, or the image of her lifeless body on that cold stone floor. As he slipped the ring on her finger, he said, "I love you, Isabelle."

Isabelle stared at the ring, saying nothing.

"Okay," Philip said, slightly unnerved by her silence, "you don't have to promise to obey. If it bothers you, we can drop the honor part, too. I am kind of stuck on the promise to love in sickness and health, however."

Isabelle looked up at the moon, then back at Philip. "Years ago, I told Tía Flora I didn't think I knew what love was. She told me to wait until I found a man who not only aroused passion, but inspired trust, offered friendship, and most of all, made me feel safe. You do all that and more, which is why," she said, "I will have no problem saying 'I do.'"

He drew her close and kissed her. "Are the ghosts gone?" he asked.

Her expression turned contemplative. "I think finding my mother's killer and clearing my father's name chased them away." Suddenly she threw back her head and laughed. "Think of it! I went fifteen rounds with a homicidal maniac, yet I can state unequivocally that this is absolutely, positively, one of the happiest nights of my life!"

Bursting with elation, she giggled, took his face in her hands, and kissed him, her own mouth still caught in a smile.

"Finally, after twenty-seven years, the cloud that's hung over my head is gone. Finally, I can come out of the blue!"

ACKNOWLEDGMENTS

One of the most joyful rewards of researching a book is discovering something new either about a subject so intriguing I wanted to know more, or about a person I wanted to know better. I'd like to acknowledge those who gifted me with their time and enlightened me with their expertise and insights. The information was invaluable, the process of attainment pure pleasure.

My heartfelt thanks to Nancy Reinish, who continues to dazzle me with her intellect and her passion for art; to Phyllis Mack, Bonnie Englebardt, Phyllis Rosen, and Paula Allen, women who not only opened the doors of the art world to me, but opened my mind as well; to Dr. Stanley Hordes of the New Mexico Jewish Historical Society; to Maureen Cogan and Amy Page of *Art & Auction* magazine; to Alan Finger of Yoga Zone; to Evelyn Goldfeier, Dr. Richard Katz, and Cynthia and Daniel Levy; to Peter Lampack for going above and beyond, again; to my friends at Crown, Betty A. Prashker and Michelle Sidrane; and last, but always first, my children, Lisa and Alex, and my husband, David—without them, I wouldn't be me.